JAMES MATTHEW BARRIE was born at Kirriemuir in Angus, Scotland, in 1860. After attending Dumfries Academy and Edinburgh University, he joined the *Nottingham Journal* as leader writer in 1883. Two years later he went to London to seek a living as a freelance writer. Drawing on his mother's memories of her childhood years, he achieved early success with stories about his hometown. The first such collection, *Auld Licht Idylls*, was published in 1888. His novel *The Little Minister* (1891) achieved great popularity, but from the 1890s onwards he turned most of his attention to the theatre. A succession of long-running plays brought Barrie wealth and critical acclaim. His most famous creation, Peter Pan, first appeared in the novel *The Little White Bird* (1902), and the play *Peter Pan* was first staged in 1904. *Peter and Wendy* followed seven years later. Barrie continued to enjoy great public recognition and success, but his private life was clouded by divorce and a series of bereavements, and he wrote less in his later years. His last play, *The Boy David*, was first performed in 1936, a few months before his death in 1937.

ROBERT DOUGLAS-FAIRHURST is Professor of English Literature at Oxford University and a Fellow of Magdalen College. His books include *Becoming Dickens: The Invention of a Novelist* (2011), which was awarded the Duff Cooper Prize, and *The Story of Alice: Lewis Carroll and the Secret History of Wonderland* (2015), which was shortlisted for the Costa Prize. In 2015 he was made a Fellow of the Royal Society of Literature.

OXFORD WORLD'S CLASSICS

J. M. BARRIE

The Collected Peter Pan

Edited with an Introduction and Notes by
ROBERT DOUGLAS-FAIRHURST

OXFORD
UNIVERSITY PRESS

OXFORD
UNIVERSITY PRESS

Great Clarendon Street, Oxford, OX2 6DP,
United Kingdom

Oxford University Press is a department of the University of Oxford.
It furthers the University's objective of excellence in research, scholarship,
and education by publishing worldwide. Oxford is a registered trade mark of
Oxford University Press in the UK and in certain other countries

Published in the United States of America by Oxford University Press
198 Madison Avenue, New York, NY 10016, United States of America

British Library Cataloguing in Publication Data

Data available

Library of Congress Control Number: 2023931646

ISBN 978-0-19-887838-4

Printed and bound in the UK by
Clays Ltd, Elcograf S.p.A.

for Luc

ACKNOWLEDGEMENTS

My greatest debts are to Luciana O'Flaherty and Martha Cunneen at Oxford University Press, the staff of the Beinecke Library at Yale University (particularly Tim Young) for their good-humoured efficiency during the period I spent consulting the Walter Beinecke Jnr. Collection in 2017, and Andrew Birkin, not only for his pioneering study *J. M. Barrie and the Lost Boys* (1979), but also for his generous guidance at the start and end of this project. I would also like to record my thanks to Peter Hollindale, whose work on previous editions of *Peter Pan and Other Plays* and *Peter Pan in Kensington Gardens/Peter and Wendy* for Oxford World's Classics has informed this new collected edition at every stage. For answering specific queries I am grateful to Rhiannon Easterbrook, Sos Eltis, Scott Palmer, Jeff Kattenhorn at the British Library, Jane Sellek at Eton College, and the staff of the Bodleian Library. For everything else I am grateful to Mac Castro, for reasons he knows very well.

CONTENTS

LIST OF ILLUSTRATIONS

F. D. Bedford's illustrations to the first edition of *Peter and Wendy* (Hodder & Stoughton, 1911) are reproduced on pp. 142, 157, 170, 174, 196, 204, 214, 236, 250, 256, and 275.

INTRODUCTION

'PAN,' Hook cries out towards the climax of their final battle, 'who and what art thou?' Back comes the preening reply 'I'm youth, I'm joy, I'm a little bird that has broken out of the egg', a remark that Barrie's narrator in *Peter and Wendy* dismisses as 'nonsense' (p. 257). But it would be equally nonsensical to expect any definition to fit Peter Pan without him giving it the slip. Definitions are for people and ideas that are fixed, and it is central to Pan's character that he is always on the move. Lost child, action hero, innocent icon, egotistical monster, and practical joker: you can no more pin him down than you can catch hold of your own reflection. Since his first stage appearance in 1904, he has starred in countless theatrical productions worldwide, played by both male and female actors, and in at least ten major films, which have reworked *Peter Pan* as everything from a fable about the need for business executives to rediscover their inner child (Steven Spielberg's 1992 *Hook*), to P. J. Hogan's 2003 version in which an adolescent Wendy, all shiny eyes and lip gloss, finally succeeds in giving a proper kiss to the cocky Peter, who responds by zooming up into the air with a very un-innocent whoop: the Mermaids' Lagoon reimagined as *The Blue Lagoon*. Barrie's story has been turned into science fiction (in Spielberg's 1982 film *E.T.*, a mother reads her daughter the episode in which Tinker Bell is brought back to life, shortly before her son does something similar for his extraterrestrial friend), a fable about modern gay life (it is repeatedly referenced in the US television drama *Queer as Folk*, where the gorgeous but narcissistic Brian is reassured that he will 'always be young, and always be beautiful', and is fondly nicknamed 'Peter' by a female friend he calls 'Wendy'),[1] and even a source of queasy pornography in which Wendy does far more than merely tuck in the Lost Boys at night. *Peter Pan* has inspired the creation of several statues, a type of rounded collar, a ballet, a stained glass window in Paddington's St James's Church, items of merchandise that range from cuddly toy crocodiles to glow-in-the-dark Tinker

---

[1] See David P. D. Munns, '"Gay, Innocent, and Heartless": *Peter Pan* and the Queering of Popular Culture', in Allison B. Kavey and Lester D. Friedman (eds), *Second Star to the Right: Peter Pan in the Popular Imagination* (New Brunswick, NJ: Rutgers University Press, 2009).

Bell costumes, a girl's name ('Wendy' was Barrie's posthumous trib-
ute to Margaret Henley, a little girl who could not pronounce her *r*'s
and so referred to him as her 'fwendy'), a brand of peanut butter,
a Disneyland ride, a way of referring to socially immature adults,[2] and
a 190-metre long Scandinavian car ferry. As the most famous modern
example of the *puer aeternus* (eternal boy) of classical legend, he has
stubbornly resisted all invitations to grow up, even as his cultural
presence has continued to grow ever larger and stronger. Appropriately
enough, Pan is everywhere.

His creator is equally elusive. The usual biographical account of
J. M. Barrie is that he was a child trapped in an adult's body, and that
he invented characters like Peter Pan as a way of escaping the person
he saw in the mirror every day: a meek writer with a drooping moustache and a smoker's hacking cough. Much of his life appeared to
consist of stray details rather than a straightforward plot. After his
death in 1937, what his friends recalled was not the grand sweep of his
career, with its humble beginning in rural Scotland followed by decades of fame and wealth, but much smaller things, such as his dreadful handwriting, or the pipe that he usually had firmly clamped in his
mouth. (It is one of many private jokes in *Peter Pan* that the hero plays
a pipe rather than smoking one.) In his dedication to the theatrical
version of *Peter Pan* he published in 1928, Barrie pointed out that if
you try to recall the past you end up having to force open a crammed
drawer in your mind: 'If you are searching for anything in particular
you don't find it, but something falls out at the back that is often more
interesting' (p. 334). In his own case, the something was a traumatic
event that happened in childhood and created a psychological wound
he spent the rest of his life delicately probing. In January 1867, when
Barrie was 6 years old, his older brother David was killed in a freak
skating accident on the eve of his fourteenth birthday. Barrie later
remembered little about the immediate aftermath, other than playing
with his younger sister Maggie under the table on which David's cof-
fin was resting, but he did vividly recall his mother's response. She
was broken by grief. On one occasion, Barrie tried to cheer her up by
going into her bedroom and reminding her that she still had a son:

[2] See Dan Kiley, *The Peter Pan Syndrome: Men Who Have Never Grown Up* (New York:
Dodd, Mead, and Co., 1983).

. . . the room was dark, and when I heard the door shut and no sound come from the bed I was afraid, and I stood still. I suppose I was breathing rather hard, or perhaps I was crying, for after a time I heard a listless voice that had never been listless before say, 'Is that you?' I think the tone hurt me, for I made no answer, and then the voice said more anxiously 'Is that you?' again. I thought it was the dead boy she was speaking to, and I said in a little lonely voice, 'No, it's no' him, it's just me.' Then I heard a cry, and my mother turned in bed, and though it was dark I knew that she was holding out her arms.[3]

Barrie decided 'to become so like him that even my mother would never see the difference', and to that end he practised whistling while adopting David's characteristic stance, with his legs planted wide apart and his hands thrust into his pockets. It was his first serious attempt at acting, and over the next few years he would invent several other roles for himself. In addition to the amateur theatricals he staged in his mother's washhouse, on one occasion he exchanged clothes with a friend who was in mourning, so that the boy could go and play while Barrie sat on a stone in his place and wept, 'though I knew not for whom'.[4] None of this greatly helped his mother, Margaret Ogilvy, who continued to mourn for her lost son as Barrie grew into a man, albeit one who at the age of 17 had already reached his full adult height of just five feet. 'Many a time she fell asleep speaking to him, and even while she slept her lips moved and she smiled as if he had come back to her', he later wrote. 'When I became a man . . . he was still a boy of thirteen.'[5] Even after he came to London to work as a journalist, recycling old Scottish stories with what soon became his trademark style of sentimental whimsy enlivened by touches of sly wit, it seems he never fully escaped the long shadows cast by his childhood. Cynthia Asquith, who worked as his secretary, remembered him as a 'strange, sombre, dark little man' with 'deep hoarded sadness in his blue eyes', and suggested that if he truly was an escapist, as some of his critics claimed, 'he didn't look as if he'd succeeded in escaping'. To adopt one of his own mournful quips, he appeared to have been 'barried alive'.[6] Or as Barrie also put it, in a line that could be read as

---

[3] J. M. Barrie, *Margaret Ogilvy, By Her Son* (London: Hodder & Stoughton, 1925), 10.
[4] Ibid. 13.   [5] Ibid. 12–13.
[6] Cynthia Asquith, *Portrait of Barrie* (London: James Barrie, 1954), 9, 2, 11.

either a breezy joke or a hard-won lesson in life, 'nothing that happens after we are twelve matters very much'.[7]

The only problem with this claim is that it comes from *Margaret Ogilvy*, a combined biography and autobiography first published in 1896, in which Barrie also described his brother's death, his mother's grief, and almost everything else we know about that formative period of his life. What we don't know is how true any of it is, because from the start Barrie enjoyed testing the border between reality and fantasy. When he performed to make his mother forget David's death, he reports, 'I kept a record of her laughs on a piece of paper',[8] and for the rest of his life he continued to record anything significant that was done or said around him. What changed were the uses to which he put these paper memories. Much of the time he treated his little red notebooks like flypaper. Every passing thought with the potential to be worked up into a story or article stuck to them, although usually written in the third person, which made them sound more like fictional case histories than true confessions.

In 1892, for instance, while he was courting the actress Mary Ansell, his notebooks flowered into life with ideas for a novel that had the working title of 'The Sentimentalist'. It centred on a young man who was a born actor, skilled at 'stepping into other people's shoes and remaining there until he became someone else', but who was unable to make the leap into genuine human commitment:

—This sentimentalist wants to make girl love him, bullies and orders her (this does it) yet doesn't want to marry.
—Such a man if an author, wd be studying his love affair for book. Even while proposing, the thought of how it wd read wd go thro' him.
—Literary man can't dislike any one he gets copy out of.[9]

Barrie certainly got plenty of copy out of his relationship with Mary, much of which reappeared in a lightly disguised form in his novel *Sentimental Tommy* (1896), the hero of which is a successful author who 'passes between dreams and reality as through tissue-paper',[10] and its sequel *Tommy and Grizel* (1900), in which Barrie

[7] Barrie, *Margaret Ogilvy*, 32.   [8] Ibid. 11.
[9] Cited in Andrew Birkin, *J. M. Barrie and the Lost Boys* (London: Constable, 1979), 23.
[10] J. M. Barrie's introduction to the first American edition of *Sentimental Tommy: The Story of his Boyhood* (New York: Charles Scribner's Sons, 1896), cited in Birkin, *J. M. Barrie and the Lost Boys*, 31.

continued his habit of offering passages of ruthless self-analysis at one remove:

They had a honeymoon by the sea . . . Tommy trying to become a lover by taking thought, and Grizel not letting on that it could not be done that way . . . He was a boy only. She knew that, despite all he had gone through, he was still a boy. And boys cannot love. Oh, is it not cruel to ask a boy to love? . . . He did not love her. . . . He was a boy who could not grow up . . . He gave her all his affection, but his passion, like an outlaw, had ever to hunt alone.[11]

What Mary thought about this draft, written just three years after she had married Barrie, is not recorded, although it was considerably tamer than some of his earlier efforts, such as a blackly comic story he published in 1887 in which the narrator suffers from a recurring nightmare: 'Always I see myself being married, and then I wake up with the scream of a lost soul, clammy and shivering . . .'[12] That hardly suggested great confidence in the blissful state of marriage. Yet Barrie's later soul-searching was by no means the only time he would treat life as a set of raw materials patiently waiting to be reworked into a story. Indeed, as his career continued to develop, there were times when his writing started to resemble the old clothes his thrifty mother used to recycle during his childhood, patching and decorating each item until it looked like new. Both of the forms he was now successfully pursuing had their attractions in this respect. In his fiction, he had learned to treat the page as a mask he could hide behind, allowing sentimental involvement and cool detachment to switch places from one moment to the next. Theatre was even more attractive in terms of its potential for trying on new identities and creating an unpredictable play of voices. On the stage, Barrie's characters could utter his thoughts without him having to accept responsibility for anything they said. More particularly, his plays allowed him to inhabit both sides of a conversation without him having to agree with either of them. As he later explained, dialogue was a form that 'fascinated me from the moment I fell into it and found that I could swim'.[13] It meant that he

[11] J. M. Barrie, *Tommy and Grizel* (New York: Charles Scribner's Sons, 1900), 465–86.
[12] J. M. Barrie, 'My Ghastly Dream', *Edinburgh Evening Dispatch* (1887), cited in Birkin, *J. M. Barrie and the Lost Boys*, 27.
[13] J. M. Barrie, *The Greenwood Hat, Being a Memoir of James Anon* (London: Peter Davies Ltd, 1930), 267.

could melt into other lives, like the hero of his two most successful novels so far, but he could also step outside the action and watch himself talking as if he were someone else.

In 1897, Barrie's notebooks were busy with a new subject: three young brothers he had met in Kensington Gardens. Five-year-old George and 4-year-old Jack Llewelyn Davies were easy to spot in their bright red tam-o'shanters, and soon Barrie had befriended them and their baby brother Peter, together with their nanny Mary Hodgson. If Barrie proved to be a surprisingly fascinating companion for three small boys, it is probably because he gave so few signs of realizing he was actually an adult. Wearing an overcoat that was several sizes too large for him, as if he was still secretly hoping to grow into it, and accompanied by a St Bernard dog named Porthos that made him look proportionately even smaller, he was every inch a suitable playfellow. He knew a great deal about cricket; he had a dog that could play hide-and-seek and get up on its hind legs for boxing matches; he could waggle his ears and make his eyebrows move up and down independently like trained caterpillars. He even seemed to be on intimate terms with fairies, and as he made up stories for the boys the atmosphere of Kensington Gardens subtly changed around them until it was full of invisible darting forces. Another child, who visited the Barries in Scotland, recalled the effort he put into these stories:

One evening we saw a pea-pod lying in the hollow of a great tree-trunk, and we brought it to Mr Barrie. There, inside, was a tiny letter, folded inside the pod, that a fairy had written. Mr Barrie said he could read fairy writing and read it to us. We received several more, in pea-pods, before the end of our visit.[14]

On Barrie's side, the Davies boys were good company but even better copy, and his notebooks quickly filled up with their unintentionally fascinating antics:

—George burying his face not to show crying.
—Little White Bird book described to me by George.
—*L. W. B.* Telling George what love is . . . in answer to George's inquiries abt how to write a story.
—*L. W. B.* What George said while walking me round the Round Pond (abt what to have for this birthday—ship—greek armour—book &c.)—I sneer.

---

[14] Pamela Maude, *Worlds Away* (London: Heinemann, 1964), 145.

—The queer pleasure it gives when George tells me to lace his shoes, &c.
—*L. W. B.* The boys disgrace one in shops by asking shopkeeper abt his
most private affairs. Shopkeeper &c. takes me for their father (I affect
rage).[15]

It is tempting to dismiss this sort of thing as misty-eyed or mawkish,
but in fact Barrie had a briskly no-nonsense attitude when it came to
the behaviour of small boys. He was fully aware that they were selfish
as well as loving, and that although they could become completely
absorbed in some minor task (creating a fiendishly complicated knot, or
bowling the perfect googly), they were also easily distracted, living
mostly in the present tense, and thus incapable of true loyalty. What
Barrie particularly admired was their freewheeling spirit of mockery,
which allowed them to be fiercely committed to whatever they were
doing, while also being ready at any moment to step back and poke
fun at it. This was similar to the attitude Barrie adopted towards his
own writing, so it is probably not surprising that he soon enlisted
eager but sceptical George in the act of storytelling. Before long their
relationship had become another opportunity for creative dialogue, as
they took turns to tell a story while repeatedly interrupting and inter-
preting each other. As Barrie later explained the process in *The Little
White Bird* (1902), when it came to creating a new story, 'First I tell it
to him, and then he tells it to me, the understanding being that it is
quite a different story; and then I retell it with his additions, and so
we go on until no one could say whether it is more his story or mine'
(p. 12). Soon their attention would turn to making up some adventures for George's baby brother. Peter Pan was on his way.

Meanwhile Barrie continued to cultivate his relationship with the
Davies family, after meeting the boys' mother, Sylvia, at a dinner
party and then being introduced to their barrister father Arthur. Not
unreasonably, Arthur was wary of this charming but moody author
who seemed to have unofficially adopted his sons, despite the fact that
he and his wife were still very much alive. However, eventually they
agreed that the whole family would spend part of the summer of 1901
in the village of Tilford, Surrey, a five-minute walk from Barrie's
holiday home of Black Lake Cottage. If Arthur (glum but stoic) and
Sylvia (puzzled but grateful) responded in a measured way to the hos-
pitality offered by Barrie and his wife, their sons were unapologetically

[15] Cited in Birkin, *J. M. Barrie and the Lost Boys*, 56.

gleeful. For several weeks they enjoyed a steady diet of Barrie's stories, in which pirates and desert islands mostly replaced fairies and pea-pods, together with games in the pines that surrounded Black Lake Cottage and swimming in the lake itself. After they returned home they discovered that he had produced a printed souvenir of the time they had spent as a lopsided band of brothers, something to make those warm summer days last much longer than their own fickle memories. *The Boy Castaways of Black Lake Island* was a proper book, bound in maroon cloth and printed on thick cream paper with gilt edges, published by Barrie's usual firm of Constable in a strictly limited edition of two copies. It was also one of the sweetest and strangest things Barrie ever wrote. Most of the pages were taken up with a selection of photographs, gummed in place and protected by gauzy sheets of tissue paper, which showed the boys playing outdoors. However, accompanying these photographs were blood-quickening captions, a detailed list of contents, and a mock-preface supposedly written by Peter Llewelyn Davies, all of which indicated that this was not just an ordinary photo album. It was a set of glimpses into an adventure story that had been acted out all summer, with the Davies boys as the three heroes and Porthos gamely taking on a variety of supporting roles including (after a papier-mâché mask was slipped over his head) an unusually docile tiger. Like Peter Pan looking through the nursery window at the end of the play, as Barrie squinted through the viewfinder of his camera, these photographs captured a world he could observe from the outside but from which he would always be excluded. However, they also represented a more optimistic alternative. For whether the boys were pictured posing with outsize axes ('We set out to be wrecked') or acting out a perilous rescue mission ('Jack hung suspended between heaven and earth'),[16] Barrie had stopped the clock at precisely those moments when they were at their happiest, and preserved them in glossy black and white. 'To be born is to be wrecked on an island',[17] he would later claim in a preface to a 1913 reissue of his favourite boyhood story, R. M. Ballantyne's *The Coral Island* (1858), but in *The Boy Castaways of Black Lake Island* he had created an environment in which childhood could remain forever safe

---

[16] J. M. Barrie, *The Boy Castaways of Black Lake Island* (London: privately printed, 1901), n.p.

[17] J. M. Barrie, 'Preface' to R. M. Ballantyne, *The Coral Island* (London: James Nisbet & Co. Ltd, 1913).

from the rising waters of age. Here was one group of little boys who would stay little.

For his next major play, which received its premiere in November 1902, Barrie decided to take some of these ideas and rework them into a fable about adults. The main action of *The Admirable Crichton* centres on a shipwreck that maroons a group of wealthy but shallow English men and women, together with their butler, on a desert island. Before long the artificial social order is replaced by a natural alternative in which the eponymous butler takes control. It is like watching Jeeves gravely peel off one of his white gloves to give Bertie Wooster a long-deserved slap. Yet while Crichton shows off his impressive survival skills, which include making a primitive sawmill and hooking up a set of electric lights, his previous employers soon regress to a comically infantile state. One female character, Lady Mary, behaves 'like a naughty, sulky child', and when Crichton tells her off she 'screws up her face like a baby and cries'.[18] More optimistically, as she casts off the shackles of civilization she also reinvents herself as a genuine child of nature. The first time we see her after two years on the island, she resembles a 'splendid boy, clad in skins',[19] whose weapons include a bow and arrows and a blowpipe, and who enters the family's log cabin not via the door but by leaping through a window. At the end of the play, she returns home and settles back into the grown-up world of whalebone corsets and marriage, but although she confesses that 'I am ashamed of myself',[20] Barrie continued to be charmed by the imaginative possibilities of the stage as a kind of island where an adult could play at being a child.

Add a selection of seeds planted in his earlier fiction, such as the hero of *Tommy and Grizel*, who is so afraid his parents will make him grow up that he runs into a wood 'and is running still, singing to himself because he is always to be a boy' (this 'Wandering Child' also crows 'Oh, am I not a wonder!' whenever he does anything impressive),[21] and further lingering echoes from Barrie's childhood reading, such as the crocodile that a fearful child thinks is living on the island in *The Swiss Family Robinson*, and the main elements of *Peter Pan* were starting to be assembled. The trigger seems to have been an evening

[18] J. M. Barrie, *The Admirable Crichton* (New York: Charles Scribner's Sons, 1928), 116–17.

[19] Ibid. 105.   [20] Ibid. 142.

[21] J. M. Barrie, *Tommy and Grizel* (London: Cassell and Co. Ltd, 1925), 399, 74.

in December 1901, when Barrie took the Davies boys to see Seymour Hicks's latest Christmas spectacular *Bluebell in Fairyland*. Billed as 'A Musical Dream-Play', it was a modern fairy tale in which a flower girl sees Peter the Cat outside her garret window, and decides to accompany him to Fairyland, where she meets an assortment of magical creatures, including twins Blob and Blib and an elusive fairy named Will-o'-the-Wisp. The story Barrie now started to plan under the loose working title of 'Fairy Play' would take all these ingredients, shake them together, and transform them into a new story that somehow gave every indication of having been there all along.

*

Barrie had already sketched out several possible scenarios for his 'Fairy Play' when he started to wonder if he might approach it instead through the figure of *Tommy and Grizel*'s 'Wandering Child'. In 1902 he jotted down some ideas in one of his notebooks:

> —*Play. 'The Happy Boy'*: Boy who can't grow up—runs away from pain & death—is caught *wild*. (*End* escapes)
> —*The Mother*—treated from child's point of view—how mother scolds, wheedles, &c.—children must be tickled by recognising truth of scenes.
> —Peter [Davies]: 'Mother, how did we get to know you?'
> —Peter Pan.[22]

'Pan' wasn't an altogether surprising choice of name for his hero. Since the 1890s, a minor cult of Pan had developed in certain literary circles, providing a classical alibi for writers who wanted to explore potentially risky themes of social and sexual transgression. Examples included stories by Max Beerbohm, Robert Louis Stevenson, Arthur Machen, Somerset Maugham, Algernon Blackwood, H. H. Munro ('Saki'), E. M. Forster, and a little later Kenneth Grahame, whose novel *The Wind in the Willows* (1908) includes an episode in which Ratty and Mole search the river for a missing baby otter, only to discover him happily sleeping between the hooves of a mysterious being with 'curved horns' and 'rippling muscles', after they are drawn to a flower-fringed island by 'the thin, clear happy call of the distant piping'.[23] By the turn of the century, the edge of potential danger in such encounters had largely been smoothed away, and Barrie's creation of

---

[22] Cited in Birkin, *J. M. Barrie and the Lost Boys*, 95.
[23] Kenneth Grahame, *The Wind in the Willows* (New York: Charles Scribner's Sons, 1908), 155, 151.

a boy dressed only in 'autumn leaves and cobwebs' (p. 348) reflected a common desire to turn Pan into a more youthful and playful figure. Maurice Hewlett, father of Cecco, who sometimes accompanied Barrie and the Davies boys in Kensington Gardens, had already published a play entitled *Pan and the Young Shepherd* (1899), which opened with the line, 'Boy, boy, wilt thou be a boy for ever?',[24] and similar questions echoed through several other attempts to find a place for Pan in modern life. Whereas previously he had been used to celebrate man's deep hidden connections with the natural world, the Edwardian Pan was slowly being transformed into a reminder of another potentially savage state that adults had outgrown: childhood. This chimed strongly with Barrie, who had long been fascinated by the imaginative creativity, moral carelessness, and acts of random cruelty that ordinary boys displayed every day. Grafting Pan onto one of this tribe was therefore partly a joke, but it was also a serious suggestion that boys might indeed be related to the mythic figure with a beautiful face but the shaggy hindquarters and hooves of a goat. For a boy already existed in that strange limbo state identified by Solomon Caw in Barrie's novel *The Little White Bird* (1902) when referring to Peter Pan as a 'little half-and-half' and a 'Betwixt-and-Between' (p. 15). A boy's ability to strut around like a god could not disguise the fact that he was also capable of acting like a beast.

Giving his hero the name of 'Peter', rather than Michael or George, was probably a matter of alliterative convenience (there is no more logic in him being called Peter Pan than there is in Peter Piper picking a peck of pickled peppers in the well-known tongue-twister), although the reference in Barrie's notebook to a 'Happy Boy' being 'caught *wild*' suggests he may have had an additional model in mind. Peter the Wild Boy had long been a source of fascination among those who wondered whether it might be possible for human beings to exist in a wholly natural state, and whether we would like it much if it were. According to one popular account, Peter was discovered in 1725 in a wood near Hanover 'walking on his hands and feet, climbing trees like a squirrel, and feeding on grass and moss . . . he was supposed to be about thirteen years old and could not speak'. Barrie would probably have sympathized with certain aspects of Peter's life, such as

[24] Maurice Hewlett, *Pan and the Young Shepherd* (London and New York: John Lane, The Bodley Head, 1899), 1.

his 'low stature' and the fact that he did not 'show any attention to
women . . . except when purposely or jocosely forced into an amour'.[25]
In effect, Peter the Wild Boy was a character from a fairy tale who had
accidentally wandered into real life, and his contemporaries weren't
slow to pick up on this suggestion, dressing him up in forest green
and making him the subject of stories that applauded his natural
innocence or shuddered over his cultural backwardness. Barrie might
especially have appreciated the fact that Peter remained trapped in
a kind of blank childhood state long after he had officially become an
adult. Not only was he unable to tell right from wrong, he seemed
wholly indifferent to anything that existed beyond the shifting sur-
faces of life. As Michael Newton explains in his history of feral children, summarizing a pamphlet on the case published in 1726 by the
novelist Daniel Defoe, 'nothing impresses him: everything flattens
out under his steady, unconcerned gaze, and he would watch a woman
burnt at the stake as unmoved as if he were watching a dance at the
theatre'.[26] It isn't far from this to Peter Pan's reaction, in the first draft
of Barrie's play, when Hook is swallowed by a giant crocodile rearing
up out of the Serpentine: 'Peter has been looking on unconcernedly
at the incident', reads the stage direction, 'and still whistling' (p. 137).
As for the rest of the story, if you add in a hint of Gothic menace
(there is something oddly vampire-like about the way Peter Pan flies
through windows and never seems to get any older), widespread cultural anxieties about growing up too fast (one advice manual published
a few years later recommended that the best way to handle a stroppy
teenage girl was to 'introduce her to camping, volley ball, folk-dancing,
etc., to counteract the tendency to loll, stay in the house and act like
a lady'),[27] and several other pieces of writing that appear to have
snagged in Barrie's memory (Robert Louis Stevenson's poem 'My
Shadow' describes a child being separated from its shadow, which
remains fast asleep in bed when the child gets up before sunrise),
Barrie's laconic 1902 note about 'Peter Pan' starts to look less like

[25] Henry Wilson and James Caulfield, *The Book of Wonderful Characters: Memoirs and Anecdotes of Remarkable and Eccentric Persons in All Ages and Countries* (London: Reeves and Turner, 1869), 133, 139.
[26] Michael Newton, *Savage Girls and Wild Boys: A History of Feral Children* (London: Faber and Faber, 2002), 44.
[27] William Byron Forbrush, *Guide Book to Childhood* (1921), cited in Gillian Avery, 'The Cult of Peter Pan', *Word and Image* 2:2 (1986), 182.

a character's name than the solution to an immensely complicated cultural puzzle.

By the time he wrote this note, Barrie had already tried out the character in a piece of fiction, and the experiment had been so successful that what should have been a minor role came close to hijacking the entire story. In *The Little White Bird*, Peter appears as the central figure in one of the tales told by the narrator, a 'gentle, whimsical, lonely old bachelor' named Captain W——.[28] Like Barrie, the Captain enjoys long walks in Kensington Gardens with a St Bernard dog named Porthos, and as the story develops he acts as the anonymous benefactor to a needy young couple before befriending their son David, a little boy who is closely modelled on George Llewelyn Davies, and who also happens to have the same name as Barrie's dead brother. Already there is enough material here to keep a whole team of psychoanalysts busy for years, but soon things become even more complicated. As David grows older, the Captain comes to regard him as a kind of adopted son, and himself as a loving rival to David's real parents. This manifests itself in both affectionate and more hostile ways. 'I once had a photograph taken of David being hanged on a tree', the Captain laconically informs us, which he then sends to the boy's mother. 'You can't think of all the subtle ways of grieving her I have.'[29]

Some parts of *The Little White Bird* are hard to read now, particularly a scene in which the Captain borrows David for an evening, bathes him, undresses him ('I remained wonderfully calm until I came somewhat too suddenly to his little braces, which agitated me profusely'),[30] and eventually lies awake in the same bed as his little guest, who goes to sleep tightly clutching the Captain's finger. Other parts of the story reverberate with echoes of the period Barrie had recently spent with the Davies family. Not only is Peter Pan exiled to an island in the Serpentine, becoming an outlaw at the heart of Kensington Gardens, but Barrie also found ways of incorporating memories of *The Boy Castaways of Black Lake Island* into his new book. Another of the Captain's stories begins with a shipwreck. 'I was the sole survivor of the ill-fated *Anna Pink*',[31] he explains, before going on to describe how David and another boy carry him to the safety of their island hut. This is only a minor variation on the third photograph in *The Boy*

<hr>

[28] J. M. Barrie, *The Little White Bird* (London: Hodder & Stoughton, 1902), 55.
[29] Ibid. 233.   [30] Ibid. 230.   [31] Ibid. 273.

Castaways of Black Lake Island, which showed the Davies boys happily splashing around in Black Lake, and was captioned 'We were the
sole survivors of the ill-fated brig *Anna Pink*.'[32] (Barrie's habit of
self-borrowing didn't stop there: the original draft of *The Admirable
Crichton* included Ernest exclaiming 'Wrecked, wrecked, wrecked! . . .
We are the sole survivors of Lord Loam's steam yacht Anna Pink.')[33]
Other parts of *The Little White Bird* show Barrie experimenting with
ideas that would eventually make their way into the longer version of
Peter Pan, such as Peter's use of a bird's nest as an improvised boat,
which would later bob into view again in a new scene set in the Mermaids'
Lagoon, or the fact that the schoolmaster Pilkington 'fishes all day in
the Gardens' for boys, 'baiting his hook' with the promise of allowing
them to wear real knickerbockers at his school.[34] Soon this conceit
would be translated into the cartoonish wickedness of Captain Hook,
who uses a giant version of a fishing hook to slash at his enemies and
grapple with the Lost Boys.

Most reviewers were impressed by Barrie's new publication, even
if they weren't always sure why. 'To analyse its merits and defects',
observed one critic, 'would be to vivisect a fairy.'[35] But by now Barrie's
thoughts were turning to the stage as a more natural home for Peter
Pan, the central figure in a story-within-a-story that had already grown
until it filled almost a third of *The Little White Bird*. There were several reasons for this, beyond the simple fact that the stage was an ideal
environment for depicting an island like Neverland, which has fixed
physical borders but otherwise no limits to what it might contain.
(Other popular children's books had already celebrated the fact that,
once a child's imagination got to work on it, the same physical location could contain any number of possible worlds: in *The Golden Age*
(1895), Kenneth Grahame pointed out that when adults looked at
a duck pond in the garden, they did not realize it was also a miniature
ocean for pirates to sail on, just as they unaccountably failed to spot
the Indians and bison that were lurking in the shrubbery, 'though the
whole place swarmed with such portents'.)[36] The first reason is that

[32] Barrie, *The Boy Castaways of Black Lake Island*, n.p.
[33] See Birkin, *J. M. Barrie and the Lost Boys*, 92.
[34] Barrie, *The Little White Bird*, 268.
[35] *TLS* review cited in Jacqueline Rose, *The Case of Peter Pan, or The Impossibility of
Children's Fiction*, rev. edn (Basingstoke: Palgrave Macmillan, 1994), 23.
[36] Kenneth Grahame, *The Golden Age* (London: Thomas Nelson and Sons, 1895), 6.

the theatre afforded excellent opportunities for investigating the hazy middle ground in a child's mind between what is real and what is true. In 1908, Barrie wrote a programme note for the first production of *Peter Pan* in France (see Appendix II), in which he pointed out that the action of the play is supposed to take place in that 'strange, magical half hour between day and night, between wakefulness and sleep', when a child lies in bed and 'the playing and the dreaming meet in his mind as one' (p. 412). *Peter Pan* invited audience members of all ages to return to that time, because the theatre was already a place in which the distinction between playing and real life was richly uncertain. A second reason for turning the story of Peter Pan into a play lay in theatre's ability to suspend life's usual rules. For while the crocodile that pursues Hook may be a scaly reminder of the inevitable march of time, including a quiet pun on the clock it has swallowed (it is a croco-*dial*), on the stage this idea rubs up against a magical alternative in which the clock can always be paused or made to run backwards. Real time is overlaid by story time. Age is provisional, a matter of belief rather than destiny, which is what allows an adult actor to play Peter Pan without any sense of incongruity. Even the laws of physics become optional: when Wendy and her brothers rise into the air and start to fly around the nursery, Barrie's success can be measured not in how clearly we see the wires, but in whether or not it occurs to us to look for them. Done well, the flying scenes are more than a playfully literal version of theatre's suspension of disbelief. They are a celebration of our ability to tunnel back into the past and forget what our adult eyes are telling us.

Barrie wrote his first full draft under a carefully neutral title: *A Play*. Anyone familiar with the later published script of *Peter Pan* is likely to spot many minor variants between the two versions, such as the fact that Michael Darling was originally called Alexander, possibly because of its mock-heroic associations with Alexander the Great, and Tinker Bell was Tippytoe or Tippy for short. Otherwise the first two acts already contained most of the events that would eventually find their way into the 1904 performance script: Wendy sewing on Peter Pan's shadow, the flight to Neverland (a name Barrie seems to have taken from a remote region of Australia that had already been the setting for several travel books and adventure stories, including A. W. Stirling's *The Never Never Land: A Ride in North Queensland* (1884) and Wilson Barrett's *The Never-Never Land* (1902)), the Lost

Boys, bloody skirmishes with pirates and Indians, and finally the long flight home. Then the play took an unexpected turn.

During a pantomime interlude set in Kensington Gardens, Peter and Wendy escape from Hook through Tippy's help, as she creates some human camouflage by turning all the Lost Boys into Clowns and all the passing schoolgirls into Columbines. With its slapstick violence and magical transformations, the scene might seem like an experiment with a wholly different genre, as if Barrie was a classical pianist who had paused a concerto performance to attempt a few jazz riffs. In fact it was less a variation on the play than a restoration of its home key, because from the start Barrie had intended *A Play* to be a new kind of pantomime. The hero was a version of the principal boy, usually played by a thigh-slapping actress in a skimpy costume, the crocodile needed to be performed by two actors, like a savage version of the pantomime horse, and when Nibs scornfully asks Curly 'How could a gentleman be a lady?' (p. 98), he is also alluding to the tradition of the pantomime dame.[37] Even the hints of literary burlesque in Barrie's dialogue chimed with similar effects in pantomime scripts. 'All stabbed but six, and they are prisoners' (p. 116), Tootles joyfully tells Peter after the battle with the pirates: a line of near-perfect blank verse, as if he was secretly auditioning for a role in a Shakespearean tragedy. The play's pantomime heritage was perhaps clearer to Barrie's contemporaries than it is to us now—one reviewer described it as 'Mr. Barrie's *Peter Pan*-tomime'[38]—and as a genre that had become known for its tendency to mix up vulgarity and innocence, dirty jokes and heartfelt pathos, it was the perfect theatrical home for a 'Betwixt-and-Between' character like Peter Pan. 'You know, Peter,' Wendy tells him in *A Play*, 'everybody grows up, except clowns', and Peter replies 'Then I want to be a clown' (p. 97). He is probably referring to more than just the prospect of a lifetime spent clowning around, because under their costumes and thick make-up it is impossible to tell how old a clown is; they are theatrical immortals. Pantomime fitted the strange outcrops of Barrie's imagination in other ways too. One of the most popular moments in any stage performance was the transformation scene, in

---

[37] Donna R. White and C. Anita Tarr list some of the other pantomime ingredients adopted by Barrie, including the fact that the original English Harlequin, John Rich, always portrayed his character hatching from an egg on stage; *J. M. Barrie's Peter Pan In and Out of Time* (Lanham, MD: The Scarecrow Press, 2006), pp. vii–xix.

[38] Cited in Rose, *The Case of Peter Pan*, 95.

which a pumpkin could swell into a glass coach or a set of rags froth up into a ball gown, usually accompanied by dazzling lighting effects and pieces of elaborate stage machinery clanking into place. As Dickens wrote in 'A Christmas Tree' (1850), in a pantomime 'Everything is capable, with the greatest ease, of being changed into Anything; and "Nothing is, but thinking makes it so." '[39] A similar idea lay at the heart of Barrie's play, in which the transformative abilities of the child's imagination were allied to a celebration of theatre itself: a place where imaginary foods can be eaten with as much relish as real ones, and it is possible to kill your enemies without even hurting them. The world Barrie was starting to build would indeed be one in which nothing was but thinking made it so.

The idea that everything was capable of being changed into anything also lay at the heart of Barrie's habits as a writer. For in his eyes writing was a fluid process far more than it was a fixed product, and he relentlessly tinkered with his work both before and after publication. Indeed, this may have been another reason why he was so attracted to pantomime as a theatrical model. Pantomime scripts were notoriously provisional affairs, never completed but instead being altered and added to throughout a run, and Barrie was similarly reluctant to leave the script of his new play alone. As the opening night of what he now called *Peter Pan* approached at London's 900-seat Duke of York's theatre, while the actors practised flying around the stage on their specially designed harnesses, and the complicated sets were hoisted into place, he was still finding it difficult to decide when it had reached a point that made it suitable for performance. The ending gave him particular trouble, even after he had quietly shuffled off the more obvious pantomime elements into a one-act play entitled *Pantaloon*, first performed at the Duke of York's theatre four days after the original run of *Peter Pan* ended, in which Peter's boast about being a little bird that has broken out of the egg was echoed in Barrie's description of Harlequin's patchwork costume being sewn together from fragments of cloth given to him 'when the world was so young that pieces of the original egg-shell still adhered to it'.[40] As late as 21 December, the night before *Peter Pan* was scheduled to open, a mechanical lift collapsed, taking half the scenery with it, and director Dion Boucicault was forced to postpone the opening night

---

[39] Charles Dickens, 'A Christmas Tree', *Household Words* 39 (21 December 1850), 292.
[40] J. M. Barrie, *Pantaloon*, in *Half Hours* (New York: Charles Scribner's Sons, 1914), 9.

until the 27th. The scenery for the final Kensington Gardens scene still wasn't finished, and as the carpenters refused to work over Christmas, once again Barrie had to rewrite the ending, by now his fifth attempt. Some of the scene changes were taking up to twenty minutes to complete, which required the addition of some hastily written 'front-cloth' scenes, one of which the actor playing Hook, Gerald du Maurier (Sylvia Llewelyn Davies's brother), had to pad out by doing impressions of Henry Irving. There were also fears that the emotional climax of the play, Tinker Bell's death and magical recovery, might produce merely embarrassed coughs in the auditorium, so Barrie arranged that if nobody clapped the orchestra would down their instruments and lead the applause. With its large cast, elaborate scenery, and seemingly endless technical challenges, *Peter Pan* had cost Barrie's unswervingly loyal producer Charles Frohman a small fortune to stage, and as the curtain rose on the opening night it seemed highly likely that it would prove to be an expensive flop.

What the audience saw on that night partly depended on how intimate with the author they were. For Arthur and Sylvia Llewelyn Davies, the opening scene in the nursery was a comic version of their own domestic arrangements that had become tangled up with certain aspects of Barrie's life, such as a dog closely modelled on Porthos which trotted around being a faithful nurse to children who drew much of their character, and even some of their dialogue, from the Davies boys. ('Mother, how did you get to know me?' asks Michael Darling as he is being put to bed (p. 341).) For everyone else, it was like settling down for a bedtime story and discovering that the characters had come unexpectedly to life. By the time Wendy and her brothers arrived in Neverland, the stage had transformed itself into a giant pop-up book. Barrie's script for *A Play* had included a sketch map of Neverland, showing mysterious areas marked 'wood', a giant central river, and Wendy's house puffing smoke out of its chimney, but also large blank areas that the reader's imagination had to fill in (p. 78). The Neverland depicted in the Duke of York's theatre was far busier with physical detail, but it retained the same basic mixture of the actual and the possible. Although there were 'practical' trees that acrobats could swing from, the dialogue was full of reminders that everything on show was make-believe. Part-real and part-imaginary, the theatrical Neverland was the perfect environment for play, and no character revealed this more clearly on that opening night than Peter Pan himself. Reinventing himself and his surroundings from one moment to the next, as played by the actress Nina Boucicault he was something like the spirit of play itself. And rather than just watching his adventures from afar, Barrie's play encouraged the first night audience to join in. When Tinker Bell was dying, and they helped to save her by clapping or waving their handkerchiefs, it gave them the same power that Peter himself holds over his kingdom, which comes alive and starts to look busy only when it knows he is on his way home. For a fleeting moment, watching *Peter Pan* allowed the audience to imagine what it would feel like to *be* Peter Pan. Of course the difference is that most people only believe in fairies for the time it takes to bring Tinker Bell back to life. The spell lifts and the game ends, just as the Darling children must leave Neverland and return to the nursery. But on that opening night the audience were confronted with a far more troubling alternative. After all of Barrie's rewritings, the final tableau depicted Peter Pan outside the Darlings' house, giving a last look through the nursery window as the curtain fell, forever barred from the ordinary life going on inside. It turned out that always to be a little boy and have fun wasn't a reason for crowing after all. In some ways it was a fate worse than death.

*

At his home in White Plains, just outside New York City, Charles Frohman awaited news of the first night from his London manager. According to one friend, he was like a nervous father-to-be pacing up and down outside the delivery room. 'Will it never come?' he kept repeating. Finally a cablegram arrived: 'PETER PAN ALL RIGHT. LOOKS LIKE A BIG SUCCESS.'[41] That turned out to be a major understatement. *Peter Pan* was a critical and commercial triumph. While there were one or two dissenting voices—the writer Anthony Hope responded to the first appearance of the Lost Boys by groaning 'Oh, for an hour of Herod!'—most people agreed that Barrie had created an instant classic.[42] Before long, children were writing to Wendy with their reactions to her role in the play ('you acted the best i think you Flew very well . . . When i am in bed i alweys think you and Peter Pan are coming in after me'), together with candid confessions and shy overtures of friendship. 'Have you a mummy', wrote

---

[41] Cited in Birkin, *J. M. Barrie and the Lost Boys*, 115.
[42] Cited in Roger Lancelyn Green, *Fifty Years of Peter Pan* (London: Peter Davies, 1954), 85–6.

one little girl, 'I have not. I have a nurse. I would like you for my mummy but daddy says you don't want me and he would not let me go.'[43] A number of adults enjoyed similar fantasies that in watching Barrie's play they were somehow eavesdropping on real life. 'Merry Christmas, O dear & honoured Peter Pan!' reads one card sent by Mark Twain,[44] as if Barrie had not invented his most famous character but merely plucked him out of the air.

Soon the play had become as familiar a part of the Christmas season as turkey or Santa Claus. Another reason Barrie was attracted to theatre, it seems, was that it was a world of transformations where, night after night, everything stayed reassuringly the same. 'Children should never be allowed to go to bed', announces Johnny Depp, playing a Hollywood-handsome version of Barrie in the 2004 film *Finding Neverland*, because 'they always wake up a day older'. However, in writing *Peter Pan*, Barrie had created a story that would always begin with Michael saying 'I won't go to bed' (p. 338), and would never make him. Despite Hook's grisly fate, for the most part Neverland was a world that kept its characters safe in the moment of performance. In this context, perhaps it is not surprising that, for several decades following director Dion Boucicault's original production, revivals of *Peter Pan* remained largely unchanged from one year to the next. The same sets and costumes were recycled long after they had become shabby and threadbare; the same bits of stage business were carefully copied. Even when Hook was given a new jacket, it was a theatrical tradition that the patched-up jacket of Gerald du Maurier should be worn on at least one night of each run. Increasingly, the play started to live up to its title: just as Barrie had imagined Peter Pan reappearing period-ically to take Wendy's children, and then her children's children, off to Neverland, so his play returned annually to the stage to charm new audiences with the same old stories. Meanwhile, different actors came and went. Some of them cut their teeth on the play, such as the 14-year-old Noel Coward, who acted Slightly in the 1913 revival. (One wag later observed that he only acted slightly for the rest of his career.) Others preferred to show their teeth in it, such as Ralph

[43] Valentina Bold, ' "A Love that is Real": Children's Responses to Wendy', in *Gateway to the Modern: Resituating J. M. Barrie*, ed. Valentina Bold and Andrew Nash (Glasgow: Association for Scottish Literary Studies, 2014), 169, 180.

[44] Walter Beinecke Jr. Collection at the Beinecke Rare Book and Manuscript Library, Yale University, GEN MSS 1400 16/575.

Richardson, Charles Laughton, and Boris Karloff, who all played Hook in different productions but with the same moustache-twirling menace. Not everyone lasted long in such a technically complicated play. Angela du Maurier, who performed Wendy in 1924 and 1925, once almost severed her nose in the climactic sword fight, and on another occasion lost control during a flying scene and crashed into the safety curtain like a fly splattering against a windscreen. Other actors stayed remarkably loyal to their parts: between 1906 and 1953, William Luff played the pirate Cecco for forty-five seasons, while George Shelton, who was still playing Smee when he was 78, was only half-joking when he referred to this annual stage outing as 'my old age Peter pansion'.[45] Yet even *Peter Pan* could not be wholly insulated from the relentless drift of time. 'When [the lost boys] seem to be growing up . . . Peter thins them out' (p. 180) warns the narrator of *Peter and Wendy*, and the young actors playing these parts quickly discovered that a similar rule—less lethal, but just as permanent—was applied to them too. Every December they would be measured before the start of rehearsals, and ejected from the cast if they had grown too tall. Only then could they appreciate the full pathos of that phrase 'the lost boys'; only then were they in a position to share Barrie's sense that the worst loss a boy could suffer was not his mother, or his home, but boyhood itself.

Despite the barnacles of tradition that were slowly beginning to attach themselves to his play, Barrie worked tirelessly to keep it fresh. 'I much hope you'll print it', the novelist Maurice Hewlett wrote to him after the first production,[46] but this was something Barrie resisted for many years, as if fixing *Peter Pan* onto the page would be like pinning a butterfly to a board. Long after he had revised the play for its first Broadway production in 1905, adding the Mermaids' Lagoon scene, expanding the structure to five acts, and changing a few lines to suit American tastes ('Yankee Doodle Dandy' replaced the singing of 'God Save the King' on board the pirate ship), he continued to tinker with the dialogue and refine various bits of stage business. Typically, having completed the script for 'When Wendy Grew Up: An Afterthought' in 1908 (reprinted as Appendix III), he was unable to resist adding extra afterthoughts to it in pencil, cutting out stage directions and

---

[45] Cited in Green, *Fifty Years of Peter Pan*, 145.
[46] Beinecke GEN MSS 1400 17/584.

sharpening up lines of dialogue.[47] Indeed, if one idea that is repeated with variations across his career is that life doesn't give us second chances, *Peter Pan* presented him with a far more optimistic alternative. Towards the end of his life, Barrie's secretary Cynthia Asquith observed him crouching over the fireplace in his flat at Adelphi Terrace, 'busily engrossed in mending the log fire on its great mound of ashes . . . patiently, intently, fanning grey ashes into flame'.[48] Year after year, his revisions to *Peter Pan* revealed the same nagging desire to revive what might otherwise fade and die.

Some of these changes took the form of private jokes. For example, after four of the Davies boys had become pupils at Eton, Barrie took pleasure in expanding the number of references to the school, and also wrote a spoof account of the time Captain Hook is supposed to have spent there (reprinted as Appendix V). In this way, jokes such as Hook's solemn cry 'Floreat Etona' as he is swallowed by the crocodile (p. 402) allowed Barrie to laugh at something he found genuinely distressing: the idea that the day a boy started school was also the day he stopped being a boy. That is probably why early drafts of *Peter Pan* ended with a schoolmaster named Pilkington—last seen stealing David from the narrator in *The Little White Bird*—trying to trap the Lost Boys in Kensington Gardens. For in Barrie's eyes, a schoolmaster was a grim reaper who particularly targeted children, his cane working like a scythe to slash away at their innocence and sense of fun. Other changes to the play were influenced by factors beyond Barrie's control. Some lines about fairy dust in Act 1 were added during the first run, after it was reported that several children who had seen the play were injured when they returned home and tried to fly by flinging themselves off their beds. Later, Peter Pan's line 'To die will be an awfully big adventure' (p. 379) was removed from revivals of the play during the First World War, once it became clear that this awful conflict was going to be big beyond anyone's imagination. While the poet Rupert Brooke had adored *Peter Pan*, seeing the London production at least ten times, his belief that dying for a noble cause was a heroic act—as Wendy tells the Lost Boys that 'We hope our sons will die like English gentlemen' (p. 395)—was much harder to sustain when confronted by the reality of trench warfare. Just a few weeks after the start of the conflict, Peter Pan's refusal to grow up would receive a grim echo

[47] Beinecke GEN MSS 1400 43/929.   [48] Asquith, *Portrait of Barrie*, 224.

in Lawrence Binyon's poem 'For the Fallen', published in *The Times* on 21 September 1914: 'They shall not grow old, as we that are left grow old: | Age shall not weary them, nor the years condemn.' Binyon's words were both a commemoration and a prophecy: soon it was clear that a whole generation of Lost Boys would never return to their mothers.

Barrie had recognized the tragic potential of his story from the start. In his first draft of the play 'Neverland' was 'Never, Never, Never Land', a name that was painfully close to King Lear's lament for his dead child Cordelia: 'Thou'lt come no more, | Never, never, never, never, never.'[49] It was a literary shadow that would be remorselessly fleshed out over the years. One by one, those close to Barrie died, often in ways that seemed like savage parodies of his own writing. First it was Arthur Llewelyn Davies, in 1907, after a malignant tumour was discovered on his face. An operation to remove part of his jaw and one of his cheekbones destroyed his ability to speak, meaning that he could only communicate on scraps of paper. One note, headed *Among the things I think about*, reads like a desperate echo of Barrie's jottings in his little red notebooks:

Michael going to school
Porthgwarra and S's blue dress
Burpham garden
Kirkby view across the valley . . .
Jack bathing
Peter answering chaff
Nicholas in the garden
George always

Barrie nursed him tenderly, and while Arthur slept he made some notes of his own, including an idea for a play called *The 1,000 Nightingales* that showed he still had the writer's chip of ice in his heart even when it was close to breaking: 'A hero who is dying. "Poor devil, he'll be dead in six months" . . . He is in his rooms awaiting end—schemes abandoned—still he's a man, dying a man . . . Everything going splendidly for him (love &c.) when audience hears of his doom.'[50] Soon afterwards, Sylvia was diagnosed with inoperable cancer, dying in 1910, and at that point Barrie's compulsion to revise once again got

[49] *King Lear*, 5.3.371–2.
[50] Cited in Birkin, *J. M. Barrie and the Lost Boys*, 135–6.

the better of him. Sylvia's will included a line about how she hoped
that Jenny, the sister of the children's nanny, would come to help her
look after them, but as transcribed by Barrie it was not 'Jenny' but
'Jimmy' who should step in as a surrogate parent. As he formally
adopted the boys in any case, it was hardly necessary to alter his copy
of the will in this way, but whether or not it was a deliberate act it revealed
once again the blurred line in his imagination between role-playing
and real life. Next to die was George, who went off to fight in France
with a copy of *The Little White Bird* tucked into his pocket and was
shot in 1915. Later in the same year, Charles Frohman was on the
Lusitania when it was torpedoed off the Irish coast, and was reported
to have refused a place on one of the lifeboats by declaring 'Why fear
death? It is the greatest adventure in life.'[51] Then Michael, the boy for
whom Barrie had the deepest and most complicated love, drowned in
1921 while swimming in Oxford, possibly in a suicide pact with another
undergraduate. Even Peter, who survived Barrie by more than twenty
years, did not entirely succeed in escaping the gravitational pull of the
work he once described as 'that terrible masterpiece'. After a lifetime
being pursued by shouting headlines—'PETER PAN FINED FOR
SPEEDING', 'PETER PAN GETS MARRIED', 'PETER PAN BECOMES
PUBLISHER'—in 1960 he committed suicide by throwing himself in
front of a London underground train.[52] Under the ground: the place
where the lost boys live.

    Surrounded by so much unhappiness, Barrie's inability to leave his
most famous creation alone became far more understandable. Peter
Pan was the one boy who would never leave him, and after republish-
ing the central chapters of *The Little White Bird* separately in 1906
as a handsomely illustrated volume entitled *Peter Pan in Kensington
Gardens*, he set about developing his story in ways that would see it
return in many different forms over the following years. 'Mr Barrie
has often been asked to write a short narrative or libretto of his
immortal children's play', reported *The Bookman* in January 1907,
'and has as often refused.'[53] Not until 1911 did Barrie finally publish
Peter and Wendy, a version that lifted most of its dialogue from the
still unpublished play, and filtered everything through a narrator who
teeters between a simple child's-eye view of events ('Wendy came first,
then John, then Michael' (p. 144)) and an adult perspective that is

[51] Ibid. 247.   [52] Ibid. 1.   [53] Cited in Rose, *The Case of Peter Pan*, 66.

thickly veined with irony. The narrator's repeated use of 'we' further complicates this picture, as it is never altogether clear whether he is referring to adults, children, or some kind of wistfully imagined hybrid—figures like Wendy, perhaps, who enjoys playing at being a grown-up by scolding the Lost Boys and telling them bedtime stories, or like Barrie himself, who was never happier than when shrugging off adulthood like a snake shedding its skin. (One of the few surviving letters he wrote to Peter and Michael Llewelyn Davies wistfully adopts the persona of a clumsy schoolboy, signing off 'i am your frend J. M. Barrie'.)[54] The overall effect is a kind of narrative double vision, in which the reader is encouraged to recapture the innocent excitement of playing a game while repeatedly being reminded of the rules.

Nor was that the end of Barrie's busy-fingered rewritings of his story. For many years he had been fascinated by cinema, even devoting part of summer 1914 to making a film in which several other writers, including George Bernard Shaw and G. K. Chesterton, dressed up as cowboys and acted out a spoof Western in the wilds of Hertfordshire. Between 1918 and 1921, Barrie painstakingly wrote several drafts of a silent film treatment for *Peter Pan* that showed off his interest in the technological possibilities of this new medium, although it was never made. (The first full-length adaptation to appear on screen was released by Paramount Pictures in 1924; Barrie's friend Sir William Wiseman loyally claimed it was 'the best picture I have ever seen'.)[55] Barrie was especially interested in cinema's games of scale: just as the diminutive Tinker Bell could fill a whole screen, so a small child could be made even smaller through use of technical trickery. In Barrie's film script, Wendy is 'subjected to alteration' by Peter and the Lost Boys: 'Their object is to make her shorter, so she is laid down and Peter pushes her feet and Slightly her head with the result that she is telescoped' (p. 299). Cinema was a new Neverland in which reality was subject to the whims of the imagination. Barrie also continued to pursue similar themes in more traditional forms. As early as 1905, he had written some notes under the heading of 'Character' about a man 'who fails to develop normally, whose spirit remains young in an ageing body, constantly upset by the painful astonishment known to all of us when some outlawed proof suddenly jars our inward conviction of perpetual

---

[54] Beinecke GEN MSS 1400 11/315.
[55] Letter to Adolph Zukor (22 December 1924), Beinecke GEN MSS 1400 8/231.

youth'. That idea remained only an embryonic sketch, but others that
got as far as the theatre included *Mary Rose* (1920), which reverses
the situation of *Peter Pan* by following the fortunes of a man who
returns every year to an enchanted island in the search for a woman
who never grows any older, and *The Boy David* (1936), which depicts
the biblical David as a 12-year-old being hunted down by the Hook-
like figure of Saul. Not until 1928 did Barrie finally publish a play text
of *Peter Pan*, and anyone who bought it was unlikely to have been
surprised by what it contained. By that point the 'stranger' Wendy
encounters in the nursery had become more like an old friend.

Meanwhile several other writers were also busy producing adapta-
tions of Barrie's story, often with his approval. This was a natural
development of the fact that *A Play* had supposedly been written by
'Anon', and as late as 1928 the author of *Peter Pan* was pretending not
to have any recollection of having written a story that already seemed
to be as timeless and impersonal as a myth. Indeed, if one of the seeds
of *Peter Pan* had been the 'Wandering Child' episode in *Tommy and
Grizel*, after the first production in 1904 he was apparently content
for his characters to wander off in more or less any direction they
liked. Soon there were simplified versions of the story for young children, songs, poems including an 'Ode to Peter Pan', magic lantern
slides, a comedian who adopted 'Peter Pan' as his stage name, dolls
to play with, Wendy houses to play in, a 'Peter Pan' restaurant on
Shaftesbury Avenue, Henry Dellafield's *Peter Pan Suite* for piano,
Christmas crackers containing mottos culled from the play (Barrie
helpfully provided the makers with a list of suitable quotations), wobbly
cardboard figures for a toy theatre, and even a Peter Pan Golf Club
founded for the theatrical company in 1906, with Barrie paying for
forty sets of clubs in bags marked 'P.P.G.C.'. The story's iconography
also refused to settle down into just one shape, with illustrations that
ranged from the tangled wildness of Arthur Rackham's watercolours
in *Peter Pan in Kensington Gardens*, to the 'dimpled cuteness' of Mabel
Lucie Attwell's figures in May Byron's abridged 1926 version of *Peter
and Wendy*.[56]

Yet while Neverland was expanding its borders, Barrie was shrinking further inside himself. 'There was something very sinister about
him, rather shivery', George Llewelyn Davies's sister-in-law observed,

***

[56] Avery, 'The Cult of Peter Pan', 173.

while one of Michael's friends remembered that on meeting Barrie 'the most self-confident people in the world became as if they had a raw lemon in their mouths'.[57] Perhaps the sourest sense of disappointment was felt by anyone who expected Barrie somehow to *be* Peter Pan: witty, wild, and crackling with mischief. But Barrie could never bring himself to be as unselfconscious as his hero. 'Thus it will go on', the last sentence of *Peter and Wendy* promised, 'so long as children are gay and innocent and heartless' (p. 276). It was a cry from the heart of a man who worried he did not have a heart. 'It is as if long after writing "P. Pan" its true meaning came to me', he wrote in a 1922 notebook. 'Desperate attempt to grow up but can't.'[58]

It is these competing desires—to retain the wide eyes of the child while developing the wiser eyes of the adult—that weave in and out of each other throughout Barrie's writing. They form the double helix of his imagination. They are also the main reason why, over the course of more than a century, his most famous play has managed to age so gracefully. Indeed, since the final mothballing of Boucicault's original production, Barrie's play has been reinvented so often it has become something of a cultural mirror, used to catch our changing reflections on everything from the benefits of moisturizer to the Neverland ranch that was home to Michael Jackson, the musical man-child who for many years was described—with both admiration and scorn—as the 'Peter Pan of pop'. Flitting here and there, alternately flattering and mocking, *Peter Pan* has become the perfect self-image of an age that is obsessed with age. Every time its hero seems to have gone for good, he reappears on the windowsill asking us to come back and play. 'To't again!' (p. 401) as Hook cries after Peter has told him that he is a little bird that has broken out of the egg. 'To't again!'

[57] Birkin, *J. M. Barrie and the Lost Boys*, 214, 201.   [58] Ibid. 297.

NOTE ON THE TEXT

ALTHOUGH Peter Pan tells Wendy that Neverland isn't hard to find—
'Second to the right and then straight on till morning'—Barrie's play had
a far more complicated journey into print, one that was full of creative
detours and dead ends. The texts printed here reveal the main stages in
this journey, but Barrie's itchy-fingered impulse to revise means that
many interim versions survive in draft form. An edition that included
every variant would run to several volumes; instead, this *Collected Peter
Pan* shows how Barrie took the flighty character he first introduced in
The Little White Bird, and turned him into the hero of a play sketched
out in six scenes (the earliest surviving full draft), a prose story (*Peter
and Wendy*, 1911), a silent film treatment (1921), and finally the defini-
tive theatrical version of *Peter Pan* (1928), in addition to several shorter
sequels and supplements. The published texts reprinted here are taken
from first editions wherever possible; obvious printing errors have been
silently corrected. *The Little White Bird* was first published by Hodder
& Stoughton in 1902; the Peter Pan episode comprised chapters 13–18.
A Play (1903–4) is printed from the only surviving complete manuscript
copy, now housed in the Lilly Library, University of Indiana. (A typescript for the original 1904 production of *Peter Pan*, which includes
handwritten lighting cues and Barrie's last-minute revisions, is
housed in the Walter Beinecke Jr. Collection at the Beinecke Rare
Book and Manuscript Library, Yale University, but the final few pages
are missing. The version of Barrie's production script submitted to
the Lord Chamberlain's Office for approval has since been lost or
stolen: it should be item no. 482 in LCP 1904/Box 29, but when last
checked by a curator at the British Library the contents of this box
jumped from no. 481 to no. 483.) *Peter and Wendy* was first published
by Hodder & Stoughton in 1911. *Scenario for a Proposed Film of Peter
Pan* (1921) is reprinted from a typescript copy in the Walter Beinecke
Jr Collection. *Peter Pan, or The Boy Who Would Not Grow Up* is
reprinted from *The Plays of J. M. Barrie*, published in one volume by
Hodder & Stoughton in 1928. 'On the Acting of a Fairy Play' (1904)
is reprinted from Barrie's incomplete typescript of the original
London production of *Peter Pan*, in the Walter Beinecke Jr Collection.
J. M. Barrie's production note (1908) is taken from a synopsis of *Peter

Pan written for a series of performances at the Vaudeville Theatre, Paris, where (translated into French) it was given away as a twelve-page booklet entitled *L'Histoire de Peter Pan, ou le petit garcon qui ne voulait pas grandir*. This text reprints the opening page of the incomplete manuscript in the Walter Beinecke Jr Collection, supplemented by two sentences translated from the published booklet; the remainder of Barrie's note largely consists of a plot summary. 'When Wendy Grew Up: An Afterthought' (1908) was performed only once in Barrie's lifetime, on 22 February 1908, when it followed on from the scene which ends with Mrs Darling closing and barring the nursery window, and it was first published in *When Wendy Grew Up: An Afterthought* (Nelson, 1957). 'The Blot on Peter Pan' (1926) is reprinted from *The Treasure Ship: A Book of Prose and Verse*, ed. Cynthia Asquith, published by S. W. Partridge & Co. in 1926. 'Captain Hook at Eton' is based on Barrie's unpublished short story 'Jas. Hook at Eton'; it was delivered by him as a speech to the First Hundred at Eton College on 7 July 1927, and is reprinted here from the text published in *The Times* the following day.

SELECT BIBLIOGRAPHY

Biography

Cynthia Asquith, *Portrait of Barrie* (London: James Barrie, 1954)

Andrew Birkin, *J. M. Barrie and the Lost Boys* (London: Constable, 1979)

Lisa Chaney, *Hide-and-Seek with Angels: A Life of J. M. Barrie* (London: Hutchinson, 2005)

Janet Dunbar, *J. M. Barrie: The Man Behind the Image* (London: Collins, 1970)

Denis Mackail, *The Story of J. M. B.* (London: Peter Davies, 1941)

Criticism

Gillian Avery, 'The Cult of Peter Pan', *Word and Image* 2:2 (1986)

Valentina Bold and Andrew Nash (eds), *Gateway to the Modern: Resituating J. M. Barrie* (Glasgow: Association for Scottish Literary Studies, 2014)

Humphrey Carpenter, *Secret Gardens: A Study of the Golden Age of Children's Literature* (1985, repr. London: Faber and Faber, 2009)

Lester D. Friedman and Allison Kavey (eds), *Second Star to the Right: Peter Pan in the Popular Imagination* (New Brunswick, NJ: Rutgers University Press, 2009)

Marah Gubar, *Artful Dodgers: Reconceiving the Golden Age of Children's Literature* (Oxford: Oxford University Press, 2009)

Peter Hollindale, 'Peter Pan: The Text and the Myth', *Children's Literature in Education* 24:1 (1993)

Peter Hollindale, 'A Hundred Years of Peter Pan', *Children's Literature in Education* 36:3 (2005)

R. D. S. Jack, 'The Manuscript of Peter Pan', *Children's Literature* 18 (1990)

R. D. S. Jack, *The Road to the Never Land: A Reassessment of J. M. Barrie's Dramatic Art* (Aberdeen: Aberdeen University Press, 1991)

Anthony Lane, 'Lost Boys', *New Yorker* 80:36 (2004)

Roger Lancelyn Green, *Fifty Years of Peter Pan* (London: Peter Davies, 1954)

Jonathan Padley, 'Peter Pan: Indefinition Defined', *The Lion and the Unicorn* 36:3 (2012)

Jacqueline Rose, *The Case of Peter Pan, or, The Impossibility of Children's Fiction* (1984, rev. edn Basingstoke: Macmillan, 1994)

Chris Roth, 'Peter Pan: Flawed or Fledgling "hero"?', *A Necessary Fantasy? The Heroic Figure in Children's Popular Culture*, ed. Dudley Jones and Tony Watkins (New York: Garland, 2000)

Maria Tatar (ed.), *The Annotated Peter Pan: The Centennial Edition* (New York and London: W. W. Norton, 2011)

Donna R. White and C. Anita Tarr (eds), *Peter Pan In and Out of Time: A Children's Classic at 100* (Lanham, MD, and Oxford: The Scarecrow Press, 2006)

Selected Adaptations and Sequels
(in chronological order)

D. S. O'Connor, *Peter Pan Keepsake, the Story of Peter Pan retold from Mr. Barrie's Dramatic Fantasy* (London: Chatto & Windus, 1907)

D. S. O'Connor and Alice B. Woodward, *The Peter Pan Picture Book* (London: G. Bell, 1907)

G. D. Drennan, *Peter Pan, His Book, His Pictures, His Career, His Friends* (London: Mills & Boon, 1909)

Frederick Orville Perkins, *Peter Pan: the Boy Who Would Never Grow Up to Be a Man* (Boston: Silver, Burdett, 1916)

May Byron, *J. M. Barrie's Peter Pan and Wendy, Retold by May Byron for Boys and Girls, with the Approval of the Author* (London: Hodder & Stoughton, 1926)

Gilbert Adair, *Peter Pan and the Only Children* (London: Macmillan, 1987)

Beryl Bainbridge, *An Awfully Big Adventure* (London: Duckworth, 1989)

Terry Brooks, *Hook* (New York: Ballantine, 1991)

Laurie Fox, *The Lost Girls* (New York: Simon & Schuster, 2003)

Geraldine McCaughrean, *Peter Pan in Scarlet* (Oxford: Oxford University Press, 2006)

J. V. Hart, *Capt. Hook: The Adventures of a Notorious Youth* (New York: HarperCollins, 2007)

John Logan, *Peter and Alice* (London: Oberon Books, 2013)

Christina Henry, *Lost Boy* (London: Titan Books, 2017)

Further Reading in Oxford World's Classics

Baden-Powell, Robert, *Scouting for Boys: A Handbook for Instruction in Good Citizenship*, ed. Elleke Boehmer.

Barrie, J. M., *Peter Pan and Other Plays*, ed. Peter Hollindale.

Barrie, J. M., *Peter Pan in Kensington Gardens / Peter and Wendy*, ed. Peter Hollindale.

Baum, L. Frank, *The Wonderful Wizard of Oz*, ed. Susan Wolstenholme.

Carroll, Lewis, *Alice's Adventures in Wonderland and Through the Looking-Glass*, ed. Peter Hunt.

Victorian Fairy Tales, ed. Michael Newton.

A CHRONOLOGY OF J. M. BARRIE

1860   James Matthew Barrie born 9 May, at Kirriemuir in Angus, Scotland, third son and seventh surviving child of David Barrie and Margaret Ogilvy.

1867   Brother David dies of fractured skull after skating accident, on eve of his fourteenth birthday.

1868   Attends Glasgow Academy, living with elder brother Alec, who teaches there.

1871   Attends Forfar Academy and lives at family home in Forfar, following brother's resignation and prospective appointment to HM Inspectorate.

1873   Attends Dumfries Academy, again living with brother Alec.

1877   First play, *Bandelero the Bandit*, performed by Dumfries Amateur Dramatic Club.

1878   Enters Edinburgh University.

1882   Graduates with MA.

1883   Joins *Nottingham Journal* as leader writer.

1884   Dismissed by *Nottingham Journal* (Oct.); 'An Auld Licht Community'published by *St James's Gazette* (Nov.).

1885   Leaves Kirriemuir to seek living as freelance writer in London (Mar.).

1887   *Better Dead*. Founds his private cricket team, the Allahakbarries.

1888   *Auld Licht Idylls. When a Man's Single*.

1889   *A Window in Thrums*.

1890   *My Lady Nicotine*.

1891   *The Little Minister. Richard Savage* (written with H. B. Marriott Watson) and *Ibsen's Ghost* first performed.

1892   *Walker, London* first performed, with Mary Ansell in a leading role. *The Professor's Love Story* first performed, in New York.

1893   *A Powerful Drug and Other Stories. A Tillyloss Scandal. Two of Them.*

1894   Marries Mary Ansell. Moves into 133 Gloucester Road (near Kensington Gardens). *A Lady's Shoe. Life in a Country Manse.*

1895   6 Sept., death of Margaret Ogilvy.

1896   *Margaret Ogilvy. Sentimental Tommy.* Visits America for first time to meet Charles Frohman, eventual producer of *Peter Pan*.

1897   First meeting with the family of Arthur and Sylvia Llewelyn Davies,
        first with boys George and Jack in Kensington Gardens, later with
        Mrs Llewelyn Davies, daughter of novelist George du Maurier and
        sister of actor Gerald du Maurier. Subsequently becomes regular
        and frequent visitor at Davies' home, 31 Kensington Park Gardens.
        Dramatized version of *The Little Minister* first performed.

1898   *Jess.*

1900   *Tommy and Grizel. The Wedding Guest* first performed. Mary Barrie
        leases Black Lake Cottage, near Farnham, Surrey. Michael Llewelyn
        Davies born.

1901   *The Boy Castaways of Black Lake Island.*

1902   *The Little White Bird. Quality Street* and *The Admirable Crichton* first
        performed. Barries move to Leinster Corner, near Kensington
        Gardens. Death of Barrie's father.

1903   *Little Mary* first performed.

1904   *Peter Pan* first performed (27 Dec.), at Duke of York's Theatre.
        Llewelyn Davies family moves to Egerton House, Berkhamsted.

1905   *Alice-Sit-by-the-Fire* and *Pantaloon* first performed.

1906   *Peter Pan in Kensington Gardens.*

1907   Death of Arthur Llewelyn Davies. Barrie involved in campaign for
        reform of theatre censorship, following Lord Chamberlain's refusal
        of licence to Harley Granville-Barker's *Waste*.

1908   Sole performance of *When Wendy Grew Up: An Afterthought* (22
        Feb.). *What Every Woman Knows* first performed.

1909   Barrie divorces Mary on grounds of her adultery with Gilbert
        Cannan. Moves to flat at 3 Adelphi Terrace House, overlooking
        Embankment. Refuses knighthood. Accepts invitation from Captain
        R. F. Scott (Scott of the Antarctic) to be godfather to his son Peter.
        Hon. LLD Edinburgh.

1910   Death of Sylvia Llewelyn Davies. Barrie becomes guardian of the
        five Llewelyn Davies boys.

1911   *Peter and Wendy.*

1913   *The Adored One* and *Half an Hour* first performed. Baronetcy.

1914   Visits America on diplomatically embarrassing effort to raise sup-
        port for the allies.

1915   George Llewelyn Davies killed in action (15 Mar.). Visits war zone,
        near Reims. Charles Frohman dies when *Lusitania* is torpedoed.

1916   *A Kiss for Cinderella* first performed.

1917 *Dear Brutus* first performed.

1918 *What Every Woman Knows* first performed. Visits France as guest of the American army, and is in Paris for the Armistice.

1919 Elected Rector of St Andrews University.

1920 *Mary Rose* first performed.

1921 *Shall We Join the Ladies?* first performed. 19 May, death by drowning of Michael Llewelyn Davies.

1922 Order of Merit.

1928 *Peter Pan* (play) first published. President of the Society of Authors. *Shall We Join the Ladies?*

1929 Gift of royalties on *Peter Pan* to Great Ormond Street Hospital for Sick Children.

1930 Hon. LLD, Cambridge University. Installation as Chancellor of Edinburgh University (25 Oct.). *The Greenwood Hat.*

1931 *Farewell, Miss Julie Logan* circulated with *The Times* at Christmas.

1936 *The Boy David* first performed.

1937 Dies, 19 June. Buried with family at Kirriemuir.

PETER PAN

PETER PAN

THE LITTLE WHITE BIRD
(1902)

You must see for yourselves that it will be difficult to follow our adventures unless you are familiar with the Kensington Gardens,* as they now became known to David.* They are in London, where the King* lives, and you go to them every day unless you are looking decidedly flushed, but no one has ever been in the whole of the Gardens, because it is so soon time to turn back. The reason it is soon time to turn back is that you sleep from twelve to one. If your mother was not so sure that you sleep from twelve to one, you could most likely see the whole of them.

The Gardens are bounded on one side by a never-ending line of omnibuses,* over which Irene has such authority that if she holds up her finger to any one of them it stops immediately. She then crosses

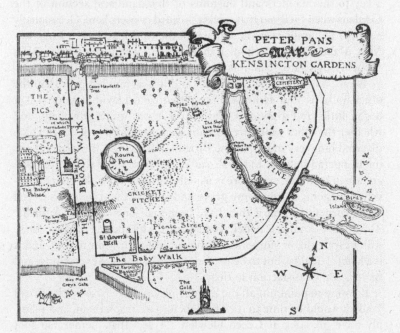

FIGURE 1 Arthur Rackham, 'Peter Pan's Map of Kensington Gardens', from *Peter Pan in Kensington Gardens* (Hodder & Stoughton, 1906).

with you in safety to the other side. There are more gates to the Gardens than one gate, but that is the one you go in at, and before you go in you speak to the lady with the balloons, who sits just outside. This is as near to being inside as she may venture, because, if she were to let go her hold of the railings for one moment, the balloons would lift her up, and she would be flown away. She sits very squat, for the balloons are always tugging at her, and the strain has given her quite a red face. Once she was a new one, because the old one had let go, and David was very sorry for the old one, but as she did let go, he wished he had been there to see.

The Gardens are a tremendous big place, with millions and hundreds of trees; and first you come to the Figs,* but you scorn to loiter there, for the Figs is the resort of superior little persons, who are forbidden to mix with the commonalty,* and is so named, according to legend, because they dress in full fig.* These dainty ones are themselves contemptuously called Figs by David and other heroes, and you have a key to the manners and customs of this dandiacal section of the Gardens when I tell you that cricket is called crickets here. Occasionally a rebel Fig climbs over the fence into the world, and such a one was Miss Mabel Grey, of whom I shall tell you when we come to Miss Mabel Grey's gate.* She was the only really celebrated Fig.

We are now in the Broad Walk,* and it is as much bigger than the other walks as your father is bigger than you. David wondered if it began little, and grew and grew, until it was quite grown up, and whether the other walks are its babies, and he drew a picture, which diverted him very much, of the Broad Walk giving a tiny walk an airing in a perambulator. In the Broad Walk you meet all the people who are worth knowing, and there is usually a grown-up with them to prevent their going on the damp grass, and to make them stand disgraced at the corner of a seat if they have been mad-dog or Mary-Annish.* To be Mary-Annish is to behave like a girl, whimpering because nurse won't carry you, or simpering with your thumb in your mouth, and it is a hateful quality; but to be mad-dog is to kick out at everything, and there is some satisfaction in that.

If I were to point out all the notable places as we pass up the Broad Walk, it would be time to turn back before we reach them, and I simply wave my stick at Cecco Hewlett's Tree,* that memorable spot where a boy called Cecco lost his penny, and, looking for it, found twopence. There has been a good deal of excavation going on there ever since. Farther up the walk is the little wooden house in which Marmaduke Perry hid. There is no more awful story of the Gardens than this of Marmaduke Perry, who had been Mary-Annish three days in succession, and was sentenced to appear in the Broad Walk dressed in his sister's clothes. He hid in the little wooden house, and refused to emerge until they brought him knicker-bockers with pockets.

You now try to go to the Round Pond, but nurses hate it, because they are not really manly, and they make you look the other way, at the Big Penny* and the Baby's Palace.* She was the most celebrated baby of the Gardens, and lived in the palace all alone, with ever so many dolls, so people rang the bell, and up she got out of her bed, though it was past six o'clock, and she lighted a candle and opened the door in her nighty, and then they all cried with great rejoicings, 'Hail, Queen of England!' What puzzled David most was how she knew where the matches were kept. The Big Penny is a statue about her.

Next we come to the Hump,* which is the part of the Broad Walk where all the big races are run; and even though you had no intention of running you do run when you come to the Hump, it is such a fascinating, slide-down kind of place. Often you stop when you have run about half-way down it, and then you are lost; but there is another little wooden house near here, called the Lost House, and so you tell the man that you are lost and then he finds you. It is glorious fun racing down the Hump, but you can't do it on windy days because then you are not there, but the fallen leaves do it instead of you. There is almost nothing that has such a keen sense of fun as a fallen leaf.

From the Hump we can see the gate that is called after Miss Mabel Grey, the Fig I promised to tell you about. There were always two nurses with her, or else one mother and one nurse, and for a long time she was a pattern-child* who always coughed off the table and said, 'How do you do?' to the other Figs, and the only game she played at was flinging a ball gracefully and letting the nurse bring it back to her. Then one day she tired of it all and went mad-dog, and, first, to show that she really was mad-dog, she unloosened both her bootlaces and put out her tongue east, west, north, and south. She then flung her sash into a puddle and danced on it till dirty water was squirted over her frock, after which she climbed the fence and had a series of incredible adventures, one of the least of which was that she kicked off both her boots. At last she came to the gate that is now called after her, out of which she ran into streets David and I have never been in though we have heard them roaring, and still she ran on and would never again have been heard of had not her mother jumped into a 'bus and thus overtaken her. It all happened, I should say, long ago, and this is not the Mabel Grey whom David knows.

Returning up the Broad Walk we have on our right the Baby Walk, which is so full of perambulators that you could cross from side to side stepping on babies, but the nurses won't let you do it. From this walk a passage called Bunting's Thumb,* because it is that length, leads into Picnic Street, where there are real kettles, and chestnut-blossom falls into your mug as you are drinking. Quite common children picnic here also, and the blossom falls into their mugs just the same.

Next comes St. Govor's Well,* which was full of water when Malcolm the Bold fell into it. He was his mother's favourite, and he let her put her arm round his neck in public because she was a widow; but he was also partial to adventures, and liked to play with a chimney-sweep* who had killed a good many bears. The sweep's name was Sooty, and one day, when they were playing near the well, Malcolm fell in and would have been drowned had not Sooty dived in and rescued him; and the water had washed Sooty clean, and he now stood revealed as Malcolm's long-lost father. So Malcolm would not let his mother put her arm round his neck any more.

Between the well and the Round Pond are the cricket-pitches, and frequently the choosing of sides exhausts so much time that there is scarcely any cricket. Everybody wants to bat first, and as soon as he is out he bowls unless you are the better wrestler, and while you are wrestling with him the fielders have scattered to play at something else. The Gardens are noted for two kinds of cricket: boy cricket, which is real cricket with a bat, and girl cricket, which is with a racquet and the governess. Girls can't really play cricket, and when you are watching their futile efforts you make funny sounds at them. Nevertheless, there was a very disagreeable incident one day when some forward girls challenged David's team, and a disturbing creature called Angela Clare sent down so many Yorkers* that—However, instead of telling you the result of that regrettable match I shall pass on hurriedly to the Round Pond, which is the wheel that keeps all the Gardens going.

It is round because it is in the very middle of the Gardens, and when you are come to it you never want to go any farther. You can't be good all the time at the Round Pond,* however much you try. You can be good in the Broad Walk all the time, but not at the Round Pond, and the reason is that you forget, and, when you remember, you are so wet that you may as well be wetter. There are men who sail boats on the Round Pond, such big boats that they bring them in barrows, and sometimes in perambulators, and then the baby has to walk. The bow-legged children in the Gardens are those who had to walk too soon because their father needed the perambulator.

You always want to have a yacht to sail on the Round Pond, and in the end your uncle gives you one; and to carry it to the Pond the first day is splendid, also to talk about it to boys who have no uncle is splendid, but soon you like to leave it at home. For the sweetest craft that slips her moorings in the Round Pond is what is called a stick-boat, because she is rather like a stick until she is in the water and you are holding the string. Then as you walk round, pulling her, you see little men running about her deck, and sails rise magically and catch the breeze, and you put in on dirty nights at snug harbours which are unknown to the lordly yachts. Night passes in a twink, and again your rakish craft noses for the wind, whales spout, you glide over buried cities, and have brushes with pirates, and cast anchor on coral isles. You are a solitary boy while all this is taking place, for two boys together cannot adventure far upon the Round Pond, and though you may talk to yourself throughout the voyage, giving orders and executing them with despatch, you know not, when it is time to go home, where you have been or what swelled your sails; your treasure-trove is all locked away in your hold, so to speak, which will be opened, perhaps, by another little boy many years afterwards.

But those yachts have nothing in their hold. Does any one return to this haunt of his youth because of the yachts that used to sail it? Oh no. It is the stick-boat that is freighted with memories. The yachts are toys, their owner a fresh-water mariner; they can cross and recross a pond only while the stick-boat goes to sea. You yachtsmen with your wands, who think we are all there to gaze on you, your ships are only accidents of this place, and were they all to be boarded and sunk by the ducks, the real business of the Round Pond would be carried on as usual.

Paths from everywhere crowd like children to the pond. Some of them are ordinary paths, which have a rail on each side, and are made by men with their coats off, but others are vagrants, wide at one spot, and at another so narrow that you can stand astride them. They are called Paths that have Made Themselves, and David did wish he could see them doing it. But, like all the most wonderful things that happen in the Gardens, it is done, we concluded, at night after the gates are closed. We have also decided that the paths make themselves because it is their only chance of getting to the Round Pond.

One of these gypsy paths comes from the place where the sheep get their hair cut. When David shed his curls at the hairdresser's, I am told, he said good-bye to them without a tremor, though Mary has never been quite the same bright creature since; so he despises the sheep as they run from their shearer, and calls out tauntingly, 'Cowardy, cowardy custard!'* But when the man grips them between his legs David shakes a fist at him for using such big scissors. Another startling moment is when the man turns back the grimy wool from the sheeps' shoulders and they look suddenly like ladies in the stalls of a theatre. The sheep are so frightened by the shearing that it makes them quite white and thin, and as soon as they are set free they begin to nibble the grass at once, quite anxiously, as if they feared that they would never be worth eating. David wonders whether they know each other, now that they are so different, and if it makes them fight with the wrong ones. They are great fighters, and thus so unlike country sheep that every year they give Porthos* a shock. He can make a field of country sheep fly by merely announcing his approach, but these town sheep come toward him with no promise of gentle entertainment, and then a light from last year breaks upon Porthos. He cannot with dignity retreat, but he stops and looks about him as if lost in admiration of the scenery, and presently he strolls away with a fine indifference and a glint at me from the corner of his eye.

The Serpentine begins near here. It is a lovely lake, and there is a drowned forest at the bottom of it. If you peer over the edge you can see the trees all growing upside down, and they say that at night there are also drowned stars in it. If so, Peter Pan sees them when he is sailing across the lake in the Thrush's Nest. A small part only of the Serpentine is in the Gardens, for soon it passes beneath a bridge to far away where the island is on which all the birds are born that become baby boys and girls. No one who is human, except Peter Pan (and he is only half human), can land on the island, but you may write what you want (boy or girl, dark or fair) on a piece of paper, and then twist it into the shape of a boat and slip it into the water, and it reaches Peter Pan's island after dark.

We are on the way home now, though of course, it is all pretence that we can go to so many of the places in one day. I should have had to be carrying David long ago, and resting on every seat like old

Mr. Salford. That was what we called him, because he always talked to us of a lovely place called Salford* where he had been born. He was a crab-apple of an old gentleman who wandered all day in the Gardens from seat to seat trying to fall in with somebody who was acquainted with the town of Salford, and when we had known him for a year or more we actually did meet another aged solitary who had once spent Saturday to Monday in Salford. He was meek and timid, and carried his address inside his hat, and whatever part of London he was in search of he always went to Westminster Abbey first as a starting-point. Him we carried in triumph to our other friend, with the story of that Saturday to Monday, and never shall I forget the gloating joy with which Mr. Salford leapt at him. They have been cronies ever since, and I notice that Mr. Salford, who naturally does most of the talking, keeps tight grip of the other old man's coat.

The two last places before you come to our gate are the Dog's Cemetery* and the chaffinch's nest, but we pretend not to know what the Dog's Cemetery is, as Porthos is always with us. The nest is very sad. It is quite white, and the way we found it was wonderful. We were having another look among the bushes for David's lost worsted ball,* and instead of the ball we found a lovely nest made of the worsted, and containing four eggs, with scratches on them very like David's handwriting, so we think they must have been the mother's love-letters to the little ones inside. Every day we were in the Gardens we paid a call at the nest, taking care that no cruel boy should see us, and we dropped crumbs, and soon the bird knew us as friends, and sat in the nest looking at us kindly with her shoulders hunched up. But one day when we went there were only two eggs in the nest, and the next time there were none. The saddest part of it was that the poor little chaffinch fluttered about the bushes, looking so reproachfully at us that we knew she thought we had done it; and though David tried to explain to her, it was so long since he had spoken the bird language that I fear she did not understand. He and I left the Gardens that day with our knuckles in our eyes.

PETER PAN

IF you ask your mother whether she knew about Peter Pan when she was a little girl, she will say, 'Why, of course I did, child'; and if you ask her whether he rode on a goat in those days, she will say, 'What a foolish question to ask; certainly he did.' Then if you ask your grandmother whether she knew about Peter Pan when she was a girl, she also says, 'Why, of course I did, child,' but if you ask her whether he rode on a goat in those days, she says she never heard of his having a goat. Perhaps she has forgotten, just as she sometimes forgets your name and calls you Mildred, which is your mother's name. Still, she could hardly forget such an important thing as the goat. Therefore there was no goat when your grandmother was a little girl. This shows that, in telling the story of Peter Pan, to begin with the goat (as most people do) is as silly as to put on your jacket before your vest.

Of course, it also shows that Peter is ever so old, but he is really always the same age, so that does not matter in the least. His age is one week, and though he was born so long ago he has never had a birthday, nor is there the slightest chance of his ever having one. The reason is that he escaped from being a human when he was seven days old; he escaped by the window and flew back to the Kensington Gardens.

If you think he was the only baby who ever wanted to escape, it shows how completely you have forgotten your own young days. When David heard this story first he was quite certain that he had never tried to escape, but I told him to think back hard, pressing his hands to his temples, and when he had done this hard, and even harder, he distinctly remembered a youthful desire to return to the tree-tops, and with that memory came others, as that he had lain in bed planning to escape as soon as his mother was asleep, and how she had once caught him half-way up the chimney. All children could have such recollections if they would press their hands hard to their temples, for, having been birds before they were human, they are naturally a little wild during the first few weeks, and very itchy at the shoulders, where their wings used to be. So David tells me.

I ought to mention here that the following is our way with a story: First I tell it to him, and then he tells it to me, the understanding being that it is quite a different story; and then I retell it with his additions, and so we go on until no one could say whether it is more his story or mine. In this story of Peter Pan, for instance, the bald narrative and most of the moral reflections are mine, though not all, for this boy can be a stern moralist; but the interesting bits about the ways and customs of babies in the bird-stage are mostly reminiscences of David's, recalled by pressing his hands to his temples and thinking hard.

Well, Peter Pan got out by the window, which had no bars. Standing on the ledge he could see trees far away, which were doubtless the Kensington Gardens, and the moment he saw them he entirely forgot that he was now a little boy in a nightgown, and away he flew, right over the houses to the Gardens. It is wonderful that he could fly without wings, but the place itched tremendously, and—and—perhaps we could all fly if we were as dead-confident-sure of our capacity to do it as was bold Peter Pan that evening.

He alighted gaily on the open sward,* between the Baby's Palace and the Serpentine, and the first thing he did was to lie on his back and kick. He was quite unaware already that he had ever been human, and thought he was a bird, even in appearance, just the same as in his early days, and when he tried to catch a fly he did not understand that the reason he missed it was because he had attempted to seize it with his hand, which, of course, a bird never does. He saw, however, that it must be past Lock-out Time,* for there were a good many fairies about, all too busy to notice him; they were getting breakfast ready, milking their cows, drawing water, and so on, and the sight of the water-pails made him thirsty, so he flew over to the Round Pond to have a drink. He stooped and dipped his beak in the pond; he thought it was his beak, but, of course, it was only his nose, and therefore, very little water came up, and that not so refreshing as usual, so next he tried a puddle, and he fell flop into it. When a real bird falls in flop, he spreads out his feathers and pecks them dry, but Peter could not remember what was the thing to do, and he decided rather sulkily to go to sleep on the weeping beech in the Baby Walk.

At first he found some difficulty in balancing himself on a branch, but presently he remembered the way, and fell asleep. He awoke long before morning, shivering, and saying to himself, 'I never was out on such a cold night'; he had really been out on colder nights when he was a bird, but, of course, as everybody knows, what seems a warm night to a bird is a cold night to a boy in a nightgown. Peter also felt strangely uncomfortable, as if his head was stuffy; he heard loud noises that made him look round sharply, though they were really himself sneezing. There was something he wanted very much, but, though he knew he wanted it, he could not think what it was. What he wanted so much was his mother to blow his nose, but that never struck him, so he decided to appeal to the fairies for enlightenment. They are reputed to know a good deal.

There were two of them strolling along the Baby Walk, with their arms round each other's waists, and he hopped down to address them. The fairies have their tiffs with the birds, but they usually give a civil answer to a civil question, and he was quite angry when these two ran away the moment they saw him. Another was lolling on a garden chair, reading a postage-stamp which some human had let fall, and when he heard Peter's voice he popped in alarm behind a tulip.

To Peter's bewilderment he discovered that every fairy he met fled from him. A band of workmen, who were sawing down a toadstool, rushed away, leaving their tools behind them. A milkmaid turned her pail upside down and hid in it. Soon the Gardens were in an uproar. Crowds of fairies were running this way and that, asking each other stoutly who was afraid; lights were extinguished, doors barricaded, and from the grounds of Queen Mab's palace* came the rub-a-dub of drums, showing that the royal guard had been called out. A regiment of Lancers* came charging down the Broad Walk, armed with holly-leaves, with which they jag the enemy horribly in passing. Peter heard the little people crying everywhere that there was a human in the Gardens after Lock-out Time, but he never thought for a moment that he was the human. He was feeling stuffier and stuffier, and more and more wistful to learn what he wanted done to his nose, but he pursued them with the vital question in vain; the timid creatures ran from him, and even the Lancers, when he approached them up the Hump, turned swiftly into a side-walk, on the pretence that they saw him there.

Despairing of the fairies, he resolved to consult the birds, but now he remembered, as an odd thing, that all the birds on the weeping-beech had flown away when he alighted on it, and though this had not troubled him at the time, he saw its meaning now. Every living thing was shunning him. Poor little Peter Pan! he sat down and cried, and even then he did not know that, for a bird, he was sitting on his wrong part. It is a blessing that he did not know, for otherwise he would have lost faith in his power to fly, and the moment you doubt whether you can fly, you cease for ever to be able to do it. The reason birds can fly and we can't is simply that they have perfect faith, for to have faith is to have wings.

Now, except by flying, no one can reach the island in the Serpentine, for the boats of humans are forbidden to land there, and there are stakes round it, standing up in the water, on each of which a bird-sentinel sits by day and night. It was to the island that Peter now flew to put his strange case before old Solomon* Caw, and he alighted on it with relief, much heartened to find himself at last at home, as the birds call the island. All of them were asleep, including the sentinels, except Solomon, who was wide awake on one side, and he listened quietly to Peter's adventures, and then told him their true meaning.

'Look at your nightgown, if you don't believe me,' Solomon said; and with staring eyes Peter looked at his nightgown, and then at the sleeping birds. Not one of them wore anything.

'How many of your toes are thumbs?' said Solomon a little cruelly, and Peter saw to his consternation, that all his toes were fingers. The shock was so great that it drove away his cold.

'Ruffle your feathers,' said that grim old Solomon, and Peter tried most desperately hard to ruffle his feathers, but he had none. Then he rose up, quaking, and for the first time since he stood on the window ledge, he remembered a lady who had been very fond of him.

'I think I shall go back to mother,' he said timidly.

'Good-bye,' replied Solomon Caw with a queer look.

But Peter hesitated. 'Why don't you go?' the old one asked politely.

'I suppose,' said Peter huskily, 'I suppose I can still fly?'

You see, he had lost faith.

'Poor little half-and-half!' said Solomon, who was not really hard-hearted, 'you will never be able to fly again, not even on windy days. You must live here on the island always.'

'And never even go to the Kensington Gardens?' Peter asked tragically.

'How could you get across?' said Solomon. He promised very kindly, however, to teach Peter as many of the bird ways as could be learned by one of such an awkward shape.

'Then I shan't be exactly a human?' Peter asked.

'No.'

'Nor exactly a bird?'

'No.'

'What shall I be?'

'You will be a Betwixt-and-Between,' Solomon said, and certainly he was a wise old fellow, for that is exactly how it turned out.

The birds on the island never got used to him. His oddities tickled them every day, as if they were quite new, though it was really the birds that were new. They came out of the eggs daily, and laughed at him at once; then off they soon flew to be humans, and other birds came out of other eggs; and so it went on for ever. The crafty mother-birds, when they tired of sitting on their eggs, used to get the young ones to break their shells a day before the right time by whispering to them that now was their chance to see Peter washing or drinking or eating. Thousands gathered round him daily to watch him do these things, just as you watch the peacocks, and they screamed with delight when he lifted the crusts they flung him with his hands instead of in the usual way with the mouth. All his food was brought to him from the Gardens at Solomon's orders by the birds. He would not eat worms or insects (which they thought very silly of him), so they brought him bread in their beaks. Thus, when you cry out, 'Greedy! Greedy!' to the bird that flies away with the big crust, you know now that you ought not to do this, for he is very likely taking it to Peter Pan.

Peter wore no nightgown now. You see, the birds were always begging him for bits of it to line their nests with, and, being very good-natured, he could not refuse, so by Solomon's advice he had hidden what was left of it. But, though he was now quite naked, you must not think that he was cold or unhappy. He was usually very happy and gay, and the reason was that Solomon had kept his promise and taught him many of the bird ways. To be easily pleased, for instance, and always to be really doing something, and to think that whatever he was doing was a thing of vast importance. Peter became very clever at helping the birds to build their nests; soon he could build better than a wood-pigeon, and nearly as well as a blackbird, though never did he satisfy the finches, and he made nice little water-troughs near the nests and dug up worms for the young ones with his fingers. He also became very learned in bird-lore, and knew an east wind from a west wind by its smell, and he could see the grass growing and hear the insects walking about inside the tree-trunks. But the best thing Solomon had done was to teach him to have a glad heart. All birds have glad hearts unless you rob their nests, and so as they were the only kind of heart Solomon knew about, it was easy to him to teach Peter how to have one.

Peter's heart was so glad that he felt he must sing all day long, just as the birds sing for joy, but, being partly human, he needed an instrument, so he made a pipe of reeds, and he used to sit by the shore of the island of an evening, practising the sough* of the wind and the ripple of the water, and catching handfuls of the shine of the moon, and he put them all in his pipe and played them so beautifully that even the birds were deceived, and they would say to each other, 'Was that a fish leaping in the water or was it Peter playing leaping fish on his pipe?' And sometimes he played the birth of birds, and then the mothers would turn round in their nests to see whether they had laid an egg. If you are a child of the Gardens you must know the chestnut-tree near the bridge, which comes out in flower first of all the chestnuts, but perhaps you have not heard why this tree leads the way. It is because Peter wearies for summer and plays that it has come, and the chestnut being so near, hears him and is cheated.

But as Peter sat by the shore tootling divinely on his pipe he sometimes fell into sad thoughts, and then the music became sad also, and the reason of all this sadness was that he could not reach the Gardens, though he could see them through the arch of the bridge. He knew he could never be a real human again, and scarcely wanted to be one, but oh! how he longed to play as other children play, and of course there is no such lovely place to play in as the Gardens. The birds brought him news of how boys and girls play, and wistful tears started in Peter's eyes.

Perhaps you wonder why he did not swim across. The reason was that he could not swim. He wanted to know how to swim, but no one on the island knew the way except the ducks, and they are so stupid. They were quite willing to teach him, but all they could say about it was, 'You sit down on the top of the water in this way, and then you kick out like that.' Peter tried it often, but always before he could kick out he sank. What he really needed to know was how you sit on the water without sinking, and they said it was quite impossible to explain such an easy thing as that. Occasionally swans touched on the island, and he would give them all his day's food and then ask them how they sat on the water, but as soon as he had no more to give them the hateful things hissed at him and sailed away.

Once he really thought he had discovered a way of reaching the Gardens. A wonderful white thing, like a runaway newspaper, floated high over the island and then tumbled, rolling over and over after the manner of a bird that has broken its wing. Peter was so frightened that he hid, but the birds told him it was only a kite, and what a kite is, and that it must have tugged its string out of a boy's hand, and soared away. After that they laughed at Peter for being so fond of the kite; he loved it so much that he even slept with one hand on it, and I think this was pathetic and pretty, for the reason he loved it was because it had belonged to a real boy.

To the birds this was a very poor reason, but the older ones felt grateful to him at this time because he had nursed a number of fledglings through the German measles, and they offered to show him how birds fly a kite. So six of them took the end of the string in their beaks and flew away with it; and to his amazement it flew after them and went even higher than they.

Peter screamed out, 'Do it again!' and with great good-nature they did it several times, and always instead of thanking them he cried 'Do it again!' which shows that even now he had not quite forgotten what it was to be a boy.

At last, with a grand design burning within his brave heart, he begged them to do it once more with him clinging to the tail, and now a hundred flew off with the string, and Peter clung to the tail, meaning to drop off when he was over the Gardens. But the kite broke to pieces in the air, and he would have been drowned in the Serpentine had he not caught hold of two indignant swans and made them carry him to the island. After this the birds said that they would help him no more in his mad enterprise.

Nevertheless, Peter did reach the Gardens at last by the help of Shelley's boat, as I am now to tell you.

THE THRUSH'S NEST

SHELLEY* was a young gentleman and as grown-up as he need ever expect to be. He was a poet; and they are never exactly grown-up. They are people who despise money except what you need for today, and he had all that and five pounds over. So, when he was walking in the Kensington Gardens, he made a paper boat of his bank-note, and sent it sailing on the Serpentine.

It reached the island at night: and the look-out brought it to Solomon Caw, who thought at first that it was the usual thing, a message from a lady, saying she would be obliged if he could let her have a good one. They always ask for the best one he has, and if he likes the letter he sends one from Class A, but if it ruffles him he sends very funny ones indeed. Sometimes he sends none at all, and at another time he sends a nestful; it all depends on the mood you catch him in. He likes you to leave it all to him, and if you mention particularly that you hope he will see his way to making it *a boy this time*, he is almost sure to send another girl. And whether you are a lady or only a little boy who wants a baby-sister, always take pains to write your address clearly. You can't think what a lot of babies Solomon has sent to the wrong house.

Shelley's boat, when opened, completely puzzled Solomon, and he took counsel of his assistants, who having walked over it twice, first with their toes pointed out, and then with their toes pointed in, decided that it came from some greedy person who wanted five. They thought this because there was a large five printed on it. 'Preposterous!' cried Solomon in a rage, and he presented it to Peter; anything useless which drifted upon the island was usually given to Peter as a plaything.

But he did not play with his precious bank-note, for he knew what it was at once, having been very observant during the week when he was an ordinary boy. With so much money, he reflected, he could surely at last contrive to reach the Gardens, and he considered all the possible ways, and decided (wisely, I think) to choose the best way. But, first, he had to tell the birds of the value of Shelley's boat; and though they were too honest to demand it back, he saw that they were galled, and they cast such black looks at Solomon, who was rather vain of his cleverness, that he flew away to the end of the island, and sat there very depressed with his head buried in his wings. Now Peter knew that unless Solomon was on your side, you never got anything done for you in the island, so he followed him and tried to hearten him.

Nor was this all that Peter did to gain the powerful old fellow's good-will. You must know that Solomon had no intention of remaining in office all his life. He looked forward to retiring by and by, and devoting his green old age to a life of pleasure on a certain yew-stump in the Figs which had taken his fancy, and for years he had been quietly filling his stocking. It was a stocking belonging to some bathing person which had been cast upon the island, and at the time I speak of it contained a hundred and eighty crumbs, thirty-four nuts, sixteen crusts, a pen-wiper, and a boot-lace. When his stocking was full, Solomon calculated that he would be able to retire on a competency.* Peter now gave him a pound. He cut it off his bank-note with a sharp stick.

This made Solomon his friend for ever, and after the two had consulted together they called a meeting of the thrushes. You will see presently why thrushes only were invited.

The scheme to be put before them was really Peter's, but Solomon did most of the talking, because he soon became irritable if other people talked. He began by saying that he had been much impressed by the superior ingenuity shown by the thrushes in nest-building, and this put them into good-humour at once, as it was meant to do; for all the quarrels between birds are about the best way of building nests. Other birds, said Solomon, omitted to line their nests with mud, and as a result they did not hold water. Here he cocked his head as if he had used an unanswerable argument; but, unfortunately, a Mrs. Finch had come to the meeting uninvited, and she squeaked out, 'We don't build nests to hold water, but to hold eggs,' and then the thrushes stopped cheering, and Solomon was so perplexed that he took several sips of water.

'Consider,' he said at last, 'how warm the mud makes the nest.'

'Consider,' cried Mrs. Finch, 'that when water gets into the nest it remains there and your little ones are drowned.'

The thrushes begged Solomon with a look to say something crushing in reply to this, but again he was perplexed.

'Try another drink,' suggested Mrs. Finch pertly. Kate was her name, and all Kates are saucy.*

Solomon did try another drink, and it inspired him. 'If,' said he, 'a finch's nest is placed on the Serpentine it fills and breaks to pieces, but a thrush's nest is still as dry as the cup of a swan's back.'

How the thrushes applauded! Now they knew why they lined their nests with mud, and when Mrs. Finch called out, 'We don't place our nests on the Serpentine,' they did what they should have done at first—chased her from the meeting. After this it was most orderly. What they had been brought together to hear, said Solomon, was this: their young friend, Peter Pan, as they well knew, wanted very much to be able to cross to the Gardens, and he now proposed, with their help, to build a boat.

At this the thrushes began to fidget, which made Peter tremble for his scheme.

Solomon explained hastily that what he meant was not one of the cumbrous boats that humans use; the proposed boat was to be simply a thrush's nest large enough to hold Peter.

But still, to Peter's agony, the thrushes were sulky. 'We are very busy people,' they grumbled, 'and this would be a big job.'

'Quite so,' said Solomon, 'and, of course, Peter would not allow you to work for nothing. You must remember that he is now in comfortable circumstances, and he will pay you such wages as you have never been paid before. Peter Pan authorises me to say that you shall all be paid sixpence a day.'

Then all the thrushes hopped for joy, and that very day was begun the celebrated Building of the Boat. All their ordinary business fell into arrears. It was the time of the year when they should have been pairing, but not a thrush's nest was built except this big one, and so Solomon soon ran short of thrushes with which to supply the demand from the mainland. The stout, rather greedy children, who look so well in perambulators but get puffed* easily when they walk, were all young thrushes once, and ladies often ask specially for them. What do you think Solomon did? He sent over to the housetops for a lot of sparrows and ordered them to lay their eggs in old thrushes' nests, and sent their young to the ladies and swore they were all thrushes! It was known afterwards on the island as the Sparrow's Year; and so, when you meet grown-up people in the Gardens who puff and blow as if they thought themselves bigger than they are, very likely they belong to that year. You ask them.

Peter was a just master, and paid his workpeople every evening. They stood in rows on the branches, waiting politely while he cut the paper sixpences out of his bank-note, and presently he called the roll, and then each bird, as the names were mentioned, flew down and got sixpence. It must have been a fine sight.

And at last, after months of labour, the boat was finished. O the deportment of Peter as he saw it growing more and more like a great thrush's nest! From the very beginning of the building of it he slept by its side, and often woke up to say sweet things to it, and after it was lined with mud and the mud had dried he always slept in it. He sleeps in his nest still, and has a fascinating way of curling round in it, for it is just large enough to hold him comfortably when he curls round like a kitten. It is brown inside, of course, but outside it is mostly green, being woven of grass and twigs, and when these wither or snap the walls are thatched afresh. There are also a few feathers here and there, which came off the thrushes while they were building.

The other birds were extremely jealous, and said that the boat would not balance on the water, but it lay most beautifully steady; they said the water would come into it, but no water came into it. Next they said that Peter had no oars, and this caused the thrushes to look at each other in dismay; but Peter replied that he had no need of oars, for he had a sail, and with such a proud, happy face he produced a sail which he had fashioned out of his nightgown, and though it was still rather like a nightgown it made a lovely sail. And that night, the moon being full, and all the birds asleep, he did enter his coracle* (as Master Francis Pretty* would have said) and depart out of the island. And first, he knew not why, he looked upward, with his hands clasped, and from that moment his eyes were pinned to the west.

He had promised the thrushes to begin by making short voyages, with them to his guides, but far away he saw the Kensington Gardens beckoning to him beneath the bridge, and he could not wait. His face was flushed, but he never looked back; there was an exultation in his little breast that drove out fear. Was Peter the least gallant of the English mariners who have sailed westward to meet the Unknown?

At first, his boat turned round and round, and he was driven back to the place of his starting, whereupon he shortened sail, by removing one of the sleeves, and was forthwith carried backwards by a contrary breeze, to his no small peril. He now let go the sail, with the result that he was drifted towards the far shore, where are black shadows he knew not the dangers of, but suspected them, and so once more hoisted his nightgown and went roomer of the shadows* until he caught a favouring wind, which bore him westward, but at so great a speed that he was like to be broke against the bridge. Which, having avoided, he passed under the bridge and came, to his great rejoicing, within full sight of the delectable Gardens. But having tried to cast anchor, which was a stone at the end of a piece of the kite-string, he found no bottom, and was fain to hold off, seeking for moorage;* and, feeling his way, he buffeted against a sunken reef that cast him overboard by the greatness of the shock, and he was near to being drowned, but clambered back into the vessel. There now arose a mighty storm, accompanied by roaring of waters, such as he had never heard the like, and he was tossed this way and that, and his hands so numbed with the cold that he could not close them. Having escaped the danger of which, he was mercifully carried into a small bay, where his boat rode at peace.

Nevertheless, he was not yet in safety; for, on pretending* to disembark, he found a multitude of small people drawn up on the shore to contest his landing, and shouting shrilly to him to be off, for it was long past Lock-out Time. This, with much brandishing of their holly-leaves, and also a company of them carried an arrow which some boy had left in the Gardens, and this they were prepared to use as a battering-ram.

Then Peter, who knew them for the fairies, called out that he was not an ordinary human and had no desire to do them displeasure, but to be their friend; nevertheless, having found a jolly harbour, he was in no temper to draw off therefrom, and he warned them if they sought to mischief him to stand to their harms.*

So saying, he boldly leapt ashore,* and they gathered around him with intent to slay him, but there then arose a great cry among the women, and it was because they had now observed that his sail was a baby's nightgown. Whereupon, they straightway loved him, and grieved that their laps were too small, the which I cannot explain, except by saying that such is the way of women. The men-fairies now sheathed their weapons on observing the behaviour of their women, on whose intelligence they set great store, and they led him civilly to their queen, who conferred upon him the courtesy of the Gardens after Lock-out Time, and henceforth Peter could go whither he chose, and the fairies had orders to put him in comfort.

Such was his first voyage to the Gardens, and you may gather from the antiquity of the language that it took place a long time ago. But Peter never grows any older, and if we could be watching for him under the bridge to-night (but, of course, we can't), I dare say we should see him hoisting his nightgown and sailing or paddling towards us in the Thrush's Nest. When he sails, he sits down, but he stands up to paddle. I shall tell you presently how he got his paddle.

Long before the time for the opening of the gates comes he steals back to the island, for people must not see him (he is not so human as all that), but this gives him hours for play, and he plays exactly as real children play. At least he thinks so, and it is one of the pathetic things about him that he often plays quite wrongly.

You see, he had no one to tell him how children really play, for the fairies are all more or less in hiding until dusk, and so know nothing, and though the birds pretended that they could tell him a great deal, when the time for telling came, it was wonderful how little they really knew. They told him the truth about hide-and-seek, and he often plays it by himself, but even the ducks on the Round Pond could not explain to him what it is that makes the pond so fascinating to boys. Every night the ducks have forgotten all the events of the day, except the number of pieces of cake thrown to them. They are gloomy creatures, and say that cake is not what it was in their young days.

So Peter had to find out many things for himself. He often played ships at the Round Pond, but his ship was only a hoop which he had found on the grass. Of course, he had never seen a hoop, and he wondered what you play at with them, and decided that you play at pretending they are boats. This hoop always sank at once, but he waded in for it, and sometimes he dragged it gleefully round the rim of the pond, and he was quite proud to think that he had discovered what boys do with hoops.

Another time, when he found a child's pail, he thought it was for sitting in, and he sat so hard in it that he could scarcely get out of it. Also he found a balloon. It was bobbing about on the Hump, quite as if it was having a game by itself, and he caught it after an exciting chase. But he thought it was a ball, and Jenny Wren* had told him that boys kick balls, so he kicked it; and after that he could not find it anywhere.

Perhaps the most surprising thing he found was a perambulator. It was under a lime-tree, near the entrance to the Fairy Queen's Winter Palace (which is within the circle of the seven Spanish chestnuts), and Peter approached it warily, for the birds had never mentioned such things to him. Lest it was alive, he addressed it politely, and then, as it gave no answer, he went nearer and felt it cautiously. He gave it a little push, and it ran from him, which made him think it must be alive after all; but, as it had run from him, he was not afraid. So he stretched out his hand to pull it to him, but this time it ran at him, and he was so alarmed that he leapt the railing and scudded away to his boat. You must not think, however, that he was a coward, for he came back next night with a crust in one hand and a stick in the other, but the perambulator had gone, and he never saw another one. I have promised to tell you also about his paddle. It was a child's spade which he had found near St. Govor's Well, and he thought it was a paddle.

Do you pity Peter Pan for making these mistakes? If so, I think it rather silly of you. What I mean is that, of course, one must pity him now and then, but to pity him all the time would be impertinence. He thought he had the most splendid time in the Gardens, and to think you have it is almost quite as good as really to have it. He played without ceasing, while you often waste time by being mad-dog or Mary-Annish. He could be neither of these things, for he had never heard of them, but do you think he is to be pitied for that?

Oh, he was merry! He was as much merrier than you, for instance, as you are merrier than your father. Sometimes he fell, like a spinning-top,

from sheer merriment. Have you seen a greyhound leaping the fences
of the Gardens? That is how Peter leaps them.

And think of the music of his pipe. Gentlemen who walk home at
night write to the papers to say they heard a nightingale in the
Gardens, but it is really Peter's pipe they hear. Of course, he had no
mother—at least, what use was she to him? You can be sorry for him
for that, but don't be too sorry, for the next thing I mean to tell you is
how he revisited her. It was the fairies who gave him the chance.

LOCK-OUT TIME

IT is frightfully difficult to know much about the fairies, and almost
the only thing known for certain is that there are fairies wherever
there are children. Long ago children were forbidden the Gardens,
and at that time there was not a fairy in the place; then the children
were admitted, and the fairies came trooping in that very evening.
They can't resist following the children, but you seldom see them,
partly because they live in the daytime behind the railings, where you
are not allowed to go, and also partly because they are so cunning.
They are not a bit cunning after Lock-out, but until Lock-out, my
word!

When you were a bird you knew the fairies pretty well, and you
remember a good deal about them in your babyhood, which it is
a great pity you can't write down, for gradually you forget, and I have
heard of children who declared that they had never once seen a fairy.
Very likely if they said this in the Kensington Gardens, they were
standing looking at a fairy all the time. The reason they were cheated
was that she pretended to be something else. This is one of their best
tricks. They usually pretend to be flowers, because the court sits in
the Fairies' Basin, and there are so many flowers there, and all along
the Baby Walk,* that a flower is the thing least likely to attract attention. They dress exactly like flowers, and change with the seasons,
putting on white when lilies are in and blue for bluebells, and so on.
They like crocus and hyacinth time best of all, as they are partial to
a bit of colour, but tulips (except white ones, which are the fairy cra-
dles) they consider garish, and they sometimes put off dressing like
tulips for days, so that the beginning of the tulip weeks is almost the
best time to catch them.

When they think you are not looking they skip along pretty lively, but if you look, and they fear there is no time to hide, they stand quite still, pretending to be flowers. Then, after you have passed without knowing that they were fairies, they rush home and tell their mothers they have had such an adventure. The Fairy Basin, you remember, is all covered with ground-ivy (from which they make their castor-oil), with flowers growing in it here and there. Most of them really are flowers, but some of them are fairies. You never can be sure of them, but a good plan is to walk by looking the other way, and then turn round sharply. Another good plan, which David and I sometimes follow, is to stare them down. After a long time they can't help winking, and then you know for certain that they are fairies.

There are also numbers of them along the Baby Walk, which is a famous gentle place, as spots frequented by fairies are called. Once twenty-four of them had an extraordinary adventure. They were a girls' school out for a walk with the governess, and all wearing hyacinth gowns, when she suddenly put her finger to her mouth, and then they all stood still on an empty bed and pretended to be hyacinths. Unfortunately what the governess had heard was two gardeners coming to plant new flowers in that very bed. They were wheeling a handcart with the flowers in it, and were quite surprised to find the bed occupied. 'Pity to lift them hyacinths,' said the one man. 'Duke's orders,' replied the other, and, having emptied the cart, they dug up the boarding-school and put the poor, terrified things in it in five rows. Of course, neither the governess nor the girls dare let on that they were fairies, so they were carted far away to a potting-shed, out of which they escaped in the night without their shoes, but there was a great row about it among the parents, and the school was ruined.

As for their houses, it is no use looking for them, because they are the exact opposite of our houses. You can see our houses by day but you can't see them by dark. Well, you can see their houses by dark, but you can't see them by day, for they are the colour of night, and I never heard of any one yet who could see night in the daytime. This does not mean that they are black, for night has its colours just as day has, but ever so much brighter. Their blues and reds and greens are like ours with a light behind them. The palace is entirely built of many-coloured glasses, and it is quite the loveliest of all royal residences, but the queen sometimes complains because the common people will peep in to see what she is doing. They are very inquisitive folk, and press quite hard against the glass, and that is why their noses are mostly snubby. The streets are miles long and very twisty, and have paths on each side made of bright worsted. The birds used to steal the worsted for their nests, but a policeman has been appointed to hold on at the other end.

One of the great differences between the fairies and us is that they never do anything useful. When the first baby laughed for the first time, his laugh broke into a million pieces, and they all went skipping about. That was the beginning of fairies. They look tremendously busy, you know, as if they had not a moment to spare, but if you were to ask them what they are doing, they could not tell you in the least. They are frightfully ignorant, and everything they do is make-believe. They have a postman, but he never calls except at Christmas with his little box, and though they have beautiful schools, nothing is taught in them; the youngest child being chief person is always elected mistress, and when she has called the roll, they all go out for a walk and never come back. It is a very noticeable thing that, in fairy families, the youngest is always chief person, and usually becomes a prince or princess; and children remember this, and think it must be so among humans also, and that is why they are often made uneasy when they come upon their mother furtively putting new frills on the basinette.*

You have probably observed that your baby-sister wants to do all sorts of things that your mother and her nurse want her not to do—to stand up at sitting-down time, and to sit down at stand-up time, for instance, or to wake up when she should fall asleep, or to crawl on the floor when she is wearing her best frock, and so on, and perhaps you put this down to naughtiness. But it is not; it simply means that she is doing as she has seen the fairies do; she begins by following their ways, and it takes about two years to get her into the human ways. Her fits of passion, which are awful to behold, and are usually called teething, are no such thing; they are her natural exasperation, because we don't understand her, though she is talking an intelligible language. She is talking fairy. The reason mothers and nurses know what her remarks mean, before other people know, as that 'Guch' means 'Give it to me at once,' while 'Wa' is 'Why do you wear such a funny hat?' is because, mixing so much with babies, they have picked up a little of the fairy language.

Of late David has been thinking back hard about the fairy tongue, with his hands clutching his temples, and he has remembered a number of their phrases which I shall tell you some day if I don't forget. He had heard them in the days when he was a thrush, and though I suggested to him that perhaps it is really bird language he is remembering, he says not, for these phrases are about fun and adventures, and the birds talked of nothing but nest-building. He distinctly remembers that the birds used to go from spot to spot like ladies at shop windows, looking at the different nests and saying, 'Not my colour, my dear,' and 'How would that do with a soft lining?' and 'But will it wear?' and 'What hideous trimming!' and so on.

The fairies are exquisite dancers, and that is why one of the first things the baby does is to sign to you to dance to him and then to cry when you do it. They hold their great balls in the open air, in what is called a fairy ring.* For weeks afterwards you can see the ring on the grass. It is not there when they begin, but they make it by waltzing round and round. Sometimes you will find mushrooms inside the ring, and these are fairy chairs that the servants have forgotten to clear away. The chairs and the rings are the only tell-tale marks these little people leave behind them, and they would remove even these were they not so fond of dancing that they toe it till the very moment of the opening of the gates. David and I once found a fairy ring quite warm.

But there is also a way of finding out about the ball before it takes place. You know the boards which tell at what time the Gardens are to close to-day. Well, these tricky fairies sometimes slyly change the board on a ball night, so that it says the Gardens are to close at six-thirty, for instance, instead of at seven. This enables them to get begun half an hour earlier.

If on such a night we could remain behind in the Gardens, as the famous Maimie Mannering did, we might see delicious sights, hundreds of lovely fairies hastening to the ball, the married ones wearing their wedding rings round their waists, the gentlemen, all in uniform, holding up the ladies' trains, and linkmen* running in front carrying winter cherries, which are the fairy-lanterns, the cloakroom where they put on their silver slippers and get a ticket for their wraps, the flowers streaming up from the Baby Walk to look on, and always welcome because they can lend a pin, the supper-table, with Queen Mab at the head of it, and behind her chair the Lord Chamberlain, who carries a dandelion on which he blows when her Majesty wants to know the time.

The tablecloth varies according to the seasons, and in May it is made of chestnut blossom. The way the fairy servants do is this: The men, scores of them, climb up the trees and shake the branches, and the blossom falls like snow. Then the lady servants sweep it together by whisking their skirts until it is exactly like a tablecloth, and that is how they get their tablecloth.

They have real glasses and real wine of three kinds, namely, blackthorn wine, berberris* wine, and cowslip wine, and the Queen pours out, but the bottles are so heavy that she just pretends to pour out. There is bread-and-butter to begin with, of the size of a three-penny bit; and cakes to end with, and they are so small that they have no crumbs. The fairies sit round on mushrooms, and at first they are well-behaved and always cough off the table, and so on, but after a bit they are not so well-behaved and stick their fingers into the butter, which is got from the roots of old trees, and the really horrid ones crawl over the tablecloth chasing sugar or other delicacies with their tongues. When the Queen sees them doing this she signs to the servants to wash up and put away, and then everybody adjourns to the dance, the Queen walking in front while the Lord Chamberlain walks behind her, carrying two little pots, one of which contains the juice of wallflower and the other the juice of Solomon's seals.* Wallflower juice is good for reviving dancers who fall to the ground in a fit, and Solomon's seals juice is for bruises. They bruise very easily, and when Peter plays faster and faster they foot it till they fall down in fits. For, as you know without my telling you, Peter Pan is the fairies' orchestra. He sits in the middle of the ring, and they would never dream of having a smart dance nowadays without him. 'P. P.' is written on the corner of the invitation-cards sent out by all really good families. They are grateful little people, too, and at the princess's coming-of-age ball (they come of age on their second birthday and have a birthday every month) they gave him the wish of his heart.

The way it was done was this. The Queen ordered him to kneel, and then said that for playing so beautifully she would give him the wish of his heart. Then they all gathered round Peter to hear what was the wish of his heart, but for a long time he hesitated, not being certain what it was himself.

'If I chose to go back to mother,' he asked at last, 'could you give me that wish?'

Now this question vexed them, for were he to return to his mother they should lose his music, so the Queen tilted her nose contemptuously and said, 'Pooh! ask for a much bigger wish than that.'

'Is that quite a little wish?' he inquired.

'As little as this,' the Queen answered, putting her hands near each other.

'What size is a big wish?' he asked.

She measured it off on her skirt and it was a very handsome length.

Then Peter reflected and said, 'Well, then, I think I shall have two little wishes instead of one big one.'

Of course, the fairies had to agree, though his cleverness rather shocked them, and he said that his first wish was to go to his mother, but with the right to return to the Gardens if he found her disappointing. His second wish he would hold in reserve.

They tried to dissuade him, and even put obstacles in the way.

'I can give you the power to fly to her house,' the Queen said, 'but I can't open the door for you.'

'The window I flew out at will be open,' Peter said confidently. 'Mother always keeps it open in the hope that I may fly back.'

'How do you know?' they asked, quite surprised, and, really, Peter could not explain how he knew.

'I just do know,' he said.

So as he persisted in his wish, they had to grant it. The way they gave him power to fly was this: They all tickled him on the shoulder, and soon he felt a funny itching in that part, and then up he rose higher and higher, and flew away out of the Gardens and over the housetops.

It was so delicious that instead of flying straight to his old home he skimmed away over St. Paul's to the Crystal Palace and back by the river and Regent's Park, and by the time he reached his mother's window he had quite made up his mind that his second wish should be to become a bird.

The window was wide open, just as he knew it would be, and in he fluttered, and there was his mother lying asleep. Peter alighted softly on the wooden rail at the foot of the bed and had a good look at her. She lay with her head on her hand, and the hollow in the pillow was like a nest lined with her brown wavy hair. He remembered, though he had long forgotten it, that she always gave her hair a holiday at night. How sweet the frills of her nightgown were! He was very glad she was such a pretty mother.

But she looked sad, and he knew why she looked sad. One of her arms moved as if it wanted to go round something, and he knew what it wanted to go round.

'O mother!' said Peter to himself, 'if you just knew who is sitting on the rail at the foot of the bed.'

Very gently he patted the little mound that her feet made, and he could see by her face that she liked it. He knew he had but to say 'Mother' ever so softly, and she would wake up. They always wake up at once if it is you that says their name. Then she would give such a joyous cry and squeeze him tight. How nice that would be to him, but oh! how exquisitely delicious it would be to her. That, I am afraid, is how Peter regarded it. In returning to his mother he never doubted that he was giving her the greatest treat a woman can have. Nothing can be more splendid, he thought, than to have a little boy of your own. How proud of him they are! and very right and proper, too.

But why does Peter sit so long on the rail; why does he not tell his mother that he has come back?

I quite shrink from the truth, which is that he sat there in two minds. Sometimes he looked longingly at his mother, and sometimes he looked longingly at the window. Certainly it would be pleasant to be her boy again, but on the other hand, what times those had been in the Gardens! Was he so sure that he should enjoy wearing clothes again? He popped off the bed and opened some drawers to have a look at his old garments. They were still there, but he could not remember how you put them on. The socks, for instance, were they worn on the hands or on the feet? He was about to try one of them on his hand, when he had a great adventure. Perhaps the drawer had creaked; at any rate, his mother woke up, for he heard her say 'Peter,' as if it was the most lovely word in the language. He remained sitting on the floor and held his breath, wondering how she knew that he had come back. If she said 'Peter' again, he meant to cry 'Mother' and run to her. But she spoke no more, she made little moans only, and when he next peeped at her she was once more asleep, with tears on her face.

It made Peter very miserable, and what do you think was the first thing he did? Sitting on the rail at the foot of the bed, he played a beautiful lullaby to his mother on his pipe. He had made it up himself out of the way she said 'Peter,' and he never stopped playing until she looked happy.

He thought this so clever of him that he could scarcely resist wakening her to hear her say, 'O Peter, how exquisitely you play!' However, as she now seemed comfortable, he again cast looks at the window. You must not think that he meditated flying away and never coming back. He had quite decided to be his mother's boy, but hesitated about beginning to-night. It was the second wish which troubled him. He no longer meant to make it a wish to be a bird, but not to ask for a second wish seemed wasteful, and, of course, he could not ask for it without returning to the fairies. Also, if he put off asking for his wish too long it might go bad. He asked himself if he had not been hard-hearted to fly away without saying good-bye to Solomon. 'I should like awfully to sail in my boat just once more,' he said wistfully to his sleeping mother. He quite argued with her as if she could hear him. 'It would be so splendid to tell the birds of this adventure,' he said coaxingly. 'I promise to come back,' he said solemnly, and meant it, too.

And in the end, you know, he flew away. Twice he came back from the window, wanting to kiss his mother, but he feared the delight of it might waken her, so at last he played her a lovely kiss on his pipe, and then he flew back to the Gardens.

Many nights, and even months, passed before he asked the fairies for his second wish; and I am not sure that I quite know why he delayed so long. One reason was that he had so many good-byes to say, not only to his particular friends, but to a hundred favourite spots. Then he had his last sail, and his very last sail, and his last sail of all, and so on. Again, a number of farewell feasts were given in his honour; and another comfortable reason was that, after all, there was no hurry, for his mother would never weary of waiting for him. This last reason displeased old Solomon, for it was an encouragement to the birds to procrastinate. Solomon had several excellent mottoes for keeping them at their work, such as 'Never put off laying to-day, because you can lay tomorrow,' and 'In this world there are no second chances,'* and yet here was Peter gaily putting off and none the worse for it. The birds pointed this out to each other, and fell into lazy habits.

But, mind you, though Peter was so slow in going back to his mother, he was quite decided to go back. The best proof of this was his caution with the fairies. They were most anxious that he should remain in the Gardens to play to them, and to bring this to pass they tried to trick him into making such a remark as 'I wish the grass was not so wet,' and some of them danced out of time in the hope that he might cry, 'I do wish you would keep time!' Then they would have said that this was his second wish. But he smoked their design, and though on occasions he began, 'I wish——' he always stopped in time. So when at last he said to them bravely, 'I wish now to go back to mother for ever and always,' they had to tickle his shoulders and let him go.

He went in a hurry in the end, because he had dreamt that his mother was crying, and he knew what was the great thing she cried for, and that a hug from her splendid Peter would quickly make her to smile. Oh! he felt sure of it, and so eager was he to be nestling in her arms that this time he flew straight to the window, which was always to be open for him.

But the window was closed, and there were iron bars on it, and peering inside he saw his mother sleeping peacefully with her arm round another little boy.

Peter called, 'Mother! mother!' but she heard him not; in vain he beat his little limbs against the iron bars. He had to fly back, sobbing, to the Gardens, and he never saw his dear again. What a glorious boy he had meant to be to her! Ah, Peter! we who have made the great mistake, how differently we should all act at the second chance. But Solomon was right—there is no second chance, not for most of us. When we reach the window it is Lock-out Time. The iron bars are up for life.*

THE LITTLE HOUSE

EVERYBODY has heard of the Little House in the Kensington Gardens, which is the only house in the whole world that the fairies have built for humans. But no one has really seen it, except just three or four, and they have not only seen it but slept in it, and unless you sleep in it you never see it. This is because it is not there when you lie down, but it is there when you wake up and step outside.

In a kind of way every one may see it, but what you see is not really it, but only the light in the windows. You see the light after Lock-out Time. David, for instance, saw it quite distinctly far away among the trees as we were going home from the pantomime, and Oliver Bailey saw it the night he stayed so late at the Temple, which is the name of his father's office. Angela Clare, who loves to have a tooth extracted because then she is treated to tea in a shop, saw more than one light, she saw hundreds of them all together; and this must have been the fairies building the house, for they build it every night, and always in a different part of the Gardens. She thought one of the lights was bigger than the others, though she was not quite sure, for they jumped about so, and it might have been another one that was bigger. But if it was the same one, it was Peter Pan's light. Heaps of children have seen the light, so that is nothing. But Maimie Mannering was the famous one for whom the house was first built.

Maimie was always rather a strange girl, and it was at night that she was strange. She was four years of age, and in the daytime she was the ordinary kind. She was pleased when her brother Tony, who was a magnificent fellow of six, took notice of her, and she looked up to him in the right way, and tried in vain to imitate him, and was flattered rather than annoyed when he shoved her about. Also, when she was batting, she would pause though the ball was in the air to point out to you that she was wearing new shoes. She was quite the ordinary kind in the daytime.

But as the shades of night fell, Tony, the swaggerer, lost his contempt for Maimie and eyed her fearfully; and no wonder, for with dark there came into her face a look that I can describe only as a leary* look. It was also a serene look that contrasted grandly with Tony's uneasy glances. Then he would make her presents of his favourite toys (which he always took away from her next morning), and she accepted them with a disturbing smile. The reason he was now become so wheedling and she so mysterious was (in brief) that they knew they were about to be sent to bed. It was then that Maimie was terrible. Tony entreated her not to do it to-night, and the mother and their coloured nurse threatened her, but Maimie merely smiled her agitating smile. And by and by when they were alone with their nightlight she would start up in bed crying 'Hsh! what was that?' Tony beseeches her, 'It was nothing—don't, Maimie, don't!' and pulls the sheet over his head. 'It is coming nearer!' she cries. 'Oh, look at it, Tony! It is feeling your bed with its horns—it is boring for you, O Tony, oh!' and she desists not until he rushes downstairs in his combinations,* screeching. When they came up to whip Maimie they usually found her sleeping tranquilly—not shamming, you know, but really sleeping, and looking like the sweetest little angel, which seems to me to make it almost worse.

But of course it was daytime when they were in the Gardens, and then Tony did most of the talking. You could gather from his talk that he was a very brave boy, and no one was so proud of it as Maimie. She would have loved to have a ticket on her saying that she was his sister. And at no time did she admire him more than when he told her, as he often did with splendid firmness, that one day he meant to remain behind in the Gardens after the gates were closed.

'O Tony,' she would say with awful respect, 'but the fairies will be so angry!'

'I dare say,' replied Tony carelessly.

'Perhaps,' she said, thrilling, 'Peter Pan will give you a sail in his boat!'

'I shall make him,' replied Tony; no wonder she was proud of him.

But they should not have talked so loudly, for one day they were overheard by a fairy who had been gathering skeleton leaves, from which the little people weave their summer curtains, and after that Tony was a marked boy. They loosened the rails before he sat on them, so that down he came on the back of his head; they tripped him up by catching his bootlace and bribed the ducks to sink his boat. Nearly all the nasty accidents you meet with in the Gardens occur because the fairies have taken an ill-will to you, and so it behoves you to be careful what you say about them.

Maimie was one of the kind who like to fix a day for doing things, but Tony was not that kind, and when she asked him which day he was to remain behind in the Gardens after Lock-out he merely replied, 'Just some day'; he was quite vague about which day except when she asked, 'Will it be to-day?' and then he could always say for certain that it would not be to-day. So she saw that he was waiting for a real good chance.

This brings us to an afternoon when the Gardens were white with snow, and there was ice on the Round Pond; not thick enough to skate on, but at least you could spoil it for to-morrow by flinging stones, and many bright little boys and girls were doing that.

When Tony and his sister arrived they wanted to go straight to the pond, but their ayah* said they must take a sharp walk first, and as she said this she glanced at the time-board to see when the Gardens closed that night. It read half-past five. Poor ayah! she is the one who laughs continuously because there are so many white children in the world, but she was not to laugh much more that day.

Well, they went up the Baby Walk and back, and when they returned to the time-board she was surprised to see that it now read five o'clock for closing-time. But she was unacquainted with the tricky ways of the fairies, and so did not see (as Maimie and Tony saw at once) that they had changed the hour because there was to be a ball to-night. She said there was only time now to walk to the top of the Hump and back, and as they trotted along with her she little guessed what was thrilling their little breasts. You see the chance had come of seeing a fairy ball. Never, Tony felt, could he hope for a better chance.

He had to feel this for Maimie so plainly felt it for him. Her eager eyes asked the question, 'Is it to-day?' and he gasped and then nodded. Maimie slipped her hand into Tony's, and hers was hot, but his was cold. She did a very kind thing; she took off her scarf and gave it to him. 'In case you should feel cold,' she whispered. Her face was aglow, but Tony's was very gloomy.

As they turned on the top of the Hump he whispered to her, 'I'm afraid Nurse would see me, so I shan't be able to do it.'

Maimie admired him more than ever for being afraid of nothing but their ayah, when there were so many unknown terrors to fear, and she said aloud, 'Tony, I shall race you to the gate,' and in a whisper, 'Then you can hide,' and off they ran.

Tony could always outdistance her easily, but never had she known him speed away so quickly as now, and she was sure he hurried that he might have more time to hide. 'Brave, brave!' her doting eyes were crying when she got a dreadful shock; instead of hiding, her hero had run out at the gate! At this bitter sight Maimie stopped blankly, as if all her lapful of darling treasures were suddenly spilled, and then for very disdain she could not sob; in a swell of protest against all puling cowards she ran to St. Govor's Well and hid in Tony's stead.

When the ayah reached the gate and saw Tony far in front she thought her other charge was with him and passed out. Twilight crept over the Gardens, and hundreds of people passed out, including the last one, who always has to run for it, but Maimie saw them not. She had shut her eyes tight and glued them with passionate tears. When she opened them something very cold ran up her legs and up her arms and dropped into her heart. It was the stillness of the Gardens. Then she heard *clang*, then from another part *clang*, then *clang, clang* far away. It was the Closing of the Gates.

Immediately the last clang had died away Maimie distinctly heard a voice say, 'So that's all right.' It had a wooden sound and seemed to come from above, and she looked up in time to see an elm-tree stretching out its arms and yawning.

She was about to say, 'I never knew you could speak!' when a metallic voice that seemed to come from the ladle at the well remarked to the elm, 'I suppose it is a bit coldish up there?' and the elm replied, 'Not particularly, but you do get numb standing so long on one leg,' and he flapped his arms vigorously just as the cabmen do before they drive off. Maimie was quite surprised to see that a number of other tall trees were doing the same sort of thing, and she stole away to the Baby Walk and crouched observantly under a Minorca holly which shrugged its shoulders but did not seem to mind her.

She was not in the least cold. She was wearing a russet-coloured pelisse* and had the hood over her head, so that nothing of her showed except her dear little face and her curls. The rest of her real self was hidden far away inside so many warm garments that in shape she seemed rather like a ball. She was about forty round the waist.

There was a good deal going on in the Baby Walk, where Maimie arrived in time to see a magnolia and a Persian lilac step over the railing and set off for a smart walk. They moved in a jerky sort of way certainly, but that was because they used crutches. An elderberry hobbled across the walk, and stood chatting with some young quinces, and they all had crutches. The crutches were the sticks that are tied to young trees and shrubs. They were quite familiar objects to Maimie, but she had never known what they were for until to-night.

She peeped up the walk and saw her first fairy. He was a street boy fairy who was running up the walk closing the weeping trees. The way he did it was this: he pressed a spring in the trunks and they shut like umbrellas, deluging the little plants beneath with snow. 'O you naughty, naughty child!' Maimie cried indignantly, for she knew what it was to have a dripping umbrella about your ears.

Fortunately the mischievous fellow was out of earshot, but a chrysanthemum heard her, and said so pointedly, 'Hoity-toity, what is this?' that she had to come out and show herself. Then the whole vegetable kingdom was rather puzzled what to do.

'Of course it is no affair of ours,' a spindle-tree said after they had whispered together, 'but you know quite well you ought not to be here, and perhaps our duty is to report you to the fairies; what do you think yourself?'

'I think you should not,' Maimie replied, which so perplexed them that they said petulantly there was no arguing with her. 'I wouldn't ask it of you,' she assured them, 'if I thought it was wrong,' and of course after this they could not well carry tales. They then said, 'Well-a-day,'* and 'Such is life,' for they can be frightfully sarcastic; but she felt sorry for those of them who had no crutches, and she said good-naturedly, 'Before I go to the fairies' ball, I should like to take you for a walk one at a time; you can lean on me, you know.'

At this they clapped their hands, and she escorted them up the Baby Walk and back again, one at a time, putting an arm or a finger round the very frail, setting their leg right when it got too ridiculous, and treating the foreign ones quite as courteously as the English, though she could not understand a word they said.

They behaved well on the whole, though some whimpered that she had not taken them as far as she took Nancy or Grace or Dorothy, and others jagged* her, but it was quite unintentional, and she was too much of a lady to cry out. So much walking tired her, and she was anxious to be off to the ball, but she no longer felt afraid. The reason she felt no more fear was that it was now night-time, and in the dark, you remember, Maimie was always rather strange.

They were now loth to let her go, for, 'If the fairies see you,' they warned her, 'they will mischief you—stab you to death, or compel you to nurse their children,* or turn you into something tedious, like an evergreen oak.' As they said this they looked with affected pity at an evergreen oak, for in winter they are very envious of the evergreens.

'Oh, la!' replied the oak bitingly, 'how deliciously cosy it is to stand here buttoned to the neck and watch you poor naked creatures shivering.'

This made them sulky, though they had really brought it on themselves, and they drew for Maimie a very gloomy picture of the perils that would face her if she insisted on going to the ball.

She learned from a purple filbert that the court was not in its usual good temper at present, the cause being the tantalising heart of the Duke of Christmas Daisies. He was an Oriental fairy, very poorly of a dreadful complaint, namely, inability to love, and though he had tried many ladies in many lands he could not fall in love with one of them. Queen Mab, who rules in the Gardens, had been confident that her girls would bewitch him, but alas! his heart, the doctor said, remained cold. This rather irritating doctor, who was his private physician, felt the Duke's heart immediately after any lady was presented, and then always shook his bald head and murmured, 'Cold, quite cold.' Naturally Queen Mab felt disgraced, and first she tried the effect of ordering the court into tears for nine minutes, and then she blamed the Cupids and decreed that they should wear fools' caps until they thawed the Duke's frozen heart.

'How I should love to see the Cupids in their dear little fools' caps!' Maimie cried, and away she ran to look for them very recklessly, for the Cupids hate to be laughed at.

It is always easy to discover where a fairies' ball is being held, as ribbons are stretched between it and all the populous parts of the Gardens, on which those invited may walk to the dance without wetting their pumps. This night the ribbons were red, and looked very pretty on the snow.

Maimie walked alongside one of them for some distance without meeting anybody, but at last she saw a fairy cavalcade approaching. To her surprise they seemed to be returning from the ball, and she had just time to hide from them by bending her knees and holding out her arms and pretending to be a garden chair. There were six horsemen in front and six behind; in the middle walked a prim lady wearing a long train held up by two pages, and on the train, as if it were a couch, reclined a lovely girl, for in this way do aristocratic fairies travel about. She was dressed in golden rain, but the most enviable part of her was her neck, which was blue in colour and of a velvet texture, and of course showed off her diamond necklace as no white throat could have glorified it. The high-born fairies obtain this admired effect by pricking their skin, which lets the blue blood come through and dye them, and you cannot imagine anything so dazzling unless you have seen the ladies' busts in the jewellers' windows.

Maimie also noticed that the whole cavalcade seemed to be in a passion, tilting their noses higher than it can be safe for even fairies to tilt them, and she concluded that this must be another case in which the doctor had said, 'Cold, quite cold.'

Well, she followed the ribbon to a place where it became a bridge over a dry puddle into which another fairy had fallen and been unable to climb out. At first this little damsel was afraid of Maimie, who most kindly went to her aid, but soon she sat in her hand chatting gaily and explaining that her name was Brownie,* and that though only a poor street singer she was on her way to the ball to see if the Duke would have her.

'Of course,' she said, 'I am rather plain,' and this made Maimie uncomfortable, for indeed the simple little creature was almost quite plain for a fairy.

It was difficult to know what to reply.

'I see you think I have no chance,' Brownie said falteringly.

'I don't say that,' Maimie answered politely; 'of course your face is just a tiny bit homely, but——' Really it was quite awkward for her.

Fortunately she remembered about her father and the bazaar. He had gone to a fashionable bazaar where all the most beautiful ladies in London were on view for half a crown the second day, but on his return home, instead of being dissatisfied with Maimie's mother, he had said, 'You can't think, my dear, what a relief it is to see a homely face again.'

Maimie repeated this story, and it fortified Brownie tremendously, indeed she had no longer the slightest doubt that the Duke would choose her. So she scudded away up the ribbon, calling out to Maimie not to follow lest the Queen should mischief her.

But Maimie's curiosity tugged her forward, and presently at the seven Spanish chestnuts she saw a wonderful light. She crept forward until she was quite near it, and then she peeped from behind a tree.

The light, which was as high as your head above the ground, was composed of myriads of glowworms all holding on to each other, and so forming a dazzling canopy over the fairy ring. There were thousands of little people looking on, but they were in shadow and drab in colour compared to the glorious creatures within that luminous circle, who were so bewilderingly bright that Maimie had to wink hard all the time she looked at them.

It was amazing and even irritating to her that the Duke of Christmas Daisies should be able to keep out of love for a moment: yet out of love his dusky grace still was: you could see it by the shamed looks of the Queen and court (though they pretended not to care), by the way darling ladies brought forward for his approval burst into tears as they were told to pass on, and by his own most dreary face.

Maimie could also see the pompous doctor feeling the Duke's heart and hear him give utterance to his parrot cry, and she was particularly sorry for the Cupids, who stood in their fools' caps in obscure places and, every time they heard that 'Cold, quite cold,' bowed their disgraced little heads.

She was disappointed not to see Peter Pan, and I may as well tell you now why he was so late that night. It was because his boat had got wedged on the Serpentine between fields of floating ice, through which he had to break a perilous passage with his trusty paddle.

The fairies had as yet scarcely missed him, for they could not dance, so heavy were their hearts. They forget all the steps when they are sad, and remember them again when they are merry. David tells me that fairies never say, 'We feel happy': what they say is, 'We feel *dancey*.'

Well, they were looking very undancey indeed, when sudden laughter broke out among the on-lookers, caused by Brownie, who had just arrived and was insisting on her right to be presented to the Duke.

Maimie craned forward eagerly to see how her friend fared, though she had really no hope; no one seemed to have the least hope except Brownie herself, who, however, was absolutely confident. She was led before his grace, and the doctor putting a finger carelessly on the ducal heart, which for convenience' sake was reached by a little trap-door in his diamond shirt, had begun to say mechanically, 'Cold, qui—,' when he stopped abruptly.

'What's this?' he cried, and first he shook the heart like a watch, and then he put his ear to it.

'Bless my soul!' cried the doctor, and by this time of course the excitement among the spectators was tremendous, fairies fainting right and left.

Everybody stared breathlessly at the Duke, who was very much startled, and looked as if he would like to run away. 'Good gracious me!' the doctor was heard muttering, and now the heart was evidently on fire, for he had to jerk his fingers away from it and put them in his mouth.

The suspense was awful.

Then in a loud voice, and bowing low, 'My Lord Duke,' said the physician elatedly, 'I have the honour to inform your excellency that your grace is in love.'

You can't conceive the effect of it. Brownie held out her arms to the Duke and he flung himself into them, the Queen leapt into the arms of the Lord Chamberlain, and the ladies of the court leapt into the arms of her gentlemen, for it is etiquette to follow her example in everything. Thus in a single moment about fifty marriages took place, for if you leap into each other's arms it is a fairy wedding. Of course a clergyman has to be present.

How the crowd cheered and leapt! Trumpets brayed, the moon came out, and immediately a thousand couples seized hold of its rays as if they were ribbons in a May dance and waltzed in wild abandon round the fairy ring. Most gladsome sight of all, the Cupids plucked the hated fools' caps from their heads and cast them high in the air. And then Maimie went and spoiled everything.

She couldn't help it. She was crazy with delight over her little friend's good fortune, so she took several steps forward and cried in an ecstasy, 'O Brownie, how splendid!'

Everybody stood still, the music ceased, the lights went out, and all in the time you may take to say, 'Oh dear!' An awful sense of her peril came upon Maimie; too late she remembered that she was a lost child in a place where no human must be between the locking and the opening of the gates; she heard the murmur of an angry multitude; she saw a thousand swords flashing for her blood, and she uttered a cry of terror and fled.

How she ran! and all the time her eyes were starting out of her head. Many times she lay down, and then quickly jumped up and ran on again. Her little mind was so entangled in terrors that she no longer knew she was in the Gardens. The one thing she was sure of was that she must never cease to run, and she thought she was still running long after she had dropped in the Figs and gone to sleep. She thought the snowflakes falling on her face were her mother kissing her good-night. She thought her coverlet of snow was a warm blanket, and tried to pull it over her head. And when she heard talking through her dreams she thought it was mother bringing father to the nursery door to look at her as she slept. But it was the fairies.

I am very glad to be able to say that they no longer desired to mischief her. When she rushed away they had rent the air with such cries as 'Slay her!' 'Turn her into something extremely unpleasant!' and so on, but the pursuit was delayed while they discussed who should march in front, and this gave Duchess Brownie time to cast herself before the Queen and demand a boon.*

Every bride has a right to a boon, and what she asked for was Maimie's life. 'Anything except that,' replied Queen Mab sternly, and all the fairies echoed, 'Anything except that.' But when they learned how Maimie had befriended Brownie and so enabled her to attend the ball to their great glory and renown, they gave three huzzas for the little human, and set off, like an army, to thank her, the court advancing in front and the canopy keeping step with it. They traced Maimie easily by her footprints in the snow.

But though they found her deep in snow in the Figs, it seemed impossible to thank Maimie, for they could not waken her. They went through the form of thanking her—that is to say, the new King stood on her body and read her a long address of welcome, but she heard not a word of it. They also cleared the snow off her, but soon she was covered again, and they saw she was in danger of perishing of cold.

'Turn her into something that does not mind the cold,' seemed a good suggestion of the doctor's, but the only thing they could think of that does not mind cold was a snowflake. 'And it might melt,' the Queen pointed out, so that idea had to be given up.

A magnificent attempt was made to carry her to a sheltered spot, but though there were so many of them she was too heavy. By this time all the ladies were crying in their handkerchiefs, but presently the Cupids had a lovely idea. 'Build a house round her,' they cried, and at once everybody perceived that this was the thing to do; in a moment a hundred fairy sawyers were among the branches, architects were running round Maimie, measuring her; a bricklayer's yard sprang up at her feet, seventy-five masons rushed up with the foundation-stone, and the Queen laid it, overseers were appointed to keep the boys off, scaffoldings were run up, the whole place rang with hammers and chisels and turning-lathes, and by this time the roof was on and the glaziers were putting in the windows.

The house was exactly the size of Maimie, and perfectly lovely. One of her arms was extended, and this had bothered them for a second, but they built a verandah round it, leading to the front door. The windows were the size of a coloured picture-book and the door rather smaller, but it would be easy for her to get out by taking off the roof. The fairies, as is their custom, clapped their hands with delight over their cleverness, and they were so madly in love with the little house that they could not bear to think they had finished it. So they gave it ever so many little extra touches, and even then they added more extra touches.

For instance, two of them ran up a ladder and put on a chimney.

'Now we fear it is quite finished,' they sighed.

But no, for another two ran up the ladder, and tied some smoke to the chimney.

'That certainly finishes it,' they said reluctantly.

'Not at all,' cried a glow-worm; 'if she were to wake without seeing a night-light she might be frightened, so I shall be her night-light.'

'Wait one moment,' said a china merchant, 'and I shall make you a saucer.'

Now, alas! it was absolutely finished.

Oh, dear no!

'Gracious me!' cried a brass manufacturer, 'there's no handle on the door,' and he put one on.

An ironmonger added a scraper, and an old lady ran up with a door-mat. Carpenters arrived with a water-butt, and the painters insisted on painting it.

Finished at last!

'Finished! how can it be finished,' the plumber demanded scornfully, 'before hot and cold are put in?' and he put in hot and cold. Then an army of gardeners arrived with fairy carts and spades and seeds and bulbs and forcing-houses,* and soon they had a flower-garden to the right of the verandah, and a vegetable garden to the left, and roses and clematis on the walls of the house, and in less time than five minutes all these dear things were in full bloom.

Oh, how beautiful the little house was now! But it was at last finished true as true, and they had to leave it and return to the dance. They all kissed their hands to it as they went away, and the last to go was Brownie. She stayed a moment behind the others to drop a pleasant dream down the chimney.

All through the night the exquisite little house stood there in the Figs taking care of Maimie, and she never knew. She slept until the dream was quite finished, and woke feeling deliciously cosy just as morning was breaking from its egg, and then she almost fell asleep again, and then she called out, 'Tony,' for she thought she was at home in the nursery. As Tony made no answer, she sat up, whereupon her head hit the roof, and it opened like the lid of a box, and to her bewilderment she saw all around her the Kensington Gardens lying deep in snow. As she was not in the nursery she wondered whether this was really herself, so she pinched her cheeks, and then she knew it was herself, and this reminded her that she was in the middle of a great adventure. She remembered now everything that had happened to her from the closing of the gates up to her running away from the fairies, but however, she asked herself, had she got into this funny place? She stepped out by the roof, right over the garden, and then she saw the dear house in which she had passed the night. It so entranced her that she could think of nothing else.

'O you darling! O you sweet! O you love!' she cried.

Perhaps a human voice frightened the little house, or maybe it now knew that its work was done, for no sooner had Maimie spoken than it began to grow smaller; it shrank so slowly that she could scarce believe it was shrinking, yet she soon knew that it could not contain her now. It always remained as complete as ever, but it became smaller and smaller, and the garden dwindled at the same time, and the snow crept closer, lapping house and garden up. Now the house was the size of a little dog's kennel, and now of a Noah's Ark, but still you could see the smoke and the door-handle and the roses on the wall, every one complete. The glow-worm light was waning too, but it was still there. 'Darling, loveliest, don't go!' Maimie cried, falling on her knees, for the little house was now the size of a reel of thread, but still quite complete. But as she stretched out her arms imploringly the snow crept up on all sides until it met itself, and where the little house had been was now one unbroken expanse of snow.

Maimie stamped her foot naughtily, and was putting her fingers to her eyes, when she heard a kind voice say, 'Don't cry, pretty human, don't cry,' and then she turned round and saw a beautiful little naked boy regarding her wistfully. She knew at once that he must be Peter Pan.

PETER'S GOAT

MAIMIE felt quite shy, but Peter knew not what shy was.

'I hope you have had a good night,' he said earnestly.

'Thank you,' she replied, 'I was so cosy and warm. But you'—and she looked at his nakedness awkwardly—'don't you feel the least bit cold?'

Now cold was another word Peter had forgotten, so he answered, 'I think not, but I may be wrong: you see I am rather ignorant. I am not exactly a boy; Solomon says I am a Betwixt-and-Between.'

'So that is what it is called,' said Maimie thoughtfully.

'That's not my name,' he explained, 'my name is Peter Pan.'

'Yes, of course,' she said, 'I know, everybody knows.'

You can't think how pleased Peter was to learn that all the people outside the gates knew about him. He begged Maimie to tell him what they knew and what they said, and she did so. They were sitting by this time on a fallen tree; Peter had cleared off the snow for Maimie, but he sat on a snowy bit himself.

'Squeeze closer,' Maimie said.

'What is that?' he asked, and she showed him, and then he did it. They talked together and he found that people knew a great deal about him, but not everything, not that he had gone back to his mother and been barred out, for instance, and he said nothing of this to Maimie, for it still humiliated him.

'Do they know that I play games exactly like real boys?' he asked very proudly. 'O Maimie, please tell them!' But when he revealed how he played, by sailing his hoop on the Round Pond, and so on, she was simply horrified.

'All your ways of playing,' she said with her big eyes on him, 'are quite, quite wrong, and not in the least like how boys play.'

Poor Peter uttered a little moan at this, and he cried for the first time for I know not how long. Maimie was extremely sorry for him, and lent him her handkerchief, but he didn't know in the least what to do with it, so she showed him, that is to say, she wiped her eyes, and then gave it back to him, saying, 'Now you do it,' but instead of wiping his own eyes he wiped hers, and she thought it best to pretend that this was what she had meant.

She said out of pity for him, 'I shall give you a kiss if you like,' but though he once knew, he had long forgotten what kisses are, and he replied, 'Thank you,' and held out his hand, thinking she had offered to put something into it. This was a great shock to her, but she felt she could not explain without shaming him, so with charming delicacy she gave Peter a thimble which happened to be in her pocket, and pretended that it was a kiss. Poor little boy! he quite believed her, and to this day he wears it on his finger, though there can be scarcely any one who needs a thimble so little. You see, though still a tiny child, it was really years and years since he had seen his mother, and I dare say the baby who had supplanted him was now a man with whiskers.

But you must not think that Peter Pan was a boy to pity rather than to admire; if Maimie began by thinking this, she soon found she was very much mistaken. Her eyes glistened with admiration when he told her of his adventures, especially of how he went to and fro between the island and the Gardens in the Thrush's Nest.

'How romantic!' Maimie exclaimed, but this was another unknown word, and he hung his head thinking she was despising him.

'I suppose Tony would not have done that?' he said very humbly.

'Never, never!' she answered with conviction, 'he would have been afraid.'

'What is afraid?' asked Peter longingly. He thought it must be some splendid thing. 'I do wish you would teach me how to be afraid, Maimie,' he said.

'I believe no one could teach that to you,' she answered adoringly, but Peter thought she meant that he was stupid. She had told him about Tony and of the wicked thing she did in the dark to frighten him (she knew quite well that it was wicked), but Peter misunderstood her meaning and said, 'Oh, how I wish I was as brave as Tony!'

It quite irritated her. 'You are twenty thousand times braver than Tony,' she said; 'you are ever so much the bravest boy I ever knew.'

He could scarcely believe she meant it, but when he did believe he screamed with joy.

'And if you want very much to give me a kiss,' Maimie said, 'you can do it.'

Very reluctantly Peter began to take the thimble off his finger. He thought she wanted it back.

'I don't mean a kiss,' she said hurriedly, 'I mean a thimble.'

'What's that?' Peter asked.

'It's like this,' she said, and kissed him.

'I should love to give you a thimble,' Peter said gravely, so he gave her one. He gave her quite a number of thimbles, and then a delightful idea came into his head. 'Maimie,' he said, 'will you marry me?'

Now, strange to tell, the same idea had come at exactly the same time into Maimie's head. 'I should like to,' she answered, 'but will there be room in your boat for two?'

'If you squeeze close,' he said eagerly.

'Perhaps the birds would be angry?'

He assured her that the birds would love to have her, though I am not so certain of it myself. Also that there were very few birds in winter. 'Of course they might want your clothes,' he had to admit rather falteringly.

She was somewhat indignant at this.

'They are always thinking of their nests,' he said apologetically, 'and there are some bits of you'—he stroked the fur on her pelisse—'that would excite them very much.'

'They shan't have my fur,' she said sharply.

'No,' he said, still fondling it, however, 'no. O Maimie,' he said rapturously, 'do you know why I love you? It is because you are like a beautiful nest.'

Somehow this made her uneasy. 'I think you are speaking more like a bird than a boy now,' she said, holding back, and indeed he was even looking rather like a bird. 'After all,' she said, 'you are only a Betwixt-and-Between.' But it hurt him so much that she immediately added, 'It must be a delicious thing to be.'

'Come and be one, then, dear Maimie,' he implored her, and they set off for the boat, for it was now very near Open-Gate time. 'And you are not a bit like a nest,' he whispered to please her.

'But I think it is rather nice to be like one,' she said in a woman's contradictory way. 'And, Peter, dear, though I can't give them my fur, I wouldn't mind their building in it. Fancy a nest in my neck with little spotty eggs in it! O Peter, how perfectly lovely!'

But as they drew near the Serpentine, she shivered a little, and said, 'Of course I shall go and see mother often, quite often. It is not as if I was saying good-bye for ever to mother, it is not in the least like that.'

'Oh no,' answered Peter, but in his heart he knew it was very like that, and he would have told her so had he not been in a quaking fear of losing her. He was so fond of her, he felt he could not live without her. 'She will forget her mother in time, and be happy with me,' he kept saying to himself, and he hurried her on, giving her thimbles by the way.

But even when she had seen the boat and exclaimed ecstatically over its loveliness, she still talked tremblingly about her mother. 'You know quite well, Peter, don't you,' she said, 'that I wouldn't come unless I knew for certain I could go back to mother whenever I want to? Peter, say it.'

He said it, but he could no longer look her in the face.

'If you are sure your mother will always want you,' he added rather sourly.

'The idea of mother's not always wanting me!' Maimie cried, and her face glistened.

'If she doesn't bar you out,' said Peter huskily.

'The door,' replied Maimie, 'will always, always be open, and mother will always be waiting at it for me.'

'Then,' said Peter, not without grimness, 'step in, if you feel so sure of her,' and he helped Maimie into the Thrush's Nest.

'But why don't you look at me,' she asked, taking him by the arm.

Peter tried hard not to look, he tried to push off, then he gave a great gulp and jumped ashore and sat down miserably in the snow.

She went to him. 'What is it, dear, dear Peter?' she said, wondering.

'O Maimie,' he cried, 'it isn't fair to take you with me if you think you can go back! Your mother'—he gulped again—'you don't know them as well as I do.'

And then he told her the woeful story of how he had been barred out, and she gasped all the time. 'But my mother,' she said, '*my* mother——'

'Yes, she would,' said Peter, 'they are all the same. I dare say she is looking for another one already.'

Maimie said aghast, 'I can't believe it. You see, when you went away your mother had none, but my mother has Tony, and surely they are satisfied when they have one.'

Peter replied bitterly, 'You should see the letters Solomon gets from ladies who have six.'

Just then they heard a grating *creak*, followed by *creak*, *creak*, all round the Gardens. It was the Opening of the Gates, and Peter jumped nervously into his boat. He knew Maimie would not come with him now, and he was trying bravely not to cry. But Maimie was sobbing painfully.

'If I should be too late,' she said in agony, 'O Peter, if she has got another one already!'

Again he sprang ashore as if she had called him back. 'I shall come and look for you to-night,' he said, squeezing close, 'but if you hurry away I think you will be in time.'

Then he pressed a last thimble on her sweet little mouth, and covered his face with his hands so that he might not see her go.

'Dear Peter!' she cried.

'Dear Maimie!' cried the tragic boy.

She leapt into his arms, so that it was a sort of fairy wedding, and then she hurried away. Oh, how she hastened to the gates! Peter, you may be sure, was back in the Gardens that night as soon as Lock-out sounded, but he found no Maimie, and so he knew she had been in time. For long he hoped that some night she would come back to him; often he thought he saw her waiting for him by the shore of the Serpentine as his bark drew to land, but Maimie never went back. She wanted to, but she was afraid that if she saw her dear Betwixt-and-Between again she would linger with him too long, and besides the ayah now kept a sharp eye on her. But she often talked lovingly of Peter, and she knitted a kettle-holder* for him, and one day when she was wondering what Easter present he would like, her mother made a suggestion.

'Nothing,' she said thoughtfully, 'would be so useful to him as a goat.'

'He could ride on it,' cried Maimie, 'and play on his pipe at the same time.'

'Then,' her mother asked, 'won't you give him your goat, the one you frighten Tony with at night?'

'But it isn't a real goat,' Maimie said.

'It seems very real to Tony,' replied her mother.

'It seems frightfully real to me too,' Maimie admitted, 'but how could I give it to Peter?'

Her mother knew a way, and next day, accompanied by Tony (who was really quite a nice boy, though of course he could not compare), they went to the Gardens, and Maimie stood alone within a fairy ring, and then her mother, who was a rather gifted lady, said—

> *'My daughter, tell me, if you can,*
> *What have you got for Peter Pan?'*

To which Maimie replied—

> *'I have a goat for him to ride,*
> *Observe me cast it far and wide.'*

She then flung her arms about as if she were sowing seed, and turned round three times.

Next Tony said—

> *'If P. doth find it waiting here,*
> *Wilt ne'er again make me to fear?'*

And Maimie answered—

> *'By dark or light I fondly swear*
> *Never to see goats anywhere.'*

She also left a letter to Peter in a likely place, explaining what she had done, and begging him to ask the fairies to turn the goat into one convenient for riding on. Well, it all happened just as she hoped, for Peter found the letter, and of course nothing could be easier for the fairies than to turn the goat into a real one, and so that is how Peter got the goat on which he now rides round the Gardens every night playing sublimely on his pipe. And Maimie kept her promise, and never frightened Tony with a goat again, though I have heard that she created another animal. Until she was quite a big girl she continued to leave presents for Peter in the Gardens (with letters explaining how humans play with them), and she is not the only one who has done this. David does it, for instance, and he and I know the likeliest place for leaving them in, and we shall tell you if you like, but for mercy's sake don't ask us before Porthos, for were he to find out the place he would take every one of them.

Though Peter still remembers Maimie he is become as gay as ever, and often in sheer happiness he jumps off his goat and lies kicking merrily on the grass. Oh, he has a joyful time! But he has still a vague memory that he was a human once, and it makes him especially kind to the house-swallows when they visit the island, for house-swallows are the spirits of little children who have died. They always build in the eaves of the houses where they lived when they were humans, and sometimes they try to fly in at a nursery window, and perhaps that is why Peter loves them best of all the birds.

And the little house? Every lawful night (that is to say, every night except ball nights) the fairies now build the little house lest there should be a human child lost in the Gardens, and Peter rides the marches looking for lost ones, and if he finds them he carries them on his goat to the little house, and when they wake up they are in it, and when they step out they see it. The fairies build the house merely because it is so pretty, but Peter rides round in memory of Maimie, and because he still loves to do just as he believes real boys would do.

But you must not think that, because somewhere among the trees the little house is twinkling, it is a safe thing to remain in the Gardens after Lock-out time. If the bad ones among the fairies happen to be out that night they will certainly mischief you, and even though they are not, you may perish of cold and dark before Peter Pan comes round. He has been too late several times, and when he sees he is too late he runs back to the Thrush's Nest for his paddle, of which Maimie had told him the true use, and he digs a grave for the child and erects a little tombstone, and carves the poor thing's initials on it. He does this at once because he thinks it is what real boys would do, and you must have noticed the little stones, and that there are always two together. He puts them in twos because they seem less lonely. I think that quite the most touching sight in the Gardens is the two tombstones* of Walter Stephen Matthews and Phœbe Phelps. They stand together at the spot where the parish of Westminster St. Mary's is said to meet the parish of Paddington. Here Peter found the two babes, who had fallen unnoticed from their perambulators, Phœbe aged thirteen months and Walter probably still younger, for Peter seems to have felt a delicacy about putting any age on his stone. They lie side by side, and the simple inscriptions read

W. St. M.	and	13a P. P. 1841.

David sometimes places white flowers on these two innocent graves.

But how strange for parents, when they hurry into the Gardens at the opening of the gates looking for their lost one, to find the sweetest little tombstone instead. I do hope that Peter is not too ready with his spade. It is all rather sad.

ANON: A PLAY
(1903–4)

CHARACTERS

Mr Darling

Peter Pan

John Frederick Darling

Alexander Roger Darling

Tootles

Nibs

Slightly

Curly

First Twin

Second Twin

Captain Hook

Starkey

Mrs Darling

Tiger Lily

Tippy (The Last Fairy)

Wendy Maria Elizabeth Darling

Pirates, Redskins, Beautiful Mothers &c., a crocodile, a lion, a jaguar and a band of wolves.

SCENE 1

THE NIGHT NURSERY

(The Room is shaped as in Diagram, and if set on a large stage it should be made to look as snug and small as possible. Thus it should not be a deep scene. The chief articles of furniture are indicated above, but all the accessories of a cosy nursery in a middle-class family are to be included. There is a frieze around the walls, representing pictorially a fairy tale. The wall, where Fire is, takes an angle as in diagram, so that a person could sit naturally at it and yet be well seen by audience. In front of fire the usual tall guard-fender. The house is in a London street in Bloomsbury and the houses opposite may be vaguely seen through the windows. It is winter time, but there is no snow. The fire is burning brightly and gives a certain light to the room, which is otherwise obscure, the hour being early evening. Time—the present.

Curtain rises on NANA, the nurse, on hearth-rug by the fire asleep. Nana is a Newfoundland dog of the black-and-white variety called Landseers. Throughout the play though she has unusual things to do. She must do them strictly as a real dog of brains would act and never as a gymnast. The part will be played by a boy, and he must be drilled into acting as a dog would act—he must never do anything that a clever dog could not

*be trained to do. Unless when otherwise indicated in this text he must
always walk on four legs, and if he is ever on two legs only he must be as
awkward on them as the real dog would be. Naturalness must be his one
aim from first to last. But, despite this he acts throughout like an ordinary
nurse, not like one new to the business, but who does tonight precisely as he
has been doing every night for the last year.*

*The light of the fire shows Nana vividly—he is dreaming and makes
the sounds dogs make at such times. It is not a bark. He wakes up, slightly
changes position lazily, and sleeps again. The grandfather clock at back
gives the warning whirr common to such clocks before they strike. Nana
jumps up suddenly wide awake with the lightning rapidity of dogs, looks
straight before him for a moment, then walks slowly to R. down stage and
putting front paws against wall by side of door switches on electric light
with his mouth. He does not do this, or anything else, as a feat, but simply
as part of his daily humdrum work. He then goes nearer clock and listens
to its striking. At each strike he gives one wag of his tail which shows that
he is counting. His back is to the audience. Clock strikes six. He next (in
the ordinary quiet business-like way of a nurse) turns down the bed clothes
with his mouth from all three beds, brings in his mouth from child's cot
a suit of pyjamas for a child (all in one piece), hangs this over fender to air
it. He throws open door of bathroom in same way as he had switched on
light. The door being open, the bath and taps are seen. He turns on a tap
with his mouth and water is seen pouring into bath. Steam rises, showing
it is hot water. He puts paw to water to test it: evidently it is hot, for he
scalds his hands. He turns on another tap of cold water, and lets the two
run together. He takes in his mouth a tin,* and sprinkles (as from
pepper-pot) into bath. He gets from bathroom a wire arrangement containing soap and a sponge and hangs it on edge of bath, lays out a large
bath towel conveniently, then walks across room and exits at door L. He
re-enters accompanied by ALEXANDER DARLING. Alex is as
small a boy as possible, and his manners, dress and speech are those of
a boy of seven. He and Nana enter side by side. Nana is not holding him
but keeps close to him. They walk to C.)*

ALEX *(sulkily)* I won't go to bed—I won't, I won't. *(Argumentatively.)*
  Nana, it isn't six o'clock yet—it isn't six o'clock. Nana, Nana, it
  isn't six o'clock. *(Nana like experienced nurses pays no attention to
  his words, has pushed him into a chair and is unloosening his boots with
  mouth—he beats her in sudden passion, but she placidly goes on taking*

off his boots.) I shan't love you any more Nana—Nana I shan't love you any more, I shan't love you, Nana—I shan't, I shan't. *(He is standing now and she is taking off his belt, pinafore and an under garment. He is now in shirt and braces and breeches.)* I won't be bathed, I tell you I *won't* be bathed—Nana, I just tell you I won't be bathed. I just *won't*.

(Nana picks up his pyjamas in mouth, and he gets on her back still complaining and she walks to bathroom, for though she neither pulls nor pushes him her moral influence is irresistible. When they have entered bathroom she shuts door. Outside the window C. at back PETER PAN is seen mysteriously—he pulls himself on to ledge—his hands finger window as if he was seeking for a way of opening it. At that moment enters MRS DARLING R. She is a young, beautiful woman in evening dress and is coming forward gaily when she sees the face at the window.)

MRS DARLING *(stopping in alarm)* Who are you? *(Peter disappears—she runs to window, opens it, looks out, shuts window, crosses slowly)*. No one there—and yet I felt sure I saw a face. *(With sudden alarm.)* My children! Are they safe?

(Opens bathroom door. Alex's head is seen over top of bath—he sprays water and calls 'Mummy!' She blows kisses to him, shuts bathroom door and calls L. anxiously 'Wendy—John.' Wendy calls unseen 'Coming Mother!' Mrs D. says 'All safe!' Enter WENDY* and JOHN arm in arm acting grown-up people.)

WENDY *(breaking away)* Oh, Mummy, let me look! The beauty, beauty frock and the lovely mummy.

MRS D. I'm so glad you like it, Wendy.

JOHN *(annoyed at this interruption)* You mustn't call her Wendy. We are playing at being you and father. I'm father *(imitating a father)*. A little less noise there—little less noise. I can't find my shaving soap anywhere. I put it down just there, and it's gone. I never saw such a house.

WENDY Why, you foolish dear, it is in your hand. *(Imitating a mother.)*

JOHN So it is. Very strange thing. Women are so unreasonable. Now let's have a baby. *(This in own voice.)*

WENDY *(in own voice)* You tell me first.

JOHN I am happy to inform of you, Mrs Darling, you are now a mother.

WENDY Oo! oo! oo! *(Jumps with joy.)*

JOHN You missed the chief thing. You haven't asked, Boy or Girl.

WENDY I'm so glad to have one at all, I don't care which it is.

JOHN That's just the difference between gentlemen and ladies. Now you tell me.

WENDY I am happy to acquaint you, Mr Darling, you are now a father.

JOHN Boy or girl?

WENDY Girl. *(John straddles legs, puts hands in pockets and is picture of depression.)* You horrid!

JOHN *(sternly)* Go on.

WENDY I am happy to acquaint you, Mr Darling, you are again a father.

JOHN Boy or girl?

WENDY Boy. *(John struts gloriously.)* Mummy, it's hateful of him. *(Alex has come from bathroom in his pyjamas and is looking on eagerly.)*

ALEX Now, John, have me.

JOHN We don't want any more.

ALEX *(plaintively)* Am I not to be born at all?

JOHN Two's enough.

ALEX Come, John—Boy, John.

JOHN Oh, rot.

ALEX *(sadly)* Nobody wants me.

MRS D. I do. I *so* want to have a third child.

ALEX Boy or girl?

MRS D. Boy.

ALEX *(in shy rapture)* I am happy to inform of you, Mrs Darling, it is a boy.

MRS D. Oh, how I wonder what his name is.

ALEX *(shyly)* Alexander! *(She seizes him in her arms and hugs him—he speaks with grave curiosity.)* Mummy, how did you get to know me?

(Enter R. MR DARLING in evening dress, except that he is without a coat and carries his white tie not made up in his hand.)

DARLING *(implying that he has been looking for his wife everywhere)* Oh, here you are mother!

MRS D. Why, what's the matter, Father dear?

DARLING Mother! The matter is that I'm a desperate man. This tie—it *will not* tie. Not round my neck. Round the bed-post, oh yes, twenty times have I made it up round the post—but round my neck, no! *(With savage politeness to tie.)* Oh, dear no—begs to be excused!

ALEX *(delighted with father's funny voice and manner)* Say it again, Favver, say it again!

DARLING *(with awful politeness to Alex)* Thank you! *(Mother seizes Alex.)* I warn you of this, mother, that unless this is round my neck we don't go out to dinner tonight, and if I don't go out to dinner tonight I never go to the office again, and if I don't go to the office again you and I starve, and our children will be flung out into the streets. *(The children weep.)*

MRS D. *(placidly)* Let me try, dear. *(She proceeds to tie it round his neck while the children stand around in an agony of suspense—she succeeds.)* There!

DARLING *(carelessly)* Thanks. *(The children skip with joy. Darling is now in indulgent good humour.)* Little less noise there—isn't it time for somebody to go to by-by?* *(Lifts Alex on to his shoulders.)*

ALEX I'm bigger than Favver! *(Nana appears at bathroom door.)*

MRS D.　John, nurse is ready for you.

JOHN　Bother! *(Nana comes and undresses him to an extent L.)*

MRS D.　And Wendy, it's your time, too, you know.

WENDY　Mummy, couldn't I stay up just a teeny bit longer?

MRS D.　Sweetheart, I want to tuck you all in before I go. *(Exit Wendy L.)*

ALEX *(whom Father has dropped into bed)* Look Favver! *(Tries to stand on head, fails, but looks up gloriously.)*

MRS D.　Alexander! *(She tucks him in—then sweetly modest to Mr D.)* They are rather sweet, don't you think, Father?

DARLING *(stoutly)* They are great.

MRS D.　Are you proud of your children, George?

DARLING *(patting her fondly)* Ah! *(On way to bathroom with John Nana strikes against Mr D. He is pettish.)* Mother, just look at this! Covered with hairs! It's too bad! *(John has gone on to bathroom, but Nana brings a brush in mouth and stands beside Mr D. with it. He takes it a matter of course way. Nana exits into bathroom, slowly, looking round at times and finding Mr D. looking sulkily at her.*)* Clumsy— clumsy! *(Exit Nana with tail between her legs.)*

MRS D.　Let me brush you, dear. *(Does so.)*

DARLING　Mother: I sometimes think it's a mistake to have a dog for a nurse.

MRS D.　George, Nana is a treasure.

DARLING　No doubt, but—I have an uneasy feeling at times that she looks upon the children as puppies.

MRS D.　Oh no, dear me, I am sure she knows they have souls.

DARLING *(meditatively)* I wonder. I wonder, Mary.

MRS D. *(anxious)* George, we *must* keep Nana—I shall tell you why. *(She signs to him to come further from Alex. They go to fire.)*

DARLING　Well?

MRS D.　George, when I came into the room tonight, I saw—a face at the window.

DARLING A face at a window four floors up?

MRS D. It was the face of a little boy—he was trying to get in.

DARLING Impossible! You can't be well, Mary. How many fingers am I holding up? *(Holds up a whole hand.)*

MRS D. Five.

DARLING How many now? *(Holds up one finger.)*

MRS D. One.

DARLING You seem to be all right.

MRS D. Oh George, this is not the first time I have seen that boy.

DARLING Oho!

MRS D. The first time was a week ago. I had been drowsing here by the fire when suddenly I felt a draught—as if the window was open. I looked round and saw that boy in the room!

DARLING *In* the *room?*

MRS D. I screamed. Nana was in her kennel over there—she sprang up, and with a fierce bark sprang at him. The boy leapt at the window. Nana pulled it down quickly, but was too late to catch him.

DARLING I thought so.

MRS D. Wait. *He* escaped, but his shadow hadn't time to get out. Down came the window and cut it clean off.

DARLING Mary, Mary, why didn't you keep that shadow?

MRS D. I did. I rolled it up, Father—and here it is. *(Produces shadow from drawers L. down stage. It is dark and made of some material so light that when unrolled it floats. She unrolls it.)*

DARLING *(examining)* Ha! ha! It's nobody I know—but he does look a scoundrel.

MRS D. I think he comes back trying to get his shadow, George.

DARLING I daresay—I daresay!

MRS D. Perhaps I should fling it out of the window?

DARLING Certainly not: there's money in this, my love. *(He puts it back in drawers.)* I shall take it to the British Museum* tomorrow and have it priced.

MRS D. Father, I haven't told you quite all. I am afraid to.

DARLING Little cowardy custard!*

MRS D. The boy was not quite alone. He was accompanied by—I don't know how to describe it—by a ball of light—it was like a flame that had escaped from the fire. Not as big as your hand, but it darted about the room like a living thing.

DARLING That's very unusual. It escaped with the boy?

MRS D. Yes, Father, what can all this mean?

DARLING *(after seeming about to say a profound thing)* What, indeed! *(Bathroom door opens.)*

MRS D. Don't alarm the children.

DARLING Not a word. *(Nana comes in with a bottle in mouth—John is seen in bathroom enveloped in a towel.)*

MRS D. What is that, Nana? *(Takes bottle.)* Of course—the medicine. *(Returns it to Nana.)* Alexander, it is your medicine.

ALEX *(in cot)* Won't take it. Boo—oo—oo.

MRS D. My precious, it is to make you well.

DARLING Be a man, Alexander.

(Nana has put spoon on chair, poured into it from bottle in mouth, and brings spoon in mouth to Alex. John has now disappeared in bathroom.)

ALEX Won't—won't.

MRS D. Here's a lovely big chocky* to take after it.

ALEX It's not a very big one.

DARLING Mother, don't pamper him. Alexander, when I was your age I took medicine without a murmur. I said 'Thank you, kind parents, for giving me bottles to make me well.' *(Wendy has come in nightgown and John in pyjamas from bathroom.)*

WENDY *(quite honestly)* That medicine you sometimes take, Father, is much nastier, isn't it?

DARLING Ever so much nastier.

ALEX Let me see you take it.

DARLING I would take it, Alexander, with pleasure, just as an example to you my lad, but somehow it has got lost—very annoying.

WENDY *(innocently)* I know where it is, Father, it's beneath your bed.

DARLING Now who could have put it there?

MRS D. George!

WENDY Mummy, come and see. Father, I shall bring it to you. *(Exeunt Mrs D. and Wendy R.)*

DARLING John, it's the most beastly stuff! It's that—that—sticky sweet kind!

JOHN It'll soon be over, Father. *(Wendy runs in with a wine-glass and bottle containing whitish liquid.)*

WENDY I've been as quick as I could.

DARLING *(with vindictive politeness)* You have been wonderfully quick—precious quick.

WENDY *(pouring it into wine-glass and giving it to Father and still under impression that Father is grateful to her)* Now, Alexander, you will see how Father takes it.

DARLING Alexander first.

ALEX Favver first.

DARLING *(threateningly)* It will make me sick, you know.

JOHN Come on, Father.

DARLING Hold your tongue.

ALEX Favver, I'm waiting.

DARLING It's easy to say you're waiting—so am I waiting.

WENDY I thought you took it quite easily, Father.

DARLING That's not the point—the point is there's more in my glass than in Alexander's spoon. *(Fiercely.)* And it isn't fair. I say it, though it was with my last breath, it isn't fair.

WENDY Why not both take it at the same time?

DARLING Certainly. Are you ready, Alexander? One—two *(Suspiciously.)* I don't believe you're going to take it.

ALEX *(with mouth over spoon)* I am—I am.

WENDY One—two—three. *(Darling pretends to take it—Alex takes his.)*

ALEX *(quickly)* Chocky! *(Wendy gets him a chocolate and Nana returns to bathroom where she is seen rinsing spoon.)*

JOHN Father hasn't taken his!

ALEX Boo—oo—oo! *(Weeps.)*

WENDY Oh, Father!

DARLING What do you mean by 'Oh, Father'? Stop that row, Alexander. I meant to take mine, but I missed it.

JOHN You promised.

DARLING No use my taking it *now. (Alex howls.)* Stop it! *(Craftily.)* I say, look here—all of you—I've just thought of a splendid joke! *(They are eager.)* You see this medicine is rather like milk to look at. Well, I shall pour it into Nana's bowl, and she'll drink it, thinking it's milk! *(They hang their heads in shame.)* What do you mean, you silly little things! *(He pours medicine into dog's bowl on floor—it has NURSE printed on it instead of DOG.)* What a joke!

WENDY Darling Nana!

DARLING To your beds, every one of you—I am *ashamed* of you. *(They get into their beds—Enter Mrs D. R.)*

MRS D. Well, is it over?

DARLING All over, Mother—quite satisfactory.

ALEX Favver—

DARLING *(aside)* Alexander, if you don't tell on me I'll give you a knife on Monday. *(Nana comes down.)* Nana, good dog! *(Pats Nana.)* Good old girl. I have put a little milk in your bowl, Nana. *(Nana shakes hands gratefully and licks his hand, then hurries to bowl, begins to lap, breaks away, and goes into kennel, looks reproachfully at Mr D.—children ashamed—he tries to brazen it out.)*

MRS D. What's the matter, Nana?

DARLING Nothing, Nothing!

MRS D. *(examining bowl)* George, it's your medicine! *(Children sob.)*

DARLING It was only a joke. Much good my wearing myself to the bone trying to be funny in this house. *(Nana moans and he is savagely polite to her.)* Oh, indeed, you think so, do you? You are so mighty fine, I suppose! Who has to walk on four legs! Who has no pockets!

WENDY *(hugging dog)* Father, she's crying!

DARLING Cuddle her! Nobody cuddles me! Oh, dear no, I am only the breadwinner, why should I be cuddled? Why, why, why? *(Loudly.)*

MRS D. George, not so loud—the servants will hear you.

DARLING *(wildly)* Let them. Bring them in, bring in the whole world. I never enter this room but I see *her* looking at me with the cold eye of disapproval. And why not? says my wife, why not? say my children. Very well, then, the worm turns, and I refuse to allow that *dog* to lord it in my nursery for one hour longer. *(Nana begs to him.)* In vain, in vain, the proper place for you is the yard, and there you go to be tied up this instant. *(Sensation—the children have arms around Nana.)*

MRS D. George, George, remember what I told you—that boy!

DARLING Pooh—pshaw! Am I master in this house or is she? Come along. Come! *(He wheedles 'Good dog' &c.—she emerges deceived, he seizes her. Exit R. dragging dog. Agony of children.)*

MRS D. Come, dears, come to by-by. Don't cry. I'm sure Father will let Nana come back in the morning. *(She carries Alex to bed, and the others get into theirs.)* Wendy, be brave.

WENDY   He's chaining Nana up. *(Mrs D. lights three night-lights, one at top of each bed—Nana is heard barking.)*

JOHN   She's awfully unhappy.

WENDY   That's not Nana's unhappy bark. That's her bark when she smells danger.

MRS D.   Danger! Are you sure, Wendy?

WENDY   Oh yes. *(Mrs D. looks out nervously at window.)* Is there anything there, Mama?

MRS D.   All quite quiet and still. Oh, how I wish I wasn't going out to dinner.

ALEX   Can anything harm us, Mummy, after the night-lights are lit?

MRS D.   Nothing, precious. They are the eyes a mother leaves behind her to guard her children. *(She sings lullaby song about night-lights, beginning at foot of Alex's bed, then when he's asleep kissing him and continuing at John's bed, then at Wendy's—all are now asleep.)* Dear night-lights that protect my sleeping babies, burn clear and steadfast tonight. *(She steals to door R., turns out electric light, and exits R. closing door.)*

(The room is now dimly lit by night-lights and fire. Pause. Then night-lights go out one by one, a slight noise of window opening is heard. Suspense. Then TIPPYTOE darts in. All that enters under this name is a gleam of light not much larger than a human finger—it flashes about the room zigzagging hither and thither in the air, then for a moment comes to rest. For that microsecond while it is standing still there is seen as it were within this light a tiny figure of a fairy woman. In actual working it is merely a flash-light that moves about. The little figure is pushed unseen, this work to be visible only when light stands still behind it, but the illusion is that the figure is always in the light, a living fairy. Having done this, Tippytoe (which name we shall give to the flame) pops into a vase on cupboard R. upstage. The vase is now vaguely lighted—no figure is seen. Nana is barking excitedly.

Enter at window PETER PAN, an elfish-looking boy in woodland garments, picturesquely ragged. In this scene the lighting must be such that he casts no shadow. A flying wire is attached to him at present, but in the gloom it is not visible. He is of extraordinary quick movements, as if made of air. He steals forward cautiously on his feet. John moves in sleep. Peter flies for first time to top of clock where he sits. He then flies and alights on foot of John's bed. Wendy moves. Peter flies behind window curtains. While here the wire is removed from him—he re-enters, looks about him cautiously.)

PETER *(in low voice)* Tippytoe! Tippy, where are you? *(A musical tinkle of plaintive little bells is heard in answer. This is Tippytoe's reply in fairy language, which Peter understands.)* Oh, there! Do come out of that jug. *(Tippy darts out this way and that.)* Tippy, do you know where they put it? *(Bells reply.)* Which big box? *(Bells reply.)* This one here? *(Examining drawers L. down stage.)* But which drawer? *(Bells reply.)* Yes, do show me. *(The light darts at a drawer.)* Ah! *(Peter pulls drawer open, flings other articles on to floor, seizes his shadow and closes drawer, unknowingly with Tippy inside it. With great delight he tries to fix on his shadow to his foot. He fails. He glides to wash-stand, gets soap, returns to hearth-rug, tries to gum on his shadow to his foot with soap, fails, loses hope, sits bowed on hearth-rug sobbing audibly. This wakens Wendy, she sits up in bed, sees the stranger, gets out of bed, and is going to door R., changes mind, and crossing goes to Peter, who is still sobbing and ignorant that anyone has awaked.)*

WENDY Boy, why are you crying? *(Peter jumps up, not frightened but with the politeness of one addressed by a lady, and lifts his cap to her, keeps it in his hand. She is surprised but pleased by this politeness and curtseys to him.)*

PETER What's your name?

WENDY Wendy Maria Elizabeth Darling. What is your name?

PETER Peter Pan.

WENDY Is that all?

PETER *(ashamed)* Yes.

WENDY *(kindly)* I'm *so* sorry.

PETER *(bravely stifling shame)* It doesn't matter.

WENDY Where do you live?

PETER Second to the right and then straight on, till morning.

WENDY What a funny address!

PETER *(tartly)* No, it isn't.

WENDY I mean, is that what they put on the letters?

PETER Don't get any letters.

WENDY But your mother gets letters.

PETER Don't have a mother.

WENDY *(in tragic pity)* Oh, Peter!

PETER *(with a gulp)* Doesn't matter.

WENDY No wonder you were crying!

PETER Wasn't crying about that. Was crying because—I can't get my shadow to stick on.

WENDY *(examining it)* It has come off! How awful! Why, Peter, you have been trying to stick it on with soap!

PETER *(touchily)* Well then?

WENDY It must be sewn on.

PETER What's sew?

WENDY You're dreadfully ignorant.

PETER *(hotly)* No, I'm not.

WENDY *(in matronly matter)* *I* shall sew it on for you, my little man.

PETER *(from his soul)* Thank you!

WENDY *(crossing and now very womanly)* But we must have a little more light. *(Turns up electric light—brings her housewife.*)* Sit there. *(He sits in chair and she kneels, and taking up one foot proceeds to sew on his shadow.)* I daresay it will hurt a little.

PETER I shan't cry. *(He winces a little, but is brave—she sews—business.)*

WENDY There! *(Peter jumps about making gleeful sounds, then seeing shadow doesn't properly respond.)*

PETER Wendy, it won't *do* anything. *(Huskily.)* Do you think it's dead?

WENDY I see what's the matter: it's all crinkled from being rolled up. Peter: I shall iron it! *(Gets iron from fire, prepares it in business like manner, irons shadow—the heat of it on shadow makes Peter wince, but he knits teeth and endures.)* It *looks* better now. Move about slowly, Peter. *(He does so, going up stage.)*

PETER Wendy, I believe it moved its arm!

WENDY Of course it would naturally be stiff at first, Peter.

PETER Oh, it's much better. *(He has got towards door L. practising it. Here it is removed, unseen by the audience and the lights are flung so that his real shadow takes its place. As he comes into view of audience it should look as like as possible to the same shadow and he pulls it along without moving arms or head.)* It's quite lively! Wendy, I shall make it go up this wall! *(He does so but makes it stick where floor and wall meet.)* It's stuck!

WENDY Dear, dear shadow, *do* climb!

PETER *(backing into middle of room)* Won't do it.

WENDY Peter, it might follow mine. *(She moves toward wall, with her shadow in front of his.)* Come along, that's beautiful, oh how nicely you move, you clever thing.

PETER *(despairing)* Stuck again! Wendy, pull it up. *(She seems to pull shadow up wall.)* Done it! Look at it! Look! *(Dances.)* I'm clever! Oh the cleverness of me! *(He crows like a rooster once—it seems to come out of him without his knowing.)*

WENDY You conceit! Of course *I* did nothing!

PETER You did a little.

WENDY A little! If I am no use I can at least withdraw. *(Bows and with dignity gets into bed and retires beneath the blankets, head and all.)*

PETER Wendy! *(He sits on end of bed and cajoles.)* Wendy, don't withdraw. I can't help crowing, Wendy, when I'm very pleased with myself. I don't *mean* to do it. It's just as if a rooster wakes up inside me. Wendy, one girl is more use than twenty boys.

WENDY *(looking out gratified)* Do you really think so, Peter?

PETER *(stoutly)* Yes, I do.

WENDY I think it's perfectly sweet of you, and I'll get up again. *(They sit together on side of bed, legs dangling.)* I shall give you a kiss, Peter, if you like.

PETER Thank you. *(Holds out hand.)*

WENDY *(aghast)* Don't you know what a kiss is?

PETER I shall know when you give it to me. *(Not to hurt his feelings she gives him a thimble off her finger—he gravely puts it on his finger.)* Now shall I give you a kiss?

WENDY If you please. *(He gives her button off his clothes.)* Peter, I shall wear it on this chain around my neck. *(She puts it on chain. Sorry for him.)* But oh, Peter, where were you brought up?

PETER I was never brought up.

WENDY How sad!

PETER Doesn't matter. I was born all right, Wendy, in a room like this—long, long ago. *(Fearfully.)* Not very long ago. I'm quite young. *(Eager.)* Wendy, say I'm quite a little boy—quick!

WENDY Yes, of course—but how old are you?

PETER I don't know—but *quite* young. Wendy, I flew away!

WENDY Flew!

PETER You see I hadn't been weighed. You know babies can fly until they are weighed. That is why mothers are so quick to weigh them.

WENDY Yes, I know.

PETER Well, my mother forgot to weigh me.

WENDY *(indignant)* Oh careless, careless! Why did you fly away, Peter?

PETER *(violently agitated)* Because I heard Father and Mother talking about what I was to be when I became a man. Wendy, I was frightened, I didn't want to be a man—I want always to be a little boy and have fun. So I flew away, and I lived a long, long time among the fairies.

WENDY *(delirious with admiration)* Peter! You know fairies!

PETER I have known millions of them.

WENDY Oh! Don't you know them still?

PETER They are nearly all dead now. You see, Wendy, whenever a baby laughs for the first time, a fairy is born, and so there ought to be one fairy for every boy and girl.

WENDY Ought to be? Isn't there?

PETER *(shakes head)* You see children know such a lot now. They soon don't believe in fairies, and every time a child says 'I don't believe in fairies' there is a fairy somewhere that falls down dead. They just crumple up like that. *(Bending a finger.)*

WENDY How tragic!

PETER There's only the one fairy left now.

WENDY Only one?

PETER *(restless)* I can't think where she has gone to. *(Calls.)* Tippy—Tippy!

WENDY *(clutching him)* Peter, you don't mean to tell me that there is a fairy in this room!

PETER She *was* here. *(Suddenly.)* Wendy, you believe in fairies, don't you?

WENDY Yes, indeed.

PETER *(relieved)* I'm glad because if she happened to be *your* fairy—

WENDY Oh, how delicious!

PETER And if you had said you didn't believe in them, she would be lying all crumpled by this time.

WENDY Oh!

PETER Tippy! You don't hear her, do you?

WENDY No, the only sound I hear is—like a tinkle of bells.

PETER That's Tippy—that's the fairy language. I hear it too! Tippy!

WENDY It seems to come from over there! *(Pointing to drawers L. down stage.)*

PETER Wendy! I believe I shut her up in the drawer! *(He opens drawer—Tippy darts out and flashes this way and that, and ring talking—i.e. ringing bells—in a rage.*) You needn't say that. I'm very sorry, but how could I know you were in the drawer?

WENDY   Oh, Peter, if she would only stand still and let me see her.

PETER   She hardly ever stands still. *(For a moment Tippy is still and her figure is seen.)*

WENDY   I see her! The lovely! *(Tippy darts again and disappears.)* Where is she now?

PETER   She's behind the basin. *(To Tippy unseen.)* Tippy, this lady thinks that perhaps you are her fairy. *(Bells reply.)*

WENDY   What did she say?

PETER   *(awkwardly)* She's not very polite. She says you are a great ugly girl—and that she's *my* fairy.

WENDY   Oh!

PETER   You know you can't be *my* fairy, Tippy, because I'm a gentleman and you're a lady. *(Bells reply.)* Oh, indeed!

WENDY   What did she say?

PETER   She said 'You silly ass!'

WENDY   Oh! Peter, if you don't live with the fairies now, where *do* you live?

PETER   I live with the lost children.

WENDY   *(sitting beside him on same chair at fire—their legs dangle)*   Who are *they*?

PETER   They are the children who fall out of their perambulators when the nurse is looking the other way. If they are not claimed in seven days they are sent far away to the Never Never Never Land to defray expenses. I'm Captain.

WENDY   What fun it must be!

PETER   Yes, but we're rather lonely. You see we have no female companionship.

WENDY   Are none of the others girls?

PETER Oh no—girls you know are much too clever to fall out.

WENDY Peter, it's perfectly lovely the way you talk about girls. John, there, just despises us. *(Peter rises gravely and kicks John out of bed. John continues to sleep on floor.)* Peter, you wicked! You're not captain here! *(Peter is abject—she relents.)* After all he hasn't waked, and you meant to be kind—Peter, you may give me a kiss.

PETER *(little bitterly)* I thought you would want it back. *(Offers her the thimble.)*

WENDY Oh, dear! Peter, I don't mean a kiss—I mean a thimble.

PETER What's that?

WENDY It's like this. *(Kisses him.)*

PETER *(stolidly)* Now shall I give you a thimble?

WENDY If you please. *(He kisses her, pauses, then Tippy darts at Wendy and vanishes. Wendy jumps up, screaming.)*

PETER What is it?

WENDY It was exactly as if somebody was pulling my hair.

PETER That must have been Tippy. Never knew her so naughty. *(Bells speak.)* Oh, is that it?

WENDY What does she say?

PETER She says she'll do that to you every time I give you a thimble.

WENDY But, why?

PETER Why, Tippy? *(Bells.)* She says 'You silly ass' again.

WENDY She's very unkind. *(Goes further off.)* Peter, did you come here to see *me*?

PETER I didn't know there was you. I came to listen at nursery windows.

WENDY Why?

PETER To try to hear stories. I don't know any stories. None of the lost boys know any stories.

WENDY How perfectly awful!

PETER Do you know why swallows build in houses? It is to listen to the stories. Oh, Wendy, your mother was telling you such a lovely story—and I do so want to know the end. That's what I came here for.

WENDY Which story is it?

PETER The Prince couldn't find the lady who wore the glass slipper.

WENDY That's Cinderella!* Peter, he found her, and they were happy ever after!

PETER *(immensely relieved)* I *am* glad. *(He is going.)*

WENDY Where are you going, Peter.

PETER To tell the other boys. They are so frightfully anxious about Cinderella.

WENDY Don't go, Peter. I know such lots and lots of stories.

PETER *(breathless)* Do you! *(His hands begin to claw her.)*

WENDY The stories I could tell to the boys!

PETER Wendy, come with me and tell them.

WENDY Oh, dear, I can't. Think of Mummy.

PETER You shall—you shall! *(Seizes her.)*

WENDY Let go, Peter Pan. *(He does so dejectedly.)* Besides, I can't fly.

PETER It's so easy. Wendy, I'll teach you.

WENDY How lovely to fly! But though I learn, mind, I won't go away with you.

PETER You won't be able to help it—it's so delicious to fly.

WENDY Then I won't learn.

PETER Oh, Wendy, how we should all *respect* you. You would tuck us in at night, Wendy. Not one of us has ever been tucked in at night.

WENDY *(hesitating)* Of course, it's awfully *fascinating*.

PETER Wendy, I have just to rub your shoulders, and then you can fly.

WENDY Oh! Will you teach John and Alexander, also?

PETER *(indifferent)* If you like.

WENDY Mind you, I don't promise to go away with you. I don't think there's the least chance of my going.

PETER *(craftily)* All right.

WENDY *(wakening John)* John, wake up. There is a boy here who is going to teach us how to fly.

JOHN Is there? Then I shall get up. *(Finds that he is on the floor.)* I say, I am up!

WENDY Alexander, this boy is to teach us to fly. *(Nana begins to bark again. Wendy is conscience-stricken.)* Nana doesn't want us to learn!

PETER H'sh! Someone's coming!

JOHN Out with the light. *(He turns it off.)* Hide—quick! *(Wendy and Peter exeunt L. John and Alex into bathroom. Enter R. HELEN, a servant, holding Nana by collar—Nana growling. They remain near door R.)*

HELEN There you suspicious brute! They are perfectly safe, aren't they! Every one of the little angels sound asleep in bed—listen to their gentle breathing. *(Nana growls.)* Now no more of it, Nana. I warn you if you bark again I shall go straight for Master and Missus and bring them home from the party, and then, oh, won't Master whip you *just*! *(Tippy darts at her leg.)* Oh! Oh! What's that nipping my leg? *(Tippy darts at her head.)* Oh! Oh! Come along, you growling brute! *(She exits, dragging Nana with her—the children emerge—the wires* are now attached to them and are invisible in the gloom.)*

ALEX What was it nipped Helen?

PETER It *had* been Tippy.

JOHN Who's Tippy?

WENDY John! She's a fairy!

JOHN Oh, rot, there are no fairies. *(Tippy darts at him, he staggers back.)* Who did that? Who hit me here? *(Covering his stomach.)*

PETER It had been Tippy.

JOHN *(Tippy darts—staggering again)* There it is again.

WENDY John, quick, say you believe in fairies and then she may stop.

JOHN I don't. *(Gets another whack.)* Yes, I do—I do. *(The persecution stops.)* I say, can you really fly? *(Peter flies.)* How splendid!

WENDY Oh, how sweet!

PETER *(in ecstasy as he flies)* I'm sweet, sweet—oh I *am* sweet!

JOHN *(trying to fly)* How do you do it?

PETER I must rub you first. *(He rubs their shoulders with his.)* Now try—try from the bed.

ALEX Me first!

JOHN *(pushing Alex down)* Me first! *(Tries to launch himself into space—jumps down tamely.)*

PETER *(flying)* Just wriggle your shoulders this way, and then let go. *(Wendy does as John did—Alex flies a yard.)*

ALEX I flewed! *(The three jump on to different beds to practice. Amid exclamations of delight they begin to be able to fly—at first awkwardly. Then they get better at it.)*

JOHN *(sailing round)* Look at me—look—look!

ALEX Look at me!

JOHN I say, why shouldn't we go out!

WENDY No, no, we mustn't—oh, it's heavenly! But we mustn't. That's what he wants, to take us far away over the sea.

PETER There are pirates!

JOHN Pirates! Let's go at once!

WENDY No, John, no.

JOHN You stay at home—girls are only in the way.

PETER No, they're not.

JOHN You like girls? Oh, you muff!*

ALEX Muff, muff, muff!

WENDY Peter, it's sweet of you. *(He and she fly together—all circle round.)*

PETER Tippy, Tippy, come along. *(Tippy's light darts about and trembles—bells ring, plaintively.)* That's Tippy crying!

WENDY Oh!

PETER She says she's crying because I am holding your hand. *(Bells again.)* She says she'll come if I let go your hand. *(Wendy and Peter let go hands. Bell rings gaily.)* She's happy now. *(All circle round with cries of delight—Tippy's light does as they do. Finally all stream out of window and disappear. Nana has been barking fiercely again. She now bursts through door R., wrecking it, with broken chain attached to her, rushes to window and stands with front feet up looking out. Mrs D. and Darling have rushed in after her. Darling turns up electric light—all are just in time to see the last of the children disappear.)*

MRS D. *(distraught)* My children! All gone—all gone!

DARLING *(equally distressed)* Oh, Mother!

MRS D. They would all have been here if you had left Nana to take care of them! Oh, why do men interfere in the affairs of the nursery! *(She half falls, leaning on kennel.)*

DARLING *(full of remorse)* My fault; my fault; *mea culpa**—my fault! Mary, from this hour, until my children come back Nana and I change places. She becomes head of the house and I go into the kennel. *(He goes into kennel and sits with head out. Nana comes down and stands looking at him.)*

CURTAIN

SCENE 2

THE HOUSE THEY BUILT FOR WENDY

(The scene is a mysterious Forest with a river running through it as in diagram. On back cloth another twist of the river is seen. The time is

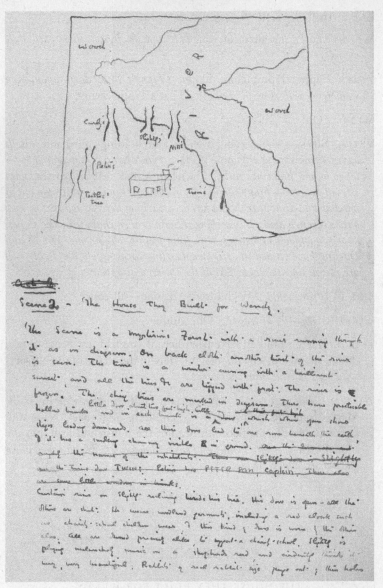

FIGURE 2　J. M. Barrie, sketch of Neverland, from *Anon: A Play* (1903–4).

a winter evening with a brilliant sunset, and all the trees &c. are tipped with frost. The river is frozen. The chief trees are marked in diagram. These have practicable* hollow trunks, and in each trunk is a little door about two feet high, which when open shows steps leading downward. All these doors lead to one room beneath the earth, and it has a smoking chimney visible R. in ground.

Curtain rises on SLIGHTLY reclining beside his tree. His door is open—all the others are shut. He wears woodland garments, including a red cloak such as charity-children wear,* and this kind of dress is worn by the others also. All are dressed precisely alike, to suggest a charity-school. Slightly is playing melancholy music on a shepherd's reed, and evidently thinks it very, very beautiful. Rabbits of real rabbit size* peep out of their holes at him. Two squirrels run up Peter's tree and disappear. A bird large enough to be played by a boy waddles on and mimics Slightly. He threatens it and it goes. He thinks it is in front of him and stalks it—it is really following him humorously. Suddenly an eerie wail is heard—it might be of some strange bird. Slightly, alarmed, looks L. down stage, quickly puts a hollow trunk over chimney to prevent smoke coming out, and climbs up his tree and watches in terror.

From L. down stage appears TIGER LILY, an Indian girl, and glides to point marked X in diagram, which is a projection, where she stands, a statuesque figure, looking this way and that. She sees marks on the ice that excite her—she makes the cry already heard, and OTHER INDIANS, both men and women, glide on. She points to marks—excitement.)

TIGER LILY Palefaces!

SEVERAL Wah! Wah! Wah! *(They examine, on knees &c.)*

TIGER LILY Tiger Lily have war council! *(All squat quickly on river in a circle. A pipe is passed around at which each takes one puff.)* Me Tiger Lily, you Tiger Lily's braves. Palefaces come, take my land—what me do now? Tiger Lily has spoken. *(Sits.)*

PANTHER *(played by a man)* Me Great Big Little Panther. Me heap brave man. Me say: sleep no more, eat no more, drink no more. Kill Paleface scalp hang here. Great Big Little Panther has spoken. *(Several shouts of approval &c., 'Wah—ugh, ugh', brandishing of weapons and they dance the war-dance to music of tom-tom. Finally all exeunt up river in single file after Tiger Lily and following tracks.*

Slightly comes down tree terrified, looks after them. NIBS, wearing skates, rises from brushwood on other side of river. They talk across river.)

SLIGHTLY Nibs, they are following the marks of your skates!

NIBS Oh, Slightly, they'll scalp me! I would rather be caught by the Pirates than by Redskins. How I wish Peter was back.

SLIGHTLY What's to be done, Nibs?

NIBS What would Peter tell us to do? That's the thing to do.

SLIGHTLY I'm sure Peter would say to me, 'Go into your tree, Slightly, and hide', and to you, 'Nibs, go up the river and scout.'

NIBS But I'm frightened.

SLIGHTLY *I'm* to obey Peter's orders—*you* can do as you choose.

(Exit Slightly into his tree. Nibs hesitatingly skates out of sight up river. From R. FOUR PIRATES come into sight. CAPTAIN HOOK is a fearsome, black-bearded man, sometimes very fierce and at other times horribly oily in manner. The most dreadful part of him is an iron hook fixed in his right elbow, at which point his arm has been cut off. He can brandish this and grip people with it. STARKEY, his lieutenant, is thin and wizened, and all his movements are wriggles. SMEE is an English pirate and CECCO an Italian. Cecco, seeing Nibs disappearing, kneels on river to fire at him with pistol, but Hook grips Cecco with his hook.)

CECCO *(groaning)* Captain, let go!

HOOK Put back that pistol first. *(Cecco does so and Hook releases him.)*

CECCO It was one of those boys you hate. I could have shot him dead.

HOOK Ay, and have brought Tiger Lily's Redskins upon us!

STARKEY That's true. Shall I after him, Captain, and tickle him with Johnny Corkscrew? *(Wriggling cutlass.)* Johnny's a silent fellow!

HOOK Not now. He's only one, and I want all the seven. They must live somewhere near here. Scatter and look for them. *(Smee and Cecco exeunt R. and L., while Hook and Starkey move towards the trees.)* Most of all I want their captain, Peter Pan. T'was he cut off my arm. I've waited long to shake his hand with this. *(Brandishing hook.)* Oh, I'll tear him!

STARKEY Yet I've oft hear you say that hook was worth a score of arms.

HOOK Ay, if I was a mother, Starkey, I'd pray to have my children born with this *(indicating hook)* instead of that *(indicating left hand)*.

STARKEY Then why such ill-will to Peter Pan for cutting off your arm?

HOOK Not for cutting it off, but for what he did with it when 'twas off. He flung it, Starkey, to a crocodile that was looking on.

STARKEY I have often noticed that you, who are afraid of nothing else, have a strange dread of crocodiles.

HOOK Not of crocodiles, but of that one crocodile. *(Agitated.)* He liked my arm so much, Starkey, that he has followed me ever since. From sea to sea, he follows the ship, licking his lips for the rest of me.

STARKEY In a way it's a sort of compliment.

HOOK I want no such compliments. I want Peter Pan, who first gave the beast its taste for me. *(He has been sitting on root that is over chimney.)* This seat's hot—it's very hot! *(Rises, lifts root, smoke emerges—sensation—then realises situation, points to doors in trees &c. They listen down chimney.)*

STARKEY You hear! They say Redskins passed this way.

HOOK Ay, but they also say Peter Pan's from home. Call back the men.

STARKEY *(whistling for men)* What's your plan, Captain?

HOOK To watch in the wood until they are all in their hole. Starkey, there can be but one room down here, for there's but one chimney. The little fools hadn't the sense to see that they didn't need a door apiece. That shows they've no mother! When Peter has come home, and they are hot and excited, we'll creep back carrying a pail of ice-cold water. We'll leave it here. They'll drink it, because having no mother they don't know how dangerous 'tis to drink cold water when you're hot!* They'll die!

STARKEY It's the wickedest cleverest plot ever I heard of.

HOOK   Shake hands on't Starkey. *(Clawing with hook.)*

STARKEY *(terrified)* No, Captain, no! *(In the meantime a great croco-dile has emerged from side of river and almost reached them.)*

HOOK   That's him! That's him! *(They rush off up stage R., crocodile slowly after them. TOOTLES comes out of his door and sits gloomily. He is meek and sweet-faced. The TWINS emerge from their tree.)*

FIRST TWIN *(hearing Tootles groan)* What's the matter, Tootles?

TOOTLES   Twin, I'm suffering from severe depression.*

SECOND TWIN   What *is* depression?

TOOTLES   I don't know—that's the awful thing about it. *(Enter Slightly from his tree.)*

FIRST TWIN   Slightly, Tootles has severe depression.

SLIGHTLY   That's because I told you the Redskins were here.

TOOTLES   No, I don't think they will come back. I think it's because I can't get that poor Cinderella out of my head. I do hope Peter has heard what became of her. *(All are sitting.)*

SECOND TWIN   I dreamed last night that the Prince found her. *(CURLY comes from his tree.)*

FIRST TWIN   Twin, I think you shouldn't have dreamt that for *I* didn't, and I fear Peter will say we oughtn't to dream differ-ently—being twins, you know.

CURLY   I have always hoped that the slipper would help the Prince to find her. *(They are all seated by this time.)*

SLIGHTLY *(cynically)* How could it, Curly!

CURLY   I don't know.

SECOND TWIN   Poor Cinderella, she was so gay that night at the ball.

TOOTLES   She was so awfully fond of him, Twin.

SLIGHTLY   Perhaps Peter has heard that she married some other body.

TOOTLES   I couldn't bear that. *(Sober.)* You see, not knowing any-thing about my own mother, I am fond of thinking that she was rather like Cinderella.

CURLY All I remember about *my* mother is that she often said to Father, 'Oh how I wish I had a cheque book of my own!' I don't know what a cheque book is, but I should just love to give my mother one.

SLIGHTLY My mother was fonder of me than your mothers were of you.

FIRST TWIN No, she wasn't.

SLIGHTLY Yes, she was. Peter had to make up names for you, but my mother had wrote my name on the pinafore I was lost in. 'Slightly Soiled'—that's my name. *(Gives himself airs.)*

SECOND TWIN H'sh! *(All stand up as a distant baying of wild animals is heard from up river.)* It's wolves! *(They rush towards Tootles' tree, all except Curly who has stolen to river and looked up it.)*

CURLY The wolves! And they're chasing Nibs!

(He runs to the others—the baying increases in volume. Then Nibs appears, skating for his life down river, pursued by at least a dozen wolves—played by boys. He flings himself on bank between Nibs' tree and that of the twins, and lies gasping while the wolves snap and growl very close to him.)

NIBS Save me! Save me!

SLIGHTLY What should we do?

SECOND TWIN What would Peter do?

TOOTLES Peter would look at them through his legs.

CURLY Let's do what Peter would do.

(All quickly present backs to wolves and look at them through legs. The wolves hang back in alarm. The boys march on them in this position—the wolves break. The boys go thus up river after them. The wolves exeunt up river in terror. They come back cockily, address Nibs from river.)

FIRST TWIN We've saved you, Nibs. Did you follow the Redskins?

NIBS *(taking off skates)* Yes, I lost sight of them but I saw a wonderfuller thing, Twin.

SLIGHTLY What?

NIBS The loveliest great white bird. It's flying this way.

TOOTLES What kind of bird, d'you think?

NIBS I know not, but it looks so wearied and as it flies it moans 'Poor Wendy!'

SECOND TWIN Poor Wendy?

SLIGHTLY My name being writ upon my clothes, I remember things better than you do and I remember now there are birds called Wendies.

FIRST TWIN See, it comes—the Wendy. How white it is!

SECOND TWIN The snow is coming with it. *(A few flakes begin to fall.)*

TOOTLES Perhaps it's the mother of snow!

CURLY You are always thinking of mothers.

(Wendy flies on aloft. She may be some other person disguised to look like the actress of Wendy. She flies wearily and undecided like one who has lost her way. She comes from L. upstage and Tippy darts after pecking her viciously—i.e. the light makes darts at her.)

CURLY It's Tippy! Tippy is trying to hurt the Wendy! Hallo Tippy! *(Bells answer.)* She says Peter wants us to shoot the Wendy.

NIBS Let's do what Peter wishes!

SLIGHTLY Ay, shoot it! Quick, bows and harries! *(All disappear into their trees except Tootles who has his bow and arrows on him.)*

TOOTLES Tippy, out of the way—I'll shoot it. *(Tootles fires—an arrow is seen in Wendy's chest. She flutters to ground in such a spot that the real Wendy can come on in her place, stagger forward and fall in centre ground between the boys' trees.)* Tippy, I've shot the Wendy. Peter will be so pleased with me. *(Tippy rings.)* Why do you say I'm a silly ass? *(Tippy darts out of sight as the boys emerge with bows.)* I've killed it! *(Slightly is the first to reach the fallen Wendy. He realises what has happened and pulls off his cap. A slight snow is now falling.)*

SLIGHTLY This is no bird. I think it must be a lady!

TOOTLES A lady!

NIBS And we have killed her. *(All take off hats.)*

CURLY Now I see! Peter was bringing her to us.

SECOND TWIN A lady—to take care of us at last! And you have killed her!

FIRST TWIN Oh, Tootles!

TOOTLES *(huskily)* I did it! *(Quietly.)* Friends, in all these years I have thought of ladies with loving respect, and when they came to me in dreams I said 'Pretty mother, pretty mother!' But when at last a lady came—I shot her. Oh, now may my mother never again come to me, even in my dreams, lest in her heart I see an arrow which I have fired. Friends, goodbye!

FIRST TWIN Don't go away.

TOOTLES I must—I am so afraid of Peter.

(He is going L. and is on middle of river when Peter is heard crowing. All cry 'Peter!' He appears on other side of river, supporting John and Alex who are both dazed with weariness.)

PETER *(grandly, L.)* Greeting, my boys!

SEVERAL Peter! *(Uneasily.)*

PETER I'm back—why do you not cheer? *(They get in front of Wendy to hide her from him.)* Why do you stand so? Great news, boys! I have brought at last the thing we've always longed for—a mother for us all!

TOOTLES Ah me!

CURLY These sleeping boys? *(John and Alex have fallen asleep against him.)*

PETER Are they asleep again? Well, let them sleep, they are dog-weary. They are her brothers and I fell behind her because they clung to me as we flew across the sea. But Wendy—she came this way, have you not seen her? *(Coming near Tootles.)*

FIRST TWIN Oh, mournful day!

TOOTLES Peter, I'll show her to you. *(They would prevent.)* No, Twins, back—let Peter see! *(Peter sees.)*

PETER Wendy—Wendy! An arrow in her heart! *(Is overcome—takes out the arrow—is stern.)* Whose arrow?

TOOTLES *(on river)* Mine, Peter.

PETER Oh, dastard* hand! *(Raises arrow to use it as dagger.)*

TOOTLES *(exposing breast)* Strike, Peter—strike true. *(Wendy's arm rises unseen.)*

PETER *(whose back is to her)* I cannot strike. *(Drops arrow.)* There's something stays my hand.

NIBS It's she—the Wendy lady. See, her arm. I think she said 'Poor Tootles.'

PETER She lives!

SLIGHTLY The Wendy lady lives.

PETER *(holding up the button on chain)* See, the arrow struck against this. It is a kiss I gave her. It has saved her life!

SLIGHTLY I remember kisses—let me see it—ay, that's a kiss. *(Tippy darts about, and the bells ring gaily.)*

CURLY Hear Tippy singing—it's because she thinks the Wendy's dead! Tippy, the Wendy lives! *(The bells are now sorrowful.)* She's crying now because the Wendy lives!

PETER What's that?

FIRST TWIN She hates the Wendy—she was pecking at her.

SECOND TWIN It was she cried to us Peter wants you to shoot the Wendy!

PETER Tippy did that! Then Tippy, listen—I am your friend no more. *(Tippy rings sorrowfully.)* Begone from me forever. *(Tippy rings plaintively.)*

TOOTLES She says she's *your* fairy.

PETER If you're my fairy I have you in my power, for if you don't go at once I'll say I don't believe in fairies, and then you'll drop down dead. *(She rings.)* Begone, begone—well not for ever but for a whole week. *(Tippy flies away ringing mournfully.)* Now what should we do with Wendy?

CURLY Let's carry her down into the house . . .

SLIGHTLY Ay, that's what one does with ladies.

PETER No, no, you mustn't touch her—it wouldn't be sufficiently respectful.

SLIGHTLY That's what *I* was thinking.

TOOTLES But if she lies there she'll die.

SLIGHTLY Ay, she'll die. It's a pity, but there's no way out.

PETER Yes, there is. Let's build a house round her!

CURLY A house?

PETER Leave all to me. Quick, bring me each the best of what we have. Gut our house. Be sharp! *(All disappear into their trees. Alex totters and it wakes him up.)*

ALEX John, John, wake up. Where's Nana, John, and Mother?

JOHN *(rubbing his eyes)* It's true—we did fly! There's Peter! Peter, is this the place?

PETER Yes.

ALEX Where's Wendy?

PETER Here. *(They cross.)*

JOHN Is she asleep?

PETER Yes.

ALEX John, let's wake her and get her to make supper for us. *(The six emerge from trees, carrying furniture, pieces of walls, etc.)* Look at them!

PETER Curly, take these boys within. Give each a cloak, then see that they help in the building of the house.

JOHN Build a house?

CURLY For the Wendy.

JOHN For Wendy? Why, she's just a girl.

CURLY That is why we are her servants.

JOHN *You*—Wendy's servants?

PETER And you also, henceforth—away with them. *(Curly marches John and Alex into his tree. Peter measures, directs, &c.)* Chairs, rugs, and a fender first. Then we'll build the walls around them.

SLIGHTLY Ay, that's how a house is built—it all comes back to me.

(They place things for a house about 4ft by 6ft. The furniture is home made and of quaintly small size, and as it is placed Tippy flies back but is waved away by Peter. Among the articles brought is a red umbrella, the covering oblong in shape instead of round, and Peter hands it to Alex.)

PETER Hold this over her till we raise a roof. *(Rejects some articles.)* These are not good enough for Wendy. How I wish I knew the kind of house that Wendy would prefer.

JOHN I like them large and showy.

PETER Then we'll be safe to make it small and modest. *(Some are by this time erecting back and side walls.)* But the decorations! In London as soon as one style's in, it's out, and if you follow it they say you live at chophouses.* Oh, how I wish I knew the correct artistic thing for this evening!

FIRST TWIN Peter, she's moving in her sleep.

TOOTLES Her mouth opens. Oh, lovely!

PETER Perhaps she's to sing in her sleep. Oh, Wendy, sing the kind of house you would like to have!

(This part of scene will be written more exactly when the time necessary for building house is known. It will be about five minutes, and the scene will be on the following lines. Wendy's song is in three verses, and they sing chorus to it, and the harmonizing &c. is also in chorus. When she mentions that she likes her room to have green walls, one dashes in with green paint-pot and is busy painting till the building hides him from view. So in other details. She sings of liking flowers outside, and they are made—walls with red caps &c. after the way such things have been done in music halls. When she sings of loving to have children playing outside they take this to mean themselves. There are several finishing touches, such as a door-knocker which is really the sole of one of Tootles' shoes. A second umbrella put at an angle to first makes red roof. The last touch is the chimney. John has come in his tall Eton hat. The top is knocked in, hat is hoisted on end of house, and immediately*

smoke begins to come out of it. They are delighted with this cleverness. Peter signs that all is complete, then he knocks.)

PETER *(whispering)* Look your best—the first impression is awfully important.

FIRST TWIN What's impression? *(All look their best. The snow has now ceased to fall. The sun is now setting brilliantly. Wendy opens door. All whip off caps.)*

WENDY *(surprised)* Where am I?

SLIGHTLY Wendy lady, for you we built this house!

NIBS Oh, say you're pleased.

WENDY Lovely, darling house!

FIRST TWIN And we're your children.

CURLY Oh, Wendy lady, be our mother! *(They go on knees, backs to audience.)*

WENDY Ought I? Of course it's frightfully fascinating. But you see I am only a little girl. I have no real experience.

TOOTLES That doesn't matter. What we so sorely need is just a nice motherly person.

WENDY Oh dear! You see, I feel that's just exactly what I am.

SEVERAL It is—it is—we saw it at once.

WENDY Very well, then I shall do my best. *(In motherly manner.)* Come inside at once, you naughty children. I am sure your feet are damp. And before I put you to bed I have just time to finish the story of Cinderella.

(All follow her into house simpering with happiness. The door is shut and blinds pulled, and the house is lit from inside, sun having now set. Far away in wood R. upstage a tiny light moves. As it comes near it proves to be a lamp carried by Captain Hook. He waves it as signal and the other Pirates steal forward, two carrying a pail of water. There is a skull and crossbones painted on the pail. There is sensation when they see the house. Hook signs to Starkey who peeps through board of house, then whispers to Hook.)

HOOK *(in reply)* They are all there? *(Starkey nods.)* Peter too? *(Starkey nods.)* And all hot and flushed? *(Starkey nods.)* Then we have them!

STARKEY No, Captain, no—the game's up. They've found a mother.

HOOK A mother! Then that water's no use—she won't let them drink it. A mother! Foiled! *(All grind teeth.)* Ha, another plan! That dry grass. Pile it here, then we'll set the house afire and smoke them out: when they come running out, give them Johnny Corkscrew! But leave Peter Pan to me! *(They pile dry grass round house. As they do so some strange cry is heard in the wood that heralds the approach of the Indians. Then silence.)*

STARKEY What was that?

HOOK Only some night bird. *(Strikes light, gives it to Starkey who creeps forward to set fire to grass. He suddenly moans—shows an arrow in his side, the effect got as in 'Ulysses.'*)* What's the matter? Shot?

STARKEY The Redskins! *(On opposite side of the river the Indians are seen vaguely brandishing weapons. They should be as shadowy as possible.)*

SMEE They're four to one—we're lost. Oh! *(An arrow is seen in him.)*

HOOK Back to the ship. Keep together.

(They disappear R. upstage. For a moment they are seen trying to cross river higher up. Indians dart at them. There is a moment's struggle then Pirates fly, Indians pursuing. Indians reappear stealing to house threateningly with tomahawks and knives.)

PANTHER *(pointing to house)* More Palefaces—take scalps!

TIGER LILY *(after peering in)* No men—papooses—little boys. Tiger Lily's braves no scalp little boys. *(They put aside weapons.)*

PANTHER *(after listening)* Lil' white squaw tell boys story—lovely story!

OTHERS Story! Story!

TIGER LILY Red men sit here listen lovely story. No let Pirates hurt lil' boys. *(All hunker and listen round walls.)*

PANTHER Red man come here every night, protect lil' boys and listen white squaw's lovely stories! *(All listen delighted.)*

OTHERS Wah! Wah! Ugh! Ugh! *(Perhaps also animals come and listen.)*

CURTAIN

SCENE 3

A SATURDAY NIGHT

(The scene is as it were on two floors. Below (i.e. on stage level) is the children's underground home, and above is the upper world, viz. the wood, river, little house &c. of Scene 1 of this act. The underground room should be a shallow room to enable gallery &c. to see it, and the action above ground takes place well down stage so that it is visible to front of stalls. The height of underground room and the slope of ground above must be treated with regard to the seeing capacity of the various parts of the house.* As no action will take place above ground except well down stage the back part need not be strong, but the part actually above room must be strong to support people.

The underground room is an irregular semi-circle with walls of earth and rock kept in place by the roots of the trees in a fantastic manner. Each tree has a door, and it is seen that by entering and ascending you would emerge by the door in the same tree above. There are no windows in the walls proper, but the roof slopes and in it is one small sky-light window. The room of course occupies the whole breadth of the stage, and in L.C. of it stands a hollow tree trunk, the continuation of which above-ground is the chimney. In this trunk is fire-place with a great fire burning and in front of it suspended on a string are articles of boys' clothing, such as stockings, shirt &c. Through the room flows a tiny stream, not more than two feet wide. It comes out of back wall with a fall of two feet and exits R. down stage. The effect is got by lighting. In back wall C. at such a height as to be visible from all parts of the house is a room about two feet square and one foot deep, which is at present closed by a little curtain, but is really Tippy's bedroom—a sort of doll's room. The room is lighted by night-lights in saucers.

Curtain rises, and above are seen a dozen Redskins both men and women sitting in semi-circle and listening through ground to what is going on below. Tiger Lily is conspicuous among them. Down below, Wendy and all the boys except Peter are sitting at an imaginary tea. The table is a removable oblong board standing on a tree trunk in the middle of the room, and this tree trunk has certain peculiar properties to be explained presently. Wendy wears romantic woodland garments of her own devising, and the boys are also quaintly dressed. She is sitting at L. end of table. The seat at R. end is empty. There are rough arm-chairs. The boys sit around on stools. Curly is on a sort of baby chair next to Wendy. The whole meal is entirely make-believe, there being nothing whatever on the table, but all pretend to eat imaginary food and to drink from imaginary cups. Wendy has the airs of a mother presiding at imaginary tea-tray. All make-believe very realistically.)

WENDY Is your mug empty, Slightly darling?

SLIGHTLY Not quite empty yet.

NIBS Mummy, he hasn't even *begun* to drink his milk!

WENDY Slightly, how very naughty of you! *(Slightly takes great gulps and passes up imaginary mug, which Wendy fills. John holds up hand.)* Well?

JOHN May I sit in Peter's chair, as he's not here?

WENDY In your father's chair? Certainly not.

JOHN *(bitterly)* He's not really our father. He didn't even know how to be a father till I showed him.

WENDY John! *(Tootles holds up hand.)* Well, dear?

TOOTLES *(rising as if to make a speech)* I don't suppose *I* could be father?

WENDY No, Tootles.

TOOTLES As I can't be father, I don't suppose, Curly, you would let me be baby.

CURLY No I won't.

TOOTLES As I can't be baby, do you think I could be a twin?

FIRST TWIN Not you. It's awfully difficult to be a twin.

TOOTLES As I can't be anything important, would any of you like to see me do a trick?

BOYS No!

TOOTLES *(sweetly but sadly)* I hadn't really any hope. *(Resumes seat.)*

SECOND TWIN Alexander is coughing on the table!

ALEX The twins *began* with cheese-cakes!

NIBS Curly is taking *both* butter and honey!

CURLY　Nibs is speaking with his mouth full!

WENDY　Oh dear, oh dear, I'm sure I sometimes think that youngsters are to be envied. Alexander, we are waiting for you. *(Alex goes to her side.)*

ALEX　*(simply)*

> Here a little child I stand
> Heaving up my either hand
> Cold as paddocks though they be
> Here I lift them up to thee
> For a benison to fall
> On our meat and on us all.* Amen.

WENDY　*(rising)* Now you may clear away. Slightly, bring me my work-basket.

(While the others are clearing she goes to chair by fire, where Slightly brings her a great basket full of stockings. She lifts a pile.) And every heel with a hole in it! *(She sits happily darning while the boys skip about as light as fairies, putting away imaginary dishes, folding up imaginary table cloth, &c. They also lift the table board and stools out of the way. Then they get rid of the tree trunk which formed support of table by pushing it down. It collapses like a concertina or opera-hat, but is very stiff, and once it springs up, sending two boys on top of it sprawling. At last they get it level with the ground and put a bolt in. During this silent scene an incident takes place above. Peter enters from L. carrying gun and game bag and the Indians prostrate themselves before him.)*

PETER　*(a little lordly in manner)* The Great White Father is glad to see the Piccaninny* warriors protecting his wigwam from the pirates.

SEVERAL OF INDIANS　Wah! It is good.

TIGER LILY　These Tiger Lily's braves—me Tiger Lily.

PETER　Yes, lady, the Great White Father knows that these are your braves.

TIGER LILY　Me great lady—you great man.

PETER　Yes, I know.

TIGER LILY　*(devoted to Peter)* Sometimes Injin girl runs into wood, Injin brave runs after her—Injin brave catch her. Then she Injin brave's squaw. Is it not so? *(To Indians.)*

INDIANS Ugh! Ugh!

TIGER LILY If Paleface runs after Injin girl—catch her—then she Paleface's squaw.

INDIANS Ugh! Ugh!

TIGER LILY Suppose Tiger Lily runs into wood—Peter Paleface catch her—what then?

PETER *(bewildered)* Paleface can never catch Indian girls, they run so fast.

TIGER LILY If Peter Paleface chases Tiger Lily, she no run very fast—she tumble in a heap, what then? *(Peter puzzled. She addresses Indians.)* What then?

AN INDIAN She him's squaw.

ALL Wah! Ugh! Ugh!

PETER The great father of the Palefaces doesn't quite understand what you mean. Are you wanting to be my mother, Tiger Lily?

TIGER LILY No mother!

PETER Then I don't understand you. Goodnight, Tiger Lily. Goodnight, braves. *(Tiger Lily is disconsolate. Peter goes into tree.)*

PANTHER *(distressed because Tiger Lily is weeping)* Tiger Lily's braves bring Paleface back! *(Lifting weapon.)*

TIGER LILY No—no hurt him. Him no understand—Tiger Lily explain more clear next time.

INDIAN Huh! *(Meaning that something is happening beneath. All listen. Wendy has started up.)*

WENDY Children, I hear your father's step! He likes you to meet him at the door.

(All boys except John and Alex run to door and meet Peter entering below by his tree. He has the manner of a cheery father returning from the day's toil.)

ALL Dad, Dad!

PETER You rogues—no, I won't let one of you into my pockets till I know whether you have been good boys.

SEVERAL We have—we have!

PETER Then in you go! *(Several get fruit from his pockets.)*

WENDY *(standing smiling at fire)* Peter, you just spoil them, you know.

PETER *(laying aside gun and bag and going to her)* Ah, old lady.

JOHN *(to Alex)* It was me told him mothers are called old lady.

PETER Got a thimble for me, little woman? *(Kisses her.)*

ALEX *(to John)* It was me told him they are called little woman.

FIRST TWIN Father! We want to dance.

PETER Dance away, my little man.

FIRST TWIN But we want you to dance.

PETER Me? My old bones would rattle.

NIBS And Mummy too.

WENDY *(scandalized)* A pretty figure I should cut dancing! The mother of such an armful dance!

SLIGHTLY But on a Saturday night?

WENDY *(hesitating)* Of course, it *is* Saturday night, Peter?

PETER People of our figure, Wendy!

WENDY But it's only among our own progeny.*

PETER True, true! But mind you, you must all promise to go to bed immediately afterwards.

ALL We promise.

PETER Well, well, well.

NIBS We'll sing too.

WENDY But what?

NIBS 'Of all the girls that are so smart';* and, mother, you'll be *Sally*.

(They sing, either an original song or 'Sally in our Alley', different ones singing different verses and with business of marching and dancing between*

verses. Above the Indians join in, the music being from their tom-toms, and Tiger Lily sings a verse of 'Sally' in Indian. The children below listen and join in, and all ends in a dance both above and below, at end of which all below exeunt into trees except Peter and Wendy, while the Indians suddenly become solemn again. Wendy and Peter still feeling themselves an aged couple have returned to fire, Peter sitting in nook on L. of it.)

WENDY And now, Peter, your slippers. *(She affects to take off his boots and put on his slippers.)* And your pipe, Peter: I love to fill it. *(She fills imaginary pipe, gives it him, holds a real lighted paper and he affects to light and smoke with enjoyment. She sits with darning in the other nook by the fire.)*

PETER Ah, old lady, there's nothing pleasanter of an evening when the day's toil is over than to sit by the fire with one's smiling missus in the opposite chair and the little ones clustered round me.

WENDY *(beaming)* It *is* sweet, Peter, isn't it! Peter, I think Curly has your nose.

PETER Nibs takes after you.

WENDY Dear Peter, with such a large family, of course I have now passed my best, but you don't want to change me, do you? We are an old couple now, Peter, but am I still your Jo?

PETER Always my Jo, Wendy.

(Sitting by the fire, Wendy sings the first verse of 'John Anderson, My Jo John,'* and Peter sings the second verse, changing the word John to Jean. Up above the Indians in couples, a woman and a man in each, go through the pantomime of the scene. When the song finishes Peter moves away, looking scared, as if he had wakened up.)

WENDY *(going to him)* Peter, what is it?

PETER I was just thinking—it's only make-believe, isn't it, that I'm their father?

WENDY *(pained)* Oh, yes.

PETER You see it would make *me* so old to be their real father.

WENDY But they are ours, Peter, yours and mine.

PETER *(anxious)* But not really?

WENDY *(bravely)* Not if you don't wish it. You know, Peter, everybody grows up, except clowns.

PETER Then I want to be a clown. How can one become a clown, Wendy?

WENDY I'm not sure. I think if you are funny too long you just can't help becoming a clown.

PETER It sounds easy!

WENDY But it's not very dignified, and oh Peter I have other views for you. Peter, what are your exact feelings for me?

PETER Those of a devoted son, Wendy.

WENDY I thought so! *(Crosses sadly to fire.)*

PETER You love me as a mother, don't you?

WENDY If that's all you wish, Peter.

PETER *All* I wish? What could be nicer, Wendy, than to be my mother?

WENDY Oh, Peter!

PETER You're so puzzling. Tiger Lily's just the same. There's something *she* wants to be to me, but she says it's not my mother.

WENDY No, it isn't. Indeed it isn't! *(Tiger Lily is listening eagerly.)*

PETER Wendy, what is it you want to be to me?

WENDY That's a question no gentleman ought to put to a lady.

PETER *(huffily)* Oh, very well. Perhaps Tippy will tell me.

WENDY *(with spirit)* Oh yes, Tippy will tell you. *She* has no scruples. *She* hugs you openly, though she can't go a twentieth part of the way round. Tippy's an abandoned little creature! *(Tippy darts about.)*

PETER She has been listening! *(Tippy rings.)* She says she knows she's an abandoned little creature, and that like a true woman, she glories in it. I suppose she means that she wants to be my mother. *(Tippy rings 'You silly ass', which the audience can now understand for itself.)*

WENDY *(with spirit)* I almost agree with her! *(Peter is hurt. Tippy darts at Wendy and evidently pinches and pulls her hair.)* Oh! Oh! Oh!

PETER Stop it, Tippy! I'm very angry. Go to bed at once—you're in disgrace. *(Tippy rings defiantly.)* But you *shall* go! *(Pulls curtain of recess open, disclosing Tippy's room.)* Come! Do you hear. *(Tippy at last flies into recess, and curtains are pulled from inside as if she were in a passion. The children all come running in wearing pyjamas.)*

NIBS Now, Mums, you promised to tell us a story as soon as we got into bed.

WENDY I *may* be wrong, children, but as far as *I* can see you are not into bed yet.

SEVERAL The bed! The bed!

(Rushing about like gay sprites they bring the bed into view. This is done by releasing ropes and pulling it down from ceiling, which would be the best way, or it is pulled out from wall. But whichever it is, it must come as a surprise to the audience, who have been unaware of its existence. It is on R. of stage, and all except Peter and Wendy jump into it. It is large enough to hold the eight, packed like sardines. Wendy takes a stool beside them, but Peter remains thinking by fire though sometimes the interest of the story draws him forward. The Indians listen to the story through the ground entranced.)

CURLY I *do* hope there will be a mother in the story.

WENDY Quiet, Curly. Well, there was once a gentleman—

CURLY I had rather he had been a lady.

NIBS Do be quiet, Curly, how could a gentleman be a lady?

WENDY You mustn't interrupt. And there was a lady also.

CURLY Oho, there *was* a lady!

FIRST TWIN Excuse my interrupting you, Mummy, but you say there *was* a lady. You mean that there *is* a lady also, don't you? *(Anxiously.)* She's not dead, is she?

WENDY Oh, no.

TOOTLES I'm awfully glad she's not dead. Are you glad, John?

JOHN Of course I am.

TOOTLES Are you glad, Slightly?

SLIGHTLY Rather!

TOOTLES Are you glad, twins?

SECOND TWIN We are just glad.

WENDY Oh, dear!

PETER Little less noise there.

WENDY The gentleman's name was Mr Darling, and her name was Mrs Darling.

JOHN I knew them.

ALEX I think I knew them.

WENDY They were married, you know, and what do you think they had?

TOOTLES It's awfully puzzling.

WENDY They had three descendants.

SLIGHTLY What's descendants?

WENDY Well—you are one.

SLIGHTLY *(conceited)* You hear that, Twins? I am a descendant.

JOHN Descendants are just children.

CURLY I had rather they had been white rats.

WENDY Well, they are descendants also, almost everything's a descendant. Now these three children had a dear faithful nurse called Nana, but Mr Darling was angry with her so he chained her up in the yard, and so all the children flew away.

NIBS It's an awfully good story.

WENDY They flew away to the Never Never Never Land, where the lost children are.

CURLY *(excited)* I just thought they did—I don't know how it is, but I just thought they did.

TOOTLES Oh, Wendy, was one of the lost children called Tootles?

WENDY Yes, he was.

TOOTLES Am I in a story? Slightly, I'm in a story! Wendy, tell us what Tootles did, tell us what Tootles said, tell us what Tootles was like!

WENDY No, I want you to consider the feelings of the unhappy parents with all the children flown away. Oh, think of the empty beds! Oh, think of the poor Mummy! Oh, think!

FIRST TWIN It's awfully sad!

SECOND TWIN I don't see how it *can* have a happy ending—do you, Nibs?

NIBS I'm frightfully anxious.

WENDY If you knew how great is a mother's love you would have no fear.

CURLY I do like a mother's love. Do you like a mother's love, Slightly?

SLIGHTLY I do just.

WENDY You see our heroine knew that the mother would always leave the window open for her children to fly back by. So they stayed away for years, and had a lovely time.

FIRST TWIN Did they ever go back?

WENDY Let us now take a peep into the future. Years have rolled by, and who is this elegant lady of uncertain age, alighting at London station?

NIBS Oh, Wendy, who is she?

WENDY Can it be—yes—no—it is—the fair Wendy! Who are the two noble portly figures accompanying her, now grown to man's estate? Can they be John and Alexander? They are! 'See, dear brothers,' says Wendy, pointing upward. 'There is the window still standing open. Ah, now we are rewarded for our sublime faith in a mother's love.' So up they flew to their mummy and their daddy, and pen cannot describe the happy scene, over which we draw a veil. *(Peter who has come forward, listening intently, now gives utterance to a cry—Wendy goes to him.)* Peter, what is it? *(He gulps.)* Peter, *where* is it? *(Feeling him like a mother searching him for the seat of pain.)*

PETER It isn't *that* kind of pain.

WENDY Then what—oh what is it?

PETER Oh, Wendy, you are wrong about mothers. Long ago I thought, like you, that my mother would always keep the window open for me, so I stayed away for years, and then I flew back, but the window was barred, for Mother had forgotten all about me, and there was another little boy sleeping in my bed.

JOHN Wendy, let's go home!

WENDY Are you sure mothers are like that?

PETER Yes.

WENDY John, Alexander! *(Clutching them.)*

FIRST TWIN You are not to leave us, Wendy!

WENDY I must!

NIBS Not tonight?

WENDY I'm frightened to stay another moment. Peter, will you make all the necessary arrangements?

PETER *(huskily)* If you wish it.

(He exits and is seen emerging on top and arranging things with the Indians, who have followed all the incidents below with as much interest as the children.)

TOOTLES If there is anything we could do, Wendy, to make you more comfortable.

CURLY We would darn our own stockings, Wendy.

SLIGHTLY We would build you a bigger house.

WENDY I love my little house!

FIRST TWIN It will be worse than before she came!

SLIGHTLY We shan't let her go!

NIBS Let's keep her prisoner.

FIRST TWIN Let's chain her.

SECOND TWIN Wendy, it's because we love you so. *(They are threatening.)*

WENDY Oh back! Tootles, I appeal to you.

TOOTLES *(much moved)* I'm just Tootles, and nobody minds *me* much. But the first who does not behave to Wendy like an English gentleman, I will blood him *severely*. *(Draws knife.)* What are you, Slightly?

SLIGHTLY English gentleman.

TOOTLES What are you, Nibs?

NIBS English gentleman.

TOOTLES What are you, Curly?

CURLY English gentleman.

TOOTLES What are you, Twins?

TWINS English gentlemen.

WENDY Dear, dear boys! *(Peter re-enters.)*

PETER Wendy, I have asked the Redskins to guide you through the wood, as flying tires you so.

WENDY Thank you, Peter.

PETER They will put you into a boat when you come to the sea, and Tippy will take it to London. Wake her, Nibs.

NIBS *(knocking at side of recess)* Tippy! Tippy! You are to get up, and take Wendy on a journey. *(Bells.)* She says she won't.

PETER *(at curtain)* Tippy, if you don't get up and dress at once I shall open the curtains, and then we shall all see you in your *negligée.** *(Bells.)* She says she's getting up.

WENDY Dear ones, I have had such a splendid thought. If you will all come with me, I feel almost sure I can find your mothers for you!

SEVERAL Oh! Oh!

WENDY You see I know a good deal about them already. They are the loveliest mothers in the world—you all say you remember that.

TOOTLES Mine was lovely. What was yours like, Nibs?

NIBS Lovely. What was yours like, Curly?

CURLY Lovely. What was yours like, Twins?

TWINS Lovely. What was yours like, Slightly?

SLIGHTLY Lovely.

WENDY That will be a help. I shall gather all the loveliest mothers together and then watch them, and if they do the slightest thing wrong they are not your mothers, but if they do everything just so, then they *are* your mothers.

SECOND TWIN Oh, Peter, can we go?

PETER All right!

TOOTLES Let's put on our blacks*—first impressions are so important.

WENDY No—your mothers will excuse your pyjamas, but there is one thing you must all bring—the baby clothes you were lost in.

SLIGHTLY Let's make parcels of them! *(All exeunt by different doors except Wendy and Peter.)*

WENDY Get yours too, Peter.

PETER But I'm not going with you, Wendy.

WENDY Yes, Peter.

PETER Oh no.

WENDY Peter, to find your mother.

PETER *(frightened)* No—no—perhaps she would say I was old, Wendy! I just want *you* to be my mother.

WENDY Your *mother*! Oh dear!

(All the children come bounding back, each carrying a stick over shoulder with bundle tied in handkerchief on it. John and Alexander have no bundles.)

NIBS They are in our handkerchiefs, Wendy.

WENDY But—but Peter isn't coming!

SEVERAL Peter not coming?

PETER No. Now then, no fuss—no blubbering. Are you ready, Tippy? *(Tippy pulls back curtains and flies out ringing.)* Lead the way.

(Tippy exits at Peter's door but does not appear above. In the meantime the Pirates—about a dozen of them—have crept unseen upon the Indians, and suddenly the air is full of cries as the two parties engage in mortal conflict with cutlasses and tomahawks. Consternation below.)

TOOTLES It must be the pirates!

PETER The Indians are fighting them! I must help them!

WENDY Peter, don't leave me!

SEVERAL Don't leave us, Peter!

(Peter with drawn knife stands ready to defend all. They listen breath-lessly. The fight is grim and realistic, and Capt. Hook's hook plays a prominent part, but soon it is over. The Indians wounded &c., fly away R. Pirates remain victorious. There is sudden stillness—Pirates sign caution and listen to what is going on below.)

PETER It's over!

WENDY But who has won?

SLIGHTLY If the Pirates have they will attack us!

PETER H'sh! If the Indians have won they will beat the tom-tom. That's always their sign of victory. Listen! *(Hook signs triumphantly to Starkey, who brings him tom-tom flung down by Indians. Hook beats it.)* The tom-tom! An Indian victory.

ALL *(below)* Hurrah! Hurrah!

PETER You are quite safe now, Wendy, for the Redskins will guide you safely. Boys, goodbye, I hope you will like your mothers. Wendy—*(He breaks down.)*

HOOK *(whispering)* A man to every tree.

STARKEY Shall we give them Johnny Corkscrew?

HOOK No. Gag them, and take them to the ship. *(At a sign a man steals to each tree.)*

PETER *(to boys)* All turn away your faces, so that you can't see your Captain crying. *(They do so.)* Goodbye, Wendy. *(Kisses her.)*

WENDY Peter, you will remember about changing your flannels,* won't you?

PETER Yes.

WENDY And that is your medicine, you know. *(Pointing to bottle.)*

PETER I won't forget it.

WENDY   I shall sometimes come back to see you, Peter.

PETER   You will never come back.

WENDY   You will sometimes come to my window, won't you?

PETER   Sometimes, but I shall never let you know I'm there.

WENDY   Peter, what are you to me? You are my—what?

PETER   Your son, Wendy.

WENDY   Oh! Goodbye.

(All exeunt by various trees leaving Peter alone—he sits gloomily head in hand. As each emerges he is seized by Pirates, gagged and thrust into the little house and door locked. The children get out of house at back unknown to audience, and the house for a reason presently to be seen has now a floor. Peter unaware of what has happened above locks all the doors, pours his medicine into glass and puts it near bed but forgets to take it. He puts out all lights except one near bed, gets into bed sadly and sleeps. Hook signs to his men and they go down trees trying to get Peter and rattle the lower doors but can't open them. Hook's right arm and hook are inserted at window, clawing for Peter, but just fail to reach him. Cecco appears on top carrying a tin cup.)

STARKEY   What's that?

CECCO   Ice cold water—the captain wants it for Peter Pan. *(Disappears at back.)*

STARKEY   I see! The captain's to pour it into his medicine glass. Peter will drink it, for he has no mother now, and the boy who when he's flushed drinks cold water dies. It works like poison.

(Hook is seen through window emptying medicine glass and pouring cold water into it. He reappears above exulting, signs to his men, four of them lift the little house like a sedan chair, and exeunt all Pirates carrying it L. The crocodile appears R. and exits after them L. There is a cautious tapping at Peter's door below.)

PETER   *(waking up)* Who's that? *(No answer—then a knock.)* Is anyone there? *(Silence—then more knocking.)* I won't open unless you speak. *(Silence—knocking. He gets pistol—cautiously opens door—*

Tippy darts in ringing. It should be noticed that Tippy has not emerged on top. She rings excitedly.) What! The Redskins were defeated and Wendy and the boys have been captured by the Pirates! Oh! Oh! I'll rescue her—I'll rescue her. *(Rushes about getting weapons. Tippy rings.)* What? Oh, it's just my medicine. *(Bells.)* Poisoned? Nonsense! Who could have poisoned it? I promised Wendy to take it and I'm going to as soon as I've sharpened my dagger. *(He is sharpening it on a revolving grindstone. Tippy darts to glass and is seen apparently drinking it, but the poison really goes down stem.)* Now then! Tippy, you've drunk my medicine. *(Tippy darts about strangely.)* What's the matter with you? *(Bells.)* It *was* poison! You drank it to save my life? Tippy, dear Tippy, are you dying! *(Tippy flies to her little room and to bed—rings feebly.)* She's dying! *(To audience.)* Her light's growing faint, and if it goes out that means she's dead. Her voice is so low I can scarcely tell what she's saying. *(Weak bells—he runs between her and audience.)* She says she thinks she could get well again if children believed in fairies. Do you believe? Say quick that you believe! *(The light has been flickering, but now children in audience are expected to begin to demonstrate.)* Wave your handkerchiefs so that she may *see* you believe. Don't let Tippy die. The light's getting stronger—wave, wave, wave. She's much better. She's all right now—oh thank you, thank you, and now, to rescue Wendy!

(He puts a mask over his face, rushes upstairs and off L. looking for track. Tippy darts about gaily, ringing in bell language the air of 'Sally in our Alley', then darts upstairs and off L.)

CURTAIN

SCENE 4

THE PIRATE RIVER

(Curtain rises on a scene shrouded in mist, and as this slowly breaks the scene is disclosed as a mysterious river of the South American kind. The river (which should perhaps be red) flows slowly and sullenly from R. to L.—it is not real water but merely an effect of lighting, and the direction of the flow is indicated by drift-wood, broken water plants, &c. The river is nearly the whole depth of the stage but not quite. On the far bank is

practical* *ground much covered by reeds &c. Beyond this—on back cloth—is the boundless gloomy forest. On the near bank of river is also a strip of practical ground with reeds &c. growing on it, and at L. and R. down stage two trees, whose branches meet high overhead, and from these hang parasitical growth, through which (it merely consists of long thin dangling streamers) the audience looks upon the river. In the water, near centre of stage a tree is growing, from which a branch stretches to the far bank, and this branch is strong enough for certain feats that are to be performed on it. To help certain business two clumps of grass are growing in the water, and on the clump near this tree a great bird has a nest on which it is sitting at rise of curtain. This bird is played by an actor supported by flying wires. Water lilies of great size grow in the other clump. The time is evening. A deadly stillness pervades the scene, and not a sound should be heard except when especially indicated.*

Among the brushwood on far side of river some wolves are seen passing. The effect here will be increased the more vaguely the animals are seen, half hidden by the undergrowth, stealing about like shadows, &c. After they disappear a lion comes and drinks. The great bird flies away down river out of sight. A snake which has been twined round the tree growing in water drops into river with a soft plop and disappears. The lion goes away. A crocodile's head rises near second clump of grass and disappears. From L. a raft comes into view, lit by a pirate lantern. In the front are piled like a load of merchandise all the boys gagged. In the stern sits Capt. Hook with Wendy gagged. Starkey is punting. Hook whistles as a signal, and Cecco appears on near bank and Smee on far bank. Hook signs to them to hide, and the raft goes on out of sight. Smee disappears on his bank, but Cecco crouches in reeds, partly visible to audience. The great bird flies up river and out of sight. Suddenly and with no warning to the audience a jaguar which has been, unknown to them, crouching in a tree on near side of the river leaps upon Cecco. They disappear together, presumably into water. There is no scream from Cecco, all is stillness.

Peter in a small boat with sails appears L. He is wearing his mask, and the reason for the mask is that his place is now taken by a substitute who passes to the audience as Peter while really a gymnast. As he appears a crocodile raises its open mouth, barring the way, and Peter saves himself by leaping and catching the branch overhanging river, to which he hangs. The bow of boat goes into crocodile's mouth which breaks it in pieces. The bits of boat are borne backwards out of sight, crocodile sinks in river, and Peter works his way along branch to far side of river and alights on ground.

He disappears for a second in wood and reappears. This is to let the real Peter take his place. Tiger Lily appears L. standing erect, paddle in hand, in bark canoe.)

PETER H'sh!

TIGER LILY Peter Paleface! *(She brings canoe close to bank on far side.)*

PETER The heart of the great white chief is sad, for he has lost his boat.

TIGER LILY Sad is the heart of Tiger Lily for the pirates have killed many of her braves. *(She lands.)* Wah-wah-wah! *(This is a dirge for the dead. Peter takes her hand. She becomes cheerful.)* Us no be sad no more. Tiger Lily with Peter Paleface—Peter Paleface with Tiger Lily—now we rub noses. *(Does so.)* Now us dance with joy!

PETER Not till I save Wendy! *(She stamps angrily.)* Will Tiger Lily give the great white chief her canoe that he may rescue Wendy?

TIGER LILY Tiger Lily take Peter Paleface in her canoe.

PETER Oh, thank you, Tiger Lily—I'll rub noses again. *(They do so.)*

TIGER LILY Tiger Lily take Peter Paleface in her canoe that way. *(Pointing L.)*

PETER No, the pirates took her that way. *(Pointing R.)*

TIGER LILY This Wendy. (*Pointing to herself.)*

PETER No, you're not.

TIGER LILY *(cajoling)* Tiger Lily wants to be your Wendy! Peter Paleface come with me, be great Indian white chief, and this *(pointing to herself)* your squaw.

PETER Desert Wendy? Never!

TIGER LILY *(fiercely)* No let Wendy have you! *(Claps hands—two Indians appear on far bank.)* Tie him tree. *(They seize Peter and tie him to tree, threaten, dancing round him with tomahawks.)*

INDIANS Have him's scalp?

TIGER LILY Go—wait. *(They disappear down bank.)* Tiger Lily love Peter Paleface.

PETER You have a queer way of showing it.

TIGER LILY This Indian girl's way. Me cut cord if you come with me.

PETER Never!

TIGER LILY Me scalp you myself if you no nice to me!

PETER I don't care. Wendy is my only mother.

TIGER LILY Then Tiger Lily leave you here—you starve or else wild beasts come eat you—little bit here, little bit there.

PETER Whatever happens I'll be true to Wendy! *(She meditates tomahawking him, but eventually goes away in canoe, back the way she had come. The cries of wild beasts are now heard in distance. Then Tippy comes into view L. darting up river—Peter sees her.)* Tippy! *(She darts to him, ringing.)* Tippy, Tippy, do you think your little teeth could bite through these cords? (Tippy alights on cords and is seen moving about them. The cries of beasts increase. Peter is soon free.) Dear, dear Tippy! (Bells.) I can't tell you now, but come into my pocket, and I'll tell you as we go.*

(Tippy gets into his pocket. He rushes off R. but immediately reappears (it is the substitute who comes now) evidently pursued. He springs on the branch and works his way along it to the tree in middle of stream. He is pursued by Smee, knife in mouth, and a chase among the trees takes place. When Smee is out of sight Peter comes down the trunk in river and leaps onto grass where great nest is. There are 3 eggs in it. He puts his hat on grass, puts eggs in it, gets into nest, and with a stick he finds there punts himself off with difficulty R. out of sight and uttering a crow. The great bird flies back and sits on hat.

Mist again falls. Now is heard drawing near a rabble of wicked song and music, which when the mist clears is seen to come from the pirate ship, which now occupies most of the stage. It is as far back as possible, to allow of there being some of the river between it and the near bank. Not all of it is seen, as the stern is out of sight L. The ship—to be described in full afterward—is an evil-looking, rakish craft, and its side is presented to audience. Level with the stage is (R.) the bow of the ship and (C.) the cabin which is open to the audience's view (i.e. there are no windows to it). Also (L.) is a hold which is closed to view. A door from cabin leads into it. It has a small round window space facing audience, but through this nothing can be seen save blackness. Above cabin and hold and stretching

L. out of sight is upper deck. It is reached by a ladder from bow. The ship is flying the skull and crossbones. On deck Starkey is keeping watch and two pirates loll about. At bow are a number of pirates singing to accordion played by COOKSON, a pirate. Others play cards. In cabin Capt. Hook seated at small table with two pirates beside him is questioning the eight boys whose hands and legs are tied but mouths free.)

HOOK *(starting up and threatening singers)* Quiet, you dogs, or I'll cast anchor in you! *(Raising hook—they are very afraid of him and stop singing, but the card playing goes on. He returns to boys.)* Now then, I've told you, six of you walks the plank this night, but I have room for two cabin-boys—which of you is it to be?

TOOTLES You see, sir, I don't think my mother would like me to be a pirate. Would your mother like you to be a pirate, Slightly?

SLIGHTLY I don't think so. Would your mother like you to be a pirate, Twin?

FIRST TWIN I don't think so. Nibs, would your mother—

HOOK Stow this gab!* You boy, *(to John)* you look as if you had a little pluck in you. Didst ever want to be a pirate, my hearty?

JOHN When I was at school I rather wanted to be a pirate. I thought of calling myself Red Handed Jack.

HOOK And a good name too. We'll call you that here, Bully,* if you join.

JOHN Alexander, what do you think?

ALEX What would you call me if I join?

HOOK You should be Blackbeard Joe.

ALEX John, what do you think?

JOHN Shall we still be loyal subjects of King Edward?*

HOOK You would have to swear, 'Down with King Edward.'

JOHN *(banging table)* Then I refuse.

ALEX *(banging table)* And I refuse.

TOOTLES *(excitedly)* Rule Britannia. *(Pirates buffet* him.)*

HOOK That seals your doom. *(To pirate.)* Bring in their mother. *(Exit pirate into hold L.)* Get the plank ready. *(To those at bow.)*

BOATSWAIN Ay, ay, sir—tumble up, you lubbers.* *(Several hurry up ladder to deck, and get plank ready—it protrudes from deck towards audience. Wendy is brought into cabin from hold.)*

ALEX *(running to her)* Wendy! *(All boys gather round her for protection.)*

WENDY You wicked man, why have you sent for me?

HOOK I thought, my hearty,* you would like to say goodbye to your cubs.

WENDY Are they to die?

SECOND TWIN Wendy, he is to make us walk the plank.

WENDY What's that?

JUKES She don't know what it is, Captain!

MULLINS Here's ignorance!

JUKES Shall I take her up on deck and then she'll see Johnny Plank?

HOOK Ay, but silence, first, for a mother's last words to her children.

WENDY These are my last words. Dear, dear boys, I feel that I have a message to you from your real mothers, and it's this: we hope our sons will die like English gentlemen.* *(She is thrust up on to deck.)*

TOOTLES I'm going to do what my mother hopes. What are you to do, Nibs?

NIBS What my mother hopes. What are you to do, Curly?

CURLY What my mother hopes. John, what are—

HOOK Silence!

STARKEY *(on deck to Wendy)* Ay, that's Johnny Plank.

WENDY Oh, horrible.

STARKEY See here, honey, I'll save *you* if you tell me a story. Tell me about the Babes in the Wood.*

WENDY Tell a story to such as you! I'd rather die.

STARKEY Then die you shall! *(He ties her to mast—during this scene between Wendy and Starkey, Peter steals alongside vessel below from*

L. with a knife in his mouth, climbs in at port hole of hold and is lost to view.) Avast* there, the plank is waiting.

COOKSON All's ready, Captain.

HOOK *(drinking)* Then, here's to Johnny Plank. *(Sings.)*

> Oh tooral loo the English brig
> We took and quickly sank,
> And for a warning to the crew
> We made them walk the plank.
> Yo ho, yo ho, the frisky plank
> You walks along it so,
> Till it goes down and you goes down
> To tooral looral lo.

(All Pirates wherever they are repeat the last lines with actions—when it's finished the boys strike up 'God Save the King.')

HOOK Stow that! D'you want a touch of the cat* to make you skip up the ladder? Fetch it, Jukes—it's in the hold. *(Exit Jukes L. into hold with lighted match.)*

> Yo ho, yo ho, the scratching cat
> Its tails are nine, you know,
> And when they're writ upon your back
> You're fit to go below.
> So here's to—

(Peter's victorious crow is heard from hold—pirates are startled, for they don't understand what it means though the boys do.)

WENDY *(to herself)* Peter!

HOOK What was that? *(Mullins rushes into hold. He staggers out.)* What's the matter with Bill Jukes, you dog?

MULLINS The matter wi' him is he's dead—he's lying stark there wi' a knife in him. *(Sensation.)*

COOKSON Bill Jukes—him as was here this minute a hearty man—dead!

MULLINS The hold's as black as a pit, but there's something terrible in there—the thing you heard crowing.

HOOK Ay, Mullins, go back and fetch me out that doodle-doo.

MULLINS *(frightened)* Captain!

HOOK *(with horrible softness)* Did you say you would go, Mullins? *(Mullins re-enters hold in fear. Pause. Then crowing again. Panic.)* Who is to bring me that doodle-doo?

COOKSON Wait till Bill Mullins comes out.

SEVERAL Ay, wait for Bill.

HOOK I think I heard you volunteer, Cookson?

COOKSON No, by thunder!

HOOK *(softly)* My hook thinks you did—I wonder if it wouldn't be advisable, Cookson, to humour the hook?

COOKSON I'll swing* before I go in there.

SEVERAL And so say we.

HOOK Is't mutiny? *(They murmur threateningly.)* Cookson's ring-leader! Shake hands, Cookson. *(Offering hook. Cookson recoils. Hook follows. Cookson in terror jumps overboard.)* Your hand, Cookson, your hand! *(Cookson disappears.)* Who else said mutiny? *(They cower before him. He seizes lamp.)* I'll bring out that doodle-doo. *(He enters hold. Suspense. He returns looking scared. Light of lantern out.)* Something blew out the light.

FIRST PIRATE Some *thing*?

SECOND PIRATE What of Bill Mullins?

HOOK He's dead. *(Panic.)*

THIRD PIRATE They do say as the surest sign a ship's accurst is when there's one on board more than can be accounted for.

FIRST PIRATE I've heard he allus boards the pirate craft at last. Had he a tail, Captain?

SECOND PIRATE They say that when he comes it's in the likeness of the wickedest man aboard.

THIRD PIRATE Had he a hook, Captain?

SEVERAL The ship's doomed. *(The captain sees boys looking delighted.)*

HOOK *(fiercely)* *You* like it do you! *(To pirates.)* Lads, here's a notion. Open the door —drive *them* in. Let *them* fight the doodle-doo for their lives. If they kill him we're so much the better—if he kills them we're none the worse.

FIRST PIRATE Ay, that's a notion!

SEVERAL In with them! *(The boys pretending fear are driven into hold and door shut on them.)*

HOOK Listen!

SEVERAL No! No!

(All put hands over ears, retreat to bow—business, half listening &c. In this silence all the boys preceded by Peter and now untied creep out at hold window with knives in their mouths and disappear along side of ship L.)

STARKEY *(on deck to Wendy)* Tell me a story, missy, and I'll save you yet. Tell me of men who go to church on Sundays, and unbelievable things like that.

WENDY Begone, bad man. Oh, Peter, Peter, Peter!

STARKEY Ay, *that* for Peter. *(Snaps fingers.)*

FIRST PIRATE Not a sound!

SECOND PIRATE I tell you, they're all lying there stark.* The ship's bewitched.

HOOK I've thought it out. There's a Jonah* aboard!

THIRD PIRATE Ay, a man wi' a hook. *(They look at Hook threateningly.)*

HOOK No, lads, no—it's the girl. Never was luck on a pirate ship wi' a woman on board.

FIRST PIRATE Ay, Blackbeard and Kidd,* they both said that.

HOOK We'll right the ship when she's gone overboard.

SECOND PIRATE It's worth trying.

HOOK *(calling)* Starkey!

STARKEY Ay, ay!

HOOK Fling the girl overboard.

STARKEY Ay, ay. Come, missy, Davy Jones* is calling.

WENDY Peter, Peter, Peter!

(Peter steals along deck from L.—he seizes Starkey. The real Starkey has disappeared—a stuffed figure like him is in its place. It is this that Peter seizes. He flings it far out into the river—it goes down with a splash. Peter crows. Panic among pirates below. Peter disappears L. with Wendy.)

HOOK *(trying to drive pirates up ladder)* On deck—on deck!

SEVERAL Back—back—the ship's accurst!

PETER *(head unseen)* Down with them—no quarter to the pirates!

(He and the boys rush along deck. Pirates fall down ladder—cries of fear. They rush through cabin and into hold, and the idea is that they get through hold to stern out of sight, pursued by boys. Wendy appears on deck from L. excitedly—three pirates pursued by Tootles and the twins rush from the hold to bow and overboard, where pursuers do not follow them. Alexander appears on deck from L. with a knife and drunk with valour.)

WENDY Oh, Alexander, stay with me, protect me!

ALEX Wendy, I've killed a pirate!

WENDY It's awful, awful!

ALEX No, it's not, I like it! Oh, Wendy I like it very, very much!

(Disappears L. as Capt. Hook is driven forward L. by Curly, Nibs and Slightly. Peter appears.)

PETER *(with authority to his boys)* Put up your knives—this man's mine. *(He and Capt. H. face each other.)*

HOOK So it's you, Pan—it's all *your* doing!

PETER Ay, it's my doing, Hook—Peter Pan, the avenger!

HOOK Proud and insolent youth, prepare to meet thy fate.

PETER Dark and sinister man, have at thee!

(They fight. Mist falls. When it rises Hook is stealing away with Wendy flung over his shoulder.)

WENDY Peter!

(Fight resumes, Wendy still on Hook's shoulder. Mist again. When it clears they are still fighting but Wendy is now on Peter's shoulder. Finally Hook leaps overboard. The crocodile rears its head in water.)

PETER   Leave him to the crocodile. *(Peter is very swollen with pride in himself.)* Forward Tootles. *(Tootles rushes forward and goes on his knees. Like all the others he has become very nautical in manner, wearing pirate's boots &c.)* What's your name, my man?

TOOTLES   Tootles.

PETER   Rise, Lieutenant Tootles. I shall mention you in dispatches. How goes the day?

TOOTLES   All stabbed but six, and they are prisoners.

PETER   Bring the prisoners forward.

TOOTLES   Ay, ay, Captain. *(Exit L.—the others are gazing admiringly at Peter.)*

WENDY   Oh, Peter, I think you are the bravest boy in all the world!

PETER   Yes, I am—I am—the bravest and the cleverest! Oh, I'm a wonder—oh, the wonder that I am! *(He struts deck and they gaze, reproducing the picture of Napoleon on the Bellerophon. Peter crows. Tootles &c. push forward the six prisoners through cabin to bow.)* You dogs, there, do you repent of all your wicked piracies?

ALEX   *(wandering about with a knife)*   Let me repent them, Peter, with Johnny Corkscrew!

PIRATES   We repent! Mercy, we repent!

PETER   They repent! Rule Britannia! *(The boys and Wendy sing the chorus of Rule Britannia.)**

WENDY   I'm so glad they didn't die before they repented.

PETER   Ay, ay, and now drown them all before they have time to stop repenting!

(Pirates are pushed into water. Again Rule Britannia is sung, and while singing the boys hit with oars &c. the pirates' heads bobbing up and down in water. The skull and crossbones is pulled down at same time, and Union Jack hoisted.)

CURTAIN

SCENE 5*

(The Scene is the night nursery again, and everything is as before. It is again early evening. The window is open. In arm chair by the fire Mrs Darling sits dozing. Nana lies asleep at foot of Wendy's bed—on the bed. The children's pyjamas are airing on fender. The light is on. Mrs D. is dreaming of her children.)

MRS D. *(starting up in transport of delight)* Wendy, John, Alexander— my children! *(Nana jumps off bed. Mrs D. realises it is only a dream.)* Oh, Nana, it is only a dream! *(Sits again.)* I dreamt my children had come back! *(Nana sits beside her and puts a paw on her lap. Mrs D. sees night-clothes on fender.)* You have put their night-things out again! Oh, Nana, it has touched my heart to see you do that night after night, as if you expected my children to come back—but they will never come back! *(They weep together, using the same hand-kerchief. Enter Helen R.)*

HELEN Nana's dinner is served. *(Exit Nana sedately R.)*

MRS D. Is the master's own dinner ready yet, Helen?

HELEN *(pointing to a bowl on table)* It's there.

MRS D. *(with gentle reproof)* On the table! Why not put it in the only place where you know he will take it? *(Helen indignantly puts the bowl on floor.)* And his water dish? *(Helen pushes dog's water dish near the bowl and puts a bottle of stout beside it.)*

HELEN *(bursting forth)* I want to give notice!

MRS D. *(pained)* Oh, Helen—is it the stairs?

HELEN No, Ma'am, it's the master. A master as lives in a dog-kennel!

MRS D. Out of remorse, Helen.

HELEN And goes to his office in a kennel—on top of a cab—with all the street-boys running along side cheering! *(Cheers outside.)* There! That's him come back!

(Enter a cabby and a street-hoist carrying kennel in which is Mr Darling in his office clothes. They are exhausted, but he is in imperturbable good humour.)

DARLING Thank you, my men. *(They exeunt. He addresses wife gaily from kennel.)* Ah, old lady, got any little trifle for me? *(She stoops and gives him a kiss.)* That's right. Helen, if you will be so good. *(Taking off coat and silk hat and giving them to her while she gives him a house jacket. More cheering.)* Listen to them! It's very gratifying!

HELEN Lot of little boys!

DARLING There are several adults today.

HELEN Poof! *(Exits scornfully.)*

DARLING Jealous cat! *(He falls to with relish on his meal, supping from bowl with spoon. In basin is a saucer from which he drinks.)*

MRS D. *(sitting on a low stool beside him)* What sort of day have you had, George?

DARLING Superb! There was never less than a hundred running alongside the cab, and when we were passing the Stock Exchange the whole of the members came out and cheered me. They simply *would* have a speech.

MRS D. I am so proud, dear.

DARLING The papers are finding me out—seven interviewers! And a deputation of ladies, so affected by my receiving them in the kennel that they wept. Twelve autograph books and six invitations to dinner from leaders of society, all saying '*Do* come in the kennel.' I think you've married pretty well, Mary, pretty well—ah?—ha?—ah?

MRS D. I do hope your head won't be turned, George.

DARLING If I had been a weak man, my dear—good heavens, if I had been a weak man! Where's my pipe—where's my baccy?* I never knew such a kennel! *(Finds them in it. Lights pipe.)* Ah! Mary, we should never have been such celebrities if the children hadn't flown away. How strangely things turn out for the best.

MRS D. Oh, George, you are sorry the children have gone aren't you?

DARLING Sorry! Isn't all this dreadful punishment for them!

MRS D. You are sure it *is* punishment, George? You are sure you are not enjoying it, dear?

DARLING Mary, how can you?

MRS D. Forgive me, dear one.

DARLING There, there! And now I feel like a snooze. Won't you play me to sleep on the nursery piano?

MRS D. *(rising)* Very well.

DARLING And shut that window. I feel a draught.

MRS D. Oh, George, never ask me to do that. The window must always be left open for them. *(Hesitating.)* George, those ladies who wept over you—you didn't kiss them, did you?

DARLING My love, they kept asking for something to remember me by—and I am a poor man.

(Mrs D. exits into day nursery, from which unseen she is heard playing 'Home, Sweet Home.'* Darling retires into kennel and sleeps. The music goes on while Wendy, John and Alexander enter by window. Wendy and John in suppressed excitement—Alex dazed.)

ALEX *(speaking in a low voice, as the others do also)* John, I think I have been here before.

JOHN It's your home, you silly.

WENDY There is your old bed, Alexander!

ALEX I had nearly forgotten.

JOHN I say! The kennel!

WENDY How odd! Perhaps Nana's in it.

JOHN *(peeping)* There's a man asleep in it.

WENDY It's Father.

JOHN So it is!

ALEX Let me see Father. He's not so big as the pirate I killed.

JOHN Wendy, surely Father didn't use to sleep in a kennel?

WENDY Oh, John, I'm so afraid that perhaps we don't remember the old life as well as we thought we did!

JOHN *(chilled)* It's very careless of Mother not to be here when we come back.

WENDY H'sh! *(Pointing through door L.)* That's her playing.

ALEX *(looking)* Who is that lady?

JOHN It's Mother.

ALEX Then are you not really our mother, Wendy?

WENDY Oh dear! It was quite time we came back.

JOHN Let's creep in and put our hands over her eyes.

WENDY No, she mustn't know we are back all at once. Let us break it to her gently.

(She whispers a plan to them. Then all get into their own beds and cover selves with the clothes except their heads. They lie with eyes open exulting till music stops. Then at sign from Wendy they shut eyes and pretend to sleep. Enter Mrs D. R.)

MRS D. *(softly)* Are you asleep, George? *(She sees Wendy in bed and puts her hand to her heart, for she does not believe that it is really Wendy. She repeats same action on seeing John and Alex. She looks away from them.)* I see them in their beds, so often, in my dreams, that I seem still to see them when I am awake, and all the time I know they are not there. *(Sits C.)* I'll not look again. So often in my dreams their silver* voices call me.

WENDY *(softly)* Mother!

MRS D. *(without looking—mournfully)* That's Wendy!

JOHN *(softly)* Mother!

MRS D. Now it's John!

ALEX *(softly)* Mother!

MRS D. Now little Alexander! *(As they speak they sit up with outstretched arms, but she is not looking at them.)* And when they call I stretch out my arms to them *(does so—brings arms together, drops them)*, but they never come. They never come!

(Again her arms are outstretched. The children have risen and stolen towards her. Wendy slips into the space between her arms, then John,

then Alex, so that her arms close on the three of them. Rapture, or possibly there may be a dramatic song here.)

CHILDREN Mother, Mother, Mother!

MRS D. It can't be true!

ALEX Mummy, pinch me and I'll pinch you—and so you see it's true. *(Repeated endearments. Darling peeps out of kennel.)*

MRS D. George, they have come back!

WENDY Father, why are you in the kennel?

DARLING It's a long story, Wendy, but—

WENDY If it's very long, Father, we'll excuse your telling it, but do come out! *(He is reluctant.)*

MRS D. George! *(She makes the sounds with which one wheedles a dog. So do the others. John whistles. Darling slowly emerges with some straw sticking on him.)*

DARLING *(feeling awkward)* I feel as if I were standing on my hind legs.

MRS D. Dear, the children are waiting.

DARLING One moment, while I say goodbye to an old friend. *(Looking at kennel.)* In those days of hard competition, it was rather jolly in there. *(Putting hand on kennel.)* Old friend—old home—never again! *(Stretching out arms.)* My children! *(Embraces them. Nana enters R.)*

CHILDREN Nana, it's yours again. *(Nana joyfully goes into kennel—looks out with French novel in mouth.)*

DARLING *(taking it)* Thank you.

JOHN Father, we've had such adventures!

ALEX I killed a pirate, father!

DARLING *(a little bitterly)* Alexander will sign the autograph books now!

TOOTLES *(appearing at window)* Wendy—we can't hold on to the spout any longer.

MRS D. *(startled)* Why—who—what—

WENDY It's all right, Mummy, they are just a few motherless boys we have brought back with us.

MRS D. But, my love—

WENDY Come in, boys. *(All come in hat in hand and carrying their bundles. They stand timidly in a respectful row.)* Boys, this is my mother.

SLIGHTLY She's a beauty!

TOOTLES I choose that one—which one do you choose, Nibs?

NIBS That one. Which one do you choose, Curly?

CURLY That one. Twin, which—

WENDY Boys, I'm very disappointed in you after all I've told you. You don't choose a real mother—you—you just get her. Isn't that the way, Father?

DARLING That's the usual way, boys, and if you will—ah—sit down—

TOOTLES Please, sir, we think Peter wouldn't like us to sit down till he tells us.

DARLING Peter? Is there another one?

WENDY Oh yes, Father, and *he's* frightfully important. *(The noise of a great crowd is heard without. Darling runs to window and looks out.)*

DARLING The street is crowded with ladies—all trying to get in at our door!

WENDY That's the beautiful mothers. We advertised that if the twenty most beautiful mothers would come to this house they would hear something to their advantage.

DARLING Twenty! There are thousands of them. Helen and the cook are charging them with brooms, and some of them are not so beautiful as they were. There's a little boy, what's he doing?

WENDY That's Peter, and he's picking out the twenty prettiest ones. Of course you'll be careful what you say to Peter—he doesn't like to be contradicted.

DARLING I shall be very careful.

WENDY And Mummy, Peter thinks he knows all about mothers but he—he doesn't. *I* shall really find their mothers for them, but I must *pretend* to think it's *he* who finds.

MRS D. Very well, Wendy—I know the kind of man. Wendy, shall I give Peter a kiss?

WENDY He calls kisses thimbles. But I think, Mother, it would be better—perhaps—to let him take the first step. *(Helen enters R.)*

HELEN Captain Pan. *(Enter Peter importantly.)*

DARLING Proud to see you here, Captain.

PETER Thank you. Is this your mother, Wendy?

WENDY *(anxiously)* Yes.

PETER *(after examining her)* I like her.

WENDY *(relieved)* You can do it now, Mummy. *(Mrs D. kisses him.)*

PETER Thank you, Granny.

MRS D. Granny?

PETER You are my granny, aren't you? Wendy's my mother, you know.

DARLING No, we didn't know. Then I—

PETER You're Grandpa.

DARLING Oh!

PETER We're all ready, Wendy—stand back everybody—I'm captain, you see—servant, show them in.

HELEN *(announcing)* The Countess of Copley. *(Enters countess. Peter and Wendy shake hands with her like host and hostess.)*

NIBS Oh, what a lovely one—that's my one. Is that your one, Twin?

FIRST TWIN Yes, she is. Curly, is that—

PETER Silence—over there, lady. *(Points to back L. children being back R.)*

HELEN Mrs Fitz Reynolds. *(Business repeated as this lady enters.)* Madame Villon. *(Third enters.)* Lady Eliza Verral. *(Fourth enters.)*

SLIGHTLY That's mine—Tootles you mustn't speak to me when I'm a lord.

PETER Silence.

HELEN Mrs William P. Danks. *(Fifth enters.)* Prefers to remain anonymous. *(Sixth enters.)*

PETER You needn't say their names, servant. *(The remainder of the twenty are ushered in and go up L. so that Wendy and Peter have down stage and especially L. down stage to themselves.)* Now ladies you are not to say a word—I'm captain. *(To Wendy.)* What next?

WENDY *(whispers)* Those who are not affected by the sight of baby clothes can't be true mothers.

PETER Oh, yes. *(To boys.)* Baby clothes! *(Boys display contents of their bundles. Peter and Wendy watch affect on mothers—most are affected, cry 'oh' &c.)* That green one's not affected.

WENDY Nor the little one.

TOOTLES Peter, the yellow one is just yawning!

PETER You green one, you yellow one, and you little one, come here. *(They step forward.)* You are not true mothers—the door! Servant! *(The three indignant are shown out.)* Curly, come. *(Curly steps forward.)* What next?

WENDY A true mother always thinks her own boy the prettiest, so the one who thinks Curly the prettiest, that one will be his mother.

PETER The lady who thinks this boy the prettiest, forward. *(Four ladies come.)* Four of them!

WENDY *(aside to Peter)* A true mother has shiny eyes when she looks at her offspring.

PETER Oho! All you four look hard at Curly. *(They do so.)* Harder—harder! *(Their eyes nearly stand out of their heads. Peter and Wendy examine them.)* You one—and you one who don't have shiny eyes—go away! Servant! *(Two exeunt.)* There's two yet!

WENDY *(after thinking hard)* Curly, lie down on that bed—and sleep. *(He does so. To ladies.)* Now we want to see you give that sleeping boy a—a thimble.

ONE LADY A thimble?

PETER It's like this. *(Kisses her.)*

LADY Oh! *(She gives Curly such a smack of a kiss that he sits up.)*

PETER That's her, that's Curly's one.

TOOTLES Curly's got his!

WENDY Wait! This other one must get her chance. Sleep again, Curly. *(He does so.)* Now! *(Second lady kisses Curly so softly that he doesn't open his eyes.)* There! *(Peter is puzzled. Wendy whispers to him.)*

PETER Oh! *(Publicly.)* You see this lady gave him a smack that wakened him—but a true mother does it without wakening him. *(To first lady.)* Go away, lady. *(She goes. To Curly.)* Curly, this is your mother—lady, this is your long lost son. Go and hug him in the day nursery. *(Lady exits L. with happy Curly and other boys cheer.)* Nibs next. *(Nibs comes down.)* Come here those who think Nibs the prettiest. *(Three come.)* The others turn your backs. *(They do so. To Wendy.)* Shall we have animal instincts this time?

WENDY Yes.

PETER *(to ladies)* Do animal instincts! *(They are puzzled.)* They're not doing them.

WENDY You forgot—the fire!

PETER Oh! Nibs stand here. *(Indicating inside fender. Nibs does so.)* Nibs is being burned! *(All three rush forward and save him.)* They all did it, Wendy!

WENDY *(whispering)* You see any kind lady would do it if she wasn't in danger herself, but— *(Whispers.)*

PETER Yes! All stand here—you too, Nibs. *(All get inside fender.)* You are all being burned! Save yourselves! *(Two rush out of danger, but the third helps Nibs before herself.)* Nibs, this is your mother! *(Waves them to day nursery.)* You two, go home. *(They exeunt. Cheer from boys.)* Slightly next. *(Slightly comes down hopefully.)*

WENDY Oh, you naughty Slightly, you have been biting your knuckles again—see how they are bleeding!

PETER Those who think Slightly is the prettiest, come. *(Slightly is expectant, but nobody comes.)* Oh!

WENDY Oh dear! *(Slightly nearly cries.)*

PETER Those who write their names on their children's clothes, come. *(Lady Elizabeth and another come.)*

SLIGHTLY *(proud of Lady Elizabeth)* I knew that was my one, Peter, shall she take me into the day nursery and hug me?

PETER Silence! Wendy, what next?

WENDY *(whispering)* His knuckles are bleeding. Now a true mother would know *at once* if her boy's knuckles were bleeding.

PETER *(to the two)* Do you notice anything about Slightly? *(They notice nothing.)* Go away. *(They exeunt.)* It's not going to do this time, Wendy.

WENDY Oh dear! Slightly, walk past those other ladies—just in case it should be one of them. *(Slightly does so—in vain. He is a forlorn figure.)* It's very disappointing, Peter.

PETER Servant, put this boy out.

HELEN *(about to do so)* Oh, Miss Wendy, his poor little knuckles are bleeding!

PETER *(quickly)* When did you see they were bleeding?

HELEN I didn't see it—I just feel it in my bones.

PETER Servant, you are his mother! Day nursery! *(They go.)* First Twin next. *(First Twin comes.)*

WENDY Both twins!

PETER We can't do more than one at a time.

WENDY *(not knowing how to explain)* Oh dear!

PETER Come here those who think this boy the prettiest. *(One comes.)* There's just one, so she's your mother. Lady, take him into the day nursery. *(She is going.)* Second Twin. *(Second Twin comes.)*

WENDY But, Peter, we—they are twins, you know.

PETER Of course they are twins.

WENDY Yes, but you see—twins—it's so awkward to me to have to explain. You know what twins are, don't you, Peter?

PETER Nobody really knows what twins are.

WENDY Oh! Father!

DARLING *(coming to her assistance)* With regard to this subject, Captain, you see, life is like this, sometimes it's one at a time, and sometimes it's two at a time. Oh, if that doesn't make it clear to you I give it up.

WENDY Mummy!

MRS D. Peter, when a lady—Wendy, I can't, his innocence is so touching.

WENDY Isn't it dear of him, Mummy, not to know? It's quite a woman's subject, isn't it?

PETER *(to stand no more nonsense)* Those who think this boy the prettiest, come.

DARLING There will be a grave miscarriage of justice here. *(The same lady comes with First Twin.)*

PETER You've had one already. All turn backs. *(They do so.)* Wendy, she has had the other twin but she's the only one who stepped forward, so what do you say to pretending she's the second twin's mother too!

WENDY Yes, Peter, yes!

PETER Lady, you are the mother of both the twins. *(She takes both L. to Peter's entertainment.)* Oh, what a joke! Tootles is the last.

(Tootles comes.) Now all you ladies lie down on the beds and sleep. *(The seven ladies left do so.)* Now Tootles, stand here and say in a whisper so low that nobody can hear it, 'Mother, I feel flushed!' But how can that help, Wendy?

WENDY   You see though a mother is sleeping ever so soundly if her boy says 'I feel flushed' it wakes her up at once.

PETER   Say it, Tootles. *(Tootles' lips are seen saying it. Three ladies start up. Peter addresses the four who remain sleeping.)* Ladies, wake up and go home. *(The four exeunt.)*

WENDY   Shoe now, Peter.

PETER   Oh, yes. Tootles— *(Whispers to him. Tootles sits down and kicks off one shoe. Peter addresses a lady.)* You, lady, put on Tootles' shoe. *(She does so. He again kicks it off. He puts it on. This is repeated.)*

LADY   *(angrily)*   Oh, I've lost patience with you.

PETER   Then you are not his mother—go.

TOOTLES   I'm very sorry for you, lady. *(She goes.)*

PETER   There's two yet. You can't have two mothers, can you?

WENDY   No, not in England.

PETER   Now, then, Tootles, go to these ladies, and box their ears hard.

TOOTLES   Oh Peter!

PETER   This is your last chance. *(Tootles apparently cuffs a lady hard.)*

LADY   *(taken aback indignantly)*   How dare you, boy!

PETER   Lady—*(Signs the door. She goes.)* I don't believe you are to get one, Tootles—but try this lady.

TOOTLES   Peter, I don't know how it is, but I feel I can't hit that one.

PETER   That shows she can't be your mother. *(Tootles cuffs her—she is the countess.)*

COUNTESS   Oh, Tootles dear, I hope you haven't hurt your hand!

WENDY   She's his mother, Peter!

PETER Tootles, you're a lord. That's them all, Wendy.

DARLING Captain, I congratulate you heartily.

PETER Thank you, Grandpa. *(Darling winces.)* Wendy, you didn't have to help me a bit! I did it all myself!

WENDY Yes, Peter.

(Peter crows. The happy mothers and their children return from R., the boys wrapped in cravats &c. of John's. Possibly song and dance here.)

COUNTESS Do you think I could have a cab now?

DARLING Certainly.

PETER *(brushing him aside)* H'sh! Yes, lady, you can have a cab. You can all have cabs.

DARLING *(annoyed)* See here, Peter, this is my house, and I naturally expect to be captain here.

WENDY Oh, Father, is this reasonable!

PETER *(fixing him)* Go at once and whistle for five cabs. *(Darling would like to rebel but dare not.)*

COUNTESS Four-wheelers, please.

NIBS A hansom,* Mother.

FIRST TWIN I do so want a hansom.

PETER Five hansoms. *(Darling would like to defy him, then exits R. cowed.)*

TOOTLES *(in loud voice that all hear)* I'm awfully fond of my mother. Are you fond of yours, Curly?

CURLY Awfully! Are you fond of yours, Slightly?

SLIGHTLY Awfully. What's yours like, Nibs?

NIBS I've an awfully good one. Have you a good one, Twin?

SECOND TWIN Awfully good. *(Whistling for hansoms is heard.)*

NIBS My mother says I'm going to school.

SLIGHTLY My mother says I'm done with school.

TOOTLES My mother says I'm nearly a man.

PETER *(startled)* Does she! *(He is suddenly subdued.)* Goodbye all of you. I'm glad you like your mothers. I hope you'll go on liking them. I hope you'll like—going to school and—growing into men. *(They salute—enter Darling R.)*

DARLING Five hansoms.

WENDY Goodbye, dear dear boys—oh, this parting is terrible! *(They weep.)*

DARLING Courage, Wendy—you must remember that it is their bread and butter.

TOOTLES *(appealing)* You see it's our bread and butter, Wendy.

WENDY I know. *(To mothers.)* You'll take great care of them, won't you? *(Aside to Helen.)* I tied Slightly's ears back at night. They are rather prominent. *(Breaking down.)* Boys, goodbye.

(She kisses them. All mothers and sons exeunt. John and Alex go into room L. Peter is standing L. down stage still crushed. Wendy goes to him, and Darling at sign from Mrs D. goes with her up stage.)

PETER Oh, Wendy, did you hear what Tootles' mother said, that he would soon be a man! *(In agony.)* Wendy, I've never told you, but I think I am nearly as old as Tootles!

WENDY I wish you hadn't been so afraid of being a man, Peter—it's—rather hard on me.

PETER I want always just to be a wonderful boy, and to have fun.

WENDY That's what you'll always be, dear Peter.

MRS D. Poor Wendy, I see now what her secret sorrow is! *(Wendy signs silence.)*

DARLING *I* don't see.

MRS D. Ah, my dear, you are only a man.

DARLING My love, I don't quite like that phrase.

PETER I didn't know you were there—goodbye.

MRS D. But we hoped you were to make a long stay, Peter.

PETER I'm going to live with Tippy in a little house we built for Wendy. Tippy is bringing it to Kensington Gardens, so that Wendy may sometimes come to see me.

DARLING Might I ask who Tippy is?

PETER She's a fairy, you know.

DARLING No, I didn't know.

PETER Goodbye, Wendy.

WENDY *(huskily)* Goodbye.

PETER *(huskily)* I'm going away, Wendy.

WENDY I don't see how—you can go alone—you're so subject to draughts—and you're sure to forget to put on your chest protector.*

PETER It's just a mother that can remember these things.

WENDY *(who is sitting, pulls him on to her knee)* My boy—my boy, Peter!

PETER Wendy, come and take care of me!

WENDY Mother—Father—may I? *(Parents are genuinely affected.)*

MRS D. Heaven forbid that *I* should ever interfere between a mother and her child.

DARLING Or I in the affairs of the nursery. If there is a father anywhere who thinks he is captain in the nursery, I am willing to lend him the kennel.

WENDY Peter, it's all right. I'm going with you!

PETER And you'll never send me to school, Mother?

WENDY Never! Father, do you think we could have a hansom?

DARLING Certainly, my dear. *(Exit R.)*

MRS D. I'll often come to see you. *(Embracing.)*

WENDY Oh, Mother, there's just one thing—we don't have any money, and I think the fare to Kensington Gardens is one and six.* *(Whistling for cab heard.)*

MRS D.   I'm so sorry, my love, but—we have only twopence in the house.

PETER   Wendy, you can give the cabman a thimble. I'm sure he will like it much better than money.

WENDY   What do you think, Mother?

MRS D.   My pet! I'm told it's sometimes done.

(They exeunt R. together. Clock begins to strike six. Nana comes out of kennel—goes to bathroom, lights it, turns on water and prepares to bathe John and Alexander.)

CURTAIN

SCENE 6

KENSINGTON GARDENS

(First a front scene with one of the garden walks running from R. to L. On back cloth a view of the Round Pond. Two boys run by with hoops. A ticket collector hurries by.

A boarding school of six girls passes with a starchy governess—all are played by the mothers of previous scene. A scavenger from R. sweeps leaves and rubbish into a heap C., leaves them and exits L. sweeping, as enter R. nurse wheeling pram. A soldier enters L. in military uniform, he smiles as passes nurse, both look behind at each other—he sniggers proudly and exits R.—she leaves pram and exits after him admiringly. A man carrying yacht which is too heavy for him enters R., sees pram, lays the baby in it on ground, puts yacht in baby's place and exits thankfully wheeling pram L. Scavenger returns L. still sweeping—sweeps all rubbish into the pile he has left, including the baby, and exits sweeping R. The twins in Eton suits* enter R. with their mother and meet Slightly—entering L. He is a street arab* carrying a cluster of balloons.)

SLIGHTLY   Buy a b'loon, ma'am?

LADY   Go away, vulgar boy.

SLIGHTLY   My wife is ill, ma'am, and I have ten starving children.

FIRST TWIN *(now very classy)*   Mama, it's Slightly!

SECOND TWIN Hello, Slightly!

SLIGHTLY *(mimicking them)* How de do,* Twins?

LADY How often have I forbid you to talk to that vulgar boy! You may give him a penny, but you mustn't talk to him.

(She gives them pennies which they give him. As they exeunt L. Peter steals on dressed and made up as Clown* and rubs them with red-hot poker*—they jump and he behaves in traditional clown manner. Slightly sits depressed on rail. Enter Tootles R.—a man of fashion—cane, cigarette, small moustache. Neither of them sees Peter.)

TOOTLES Do, Slightly? Don't you know me, Slightly?

SLIGHTLY Yes, my lord, but you being a swell* now I thought your lordship wouldn't like me to let on as I knowed you.

TOOTLES Rot! I say, Slightly, there's nobody looking, I'll shake hands with you. *(Does so.)* And you can have that. *(Gives him cigarette end.)* How do I look, Slightly?

SLIGHTLY Splendid, your lordship.

TOOTLES Look at that, Slightly, and that. *(Pointing to his moustache. A prim lady and gentleman enter R.—he is holding parasol over her.)* Excuse me, lady and gentleman, I don't have the pleasure of knowing you, but look at that, and that! *(Exits R. delighted with himself and exit Slightly L. much admiring.)*

LADY The impertinence!

GENTLEMAN Outrageous!

(Peter from behind takes parasol and puts poker in its place without their knowing. They exeunt L. the man holding up poker—Peter grins. Wendy dances on from R. dressed as a Columbine.)*

WENDY *(suddenly)* Peter, the keeper!

PETER Hide, Wendy!

(They hide at each side as enter Keeper L. He meets Hook entering R. dressed as schoolmaster in cap and gown and carrying birch. The hook is hidden.)

STARKEY *(shaking)* Captain Hook! *(Goes on knees.)*

HOOK You know me! Who are you? *(Starkey pulls off his beard.)* Starkey! So you escaped also!

STARKEY Ay, I swam ashore, but I thought your crocodile had got you.

HOOK No, I gave him this in the eye *(holding up hook)* and he had to let go. Starkey, you're now an honest man—for shame!

STARKEY *(cringing)* Times are so hard. T'was those boys did for us.

HOOK That's why I'm a schoolmaster—to revenge myself on boys! I hook them so, Starkey *(indicating how he lifts them by waist)* and then I lay on like this! When it was found out what a useful hook I had every school in merry England clamoured for my services.

STARKEY What's clamoured?

HOOK Yelled. But that's not enough—I want Peter Pan himself. Starkey, I dream at nights that I'm laying on to Peter Pan. I'll have him yet—he's here!

STARKEY Here?

HOOK He paints his face that none may recognise him as a boy who ought to be at school.

STARKEY A boy who, they say, lives here both night and day?

HOOK In some magic house. That's Peter.

STARKEY Now I know him—and his mother too.

HOOK That's Wendy, and she has broke the law by not sending her boy to school. Come, bully,* let's catch them—Peter *I'll* look after, and Mother Wendy, she shall go to jail! They can't escape me, I have assistant masters watching at all the gates. *(Exeunt L. Peter and Wendy emerge quaking—Tippy has been darting about.)*

PETER He's bound to get us! Oh, I wish I hadn't become a clown. Boys oughtn't to be too funny, but just funny enough.

WENDY Our dress makes us so conspicuous.

PETER What's conspicuous?

WENDY Easy to pick out.

PETER   School, Wendy.

WENDY   Jail, Peter! Tippy alone can save us.

PETER   Tippy! *(They go on knees to Tippy, who has alighted in grass—Tippy rings.)* She says she will save me but not you.

WENDY   Oh!

PETER   *(rising)* Tippy, I refuse.

WENDY   Where are you going?

PETER   To give myself up to Hook if he promises to spare you.

WENDY   No, Peter, no, take Tippy's help and let me go to jail.

PETER   Never! Goodbye! *(They embrace tragically—bells.)* She says 'Stop that thimbling and I'll save you both!'

WENDY   Dear fairy!

PETER   Tippy, be quick. *(Tippy darts away L.)*

WENDY   I wonder how she'll do it? *(A sound as of a cracker being pulled is heard.)* What's that? It sounds like someone pulling crackers! *(Another—then the two boys with hoops run by—they are now in Clown make-up and dress.)*

PETER   Wendy, I believe she's making them all like me, so that Hook won't be able to pick me out. *(Another cracker.)* Oh, look! *(A nursery maid dressed as Columbine enters L. with pram.)* Do you think she knows she's like that?

WENDY   Excuse me, nurse—do you know you're like that?

NURSE   Like what? *(Looks down and is astounded.)* Lawks! *(She dances, then in sudden alarm lifts child in pram—it is now a Clown.)* Oh! What will missus say!

(Exits R.—a fusillade of crackers, and the boarding school walks by, all as Columbines and prim mistress as a Harlequin.)

LADY   *(looking behind)* What disgraceful dresses for school-girls, Charles!

GENTLEMAN   Monstrous, my love.

WENDY Peter, you can break it to that one.

PETER Lady, look down. *(Sensation.)*

LADY Charles!

GENTLEMAN Katie, for shame.

LADY Charles, take me home!

GENTLEMAN No, Katie, for the children's sake I can never take you home again. Farewell, for ever! *(Exit L.)*

LADY Charles! *(Rushes after him.)*

PETER *(imitating her)* Charles—Charles—

(Exits after with comic burlesque of her—and seems to return still burlesquing her, but not quaking. It is, however, another Clown like him in appearance who comes on—the idea being to deceive the audience into thinking this is still Peter.)

WENDY Oh, Peter, how naughty of you! *(She suddenly sees Hook coming L.)* Run, Peter, run!

(As Hook enters L. Wendy rushes off R. eluding Starkey who enters R. Hook and Starkey bar Peter's way—he dodges, &c. but they at last clutch him.)

HOOK I have him now!

STARKEY Are you sure it's Peter?

HOOK I'll soon show you it's Peter. *(Wipes the make-up off boy's face and he stands revealed as another boy—perhaps Alex, John or one of the lost children. Hook and Starkey stare—exit boy impudently.)* I'll have him yet!

(Signs L. and a number of assistant masters in cap and gown and birch* enter and follow him and Starkey out R. stealthily, and with pantomime business. The crocodile appears and exits doggedly after them.

The Scene changes to another scene in the Kensington Gardens, the whole stage now being used, and this is got merely by raising back cloth of first scene. The Serpentine is new scene on back cloth—up stage C. is the little house. The centre is turf under trees, and it is covered with Clowns, Pantaloons, Columbines and Harlequins, very gay and animated and all engaged in a dance in character, i.e. it is a dance in which

Clowns do polka business, Columbines run up Harlequins, Pantaloons are knocked down &c. Hook is seen hiding in a practical* tree R. half down stage. As the dance goes on, assistant masters occasionally rush forward, capture a Clown and rub his face when he always turns out not to be Peter. There is a dramatic pause in the dance at these times, and then it is gaily resumed. Suddenly a 'clang' makes all stop.)

ONE *(as in 'Crichton')* Was that a ship's gun, Gov? *('Clang.')*

ANOTHER It was the closing of the gates!

TOOTLES I don't want to be shut up here all night—do you, Twins?

FIRST TWIN Rather not.

TOOTLES Do you, Curly?

CURLY Rather not.

TOOTLES Do you, John?

JOHN Rather not.

TOOTLES Do you, Alexander?

ALEX Rather not.

TOOTLES Do you, Peter?

(Dramatic pause as masters creep forward to see who will answer—'clang' of gates and everybody rushes away except Hook in tree. Peter with face clean comes out of little house and sits at door playing childishly on a whistle—Hook is triumphant and prepares to come down tree and seize him. The crocodile emerges from Serpentine, comes down and rears forepart of his monstrous body against tree with great mouth open. Hook unconscious of his danger comes down feet foremost, his feet, legs &c. enter crocodile—he just realises his position as his head is also going down. Crocodile closes mouth. Peter has been looking on unconcernedly at the incident and still whistling. On crocodile's way back to Serpentine it opens its mouth and Hook looks out.)

HOOK *(to Peter)* No words of mine can indicate my utter contempt for you.

PETER Thou not altogether unheroic figure, farewell.

HOOK Peter, do you think you could get me a pack of cards quick, Peter?

(Crocodile shuts mouth—Peter crows—Crocodile disappears in Serpentine. The little house lights up from inside and Wendy and Mrs D. emerge. The latter is in ordinary dress—all has been fantastic so far, but now they are strictly matter of fact.)

MRS D.   Well, goodbye, Wendy—I'm very glad to find you so comfortable.

WENDY   You really do like the house?

MRS D.   Immensely. Of course it's small, Wendy.

WENDY   It is small—Peter, don't bite your nails. But you see, Mother, I didn't want a tall house. Stairs are such a bother to servants.

MRS D.   Yes indeed. Still, as you don't *have* any servants, my love?

WENDY   True, true. But you see, Mummy, it isn't as if we meant to entertain.

MRS D.   Quite so. And after all, you're a small family.

WENDY   That's just what I say. Most people our size wouldn't have a house at all. Peter, where do boys who touzle* their hair go to? *(Darling comes from house in ordinary clothes.)*

DARLING   I like your house, Wendy. Gravel soil—south aspect.

WENDY   And the cupboard accommodation is so good, Father. I made a point of that. Besides, we pay no rent.

DARLING   And that's a consideration. Though how the keepers allow it, Wendy—

WENDY   They don't, but when they try to meddle, Tippy makes the house disappear, you know.

DARLING   She's certainly a clever little creature. *(Tippy darts and rings.)*

PETER   Tippy says she'll let you out if you go now, Grandpa.

DARLING   Grandpa! Yes, well, bye bye, Peter—Wendy, a penny?

WENDY   Thank you, Father, it will be very useful—of course our expenses are rather heavy just now.

MRS D.   But where is Nana? *(Calling.)* Nana, we are going. I must say Nana hasn't been nearly such a good nurse since she had puppies of her own.

(Enter Nana followed by two real Newfoundland puppies—leave-takings and exeunt all but Peter and Wendy who kiss hands and wave. Clock in little house strikes six.)

WENDY   Peter, sweetest, bath time! *(Lifts him up in her arms.)*

PETER   Are you glad, glad glad, Mummy, that I'm your son?

WENDY   Peter, I consider it such a privilege!

(Hugs him in motherly way. They wave handkerchiefs to audience, as it were, from door of little house. There is no moon but many stars—these twinkle violently. For a moment many go out leaving stage dark, and in this moment the house is removed and Peter and Wendy exeunt. At the same time the house is flung on stage by the Pepper's ghost* 'illusion,' and also Peter and Wendy are flung by the same 'illusion' so that as stars beam again it seems to audience that the house is still there and that the children are still at the door waving. Footsteps are heard. They are the steps of Starkey as keeper with lantern. As he appears trudging by the house and children are no longer there. When he has passed, they are there again. Stars all go out. Blackness.)

CURTAIN

PETER AND WENDY
(1911)

THE NEVER NEVER LAND

CHAPTER 1

PETER BREAKS THROUGH

ALL children, except one, grow up. They soon know that they will grow up, and the way Wendy knew was this. One day when she was two years old she was playing in a garden, and she plucked another flower and ran with it to her mother. I suppose she must have looked rather delightful, for Mrs Darling put her hand to her heart and cried, 'Oh, why can't you remain like this for ever!' This was all that passed between them on the subject, but henceforth Wendy knew that she must grow up. You always know after you are two. Two is the beginning of the end.

Of course they lived at 14, and until Wendy came her mother was the chief one. She was a lovely lady, with a romantic mind and such a sweet mocking mouth. Her romantic mind was like the tiny boxes, one within the other, that come from the puzzling East,* however many you discover there is always one more; and her sweet mocking mouth had one kiss on it that Wendy could never get, though there it was, perfectly conspicuous in the right-hand corner.

The way Mr Darling won her was this: the many gentlemen who had been boys when she was a girl discovered simultaneously that they loved her, and they all ran to her house to propose to her except Mr Darling, who took a cab and nipped in first, and so he got her. He got all of her, except the innermost box and the kiss. He never knew about the box, and in time he gave up trying for the kiss. Wendy thought Napoleon* could have got it, but I can picture him trying, and then going off in a passion, slamming the door.

Mr Darling used to boast to Wendy that her mother not only loved him but respected him. He was one of those deep ones who know about stocks and shares. Of course no one really knows, but he quite seemed to know, and he often said stocks were up and shares were down in a way that would have made any woman respect him.

Mrs Darling was married in white, and at first she kept the books perfectly, almost gleefully, as if it were a game, not so much as a brussels sprout was missing; but by and by whole cauliflowers dropped out, and instead of them there were pictures of babies without faces. She drew them when she should have been totting up. They were Mrs Darling's guesses.

Wendy came first, then John, then Michael.

For a week or two after Wendy came it was doubtful whether they would be able to keep her, as she was another mouth to feed. Mr Darling was frightfully proud of her, but he was very honourable, and he sat on the edge of Mrs Darling's bed, holding her hand and calculating expenses, while she looked at him imploringly. She wanted to risk it, come what might, but that was not his way; his way was with a pencil and a piece of paper, and if she confused him with suggestions he had to begin at the beginning again.

'Now don't interrupt,' he would beg of her. 'I have one pound seventeen* here, and two and six at the office; I can cut off my coffee at the office, say ten shillings, making two nine and six, with your eighteen and three makes three nine seven, with five naught naught in my cheque-book makes eight nine seven—who is that moving?—eight nine seven, dot and carry seven—don't speak, my own—and the pound you lent to that man who came to the door—quiet, child—dot and carry child—there, you've done it!—did I say nine nine seven? yes, I said nine nine seven; the question is, can we try it for a year on nine nine seven?'

'Of course we can, George,' she cried. But she was prejudiced in Wendy's favour, and he was really the grander character of the two.

'Remember mumps,' he warned her almost threateningly, and off he went again. 'Mumps one pound, that is what I have put down, but I dare say it will be more like thirty shillings—don't speak—measles one five, German measles half a guinea, makes two fifteen six—don't waggle your finger—whooping-cough, say fifteen shillings'—and so on it went, and it added up differently each time; but at last Wendy just got through, with mumps reduced to twelve six, and the two kinds of measles treated as one.

There was the same excitement over John, and Michael had an even narrower squeak; but both were kept, and soon you might have seen the three of them going in a row to Miss Fulsom's Kindergarten school, accompanied by their nurse.

Mrs Darling loved to have everything just so, and Mr Darling had a passion for being exactly like his neighbours; so, of course, they had a nurse. As they were poor, owing to the amount of milk the children drank, this nurse was a prim Newfoundland dog,* called Nana, who had belonged to no one in particular until the Darlings engaged her. She had always thought children important, however, and the Darlings had become acquainted with her in Kensington Gardens, where she spent most of her spare time peeping into perambulators, and was much hated by careless nursemaids, whom she followed to their homes and complained of to their mistresses. She proved to be quite a treasure of a nurse. How thorough she was at bath-time; and up at any moment of the night if one of her charges made the slightest cry. Of course her kennel was in the nursery. She had a genius for knowing when a cough is a thing to have no patience with and when it needs stocking round your throat. She believed to her last day in old-fashioned remedies like rhubarb leaf, and made sounds of contempt over all this new-fangled talk about germs, and so on. It was a lesson in propriety to see her escorting the children to school, walking sedately by their side when they were well behaved, and butting them back into line if they strayed. On John's footer* days she never once forgot his sweater, and she usually carried an umbrella in her mouth in case of rain. There is a room in the basement of Miss Fulsom's school where the nurses wait. They sat on forms, while Nana lay on the floor, but that was the only difference. They affected to ignore her as of an inferior social status to themselves, and she despised their light talk. She resented visits to the nursery from Mrs Darling's friends, but if they did come she first whipped off Michael's pinafore and put him into the one with blue braiding, and smoothed out Wendy and made a dash at John's hair.

No nursery could possibly have been conducted more correctly, and Mr Darling knew it, yet he sometimes wondered uneasily whether the neighbours talked.

He had his position in the City to consider.

Nana also troubled him in another way. He had sometimes a feeling that she did not admire him. 'I know she admires you tremendously, George,'* Mrs Darling would assure him, and then she would sign to the children to be specially nice to father. Lovely dances followed, in which the only other servant, Liza, was sometimes allowed to join. Such a midget she looked in her long skirt and maid's cap, though she had sworn, when engaged, that she would never see ten again. The gaiety of those romps! And gayest of all was Mrs Darling, who would pirouette so wildly that all you could see of her was the kiss, and then if you had dashed at her you might have got it. There never was a simpler, happier family until the coming of Peter Pan.

Mrs Darling first heard of Peter when she was tidying up her children's minds. It is the nightly custom of every good mother after her children are asleep to rummage in their minds and put things straight for next morning, repacking into their proper places the many articles that have wandered during the day. If you could keep awake (but of course you can't) you would see your own mother doing this, and you would find it very interesting to watch her. It is quite like tidying up drawers. You would see her on her knees, I expect, lingering humorously over some of your contents, wondering where on earth you had picked this thing up, making discoveries sweet and not so sweet, pressing this to her cheek as if it were as nice as a kitten, and hurriedly stowing that out of sight. When you wake in the morning, the naughtinesses and evil passions with which you went to bed have been folded up small and placed at the bottom of your mind; and on the top, beautifully aired, are spread out your prettier thoughts, ready for you to put on.

I don't know whether you have ever seen a map of a person's mind. Doctors sometimes draw maps of other parts of you, and your own map can become intensely interesting, but catch them trying to draw a map of a child's mind, which is not only confused, but keeps going round all the time. There are zigzag lines on it, just like your temperature on a card, and these are probably roads in the island; for the Neverland* is always more or less an island, with astonishing splashes of colour here and there, and coral reefs and rakish-looking craft in the offing, and savages and lonely lairs, and gnomes who are mostly tailors,* and caves through which a river runs, and princes with six elder brothers,* and a hut fast going to decay, and one very small old lady with a hooked nose. It would be an easy map if that were all; but there is also first day at school, religion, fathers, the Round Pond, needlework, murders, hangings, verbs that take the dative, chocolate-pudding day, getting into braces, say ninety-nine, threepence for pulling out your tooth yourself, and so on; and either these are part of the island or they are another map showing through, and it is all rather confusing, especially as nothing will stand still.

Of course the Neverlands vary a good deal. John's, for instance, had a lagoon with flamingoes flying over it at which John was shooting, while Michael, who was very small, had a flamingo with lagoons flying over it. John lived in a boat turned upside down on the sands, Michael in a wigwam, Wendy in a house of leaves deftly sewn together.

John had no friends, Michael had friends at night, Wendy had a pet wolf forsaken by its parents; but on the whole the Neverlands have a family resemblance, and if they stood still in a row you could say of them that they have each other's nose, and so forth. On these magic shores children at play are for ever beaching their coracles. We too have been there; we can still hear the sound of the surf, though we shall land no more.

Of all delectable islands the Neverland is the snuggest and most compact; not large and sprawly, you know, with tedious distances between one adventure and another, but nicely crammed. When you play at it by day with the chairs and table-cloth, it is not in the least alarming, but in the two minutes before you go to sleep it becomes very nearly real. That is why there are night-lights.

Occasionally in her travels through her children's minds Mrs Darling found things she could not understand, and of these quite the most perplexing was the word Peter. She knew of no Peter, and yet he was here and there in John and Michael's minds, while Wendy's began to be scrawled all over with him. The name stood out in bolder letters than any of the other words, and as Mrs Darling gazed she felt that it had an oddly cocky appearance.

'Yes, he is rather cocky,' Wendy admitted with regret. Her mother had been questioning her.

'But who is he, my pet?'

'He is Peter Pan, you know, mother.'

At first Mrs Darling did not know, but after thinking back into her childhood she just remembered a Peter Pan who was said to live with the fairies. There were odd stories about him; as that when children died he went part of the way with them, so that they should not be frightened. She had believed in him at the time, but now that she was married and full of sense she quite doubted whether there was any such person.

'Besides,' she said to Wendy, 'he would be grown up by this time.'

'Oh no, he isn't grown up,' Wendy assured her confidently, 'and he is just my size.' She meant that he was her size in both mind and body; she didn't know how she knew it, she just knew it.

Mrs Darling consulted Mr Darling, but he smiled pooh-pooh. 'Mark my words,' he said, 'it is some nonsense Nana has been putting into their heads; just the sort of idea a dog would have. Leave it alone, and it will blow over.'

But it would not blow over; and soon the troublesome boy gave Mrs Darling quite a shock.

Children have the strangest adventures without being troubled by them. For instance, they may remember to mention, a week after the event happened, that when they were in the wood they met their dead father and had a game with him. It was in this casual way that Wendy one morning made a disquieting revelation. Some leaves of a tree had been found on the nursery floor, which certainly were not there when the children went to bed, and Mrs Darling was puzzling over them when Wendy said with a tolerant smile:

'I do believe it is that Peter again!'

'Whatever do you mean, Wendy?'

'It is so naughty of him not to wipe,'* Wendy said, sighing. She was a tidy child.

She explained in quite a matter-of-fact way that she thought Peter sometimes came to the nursery in the night and sat on the foot of her bed and played on his pipes to her. Unfortunately she never woke, so she didn't know how she knew, she just knew.

'What nonsense you talk, precious. No one can get into the house without knocking.'

'I think he comes in by the window,' she said.

'My love, it is three floors up.'

'Were not the leaves at the foot of the window, mother?'

It was quite true; the leaves had been found very near the window.

Mrs Darling did not know what to think, for it all seemed so natural to Wendy that you could not dismiss it by saying she had been dreaming.

'My child,' the mother cried, 'why did you not tell me of this before?'

'I forgot,' said Wendy lightly. She was in a hurry to get her breakfast. Oh, surely she must have been dreaming.

But, on the other hand, there were the leaves. Mrs Darling examined them carefully; they were skeleton leaves, but she was sure they did not come from any tree that grew in England. She crawled about the floor, peering at it with a candle for marks of a strange foot. She rattled the poker up the chimney and tapped the walls. She let down a tape from the window to the pavement, and it was a sheer drop of thirty feet, without so much as a spout to climb up by.

Certainly Wendy had been dreaming.

But Wendy had not been dreaming, as the very next night showed, the night on which the extraordinary adventures of these children may be said to have begun.

On the night we speak of all the children were once more in bed. It happened to be Nana's evening off, and Mrs Darling had bathed them and sung to them till one by one they had let go her hand and slid away into the land of sleep.

All were looking so safe and cosy that she smiled at her fears now and sat down tranquilly by the fire to sew.

It was something for Michael, who on his birthday was getting into shirts.* The fire was warm, however, and the nursery dimly lit by three night-lights, and presently the sewing lay on Mrs Darling's lap. Then her head nodded, oh, so gracefully. She was asleep. Look at the four of them, Wendy and Michael over there, John here, and Mrs Darling by the fire. There should have been a fourth night-light.

While she slept she had a dream. She dreamt that the Neverland had come too near and that a strange boy had broken through from it. He did not alarm her, for she thought she had seen him before in the faces of many women who have no children. Perhaps he is to be found in the faces of some mothers also. But in her dream he had rent the film that obscures the Neverland, and she saw Wendy and John and Michael peeping through the gap.

The dream by itself would have been a trifle, but while she was dreaming the window of the nursery blew open, and a boy did drop on the floor. He was accompanied by a strange light, no bigger than your fist, which darted about the room like a living thing; and I think it must have been this light that wakened Mrs Darling.

She started up with a cry, and saw the boy, and somehow she knew at once that he was Peter Pan. If you or I or Wendy had been there we should have seen that he was very like Mrs Darling's kiss. He was a lovely boy, clad in skeleton leaves and the juices that ooze out of trees; but the most entrancing thing about him was that he had all his first teeth. When he saw she was a grown-up, he gnashed the little pearls at her.

CHAPTER 2

THE SHADOW

MRS DARLING screamed, and, as if in answer to a bell, the door opened, and Nana entered, returned from her evening out. She growled and sprang at the boy, who leapt lightly through the window. Again Mrs Darling screamed, this time in distress for him, for she thought he was killed, and she ran down into the street to look for his little body, but it was not there; and she looked up, and in the black night she could see nothing but what she thought was a shooting star.

She returned to the nursery, and found Nana with something in her mouth, which proved to be the boy's shadow. As he leapt at the window Nana had closed it quickly, too late to catch him, but his shadow had not had time to get out; slam went the window and snapped it off.

You may be sure Mrs Darling examined the shadow carefully, but it was quite the ordinary kind.

Nana had no doubt of what was the best thing to do with this shadow. She hung it out at the window, meaning 'He is sure to come back for it; let us put it where he can get it easily without disturbing the children.'

But unfortunately Mrs Darling could not leave it hanging out at the window; it looked so like the washing and lowered the whole tone of the house. She thought of showing it to Mr Darling, but he was totting up winter great-coats for John and Michael, with a wet towel round his head to keep his brain clear, and it seemed a shame to trouble him; besides, she knew exactly what he would say: 'It all comes of having a dog for a nurse.'

She decided to roll the shadow up and put it away carefully in a drawer, until a fitting opportunity came for telling her husband. Ah me!

The opportunity came a week later, on that never-to-be-forgotten Friday. Of course it was a Friday.

'I ought to have been specially careful on a Friday,' she used to say afterwards to her husband, while perhaps Nana was on the other side of her, holding her hand.

'No, no,' Mr Darling always said, 'I am responsible for it all. I, George Darling, did it. *Mea culpa, mea culpa*.'* He had had a classical education.

They sat thus night after night recalling that fatal Friday, till every detail of it was stamped on their brains and came through on the other side like the faces on a bad coinage.

'If only I had not accepted that invitation to dine at 27,' Mrs Darling said.

'If only I had not poured my medicine into Nana's bowl,' said Mr Darling.

'If only I had pretended to like the medicine,' was what Nana's wet eyes said.

'My liking for parties, George.'

'My fatal gift of humour, dearest.'

'My touchiness about trifles, dear master and mistress.'

Then one or more of them would break down altogether; Nana at the thought, 'It's true, it's true, they ought not to have had a dog for a nurse.' Many a time it was Mr Darling who put the handkerchief to Nana's eyes.

'That fiend!' Mr Darling would cry, and Nana's bark was the echo of it, but Mrs Darling never upbraided Peter; there was something in the right-hand corner of her mouth that wanted her not to call Peter names.

They would sit there in the empty nursery, recalling fondly every smallest detail of that dreadful evening. It had begun so uneventfully, so precisely like a hundred other evenings, with Nana putting on the water for Michael's bath and carrying him to it on her back.

'I won't go to bed,' he had shouted, like one who still believed that he had the last word on the subject, 'I won't, I won't. Nana, it isn't six o'clock yet. Oh dear, oh dear, I shan't love you any more, Nana. I tell you I won't be bathed, I won't, I won't!'

Then Mrs Darling had come in, wearing her white evening-gown. She had dressed early because Wendy so loved to see her in her evening-gown, with the necklace George had given her. She was wearing Wendy's bracelet on her arm; she had asked for the loan of it. Wendy so loved to lend her bracelet to her mother.

She had found her two older children playing at being herself and father on the occasion of Wendy's birth, and John was saying:

'I am happy to inform you, Mrs Darling, that you are now a mother,' in just such a tone as Mr Darling himself may have used on the real occasion.

Wendy had danced with joy, just as the real Mrs Darling must have done.

Then John was born, with the extra pomp that he conceived due to the birth of a male, and Michael came from his bath to ask to be born also, but John said brutally that they did not want any more.

Michael had nearly cried. 'Nobody wants me,' he said, and of course the lady in evening-dress could not stand that.

'I do,' she said, 'I so want a third child.'

'Boy or girl?' asked Michael, not too hopefully.

'Boy.'

Then he had leapt into her arms. Such a little thing for Mr and Mrs Darling and Nana to recall now, but not so little if that was to be Michael's last night in the nursery.

They go on with their recollections.

'It was then that I rushed in like a tornado, wasn't it?' Mr Darling would say, scorning himself; and indeed he had been like a tornado.

Perhaps there was some excuse for him. He, too, had been dressing for the party, and all had gone well with him until he came to his tie. It is an astounding thing to have to tell, but this man, though he knew about stocks and shares, had no real mastery of his tie. Sometimes the thing yielded to him without a contest, but there were occasions when it would have been better for the house if he had swallowed his pride and used a made-up tie.

This was such an occasion. He came rushing into the nursery with the crumpled little brute of a tie in his hand.

'Why, what is the matter, father dear?'

'Matter!' he yelled; he really yelled. 'This tie, it will not tie.' He became dangerously sarcastic. 'Not round my neck! Round the bed-post! Oh yes, twenty times have I made it up round the bedpost, but round my neck, no! Oh dear no! begs to be excused!'

He thought Mrs Darling was not sufficiently impressed, and he went on sternly, 'I warn you of this, mother, that unless this tie is round my neck we don't go out to dinner tonight, and if I don't go out to dinner tonight, I never go to the office again, and if I don't go to the office again, you and I starve, and our children will be flung into the streets.'

Even then Mrs Darling was placid. 'Let me try, dear,' she said, and indeed that was what he had come to ask her to do; and with her nice cool hands she tied his tie for him, while the children stood around to see their fate decided. Some men would have resented her being able to do it so easily, but Mr Darling was far too fine a nature for that; he thanked her carelessly, at once forgot his rage, and in another moment was dancing round the room with Michael on his back.

'How wildly we romped!' says Mrs Darling now, recalling it.

'Our last romp!' Mr Darling groaned.

'O George, do you remember Michael suddenly said to me, "How did you get to know me, mother?"'

'I remember!'

'They were rather sweet, don't you think, George?'

'And they were ours, ours, and now they are gone.'

The romp had ended with the appearance of Nana, and most unluckily Mr Darling collided against her, covering his trousers with hairs. They were not only new trousers, but they were the first he had ever had with braid on them, and he had to bite his lip to prevent the tears coming. Of course Mrs Darling brushed him, but he began to talk again about its being a mistake to have a dog for a nurse.

'George, Nana is a treasure.'

'No doubt, but I have an uneasy feeling at times that she looks upon the children as puppies.'

'Oh no, dear one, I feel sure she knows they have souls.'

'I wonder,' Mr Darling said thoughtfully, 'I wonder.' It was an opportunity, his wife felt, for telling him about the boy. At first he pooh-poohed the story, but he became thoughtful when she showed him the shadow.

'It is nobody I know,' he said, examining it carefully, 'but he does look a scoundrel.'

'We were still discussing it, you remember,' says Mr Darling, 'when Nana came in with Michael's medicine. You will never carry the bottle in your mouth again, Nana, and it is all my fault.'

Strong man though he was, there is no doubt that he had behaved rather foolishly over the medicine. If he had a weakness, it was for thinking that all his life he had taken medicine boldly; and so now, when Michael dodged the spoon in Nana's mouth, he had said reprovingly, 'Be a man, Michael.'

'Won't, won't,' Michael cried naughtily. Mrs Darling left the room to get a chocolate for him, and Mr Darling thought this showed want of firmness.

'Mother, don't pamper him,' he called after her. 'Michael, when I was your age I took medicine without a murmur. I said, "Thank you, kind parents, for giving me bottles to make me well." '

He really thought this was true, and Wendy, who was now in her nightgown, believed it also, and she said, to encourage Michael, 'That medicine you sometimes take, father, is much nastier, isn't it?'

'Ever so much nastier,' Mr Darling said bravely, 'and I would take it now as an example to you, Michael, if I hadn't lost the bottle.'

He had not exactly lost it; he had climbed in the dead of night to the top of the wardrobe and hidden it there. What he did not know was that the faithful Liza had found it, and put it back on his washstand.

'I know where it is, father,' Wendy cried, always glad to be of service. 'I'll bring it,' and she was off before he could stop her. Immediately his spirits sank in the strangest way.

'John,' he said, shuddering, 'it's most beastly stuff. It's that nasty, sticky, sweet kind.'

'It will soon be over, father,' John said cheerily, and then in rushed Wendy with the medicine in a glass.

'I have been as quick as I could,' she panted.

'You have been wonderfully quick,' her father retorted, with a vindictive politeness that was quite thrown away upon her. 'Michael first,' he said doggedly.

'Father first,' said Michael, who was of a suspicious nature.

'I shall be sick, you know,' Mr Darling said threateningly.

'Come on, father,' said John.

'Hold your tongue, John,' his father rapped out.

Wendy was quite puzzled. 'I thought you took it quite easily, father.'

'That is not the point,' he retorted. 'The point is, that there is more in my glass than in Michael's spoon.' His proud heart was nearly bursting. 'And it isn't fair; I would say it though it were with my last breath; it isn't fair.'

'Father, I am waiting,' said Michael coldly.

'It's all very well to say you are waiting; so am I waiting.'

'Father's a cowardy custard.'*

'So are you a cowardy custard.'

'I'm not frightened.'

'Neither am I frightened.'

'Well, then, take it.'

'Well, then, you take it.'

Wendy had a splendid idea. 'Why not both take it at the same time?'

'Certainly,' said Mr Darling. 'Are you ready, Michael?'

Wendy gave the words, one, two, three, and Michael took his medicine, but Mr Darling slipped his behind his back.

There was a yell of rage from Michael, and 'O father!' Wendy exclaimed.

'What do you mean by "O father"?' Mr Darling demanded. 'Stop that row, Michael. I meant to take mine, but I—I missed it.'

It was dreadful the way all the three were looking at him, just as if they did not admire him. 'Look here, all of you,' he said entreatingly, as soon as Nana had gone into the bathroom, 'I have just thought of a splendid joke. I shall pour my medicine into Nana's bowl, and she will drink it, thinking it is milk!'

It was the colour of milk; but the children did not have their father's sense of humour, and they looked at him reproachfully as he poured the medicine into Nana's bowl. 'What fun,' he said doubtfully, and they did not dare expose him when Mrs Darling and Nana returned.

'Nana, good dog,' he said, patting her. 'I have put a little milk into your bowl, Nana.'

Nana wagged her tail, ran to the medicine, and began lapping it. Then she gave Mr Darling such a look, not an angry look: she showed him the great red tear that makes us so sorry for noble dogs, and crept into her kennel.

Mr Darling was frightfully ashamed of himself, but he would not give in. In a horrid silence Mrs Darling smelt the bowl. 'O George,' she said, 'it's your medicine!'

'It was only a joke,' he roared, while she comforted her boys, and Wendy hugged Nana. 'Much good,' he said bitterly, 'my wearing myself to the bone trying to be funny in this house.'

And still Wendy hugged Nana. 'That's right,' he shouted. 'Coddle her! Nobody coddles me. Oh dear no! I am only the breadwinner, why should I be coddled, why, why, why!'

'George,' Mrs Darling entreated him, 'not so loud; the servants will hear you.' Somehow they had got into the way of calling Liza the servants.

'Let them,' he answered recklessly. 'Bring in the whole world. But I refuse to allow that dog to lord it in my nursery for an hour longer.'

The children wept, and Nana ran to him beseechingly, but he waved her back. He felt he was a strong man again. 'In vain, in vain,' he cried; 'the proper place for you is the yard, and there you go to be tied up this instant.'

'George, George,' Mrs Darling whispered, 'remember what I told you about that boy.'

Alas, he would not listen. He was determined to show who was master in that house, and when commands would not draw Nana from the kennel, he lured her out of it with honeyed words, and seizing her roughly, dragged her from the nursery. He was ashamed of himself, and yet he did it. It was all owing to his too affectionate nature, which craved for admiration. When he had tied her up in the back-yard, the wretched father went and sat in the passage, with his knuckles to his eyes.

In the meantime Mrs Darling had put the children to bed in unwonted silence and lit their night-lights. They could hear Nana barking, and John whimpered, 'It is because he is chaining her up in the yard,' but Wendy was wiser.

'That is not Nana's unhappy bark,' she said, little guessing what was about to happen; 'that is her bark when she smells danger.'

Danger!

'Are you sure, Wendy?'

'Oh yes.'

Mrs Darling quivered and went to the window. It was securely fastened. She looked out, and the night was peppered with stars. They were crowding round the house, as if curious to see what was to take place there, but she did not notice this, nor that one or two of the smaller ones winked at her. Yet a nameless fear clutched at her heart and made her cry, 'Oh, how I wish that I wasn't going to a party tonight!'

Even Michael, already half asleep, knew that she was perturbed, and he asked, 'Can anything harm us, mother, after the night-lights are lit?'

'Nothing, precious,' she said; 'they are the eyes a mother leaves behind her to guard her children.'

She went from bed to bed singing enchantments over them, and little Michael flung his arms round her. 'Mother,' he cried, 'I'm glad of you.' They were the last words she was to hear from him for a long time.

PETER FLEW IN

No. 27 was only a few yards distant, but there had been a slight fall of snow, and Father and Mother Darling picked their way over it deftly not to soil their shoes. They were already the only persons in the street, and all the stars were watching them. Stars are beautiful, but they may not take an active part in anything, they must just look

on for ever. It is a punishment put on them for something they did so
long ago that no star now knows what it was. So the older ones have
become glassy-eyed and seldom speak (winking is the star language),
but the little ones still wonder. They are not really friendly to Peter,
who has a mischievous way of stealing up behind them and trying to
blow them out; but they are so fond of fun that they were on his side
tonight, and anxious to get the grown-ups out of the way. So as soon
as the door of 27 closed on Mr and Mrs Darling there was a commotion in the firmament, and the smallest of all the stars in the Milky
Way screamed out:

'Now, Peter!'

CHAPTER 3

COME AWAY, COME AWAY!

FOR a moment after Mr and Mrs Darling left the house the night-lights by the beds of the three children continued to burn clearly. They were awfully nice little night-lights, and one cannot help wishing that they could have kept awake to see Peter; but Wendy's light blinked and gave such a yawn that the other two yawned also, and before they could close their mouths all the three went out.

There was another light in the room now, a thousand times brighter than the night-lights, and in the time we have taken to say this, it has been in all the drawers in the nursery, looking for Peter's shadow, rummaged the wardrobe, and turned every pocket inside out. It was not really a light; it made this light by flashing about so quickly, but when it came to rest for a second you saw it was a fairy, no longer than your hand, but still growing. It was a girl called Tinker Bell exquisitely gowned in a skeleton leaf, cut low and square, through which her figure could be seen to the best advantage. She was slightly inclined to *embonpoint*.*

A moment after the fairy's entrance the window was blown open by the breathing of the little stars, and Peter dropped in. He had carried Tinker Bell part of the way, and his hand was still messy with the fairy dust.

'Tinker Bell,' he called softly, after making sure that the children were asleep, 'Tink, where are you?' She was in a jug for the moment, and liking it extremely; she had never been in a jug before.

'Oh, do come out of that jug, and tell me, do you know where they put my shadow?'

The loveliest tinkle as of golden bells answered him. It is the fairy language. You ordinary children can never hear it, but if you were to hear it you would know that you had heard it once before.

Tink said that the shadow was in the big box. She meant the chest of drawers, and Peter jumped at the drawers, scattering their contents to the floor with both hands, as kings toss ha'pence to the crowd.* In a moment he had recovered his shadow, and in his delight he forgot that he had shut Tinker Bell up in the drawer.

If he thought at all, but I don't believe he ever thought, it was that he and his shadow, when brought near each other, would join like drops of water; and when they did not he was appalled. He tried to stick it on with soap from the bathroom, but that also failed. A shudder passed through Peter, and he sat on the floor and cried.

His sobs woke Wendy, and she sat up in bed. She was not alarmed to see a stranger crying on the nursery floor; she was only pleasantly interested.

'Boy,' she said courteously, 'why are you crying?'

Peter could be exceedingly polite also, having learned the grand manner at fairy ceremonies, and he rose and bowed to her beautifully. She was much pleased, and bowed beautifully to him from the bed.

'What's your name?' he asked.

'Wendy Moira Angela Darling,' she replied with some satisfaction. 'What is your name?'

'Peter Pan.'

She was already sure that he must be Peter, but it did seem a comparatively short name.

'Is that all?'

'Yes,' he said rather sharply. He felt for the first time that it was a shortish name.

'I'm so sorry,' said Wendy Moira Angela.

'It doesn't matter,' Peter gulped.

She asked where he lived.

'Second to the right,' said Peter, 'and then straight on till morning.'

'What a funny address!'

Peter had a sinking. For the first time he felt that perhaps it was a funny address.

'No, it isn't,' he said.

'I mean,' Wendy said nicely, remembering that she was hostess, 'is that what they put on the letters?'

He wished she had not mentioned letters.

'Don't get any letters,' he said contemptuously.

'But your mother gets letters?'

'Don't have a mother,' he said. Not only had he no mother, but he had not the slightest desire to have one. He thought them very over-rated persons. Wendy, however, felt at once that she was in the presence of a tragedy.

'O Peter, no wonder you were crying,' she said, and got out of bed and ran to him.

'I wasn't crying about mothers,' he said rather indignantly. 'I was crying because I can't get my shadow to stick on. Besides, I wasn't crying.'

'It has come off?'

'Yes.'

Then Wendy saw the shadow on the floor, looking so draggled, and she was frightfully sorry for Peter. 'How awful!' she said, but she could not help smiling when she saw that he had been trying to stick it on with soap. How exactly like a boy!

Fortunately she knew at once what to do. 'It must be sewn on,' she said, just a little patronizingly.

'What's sewn?' he asked.

'You're dreadfully ignorant.'

'No, I'm not.'

But she was exulting in his ignorance. 'I shall sew it on for you, my little man,' she said, though he was as tall as herself; and she got out her housewife,* and sewed the shadow on to Peter's foot.

'I dare say it will hurt a little,' she warned him.

'Oh, I shan't cry,' said Peter, who was already of opinion that he had never cried in his life. And he clenched his teeth and did not cry; and soon his shadow was behaving properly, though still a little creased.

'Perhaps I should have ironed it,' Wendy said thoughtfully; but Peter, boylike, was indifferent to appearances, and he was now jumping about in the wildest glee. Alas, he had already forgotten that he owed his bliss to Wendy. He thought he had attached the shadow himself. 'How clever I am,' he crowed rapturously, 'oh, the cleverness of me!'

It is humiliating to have to confess that this conceit of Peter was one of his most fascinating qualities. To put it with brutal frankness, there never was a cockier boy.

But for the moment Wendy was shocked. 'You conceit,'* she exclaimed, with frightful sarcasm; 'of course I did nothing!'

'You did a little,' Peter said carelessly, and continued to dance.

'A little!' she replied with hauteur; 'if I am no use I can at least withdraw'; and she sprang in the most dignified way into bed and covered her face with the blankets.

To induce her to look up he pretended to be going away, and when this failed he sat on the end of the bed and tapped her gently with his foot. 'Wendy,' he said, 'don't withdraw. I can't help crowing, Wendy, when I'm pleased with myself.' Still she would not look up, though she was listening eagerly. 'Wendy,' he continued, in a voice that no woman has ever yet been able to resist, 'Wendy, one girl is more use than twenty boys.'

Now Wendy was every inch a woman, though there were not very many inches, and she peeped out of the bedclothes.

'Do you really think so, Peter?'

'Yes, I do.'

'I think it's perfectly sweet of you,' she declared, 'and I'll get up again'; and she sat with him on the side of the bed. She also said she would give him a kiss if he liked, but Peter did not know what she meant, and he held out his hand expectantly.

'Surely you know what a kiss is?' she asked, aghast.

'I shall know when you give it to me,' he replied stiffly; and not to hurt his feelings she gave him a thimble.

'Now,' said he, 'shall I give you a kiss?' and she replied with a slight primness, 'If you please.' She made herself rather cheap by inclining her face toward him, but he merely dropped an acorn button into her hand; so she slowly returned her face to where it had been before, and said nicely that she would wear his kiss on the chain round her neck. It was lucky that she did put it on that chain, for it was afterwards to save her life.

When people in our set* are introduced, it is customary for them to ask each other's age, and so Wendy, who always liked to do the correct thing, asked Peter how old he was. It was not really a happy question to ask him; it was like an examination paper that asks grammar, when what you want to be asked is Kings of England.

'I don't know,' he replied uneasily, 'but I am quite young.' He really knew nothing about it; he had merely suspicions, but he said at a venture,* 'Wendy, I ran away the day I was born.'

Wendy was quite surprised, but interested; and she indicated in the charming drawing-room manner, by a touch on her nightgown, that he could sit nearer her.

'It was because I heard father and mother,' he explained in a low voice, 'talking about what I was to be when I became a man.' He was extraordinarily agitated now. 'I don't want ever to be a man', he said with passion. 'I want always to be a little boy and to have fun. So I ran away to Kensington Gardens and lived a long long time among the fairies.'

She gave him a look of the most intense admiration, and he thought it was because he had run away, but it was really because he knew fairies. Wendy had lived such a home life that to know fairies struck her as quite delightful. She poured out questions about them, to his surprise, for they were rather a nuisance to him, getting in his way and so on, and indeed he sometimes had to give them a hiding.* Still, he liked them on the whole, and he told her about the beginning of fairies.

'You see, Wendy, when the first baby laughed for the first time, its laugh broke into a thousand pieces, and they all went skipping about, and that was the beginning of fairies.'

Tedious talk this, but being a stay-at-home she liked it.

'And so,' he went on good-naturedly, 'there ought to be one fairy for every boy and girl.'

'Ought to be? Isn't there?'

'No. You see, children know such a lot now, they soon don't believe in fairies, and every time a child says, "I don't believe in fairies," there is a fairy somewhere that falls down dead.'

Really, he thought they had now talked enough about fairies, and it struck him that Tinker Bell was keeping very quiet. 'I can't think where she has gone to,' he said, rising, and he called Tink by name. Wendy's heart went flutter with a sudden thrill.

'Peter,' she cried, clutching him, 'you don't mean to tell me that there is a fairy in this room!'

'She was here just now,' he said a little impatiently. 'You don't hear her, do you?' and they both listened.

'The only sound I hear,' said Wendy, 'is like a tinkle of bells.'

'Well, that's Tink, that's the fairy language. I think I hear her too.'

The sound came from the chest of drawers, and Peter made a merry face. No one could ever look quite so merry as Peter, and the loveliest of gurgles was his laugh. He had his first laugh still.

'Wendy,' he whispered gleefully, 'I do believe I shut her up in the drawer!'

He let poor Tink out of the drawer, and she flew about the nursery screaming with fury.

'You shouldn't say such things,' Peter retorted. 'Of course I'm very sorry, but how could I know you were in the drawer?'

Wendy was not listening to him. 'O Peter,' she cried, 'if she would only stand still and let me see her!'

'They hardly ever stand still,' he said, but for one moment Wendy saw the romantic figure come to rest on the cuckoo clock. 'O the lovely!' she cried, though Tink's face was still distorted with passion.

'Tink,' said Peter amiably, 'this lady says she wishes you were her fairy.'

Tinker Bell answered insolently.

'What does she say, Peter?'

He had to translate. 'She is not very polite. She says you are a great ugly girl, and that she is my fairy.'

He tried to argue with Tink. 'You know you can't be my fairy, Tink, because I am a gentleman and you are a lady.'

To this Tink replied in these words, 'You silly ass,' and disappeared into the bathroom. 'She is quite a common fairy,' Peter explained apologetically; 'she is called Tinker Bell because she mends the pots and kettles.'

They were together in the armchair by this time, and Wendy plied him with more questions.

'If you don't live in Kensington Gardens now————'

'Sometimes I do still.'

'But where do you live mostly now?'

'With the lost boys.'

'Who are they?'

'They are the children who fall out of their perambulators when the nurse is looking the other way. If they are not claimed in seven days they are sent far away to the Neverland to defray expenses. I'm captain.'

'What fun it must be!'

'Yes,' said cunning Peter, 'but we are rather lonely. You see we have no female companionship.'

'Are none of the others girls?'

'Oh no; girls, you know, are much too clever to fall out of their prams.'

This flattered Wendy immensely. 'I think,' she said, 'it is perfectly lovely the way you talk about girls; John there just despises us.'

For reply Peter rose and kicked John out of bed, blankets and all; one kick. This seemed to Wendy rather forward for a first meeting, and she told him with spirit that he was not captain in her house. However, John continued to sleep so placidly on the floor that she allowed him to remain there. 'And I know you meant to be kind,' she said, relenting, 'so you may give me a kiss.'

For the moment she had forgotten his ignorance about kisses. 'I thought you would want it back,' he said a little bitterly, and offered to return her the thimble.

'Oh dear,' said the nice Wendy, 'I don't mean a kiss, I mean a thimble.'

'What's that?'

'It's like this.' She kissed him.

'Funny!' said Peter gravely. 'Now shall I give you a thimble?'

'If you wish to,' said Wendy, keeping her head erect this time.

Peter thimbled her, and almost immediately she screeched. 'What is it, Wendy?'

'It was exactly as if someone were pulling my hair.'

'That must have been Tink. I never knew her so naughty before.'

And indeed Tink was darting about again, using offensive language.

'She says she will do that to you, Wendy, every time I give you a thimble.'

'But why?'

'Why, Tink?'

Again Tink replied, 'You silly ass.' Peter could not understand why, but Wendy understood; and she was just slightly disappointed when he admitted that he came to the nursery window not to see her but to listen to stories.

'You see I don't know any stories. None of the lost boys know any stories.'

'How perfectly awful,' Wendy said.

'Do you know', Peter asked, 'why swallows build in the eaves of houses? It is to listen to the stories. O Wendy, your mother was telling you such a lovely story.'

'Which story was it?'

'About the prince who couldn't find the lady who wore the glass slipper.'

'Peter,' said Wendy excitedly, 'that was Cinderella,* and he found her, and they lived happily ever after.'

Peter was so glad that he rose from the floor, where they had been sitting, and hurried to the window. 'Where are you going?' she cried with misgiving.

'To tell the other boys.'

'Don't go, Peter,' she entreated, 'I know such lots of stories.'

Those were her precise words, so there can be no denying that it was she who first tempted him.

He came back, and there was a greedy look in his eyes now which ought to have alarmed her, but did not.

'Oh, the stories I could tell to the boys!' she cried, and then Peter gripped her and began to draw her toward the window.

'Let me go!' she ordered him.

'Wendy, do come with me and tell the other boys.'

Of course she was very pleased to be asked, but she said, 'Oh dear, I can't. Think of mummy! Besides, I can't fly.'

'I'll teach you.'

'Oh, how lovely to fly.'

'I'll teach you how to jump on the wind's back, and then away we go.'

'Oo!' she exclaimed rapturously.

'Wendy, Wendy, when you are sleeping in your silly bed you might be flying about with me saying funny things to the stars.'

'Oo!'

'And, Wendy, there are mermaids.'

'Mermaids! With tails?'

'Such long tails.'

'Oh,' cried Wendy, 'to see a mermaid!'

He had become frightfully cunning. 'Wendy,' he said, 'how we should all respect you.'

She was wriggling her body in distress. It was quite as if she were trying to remain on the nursery floor.

But he had no pity for her.

'Wendy,' he said, the sly one, 'you could tuck us in at night.'

'Oo!'

'None of us has ever been tucked in at night.'

'Oo,' and her arms went out to him.

'And you could darn our clothes, and make pockets for us. None of us has any pockets.'

How could she resist? 'Of course it's awfully fascinating!' she cried. 'Peter, would you teach John and Michael to fly too?'

'If you like,' he said indifferently; and she ran to John and Michael and shook them. 'Wake up,' she cried, 'Peter Pan has come and he is to teach us to fly.'

John rubbed his eyes. 'Then I shall get up,' he said. Of course he was on the floor already. 'Hallo,' he said, 'I am up!'

Michael was up by this time also, looking as sharp as a knife with six blades and a saw,* but Peter suddenly signed silence. Their faces assumed the awful craftiness of children listening for sounds from the grown-up world. All was as still as salt. Then everything was right. No, stop! Everything was wrong. Nana, who had been barking distressfully all the evening, was quiet now. It was her silence they had heard.

'Out with the light! Hide! Quick!' cried John, taking command for the only time throughout the whole adventure. And thus when Liza entered, holding Nana, the nursery seemed quite its old self, very dark; and you could have sworn you heard its three wicked inmates breathing angelically as they slept. They were really doing it artfully from behind the window curtains.

Liza was in a bad temper, for she was mixing the Christmas puddings in the kitchen, and had been drawn away from them, with a raisin still on her cheek, by Nana's absurd suspicions. She thought the best way of getting a little quiet was to take Nana to the nursery for a moment, but in custody of course.

'There, you suspicious brute,' she said, not sorry that Nana was in disgrace, 'they are perfectly safe, aren't they? Every one of the little angels sound asleep in bed. Listen to their gentle breathing.'

Here Michael, encouraged by his success, breathed so loudly that they were nearly detected. Nana knew that kind of breathing, and she tried to drag herself out of Liza's clutches.

But Liza was dense. 'No more of it, Nana,' she said sternly, pulling her out of the room. 'I warn you if you bark again I shall go straight for master and missus and bring them home from the party, and then, oh, won't master whip you, just.'

She tied the unhappy dog up again, but do you think Nana ceased to bark? Bring master and missus home from the party! Why, that was just what she wanted. Do you think she cared whether she was whipped so long as her charges were safe? Unfortunately Liza returned to her puddings, and Nana, seeing that no help would come from her, strained and strained at the chain until at last she broke it. In another moment she had burst into the dining room of 27 and flung up her paws to heaven, her most expressive way of making a communication. Mr and Mrs Darling knew at once that something terrible was happening in their nursery, and without a goodbye to their hostess they rushed into the street.

But it was now ten minutes since three scoundrels had been breathing behind the curtains; and Peter Pan can do a great deal in ten minutes.

We now return to the nursery.

'It's all right,' John announced, emerging from his hiding-place. 'I say, Peter, can you really fly?'

Instead of troubling to answer him Peter flew round the room, taking in the mantelpiece on the way.

'How topping!'* said John and Michael.

'How sweet!' cried Wendy.

'Yes, I'm sweet, oh, I am sweet!' said Peter, forgetting his manners again.

It looked delightfully easy, and they tried it first from the floor and then from the beds, but they always went down instead of up.

'I say, how do you do it?' asked John, rubbing his knee. He was quite a practical boy.

'You just think lovely wonderful thoughts,' Peter explained, 'and they lift you up in the air.'

He showed them again.

'You're so nippy at it,' John said; 'couldn't you do it very slowly once?'

Peter did it both slowly and quickly. 'I've got it now, Wendy!' cried John, but soon he found he had not. Not one of them could fly an inch, though even Michael was in words of two syllables,* and Peter did not know A from Z.

Of course Peter had been trifling with them, for no one can fly unless the fairy dust has been blown on him. Fortunately, as we have mentioned, one of his hands was messy with it, and he blew some on each of them, with the most superb results.

'Now just wriggle your shoulders this way,' he said, 'and let go.'

They were all on their beds, and gallant Michael let go first. He did not quite mean to let go, but he did it, and immediately he was borne across the room.

'I flewed!' he screamed while still in mid-air.

John let go and met Wendy near the bathroom.

'Oh, lovely!'

'Oh, ripping!'

'Look at me!'

'Look at me!'

'Look at me!'

They were not nearly so elegant as Peter, they could not help kicking a little, but their heads were bobbing against the ceiling, and there is almost nothing so delicious as that. Peter gave Wendy a hand at first, but had to desist, Tink was so indignant.

Up and down they went, and round and round. Heavenly was Wendy's word.

'I say,' cried John, 'why shouldn't we all go out!'

Of course it was to this that Peter had been luring them.

Michael was ready: he wanted to see how long it took him to do a billion miles. But Wendy hesitated.

'Mermaids!' said Peter again.

'Oo!'

'And there are pirates.'

'Pirates,' cried John, seizing his Sunday hat, 'let us go at once.'

It was just at this moment that Mr and Mrs Darling hurried with Nana out of 27. They ran into the middle of the street to look up at the nursery window; and, yes, it was still shut, but the room was ablaze with light, and most heart-gripping sight of all, they could see in shadow on the curtain three little figures in night attire circling round and round, not on the floor but in the air.

Not three figures, four!

In a tremble they opened the street door. Mr Darling would have rushed upstairs, but Mrs Darling signed to him to go softly. She even tried to make her heart go softly.

Will they reach the nursery in time? If so, how delightful for them, and we shall all breathe a sigh of relief, but there will be no story. On the other hand, if they are not in time, I solemnly promise that it will all come right in the end.

They would have reached the nursery in time had it not been that the little stars were watching them. Once again the stars blew the window open, and that smallest star of all called out:

'Cave,* Peter!'

Then Peter knew that there was not a moment to lose. 'Come,' he cried imperiously, and soared out at once into the night, followed by John and Michael and Wendy.

Mr and Mrs Darling and Nana rushed into the nursery too late. The birds were flown.

THE BIRDS WERE FLOWN

CHAPTER 4

THE FLIGHT

'SECOND to the right, and straight on till morning.'

That, Peter had told Wendy, was the way to the Neverland; but even birds, carrying maps and consulting them at windy corners, could not have sighted it with these instructions. Peter, you see, just said anything that came into his head.

At first his companions trusted him implicitly, and so great were the delights of flying that they wasted time circling round church spires or any other tall objects on the way that took their fancy.

John and Michael raced, Michael getting a start.

They recalled with contempt that not so long ago they had thought themselves fine fellows for being able to fly round a room.

Not so long ago. But how long ago? They were flying over the sea before this thought began to disturb Wendy seriously. John thought it was their second sea and their third night.

Sometimes it was dark and sometimes light, and now they were very cold and again too warm. Did they really feel hungry at times, or were they merely pretending, because Peter had such a jolly new way of feeding them? His way was to pursue birds who had food in their mouths suitable for humans and snatch it from them; then the birds would follow and snatch it back; and they would all go chasing each other gaily for miles, parting at last with mutual expressions of good-will. But Wendy noticed with gentle concern that Peter did not seem to know that this was rather an odd way of getting your bread and butter, nor even that there are other ways.

Certainly they did not pretend to be sleepy, they were sleepy; and that was a danger, for the moment they popped off,* down they fell. The awful thing was that Peter thought this funny.

'There he goes again!' he would cry gleefully, as Michael suddenly dropped like a stone.

'Save him, save him!' cried Wendy, looking with horror at the cruel sea far below. Eventually Peter would dive through the air, and catch Michael just before he could strike the sea, and it was lovely the way he did it; but he always waited till the last moment, and you felt it was his cleverness that interested him and not the saving of human life.

Also he was fond of variety, and the sport that engrossed him one moment would suddenly cease to engage him, so there was always the possibility that the next time you fell he would let you go.

He could sleep in the air without falling, by merely lying on his back and floating, but this was, partly at least, because he was so light that if you got behind him and blew he went faster.

'Do be more polite to him,' Wendy whispered to John, when they were playing 'Follow my Leader'.

'Then tell him to stop showing off,' said John.

When playing Follow my Leader, Peter would fly close to the water and touch each shark's tail in passing, just as in the street you may run your finger along an iron railing. They could not follow him in this with much success, so perhaps it was rather like showing off, especially as he kept looking behind to see how many tails they missed.

'You must be nice to him,' Wendy impressed on her brothers. 'What could we do if he were to leave us?'

'We could go back,' Michael said.

'How could we ever find our way back without him?'

'Well, then, we could go on,' said John.

'That is the awful thing, John. We should have to go on, for we don't know how to stop.'

This was true; Peter had forgotten to show them how to stop.

John said that if the worst came to the worst, all they had to do was to go straight on, for the world was round, and so in time they must come back to their own window.

'And who is to get food for us, John?'

'I nipped a bit out of that eagle's mouth pretty neatly, Wendy.'

'After the twentieth try,' Wendy reminded him. 'And even though we became good at picking up food, see how we bump against clouds and things if he is not near to give us a hand.'

Indeed they were constantly bumping. They could now fly strongly, though they still kicked far too much; but if they saw a cloud in front of them, the more they tried to avoid it, the more certainly did they bump into it. If Nana had been with them, she would have had a bandage round Michael's forehead by this time.

Peter was not with them for the moment, and they felt rather lonely up there by themselves. He could go so much faster than they that he would suddenly shoot out of sight, to have some adventure in which they had no share. He would come down laughing over something fearfully funny he had been saying to a star, but he had already forgotten what it was, or he would come up with mermaid scales still sticking to him, and yet not be able to say for certain what had been happening. It was really rather irritating to children who had never seen a mermaid.

'And if he forgets them so quickly,' Wendy argued, 'how can we expect that he will go on remembering us?'

Indeed, sometimes when he returned he did not remember them, at least not well. Wendy was sure of it. She saw recognition come into his eyes as he was about to pass them the time of day and go on; once even she had to tell him her name.

'I'm Wendy,' she said agitatedly.

He was very sorry. 'I say, Wendy,' he whispered to her, 'always if you see me forgetting you, just keep on saying "I'm Wendy", and then I'll remember.'

Of course this was rather unsatisfactory. However, to make amends he showed them how to lie out flat on a strong wind that was going their way, and this was such a pleasant change that they tried it several times and found they could sleep thus with security. Indeed they would have slept longer, but Peter tired quickly of sleeping, and soon he would cry in his captain voice, 'We get off here.' So with occasional tiffs,* but on the whole rollicking, they drew near the Neverland; for after many moons they did reach it, and, what is more, they had been going pretty straight all the time, not perhaps so much owing to the guidance of Peter or Tink as because the island was out looking for them. It is only thus that anyone may sight those magic shores.

'There it is,' said Peter calmly.

'Where, where?'

'Where all the arrows are pointing.'

Indeed a million golden arrows were pointing out the island to the children, all directed by their friend the sun, who wanted them to be sure of their way before leaving them for the night.

Wendy and John and Michael stood on tiptoe in the air to get their first sight of the island. Strange to say, they all recognized it at once, and until fear fell upon them they hailed it, not as something long dreamt of and seen at last, but as a familiar friend to whom they were returning home for the holidays.

'John, there's the lagoon.'

'Wendy, look at the turtles burying their eggs in the sand.'

"LET HIM KEEP WHO CAN

'I say, John, I see your flamingo with the broken leg.'

'Look, Michael, there's your cave.'

'John, what's that in the brushwood?'

'It's a wolf with her whelps. Wendy, I do believe that's your little whelp.'

'There's my boat, John, with her sides stove in.'

'No, it isn't. Why, we burned your boat.'

'That's her, at any rate. I say, John, I see the smoke of the redskin camp.'

'Where? Show me, and I'll tell you by the way the smoke curls whether they are on the war-path.'

'There, just across the Mysterious River.'

'I see now. Yes, they are on the war-path right enough.'

Peter was a little annoyed with them for knowing so much; but if he wanted to lord it over them his triumph was at hand, for have I not told you that anon* fear fell upon them?

It came as the arrows went, leaving the island in gloom.

In the old days at home the Neverland had always begun to look a little dark and threatening by bedtime. Then unexplored patches arose in it and spread; black shadows moved about in them; the roar of the beasts of prey was quite different now, and above all, you lost the certainty that you would win. You were quite glad that the night-lights were on. You even liked Nana to say that this was just the mantelpiece over here, and that the Neverland was all make-believe.

Of course the Neverland had been make-believe in those days; but it was real now, and there were no night-lights, and it was getting darker every moment, and where was Nana?

They had been flying apart, but they huddled close to Peter now. His careless manner had gone at last, his eyes were sparkling, and a tingle went through them every time they touched his body. They were now over the fearsome island, flying so low that sometimes a tree grazed their feet. Nothing horrid was visible in the air, yet their progress had become slow and laboured, exactly as if they were pushing their way through hostile forces. Sometimes they hung in the air until Peter had beaten on it with his fists.

'They don't want us to land,' he explained.

'Who are they?' Wendy whispered, shuddering.

But he could not or would not say. Tinker Bell had been asleep on his shoulder, but now he wakened her and sent her on in front.

Sometimes he poised himself in the air, listening intently with his hand to his ear, and again he would stare down with eyes so bright that they seemed to bore two holes to earth. Having done these things, he went on again.

His courage was almost appalling. 'Do you want an adventure now,' he said casually to John, 'or would you like to have your tea first?'

Wendy said 'tea first' quickly, and Michael pressed her hand in gratitude, but the braver John hesitated.

'What kind of adventure?' he asked cautiously.

'There's a pirate asleep in the pampas* just beneath us,' Peter told him. 'If you like, we'll go down and kill him.'

'I don't see him,' John said after a long pause.

'I do.'

'Suppose,' John said a little huskily, 'he were to wake up.'

Peter spoke indignantly. 'You don't think I would kill him while he was sleeping! I would wake him first, and then kill him. That's the way I always do.'

'I say! Do you kill many?'

'Tons.'

John said 'how ripping', but decided to have tea first. He asked if there were many pirates on the island just now, and Peter said he had never known so many.

'Who is captain now?'

'Hook,' answered Peter; and his face became very stern as he said that hated word.

'Jas. Hook?'

'Aye.'

Then indeed Michael began to cry, and even John could speak in gulps only, for they knew Hook's reputation.

'He was Blackbeard's bo'sun,'* John whispered huskily. 'He is the worst of them all. He is the only man of whom Barbecue* was afraid.'

'That's him,' said Peter.

'What is he like? Is he big?'

'He is not so big as he was.'

'How do you mean?'

'I cut off a bit of him.'

'You!'

'Yes, me,' said Peter sharply.

'I wasn't meaning to be disrespectful.'

'Oh, all right.'

'But, I say, what bit?'

'His right hand.'

'Then he can't fight now?'

'Oh, can't he just!'

'Left-hander?'

'He has an iron hook instead of a right hand, and he claws with it.'

'Claws!'

'I say, John,' said Peter.

'Yes.'

'Say, "Aye, aye, sir." '

'Aye, aye, sir.'

'There is one thing', Peter continued, 'that every boy who serves under me has to promise, and so must you.'

John paled.

'It is this, if we meet Hook in open fight, you must leave him to me.'

'I promise,' John said loyally.

For the moment they were feeling less eerie, because Tink was flying with them, and in her light they could distinguish each other. Unfortunately she could not fly so slowly as they, and so she had to go round and round them in a circle in which they moved as in a halo. Wendy quite liked it, until Peter pointed out the drawback.

'She tells me,' he said, 'that the pirates sighted us before the darkness came, and got Long Tom* out.'

'The big gun?'

'Yes. And of course they must see her light, and if they guess we are near it they are sure to let fly.'

'Wendy!'

'John!'

'Michael!'

'Tell her to go away at once, Peter,' the three cried simultaneously, but he refused.

'She thinks we have lost the way,' he replied stiffly, 'and she is rather frightened. You don't think I would send her away all by herself when she is frightened!'

For a moment the circle of light was broken, and something gave Peter a loving little pinch.

'Then tell her,' Wendy begged, 'to put out her light.'

'She can't put it out. That is about the only thing fairies can't do. It just goes out of itself when she falls asleep, same as the stars.'

'Then tell her to sleep at once,' John almost ordered.

'She can't sleep except when she's sleepy. It is the only other thing fairies can't do.'

'Seems to me,' growled John, 'these are the only two things worth doing.'

Here he got a pinch, but not a loving one.

'If only one of us had a pocket,' Peter said, 'we could carry her in it.' However, they had set off in such a hurry that there was not a pocket between the four of them.

He had a happy idea. John's hat!

Tink agreed to travel by hat if it was carried in the hand. John carried it, though she had hoped to be carried by Peter. Presently Wendy took the hat, because John said it struck against his knee as he flew; and this, as we shall see, led to mischief, for Tinker Bell hated to be under an obligation to Wendy.

In the black topper* the light was completely hidden, and they flew on in silence. It was the stillest silence they had ever known, broken once by a distant lapping, which Peter explained was the wild beasts drinking at the ford, and again by a rasping sound that might have been the branches of trees rubbing together, but he said it was the redskins sharpening their knives.

Even these noises ceased. To Michael the loneliness was dreadful. 'If only something would make a sound!' he cried.

As if in answer to his request, the air was rent by the most tremendous crash he had ever heard. The pirates had fired Long Tom at them.

The roar of it echoed through the mountains, and the echoes seemed to cry savagely, 'Where are they, where are they, where are they?'

Thus sharply did the terrified three learn the difference between an island of make-believe and the same island come true.

When at last the heavens were steady again, John and Michael found themselves alone in the darkness. John was treading the air mechanically, and Michael without knowing how to float was floating.

'Are you shot?' John whispered tremulously.

'I haven't tried yet,' Michael whispered back.

We know now that no one had been hit. Peter, however, had been carried by the wind of the shot far out to sea, while Wendy was blown upwards with no companion but Tinker Bell.

It would have been well for Wendy if at that moment she had dropped the hat.

I don't know whether the idea came suddenly to Tink, or whether she had planned it on the way, but she at once popped out of the hat and began to lure Wendy to her destruction.

Tink was not all bad: or, rather, she was all bad just now, but, on the other hand, sometimes she was all good. Fairies have to be one thing or the other, because being so small they unfortunately have room for one feeling only at a time. They are, however, allowed to change, only it must be a complete change. At present she was full of jealousy of Wendy. What she said in her lovely tinkle Wendy could not of course understand, and I believe some of it was bad words, but it sounded kind, and she flew back and forward, plainly meaning 'Follow me, and all will be well.'

What else could poor Wendy do? She called to Peter and John and Michael, and got only mocking echoes in reply. She did not yet know that Tink hated her with the fierce hatred of a very woman. And so, bewildered, and now staggering in her flight, she followed Tink to her doom.

CHAPTER 5

THE ISLAND COME TRUE

FEELING that Peter was on his way back, the Neverland had again woke into life. We ought to use the pluperfect and say wakened, but woke is better and was always used by Peter.

In his absence things are usually quiet on the island. The fairies take an hour longer in the morning, the beasts attend to their young, the redskins feed heavily for six days and nights, and when pirates and lost boys meet they merely bite their thumbs at each other. But with the coming of Peter, who hates lethargy, they are all under way again: if you put your ear to the ground now, you would hear the whole island seething with life.

On this evening the chief forces of the island were disposed as follows. The lost boys were out looking for Peter, the pirates were out looking for the lost boys, the redskins were out looking for the pirates, and the beasts were out looking for the redskins. They were going round and round the island, but they did not meet because all were going at the same rate.

All wanted blood except the boys, who liked it as a rule, but tonight were out to greet their captain. The boys on the island vary, of course, in numbers, according as they get killed and so on; and when they seem to be growing up, which is against the rules, Peter thins them out; but at this time there were six of them, counting the Twins as two. Let us pretend to lie here among the sugar-cane and watch them as they steal by in single file, each with his hand on his dagger.

They are forbidden by Peter to look in the least like him, and they wear the skins of bears slain by themselves, in which they are so round and furry that when they fall they roll. They have therefore become very sure-footed.

The first to pass is Tootles, not the least brave but the most unfortunate of all that gallant band. He had been in fewer adventures than any of them, because the big things constantly happened just when he had stepped round the corner; all would be quiet, he would take the opportunity of going off to gather a few sticks for firewood, and then when he returned the others would be sweeping up the blood. This ill-luck had given a gentle melancholy to his countenance, but instead of souring his nature had sweetened it, so that he was quite the humblest of the boys. Poor kind Tootles, there is danger in the air for you tonight. Take care lest an adventure is now offered you, which, if accepted, will plunge you in deepest woe. Tootles, the fairy Tink, who is bent on mischief this night, is looking for a tool, and she thinks you the most easily tricked of the boys. 'Ware Tinker Bell.

Would that he could hear us, but we are not really on the island, and he passes by, biting his knuckles.

Next comes Nibs, the gay and debonair, followed by Slightly, who cuts whistles out of the trees and dances ecstatically to his own tunes. Slightly is the most conceited of the boys. He thinks he remembers the days before he was lost, with their manners and customs, and this has given his nose an offensive tilt. Curly is fourth; he is a pickle,* and so often has he had to deliver up his person when Peter said sternly, 'Stand forth the one who did this thing,' that now at the command he stands forth automatically whether he has done it or not. Last come the Twins, who cannot be described because we should be sure to be describing the wrong one. Peter never quite knew what twins were, and his band were not allowed to know anything he did not know, so these two were always vague about themselves, and did their best to give satisfaction by keeping close together in an apologetic sort of way.

The boys vanish in the gloom, and after a pause, but not a long pause, for things go briskly on the island, come the pirates on their track. We hear them before they are seen, and it is always the same dreadful song:

> 'Avast belay, yo ho, heave to,
> A-pirating we go,
> And if we're parted by a shot
> We're sure to meet below!'

A more villainous-looking lot never hung in a row on Execution Dock.* Here, a little in advance, ever and again with his head to the ground listening, his great arms bare, pieces of eight* in his ears as ornaments, is the handsome Italian Cecco,* who cut his name in letters of blood on the back of the governor of the prison at Gao.* That gigantic black behind him has had many names since he dropped the one with which dusky mothers still terrify their children on the banks of the Guadjo-mo.* Here is Bill Jukes, every inch of him tattooed, the same Bill Jukes who got six dozen on the *Walrus* from Flint* before he would drop the bag of moidores,* and Cookson, said to be Black Murphy's brother (but this was never proved); and Gentleman Starkey, once an usher* in a public school and still dainty in his ways of killing; and Skylights (Morgan's Skylights*); and the Irish bo'sun Smee,* an oddly genial man who stabbed, so to speak, without offence, and was the only Nonconformist* in Hook's crew; and Noodler, whose hands were fixed on backwards; and Robt. Mullins and Alf Mason* and many another ruffian long known and feared on the Spanish Main.*

In the midst of them, the blackest and largest jewel in that dark setting, reclined James Hook, or, as he wrote himself, Jas. Hook, of whom it is said he was the only man that the Sea-Cook* feared. He lay at his ease in a rough chariot drawn and propelled by his men, and instead of a right hand he had the iron hook with which ever and anon he encouraged them to increase their pace. As dogs this terrible man treated and addressed them, and as dogs they obeyed him. In person he was cadaverous and blackavised,* and his hair was dressed in long curls, which at a little distance looked like black candles, and gave a singularly threatening expression to his handsome countenance. His eyes were of the blue of the forget-me-not, and of a profound melancholy, save when he was plunging his hook into you, at which time two red spots appeared in them and lit them up horribly. In manner, something of the grand seigneur* still clung to him, so that he even ripped you up with an air, and I have been told that he was a *raconteur** of repute. He was never more sinister than when he was most polite, which is probably the truest test of breeding; and the elegance of his diction, even when he was swearing, no less than the distinction of his demeanour, showed him one of a different caste from his crew. A man of indomitable courage, it was said of him that the only thing he shied at was the sight of his own blood, which was thick and of an unusual colour. In dress he somewhat aped the attire associated with the name of Charles II, having heard it said in some earlier period of his career that he bore a strange resemblance to the ill-fated Stuarts; and in his mouth he had a holder of his own contrivance which enabled him to smoke two cigars at once. But undoubtedly the grimmest part of him was his iron claw.

Let us now kill a pirate, to show Hook's method. Skylights will do. As they pass, Skylights lurches clumsily against him, ruffling his lace collar; the hook shoots forth, there is a tearing sound and one screech, then the body is kicked aside, and the pirates pass on. He has not even taken the cigars from his mouth.

Such is the terrible man against whom Peter Pan is pitted. Which will win?

On the trail of the pirates, stealing noiselessly down the war-path, which is not visible to inexperienced eyes, come the redskins, every one of them with his eyes peeled. They carry tomahawks and knives, and their naked bodies gleam with paint and oil. Strung around them are scalps, of boys as well as of pirates, for these are the Piccaninny* tribe, and not to be confused with the softer-hearted Delawares or the Hurons.* In the van, on all fours, is Great Big Little Panther, a brave of so many scalps that in his present position they somewhat impede his progress. Bringing up the rear, the place of greatest danger, comes Tiger Lily, proudly erect, a princess in her own right. She is the most beautiful of dusky Dianas* and the belle of the Piccaninnies, coquettish, cold and amorous by turns; there is not a brave who would not have the wayward thing to wife, but she staves off the altar with a hatchet. Observe how they pass over fallen twigs without making the slightest noise. The only sound to be heard is their somewhat heavy breathing. The fact is that they are all a little fat just now after the heavy gorging, but in time they will work this off. For the moment, however, it constitutes their chief danger.

The redskins disappear as they have come, like shadows, and soon their place is taken by the beasts, a great and motley procession: lions, tigers, bears, and the innumerable smaller savage things that flee from them, for every kind of beast, and, more particularly, all the man-eaters, live cheek by jowl on the favoured island. Their tongues are hanging out, they are hungry tonight.

When they have passed, comes the last figure of all, a gigantic crocodile. We shall see for whom she is looking presently.

The crocodile passes, but soon the boys appear again, for the procession must continue indefinitely until one of the parties stops or changes its pace. Then quickly they will be on top of each other.

All are keeping a sharp look-out in front, but none suspects that the danger may be creeping up from behind. This shows how real the island was.

The first to fall out of the moving circle was the boys. They flung themselves down on the sward, close to their underground home.

'I do wish Peter would come back,' every one of them said nervously, though in height and still more in breadth they were all larger than their captain.

'I am the only one who is not afraid of the pirates,' Slightly said, in the tone that prevented his being a general favourite; but perhaps some distant sound disturbed him, for he added hastily, 'but I wish he would come back, and tell us whether he has heard anything more about Cinderella.'

They talked of Cinderella, and Tootles was confident that his mother must have been very like her.

It was only in Peter's absence that they could speak of mothers, the subject being forbidden by him as silly.

'All I remember about my mother,' Nibs told them, 'is that she often said to father, "Oh, how I wish I had a cheque-book of my own." I don't know what a cheque-book is, but I should just love to give my mother one.'

While they talked they heard a distant sound. You or I, not being wild things of the woods, would have heard nothing, but they heard it, and it was the grim song:

> 'Yo ho, yo ho, the pirate life,
> The flag o'skull and bones,
> A merry hour, a hempen rope,
> And hey for Davy Jones.'*

At once the lost boys—but where are they? They are no longer there. Rabbits could not have disappeared more quickly.

I will tell you where they are. With the exception of Nibs, who has darted away to reconnoitre,* they are already in their home under the ground, a very delightful residence of which we shall see a good deal presently. But how have they reached it? for there is no entrance to be seen, not so much as a pile of brushwood, which, if removed, would disclose the mouth of a cave. Look closely, however, and you may note that there are here seven large trees, each having in its hollow trunk a hole as large as a boy. These are the seven entrances to the home under the ground, for which Hook has been searching in vain these many moons. Will he find it tonight?

As the pirates advanced, the quick eye of Starkey sighted Nibs disappearing through the wood, and at once his pistol flashed out. But an iron claw gripped his shoulder.

'Captain, let go,' he cried, writhing.

Now for the first time we hear the voice of Hook. It was a black voice. 'Put back that pistol first,' it said threateningly.

'It was one of those boys you hate. I could have shot him dead.'

'Aye, and the sound would have brought Tiger Lily's redskins upon us. Do you want to lose your scalp?'

'Shall I after him, captain,' asked pathetic Smee, 'and tickle him with Johnny Corkscrew?' Smee had pleasant names for everything, and his cutlass was Johnny Corkscrew, because he wriggled it in the wound. One could mention many lovable traits in Smee. For instance, after killing, it was his spectacles he wiped instead of his weapon.

'Johnny's a silent fellow,' he reminded Hook.

'Not now, Smee,' Hook said darkly. 'He is only one, and I want to mischief all the seven. Scatter and look for them.'

The pirates disappeared among the trees, and in a moment their captain and Smee were alone. Hook heaved a heavy sigh; and I know not why it was, perhaps it was because of the soft beauty of the evening, but there came over him a desire to confide to his faithful bo'sun the story of his life. He spoke long and earnestly, but what it was all about Smee, who was rather stupid, did not know in the least.

Anon he caught the word Peter.

'Most of all,' Hook was saying passionately, 'I want their captain, Peter Pan. 'Twas he cut off my arm.' He brandished the hook threateningly. 'I've waited long to shake his hand with this. Oh, I'll tear him.'

'And yet,' said Smee, 'I have often heard you say that hook was worth a score of hands, for combing the hair and other homely uses.'

'Aye,' the captain answered, 'if I was a mother I would pray to have my children born with this instead of that,' and he cast a look of pride upon his iron hand and one of scorn upon the other. Then again he frowned.

'Peter flung my arm', he said, wincing, 'to a crocodile that happened to be passing by.'

'I have often', said Smee, 'noticed your strange dread of crocodiles.'

'Not of crocodiles,' Hook corrected him, 'but of that one crocodile.' He lowered his voice. 'It liked my arm so much, Smee, that it has followed me ever since, from sea to sea and from land to land, licking its lips for the rest of me.'

'In a way,' said Smee, 'it's a sort of compliment.'

'I want no such compliments,' Hook barked petulantly. 'I want Peter Pan, who first gave the brute its taste for me.'

He sat down on a large mushroom, and now there was a quiver in his voice. 'Smee,' he said huskily, 'that crocodile would have had me before this, but by a lucky chance it swallowed a clock which goes tick tick inside it, and so before it can reach me I hear the tick and bolt.' He laughed, but in a hollow way.

'Some day,' said Smee, 'the clock will run down, and then he'll get you.'

Hook wetted his dry lips. 'Aye,' he said, 'that's the fear that haunts me.'

Since sitting down he had felt curiously warm. 'Smee,' he said, 'this seat is hot.' He jumped up. 'Odds, bobs, hammer and tongs,* I'm burning.'

They examined the mushroom, which was of a size and solidity unknown on the mainland; they tried to pull it up, and it came away at once in their hands, for it had no root. Stranger still, smoke began at once to ascend. The pirates looked at each other. 'A chimney!' they both exclaimed.

They had indeed discovered the chimney of the home under the ground. It was the custom of the boys to stop it with a mushroom when enemies were in the neighbourhood.

Not only smoke came out of it. There came also children's voices, for so safe did the boys feel in their hiding-place that they were gaily chattering. The pirates listened grimly, and then replaced the mushroom. They looked around them and noted the holes in the seven trees.

'Did you hear them say Peter Pan's from home?' Smee whispered, fidgeting with Johnny Corkscrew.

Hook nodded. He stood for a long time lost in thought, and at last a curdling smile lit up his swarthy face. Smee had been waiting for it. 'Unrip* your plan, captain,' he cried eagerly.

'To return to the ship,' Hook replied slowly through his teeth, 'and cook a large rich cake of a jolly thickness with green sugar on it. There can be but one room below, for there is but one chimney. The silly moles had not the sense to see that they did not need a door apiece. That shows they have no mother. We will leave the cake on the shore of the mermaids' lagoon. These boys are always swimming about there, playing with the mermaids. They will find the cake and they will gobble it up, because, having no mother, they don't know how dangerous 'tis to eat rich damp cake.' He burst into laughter, not hollow laughter now, but honest laughter. 'Aha, they will die.'

Smee had listened with growing admiration.

'It's the wickedest, prettiest policy ever I heard of,' he cried, and in their exultation they danced and sang:

> 'Avast, belay, when I appear,
> By fear they're overtook;
> Naught's left upon your bones when you
> Have shaken claws with Hook.'

They began the verse, but they never finished it, for another sound broke in and stilled them. It was at first such a tiny sound that a leaf might have fallen on it and smothered it, but as it came nearer it was more distinct.

Tick tick tick tick.

Hook stood shuddering, one foot in the air.

'The crocodile,' he gasped, and bounded away, followed by his bo'sun.

It was indeed the crocodile. It had passed the redskins, who were now on the trail of the other pirates. It oozed on after Hook.

Once more the boys emerged into the open; but the dangers of the night were not yet over, for presently Nibs rushed breathless into their midst, pursued by a pack of wolves. The tongues of the pursuers were hanging out; the baying of them was horrible.

'Save me, save me!' cried Nibs, falling on the ground.

'But what can we do, what can we do?'

It was a high compliment to Peter that at that dire moment their thoughts turned to him.

'What would Peter do?' they cried simultaneously.

Almost in the same breath they added, 'Peter would look at them through his legs.'

And then, 'Let us do what Peter would do.'

It is quite the most successful way of defying wolves, and as one boy they bent and looked through their legs. The next moment is the long one; but victory came quickly, for as the boys advanced upon them in this terrible attitude, the wolves dropped their tails and fled.

Now Nibs rose from the ground, and the others thought that his staring eyes still saw the wolves. But it was not wolves he saw.

'I have seen a wonderfuller thing,' he cried as they gathered round him eagerly. 'A great white bird. It is flying this way.'

'What kind of a bird, do you think?'

'I don't know,' Nibs said, awestruck, 'but it looks so weary, and as it flies it moans, "Poor Wendy".'

'Poor Wendy?'

'I remember,' said Slightly instantly, 'there are birds called Wendies.'

'See, it comes,' cried Curly, pointing to Wendy in the heavens.

Wendy was now almost overhead, and they could hear her plaintive cry. But more distinct came the shrill voice of Tinker Bell. The jealous fairy had now cast off all disguise of friendship, and was darting at her victim from every direction, pinching savagely each time she touched.

'Hullo, Tink,' cried the wondering boys.

Tink's reply rang out: 'Peter wants you to shoot the Wendy.'

It was not in their nature to question when Peter ordered. 'Let us do what Peter wishes,' cried the simple boys. 'Quick, bows and arrows.'

All but Tootles popped down their trees. He had a bow and arrow with him, and Tink noted it, and rubbed her little hands.

'Quick, Tootles, quick,' she screamed. 'Peter will be so pleased.'

Tootles excitedly fitted the arrow to his bow. 'Out of the way, Tink,' he shouted; and, then he fired, and Wendy fluttered to the ground with an arrow in her breast.

CHAPTER 6

THE LITTLE HOUSE

FOOLISH Tootles was standing like a conqueror over Wendy's body when the other boys sprang, armed, from their trees.

'You are too late,' he cried proudly, 'I have shot the Wendy. Peter will be so pleased with me.'

Overhead Tinker Bell shouted 'Silly ass!' and darted into hiding. The others did not hear her. They had crowded round Wendy, and as they looked a terrible silence fell upon the wood. If Wendy's heart had been beating they would all have heard it.

Slightly was the first to speak. 'This is no bird,' he said in a scared voice. 'I think it must be a lady.'

'A lady?' said Tootles, and fell a-trembling.

'And we have killed her,' Nibs said hoarsely.

They all whipped off their caps.

'Now I see,' Curly said; 'Peter was bringing her to us.' He threw himself sorrowfully on the ground.

'A lady to take care of us at last,' said one of the twins, 'and you have killed her.'

They were sorry for him, but sorrier for themselves, and when he took a step nearer them they turned from him.

Tootles' face was very white, but there was a dignity about him now that had never been there before.

'I did it,' he said, reflecting. 'When ladies used to come to me in dreams, I said, "Pretty mother, pretty mother." But when at last she really came, I shot her.'

He moved slowly away.

'Don't go,' they called in pity.

'I must,' he answered, shaking; 'I am so afraid of Peter.'

It was at this tragic moment that they heard a sound which made the heart of every one of them rise to his mouth. They heard Peter crow.

'Peter!' they cried, for it was always thus that he signalled his return.

'Hide her,' they whispered, and gathered hastily around Wendy. But Tootles stood aloof.

Again came that ringing crow, and Peter dropped in front of them. 'Greeting, boys,' he cried, and mechanically they saluted, and then again was silence.

He frowned.

'I am back,' he said hotly, 'why do you not cheer?'

They opened their mouths, but the cheers would not come. He overlooked it in his haste to tell the glorious tidings.

'Great news, boys,' he cried. 'I have brought at last a mother for you all.'

Still no sound, except a little thud from Tootles as he dropped on his knees.

'Have you not seen her?' asked Peter, becoming troubled. 'She flew this way.'

'Ah me,' one voice said, and another said, 'Oh, mournful day.'

Tootles rose. 'Peter,' he said quietly, 'I will show her to you'; and when the others would still have hidden her he said, 'Back, twins, let Peter see.'

So they all stood back, and let him see, and after he had looked for a little time he did not know what to do next.

'She is dead,' he said uncomfortably. 'Perhaps she is frightened at being dead.'

He thought of hopping off in a comic sort of way till he was out of sight of her, and then never going near the spot any more. They would all have been glad to follow if he had done this.

But there was the arrow. He took it from her heart and faced his band.

'Whose arrow?' he demanded sternly.

'Mine, Peter,' said Tootles on his knees.

'Oh, dastard hand,' Peter said, and he raised the arrow to use it as a dagger.

Tootles did not flinch. He bared his breast. 'Strike, Peter,' he said firmly, 'strike true.'

Twice did Peter raise the arrow, and twice did his hand fall. 'I cannot strike,' he said with awe, 'there is something stays my hand.'

All looked at him in wonder, save Nibs, who fortunately looked at Wendy.

'It is she,' he cried, 'the Wendy lady; see, her arm.' Wonderful to relate, Wendy had raised her arm. Nibs bent over her and listened reverently. 'I think she said "Poor Tootles",' he whispered.

'She lives,' Peter said briefly.

Slightly cried instantly, 'The Wendy lady lives.'

Then Peter knelt beside her and found his button. You remember she had put it on a chain that she wore round her neck.

'See,' he said, 'the arrow struck against this. It is the kiss I gave her. It has saved her life.'

'I remember kisses,' Slightly interposed quickly, 'let me see it. Aye, that's a kiss.'

Peter did not hear him. He was begging Wendy to get better quickly, so that he could show her the mermaids. Of course she could not answer yet, being still in a frightful faint; but from overhead came a wailing note.

'Listen to Tink,' said Curly, 'she is crying because the Wendy lives.'

Then they had to tell Peter of Tink's crime, and almost never had they seen him look so stern.

'Listen, Tinker Bell,' he cried; 'I am your friend no more. Begone from me for ever.'

She flew on to his shoulder and pleaded, but he brushed her off. Not until Wendy again raised her arm did he relent sufficiently to say, 'Well, not for ever, but for a whole week.'

Do you think Tinker Bell was grateful to Wendy for raising her arm? Oh dear no, never wanted to pinch her so much. Fairies indeed are strange, and Peter, who understood them best, often cuffed them.

But what to do with Wendy in her present delicate state of health?

'Let us carry her down into the house,' Curly suggested.

'Aye,' said Slightly, 'that is what one does with ladies.'

'No, no,' Peter said, 'you must not touch her. It would not be sufficiently respectful.'

'That,' said Slightly, 'is what I was thinking.'

'But if she lies there,' Tootles said, 'she will die.'

'Aye, she will die,' Slightly admitted, 'but there is no way out.'

'Yes, there is,' cried Peter. 'Let us build a little house round her.'

They were all delighted. 'Quick,' he ordered them, 'bring me each of you the best of what we have. Gut our house. Be sharp.'

In a moment they were as busy as tailors the night before a wedding. They skurried this way and that, down for bedding, up for firewood, and while they were at it, who should appear but John and Michael. As they dragged along the ground they fell asleep standing, stopped, woke up, moved another step, and slept again.

'John, John,' Michael would cry, 'wake up. Where is Nana, John, and mother?'

And then John would rub his eyes and mutter, 'It is true, we did fly.'

You may be sure they were very relieved to find Peter.

'Hullo, Peter,' they said.

'Hullo,' replied Peter amicably, though he had quite forgotten them. He was very busy at the moment measuring Wendy with his feet to see how large a house she would need. Of course he meant to leave room for chairs and a table. John and Michael watched him.

'Is Wendy asleep?' they asked.

'Yes.'

'John,' Michael proposed, 'let us wake her and get her to make supper for us'; but as he said it some of the other boys rushed on carrying branches for the building of the house. 'Look at them!' he cried.

'Curly,' said Peter in his most captainy voice, 'see that these boys help in the building of the house.'

'Aye, aye, sir.'

'Build a house?' exclaimed John.

'For the Wendy,' said Curly.

'For Wendy?' John said, aghast. 'Why, she is only a girl.'

'That', explained Curly, 'is why we are her servants.'

'You? Wendy's servants!'

'Yes,' said Peter, 'and you also. Away with them.'

The astounded brothers were dragged away to hack and hew and carry. 'Chairs and a fender first,' Peter ordered. 'Then we shall build the house round them.'

'Aye,' said Slightly, 'that is how a house is built; it all comes back to me.'

Peter thought of everything. 'Slightly,' he ordered, 'fetch a doctor.'

'Aye, aye,' said Slightly at once, and disappeared, scratching his head. But he knew Peter must be obeyed, and he returned in a moment, wearing John's hat and looking solemn.

'Please, sir,' said Peter, going to him, 'are you a doctor?'

The difference between him and the other boys at such a time was that they knew it was make-believe, while to him make-believe and true were exactly the same thing. This sometimes troubled them, as when they had to make-believe that they had had their dinners.

If they broke down in their make-believe he rapped them on the knuckles.

'Yes, my little man,' anxiously replied Slightly, who had chapped knuckles.

'Please, sir,' Peter explained, 'a lady lies very ill.'

She was lying at their feet, but Slightly had the sense not to see her.

'Tut, tut, tut,' he said, 'where does she lie?'

'In yonder glade.'

'I will put a glass thing* in her mouth,' said Slightly; and he made-believe to do it, while Peter waited. It was an anxious moment when the glass thing was withdrawn.

'How is she?' inquired Peter.

'Tut, tut, tut,' said Slightly, 'this has cured her.'

'I am glad,' Peter cried.

'I will call again in the evening,' Slightly said; 'give her beef tea out of a cup with a spout to it'; but after he had returned the hat to John he blew big breaths, which was his habit on escaping from a difficulty.

In the meantime the wood had been alive with the sound of axes; almost everything needed for a cosy dwelling already lay at Wendy's feet.

'If only we knew,' said one, 'the kind of house she likes best.'

'Peter,' shouted another, 'she is moving in her sleep.'

'Her mouth opens,' cried a third, looking respectfully into it. 'Oh, lovely!'

'Perhaps she is going to sing in her sleep,' said Peter. 'Wendy, sing the kind of house you would like to have.'

Immediately, without opening her eyes, Wendy began to sing:

> 'I wish I had a pretty house,
> The littlest ever seen,
> With funny little red walls
> And roof of mossy green.'

They gurgled with joy at this, for by the greatest good luck the branches they had brought were sticky with red sap, and all the ground was carpeted with moss. As they rattled up the little house they broke into song themselves:

> 'We've built the little walls and roof
> And made a lovely door,
> So tell us, mother Wendy,
> What are you wanting more?'

To this she answered rather greedily:

> 'Oh, really, next I think I'll have
> Gay windows all about,

> With roses peeping in, you know,
> And babies peeping out.'

With a blow of their fists they made windows, and large yellow leaves were the blinds. But roses————?

'Roses,' cried Peter sternly.

Quickly they made-believe to grow the loveliest roses up the walls. Babies?

To prevent Peter ordering babies they hurried into song again:

> 'We've made the roses peeping out,
> The babes are at the door,
> We cannot make ourselves, you know,
> 'Cos we've been made before.'

Peter, seeing this to be a good idea, at once pretended that it was his own. The house was quite beautiful, and no doubt Wendy was very cosy within, though, of course, they could no longer see her. Peter strode up and down, ordering finishing touches. Nothing escaped his eagle eye. Just when it seemed absolutely finished:

'There's no knocker on the door,' he said.

They were very ashamed, but Tootles gave the sole of his shoe, and it made an excellent knocker.

Absolutely finished now, they thought.

Not a bit of it. 'There's no chimney,' Peter said; 'we must have a chimney.'

'It certainly does need a chimney,' said John importantly. This gave Peter an idea. He snatched the hat off John's head, knocked out the bottom, and put the hat on the roof. The little house was so pleased to have such a capital* chimney that, as if to say thank you, smoke immediately began to come out of the hat.

Now really and truly it was finished. Nothing remained to do but to knock.

'All look your best,' Peter warned them; 'first impressions are awfully important.'

He was glad no one asked him what first impressions are; they were all too busy looking their best.

He knocked politely; and now the wood was as still as the children, not a sound to be heard except from Tinker Bell, who was watching from a branch and openly sneering.

What the boys were wondering was, would anyone answer the knock? If a lady, what would she be like?

The door opened and a lady came out. It was Wendy. They all whipped off their hats.

She looked properly surprised, and this was just how they had hoped she would look.

'Where am I?' she said.

Of course Slightly was the first to get his word in. 'Wendy lady,' he said rapidly, 'for you we built this house.'

'Oh, say you're pleased,' cried Nibs.

'Lovely, darling house,' Wendy said, and they were the very words they had hoped she would say.

'And we are your children,' cried the twins.

Then all went on their knees, and holding out their arms cried, 'O Wendy lady, be our mother.'

'Ought I?' Wendy said, all shining. 'Of course it's frightfully fascinating, but you see I am only a little girl. I have no real experience.'

'That doesn't matter,' said Peter, as if he were the only person present who knew all about it, though he was really the one who knew least. 'What we need is just a nice motherly person.'

'Oh dear!' Wendy said, 'you see I feel that is exactly what I am.'

'It is, it is,' they all cried; 'we saw it at once.'

'Very well,' she said, 'I will do my best. Come inside at once, you naughty children; I am sure your feet are damp. And before I put you to bed I have just time to finish the story of Cinderella.'

In they went; I don't know how there was room for them, but you can squeeze very tight in the Neverland. And that was the first of the many joyous evenings they had with Wendy. By and by she tucked them up in the great bed in the home under the trees, but she herself slept that night in the little house, and Peter kept watch outside with drawn sword, for the pirates could be heard carousing far away and the wolves were on the prowl. The little house looked so cosy and safe in the darkness, with a bright light showing through its blinds, and the chimney smoking beautifully, and Peter standing on guard.

After a time he fell asleep, and some unsteady fairies had to climb over him on their way home from an orgy.* Any of the other boys obstructing the fairy path at night they would have mischiefed, but they just tweaked Peter's nose and passed on.

PETER ON GUARD

CHAPTER 7

THE HOME UNDER THE GROUND

ONE of the first things Peter did next day was to measure Wendy and John and Michael for hollow trees. Hook, you remember, had sneered at the boys for thinking they needed a tree apiece, but this was ignorance, for unless your tree fitted you it was difficult to go up and down, and no two of the boys were quite the same size. Once you fitted, you drew in your breath at the top, and down you went at exactly the right speed, while to ascend you drew in and let out alternately, and so wriggled up. Of course, when you have mastered the action you are able to do these things without thinking of them, and then nothing can be more graceful.

But you simply must fit, and Peter measures you for your tree as carefully as for a suit of clothes: the only difference being that the clothes are made to fit you, while you have to be made to fit the tree. Usually it is done quite easily, as by your wearing too many garments or too few; but if you are bumpy in awkward places or the only available tree is an odd shape, Peter does some things to you, and after that you fit. Once you fit, great care must be taken to go on fitting, and this, as Wendy was to discover to her delight, keeps a whole family in perfect condition.

Wendy and Michael fitted their trees at the first try, but John had to be altered a little.

After a few days' practice they could go up and down as gaily as buckets in a well. And how ardently they grew to love their home under the ground; especially Wendy. It consisted of one large room, as all houses should do, with a floor in which you could dig if you wanted to go fishing, and in this floor grew stout mushrooms of a charming colour, which were used as stools. A Never tree tried hard to grow in the centre of the room, but every morning they sawed the trunk through, level with the floor. By tea-time it was always about two feet high, and then they put a door on top of it, the whole thus becoming a table; as soon as they cleared away, they sawed off the trunk again, and thus there was more room to play. There was an enormous fire-place which was in almost any part of the room where you cared to light it, and across this Wendy stretched strings, made of fibre, from which she suspended her washing. The bed was tilted against the wall by day, and let down at 6.30, when it filled nearly half the room; and all the boys except Michael slept in it, lying like sardines in a tin. There was a strict rule against turning round until one gave the signal, when all turned at once. Michael should have used it also; but Wendy would have a baby, and he was the littlest, and you know what women are, and the short and the long of it is that he was hung up in a basket.

It was rough and simple, and not unlike what baby bears would have made of an underground house in the same circumstances. But there was one recess in the wall, no larger than a bird-cage, which was the private apartment of Tinker Bell. It could be shut off from the rest of the home by a tiny curtain, which Tink, who was most fastidious, always kept drawn when dressing or undressing. No woman, however large, could have had a more exquisite boudoir and bedchamber combined. The couch, as she always called it, was a genuine Queen Mab,* with club legs; and she varied the bedspreads according to what fruit-blossom was in season. Her mirror was a Puss-in-boots,* of which there are now only three, unchipped, known to the fairy dealers; the wash-stand was Pie-crust and reversible, the chest of drawers an authentic Charming the Sixth,* and the carpet and rugs of the best (the early) period of Margery and Robin.* There was a chandelier from Tiddlywinks* for the look of the thing, but of course she lit the residence herself. Tink was very contemptuous of the rest of the house, as indeed was perhaps inevitable; and her chamber, though beautiful, looked rather conceited, having the appearance of a nose permanently turned up.

I suppose it was all especially entrancing to Wendy, because those rampageous* boys of hers gave her so much to do. Really there were whole weeks when, except perhaps with a stocking in the evening, she was never above ground. The cooking, I can tell you, kept her nose to the pot. Their chief food was roasted breadfruit, yams, coconuts, baked pig, mammee-apples, tappa rolls, and bananas, washed down with calabashes of poe-poe;* but you never exactly knew whether there would be a real meal or just a make-believe, it all depended upon Peter's whim. He could eat, really eat, if it was part of a game, but he could not stodge just to feel stodgy, which is what most children like better than anything else; the next best thing being to talk about it. Make-believe was so real to him that during a meal of it you could see him getting rounder. Of course it was trying, but you simply had to follow his lead, and if you could prove to him that you were getting loose for your tree he let you stodge.

Wendy's favourite time for sewing and darning was after they had all gone to bed. Then, as she expressed it, she had a breathing time for herself; and she occupied it in making new things for them, and putting double pieces on the knees, for they were all most frightfully hard on their knees.

When she sat down to a basketful of their stockings, every heel with a hole in it, she would fling up her arms and exclaim, 'Oh dear, I am sure I sometimes think spinsters are to be envied.'

Her face beamed when she exclaimed this.

You remember about her pet wolf. Well, it very soon discovered that she had come to the island and it found her out, and they just ran into each other's arms. After that it followed her about everywhere.

As time wore on did she think much about the beloved parents she had left behind her? This is a difficult question, because it is quite impossible to say how time does wear on in the Neverland, where it is calculated by moons and suns, and there are ever so many more of them than on the mainland. But I am afraid that Wendy did not really worry about her father and mother; she was absolutely confident that they would always keep the window open for her to fly back by, and this gave her complete ease of mind. What did disturb her at times was that John remembered his parents vaguely only, as people he had once known, while Michael was quite willing to believe that she was really his mother. These things scared her a little, and nobly anxious to do her duty, she tried to fix the old life in their minds by setting them examination papers on it, as like as possible to the ones she used to do at school. The other boys thought this awfully interesting, and insisted on joining, and they made slates* for themselves, and sat round the table, writing and thinking hard about the questions she had written on another slate and passed round. They were the most ordinary questions—'What was the colour of Mother's eyes? Which was taller, Father or Mother? Was Mother blonde or brunette? Answer all three questions if possible.' '(A) Write an essay of not less than 40 words on How I spent my last Holidays, or The Characters of Father and Mother compared. Only one of these to be attempted.' Or '(1) Describe Mother's laugh; (2) Describe Father's laugh; (3) Describe Mother's Party Dress; (4) Describe the Kennel and its Inmate.'

They were just everyday questions like these, and when you could not answer them you were told to make a cross; and it was really dreadful what a number of crosses even John made. Of course the only boy who replied to every question was Slightly, and no one could have been more hopeful of coming out first, but his answers were perfectly ridiculous, and he really came out last: a melancholy thing.

Peter did not compete. For one thing he despised all mothers except Wendy, and for another he was the only boy on the island who could neither write nor spell; not the smallest word. He was above all that sort of thing.

By the way, the questions were all written in the past tense. What was the colour of Mother's eyes, and so on. Wendy, you see, had been forgetting too.

Adventures, of course, as we shall see, were of daily occurrence; but about this time Peter invented, with Wendy's help, a new game that fascinated him enormously, until he suddenly had no more interest in it, which, as you have been told, was what always happened with his games. It consisted in pretending not to have adventures, in doing the sort of thing John and Michael had been doing all their lives: sitting on stools flinging balls in the air, pushing each other, going out for walks and coming back without having killed so much as a grizzly. To see Peter doing nothing on a stool was a great sight; he could not help looking solemn at such times, to sit still seemed to him such a comic thing to do. He boasted that he had gone for a walk for the good of his health. For several suns these were the most novel of all adventures to him; and John and Michael had to pretend to be delighted also; otherwise he would have treated them severely.

He often went out alone, and when he came back you were never absolutely certain whether he had had an adventure or not. He might have forgotten it so completely that he said nothing about it; and then when you went out you found the body; and, on the other hand, he might say a great deal about it, and yet you could not find the body. Sometimes he came home with his head bandaged, and then Wendy cooed over him and bathed it in lukewarm water, while he told a dazzling tale. But she was never quite sure, you know. There were, however, many adventures which she knew to be true because she was in them herself, and there were still more that were at least partly true, for the other boys were in them and said they were wholly true. To describe them all would require a book as large as an English–Latin,

Latin–English Dictionary, and the most we can do is to give one as a specimen of an average hour on the island. The difficulty is which one to choose. Should we take the brush with the redskins at Slightly Gulch? It was a sanguinary* affair, and especially interesting as showing one of Peter's peculiarities, which was that in the middle of a fight he would suddenly change sides. At the Gulch, when victory was still in the balance, sometimes leaning this way and sometimes that, he called out, 'I'm redskin today; what are you, Tootles?' And Tootles answered, 'Redskin; what are you, Nibs?' and Nibs said, 'Redskin; what are you, Twin?' and so on; and they were all redskin; and of course this would have ended the fight had not the real redskins, fascinated by Peter's methods, agreed to be lost boys for that once, and so at it they all went again, more fiercely than ever.

The extraordinary upshot of this adventure was—but we have not decided yet that this is the adventure we are to narrate. Perhaps a better one would be the night attack by the redskins on the house under the ground, when several of them stuck in the hollow trees and had to be pulled out like corks. Or we might tell how Peter saved Tiger Lily's life in the Mermaids' Lagoon, and so made her his ally.

Or we could tell of that cake the pirates cooked so that the boys might eat it and perish; and how they placed it in one cunning spot after another; but always Wendy snatched it from the hands of her children, so that in time it lost its succulence, and became as hard as a stone, and was used as a missile, and Hook fell over it in the dark.

Or suppose we tell of the birds that were Peter's friends, particularly of the Never bird that built in a tree overhanging the lagoon, and how the nest fell into the water, and still the bird sat on her eggs, and Peter gave orders that she was not to be disturbed. That is a pretty story, and the end shows how grateful a bird can be; but if we tell it we must also tell the whole adventure of the lagoon, which would of course be telling two adventures rather than just one. A shorter adventure, and quite as exciting, was Tinker Bell's attempt, with the help of some street fairies, to have the sleeping Wendy conveyed on a great floating leaf to the mainland. Fortunately the leaf gave way and Wendy woke, thinking it was bath-time, and swam back. Or again, we might choose Peter's defiance of the lions, when he drew a circle round him on the ground with an arrow and defied them to cross it; and though he waited for hours, with the other boys and Wendy looking on breathlessly from trees, not one of them dared to accept his challenge.

Which of these adventures shall we choose? The best way will be to toss for it.

I have tossed, and the lagoon has won. This almost makes one wish that the gulch or the cake or Tink's leaf had won. Of course I could do it again, and make it best out of three; however, perhaps fairest to stick to the lagoon.

CHAPTER 8

IF you shut your eyes and are a lucky one, you may see at times a shapeless pool of lovely pale colours suspended in the darkness; then if you squeeze your eyes tighter, the pool begins to take shape, and the colours become so vivid that with another squeeze they must go on fire. But just before they go on fire you see the lagoon. This is the nearest you ever get to it on the mainland, just one heavenly moment; if there could be two moments you might see the surf and hear the mermaids singing.

The children often spent long summer days on this lagoon, swimming or floating most of the time, playing the mermaid games in the water, and so forth. You must not think from this that the mermaids were on friendly terms with them; on the contrary, it was among Wendy's lasting regrets that all the time she was on the island she never had a civil word from one of them. When she stole softly to the edge of the lagoon she might see them by the score, especially on Marooners' Rock, where they loved to bask, combing out their hair in a lazy way that quite irritated her; or she might even swim, on tiptoe as it were, to within a yard of them, but then they saw her and dived, probably splashing her with their tails, not by accident, but intentionally.

They treated all the boys in the same way, except of course Peter, who chatted with them on Marooners' Rock by the hour, and sat on their tails when they got cheeky. He gave Wendy one of their combs.

The most haunting time at which to see them is at the turn of the moon, when they utter strange wailing cries; but the lagoon is dangerous for mortals then, and until the evening of which we have now to tell, Wendy had never seen the lagoon by moonlight, less from fear, for of course Peter would have accompanied her, than because she had strict rules about every one being in bed by seven. She was often at the lagoon, however, on sunny days after rain, when the mermaids come up in extraordinary numbers to play with their bubbles. The bubbles of many colours made in rainbow water they treat as balls, hitting them gaily from one to another with their tails, and trying to keep them in the rainbow till they burst. The goals are at each end of the rainbow, and the keepers only are allowed to use their hands.

SUMMER DAYS ON THE LAGOON

Sometimes hundreds of mermaids will be playing in the lagoon at a time, and it is quite a pretty sight.

But the moment the children tried to join in they had to play by themselves, for the mermaids immediately disappeared. Nevertheless we have proof that they secretly watched the interlopers, and were not above taking an idea from them; for John introduced a new way of hitting the bubble, with the head instead of the hand, and the mermaid goal-keepers adopted it. This is the one mark that John has left on the Neverland.

It must also have been rather pretty to see the children resting on a rock for half an hour after their midday meal. Wendy insisted on their doing this, and it had to be a real rest even though the meal was make-believe. So they lay there in the sun, and their bodies glistened in it, while she sat beside them and looked important.

It was one such day, and they were all on Marooners' Rock. The rock was not much larger than their great bed, but of course they all knew how not to take up much room, and they were dozing, or at least lying with their eyes shut, and pinching occasionally when they thought Wendy was not looking. She was very busy, stitching.

While she stitched a change came to the lagoon. Little shivers ran over it, and the sun went away and shadows stole across the water, turning it cold. Wendy could no longer see to thread her needle, and when she looked up, the lagoon that had always hitherto been such a laughing place seemed formidable and unfriendly.

It was not, she knew, that night had come, but something as dark as night had come. No, worse than that. It had not come, but it had sent that shiver through the sea to say that it was coming. What was it?

There crowded upon her all the stories she had been told of Marooners' Rock, so called because evil captains put sailors on it and leave them there to drown. They drown when the tide rises, for then it is submerged.

Of course she should have roused the children at once; not merely because of the unknown that was stalking toward them, but because it was no longer good for them to sleep on a rock grown chilly. But she was a young mother and she did not know this; she thought you simply must stick to your rule about half an hour after the midday meal. So, though fear was upon her, and she longed to hear male voices, she would not waken them. Even when she heard the sound of muffled oars,* though her heart was in her mouth, she did not waken them. She stood over them to let them have their sleep out. Was it not brave of Wendy?

It was well for those boys then that there was one among them who could sniff danger even in his sleep. Peter sprang erect, as wide awake at once as a dog, and with one warning cry he roused the others.

He stood motionless, one hand to his ear.

'Pirates!' he cried. The others came closer to him. A strange smile was playing about his face, and Wendy saw it and shuddered. While that smile was on his face no one dared address him; all they could do was to stand ready to obey. The order came sharp and incisive.

'Dive!'

There was a gleam of legs, and instantly the lagoon seemed deserted. Marooners' Rock stood alone in the forbidding waters, as if it were itself marooned.

The boat drew nearer. It was the pirate dinghy, with three figures in her, Smee and Starkey, and the third a captive, no other than Tiger Lily. Her hands and ankles were tied, and she knew what was to be her fate. She was to be left on the rock to perish, an end to one of her race more terrible than death by fire or torture, for is it not written in the book of the tribe that there is no path through water to the happy hunting-ground? Yet her face was impassive; she was the daughter of a chief, she must die as a chief's daughter, it is enough.

They had caught her boarding the pirate ship with a knife in her mouth. No watch was kept on the ship, it being Hook's boast that the wind of his name guarded the ship for a mile around. Now her fate would help to guard it also. One more wail would go the round in that wind by night.

In the gloom that they brought with them the two pirates did not see the rock till they crashed into it.

'Luff, you lubber,'* cried an Irish voice that was Smee's; 'here's the rock. Now, then, what we have to do is to hoist the redskin on to it, and leave her there to drown.'

It was the work of one brutal moment to land the beautiful girl on the rock; she was too proud to offer a vain resistance.

Quite near the rock, but out of sight, two heads were bobbing up and down, Peter's and Wendy's. Wendy was crying, for it was the first tragedy she had seen. Peter had seen many tragedies, but he had forgotten them all. He was less sorry than Wendy for Tiger Lily; it was two against one that angered him, and he meant to save her. An easy way would have been to wait until the pirates had gone, but he was never one to choose the easy way.

There was almost nothing he could not do, and he now imitated the voice of Hook.

'Ahoy there, you lubbers,' he called. It was a marvellous imitation.

'The captain,' said the pirates, staring at each other in surprise.

'He must be swimming out to us,' Starkey said, when they had looked for him in vain.

'We are putting the redskin on the rock,' Smee called out.

'Set her free,' came the astonishing answer.

'Free!'

'Yes, cut her bonds and let her go.'

'But, captain————'

'At once, d'ye hear,' cried Peter, 'or I'll plunge my hook in you.'

'This is queer,' Smee gasped.

'Better do what the captain orders,' said Starkey nervously.

'Aye, aye,' Smee said, and he cut Tiger Lily's cords. At once like an eel she slid between Starkey's legs into the water.

Of course Wendy was very elated over Peter's cleverness; but she knew that he would be elated also and very likely crow and thus betray himself, so at once her hand went out to cover his mouth. But it was stayed even in the act, for 'Boat ahoy!' rang over the lagoon in Hook's voice, and this time it was not Peter who had spoken.

Peter may have been about to crow, but his face puckered in a whistle of surprise instead.

'Boat ahoy!' again came the cry.

Now Wendy understood. The real Hook was also in the water.

He was swimming to the boat, and as his men showed a light to guide him he had soon reached them. In the light of the lantern Wendy saw his hook grip the boat's side; she saw his evil swarthy face as he rose dripping from the water, and, quaking, she would have liked to swim away, but Peter would not budge. He was tingling with life and also top-heavy with conceit. 'Am I not a wonder, oh, I am a wonder!' he whispered to her; and though she thought so also, she was really glad for the sake of his reputation that no one heard him except herself.

He signed to her to listen.

The two pirates were very curious to know what had brought their captain to them, but he sat with his head on his hook in a position of profound melancholy.

'Captain, is all well?' they asked timidly, but he answered with a hollow moan.

'He sighs,' said Smee.

'He sighs again,' said Starkey.

'And yet a third time he sighs,' said Smee.

'What's up, captain?'

Then at last he spoke passionately.

'The game's up,' he cried, 'those boys have found a mother.'

Affrighted though she was, Wendy swelled with pride.

'O evil day,' cried Starkey.

'What's a mother?' asked the ignorant Smee.

Wendy was so shocked that she exclaimed, 'He doesn't know!' and always after this she felt that if you could have a pet pirate Smee would be her one.

Peter pulled her beneath the water, for Hook had started up, crying, 'What was that?'

'I heard nothing,' said Starkey, raising the lantern over the waters, and as the pirates looked they saw a strange sight. It was the nest I have told you of, floating on the lagoon, and the Never bird was sitting on it.

'See,' said Hook in answer to Smee's question, 'that is a mother. What a lesson. The nest must have fallen into the water, but would the mother desert her eggs? No.'

There was a break in his voice, as if for a moment he recalled innocent days when—but he brushed away this weakness with his hook.

Smee, much impressed, gazed at the bird as the nest was borne past, but the more suspicious Starkey said, 'If she is a mother, perhaps she is hanging about here to help Peter.'

Hook winced. 'Aye,' he said, 'that is the fear that haunts me.'

He was roused from this dejection by Smee's eager voice.

'Captain,' said Smee, 'could we not kidnap these boys' mother and make her our mother?'

'It is a princely scheme,' cried Hook, and at once it took practical shape in his great brain. 'We will seize the children and carry them to the boat: the boys we will make walk the plank, and Wendy shall be our mother.'

Again Wendy forgot herself.

'Never!' she cried, and bobbed.

'What was that?'

But they could see nothing. They thought it must have been but a leaf in the wind. 'Do you agree, my bullies?' asked Hook.

'There is my hand on it,' they both said.

'And there is my hook. Swear.'

They all swore. By this time they were on the rock, and suddenly Hook remembered Tiger Lily.

'Where is the redskin?' he demanded abruptly.

He had a playful humour at moments, and they thought this was one of the moments.

'That is all right, captain,' Smee answered complacently, 'we let her go.'

'Let her go!' cried Hook.

''Twas your own orders,' the bos'un faltered.

'You called over the water to us to let her go,' said Starkey.

'Brimstone and gall,'* thundered Hook, 'what cozening* is here?' His face had gone black with rage, but he saw that they believed their words, and he was startled. 'Lads,' he said, shaking a little, 'I gave no such order.'

'It is passing queer,' Smee said, and they all fidgeted uncomfortably. Hook raised his voice, but there was a quiver in it.

'Spirit that haunts this dark lagoon tonight,' he cried, 'dost hear me?'

Of course Peter should have kept quiet, but of course he did not. He immediately answered in Hook's voice:

'Odds, bobs, hammer and tongs, I hear you.'

In that supreme moment Hook did not blanch, even at the gills, but Smee and Starkey clung to each other in terror.

'Who are you, stranger, speak?' Hook demanded.

'I am James Hook,' replied the voice, 'captain of the *Jolly Roger*.'

'You are not; you are not,' Hook cried hoarsely.

'Brimstone and gall,' the voice retorted, 'say that again, and I'll cast anchor in you.'

Hook tried a more ingratiating manner. 'If you are Hook,' he said almost humbly, 'come, tell me, who am I?'

'A codfish,' replied the voice, 'only a codfish.'

'A codfish!' Hook echoed blankly; and it was then, but not till then, that his proud spirit broke. He saw his men draw back from him.

'Have we been captained all this time by a codfish?' they muttered. 'It is lowering to our pride.'

They were his dogs snapping at him, but, tragic figure though he had become, he scarcely heeded them. Against such fearful evidence it was not their belief in him that he needed, it was his own. He felt his ego slipping from him. 'Don't desert me, bully,'* he whispered hoarsely to it.

In his dark nature there was a touch of the feminine, as in all the great pirates, and it sometimes gave him intuitions. Suddenly he tried the guessing game.

'Hook,' he called, 'have you another voice?'

Now Peter could never resist a game, and he answered blithely in his own voice, 'I have.'

'And another name?'

'Aye, aye.'

'Vegetable?' asked Hook.

'No.'

'Mineral?'

'No.'

'Animal?'

'Yes.'

'Man?'

'No!' This answer rang out scornfully.

'Boy?'

'Yes.'

'Ordinary boy?'

'No!'

'Wonderful boy?'

To Wendy's pain the answer that rang out this time was 'Yes.'

'Are you in England?'

'No.'

'Are you here?'

'Yes.'

Hook was completely puzzled. 'You ask him some questions,' he said to the others, wiping his damp brow.

Smee reflected. 'I can't think of a thing,' he said regretfully.

'Can't guess, can't guess,' crowed Peter. 'Do you give it up?'

Of course in his pride he was carrying the game too far, and the miscreants saw their chance.

'Yes, yes,' they answered eagerly.

'Well, then,' he cried, 'I am Peter Pan.'

Pan!

In a moment Hook was himself again, and Smee and Starkey were his faithful henchmen.

'Now we have him,' Hook shouted. 'Into the water, Smee. Starkey, mind the boat. Take him dead or alive.'

He leaped as he spoke, and simultaneously came the gay voice of Peter.

'Are you ready, boys?'

'Aye, aye,' from various parts of the lagoon.

'Then lam into* the pirates.'

The fight was short and sharp. First to draw blood was John, who gallantly climbed into the boat and held Starkey. There was a fierce struggle, in which the cutlass was torn from the pirate's grasp. He wriggled overboard and John leapt after him. The dinghy drifted away.

Here and there a head bobbed up in the water, and there was a flash of steel followed by a cry or a whoop. In the confusion some struck at their own side. The corkscrew of Smee got Tootles in the fourth rib, but he was himself pinked* in turn by Curly. Farther from the rock Starkey was pressing Slightly and the twins hard.

Where all this time was Peter? He was seeking bigger game.

The others were all brave boys, and they must not be blamed for backing from the pirate captain. His iron claw made a circle of dead water round him, from which they fled like affrighted fishes.

But there was one who did not fear him: there was one prepared to enter that circle.

Strangely, it was not in the water that they met. Hook rose to the rock to breathe, and at the same moment Peter scaled it on the opposite side. The rock was slippery as a ball, and they had to crawl rather than climb. Neither knew that the other was coming. Each feeling for a grip met the other's arm: in surprise they raised their heads; their faces were almost touching; so they met.

Some of the greatest heroes have confessed that just before they fell to they had a sinking. Had it been so with Peter at that moment I would admit it. After all, this was the only man that the Sea-Cook had feared. But Peter had no sinking, he had one feeling only, gladness; and he gnashed his pretty teeth with joy. Quick as thought he snatched a knife from Hook's belt and was about to drive it home, when he saw that he was higher up the rock than his foe. It would not have been fighting fair. He gave the pirate a hand to help him up.

It was then that Hook bit him.

Not the pain of this but its unfairness was what dazed Peter. It made him quite helpless. He could only stare, horrified. Every child is affected thus the first time he is treated unfairly. All he thinks he has a right to when he comes to you to be yours is fairness. After you have been unfair to him he will love you again, but he will never afterwards be quite the same boy. No one ever gets over the first unfairness; no one except Peter. He often met it, but he always forgot it. I suppose that was the real difference between him and all the rest.

So when he met it now it was like the first time; and he could just stare, helpless. Twice the iron hand clawed him.

A few minutes afterwards the other boys saw Hook in the water striking wildly for the ship; no elation on his pestilent face now, only white fear, for the crocodile was in dogged pursuit of him. On ordinary occasions the boys would have swum alongside cheering; but now they were uneasy, for they had lost both Peter and Wendy, and were scouring the lagoon for them, calling them by name. They found the dinghy and went home in it, shouting, 'Peter, Wendy' as they went, but no answer came save mocking laughter from the mermaids. 'They must be swimming back or flying,' the boys concluded. They were not very anxious, they had such faith in Peter. They chuckled, boylike, because they would be late for bed; and it was all Mother Wendy's fault!

When their voices died away there came cold silence over the lagoon, and then a feeble cry.

'Help, help!'

Two small figures were beating against the rock; the girl had fainted and lay on the boy's arm. With a last effort Peter pulled her up the rock and then lay down beside her. Even as he also fainted he saw that the water was rising. He knew that they would soon be drowned, but he could do no more.

As they lay side by side a mermaid caught Wendy by the feet, and began pulling her softly into the water. Peter, feeling her slip from him, woke with a start, and was just in time to draw her back. But he had to tell her the truth.

'We are on the rock, Wendy,' he said, 'but it is growing smaller. Soon the water will be over it.'

She did not understand even now.

'We must go,' she said, almost brightly.

'Yes,' he answered faintly.

'Shall we swim or fly, Peter?'

He had to tell her.

'Do you think you could swim or fly as far as the island, Wendy, without my help?'

She had to admit that she was too tired.

He moaned.

'What is it?' she asked, anxious about him at once.

'I can't help you, Wendy. Hook wounded me. I can neither fly nor swim.'

'Do you mean we shall both be drowned?'

'Look how the water is rising.'

They put their hands over their eyes to shut out the sight. They thought they would soon be no more. As they sat thus something brushed against Peter as light as a kiss, and stayed there, as if saying timidly, 'Can I be of any use?'

It was the tail of a kite, which Michael had made some days before. It had torn itself out of his hand and floated away.

'Michael's kite,' Peter said without interest, but next moment he had seized the tail, and was pulling the kite toward him.

'It lifted Michael off the ground,' he cried; 'why should it not carry you?'

'Both of us!'

'It can't lift two; Michael and Curly tried.'

'Let us draw lots,' Wendy said bravely.

'And you a lady; never.' Already he had tied the tail round her. She clung to him; she refused to go without him; but with a 'Good-bye, Wendy,' he pushed her from the rock; and in a few minutes she was borne out of his sight. Peter was alone on the lagoon.

The rock was very small now; soon it would be submerged. Pale rays of light tiptoed across the waters; and by and by there was to be heard a sound at once the most musical and the most melancholy in the world: the mermaids calling to the moon.

Peter was not quite like other boys; but he was afraid at last. A tremor ran through him, like a shudder passing over the sea; but on the sea one shudder follows another till there are hundreds of them, and Peter felt just the one. Next moment he was standing erect on the rock again, with that smile on his face and a drum beating within him. It was saying, 'To die will be an awfully big adventure.'*

"TO DIE WILL BE AN AWFULLY BIG ADVENTURE?"

THE last sounds Peter heard before he was quite alone were the mermaids retiring one by one to their bed-chambers under the sea. He was too far away to hear their doors shut; but every door in the coral caves where they live rings a tiny bell when it opens or closes (as in all the nicest houses on the mainland), and he heard the bells.

Steadily the waters rose till they were nibbling at his feet; and to pass the time until they made their final gulp, he watched the only thing moving on the lagoon. He thought it was a piece of floating paper, perhaps part of the kite, and wondered idly how long it would take to drift ashore.

Presently he noticed as an odd thing that it was undoubtedly out upon the lagoon with some definite purpose, for it was fighting the tide, and sometimes winning; and when it won, Peter, always sympathetic to the weaker side, could not help clapping; it was such a gallant piece of paper.

It was not really a piece of paper; it was the Never bird, making desperate efforts to reach Peter on her nest. By working her wings, in a way she had learned since the nest fell into the water, she was able to some extent to guide her strange craft, but by the time Peter recognized her she was very exhausted. She had come to save him, to give him her nest, though there were eggs in it. I rather wonder at the bird, for though he had been nice to her, he had also sometimes tormented her. I can suppose only that, like Mrs Darling and the rest of them, she was melted because he had all his first teeth.

She called out to him what she had come for, and he called out to her what was she doing there; but of course neither of them understood the other's language. In fanciful stories people can talk to the birds freely, and I wish for the moment I could pretend that this was such a story, and say that Peter replied intelligently to the Never bird; but truth is best, and I want to tell only what really happened. Well, not only could they not understand each other, but they forgot their manners.

'I—want—you—to—get—into—the—nest,' the bird called, speaking as slowly and distinctly as possible, 'and—then—you—can—

drift—ashore, but—I—am—too—tired—to—bring—it—any—nearer—so—you—must—try—to—swim—to—it.'

'What are you quacking about?' Peter answered. 'Why don't you let the nest drift as usual?'

'I—want—you—' the bird said, and repeated it all over.

Then Peter tried slow and distinct.

'What—are—you—quacking—about?' and so on.

The Never bird became irritated; they have very short tempers.

'You dunderheaded little jay,'* she screamed, 'why don't you do as I tell you?'

Peter felt that she was calling him names, and at a venture he retorted hotly:

'So are you!'

Then rather curiously they both snapped out the same remark:

'Shut up!'

'Shut up!'

Nevertheless the bird was determined to save him if she could, and by one last mighty effort she propelled the nest against the rock. Then up she flew; deserting her eggs, so as to make her meaning clear.

Then at last he understood, and clutched the nest and waved his thanks to the bird as she fluttered overhead. It was not to receive his thanks, however, that she hung there in the sky; it was not even to watch him get into the nest; it was to see what he did with her eggs.

There were two large white eggs, and Peter lifted them up and reflected. The bird covered her face with her wings, so as not to see the last of her eggs; but she could not help peeping between the feathers.

I forget whether I have told you that there was a stave on the rock, driven into it by some buccaneers of long ago to mark the site of buried treasure. The children had discovered the glittering hoard, and when in mischievous mood used to fling showers of moidores, diamonds, pearls, and pieces of eight to the gulls, who pounced upon them for food, and then flew away, raging at the scurvy trick that had been played upon them. The stave was still there, and on it Starkey had hung his hat, a deep tarpaulin, watertight, with a broad brim. Peter put the eggs into this hat and set it on the lagoon. It floated beautifully.

The Never bird saw at once what he was up to, and screamed her admiration of him; and, alas, Peter crowed his agreement with her.

Then he got into the nest, reared the stave in it as a mast, and hung up his shirt for a sail. At the same moment the bird fluttered down upon the hat and once more sat snugly on her eggs. She drifted in one direction, and he was borne off in another, both cheering.

Of course when Peter landed he beached his barque* in a place where the bird would easily find it; but the hat was such a great success that she abandoned the nest. It drifted about till it went to pieces, and often Starkey came to the shore of the lagoon, and with many bitter feelings watched the bird sitting on his hat. As we shall not see her again, it may be worth mentioning here that all Never birds now build in that shape of nest, with a broad brim on which the youngsters take an airing.

Great were the rejoicings when Peter reached the home under the ground almost as soon as Wendy, who had been carried hither and thither by the kite. Every boy had adventures to tell; but perhaps the biggest adventure of all was that they were several hours late for bed. This so inflated them that they did various dodgy things to get staying up still longer, such as demanding bandages; but Wendy, though glorying in having them all home again safe and sound, was scandalized by the lateness of the hour, and cried, 'To bed, to bed,' in a voice that had to be obeyed. Next day, however, she was awfully tender, and gave out bandages to every one; and they played till bedtime at limping about and carrying their arms in slings.

CHAPTER 10

THE HAPPY HOME

ONE important result of the brush on the lagoon was that it made the redskins their friends. Peter had saved Tiger Lily from a dreadful fate, and now there was nothing she and her braves would not do for him. All night they sat above, keeping watch over the home under the ground and awaiting the big attack by the pirates which obviously could not be much longer delayed. Even by day they hung about, smoking the pipe of peace, and looking almost as if they wanted tit-bits to eat.

They called Peter the Great White Father, prostrating themselves before him; and he liked this tremendously, so that it was not really good for him.

'The Great White Father,' he would say to them in a very lordly manner, as they grovelled at his feet, 'is glad to see the Piccaninny warriors protecting his wigwam from the pirates.'

'Me Tiger Lily,' that lovely creature would reply. 'Peter Pan save me, me his velly nice friend. Me no let pirates hurt him.'

She was far too pretty to cringe in this way, but Peter thought it his due, and he would answer condescendingly, 'It is good. Peter Pan has spoken.'

Always when he said 'Peter Pan has spoken', it meant that they must now shut up, and they accepted it humbly in that spirit; but they were by no means so respectful to the other boys, whom they looked upon as just ordinary braves. They said 'How-do?' to them, and things like that; and what annoyed the boys was that Peter seemed to think this all right.

Secretly Wendy sympathized with them a little, but she was far too loyal a housewife to listen to any complaints against father. 'Father knows best,' she always said, whatever her private opinion must be. Her private opinion was that the redskins should not call her a squaw.

We have now reached the evening that was to be known among them as the Night of Nights, because of its adventures and their upshot. The day, as if quietly gathering its forces, had been almost uneventful, and now the redskins in their blankets were at their posts above, while, below, the children were having their evening meal;

all except Peter, who had gone out to get the time. The way you got the time on the island was to find the crocodile, and then stay near him till the clock struck.

This meal happened to be a make-believe tea, and they sat round the board, guzzling in their greed; and really, what with their chatter and recriminations, the noise, as Wendy said, was positively deafening. To be sure, she did not mind noise, but she simply would not have them grabbing things, and then excusing themselves by saying that Tootles had pushed their elbow. There was a fixed rule that they must never hit back at meals, but should refer the matter of dispute to Wendy by raising the right arm politely and saying, 'I complain of So-and-so'; but what usually happened was that they forgot to do this or did it too much.

'Silence,' cried Wendy when for the twentieth time she had told them that they were not all to speak at once. 'Is your calabash empty, Slightly, darling?'

'Not quite empty, Mummy,' Slightly said, after looking into an imaginary mug.

'He hasn't even begun to drink his milk,' Nibs interposed.

This was telling, and Slightly seized his chance.

'I complain of Nibs,' he cried promptly.

John, however, had held up his hand first.

'Well, John?'

'May I sit in Peter's chair, as he is not here?'

'Sit in father's chair, John!' Wendy was scandalized. 'Certainly not.'

'He is not really our father,' John answered. 'He didn't even know what a father does till I showed him.'

This was grumbling. 'We complain of John,' cried the twins.

Tootles held up his hand. He was so much the humblest of them, indeed he was the only humble one, that Wendy was specially gentle with him.

'I don't suppose,' Tootles said diffidently, 'that I could be father.'

'No, Tootles.'

Once Tootles began, which was not very often, he had a silly way of going on.

'As I can't be father,' he said heavily, 'I don't suppose, Michael, you would let me be baby?'

'No, I won't,' Michael rapped out. He was already in his basket.

'As I can't be baby,' Tootles said, getting heavier and heavier, 'do you think I could be a twin?'

'No, indeed,' replied the twins; 'it's awfully difficult to be a twin.'

'As I can't be anything important,' said Tootles, 'would any of you like to see me do a trick?'

'No,' they all replied.

Then at last he stopped. 'I hadn't really any hope,' he said.

The hateful telling broke out again.

'Slightly is coughing on the table.'

'The twins began with mammee-apples.'

'Curly is taking both tappa rolls and yams.'

'Nibs is speaking with his mouth full.'

'I complain of the twins.'

'I complain of Curly.'

'I complain of Nibs.'

'Oh dear, oh dear,' cried Wendy, 'I'm sure I sometimes think that children are more trouble than they are worth.'

She told them to clear away, and sat down to her workbasket: a heavy load of stockings and every knee with a hole in it as usual.

'Wendy,' remonstrated Michael, 'I'm too big for a cradle.'

'I must have somebody in a cradle,' she said almost tartly, 'and you are the littlest. A cradle is such a nice homely thing to have about a house.'

While she sewed they played around her; such a group of happy faces and dancing limbs lit up by that romantic fire. It had become a very familiar scene this in the home under the ground, but we are looking on it for the last time.

There was a step above, and Wendy, you may be sure, was the first to recognize it.

'Children, I hear your father's step. He likes you to meet him at the door.'

Above, the redskins crouched before Peter.

'Watch well, braves. I have spoken.'

And then, as so often before, the gay children dragged him from his tree. As so often before, but never again.

He had brought nuts for the boys as well as the correct time for Wendy.

'Peter, you just spoil them, you know,' Wendy simpered.

'Aye, old lady,' said Peter, hanging up his gun.

'It was me told him mothers are called old lady,' Michael whispered to Curly.

'I complain of Michael,' said Curly instantly.

The first twin came to Peter. 'Father, we want to dance.'

'Dance away, my little man,' said Peter, who was in high good humour.

'But we want you to dance.'

Peter was really the best dancer among them, but he pretended to be scandalized.

'Me! My old bones would rattle.'

'And Mummy too.'

'What,' cried Wendy, 'the mother of such an armful, dance!'

'But on a Saturday night,' Slightly insinuated.

It was not really Saturday night, at least it may have been, for they had long lost count of the days; but always if they wanted to do anything special they said this was Saturday night, and then they did it.

'Of course it is Saturday night, Peter,' Wendy said, relenting.

'People of our figure, Wendy.'

'But it is only among our own progeny.'

'True, true.'

So they were told they could dance, but they must put on their nighties first.

'Ah, old lady,' Peter said aside to Wendy, warming himself by the fire and looking down at her as she sat turning a heel, 'there is nothing more pleasant of an evening for you and me when the day's toil is over than to rest by the fire with the little ones near by.'

'It is sweet, Peter, isn't it?' Wendy said, frightfully gratified. 'Peter, I think Curly has your nose.'

'Michael takes after you.'

She went to him and put her hand on his shoulder.

'Dear Peter,' she said, 'with such a large family, of course, I have now passed my best, but you don't want to change me, do you?'

'No, Wendy.'

Certainly he did not want a change, but he looked at her uncomfortably; blinking, you know, like one not sure whether he was awake or asleep.

'Peter, what is it?'

'I was just thinking,' he said, a little scared. 'It is only make-believe, isn't it, that I am their father?'

'Oh yes,' Wendy said primly.

'You see,' he continued apologetically, 'it would make me seem so old to be their real father.'

'But they are ours, Peter, yours and mine.'

'But not really, Wendy?' he asked anxiously.

'Not if you don't wish it,' she replied; and she distinctly heard his sigh of relief. 'Peter', she asked, trying to speak firmly, 'What are your exact feelings for me?'

'Those of a devoted son, Wendy.'

'I thought so,' she said, and went and sat by herself at the extreme end of the room.

'You are so queer,' he said, frankly puzzled, 'and Tiger Lily is just the same. There is something she wants to be to me, but she says it is not my mother.'

'No, indeed, it is not,' Wendy replied with frightful emphasis. Now we know why she was prejudiced against the redskins.

'Then, what is it?'

'It isn't for a lady to tell.'

'Oh, very well,' Peter said, a little nettled. 'Perhaps Tinker Bell will tell me.'

'Oh yes, Tinker Bell will tell you,' Wendy retorted scornfully. 'She is an abandoned little creature.'

Here Tink, who was in her boudoir, eavesdropping, squeaked out something impudent.

'She says she glories in being abandoned,' Peter interpreted.

He had a sudden idea. 'Perhaps Tink wants to be my mother?'

'You silly ass!' cried Tinker Bell in a passion.

She had said it so often that Wendy needed no translation.

'I almost agree with her,' Wendy snapped. Fancy Wendy snapping. But she had been much tried, and she little knew what was to happen before the night was out. If she had known she would not have snapped.

None of them knew. Perhaps it was best not to know. Their ignorance gave them one more glad hour; and as it was to be their last hour on the island, let us rejoice that there were sixty glad minutes in it. They sang and danced in their nightgowns. Such a deliciously creepy song it was, in which they pretended to be frightened at their own shadows; little witting* that so soon shadows would close in upon them, from whom they would shrink in real fear. So uproariously gay was the dance, and how they buffeted each other on the bed and out of it! It was a pillow fight rather than a dance, and when it was finished, the pillows insisted on one bout more, like partners who know that they may never meet again. The stories they told, before it was time for Wendy's good-night story! Even Slightly tried to tell a story that night, but the beginning was so fearfully dull that it appalled even himself, and he said gloomily:

'Yes, it is a dull beginning. I say, let us pretend that it is the end.'

And then at last they all got into bed for Wendy's story, the story they loved best, the story Peter hated. Usually when she began to tell this story he left the room or put his hands over his ears; and possibly if he had done either of those things this time they might all still be on the island. But tonight he remained on his stool; and we shall see what happened.

CHAPTER 11

'LISTEN, then,' said Wendy, settling down to her story, with Michael at her feet and seven boys in the bed. 'There was once a gentleman———'

'I had rather he had been a lady,' Curly said.

'I wish he had been a white rat,' said Nibs.

'Quiet,' their mother admonished them. 'There was a lady also, and—'

'O Mummy,' cried the first twin, 'you mean that there is a lady also, don't you? She is not dead, is she?'

'Oh, no.'

'I am awfully glad she isn't dead,' said Tootles. 'Are you glad, John?'

'Of course I am.'

'Are you glad, Nibs?'

'Rather.'

'Are you glad, Twins?'

'We are just glad.'

'Oh dear,' sighed Wendy.

'Little less noise there,' Peter called out, determined that she should have fair play, however beastly a story it might be in his opinion.

'The gentleman's name,' Wendy continued, 'was Mr Darling, and her name was Mrs Darling.'

'I knew them,' John said, to annoy the others.

'I think I knew them,' said Michael rather doubtfully.

'They were married, you know,' explained Wendy, 'and what do you think they had?'

'White rats,' cried Nibs, inspired.

'No.'

'It's awfully puzzling,' said Tootles, who knew the story by heart.

'Quiet, Tootles. They had three descendants.'

'What is descendants?'

'Well, you are one, Twin.'

'Do you hear that, John? I am a descendant.'

'Descendants are only children,' said John.

'Oh dear, oh dear,' sighed Wendy. 'Now, these three children had a faithful nurse called Nana; but Mr Darling was angry with her and chained her up in the yard; and so all the children flew away.'

'It's an awfully good story,' said Nibs.

'They flew away,' Wendy continued, 'to the Neverland, where the lost children are.'

'I just thought they did,' Curly broke in excitedly. 'I don't know how it is, but I just thought they did.'

'O Wendy,' cried Tootles, 'was one of the lost children called Tootles?'

'Yes, he was.'

'I am in a story. Hurrah, I am in a story, Nibs.'

'Hush. Now, I want you to consider the feelings of the unhappy parents with all their children flown away.'

'Oo!' they all moaned, though they were not really considering the feelings of the unhappy parents one jot.

'Think of the empty beds!'

'Oo!'

'It's awfully sad,' the first twin said cheerfully.

'I don't see how it can have a happy ending,' said the second twin. 'Do you, Nibs?'

'I'm frightfully anxious.'

'If you knew how great is a mother's love,' Wendy told them triumphantly, 'you would have no fear.' She had now come to the part that Peter hated.

'I do like a mother's love,' said Tootles, hitting Nibs with a pillow. 'Do you like a mother's love, Nibs?'

'I do just,' said Nibs, hitting back.

'You see,' Wendy said complacently, 'our heroine knew that the mother would always leave the window open for her children to fly back by; so they stayed away for years and had a lovely time.'

'Did they ever go back?'

'Let us now,' said Wendy, bracing herself for her finest effort, 'take a peep into the future'; and they all gave themselves the twist that makes peeps into the future easier. 'Years have rolled by; and who is this elegant lady of uncertain age alighting at London Station?'

'O Wendy, who is she?' cried Nibs, every bit as excited as if he didn't know.

'Can it be—yes—no—it is—the fair Wendy!'

'Oh!'

'And who are the two noble portly figures accompanying her, now grown to man's estate? Can they be John and Michael? They are!'

'Oh!'

' "See, dear brothers," says Wendy, pointing upwards, "there is the window still standing open. Ah, now we are rewarded for our sublime faith in a mother's love." So up they flew to their mummy and daddy; and pen cannot describe the happy scene, over which we draw a veil.'

That was the story, and they were as pleased with it as the fair narrator herself. Everything just as it should be, you see. Off we skip like the most heartless things in the world, which is what children are, but so attractive; and we have an entirely selfish time; and then when we have need of special attention we nobly return for it, confident that we shall be embraced instead of smacked.

So great indeed was their faith in a mother's love that they felt they could afford to be callous for a bit longer.

But there was one there who knew better; and when Wendy finished he uttered a hollow groan.

'What is it, Peter?' she cried, running to him, thinking he was ill. She felt him solicitously, lower down than his chest. 'Where is it, Peter?'

'It isn't that kind of pain,' Peter replied darkly.

'Then what kind is it?'

'Wendy, you are wrong about mothers.'

They all gathered round him in affright, so alarming was his agitation; and with a fine candour he told them what he had hitherto concealed.

'Long ago,' he said, 'I thought like you that my mother would always keep the window open for me; so I stayed away for moons and moons and moons, and then flew back; but the window was barred, for mother had forgotten all about me, and there was another little boy sleeping in my bed.'

I am not sure that this was true, but Peter thought it was true; and it scared them.

'Are you sure mothers are like that?'

'Yes.'

So this was the truth about mothers. The toads!

Still it is best to be careful; and no one knows so quickly as a child when he should give in. 'Wendy, let us go home,' cried John and Michael together.

'Yes,' she said, clutching them.

'Not tonight?' asked the lost boys, bewildered. They knew in what they called their hearts that one can get on quite well without a mother, and that it is only the mothers who think you can't.

'At once,' Wendy replied resolutely, for the horrible thought had come to her: 'Perhaps mother is in half-mourning* by this time.'

This dread made her forgetful of what must be Peter's feelings, and she said to him rather sharply, 'Peter, will you make the necessary arrangements?'

'If you wish it,' he replied, as coolly as if she had asked him to pass the nuts.

Not so much as a sorry-to-lose-you between them! If she did not mind the parting, he was going to show her, was Peter, that neither did he.

But of course he cared very much; and he was so full of wrath against grown-ups, who, as usual, were spoiling everything, that as soon as he got inside his tree he breathed intentionally quick short breaths at the rate of about five to a second. He did this because there is a saying in the Neverland that every time you breathe, a grown-up dies; and Peter was killing them off vindictively as fast as possible.

Then having given the necessary instructions to the redskins he returned to the home, where an unworthy scene had been enacted in his absence. Panic-stricken at the thought of losing Wendy, the lost boys had advanced upon her threateningly.

'It will be worse than before she came,' they cried.

'We shan't let her go.'

'Let's keep her prisoner.'

'Aye, chain her up.'

In her extremity an instinct told her to which of them to turn.

'Tootles,' she cried, 'I appeal to you.'

Was it not strange? She appealed to Tootles, quite the silliest one.

Grandly, however, did Tootles respond. For that one moment he dropped his silliness and spoke with dignity.

'I am just Tootles,' he said, 'and nobody minds me. But the first who does not behave to Wendy like an English gentleman I will blood him severely.'

He drew his hanger;* and for that instant his sun was at noon. The others held back uneasily. Then Peter returned, and they saw at once that they would get no support from him. He would keep no girl in the Neverland against her will.

'Wendy,' he said, striding up and down, 'I have asked the redskins to guide you through the wood, as flying tires you so.'

'Thank you, Peter.'

'Then,' he continued in the short sharp voice of one accustomed to be obeyed, 'Tinker Bell will take you across the sea. Wake her, Nibs.'

Nibs had to knock twice before he got an answer, though Tink had really been sitting up in bed listening for some time.

'Who are you? How dare you? Go away,' she cried.

'You are to get up, Tink,' Nibs called, 'and take Wendy on a journey.'

Of course Tink had been delighted to hear that Wendy was going; but she was jolly well determined not to be her courier, and she said so in still more offensive language. Then she pretended to be asleep again.

'She says she won't,' Nibs exclaimed, aghast at such insubordination, whereupon Peter went sternly towards the young lady's chamber.

'Tink,' he rapped out, 'if you don't get up and dress at once I will open the curtains, and then we shall all see you in your *négligée*.'*

This made her leap to the floor. 'Who said I wasn't getting up?' she cried.

In the meantime the boys were gazing very forlornly at Wendy, now equipped with John and Michael for the journey. By this time they were dejected, not merely because they were about to lose her, but also because they felt that she was going off to something nice to which they had not been invited. Novelty was beckoning to them as usual.

Crediting them with a nobler feeling, Wendy melted.

'Dear ones,' she said, 'if you will all come with me I feel almost sure I can get my father and mother to adopt you.'

The invitation was meant specially for Peter; but each of the boys was thinking exclusively of himself, and at once they jumped with joy.

'But won't they think us rather a handful?' Nibs asked in the middle of his jump.

'Oh, no,' said Wendy, rapidly thinking it out, 'it will only mean having a few beds in the drawing-room; they can be hidden behind screens on first Thursdays.'*

'Peter, can we go?' they all cried imploringly. They took it for granted that if they went he would go also, but really they scarcely cared. Thus children are ever ready, when novelty knocks, to desert their dearest ones.

'All right,' Peter replied with a bitter smile; and immediately they rushed to get their things.

'And now, Peter,' Wendy said, thinking she had put everything right, 'I am going to give you your medicine before you go.' She loved to give them medicine, and undoubtedly gave them too much. Of course it was only water, but it was out of a calabash, and she always shook the calabash and counted the drops, which gave it a certain medicinal quality. On this occasion, however, she did not give Peter his draught, for just as she had prepared it, she saw a look on his face that made her heart sink.

'Get your things, Peter,' she cried, shaking.

'No,' he answered, pretending indifference, 'I am not going with you, Wendy.'

'Yes, Peter.'

'No.'

To show that her departure would leave him unmoved, he skipped up and down the room, playing gaily on his heartless pipes. She had to run about after him, though it was rather undignified.

'To find your mother,' she coaxed.

Now, if Peter had ever quite had a mother, he no longer missed her. He could do very well without one. He had thought them out, and remembered only their bad points.

'No, no,' he told Wendy decisively; 'perhaps she would say I was old, and I just want always to be a little boy and to have fun.'

'But, Peter———'

'No.'

And so the others had to be told.

'Peter isn't coming.'

Peter not coming! They gazed blankly at him, their sticks over their backs, and on each stick a bundle. Their first thought was that if Peter was not going he had probably changed his mind about letting them go.

But he was far too proud for that. 'If you find your mothers,' he said darkly, 'I hope you will like them.'

The awful cynicism of this made an uncomfortable impression, and most of them began to look rather doubtful. After all, their faces said, were they not noodles* to want to go?

'Now then,' cried Peter, 'no fuss, no blubbering; good-bye, Wendy'; and he held out his hand cheerily, quite as if they must really go now, for he had something important to do.

.She had to take his hand, as there was no indication that he would prefer a thimble.

'You will remember about changing your flannels,* Peter?' she said, lingering over him. She was always so particular about their flannels.

'Yes.'

'And you will take your medicine?'

'Yes.'

That seemed to be everything; and an awkward pause followed. Peter, however, was not the kind that breaks down before people. 'Are you ready, Tinker Bell?' he called out.

'Aye, aye.'

'Then lead the way.'

Tink darted up the nearest tree; but no one followed her, for it was at this moment that the pirates made their dreadful attack upon the redskins. Above, where all had been so still, the air was rent with shrieks and the clash of steel. Below, there was dead silence. Mouths opened and remained open. Wendy fell on her knees, but her arms were extended toward Peter. All arms were extended to him, as if suddenly blown in his direction; they were beseeching him mutely not to desert them. As for Peter, he seized his sword, the same he thought he had slain Barbecue with; and the lust of battle was in his eye.

CHAPTER 12

THE CHILDREN ARE CARRIED OFF

THE pirate attack had been a complete surprise: a sure proof that the unscrupulous Hook had conducted it improperly, for to surprise red-skins fairly is beyond the wit of the white man.

By all the unwritten laws of savage warfare it is always the redskin who attacks, and with the wiliness of his race he does it just before the dawn, at which time he knows the courage of the whites to be at its lowest ebb. The white men have in the meantime made a rude stock-ade on the summit of yonder undulating ground, at the foot of which a stream runs; for it is destruction to be too far from water. There they await the onslaught, the inexperienced ones clutching their revolvers and treading on twigs, but the old hands sleeping tranquilly until just before the dawn. Through the long black night the savage scouts wriggle, snake-like, among the grass without stirring a blade. The brushwood closes behind them as silently as sand into which a mole has dived. Not a sound is to be heard, save when they give vent to a wonderful imitation of the lonely call of the coyote. The cry is answered by other braves; and some of them do it even better than the coyotes, who are not very good at it. So the chill hours wear on, and the long suspense is horribly trying to the paleface who has to live through it for the first time; but to the trained hand those ghastly calls and still ghastlier silences are but an intimation of how the night is marching.

That this was the usual procedure was so well known to Hook that in disregarding it he cannot be excused on the plea of ignorance.

The Piccaninnies, on their part, trusted implicitly to his honour, and their whole action of the night stands out in marked contrast to his. They left nothing undone that was consistent with the reputation of their tribe. With that alertness of the senses which is at once the marvel and despair of civilized peoples, they knew that the pirates were on the island from the moment one of them trod on a dry stick; and in an incredibly short space of time the coyote cries began. Every foot of ground between the spot where Hook had landed his forces and the home under the trees was stealthily examined by braves wearing their moccasins with the heels in front. They found only one hillock with a stream at its base, so that Hook had no choice; here he must establish himself and wait for just before the dawn. Everything being thus mapped out with almost diabolical cunning, the main body of the redskins folded their blankets around them, and in the phlegmatic manner that is to them the pearl of manhood squatted above the children's home, awaiting the cold moment when they should deal pale death.

Here dreaming, though wide awake, of the exquisite tortures to which they were to put him at break of day, those confiding savages were found by the treacherous Hook. From the accounts afterwards supplied by such of the scouts as escaped the carnage, he does not seem even to have paused at the rising ground, though it is certain that in that grey light he must have seen it: no thought of waiting to be attacked appears from first to last to have visited his subtle mind; he would not even hold off till the night was nearly spent; on he pounded with no policy but to fall to. What could the bewildered scouts do, masters as they were of every warlike artifice save this one, but trot helplessly after him, exposing themselves fatally to view, the while they gave pathetic utterance to the coyote cry.

Around the brave Tiger Lily were a dozen of her stoutest warriors, and they suddenly saw the perfidious pirates bearing down upon them. Fell from their eyes then the film through which they had looked at victory. No more would they torture at the stake. For them the happy hunting-grounds* now. They knew it; but as their fathers' sons they acquitted themselves. Even then they had time to gather in a phalanx that would have been hard to break had they risen quickly, but this they were forbidden to do by the traditions of their race. It is written that the noble savage must never express surprise in the presence of the white. Thus terrible as the sudden appearance of the pirates must have been to them, they remained stationary for a moment, not a muscle moving; as if the foe had come by invitation. Then, indeed, the tradition gallantly upheld, they seized their weapons, and the air was torn with the war-cry; but it was now too late.

It is no part of ours to describe what was a massacre rather than a fight. Thus perished many of the flower of the Piccaninny tribe. Not all unavenged did they die, for with Lean Wolf fell Alf Mason, to disturb the Spanish Main no more; and among others who bit the dust were Geo. Scourie, Chas. Turley,* and the Alsatian Foggerty. Turley fell to the tomahawk of the terrible Panther, who ultimately cut a way through the pirates with Tiger Lily and a small remnant of the tribe.

To what extent Hook is to blame for his tactics on this occasion is for the historian to decide. Had he waited on the rising ground till the proper hour he and his men would probably have been butchered; and in judging him it is only fair to take this into account. What he should perhaps have done was to acquaint his opponents that he proposed to follow a new method. On the other hand this, as destroying the element of surprise, would have made his strategy of no avail, so that the whole question is beset with difficulties. One cannot at least withhold a reluctant admiration for the wit that had conceived so bold a scheme, and the fell genius* with which it was carried out.

What were his own feelings about himself at that triumphant moment? Fain would his dogs have known, as breathing heavily and wiping their cutlasses, they gathered at a discreet distance from his hook, and squinted through their ferret eyes at this extraordinary man. Elation must have been in his heart, but his face did not reflect it; ever a dark and solitary enigma, he stood aloof from his followers in spirit as in substance.

The night's work was not yet over, for it was not the redskins he had come out to destroy; they were but the bees to be smoked, so that he should get at the honey. It was Pan he wanted, Pan and Wendy and their band, but chiefly Pan.

Peter was such a small boy that one tends to wonder at the man's hatred of him. True, he had flung Hook's arm to the crocodile; but even this and the increased insecurity of life to which it led, owing to the crocodile's pertinacity, hardly account for a vindictiveness so relentless and malignant. The truth is that there was a something about Peter which goaded the pirate captain to frenzy. It was not his courage, it was not his engaging appearance, it was not—There is no beating about the bush, for we know quite well what it was, and have got to tell. It was Peter's cockiness.

This had got on Hook's nerves; it made his iron claw twitch, and at night it disturbed him like an insect. While Peter lived, the tortured man felt that he was a lion in a cage into which a sparrow had come.

The question now was how to get down the trees, or how to get his dogs down. He ran his greedy eyes over them, searching for the thinnest ones. They wriggled uncomfortably, for they knew he would not scruple to ram them down with poles.

In the meantime, what of the boys? We have seen them at the first clang of weapons, turned as it were into stone figures, open-mouthed, all appealing with outstretched arms to Peter; and we return to them as their mouths close, and their arms fall to their sides. The pandemonium above has ceased almost as suddenly as it arose, passed like a fierce gust of wind; but they know that in the passing it has determined their fate.

Which side had won?

The pirates, listening avidly at the mouths of the trees, heard the question put by every boy, and alas, they also heard Peter's answer.

'If the redskins have won,' he said, 'they will beat the tom-tom; it is always their sign of victory.'

Now Smee had found the tom-tom, and was at that moment sitting on it. 'You will never hear the tom-tom again,' he muttered, but inaudibly of course, for strict silence had been enjoined. To his amazement Hook signed to him to beat the tom-tom; and slowly there came to Smee an understanding of the dreadful wickedness of the order. Never, probably, had this simple man admired Hook so much.

Twice Smee beat upon the instrument, and then stopped to listen gleefully.

'The tom-tom,' the miscreants heard Peter cry; 'an Indian victory!'

The doomed children answered with a cheer that was music to the black hearts above, and almost immediately they repeated their goodbyes to Peter. This puzzled the pirates, but all their other feelings were swallowed by a base delight that the enemy were about to come up the trees. They smirked at each other and rubbed their hands. Rapidly and silently Hook gave his orders: one man to each tree, and the others to arrange themselves in a line two yards apart.

CHAPTER 13

DO YOU BELIEVE IN FAIRIES?

THE more quickly this horror is disposed of the better. The first to emerge from his tree was Curly. He rose out of it into the arms of Cecco, who flung him to Smee, who flung him to Starkey, who flung him to Bill Jukes, who flung him to Noodler, and so he was tossed from one to another till he fell at the feet of the black pirate. All the boys were plucked from their trees in this ruthless manner; and several of them were in the air at a time, like bales of goods flung from hand to hand.

A different treatment was accorded to Wendy, who came last. With ironical politeness Hook raised his hat to her, and, offering her his arm, escorted her to the spot where the others were being gagged. He did it with such an air, he was so frightfully *distingué*,* that she was too fascinated to cry out. She was only a little girl.

Perhaps it is tell-tale to divulge that for a moment Hook entranced her, and we tell on her only because her slip led to strange results. Had she haughtily unhanded him (and we should have loved to write it of her), she would have been hurled through the air like the others, and then Hook would probably not have been present at the tying of the children; and had he not been at the tying he would not have discovered Slightly's secret, and without the secret he could not presently have made his foul attempt on Peter's life.

They were tied to prevent their flying away, doubled up with their knees close to their ears; and for the trussing of them the black pirate had cut a rope into nine equal pieces. All went well until Slightly's turn came, when he was found to be like those irritating parcels that use up all the string in going round and leave no tags with which to tie a knot. The pirates kicked him in their rage, just as you kick the parcel (though in fairness you should kick the string); and strange to say it was Hook who told them to belay their violence. His lip was curled with malicious triumph. While his dogs were merely sweating because every time they tried to pack the unhappy lad tight in one part he bulged out in another, Hook's master mind had gone far beneath Slightly's surface, probing not for effects but for causes; and his exultation showed that he had found them. Slightly, white to the gills,

PUNG LIKE BALES

knew that Hook had surprised his secret, which was this, that no boy
so blown out* could use a tree wherein an average man need stick.
Poor Slightly, most wretched of all the children now, for he was in
a panic about Peter, bitterly regretted what he had done. Madly
addicted to the drinking of water when he was hot, he had swelled in

consequence to his present girth, and instead of reducing himself to fit his tree he had, unknown to the others, whittled his tree to make it fit him.

Sufficient of this Hook guessed to persuade him that Peter at last lay at his mercy; but no word of the dark design that now formed in the subterranean caverns of his mind crossed his lips; he merely signed that the captives were to be conveyed to the ship, and that he would be* alone.

How to convey them? Hunched up in their ropes they might indeed be rolled downhill like barrels, but most of the way lay through a morass.* Again Hook's genius surmounted difficulties. He indicated that the little house must be used as a conveyance. The children were flung into it, four stout pirates raised it on their shoulders, the others fell in behind, and singing the hateful pirate chorus the strange procession set off through the wood. I don't know whether any of the children were crying; if so, the singing drowned the sound; but as the little house disappeared in the forest, a brave though tiny jet of smoke issued from its chimney as if defying Hook.

Hook saw it, and it did Peter a bad service. It dried up any trickle of pity for him that may have remained in the pirate's infuriated breast.

The first thing he did on finding himself alone in the fast-falling night was to tiptoe to Slightly's tree, and make sure that it provided him with a passage. Then for long he remained brooding; his hat of ill omen on the sward,* so that a gentle breeze which had arisen might play refreshingly through his hair. Dark as were his thoughts his blue eyes were as soft as the periwinkle.* Intently he listened for any sound from the nether world, but all was as silent below as above; the house under the ground seemed to be but one more empty tenement in the void. Was that boy asleep, or did he stand waiting at the foot of Slightly's tree, with his dagger in his hand?

There was no way of knowing, save by going down. Hook let his cloak slip softly to the ground, and then biting his lips till a lewd* blood stood on them, he stepped into the tree. He was a brave man; but for a moment he had to stop there and wipe his brow, which was dripping like a candle. Then silently he let himself go into the unknown.

He arrived unmolested at the foot of the shaft, and stood still again, biting at his breath, which had almost left him. As his eyes became

accustomed to the dim light various objects in the home under the
trees took shape; but the only one on which his greedy gaze rested,
long sought for and found at last, was the great bed. On the bed lay
Peter fast asleep.

Unaware of the tragedy being enacted above, Peter had continued,
for a little time after the children left, to play gaily on his pipes: no
doubt rather a forlorn attempt to prove to himself that he did not
care. Then he decided not to take his medicine, so as to grieve Wendy.
Then he lay down on the bed outside the coverlet, to vex her still
more; for she had always tucked them inside it, because you never
know that you may not grow chilly at the turn of the night. Then he
nearly cried; but it struck him how indignant she would be if he
laughed instead; so he laughed a haughty laugh and fell asleep in
the middle of it.

Sometimes, though not often, he had dreams, and they were more
painful than the dreams of other boys. For hours he could not be
separated from these dreams, though he wailed piteously in them.
They had to do, I think, with the riddle of his existence. At such times
it had been Wendy's custom to take him out of bed and sit with him
on her lap, soothing him in dear ways of her own invention, and when
he grew calmer to put him back to bed before he quite woke up, so
that he should not know of the indignity to which she had subjected
him. But on this occasion he had fallen at once into a dreamless sleep.
One arm dropped over the edge of the bed, one leg was arched, and
the unfinished part of his laugh was stranded on his mouth, which
was open, showing the little pearls.

Thus defenceless, Hook found him. He stood silent at the foot of
the tree looking across the chamber at his enemy. Did no feeling of
compassion disturb his sombre breast? The man was not wholly evil;
he loved flowers (I have been told) and sweet music (he was himself
no mean performer on the harpsichord); and let it be frankly admitted, the idyllic nature of the scene stirred him profoundly. Mastered
by his better self, he would have returned reluctantly up the tree, but
for one thing.

What stayed him was Peter's impertinent appearance as he slept.
The open mouth, the drooping arm, the arched knee: they were such
a personification of cockiness as, taken together, will never again, one
may hope, be presented to eyes so sensitive to their offensiveness.
They steeled Hook's heart. If his rage had broken him into a hundred

pieces every one of them would have disregarded the incident, and leapt at the sleeper.

Though a light from the one lamp shone dimly on the bed Hook stood in darkness himself, and at the first stealthy step forward he discovered an obstacle, the door of Slightly's tree. It did not entirely fill the aperture, and he had been looking over it. Feeling for the catch, he found to his fury that it was low down, beyond his reach. To his disordered brain it seemed then that the irritating quality in Peter's face and figure visibly increased, and he rattled the door and flung himself against it. Was his enemy to escape him after all?

But what was that? The red in his eye had caught sight of Peter's medicine standing on a ledge within easy reach. He fathomed what it was straightway, and immediately he knew that the sleeper was in his power.

Lest he should be taken alive, Hook always carried about his person a dreadful drug, blended by himself of all the death-dealing rings* that had come into his possession. These he had boiled down into a yellow liquid quite unknown to science, which was probably the most virulent poison in existence.

Five drops of this he now added to Peter's cup. His hand shook, but it was in exultation rather than in shame. As he did it he avoided glancing at the sleeper, but not lest pity should unnerve him; merely to avoid spilling. Then one long gloating look he cast upon his victim, and turning, wormed his way with difficulty up the tree. As he emerged at the top he looked the very spirit of evil breaking from its hole. Donning his hat at its most rakish angle, he wound his cloak around him, holding one end in front as if to conceal his person from the night, of which it was the blackest part, and muttering strangely to himself stole away through the trees.

Peter slept on. The light guttered and went out, leaving the tenement in darkness; but still he slept. It must have been not less than ten o'clock by the crocodile, when he suddenly sat up in his bed, wakened by he knew not what. It was a soft cautious tapping on the door of his tree.

Soft and cautious, but in that stillness it was sinister. Peter felt for his dagger till his hand gripped it. Then he spoke.

'Who is that?'

For long there was no answer: then again the knock.

'Who are you?'

No answer.

He was thrilled, and he loved being thrilled. In two strides he reached his door. Unlike Slightly's door it filled the aperture, so that he could not see beyond it, nor could the one knocking see him.

'I won't open unless you speak,' Peter cried.

Then at last the visitor spoke, in a lovely bell-like voice.

'Let me in, Peter.'

It was Tink, and quickly he unbarred to her. She flew in excitedly, her face flushed and her dress stained with mud.

'What is it?'

'Oh, you could never guess,' she cried, and offered him three guesses. 'Out with it!' he shouted; and in one ungrammatical sentence, as long as the ribbons conjurers pull from their mouths, she told of the capture of Wendy and the boys.

Peter's heart bobbed up and down as he listened. Wendy bound, and on the pirate ship; she who loved everything to be just so!

'I'll rescue her,' he cried, leaping at his weapons. As he leapt he thought of something he could do to please her. He could take his medicine.

His hand closed on the fatal draught.

'No!' shrieked Tinker Bell, who had heard Hook muttering about his deed as he sped through the forest.

'Why not?'

'It is poisoned.'

'Poisoned? Who could have poisoned it?'

'Hook.'

'Don't be silly. How could Hook have got down here?'

Alas, Tinker Bell could not explain this, for even she did not know the dark secret of Slightly's tree. Nevertheless Hook's words had left no room for doubt. The cup was poisoned.

'Besides,' said Peter, quite believing himself, 'I never fell asleep.'

He raised the cup. No time for words now; time for deeds; and with one of her lightning movements Tink got between his lips and the draught, and drained it to the dregs.

'Why, Tink, how dare you drink my medicine?'

But she did not answer. Already she was reeling in the air.

'What is the matter with you?' cried Peter, suddenly afraid.

'It was poisoned, Peter,' she told him softly; 'and now I am going to be dead.'

'O Tink, did you drink it to save me?'

'Yes.'

'But why, Tink?'

Her wings would scarcely carry her now, but in reply she alighted on his shoulder and gave his chin a loving bite. She whispered in his ear, 'You silly ass'; and then, tottering to her chamber, lay down on the bed.

His head almost filled the fourth wall of her little room as he knelt near her in distress. Every moment her light was growing fainter; and he knew that if it went out she would be no more. She liked his tears so much that she put out her beautiful finger and let them run over it.

Her voice was so low that at first he could not make out what she said. Then he made it out. She was saying that she thought she could get well again if children believed in fairies.

Peter flung out his arms. There were no children there, and it was night-time; but he addressed all who might be dreaming of the Neverland, and who were therefore nearer to him than you think; boys and girls in their nighties, and naked papooses* in their baskets hung from trees.

'Do you believe?' he cried.

Tink sat up in bed almost briskly to listen to her fate.

She fancied she heard answers in the affirmative, and then again she wasn't sure.

'What do you think?' she asked Peter.

'If you believe,' he shouted to them, 'clap your hands; don't let Tink die.'

Many clapped.

Some didn't.

A few little beasts hissed.

The clapping stopped suddenly, as if countless mothers had rushed to their nurseries to see what on earth was happening; but already Tink was saved. First her voice grew strong; then she popped out of bed; then she was flashing through the room more merry and impudent than ever. She never thought of thanking those who believed, but she would have liked to get at the ones who had hissed.

'And now to rescue Wendy.'

The moon was riding in a cloudy heaven when Peter rose from his tree, begirt with weapons and wearing little else, to set out upon his perilous quest. It was not such a night as he would have chosen.

He had hoped to fly, keeping not far from the ground so that nothing unwonted should escape his eyes; but in that fitful light to have flown low would have meant trailing his shadow through the trees, thus disturbing the birds and acquainting a watchful foe that he was astir.

He regretted now that he had given the birds of the island such strange names that they are very wild and difficult of approach.

There was no other course but to press forward in redskin fashion, at which happily he was an adept. But in what direction, for he could not be sure that the children had been taken to the ship? A slight fall of snow had obliterated all footmarks; and a deathly silence pervaded the island, as if for a space Nature stood still in horror of the recent carnage. He had taught the children something of the forest lore that he had himself learned from Tiger Lily and Tinker Bell, and knew that in their dire hour they were not likely to forget it. Slightly, if he had an opportunity, would blaze the trees, for instance, Curly would drop seeds, and Wendy would leave her handkerchief at some important place. But morning was needed to search for such guidance, and he could not wait. The upper world had called him, but would give no help.

The crocodile passed him, but not another living thing, not a sound, not a movement; and yet he knew well that sudden death might be at the next tree, or stalking him from behind.

He swore this terrible oath: 'Hook or me this time.'

Now he crawled forward like a snake; and again, erect, he darted across a space on which the moonlight played: one finger on his lip and his dagger at the ready. He was frightfully happy.

CHAPTER 14

THE PIRATE SHIP

ONE green light squinting over Kidd's Creek,* which is near the mouth of the pirate river, marked where the brig, the *Jolly Roger*, lay, low in the water; a rakish-looking craft foul to the hull,* every beam in her detestable, like ground strewn with mangled feathers. She was the cannibal of the seas, and scarce needed that watchful eye, for she floated immune in the horror of her name.*

She was wrapped in the blanket of night, through which no sound from her could have reached the shore. There was little sound, and none agreeable save the whir of the ship's sewing machine at which Smee sat, ever industrious and obliging, the essence of the commonplace, pathetic Smee. I know not why he was so infinitely pathetic, unless it were because he was so pathetically unaware of it; but even strong men had to turn hastily from looking at him, and more than once on summer evenings he had touched the fount of Hook's tears and made it flow. Of this, as of almost everything else, Smee was quite unconscious.

A few of the pirates leant over the bulwarks drinking in the miasma* of the night; others sprawled by barrels over games of dice and cards; and the exhausted four who had carried the little house lay prone on the deck, where even in their sleep they rolled skilfully to this side or that out of Hook's reach, lest he should claw them mechanically in passing.

Hook trod the deck in thought. O man unfathomable. It was his hour of triumph. Peter had been removed for ever from his path, and all the other boys were on the brig, about to walk the plank.* It was his grimmest deed since the days when he had brought Barbecue to heel; and knowing as we do how vain a tabernacle is man, could we be surprised had he now paced the deck unsteadily, bellied out* by the winds of his success?

But there was no elation in his gait, which kept pace with the action of his sombre mind. Hook was profoundly dejected.

He was often thus when communing with himself on board ship in the quietude of the night. It was because he was so terribly alone. This inscrutable man never felt more alone than when surrounded by his dogs.* They were socially so inferior to him.

Hook was not his true name. To reveal who he really was would even at this date set the country in a blaze; but as those who read between the lines must already have guessed, he had been at a famous public school;* and its traditions still clung to him like garments, with which indeed they are largely concerned. Thus it was offensive to him even now to board a ship in the same dress in which he grappled her; and he still adhered in his walk to the school's distinguished slouch. But above all he retained the passion for good form.*

Good form! However much he may have degenerated, he still knew that this is all that really matters.

From far within him he heard a creaking as of rusty portals, and through them came a stern tap-tap-tap, like hammering in the night when one cannot sleep. 'Have you been good form today?' was their eternal question.

'Fame, fame, that glittering bauble, it is mine,' he cried.

'Is it quite good form to be distinguished at anything?' the tap-tap from his school replied.

'I am the only man whom Barbecue feared,' he urged; 'and Flint himself feared Barbecue.'

'Barbecue, Flint—what house?'* came the cutting retort.

Most disquieting reflection of all, was it not bad form to think about good form?

His vitals* were tortured by this problem. It was a claw within him sharper than the iron one; and as it tore him, the perspiration dripped down his tallow countenance and streaked his doublet. Oft-times he drew his sleeve across his face, but there was no damming that trickle.

Ah, envy not Hook.

There came to him a presentiment of his early dissolution.* It was as if Peter's terrible oath had boarded the ship. Hook felt a gloomy desire to make his dying speech, lest presently there should be no time for it.

'Better for Hook,' he cried, 'if he had had less ambition.' It was in his darkest hours only that he referred to himself in the third person.

'No little children love me.'

Strange that he should think of this, which had never troubled him before; perhaps the sewing machine brought it to his mind. For long he muttered to himself, staring at Smee, who was hemming placidly, under the conviction that all children feared him.

Feared him! Feared Smee! There was not a child on board the brig that night who did not already love him. He had said horrid things to them and hit them with the palm of his hand, because he could not hit with his fist; but they had only clung to him the more. Michael had tried on his spectacles.

To tell poor Smee that they thought him lovable! Hook itched to do it, but it seemed too brutal. Instead, he revolved this mystery in his mind: why do they find Smee lovable? He pursued the problem like the sleuth-hound* that he was. If Smee was lovable, what was it that made him so? A terrible answer suddenly presented itself: 'Good form?'

Had the bo'sun good form without knowing it, which is the best form of all?

He remembered that you have to prove you don't know you have it before you are eligible for Pop.*

With a cry of rage he raised his iron hand over Smee's head; but he did not tear. What arrested him was this reflection:

'To claw a man because he is good form, what would that be?'

'Bad form!'

The unhappy Hook was as impotent as he was damp,* and he fell forward like a cut flower.

His dogs thinking him out of the way for a time, discipline instantly relaxed; and they broke into a bacchanalian* dance, which brought him to his feet at once; all traces of human weakness gone, as if a bucket of water had passed over him.

'Quiet, you scugs,'* he cried, 'or I'll cast anchor in you'; and at once the din was hushed. 'Are all the children chained, so that they cannot fly away?'

'Aye, aye.'

'Then hoist them up.'

The wretched prisoners were dragged from the hold, all except Wendy, and ranged in line in front of him. For a time he seemed unconscious of their presence. He lolled at his ease, humming, not unmelodiously, snatches of a rude song, and fingering a pack of cards. Ever and anon the light from his cigar gave a touch of colour to his face.

'Now then, bullies,' he said briskly, 'six of you walk the plank tonight, but I have room for two cabin boys. Which of you is it to be?'

'Don't irritate him unnecessarily,' had been Wendy's instructions in the hold; so Tootles stepped forward politely. Tootles hated the idea of signing under such a man, but an instinct told him that it would be prudent to lay the responsibility on an absent person; and though a somewhat silly boy, he knew that mothers alone are always willing to be the buffer. All children know this about mothers, and despise them for it, but make constant use of it.

So Tootles explained prudently, 'You see, sir, I don't think my mother would like me to be a pirate. Would your mother like you to be a pirate, Slightly?'

He winked at Slightly, who said mournfully, 'I don't think so,' as if he wished things had been otherwise. 'Would your mother like you to be a pirate, Twin?'

'I don't think so,' said the first twin, as clever as the others. 'Nibs, would———?'

'Stow this gab,'* roared Hook, and the spokesmen were dragged back. 'You, boy,' he said, addressing John, 'you look as if you had a little pluck in you. Didst never want to be a pirate, my hearty?'

Now John had sometimes experienced this hankering at maths prep;* and he was struck by Hook's picking him out.

'I once thought of calling myself Red-handed Jack,' he said diffidently.

'And a good name too. We'll call you that here, bully, if you join.'

'What do you think, Michael?' asked John.

'What would you call me if I join?' Michael demanded.

'Blackbeard Joe.'

Michael was naturally impressed. 'What do you think, John?' He wanted John to decide, and John wanted him to decide.

'Shall we still be respectful subjects of the King?' John inquired.

Through Hook's teeth came the answer: 'You would have to swear, "Down with the King."'

Perhaps John had not behaved very well so far, but he shone out now.

'Then I refuse,' he cried, banging the barrel in front of Hook.

'And I refuse,' cried Michael.

'Rule Britannia!'* squeaked Curly.

The infuriated pirates buffeted them in the mouth; and Hook roared out, 'That seals your doom. Bring up their mother. Get the plank ready.'

They were only boys, and they went white as they saw Jukes and Cecco preparing the fatal plank. But they tried to look brave when Wendy was brought up.

No words of mine can tell you how Wendy despised those pirates. To the boys there was at least some glamour in the pirate calling, but all that she saw was that the ship had not been scrubbed for years. There was not a port-hole on the grimy glass of which you might not have written with your finger, 'Dirty pig'; and she had already written it on several. But as the boys gathered round her she had no thought, of course, save for them.

'So, my beauty,' said Hook, as if he spoke in syrup, 'you are to see your children walk the plank.'

Fine gentleman though he was, the intensity of his communings had soiled his ruff, and suddenly he knew that she was gazing at it. With a hasty gesture he tried to hide it, but he was too late.

'Are they to die?' asked Wendy, with a look of such frightful contempt that he nearly fainted.

'They are,' he snarled. 'Silence all,' he called gloatingly, 'for a mother's last words to her children.'

At this moment Wendy was grand. 'These are my last words, dear boys,' she said firmly. 'I feel that I have a message to you from your real mothers, and it is this: "We hope our sons will die like English gentlemen."'

Even the pirates were awed; and Tootles cried out hysterically, 'I am going to do what my mother hopes. What are you to do, Nibs?'

'What my mother hopes. What are you to do, Twin?'

'What my mother hopes. John, what are————?'

But Hook had found his voice again.

'Tie her up,' he shouted.

It was Smee who tied her to the mast. 'See here, honey,' he whispered, 'I'll save you if you promise to be my mother.'

But not even for Smee would she make such a promise. 'I would almost rather have no children at all,' she said disdainfully.

It is sad to know that not a boy was looking at her as Smee tied her to the mast; the eyes of all were on the plank; that last little walk they were about to take. They were no longer able to hope that they would walk it manfully, for the capacity to think had gone from them; they could stare and shiver only.

Hook smiled on them with his teeth closed, and took a step toward Wendy. His intention was to turn her face so that she should see the boys walking the plank one by one. But he never reached her, he never heard the cry of anguish he hoped to wring from her. He heard something else instead.

It was the terrible tick-tick of the crocodile.

They all heard it—pirates, boys, Wendy; and immediately every head was blown in one direction; not to the water whence the sound proceeded, but toward Hook. All knew that what was about to happen concerned him alone, and that from being actors they were suddenly become spectators.

Very frightful was it to see the change that came over him. It was as if he had been clipped at every joint. He fell in a little heap.

The sound came steadily nearer; and in advance of it came this ghastly thought, 'The crocodile is about to board the ship.'

Even the iron claw hung inactive; as if knowing that it was no intrinsic part of what the attacking force wanted. Left so fearfully alone, any other man would have lain with his eyes shut where he fell; but the gigantic brain of Hook was still working, and under its guidance he crawled on his knees along the deck as far from the sound as he could go. The pirates respectfully cleared a passage for him, and it was only when he brought up against the bulwarks that he spoke.

'Hide me,' he cried hoarsely.

They gathered round him; all eyes averted from the thing that was coming aboard. They had no thought of fighting it. It was Fate.

Only when Hook was hidden from them did curiosity loosen the limbs of the boys so that they could rush to the ship's side to see the crocodile climbing it. Then they got the strangest surprise of this Night of Nights; for it was no crocodile that was coming to their aid. It was Peter.

He signed to them not to give vent to any cry of admiration that might rouse suspicion. Then he went on ticking.

CHAPTER 15

ODD things happen to all of us on our way through life without our noticing for a time that they have happened. Thus, to take an instance, we suddenly discover that we have been deaf in one ear for we don't know how long, but, say, half an hour. Now such an experience had come that night to Peter. When last we saw him he was stealing across the island with one finger to his lips and his dagger at the ready. He had seen the crocodile pass by without noticing anything peculiar about it, but by and by he remembered that it had not been ticking. At first he thought this eerie, but soon he concluded rightly that the clock had run down.

Without giving a thought to what might be the feelings of a fellow-creature thus abruptly deprived of its closest companion, Peter at once considered how he could turn the catastrophe to his own use; and he decided to tick, so that wild beasts should believe he was the crocodile and let him pass unmolested. He ticked superbly, but with one unforeseen result. The crocodile was among those who heard the sound, and it followed him, though whether with the purpose of regaining what it had lost, or merely as a friend under the belief that it was again ticking itself, will never be certainly known, for, like all slaves to a fixed idea, it was a stupid beast.

Peter reached the shore without mishap, and went straight on; his legs encountering the water as if quite unaware that they had entered a new element. Thus many animals pass from land to water, but no other human of whom I know. As he swam he had but one thought: 'Hook or me this time.' He had ticked so long that he now went on ticking without knowing that he was doing it. Had he known he would have stopped, for to board the brig by the help of the tick, though an ingenious idea, had not occurred to him.

On the contrary, he thought he had scaled her side as noiseless as a mouse; and he was amazed to see the pirates cowering from him, with Hook in their midst as abject as if he had heard the crocodile.

The crocodile! No sooner did Peter remember it than he heard the ticking. At first he thought the sound did come from the crocodile, and he looked behind him swiftly. Then he realized that he was doing

HOOK OR ME THIS TIME

it himself, and in a flash he understood the situation. 'How clever of me,' he thought at once, and signed to the boys not to burst into applause.

It was at this moment that Ed Teynte the quartermaster emerged from the forecastle and came along the deck. Now, reader, time what happened by your watch. Peter struck true and deep. John clapped his hands on the ill-fated pirate's mouth to stifle the dying groan. He fell forward. Four boys caught him to prevent the thud. Peter gave the signal, and the carrion was cast overboard. There was a splash, and then silence. How long has it taken?

'One!' (Slightly had begun to count.)

None too soon, Peter, every inch of him on tiptoe, vanished into the cabin; for more than one pirate was screwing up his courage to look round. They could hear each other's distressed breathing now, which showed them that the more terrible sound had passed.

'It's gone, captain,' Smee said, wiping his spectacles. 'All's still again.'

Slowly Hook let his head emerge from his ruff, and listened so intently that he could have caught the echo of the tick. There was not a sound, and he drew himself up firmly to his full height.

'Then here's to Johnny Plank,' he cried brazenly, hating the boys more than ever because they had seen him unbend. He broke into the villainous ditty:

> 'Yo ho, yo ho, the frisky plank,
> You walks along it so,
> Till it goes down and you goes down
> To Davy Jones below!'

To terrorize the prisoners the more, though with a certain loss of dignity, he danced along an imaginary plank, grimacing at them as he sang; and when he finished he cried, 'Do you want a touch of the cat* before you walk the plank?'

At that they fell on their knees. 'No, no,' they cried so piteously that every pirate smiled.

'Fetch the cat, Jukes,' said Hook; 'it's in the cabin.'

The cabin! Peter was in the cabin! The children gazed at each other.

'Aye, aye,' said Jukes blithely, and he strode into the cabin. They followed him with their eyes; they scarce knew that Hook had resumed his song, his dogs joining in with him:

> 'Yo ho, yo ho, the scratching cat,
> Its tails are nine, you know,
> And when they're writ upon your back————'

What was the last line will never be known, for of a sudden the song was stayed by a dreadful screech from the cabin. It wailed through the ship, and died away. Then was heard a crowing sound which was well understood by the boys, but to the pirates was almost more eerie than the screech.

'What was that?' cried Hook.

'Two,' said Slightly solemnly.

The Italian Cecco hesitated for a moment and then swung into the cabin. He tottered out, haggard.

'What's the matter with Bill Jukes, you dog?' hissed Hook, towering over him.

'The matter wi' him is he's dead, stabbed,' replied Cecco in a hollow voice.

'Bill Jukes dead!' cried the startled pirates.

'The cabin's as black as a pit,' Cecco said, almost gibbering, 'but there is something terrible in there: the thing you heard crowing.'

The exultation of the boys, the lowering looks of the pirates, both were seen by Hook.

'Cecco,' he said in his most steely voice, 'go back and fetch me out that doodle-doo.'

Cecco, bravest of the brave, cowered before his captain, crying, 'No, no': but Hook was purring to his claw.

'Did you say you would go, Cecco?' he said musingly.

Cecco went, first flinging up his arms despairingly. There was no more singing, all listened now; and again came a death-screech and again a crow.

No one spoke except Slightly. 'Three,' he said.

Hook rallied his dogs with a gesture. ''Sdeath and odds fish,'* he thundered, 'who is to bring me that doodle-doo?'

'Wait till Cecco comes out,' growled Starkey, and the others took up the cry.

'I think I heard you volunteer, Starkey,' said Hook, purring again.

'No, by thunder!' Starkey cried.

'My hook thinks you did,' said Hook, crossing to him. 'I wonder if it would not be advisable, Starkey, to humour the hook?'

'I'll swing* before I go in there,' replied Starkey doggedly, and again he had the support of the crew.

'Is it mutiny?' asked Hook more pleasantly than ever. 'Starkey's ring-leader.'

'Captain, mercy,' Starkey whimpered, all of a tremble now.

'Shake hands, Starkey,' said Hook, proffering his claw.

Starkey looked round for help, but all deserted him. As he backed Hook advanced, and now the red spark was in his eye. With a despairing scream the pirate leapt upon Long Tom and precipitated himself into the sea.

'Four,' said Slightly.

'And now,' Hook asked courteously, 'did any other gentleman say mutiny?' Seizing a lantern and raising his claw with a menacing gesture, 'I'll bring out that doodle-doo myself,' he said, and sped into the cabin.

'Five.' How Slightly longed to say it. He wetted his lips to be ready, but Hook came staggering out, without his lantern.

'Something blew out the light,' he said a little unsteadily.

'Something!' echoed Mullins.

'What of Cecco?' demanded Noodler.

'He's as dead as Jukes,' said Hook shortly.

His reluctance to return to the cabin impressed them all unfavourably, and the mutinous sounds again broke forth. All pirates are superstitious; and Cookson cried, 'They do say the surest sign a ship's accurst is when there's one on board* more than can be accounted for.'

'I've heard,' muttered Mullins, 'he always boards the pirate craft at last. Had he a tail, captain?'

'They say,' said another, looking viciously at Hook, 'that when he comes it's in the likeness of the wickedest man aboard.'

'Had he a hook, captain?' asked Cookson insolently; and one after another took up the cry, 'The ship's doomed.' At this the children could not resist raising a cheer. Hook had wellnigh forgotten his prisoners, but as he swung round on them now his face lit up again.

'Lads,' he cried to his crew, 'here's a notion. Open the cabin door and drive them in. Let them fight the doodle-doo for their lives. If they kill him we're so much the better; if he kills them we're none the worse.'

For the last time his dogs admired Hook, and devotedly they did his bidding. The boys, pretending to struggle, were pushed into the cabin and the door was closed on them.

'Now, listen,' cried Hook, and all listened. But not one dared to face the door. Yes, one, Wendy, who all this time had been bound to the mast. It was for neither a scream nor a crow that she was watching; it was for the reappearance of Peter.

She had not long to wait. In the cabin he had found the thing for which he had gone in search: the key that would free the children of their manacles; and now they all stole forth, armed with such weapons as they could find. First signing to them to hide, Peter cut Wendy's bonds, and then nothing could have been easier than for them all to fly off together; but one thing barred the way, an oath, 'Hook or me this time.' So when he had freed Wendy, he whispered to her to conceal herself with the others, and himself took her place by the mast, her cloak around him so that he should pass for her. Then he took a great breath and crowed.

To the pirates it was a voice crying that all the boys lay slain in the cabin; and they were panic-stricken. Hook tried to hearten them; but like the dogs he had made them they showed him their fangs, and he knew that if he took his eyes off them now they would leap at him.

'Lads,' he said, ready to cajole or strike as need be, but never quailing for an instant, 'I've thought it out. There's a Jonah* aboard.'

'Aye,' they snarled, 'a man wi' a hook.'

'No, lads, no, it's the girl. Never was luck on a pirate ship wi' a woman on board. We'll right the ship when she's gone.'

Some of them remembered that this had been a saying of Flint's. 'It's worth trying,' they said doubtfully.

'Fling the girl overboard,' cried Hook; and they made a rush at the figure in the cloak.

'There's none can save you now, missy,' Mullins hissed jeeringly.

'There's one,' replied the figure.

'Who's that?'

'Peter Pan the avenger!' came the terrible answer; and as he spoke Peter flung off his cloak. Then they all knew who 'twas that had been undoing them in the cabin, and twice Hook essayed to speak and twice he failed. In that frightful moment I think his fierce heart broke.

At last he cried, 'Cleave him to the brisket,'* but without conviction.

'Down, boys, and at them,' Peter's voice rang out; and in another moment the clash of arms was resounding through the ship. Had the pirates kept together it is certain that they would have won; but the onset came when they were all unstrung, and they ran hither and thither, striking wildly, each thinking himself the last survivor of the crew. Man to man they were the stronger; but they fought on the defensive only, which enabled the boys to hunt in pairs and choose their quarry. Some of the miscreants leapt into the sea; others hid in dark recesses, where they were found by Slightly, who did not fight, but ran about with a lantern which he flashed in their faces, so that they were half blinded and fell an easy prey to the reeking* swords of the other boys. There was little sound to be heard but the clang of weapons, an occasional screech or splash, and Slightly monotonously counting—five—six—seven—eight—nine—ten—eleven.

I think all were gone when a group of savage boys surrounded Hook, who seemed to have a charmed life, as he kept them at bay in that circle of fire. They had done for his dogs, but this man alone seemed to be a match for them all. Again and again they closed upon him, and again and again he hewed a clear space. He had lifted up one boy with his hook, and was using him as a buckler,* when another, who had just passed his sword through Mullins, sprang into the fray.

'Put up your swords, boys,' cried the newcomer, 'this man is mine.'

Thus suddenly Hook found himself face to face with Peter. The others drew back and formed a ring round them.

For long the two enemies looked at one another; Hook shuddering slightly, and Peter with the strange smile upon his face.

'So, Pan,' said Hook at last, 'this is all your doing.'

'Aye, James Hook,' came the stern answer, 'it is all my doing.'

'Proud and insolent youth,' said Hook, 'prepare to meet thy doom.'

'Dark and sinister man,' Peter answered, 'have at thee.'

Without more words they fell to, and for a space there was no advantage to either blade. Peter was a superb swordsman, and parried with dazzling rapidity; ever and anon he followed up a feint with a lunge that got past his foe's defence, but his shorter reach stood him in ill stead, and he could not drive the steel home. Hook, scarcely his inferior in brilliancy, but not quite so nimble in wrist play, forced him back by the weight of his onset, hoping suddenly to end all with a favourite thrust, taught him long ago by Barbecue at Rio; but to his astonishment he found this thrust turned aside again and again. Then he sought to close and give the quietus* with his iron hook, which all this time had been pawing the air; but Peter doubled under it and, lunging fiercely, pierced him in the ribs. At sight of his own blood, whose peculiar colour, you remember, was offensive to him, the sword fell from Hook's hand, and he was at Peter's mercy.

"THIS MAN IS MINE"

'Now!' cried all the boys; but with a magnificent gesture Peter invited his opponent to pick up his sword. Hook did so instantly, but with a tragic feeling that Peter was showing good form.

Hitherto he had thought it was some fiend fighting him, but darker suspicions assailed him now.

'Pan, who and what art thou?' he cried huskily.

'I'm youth, I'm joy,' Peter answered at a venture, 'I'm a little bird that has broken out of the egg.'

This, of course, was nonsense; but it was proof to the unhappy Hook that Peter did not know in the least who or what he was, which is the very pinnacle of good form.

'To't again,' he cried despairingly.

He fought now like a human flail, and every sweep of that terrible sword would have severed in twain any man or boy who obstructed it; but Peter fluttered round him as if the very wind it made blew him out of the danger zone. And again and again he darted in and pricked.

Hook was fighting now without hope. That passionate breast no longer asked for life; but for one boon it craved; to see Peter bad form before it was cold for ever.

Abandoning the fight he rushed into the powder magazine* and fired it.

'In two minutes,' he cried, 'the ship will be blown to pieces.'

Now, now, he thought, true form will show.

But Peter issued from the powder magazine with the shell in his hands, and calmly flung it overboard.

What sort of form was Hook himself showing? Misguided man though he was, we may be glad, without sympathizing with him, that in the end he was true to the traditions of his race. The other boys were flying around him now, flouting, scornful; and as he staggered about the deck striking up at them impotently, his mind was no longer with them; it was slouching in the playing fields of long ago, or being sent up for good,* or watching the wall-game from a famous wall.* And his shoes were right, and his waistcoat was right, and his tie was right, and his socks were right.

James Hook, thou not wholly unheroic figure, farewell.

For we have come to his last moment.

Seeing Peter slowly advancing upon him through the air with dagger poised, he sprang upon the bulwarks* to cast himself into the sea. He did not know that the crocodile was waiting for him; for we purposely stopped the clock that this knowledge might be spared him: a little mark of respect from us at the end.

He had one last triumph, which I think we need not grudge him. As he stood on the bulwark looking over his shoulder at Peter gliding through the air, he invited him with a gesture to use his foot. It made Peter kick instead of stab.

At last Hook had got the boon for which he craved.

'Bad form,' he cried jeeringly, and went content to the crocodile.

Thus perished James Hook.

'Seventeen,' Slightly sang out; but he was not quite correct in his figures. Fifteen paid the penalty for their crimes that night, but two reached the shore: Starkey to be captured by the redskins, who made him nurse for all their papooses, a melancholy come-down for a pirate; and Smee, who henceforth wandered about the world in his spectacles, making a precarious living by saying he was the only man that Jas. Hook had feared.

Wendy, of course, had stood by taking no part in the fight, though watching Peter with glistening eyes; but now that all was over she became prominent again. She praised them equally, and shuddered delightfully when Michael showed her the place where he had killed one; and then she took them into Hook's cabin and pointed to his watch which was hanging on a nail. It said, 'half past one'!

The lateness of the hour was almost the biggest thing of all. She got them to bed in the pirates' bunks pretty quickly, you may be sure; all but Peter, who strutted up and down on deck, until at last he fell asleep by the side of Long Tom. He had one of his dreams that night, and cried in his sleep for a long time, and Wendy held him tight.

CHAPTER 16

THE RETURN HOME

By two bells that morning they were all stirring their stumps; for there was a big sea running; and Tootles, the bo'sun, was among them, with a rope's end* in his hand and chewing tobacco. They all donned pirate clothes cut off at the knee, shaved smartly, and tumbled up, with the true nautical roll and hitching their trousers.

It need not be said who was the captain. Nibs and John were first and second mate. There was a woman aboard. The rest were tars before the mast,* and lived in the fo'c'sle.* Peter had already lashed himself to the wheel;* but he piped all hands* and delivered a short address to them; said he hoped they would do their duty like gallant hearties, but that he knew they were the scum of Rio and the Gold Coast,* and if they snapped at him he would tear them. His bluff strident words struck the note sailors understand, and they cheered him lustily. Then a few sharp orders were given, and they turned the ship round, and nosed her for the mainland.

Captain Pan calculated, after consulting the ship's chart, that if this weather lasted they should strike the Azores* about the 21st of June, after which it would save time to fly.

Some of them wanted it to be an honest ship and others were in favour of keeping it a pirate; but the captain treated them as dogs, and they dared not express their wishes to him even in a round robin.* Instant obedience was the only safe thing. Slightly got a dozen* for looking perplexed when told to take soundings.* The general feeling was that Peter was honest just now to lull Wendy's suspicions, but that there might be a change when the new suit was ready, which, against her will, she was making for him out of some of Hook's wickedest garments. It was afterwards whispered among them that on the first night he wore this suit he sat long in the cabin with Hook's cigarholder in his mouth and one hand clenched, all but the forefinger, which he bent and held threateningly aloft like a hook.

Instead of watching the ship, however, we must now return to that desolate home from which three of our characters had taken heartless flight so long ago. It seems a shame to have neglected No. 14 all this time; and yet we may be sure that Mrs Darling does not blame us.

If we had returned sooner to look with sorrowful sympathy at her, she would probably have cried, 'Don't be silly; what do I matter? Do go back and keep an eye on the children.' So long as mothers are like this their children will take advantage of them; and they may lay to that.

Even now we venture into that familiar nursery only because its lawful occupants are on their way home; we are merely hurrying on in advance of them to see that their beds are properly aired and that Mr and Mrs Darling do not go out for the evening. We are no more than servants. Why on earth should their beds be properly aired, seeing that they left them in such a thankless hurry? Would it not serve them jolly well right if they came back and found that their parents were spending the weekend in the country? It would be the moral lesson they have been in need of ever since we met them; but if we contrived things in this way Mrs Darling would never forgive us.

One thing I should like to do immensely, and that is to tell her, in the way authors have, that the children are coming back, that indeed they will be here on Thursday week. This would spoil so completely the surprise to which Wendy and John and Michael are looking forward. They have been planning it out on the ship: mother's rapture, father's shout of joy, Nana's leap through the air to embrace them first, when what they ought to be preparing for is a good hiding. How delicious to spoil it all by breaking the news in advance; so that when they enter grandly Mrs Darling may not even offer Wendy her mouth, and Mr Darling may exclaim pettishly, 'Dash it all, here are those boys again.' However, we should get no thanks even for this. We are beginning to know Mrs Darling by this time, and may be sure that she would upbraid us for depriving the children of their little pleasure.

'But, my dear madam, it is ten days till Thursday week; so that by telling you what's what, we can save you ten days of unhappiness.'

'Yes, but at what a cost! By depriving the children of ten minutes of delight.'

'Oh, if you look at it in that way.'

'What other way is there in which to look at it?'

You see, the woman had no proper spirit. I had meant to say extraordinarily nice things about her; but I despise her, and not one of them will I say now. She does not really need to be told to have things ready, for they are ready. All the beds are aired, and she never leaves the house, and observe, the window is open. For all the use we are to her, we might go back to the ship. However, as we are here we may as well stay and look on. That is all we are, lookers-on. Nobody really wants us. So let us watch and say jaggy* things, in the hope that some of them will hurt.

The only change to be seen in the night-nursery is that between nine and six the kennel is no longer there. When the children flew away, Mr Darling felt in his bones that all the blame was his for having chained Nana up, and that from first to last she had been wiser than he. Of course, as we have seen, he was quite a simple man; indeed he might have passed for a boy again if he had been able to take his baldness off; but he had also a noble sense of justice and a lion courage to do what seemed right to him; and having thought the matter out with anxious care after the flight of the children, he went down on all fours and crawled into the kennel. To all Mrs Darling's dear invitations to him to come out he replied sadly but firmly:

'No, my own one, this is the place for me.'

In the bitterness of his remorse he swore that he would never leave the kennel until his children came back. Of course, this was a pity; but whatever Mr Darling did he had to do in excess; otherwise he soon gave up doing it. And there never was a more humble man than the once proud George Darling, as he sat in the kennel of an evening talking with his wife of their children and all their pretty ways.

Very touching was his deference to Nana. He would not let her come into the kennel, but on all other matters he followed her wishes implicitly.

Every morning the kennel was carried with Mr Darling in it to a cab, which conveyed him to his office, and he returned home in the same way at six. Something of the strength of character of the man will be seen if we remember how sensitive he was to the opinion of neighbours: this man whose every movement now attracted surprised attention. Inwardly he must have suffered torture; but he preserved a calm exterior even when the young criticized his little home, and he always lifted his hat courteously to any lady who looked inside.

It may have been quixotic, but it was magnificent. Soon the inward meaning of it leaked out, and the great heart of the public was touched. Crowds followed the cab, cheering it lustily; charming girls scaled it to get his autograph; interviews appeared in the better class of papers, and society invited him to dinner and added, 'Do come in the kennel.'

On that eventful Thursday week Mrs Darling was in the night-nursery awaiting George's return home: a very sad-eyed woman. Now that we look at her closely and remember the gaiety of her in the old days, all gone now just because she has lost her babes, I find I won't be able to say nasty things about her after all. If she was too fond of her rubbishy* children she couldn't help it. Look at her in her chair, where she has fallen asleep. The corner of her mouth, where one looks first, is almost withered up. Her hand moves restlessly on her breast as if she had a pain there. Some like Peter best and some like Wendy best, but I like her best. Suppose, to make her happy, we whisper to her in her sleep that the brats are coming back. They are really within two miles of the window now, and flying strong, but all we need whisper is that they are on the way. Let's.

It is a pity we did it, for she has started up, calling their names; and there is no one in the room but Nana.

'O Nana, I dreamt my dear ones had come back.'

Nana had filmy eyes, but all she could do was to put her paw gently on her mistress's lap; and they were sitting together thus when the kennel was brought back. As Mr Darling puts his head out at it to kiss his wife, we see that his face is more worn than of yore, but has a softer expression.

He gave his hat to Liza, who took it scornfully; for she had no imagination, and was quite incapable of understanding the motives of such a man. Outside, the crowd who had accompanied the cab home were still cheering, and he was naturally not unmoved.

'Listen to them,' he said; 'it is very gratifying.'

'Lot of little boys,' sneered Liza.

'There were several adults today,' he assured her with a faint flush; but when she tossed her head he had not a word of reproof for her. Social success had not spoilt him; it had made him sweeter. For some time he sat half out of the kennel, talking with Mrs Darling of this success, and pressing her hand reassuringly when she said she hoped his head would not be turned by it.

'But if I had been a weak man,' he said. 'Good heavens, if I had been a weak man!'

'And, George,' she said timidly, 'you are as full of remorse as ever, aren't you?'

'Full of remorse as ever, dearest! See my punishment: living in a kennel.'

'But it is punishment, isn't it, George? You are sure you are not enjoying it?'

'My love!'

You may be sure she begged his pardon; and then, feeling drowsy, he curled round in the kennel.

'Won't you play me to sleep,' he asked, 'on the nursery piano?' and as she was crossing to the day-nursery he added thoughtlessly, 'And shut that window. I feel a draught.'

'O George, never ask me to do that. The window must always be left open for them, always, always.'

Now it was his turn to beg her pardon; and she went into the day-nursery and played, and soon he was asleep; and while he slept, Wendy and John and Michael flew into the room.

Oh no. We have written it so, because that was the charming arrangement planned by them before we left the ship; but something must have happened since then, for it is not they who have flown in, it is Peter and Tinker Bell.

Peter's first words tell all.

'Quick, Tink,' he whispered, 'close the window; bar it. That's right. Now you and I must get away by the door; and when Wendy comes she will think her mother has barred her out; and she will have to go back with me.'

Now I understand what had hitherto puzzled me, why when Peter had exterminated the pirates he did not return to the island and leave Tink to escort the children to the mainland. This trick had been in his head all the time.

Instead of feeling that he was behaving badly he danced with glee; then he peeped into the day-nursery to see who was playing. He whispered to Tink, 'It's Wendy's mother. She is a pretty lady, but not so pretty as my mother. Her mouth is full of thimbles, but not so full as my mother's was.'

Of course he knew nothing whatever about his mother; but he sometimes bragged about her.

He did not know the tune, which was 'Home, Sweet Home',* but he knew it was saying, 'Come back, Wendy, Wendy, Wendy'; and he cried exultantly, 'You will never see Wendy again, lady, for the window is barred.'

He peeped in again to see why the music had stopped; and now he saw that Mrs Darling had laid her head on the box, and that two tears were sitting on her eyes.

'She wants me to unbar the window,' thought Peter, 'but I won't, not I.'

He peeped again, and the tears were still there, or another two had taken their place.

'She's awfully fond of Wendy,' he said to himself. He was angry with her now for not seeing why she could not have Wendy.

The reason was so simple: 'I'm fond of her too. We can't both have her, lady.'

But the lady would not make the best of it, and he was unhappy. He ceased to look at her, but even then she would not let go of him. He skipped about and made funny faces, but when he stopped it was just as if she were inside him, knocking.

'Oh, all right,' he said at last, and gulped. Then he unbarred the window. 'Come on, Tink,' he cried, with a frightful sneer at the laws of nature; 'we don't want any silly mothers'; and he flew away.

Thus Wendy and John and Michael found the window open for them after all, which of course was more than they deserved. They alighted on the floor, quite unashamed of themselves; and the youngest one had already forgotten his home.

'John,' he said, looking around him doubtfully, 'I think I have been here before.'

'Of course you have, you silly. There is your old bed.'

'So it is,' Michael said, but not with much conviction.

'I say,' cried John, 'the kennel!' and he dashed across to look into it.

'Perhaps Nana is inside it,' Wendy said.

But John whistled. 'Hullo,' he said, 'there's a man inside it.'

'It's father!' exclaimed Wendy.

'Let me see father,' Michael begged eagerly, and he took a good look. 'He is not so big as the pirate I killed,' he said with such frank disappointment that I am glad Mr Darling was asleep; it would have been sad if those had been the first words he heard his little Michael say.

Wendy and John had been taken aback somewhat at finding their father in the kennel.

'Surely,' said John, like one who had lost faith in his memory, 'he used not to sleep in the kennel?'

'John,' Wendy said falteringly, 'perhaps we don't remember the old life as well as we thought we did.'

A chill fell upon them; and serve them right.

'It is very careless of mother', said that young scoundrel John, 'not to be here when we come back.'

It was then that Mrs Darling began playing again.

'It's mother!' cried Wendy, peeping.

'So it is!' said John.

'Then are you not really our mother, Wendy?' asked Michael, who was surely sleepy.

'Oh dear!' exclaimed Wendy, with her first real twinge of remorse, 'it was quite time we came back.'

'Let us creep in,' John suggested, 'and put our hands over her eyes.'

But Wendy, who saw that they must break the joyous news more gently, had a better plan.

'Let us all slip into our beds, and be there when she comes in, just as if we had never been away.'

And so when Mrs Darling went back to the night-nursery to see if her husband was asleep, all the beds were occupied. The children waited for her cry of joy, but it did not come. She saw them, but she did not believe they were there. You see, she saw them in their beds so often in her dreams that she thought this was just the dream hanging around her still.

She sat down in the chair by the fire, where in the old days she had nursed them.

They could not understand this, and a cold fear fell upon all the three of them.

'Mother!' Wendy cried.

'That's Wendy,' she said, but still she was sure it was the dream.

'Mother!'

'That's John,' she said.

'Mother!' cried Michael. He knew her now.

'That's Michael,' she said, and she stretched out her arms for the three little selfish children they would never envelop again. Yes, they did, they went round Wendy and John and Michael, who had slipped out of bed and run to her.

'George, George,' she cried when she could speak; and Mr Darling woke to share her bliss, and Nana came rushing in. There could not have been a lovelier sight; but there was none to see it except a strange boy who was staring in at the window. He had ecstasies innumerable that other children can never know; but he was looking through the window at the one joy from which he must be for ever barred.

CHAPTER 17

I HOPE you want to know what became of the other boys. They were waiting below to give Wendy time to explain about them; and when they had counted five hundred they went up. They went up by the stair, because they thought this would make a better impression. They stood in a row in front of Mrs Darling, with their hats off, and wishing they were not wearing their pirate clothes. They said nothing, but their eyes asked her to have them. They ought to have looked at Mr Darling also, but they forgot about him.

Of course Mrs Darling said at once that she would have them; but Mr Darling was curiously depressed, and they saw that he considered six a rather large number.

'I must say,' he said to Wendy, 'that you don't do things by halves,' a grudging remark which the twins thought was pointed at them.

The first twin was the proud one, and he asked, flushing, 'Do you think we should be too much of a handful, sir? Because if so we can go away.'

'Father!' Wendy cried, shocked; but still the cloud was on him. He knew he was behaving unworthily, but he could not help it.

'We could lie doubled up,' said Nibs.

'I always cut their hair myself,' said Wendy.

'George!' Mrs Darling exclaimed, pained to see her dear one showing himself in such an unfavourable light.

Then he burst into tears, and the truth came out. He was as glad to have them as she was, he said, but he thought they should have asked his consent as well as hers, instead of treating him as a cypher* in his own house.

'I don't think he is a cypher,' Tootles cried instantly. 'Do you think he is a cypher, Curly?'

'No, I don't. Do you think he is a cypher, Slightly?'

'Rather not. Twin, what do you think?'

It turned out that not one of them thought him a cypher; and he was absurdly gratified, and said he would find space for them all in the drawing-room if they fitted in.

'We'll fit in, sir,' they assured him.

'Then follow the leader,' he cried gaily. 'Mind you, I am not sure that we have a drawing-room, but we pretend we have, and it's all the same. Hoop la!'*

He went off dancing through the house, and they all cried 'Hoop la!' and danced after him, searching for the drawing-room; and I forget whether they found it, but at any rate they found corners, and they all fitted in.

As for Peter, he saw Wendy once again before he flew away. He did not exactly come to the window, but he brushed against it in passing, so that she could open it if she liked and call to him. That was what she did.

'Hullo, Wendy, good-bye,' he said.

'Oh dear, are you going away?'

'Yes.'

'You don't feel, Peter,' she said falteringly, 'that you would like to say anything to my parents about a very sweet subject?'

'No.'

'About me, Peter?'

'No.'

Mrs Darling came to the window, for at present she was keeping a sharp eye on Wendy. She told Peter that she had adopted all the other boys, and would like to adopt him also.

'Would you send me to school?' he inquired craftily.

'Yes.'

'And then to an office?'

'I suppose so.'

'Soon I should be a man?'

'Very soon.'

'I don't want to go to school and learn solemn things,' he told her passionately. 'I don't want to be a man. O Wendy's mother, if I was to wake up and feel there was a beard!'

'Peter', said Wendy the comforter, 'I should love you in a beard'; and Mrs Darling stretched out her arms to him, but he repulsed her.

'Keep back, lady, no one is going to catch me and make me a man.'

'But where are you going to live?'

'With Tink in the house we built for Wendy. The fairies are to put it high up among the tree-tops where they sleep at nights.'

'How lovely,' cried Wendy so longingly that Mrs Darling tightened her grip.

'I thought all the fairies were dead,' Mrs Darling said.

'There are always a lot of young ones,' explained Wendy, who was now quite an authority, 'because you see when a new baby laughs for the first time a new fairy is born, and as there are always new babies there are always new fairies. They live in nests on the tops of trees; and the mauve ones are boys and the white ones are girls, and the blue ones are just little sillies who are not sure what they are.'

'I shall have such fun,' said Peter, with one eye on Wendy.

'It will be rather lonely in the evening,' she said, 'sitting by the fire.'

'I shall have Tink.'

'Tink can't go a twentieth part of the way round,' she reminded him a little tartly.

'Sneaky tell-tale!' Tink called out from somewhere round the corner.

'It doesn't matter,' Peter said.

'O Peter, you know it matters.'

'Well then, come with me to the little house.'

'May I, Mummy?'

'Certainly not. I have got you home again, and I mean to keep you.'

'But he does so need a mother.'

'So do you, my love.'

'Oh, all right,' Peter said, as if he had asked her from politeness merely; but Mrs Darling saw his mouth twitch, and she made this handsome offer: to let Wendy go to him for a week every year to do his spring-cleaning. Wendy would have preferred a more permanent arrangement; and it seemed to her that spring would be long in coming; but this promise sent Peter away quite gay again. He had no sense of time, and was so full of adventures that all I have told you about him is only a halfpenny-worth of them. I suppose it was because Wendy knew this that her last words to him were these rather plaintive ones:

'You won't forget me, Peter, will you, before spring-cleaning time comes?'

Of course Peter promised; and then he flew away. He took Mrs Darling's kiss with him. The kiss that had been for no one else Peter took quite easily. Funny. But she seemed satisfied.

Of course all the boys went to school; and most of them got into Class III, but Slightly was put first into Class IV and then into Class V. Class I is the top class. Before they had attended school a week they saw what goats they had been not to remain on the island; but it was too late now, and soon they settled down to being as ordinary as you or me or Jenkins minor. It is sad to have to say that the power to fly gradually left them. At first Nana tied their feet to the bedposts so that they should not fly away in the night; and one of their diversions by day was to pretend to fall off buses; but by and by they ceased to tug at their bonds in bed, and found that they hurt themselves when they let go of the bus. In time they could not even fly after their hats. Want of practice, they called it; but what it really meant was that they no longer believed.

Michael believed longer than the other boys, though they jeered at him; so he was with Wendy when Peter came for her at the end of the first year. She flew away with Peter in the frock she had woven from leaves and berries in the Neverland, and her one fear was that he might notice how short it had become; but he never noticed, he had so much to say about himself.

She had looked forward to thrilling talks with him about old times, but new adventures had crowded the old ones from his mind.

'Who is Captain Hook?' he asked with interest when she spoke of the arch enemy.

'Don't you remember,' she asked, amazed, 'how you killed him and saved all our lives?'

'I forget them after I kill them,' he replied carelessly.

When she expressed a doubtful hope that Tinker Bell would be glad to see her he said, 'Who is Tinker Bell?'

'O Peter,' she said, shocked; but even when she explained he could not remember.

'There are such a lot of them,' he said. 'I expect she is no more.'

I expect he was right, for fairies don't live long, but they are so little that a short time seems a good while to them.

Wendy was pained too to find that the past year was but as yesterday to Peter; it had seemed such a long year of waiting to her. But he was exactly as fascinating as ever, and they had a lovely spring-cleaning in the little house on the tree-tops.

Next year he did not come for her. She waited in a new frock because the old one simply would not meet; but he never came.

'Perhaps he is ill,' Michael said.

'You know he is never ill.'

Michael came close to her and whispered, with a shiver, 'Perhaps there is no such person, Wendy!' and then Wendy would have cried if Michael had not been crying.

Peter came next spring cleaning; and the strange thing was that he never knew he had missed a year.

That was the last time the girl Wendy ever saw him. For a little longer she tried for his sake not to have growing pains; and she felt she was untrue to him when she got a prize for general knowledge. But the years came and went without bringing the careless boy; and when they met again Wendy was a married woman, and Peter was no more to her than a little dust in the box in which she had kept her toys. Wendy was grown up. You need not be sorry for her. She was one of the kind that likes to grow up. In the end she grew up of her own free will a day quicker than other girls.

All the boys were grown up and done for by this time; so it is scarcely worth while saying anything more about them. You may see the twins and Nibs and Curly any day going to an office, each carrying a little bag and an umbrella. Michael is an engine-driver. Slightly married a lady of title, and so he became a lord.* You see that judge in a wig coming out at the iron door? That used to be Tootles. The bearded man who doesn't know any story to tell his children was once John.

Wendy was married in white with a pink sash. It is strange to think that Peter did not alight in the church and forbid the banns.*

Years rolled on again, and Wendy had a daughter. This ought not to be written in ink but in a golden splash.

She was called Jane, and always had an odd inquiring look, as if from the moment she arrived on the mainland she wanted to ask questions. When she was old enough to ask them they were mostly about Peter Pan. She loved to hear of Peter, and Wendy told her all she could remember in the very nursery from which the famous flight had taken place. It was Jane's nursery now, for her father had bought it at the three per cents* from Wendy's father, who was no longer fond of stairs. Mrs Darling was now dead and forgotten.

There were only two beds in the nursery now, Jane's and her nurse's; and there was no kennel, for Nana also had passed away. She died of old age, and at the end she had been rather difficult to get on with; being very firmly convinced that no one knew how to look after children except herself.

Once a week Jane's nurse had her evening off; and then it was Wendy's part to put Jane to bed. That was the time for stories. It was Jane's invention to raise the sheet over her mother's head and her own, thus making a tent, and in the awful darkness to whisper:

'What do we see now?'

'I don't think I see anything tonight,' says Wendy, with a feeling that if Nana were here she would object to further conversation.

'Yes, you do,' says Jane, 'you see when you were a little girl.'*

'That is a long time ago, sweetheart,' says Wendy. 'Ah me, how time flies!'

'Does it fly,' asks the artful child, 'the way you flew when you were a little girl?'

'The way I flew! Do you know, Jane, I sometimes wonder whether I ever did really fly.'

'Yes, you did.'

'The dear old days when I could fly!'

'Why can't you fly now, mother?'

'Because I am grown up, dearest. When people grow up they forget the way.'

'Why do they forget the way?'

'Because they are no longer gay and innocent and heartless. It is only the gay and innocent and heartless who can fly.'

'What is gay and innocent and heartless? I do wish I was gay and innocent and heartless.'

Or perhaps Wendy admits that she does see something. 'I do believe', she says, 'that it is this nursery.'

'I do believe it is,' says Jane. 'Go on.'

They are now embarked on the great adventure of the night when Peter flew in looking for his shadow.

'The foolish fellow', says Wendy, 'tried to stick it on with soap, and when he could not he cried, and that woke me, and I sewed it on for him.'

'You have missed a bit,' interrupts Jane, who now knows the story better than her mother. 'When you saw him sitting on the floor crying, what did you say?'

'I sat up in bed and I said, "Boy, why are you crying?"'

'Yes, that was it,' says Jane, with a big breath.

'And then he flew us all away to the Neverland and the fairies and the pirates and the redskins and the mermaids' lagoon, and the home under the ground, and the little house.'

'Yes! Which did you like best of all?'

'I think I liked the home under the ground best of all.'

'Yes, so do I. What was the last thing Peter ever said to you?'

'The last thing he ever said to me was, "Just always be waiting for me, and then some night you will hear me crowing."'

'Yes.'

'But, alas, he forgot all about me.' Wendy said it with a smile. She was as grown up as that.

'What did his crow sound like?' Jane asked one evening.

'It was like this,' Wendy said, trying to imitate Peter's crow.

'No, it wasn't,' Jane said gravely, 'it was like this'; and she did it ever so much better than her mother.

Wendy was a little startled. 'My darling, how can you know?'

'I often hear it when I am sleeping,' Jane said.

'Ah yes, many girls hear it when they are sleeping, but I was the only one who heard it awake.'

'Lucky you,' said Jane.

And then one night came the tragedy. It was the spring of the year, and the story had been told for the night, and Jane was now asleep in her bed. Wendy was sitting on the floor, very close to the fire, so as to see to darn, for there was no other light in the nursery; and while she sat darning she heard a crow. Then the window blew open as of old, and Peter dropped on the floor.

He was exactly the same as ever, and Wendy saw at once that he still had all his first teeth.

He was a little boy, and she was grown up. She huddled by the fire not daring to move, helpless and guilty, a big woman.

'Hullo, Wendy,' he said, not noticing any difference, for he was thinking chiefly of himself; and in the dim light her white dress might have been the nightgown in which he had seen her first.

'Hullo, Peter,' she replied faintly, squeezing herself as small as possible. Something inside her was crying, 'Woman, woman, let go of me.'

'Hullo, where is John?' he asked, suddenly missing the third bed.

'John is not here now,' she gasped.

'Is Michael asleep?' he asked, with a careless glance at Jane.

'Yes,' she answered; and now she felt that she was untrue to Jane as well as to Peter.

'That is not Michael,' she said quickly, lest a judgement should fall on her.

Peter looked. 'Hullo, is it a new one?'

'Yes.'

'Boy or girl?'

'Girl.'

Now surely he would understand; but not a bit of it.

'Peter,' she said, faltering, 'are you expecting me to fly away with you?'

'Of course, that is why I have come.' He added a little sternly, 'Have you forgotten that this is spring-cleaning time?'

She knew it was useless to say that he had let many spring-cleaning times pass.

'I can't come,' she said apologetically, 'I have forgotten how to fly.'

'I'll soon teach you again.'

'O Peter, don't waste the fairy dust on me.'

She had risen; and now at last a fear assailed him. 'What is it?' he cried, shrinking.

'I will turn up the light,' she said, 'and then you can see for yourself.'

For almost the only time in his life that I know of, Peter was afraid. 'Don't turn up the light,' he cried.

She let her hands play in the hair of the tragic boy. She was not a little girl heart-broken about him; she was a grown woman smiling at it all, but they were wet smiles.

Then she turned up the light, and Peter saw. He gave a cry of pain; and when the tall beautiful creature stooped to lift him in her arms he drew back sharply.

'What is it?' he cried again.

She had to tell him.

'I am old, Peter. I am ever so much more than twenty. I grew up long ago.'

'You promised not to!'

'I couldn't help it. I am a married woman, Peter.'

'No, you're not.'

'Yes, and the little girl in the bed is my baby.'

'No, she's not.'

But he supposed she was; and he took a step towards the sleeping child with his dagger upraised. Of course he did not strike. He sat down on the floor instead and sobbed; and Wendy did not know how to comfort him, though she could have done it so easily once. She was only a woman now, and she ran out of the room to try to think.

Peter continued to cry, and soon his sobs woke Jane. She sat up in bed, and was interested at once.

PETER AND JANE

'Boy,' she said, 'why are you crying?'
Peter rose and bowed to her, and she bowed to him from the bed.
'Hullo,' he said.
'Hullo,' said Jane.
'My name is Peter Pan,' he told her.

'Yes, I know.'

'I came back for my mother,' he explained, 'to take her to the Neverland.'

'Yes, I know,' Jane said, 'I've been waiting for you.'

When Wendy returned diffidently she found Peter sitting on the bedpost crowing gloriously, while Jane in her nighty was flying round the room in solemn ecstasy.

'She is my mother,' Peter explained; and Jane descended and stood by his side, with the look on her face that he liked to see on ladies when they gazed at him.

'He does so need a mother,' Jane said.

'Yes, I know,' Wendy admitted rather forlornly; 'no one knows it so well as I.'

'Good-bye,' said Peter to Wendy; and he rose in the air, and the shameless Jane rose with him; it was already her easiest way of moving about.

Wendy rushed to the window.

'No, no,' she cried.

'It is just for spring-cleaning time,' Jane said; 'he wants me always to do his spring-cleaning.'

'If only I could go with you,' Wendy sighed.

'You see you can't fly,' said Jane.

Of course in the end Wendy let them fly away together. Our last glimpse of her shows her at the window, watching them receding into the sky until they were as small as stars.

As you look at Wendy you may see her hair becoming white, and her figure little again, for all this happened long ago. Jane is now a common grown-up, with a daughter called Margaret; and every spring-cleaning time, except when he forgets, Peter comes for Margaret and takes her to the Neverland, where she tells him stories about himself, to which he listens eagerly. When Margaret grows up she will have a daughter, who is to be Peter's mother in turn; and thus it will go on, so long as children are gay and innocent and heartless.

SCENARIO
for a Proposed Film of
PETER PAN
or
The Boy Who Wouldn't Grow Up.
(1921)

(NOTE:— The music of the acted play, as specially written for it, should accompany the pictures. Thus there is the music which always heralds Peter's appearances—the Tinker Bell music—the pirate music—the redskin music—the crocodile music, etc., all of which have a dramatic significance as well as helping in the telling of the story. Other special music should be written so that all the music accompanying the play becomes really part of it. The sub-titles, i.e., the words flung on the screen, are here underlined in red. The aim has been to have as few words as possible. There are very few words in the last half hour or more of this film, and there are also about fifteen minutes of the lagoon scene without any words. Many of the chief scenes, especially those calling for novel cinema treatment, are of course not in the acted play, but where they are in it they should be acted in the same way, and to that extent the play should be a guide to the film. This scenario is very condensed: here we give only the bones of the story. The details of how to get the humour, etc., must come later. The technical matters are obviously of huge importance and difficulty, and it remains to be seen whether the cinema experts can solve them.)

The first picture is of Peter riding gaily on a goat through a wood, playing on his pipes (a reproduction of the painting in my possession).* He suddenly flies on to a tree in the inconsequential way of birds. From this he flies over a romantic river, circling it with the careless loveliness of a sea-gull. He as suddenly re-alights on his goat and rides away playing his pipes, his legs sticking out cockily. Vast practice and rehearsal will be needed to get the flying beautiful and really like a bird's. The flying must be far better and more elaborate than in the acted play, and should cover of course a far wider expanse. This incident should show at once that the film can do things for 'Peter Pan' which the ordinary stage cannot do. It should strike a note of wonder in the first picture, and whet the appetite for marvels.

There was once a poor London clerk and his wife, called Mr and Mrs Darling; but what do you think they had?

Mr and Mrs Darling who should be very tall, so as to make the children smaller, are sitting on each side of fireplace in a humble, but pleasant London sitting-room. The furniture should be of the simplest kind. There should not in this room, or any room shown in the play, be any of the massive carved furniture in heavy oak with spiral legs, etc., that is often shown in films. These are people of refined taste, but with very small means. Mr Darling is only a clerk in an office, and the humbleness of their social position should always be emphasized. She is sewing a childish garment. After a moment there come running to them one at a time their three children.

<u>Wendy, John and Michael.</u>

It is a happy domestic picture, all very loving. The children romp away and the parents are there without them. They have been boisterous and Mrs Darling is tired and over-worked. Mr Darling kindly tries to take the sewing from her, but she shakes her head. Liza, their little maid, comes in with the evening paper to Mr Darling. It should be a London paper, not an American one. Liza should be played by a child of about eight years of age, but with her hair up and a long skirt. She departs primly. Mr Darling points out an advertisement in the paper to Mrs Darling. It is shown in a close-up:— 'For nurses and nursery maids, apply Mrs S. 22 Green Street'. Evidently this is what they are in need of, but they compare money and indicate that they are too poor. Then he shows her another advertisement in close-up:— 'Newfoundland dog for sale, cheap. <u>Very fond of children</u>. Apply Dogs' Home'. He points to the underlined words in particular. She is evidently afraid, but he sees an idea in it.

Then there is a picture of Mr Darling leading a Newfoundland dog through a London street. The dog is coming willingly.

The next picture shows the result of the previous ones. We see the night nursery with three beds as in the opening of the acted play. It should be an English nursery. The Newfoundland dog, Nana, is seen going about the work of a nurse in a very practical way. We see Nana preparing the bath, bathing Michael in the bathroom very realistically, and herding the three to bed, tucking them in, etc. A long, continuous amusing picture, reproducing this incident from the play, but more fully than is possible there.

When Nana thinks they are all asleep she retires into her kennel which is in the nursery, and we see her go to sleep there with her head just out of the kennel. The naughty children are not really asleep. They jump up. Wendy makes sure that Nana is asleep, then she signs to the others, and they creep into her bed. She begins to tell them a story, while they sit up eagerly listening. It is rather dark.

(Note about Nana:—she should be generally played by a human being in a skin exactly like that of some real Newfoundland dog which is available, so that in certain scenes—as in the street scenes—this dog can be substituted for the actor.) Next we have a vision of Cinderella with her broom asleep by fire in kitchen, to show that this is the story Wendy is telling.

<u>Do you know why swallows build in the eaves of houses? It is to listen to the stories.</u>

We see Wendy telling this to her brothers. Michael goes on tip-toe to the window to 'shoo' the swallows away. Then we have an outside view of the window, with several swallows sitting on the sill, listening. Michael suddenly appears at the window, opens curtains and 'shoos' them away. He returns, grinning, to Wendy's bed, thinking himself a very clever lad.

<u>Unknown to Wendy there was sometimes another listener to the stories.</u>

From outside we see Peter listening at the window. Then we have alternate scenes of Wendy telling tales and Peter listening eagerly. (We should not see that Peter has flown here yet.)

<u>One night Nana nearly caught him, and he only escaped by leaving his shadow behind.</u>

Peter comes, stealthily, in by window to hear the story better. He crawls along the floor and listens delightedly. Nana wakes up and runs at him. He leaps out at window, but she brings down the sash so quickly that his shadow is left behind. Excitement of the children, who sit up. Mrs Darling rushes in, followed by Mr Darling. Nana has the shadow in her mouth. Mr Darling unfolds the shadow and examines it. He evidently thinks it a very naughty shadow. Mrs Darling rolls it up and puts it away in a drawer. They look out at the window, but no one can be seen. The pictures here show us that the nursery is at the top of a house in a poor, but respectable, London street.

The mystery makes them uneasy. Then Mrs Darling evidently thinks Michael is looking too excited. She looks at his tongue, puts a thermometer in his mouth and produces a bottle, which we see, in a close-up, is labelled 'Castor Oil'. She pours some in a spoon and puts the handle into Nana's mouth.

Michael is in his own bed, with the others around. Nana crosses to him with the medicine spoon in her mouth. He is naughty and won't take it, etc., as in the play, which should be consulted here for the humours of the scene.

'Be a man, my son. I would take my medicine now, as an example to you, if I hadn't lost the bottle.'

Mr Darling is saying this in his superior way.

'I know where you put it, father.'

Wendy says this, thinking she is pleasing him. She runs off. Anguish of Mr Darling, which is increased when she returns with the bottle, which we have seen her in another picture getting from the top of a cupboard in his bedroom, where he had, doubtless, hidden it. It should be a very humble bedroom. She pours some of his medicine into a glass and gives it to him. He glares. John chuckles at his father's predicament. Wendy gives the signal: one, two, three, for them to drink simultaneously. Humours of Michael and his father in this situation as in play.

Michael drinks his medicine, but Mr Darling ignobly conceals his glass behind his back. Michael sees this and cries. All are ashamed of Mr Darling, as they peep behind his back and see the glass. Nana sticks out her tail and struts contemptuously out of the room. He is annoyed at her. Then he indicates that he has a funny idea. He gets a milk bottle (which we see to be milk in a close-up) and pours a little milk on top of his medicine and then pours the white mixture into Nana's drinking bowl.

The others don't like this, but he points to it when Nana returns. She is grateful and begins to lap it up, then looks at him reproachfully and sneaks into her kennel. The children weep, and he is testy over the ill success of his joke. He orders Nana to come out, but she shrinks. Then, as in the play, he tries blandishment and lures her out, then suddenly seizes her and drags her away out at the door, to the grief of the children.

He foolishly ties Nana up in the yard, instead of leaving her in the nursery to guard his children.

In the next picture we see him tying Nana up in the yard below.

That night Mrs Darling had to go with her husband to a party.

First we see her in a bedroom tying her husband's tie, and we see him inking seams in his coat and also inking his tall hat, which shows how poor they are. Then we see her in her party frock going from bed to bed kissing the children, etc. Then lighting a night light at the head of each bedside. She has a last maternal look at them from the door, all as in play, with the accompanying music.

Then we see Mr and Mrs Darling going out, and passing the yard, where Mr Darling won't let Mrs Darling fondle Nana. Nana weeps. The two pass up the street under an umbrella, as it is snowing. The house to which they go is not far away. It is in the same street, but on the opposite side. They walk. (There are no automobiles or telephones in this play.)

Next we see the outside of the window with two or three swallows on the window-sill.

Now Nana is seen fretting in the yard, as if she smelt danger. Then the nursery again. Children asleep. The night-lights blink and go out one by one in an eerie way to the music of the play, suggesting that something strange is to happen. There should be an awful creepiness here, which the music greatly helps.

The fairy, Tinker Bell.

Now we have the outside of the window, with swallows still there. The fairy music comes now. The fairy, Tink, flies on and alights on the window-sill. The swallows remain. She should be about five inches in height, and, if the effect can be got, this should be one of the quaintest pictures of the film, the appearance of a real fairy. She is a vain little thing, and arranges her clothes to her satisfaction. She also keeps shoving the birds about so as to get the best place for herself. There should never be any close-up pictures of Tink or other fairies: we should always just see them as not more than five inches high. Finally she shoves the swallows off the sill. Then she pops through the window. We see her flying about the nursery, alighting on each bed, etc. Next we see Nana below looking at the sky and barking. Then we see Peter flying towards us. At first he is a mere speck in the distance. Then he comes closer and reaches the window.

Now the inside of the nursery, with the children still asleep. It is rather dark now. Tink is not visible. Peter comes in through window. He has come for his shadow. He makes sure they are asleep. It should all be very dramatic here—like an attempted burglary, and the music helps.

He rummages in the drawers for his shadow, finds it, sits on the floor trying to stick it on to his foot with soap, which he gets from the bathroom. It won't stick on. He sobs. Wendy hears him and sits up in bed.

'Boy, why are you crying?'

She is asking this. He rises and, standing at foot of her bed, bows politely to her. She is gratified and bows from the bed in the quaint manner of the play, in which this is a popular incident.

'Girl, what is your name?'
'Wendy. What is your name?'
'Peter Pan.'
'Where is your mother, Peter?'
'Don't have a mother, Wendy.'
'Oh!'

As the result of this conversation Wendy springs out of bed, runs to him, puts arm round him and mothers him. It should be seen that she has at once taken the mother's place. He holds up his shadow to show that this is what is worrying him. She lifts the soap and in a close-up we see that it is marked 'Soap'. She is astonished at his ignorance, puts him on a chair, and proceeds to sew the shadow on to his foot in her old-fashioned, motherly way, with the business of the play, in which he suffers agonies, but is very brave. When he finds that all is well he struts about conceitedly, showing off his shadow. He dances gaily to his shadow, and brushes her aside as of no consequence, and this annoys Wendy.

'If I am no use I can at least withdraw.'

We see Wendy saying this. She then haughtily leaps into bed and covers her body and face with the blankets all in one action, which is another popular incident of the play.

Peter is now sorry. First he pretends to go away, but hides. Then he leaps on to the rail at foot of the bed and sits on it and pokes her in a wheedling way with his foot.

'Wendy, don't withdraw. One girl is more use than twenty boys.'

He is saying this. She peeps at him smiling and forgivingly, jumps up and sits on the side of her bed and signs to him to join her. He does so. They are a very friendly pair.

When Wendy said she would give him a kiss he held out his hand for it.
He didn't know what a kiss was; and, so, not to hurt his feelings, she
gave him a thimble.

We see this incident as in the play.

'Now shall I give you a kiss?'

Peter is saying this to Wendy. She nods. He gravely pulls a button off
his clothes and gives it to her. We see it is a button in a close-up. She
pretends pleasure, but privately makes a face.

'I ran away from home, Wendy, soon after I was born. I heard my father
saying I would soon be a man; and I want always to be a little boy, and
to have fun.'

He tells her this. Then we see Peter's mother lying in bed and the
father coming in. She holds up the baby proudly (It must be a real
baby just old enough to crawl.)

The father sits on a chair talking to the mother.

Now comes another realistic picture. We have visions of what the
father is telling the mother, viz, of how the baby will rapidly grow up.
Without the background seeming to alter we see the baby changing to
a tiny boy, then to an older boy, then, through various changes to a youth
and a man with moustache, sitting like a clerk on a stool at a desk. The
clothes, socks, etc., of him at one period should seem to drop off him and
be replaced by others as he grows older, and we should actually see his
legs growing longer, and so on. It will be worthwhile to devote much
attention to this picture to get the right effect. The idea is to apply to the
growth of a child from babyhood to manhood the same sort of cinema
treatment that is sometimes given to illustrate the growth of flowers and
plants. The real baby is much alarmed by all this pictorial prediction of
his future. While the parents talk he creeps unseen by them out of bed
and under it; emerges from under it, and crawls along floor out of the
door. We see him crawling through an anteroom in which a nurse is
asleep. Then he is seen crawling downstairs. Then we might get the effect
of him crawling across a street full of traffic. He crawls into Kensington
Gardens. There, two great birds come to help and, sustaining him
between them, fly away with him. His nightgown is now much torn.

Peter tells Wendy about his friends, the fairies. 'When the first baby
laughed for the first time, its laugh broke into a thousand pieces, and
they all went skipping about: and that was the beginning of fairies.'

He tells her this. Then the scene is a primeval wood. Adam and Eve leave their child on the ground. They go. The child laughs and kicks joyously. Then the picture is full of little splashes whirling about like falling leaves, and when they come to rest they are gay little fairies. The tinkling of bells comes here also to indicate their chatter, and we also have the fairy music.

> Every time a child says 'I don't believe in fairies', there is a fairy somewhere who falls down dead.

Peter is telling this to the enraptured Wendy. Then we see another nursery, with an unpleasant boy making this remark to his nurse.

Then the scene changes to a tree, on a branch of which several fairies are sitting chattering happily. They are small like Tink. Suddenly one of them claps her hand to her heart, reels and falls to the ground. The others descend and sadly carry her remains away.

> Wendy sees her first fairy.

We see Peter and Wendy chasing Tink about. Tink alights on the clock. Wendy admires her ecstatically.

> But Tink loves Peter, and when she sees Wendy giving him a real kiss (now called a thimble) she misbehaves.

Peter and Wendy are now together on an armchair. She gives him a real kiss, and he likes it, beams, and solemnly gives her one. Then Tink rushes at her and pulls her hair, etc. Wendy screams. Peter threatens. The unseen bells which represent the fairy language ring agitatedly.

> She says she will do that every time I give you a thimble. 'But why, Tink?'

Peter is asking. The reply comes in a different kind of tinkle that should remain in the audience's memory.

> She said: 'You silly ass!'

Peter says this to Wendy. He chases Tink away, out of the window.

> 'I live in the Never, Never Land with the Lost Boys. Come with me, Wendy, and I'll teach you to fly, and you can be our mother. We do so need a mother.'

Picture of Peter urging her to this. They are now sprawling on the floor. Peter works his way along the floor to her—another comic effect in the play. Then a vision of the lost boys all perched on a branch of a tree asleep, huddled together in a row and sitting exactly like sleeping birds. They are in very ragged clothes and should look very small. Peter, himself, is one of them.

'Of course it's awfully fascinating!'

Wendy is saying this to Peter, and is screwed up in rapture as she says it.

Next a picture of little Liza asleep in the kitchen on a chair, a half-washed dish in her hands.

Then one of Nana in the yard, being annoyed by Tink, who is behaving impudently to her, teasing her, drinking from her bowl, etc. Nana makes rushes at her, but the mischievous Tink always flies out of reach.

'John, Michael, wake up. There is a boy here who is to teach us to fly and take us to the Never, Never Land. He says there are pirates and mermaids and redskins.' 'I say, let's go at once.'

Wendy is waking up Michael while Peter wafts John out of bed with his foot. Wendy is telling the great news, and John's is the enthusiastic reply. John puts on his long hat. John is in pyjamas, Michael in 'combinations' and Wendy in a white cotton nightgown.

A lesson in flying.

We should now have a fine series of film pictures without words.

First we see Peter in the nursery showing the others how to fly, while they watch him eagerly from their beds. Then Nana in the yard tearing at her chain, and looking up at the nursery window which is the only one lit up.

Then little Liza still asleep in her chair in the kitchen—in a different position.

Then a view of Peter and the others through the window on whose sill Tink is sitting.

Then Mr Darling, Mrs Darling with others at a dinner party. Then the nursery again. The children are trying to fly by jumping about and falling.

'Just think lovely wonderful thoughts, and they lift you up in the air.'

Peter is saying this to them, and shows them how to do it, but still they can't.

Then Nana is seen breaking her chain and rushing off down the street. She should be a real dog now.

'Wait till I blow the fairy dust on you.'

Peter blows fairy dust on the children. They are boastful because, as the result of this, they can fly a yard or so now, but they are still very bad at it.

Nana is next seen bursting a door open, and rushing up a stair into a room where the dining party is. She tells in barks of the goings-on at home. The people dining rush to the window and pull the curtains slightly open. They don't pull them open to anything like their full extent. About eighteen inches will be ample, and that only in the middle of the curtains, not the whole length. Through an aperture of about eighteen inches wide and deep the whole of the nursery window, about 80 yards away, will be seen. It is the only lighted window, and on it we can see the shadows of the children moving alarmingly on the nursery blind. Mr and Mrs Darling are much agitated, and rush with Nana out of the dining-room and down the stair.

Then we see the children flying in the nursery. They are clumsy compared to Peter, but are now able to revolve triumphantly round the nursery. They are in ecstasy. Then Mr and Mrs Darling hurrying with Nana along the snowy street. They point agitatedly to the window, against which the shadows of the children can be seen flying round and round.

A close-up of this awful sight.

Then inside the nursery. All are going round in a mad delirium of delight; and then comes the flight of Peter and his companions through the window.

The parents and Nana burst into nursery just in time to see them disappear.

From the window they watch the children flying away over the house-tops.

The flight to the Never, Never Land has now begun. We see the truants flying over the Thames and the Houses of Parliament. Then an ordinary sitting of the House of Commons, faithfully reproduced. A policeman rushes in to the august Chamber and interrupts proceedings with startling news of what is happening in the air. All rush out to see, the Speaker, who is easily identified by his wig, being first. They get to the Terrace of the House and excitedly watch the flying group disappear. Then the children flying over the Atlantic. The moon comes out. Wendy tires, Peter supports her.

Then they near New York. The statue of Liberty becomes prominent. They are so tired that they all alight on it. It is slippery, and they can't find a resting place. At first we should think it is a real statue. Then we should get the effect of the statue mothering them by coming to life, to the extent of making them comfortable in her arms for the night.

This should be one of the most striking pictures.

(Note:—If the play is to be divided into four parts (not called reels), this should be the end of part one).

Next we see them resume their journey. They cross America, with Niagara seen.

Then they are over the Pacific, where the Never, Never Land is.

<u>The Never, Never Land.</u>

We see the island all glorious and peaceful in a warm sun. We see the whole of it as in a map, not a modern map but the old-fashioned pictorial kind with quaintly exaggerated details. I have a map of the Never, Never Land in this style, which should be reproduced.

Then we see the sun go down and the island become dark and threatening.

Wolves are seen chasing one of the Lost Boys.

Then wild animals drinking at the ford by moonlight.

Then redskins, in the Fenimore Cooper* story manner, torturing a prisoner who is tied to a tree. He is a pirate.

<u>Tiger Lily.</u>
<u>'Every brave would have had her to wife, but she received their advances coldly.'</u>

First Tiger Lily comes into view. Then we see a redskin evidently proposing to the beautiful creature, who is the Indian princess. She whips out her hatchet and fells him. She and all the redskins should be very tall in contrast with the children.

Then Peter is seen in the air, pointing out the distant pirate ship to Wendy. Then the dreadful ship comes into view, flying the Jolly Roger. We should have a fine, wicked pirate ship of the days when they attacked the Spanish galleons—a reproduction of some notorious ship, black and sinister, with an enormous hull which Peter is to climb presently. By and bye we are to be shown various parts of the ship in detail. It is at anchor just now, and its sails are not showing. We don't see the sails until Peter gives an order much later in the play.

Jas Hook, the Pirate Captain (Eton and Balliol.)

We have here a picture of Hook dressed as he is in the play, with an iron hook instead of a right hand—a double cigar in mouth, etc. He should be very tall. (Note:— about the playing of this part. Hook should be played absolutely seriously, and the actor must avoid all temptation to play the part as if he was conscious of its humours. There is such a temptation, and in the stage play the actors of the part have sometimes yielded to it, with fatal results. He is a bloodthirsty villain, all the more so because he is an educated man. The other pirates are rough scoundrels, but he can be horribly polite when he is most wicked. He should have the manners of a beau.* But above all the part should be played with absolute seriousness and avoidance of trying to be funny. This should be insisted on throughout, and especially later in the pirate ship scene. This same warning applies to all the pirates.)

Pathetic Smee, the Nonconformist* pirate.

Smee is in spectacles, and is the hopelessly loveable-looking ruffian of the play. He is sitting on the floor in a corner of the ship. By his side are tea-pot, cup and saucer, etc. He is drinking his tea out of the saucer.

Every one of them a name of Terror on the Spanish Main.

We see the dreadful crew—about twenty in all. Starkey, Cecco, etc. Some should be dressed as in the play. The others copied from the books about buccaneers.

A pirate points out the flying children.

Then Peter in the air is giving the warning to Wendy and the others.

Then we see Long Tom, the great gun, being got ready on deck.

All the pirates must be very tall. It is fired by Hook's command.

We see Peter and his companions blown away in different directions, but evidently not damaged otherwise. They roll about in the air and then fly on. They are now separated.

The Lost Boys awaiting Peter's return.

The scene is the wood of the play with big trees that have hollow trunks. All trees should be very large to make children seem smaller. From a chimney in ground smoke is coming.

We see the children emerging above ground from their trees as in the play. First comes Slightly.

<u>Slightly Soiled.</u>

He was so called because that was the name marked on the clothes he had been lost in. Slightly comes, he is the comic figure among the boys.

<u>Tootles—Nibs—Curly—The Twins.</u>

They come up, all differentiated as in the play. All are looking in the sky for Peter.

> 'Yo ho, yo ho, the pirate life.
> The flag of skull and bones.
> A merry life, a hempen rope.
> And hey for Davy Jones!'

Now the music of this pirate song is heard, but not the words. The Lost Boys quake for they know it means that the pirates are coming.

The boys all dart down their trees out of sight, except Nibs who steals off to reconnoitre, one of them first putting a mushroom over the chimney to hide the tell-tale smoke.

The pirates are punting rafts upon a romantic river.

On one raft with cushions raising him high sits Hook regally. Several pictures of them on river. Then Hook gets off. All are looking for the boys. He signals to them to scout in different directions. They move off stealthily. Two or three of them are gigantic negroes. They are evidently villains of every race.

<u>''Twas Peter Pan cut off my arm and flung it to a crocodile that happened to be passing by. That crocodile liked my arm so much, Smee, that it has followed me about ever since, from sea to sea and from land to land, licking its lips for the rest of me.'</u>

<u>'In a way, Captain, it's a sort of compliment.'</u>

Hook is saying this to Smee horribly, near the underground house of whose existence they don't know yet. One boy's head is out of a tree trunk listening. He withdraws it, horrified. The whole scene is now shown in vision of Peter fighting Hook, cutting off his arm and flinging it to the crocodile.

The whack with which the arm is cut off should be so terrific that we see Hook 'seeing stars', but it is not 'stars' he sees; it is the trees around him all moving just for a few seconds. The same sort of curious effect as was got in my private film of 'Macbeth'* when the trees were seen chasing Macbeth.

This should be in strange and dreadful scenery, quite unlike that of the island. Then we see the dogged pursuit of Hook by the crocodile on a great globe of the world. We see an actual globe. Wherever the ship goes the crocodile is swimming after it. If Hook takes to land it still follows. Thus they go over the globe, which slowly revolves for our benefit, the figures being small, but discernible and much larger than they could really be.

> 'One day, Smee, that crocodile swallowed a clock, which goes tick-tick inside him, and so before he can reach me I hear the tick and bolt.'

Hook is telling this triumphantly. He is sitting on a large mushroom at this time, the one that conceals the chimney. Then, in a vision, we see the incident happening. Hook appears in another woodland scene near a river, but again different kind of scenery. All these scenes should be different from each other and very picturesque. He has something concealed under his cloak. He is very cunning and criminal in manner. It is a clock which he winds up. It now ticks, and we hear the ticking. He places it on the ground and hides. The crocodile comes, shoves clock about curiously and eventually swallows clock. It continues ticking, but in a more muffled way. The crocodile turns his head trying to look at his body and goes away puzzled. Hook emerges triumphant and exits in the opposite direction villanously.

Then we see Hook and Smee again. Hook rises, evidently feeling hot. They lift the big mushroom on which he has been sitting, and discover that it conceals a chimney from which smoke now comes. They point to the holes in the trees and indicate triumphantly that they have discovered the boys' secret home. They draw their pistols and cutlasses and are about to descend the trees. A boy has been watching again. He descends and tells the other boys. We now see the underground home, which will be described later. The boys there are all in terror, but they seize weapons.

Then, above ground again, Hook and Smee are about to descend trees when they hear an alarming sound, which we hear also. It is the tick-tick of the crocodile. They rush away.

Crocodile Music. The crocodile appears and plods after them. He is a sort of Nemesis,* ever plodding after Hook. It will be found best sometimes to have a real crocodile of huge size, and sometimes a theatrical property.

Now boys' heads peep out at tree trunks, watching. They disappear down trees as the redskins appear on the warpath following the pirates in single file. This is slow and creepy, to the redskin music. The redskins go off dramatically, as in the play. When they have passed the boys emerge. Nibs comes running to them excitedly pointing upwards. We now see Wendy flying alone and with difficulty. First she is seen over another part of the wood—then over the boys. Tink is also in air, dashing about.

The jealous Tink calls 'Shoot the Wendy bird!'

The bells tinkle. Tootles gets bow and arrow and shoots Wendy. We see the arrow in her. The bells ring 'You silly ass!'

Wendy falls to the ground. The boys gather round her.

'This is no bird. I think it must be a lady. Let me see, I remember ladies. Ay, that's a lady.'

Slightly, in his conceited way, shoves the others aside and makes this disturbing announcement. All take off their caps. Tootles is scared: suddenly all look up. Peter is seen flying alone. First they are delighted. Then all gather round Wendy to hide her. Peter comes flying down.

'Boys, great news! I have brought at last a mother for us all.'

They are woebegone. Tootles nobly makes them stand aside and let Peter see Wendy.

Peter is dramatic. He goes on his knees beside her and pulls out the arrow. Tootles, baring his chest, indicates that he is the guilty one. Peter raises the arrow to use it as a dagger on Tootles. Wendy's arm rises, and a Twin points this phenomenon out to Peter who examines Wendy again. Suspense of boys.

'She lives! This is the kiss I gave her. The arrow struck against it. It has saved her life.'

Peter holds up the button from her chest.

There is a close-up picture of button.

'I remember kisses. Let me see. Ay, that's a kiss.'

Slightly is shown the button and gives his confident opinion. Then a picture of Tink on a tree, and Peter sternly ordering her away. She flies away crying: 'You silly ass!'

John and Michael are now seen first flying and then tottering down. They are so tired that they fall asleep at once against a tree.

Then the children try to carry Wendy down a tree trunk. They cannot get her down. Peter confides to them a grand idea, which they proceed to put into execution. It is to build a house round her.

We now see them building a house round Wendy in the elaborate manner of the play, just about the size of herself, John and Michael being waked up to join in. The house should not be a make-believe affair of canvas as it has to be in the acted play. Here it should be a real house, though comic. We should see the boys felling trees, carpentering, etc., actually building the house with miraculous speed, much as described in 'Peter Pan in Kensington Gardens'.* We see them knocking in the posts, making doors, windows, etc. with lightning rapidity, and all this to music. When the little house is finished it is a beautiful little house of wood and moss, lop-sided and all wrong, but fascinating.

They survey the completed house. Peter evidently sees there is one thing wanting. He indicates that it is a chimney. He knocks the top out of John's tall hat (which John has been wearing since he left home) and puts it on roof as a chimney. Immediately smoke comes out of the hat.

<u>Wendy consents to be their mother.</u>

They are gathered round the little house expectantly. Peter knocks at the door. Wendy comes out in a daze. Then the scene of the play,* with its business. They go on their knees, arms outstretched, asking her to be their mother. She consents. Glee. Wendy is at once maternal in manner.

They dance round the house. All romp inside except Peter, who remains outside on guard with drawn sword. It gets dark. The little house is lighted up inside. The shadows of wild beasts pass in background. Peter drives away wolves. The last one is a baby wolf, so small and young that it does not know how to run away. He lifts it up in his arms and carries it to its mother, who goes off thankfully with it. Then Peter falls asleep by the door of the little house. Tink comes cautiously. She hops on to his knee, then on to his shoulder, kisses him. She remains there. Peter sleeps on.

One day soon after her arrival Peter took Wendy to the lagoon to see the Mermaids.

A gay procession is seen setting forth through romantic scenery. First Tootles, Nibs, Slightly, Twins, and Curly on foot gaily rollicking, leap-frogging, etc. Their clothes are now carefully darned, etc. Then Wendy sitting on a rough little home-made sledge which is pulled by a kite string, the kite being high in the air. Then John and Michael on foot and very gay. Then last Peter riding on his goat. A peculiar effect should be tried for here which may be got by the same mechanical means as the trees moving in earlier scene when Peter cut off Hook's arm. The effect wanted is that, as Peter passes along a sort of path, flowers come moving after him in a long procession.

'Look at those beastly flowers following me again!'

Peter is looking behind him and saying this indignantly. He signs to the flowers authoritatively to stop it, and they now stand still. He goes on, and as soon as he has disappeared they begin to follow again. He has only been hiding and now pops round the corner and catches them following. Again they stop—he waves to them to go back, and then we see them all go back till there are none left. They behave precisely like a dog following its master and ordered home. Peter now rides forward. (Note: We have now about twenty minutes of pictures without words)

The next incident is that the kite string breaks because John tries to sit on sledge—thus showing that the kite can't pull two. Wendy tumbles out of the sledge, and the kite disappears in the air. The sledge is abandoned. Peter gallantly dismounts to let Wendy ride the goat, and on they go. Then Peter signs caution, Wendy dismounts and they proceed stealthily on tip-toe to take the mermaids by surprise. They hide among long grass and peer at the beautiful mermaids' lagoon which now comes into view. It should be a lovely lagoon in a coral island; coral reefs and Pacific vegetation. There are no mermaids at present. Peter points out objects of interest to Wendy, the chief one being a rock in the water called Marooners' Rock, of which we are to see more presently.

Then they are excited over an incident that takes place. A branch of a tree on which is a great nest breaks off and falls into the water. The mother bird is on the nest and continues to sit on it as it floats away from the branch into the lagoon. Wendy kisses her hand to it in praise of its maternal behaviour.

Next we see the mermaids. The children watch from their hiding place. The mermaid pictures should be a beautiful series of considerable length. First the mermaids are far away, scores of them basking lazily by the shores of the lagoon, some in the water, some out of it. They should mostly be at a distance as in this way the illusion will carry best. We may see one nearer on a rock combing her hair if this can be done without the tail being unnatural. Excitement of Wendy, Peter signs caution. All the children dive stealthily into the water, Peter leading, with the object of catching a mermaid. Alternate pictures of mermaids, and then the children swimming craftily towards them. They jump up to catch the one combing hair, but she slips through their fingers. Peter takes a flying leap through the air and alights on her back. He is wildly gay. No one else can be so gay as Peter, nor so serious, nor so gallant, nor so cocky.

Next, at another part of the lagoon we see Tiger Lily picturesquely poised by the shore with an arrow in her bow for Smee, who is coming along in a boat. From behind a tree Starkey leaps on her, and Smee wades ashore to help him. Starkey is about to knife her when Smee proposes something more dreadful. It is shown as in a vision. We see Marooners' Rock in the vision with Tiger Lily lying bound on it. The tide rises till the rock and she are submerged. Starkey likes this vision, and in the next picture they have put her bound on the rock. They are in the boat now beside the rock, and we have two pictures, one of Hook swimming out to them, and one of Peter stealing to the rock to rescue Tiger Lily. Peter, unseen by the pirates, cuts her bonds and she slips into the water. Hook arrives and gets into the boat. They proudly point to the rock, and then, to their dismay, see that Tiger Lily has vanished. Hook threatens, and they go on their knees to him. He is looking everywhere for the possible foe, and Peter cannot resist rising in the water and jeering at him. At last, Hook thinks, he has got Peter. He and Smee dive and Starkey guards the boat.

The fight in the water begins. Mermaids and fishes are seen rushing away in fear. John and Starkey fight in the boat and go over in each other's embrace. The great fight is on the rock between Hook and Peter, which should be much as in the play. It ends with Peter rolling off the rock into the water, unfairly gashed by Hook, who triumphantly dives. Then we see Hook swimming to land and stealing off. Then, after Hook has disappeared, the crocodile is seen landing and pursuing him. Hook is ignorant on these occasions that the crocodile is following.

Next, the other boys gather round the drifting boat and get into it. They call and look everywhere for Peter and Wendy. The boat drifts away till it is lost sight of. Now no one is to be seen on the lagoon, which now looks cold and cruel. Then we see the mermaids in their romantic cave. Wendy is their prisoner. They examine her curiously. They laugh derisively at her feet, so that she has to sit on her feet. They put their fingers in her eyes and swish her with their tails, which is evidently their way of hurting people. Then they sleep. She sits there staring with affrighted eyes. Peter comes and, stepping stealthily over the mermaids, rescues her and goes off. He is evidently wounded and so is she. A mermaid wakes up and follows them, looking wicked. Next Peter, evidently wounded, drags Wendy on to Marooners' Rock, and both lie there in a faint.

The cruel mermaid comes swimming to the rock and is pulling Wendy inch by inch into the water when Peter sits up and saves her. This should be very dramatic. The mermaid disappears. We see the two children sitting there, a touching pair, to the music of the scene. Peter points to how the water is rising, but they are too exhausted to do anything.

We see that the rock is being submerged.

Then the kite comes again into view drifting in the air. First we see it over another part of the lagoon. Then nearer the rock. Peter has an idea; he grips the tail and pulls the kite toward him.

Peter nobly ties the tail round Wendy, indicating that it can't carry two. They embrace. Then she is carried over the lagoon by the kite. Peter waves to her till she is lost to sight. He shudders as he realises his situation. We see him next alone.

Then we see Wendy being carried over the island by the kite.

<u>To die will be an awfully big adventure.</u>

Peter is now standing, proudly erect. The rock is sinking. It is now moonlight. Then we see another part of the lagoon with the mother-bird still drifting on her nest.

Then Peter on the rock. He is now up to his knees in water, but still brave. Then the nest drifts toward him. He sees it. The bird quacks and flies away. Peter has an inspiration. He pulls the nest toward him and takes two big eggs out of it. At first he doesn't know what to do with them. Then he lifts Starkey's hat. On Marooners' Rock is a post on which Starkey has left his hat. Peter puts the eggs into the hat and the hat in the water. The hat drifts away. He then gets into the nest and drifts in the same direction. He makes a sail of his shirt and now he goes in another direction. He is very solemn and intense, with gleaming eyes.

Several pictures of Peter in the nest. Next we see the hat alone on the lagoon. The bird flies back and sits on it. Then we see the nest drawing near shore. Wendy wades out to meet it and they are triumphant. Peter is painfully cocky again. Last we see the hat stationary among reeds in the water. The mother bird gets off it and waddles ashore. She is presently followed by two baby birds.

(Note:— If the play is divided into parts this should be the end of part two.)

In the house under the trees they lived very like baby bears.

First we see baby bears in a cave playing around their mother. She is motherly to them, but also punishes. She brings food and they gather round it greedily. They trot about after her. They curl up on the ground against her and sleep.

Then we see the boys behaving in exactly the same way with Wendy as mother. The feeding is also very like the bears. They also trot about after Wendy. They also curl up on floor against her and sleep.

When one of them wanted to turn in bed Wendy gave the signal, and they all turned simultaneously.

Wendy is giving Curly a good washing at a basin. He is dripping, etc. Michael as the baby is in a sort of basinette,* swung from roof. All the other boys are pulling down from the wall the big bed of the play. Peter is one of them. They are in nightgowns. Curly joins the others and all get into bed, lying like sardines, some heads at top of bed and some heads at foot. After some horse-play they lie quiet. Then one holds up his hand. Wendy, who has sat down by fire to darn, gives the signal, and all turn simultaneously.

In the Never, Never Land the Seasons succeed each other more rapidly than at home.

In illustration of this we see a new scene. It is a romantic little glade, in which one fruit tree and a tiny stream of water are the chief objects. At one point the water is trickling down and Peter comes with a home-made wooden bucket which he places beneath this trickle and sits, waiting for bucket to fill slowly. The time is summer, and the fruit tree is heavy with ripe fruit. Gradually the scene changes to winter. The fruit disappears, the leaves fall off and the tree is bare. The ground becomes white with snow. The stream is frozen and an icicle hangs where the water had been trickling into bucket. Peter breaks icicle. He is cold, pulls his clothes tighter round him. Then in same way, the scene changes to a sunny day in spring. The tree becomes beautiful with blossom and leaves. The ground is a rich green. Peter is so warm that he has to undo his jacket. The trickle is running free again. The bucket is now full, and he departs with it quite unaware that anything out of the common has happened. The whole point of this picture is that the changes should be gradual—not sudden jumps from one picture to another. We should see the melting from one season to another—i.e. the actual process should be seen.

Tink, of course, had an apartment of her own.

We see Tink's exquisite tiny bedroom, with her brushing hair, etc. It opens off the big room and should be shown much more beautifully than is possible in the play.

At first the newcomers had to be pulled out of their trees like a cork, but Peter altered them, and soon they fitted.

We see John and Wendy being ignominiously pulled up by the hair of the head. They had stuck in their trees.

Then John is being held down, while Peter flattens him out with a rolling pin. He is flattened too much. He is flattened out on the ground till he covers quite a large extent—as if a hundred barrels had rolled over him. Wendy is indignant. Then Peter and the boys roll him up like a stretch of carpet and Peter works on him till he is of a correct shape and bulk. He now runs up and down the tree gaily. Wendy is then subjected to alteration. This object is to make her shorter, so she is laid down and Peter pushes her feet and Slightly her head with the result that she is telescoped. This scene takes place beside water. Wendy runs to see her reflection in the water. We see it also. She is now very short and stout. She is in distress. The boys don't know what to do. She lies down again and Peter operates on her with the rolling pin, successfully. Again she looks at her reflection in the water. Now she is delighted. She runs gaily up and down her tree. General happiness.

When you wanted to know the time you waited beside the crocodile till the clock struck.

Peter is sitting beside the crocodile waiting. The clock strikes 4. We should hear it also. Peter skips away. The next picture shows Wendy as a schoolmistress. It is the underground scene, and she has a cane in her hand. On a board she has chalked in a childish hand:

'Rite down all you can remember about your adoredable parents.'

All the boys, except First Twin, are in a row on their toadstools with slates, trying to write, but looking puzzled. Peter, indeed, has fallen asleep with a broken slate at his feet. First Twin is on a high stool in corner in disgrace with a fool's cap on his head.

Then we are shown three of their slates in a close-up. Tootles has made an O on his. On Nib's slate is written: 'All I remembers about my mother is that she useder to say: "Oh, how I wish I had a chek book of my own".'

On Michael's is written: 'Are you not our mother, Wendy?' She is troubled by this. It is painful to her that they have forgotten so much.

Wendy was one of those mothers who like their offspring to have a good romp before bed-time.

First, all the boys, including Peter, in their ordinary clothes flying about over the tree-tops, engaged in a game of football. They have a home-made football, and are arranged in sides and manage to keep ball in air. They have also absurd goal-posts, which they have tied to trees, standing out higher than the trees. It is a moonlight evening.

They had many a night of joyous revelry.

We see them in their nightgowns under ground, and they are engaged in the pillow dance just as it is done in the play, except that Peter is chief dancer in place of First Twin. Wendy is sitting on a stool darning their stockings and occasionally smiling at them in a motherly way. The dance ends with a pillow fight.

Tink and her friends were sometimes a nuisance; they got into everything.

Peter is seen in underground room putting on his long boots. Evidently something is in one of them that ought not to be there. He holds it upside down and Tink drops out. Peter is so used to this kind of thing that he expresses no surprise. He just continues to put on his boots.

Then in same room Wendy is cutting Slightly's hair like a barber. There is a pot on fire—it moves agitatedly. She lifts pot off fire and takes off lid. Tink jumps out of pot wet and indignant.

Then the same room with the bed prepared for night. Peter is sharpening a weapon. One of the pillows on bed rocks about in an odd way. Wendy is there and points this out to Peter. He seizes pillow, opens it at top and holds pillow upside down. A hundred fairies drop from pillow on to floor. Peter sweeps them away with a broom.

Then they are seen above ground flying away out of the tree-trunks.

<u>Peter loved Wendy as a son, but she wanted him to love her as something else. He could not think what it was.</u>

She is saying this lovingly to him in the underground house, but when he is puzzled she stamps her foot, then sits forlornly.

<u>'What can it be, Tink?'</u>

He is asking this above ground of Tink, who replies in her bell language: 'You silly ass!'

<u>'What can it be, Tiger Lily?'</u>

He is asking the same question of Tiger Lily. She prostrates herself before him in adoration, etc., but he can't understand. She goes away sadly. He remains hopelessly puzzled. Then he skips away indifferently.

<u>For many moons Hook cogitated over his revenge.</u>

We see him sitting in the crow's nest* of the ship, a perilous but romantic situation. There is a map of the island in his hands, and in a close-up we see quaint details with writing that marks places, such as 'Underground Home'. Little flags are stuck over map as in a war-map and he is busy using these. The moon is seen first in a quarter moon then half and so on to full moon, then it reverses the process to indicate passing of time. He also spies on the island through a telescope. We see Peter in silhouette standing motionless on a promontory watching the pirate ship in the distance. He looks very cocky.

<u>What maddened Hook beyond endurance was Peter's cockiness. In the night-time it disturbed him like an insect.</u>

We see Hook's cabin with no one in it at first. This cabin is largely furnished like a boy's room at Eton. It has a wicker chair and a desk with a row of books as in an Eton room. On the walls besides weapons are the colours* he won at school, the ribbons, etc., arranged in the eccentric Etonian way, and the old school-lists, caps and also two pictures, which when shown in close-ups are seen to be (1) Eton College (2) a photograph of an Eton football eleven; the central figure is Hook, as he was when a boy, but distinguishable, with a football in his hands and the prize cup between his knees. He and the other boys must wear correct colours. The cat-o'-nine-tails* also hangs up prominently.

Hook comes in and begins to undress. There has probably never before been much attention given to how a buccaneer retires to bed. We endeavour to supply this want. He winds up his watch, and hangs it up, etc. Presently we see him in a nightgown. He gets into bed and finds the sheets cold. He lies in bed smoking and reading the 'Eton Chronicle'* (of which a real copy must be used). He lays down the cigar-holder and blows out his candle.

Then we see him having a nightmare about Peter, brandishing his hook and scratching as if tortured by an insect. Peter is seen in a vision mocking him.

<u>Months passed, and at last Hook unripped his plot.</u>

We have now a series of pictures.

First we see the pirates, picturesque but horrible, climbing out of their ship into their two rowing-boats. They are armed to the teeth. We have a grim vision of the side of the wicked ship, old and dirty.

Next we see the redskins sitting in a circle round a fire in the open. A pipe is passed from one to another. Their wigwams are seen near by.

Then the two boats being pulled across the lagoon—Hook standing erect in one of them—Smee in the other.

Then all the children, except Peter, in the underground home. They are in their ordinary clothes, and are having a merry evening at leap-frog etc. Wendy is sitting by the fire smiling at them and sewing as usual. Stockings and other garments hang drying on a string by the fire.

Then we see the pirates landing and stealing off into the forest.

<u>Peter was away from home that night, attending a fairy wedding.</u>

Peter is seen at the fairy wedding. This should be an elaborate and beautiful picture of some length, one of the prettiest in the film. Peter is sitting against a tree playing his pipes, and fairies emerge from under big leaves into a fairy circle and go through a fairy wedding; an idea of what this should be like* can be got from my book 'Peter Pan in Kensington Gardens'. The music (which will have to be new) of this fairy scene should come from bells.

Then we see the crocodile asleep in a lonely glade beside a stream.

So preternaturally quick of hearing are all savage things that, when Smee trod on a dry twig, the sound woke the whole island into life.

We see the pirates proceeding cautiously through the wood. In a close-up we see Smee tread on a twig. Evidently the others all hear it. In a sudden stoppage of the music we should hear it also. They gape at him startled, then fling themselves among the long grass to hide. Smee is conscience-stricken. Then a series of pictures which, to have the best effect, should be short and sharp, changing quickly. They indicate the effect in different parts of the island of hearing the twig snap.

First it is heard by the children in their leap-frog games. They suddenly stop in the middle of the play, and gather scared, round Wendy. Then the redskins hear it, leap up, seize their weapons and are at once terrible scalp-hunters on the war-path. Then the fairy wedding is interrupted by Peter hearing it, and starting to his feet. The fairies suddenly disappear. Some of them are on his knee, shoulders, etc. He brushes them off like breadcrumbs. He goes off excitedly and stealthily, with Tink.

Then the crocodile starts from his sleep on hearing it, and pounds off through the forest, dogged of purpose, on his never-ending quest.

These pictures should all be short to represent the effect of Smee's blunder, and before each one we should have repeated briefly for a second or two only the picture of Smee treading on the twig.

Tiger Lily and her braves guard the home of The Great White Mother.

We see her and her redskins above the children's home, guarding it, and lying in their blankets, etc. Then Peter comes toward them through the forest, and they prostrate themselves before him. He accepts their homage as the natural thing. No one could be more cocky. He is like a king to his subjects. He descends his tree.

Then we see a pirate on top of a tree, signaling what he observes to the pirates below. They move forward furtively.

Peter found Wendy telling a story to the boys.

The children are seen, clustered in bed in their nightgowns, listening eagerly to Wendy who sits near them with Michael between her knees.

Peter is sitting on a toadstool at the other end of the underground room, whittling a stick and evidently disliking the story, putting his hands over his ears, etc. Up above, as in the play, we at times see the redskins. We now have a series of visions (reproduced from the nursery scenes) illustrating Wendy's story, which is really the tale of how Wendy, John and Michael were spirited away to the Never, Never Land.

First we see the three in their nursery being put to bed by Nana. Then the mother saying good-night to them and going off with the father to the party. Then Peter enters at window. Then he teaches them how to fly. Then they fly out at window, the parents and Nana coming just too late to catch them. These, being reproductions, are brief.

Between these varied pictures we see two of Wendy telling them the story, and the children misbehaving and whacking each other as they do in the play. Peter's uneasiness increases.

'But their adoredable mother always kept the window open for them, and when at last they flow back to her, pen cannot describe the happy scene.'

Wendy is saying this as in the play, and we have a vision of Mr and Mrs Darling welcoming the return of the children with joy. (It should not be the picture afterwards seen at end of play.) Peter starts up with a cry, which draws all attention to him.

'Wendy, you are wrong about Mothers. Long ago I flew back but the window was barred, and there was another little boy sleeping in my bed.'

We see Peter telling this. Then we have a vision of Peter looking through the window of his old nursery, and there is a baby in the basinette. The window is iron barred. He beats on the window in vain and is furious.

Then we see John and Michael cross to Wendy in terror.

'Perhaps Mother is in half mourning by this time.'

Wendy says it, alarmed; and, in a vision, we have a picture of Mr and Mrs Darling at home brightly practising a new dance to a gramophone, and not in mourning.

'We must go back at once. You can all come with me. I am sure father and mother will adopt you.'

'Won't they think us rather a handful, Wendy?'

'Oh, no, it will only mean having a few beds in the drawing-room; they can be hidden behind screens on first Thursdays.'

Wendy is saying it. Then, in a vision, we see the little drawing-room first as an ordinary, but quite humble room, and then the same room with many little beds in it, and one of the lost children in each. Then we see the boys delightedly getting their bundles to accompany Wendy, and all now dressed as in this scene in the play. All are jolly except Peter, who stands with arms folded. Wendy entreats him to get ready like the others.

'Nobody is going to make me a man; I want always to be a little boy and to have fun.'

He is saying this. He skips about, pretending heartlessness and playing his pipes. Wendy is in woe. She appeals to him in vain.

'You will remember about changing your flannels, Peter? and to take your medicine? I'll pour it out for you.'

He nods sullenly. We see her pouring out his medicine and leaving it on a ledge at the back in a glass.

'What are your exact feelings for me, Peter?'

'Those of an adoredable son, Wendy.'

She asks him lovingly, but his reply makes her stamp her foot. They are about to ascend their trees when a sudden turmoil above terrifies them. This scene has been underground only—nothing above shown.

Now the scene changes to above ground. The pirate music is heard. The redskins start up into fighting positions, and at the same moment the pirates are upon them. Now takes place the great fight between pirates and redskins, which should be a much more realistic and grim affair than in the play. There it has to be more pretence, but here we should see real redskin warfare that will be recognised as such by all readers of Fenimore Cooper, etc. Alternated with it we should see the children below listening for the result in agony. Peter has seized a sword and wants to rush up to join in the fight, but Wendy holds him back and the terrified Michael clings to his knees. Some pirates are killed, but more redskins, and the remaining redskins, including Tiger Lily are put to flight. The bodies are removed. Then the pirates gather together and listen at the trees.

'If the redskins have won they will beat the tom-tom; it is always their sign of victory.'

Peter is saying it. All the children listen eagerly. At the same time we see the scene above. Hook, listening at tree has heard Peter's remark. He sees how to deceive the children. He seizes the tom-tom and wickedly beats it.

> 'An Indian victory! You are quite safe now, Wendy. Good-bye. Tink, lead the way.'

Peter says it. All rejoice. Peter pulls the curtain of Tink's room. Tink darts about then disappears up a tree. Peter and Wendy have an affecting farewell. Peter is breaking down and the other boys look on inquisitively. He stamps and they turn their faces away in fear of him. When he is sure they are not looking he embraces Wendy, but like a child, not like a lover. Then all but Peter disappear in tree trunks. Above ground we see the pirates waiting devilishly at the trees to seize the children as they come up. Tink darts up and escapes them. She flutters around and is lost sight of. Then up their trees come the doomed children, one by one, to be immediately seized before they utter a cry. They are tossed like bales of cotton from one pirate to another, and this should be a quaint effect if exactly carried out. They should probably be on wires to get it right, but there must be no burlesquing of it. All should seem natural. The last is Wendy, to whom Hook gives his arm with horrible courtesy. She takes it in a dazed way. He gives the signal and all go except himself. He stands there, a dreadful figure in his cloak. Next a brief picture of the surviving redskins in panic, striking their tents. The squaws carry babies in the Indian way. Then we see the underground home again. Peter thinks they have all got safely away. We see him barring the doors of the trees.

> 'Who was Peter Pan? No one really knows. Perhaps he was just somebody's boy who never was born.'

We have a picture of Peter sitting, a sad, solitary figure on the side of the bed.

Then up above we see Hook listening. He produces from his pocket a bottle, and a close-up picture shows the word 'Poison' on it. Scowling horribly he begins to descend a tree. Then, below, we see Peter now lying on the bed. He has gone miserably to sleep. Hook's head appears very devilishly above the door of the tree. He can't reach the bar of the door to get in. He is foiled. Then he sees the medicine, which is within reach. He pours some poison into it. Then, with horrid triumph, he withdraws. We see him reappear at top, and now he is suddenly attacked by Tink, who flies at his face. She evidently stings him badly, but he drives her away, wraps his cloak around him and goes off villainously.

Again we see Peter on bed. Tink flies in and wakes him. She rings excitedly, and for some time. He understands the terrible news she is telling him and seizes his dagger. He vows vengeance. He sharpens the dagger on his grindstone.

'My medicine poisoned? Rot: I promised Wendy to take it, and I will.'

He is saying this to Tink, who is excitedly hopping around the glass. He takes the medicine in his hand. She bravely drinks it.

When he sees she has done this he is amazed. She begins to flutter about, and makes the bell-sounds.

'What! It was poisoned, and you drank it to save my life?'

Tink is fluttering about weakly. Peter is in distress.

'Tink, why did you do it?'

He asks despairingly. She tinkles back 'You silly ass!'

She flutters into her bedroom on to bed. Peter is in agony outside her room, looking in. Close-up picture of Tink writhing on bed. Peter's head is peering into room and will be nearly as large as the room.

'She says she thinks she could get well again if children believed in fairies. Oh, say that you believe: Wave your handkerchiefs! Don't let Tink die!'

Peter is addressing the audience. He, as it were, comes outside the scene to do so. We hope that, as in the play, the audience demonstrate. The light in the little room, which has been palpitating, grows stronger. Peter is triumphant; he thanks audience.

'And now to rescue Wendy.'

In a close-up we see Tink gaily dancing on her bed. (Note:— If the play is divided into parts this is the end of part three. The remainder of the play is part four.)

(From this point for a long time there are no words flung on screen.)

We now see Peter in pursuit of the pirates.

First he emerges from the tree. He looks for signs of which way they have gone. In a close-up we see their footmarks.

He follows these. Then we see the pirates brutally leading the chained prisoners through the wood.

Then a brief picture of the redskins departing hurriedly in their Indian canoes for some new hunting-ground.

Then Hook alone triumphantly proceeding through the wood. Then the crocodile alone (unknown to Hook) doggedly plodding after him.

Then Peter still following the trail by the footmarks. There should be a feeling of danger in the air. It is dusk. We see the shadows of prowling wild animals. We don't see the animals themselves, only their shadows, which should make the scene more creepy.

Then the two rowing boats. The children are tossed in, again like bales of cotton.

Hook comes. The boats put off. We see them drawing near the pirate ship. Hook boards first. He hauls up the children by his hook.

We see Peter arrive at the water's edge. He is looking about him when in a sudden lull of the music he hears (and we hear) the crocodile's clock striking twice, to imply that it is half past some hour of the evening. He searches and finds the crocodile, who was invisible when his clock struck. It is the striking of the clock that makes Peter know that the crocodile must be nearby. We see Peter and the crocodile together by the water's edge. Peter explains what he wants and the crocodile signifies assent. They then enter the water together.

Then we see the hold of the pirate ship with the children lying bound.

Then Hook in his cabin sitting on his bed smiling to himself. He is in great and horrible glee. We have a picture of what this desperado* is chuckling over. It is a vision of Peter underground, drinking the medicine and then writhing in death throes on the floor. Then the deck of the ship with the pirates dancing to a fiddle. Smee is sitting working at a sewing machine. Hook appears threateningly at the door of his cabin, which opens off the deck, and all stop dancing in fear of him. They shrink back. He paces the deck gloomily, a dark spirit. He is a sort of Hamlet figure in the 'To be or not to be' soliloquy.* Smee is still at his sewing machine.

A strange mood of depression comes over Hook, as if he fears his coming dissolution.* Scenes of his innocent days pass before him. He sees himself again at Eton answering at 'Absence' and on the football field and in 'Pop'*—pictures of these visions (which will be given in detail later). Then again we see him on deck brooding. Smee tears a cloth as in the play and Hook thinks an accident has happened to his trousers. He calls Starkey privately to examine him. Then Smee quite innocently does it again. Hook realises the truth this time, and threatens Smee. All the business of the play here.*

Hook sits beside a barrel, on which there are playing cards.

He gives an order and pirates descend into the hold and hoist up the manacled children. We see them first in the hold, and then being brutally hoisted up. Smee ties Wendy to the mast; he is ingratiating to her, but she scorns him. All stare at Hook, who goes on playing cards, without seeming to notice them.

Next we see Peter and the crocodile swimming side by side. Then the deck again. Hook suddenly turns on the children threateningly. They are frightened. He raises his hat and bows with fiendish politeness to Wendy, who replies with a look of contempt. He goes from one to another clawing at them, then gives an order, and, in response, the pirates get the plank ready and extend it over the water. In a close-up the terrified children are shown graphically what is meant by the phrase 'walking the plank'. To the music of the pirate song Hook shows them what is to be their fate, by walking an imaginary plank.

> Yo ho, yo ho, the frisky plank
> You walks along it so,
> Till it goes down, and you goes down
> To Davy Jones below.

We don't hear the words, but his actions give the idea, and we hear the music. The pirates at the plank at the same time show how it works. All this should be much more graphic and realistic than in the play.

Next we see Peter and the crocodile reach the side of the ship. Peter indicates to crocodile to swim round and round the ship. Peter himself then begins his heroic ascent of the vessel, dagger in mouth. He does wonderful deeds of climbing not only up the huge hulk but among the rigging.

Next we see the crocodile in the water beside the ship and we hear its clock begin to strike the hour of twelve. When it has struck three the scene changes to the deck of the ship, but the striking of the clock still goes on. It strikes 12 altogether. Hook hears it and is unmanned. He crouches at the side of the deck and some pirates gather round him to conceal him, while others look over the vessel's side for the crocodile. While this is going on Peter arrives on deck to the delight of the children.

He does not come in the simple way followed in the play. He leaps from rope to rope, crawls along perilous masts and comes down the rigging with extraordinary courage and agility. He does not carry a clock as in play, as this is not now needed. He signs caution. A pirate comes from the back and is neatly knifed and flung overboard. Always when anyone goes overboard we should have the effect of the splash. Peter steals into Hook's cabin. The pirates peering overboard indicate to Hook that the danger is past. Hook swaggers again. He sees Slightly jeering at him, seizes him and is about to make him walk the plank at once when he has an idea. We have a vision of this idea. The vision is of the cat-o'-nine-tails hanging up in his cabin. We have a close-up picture of it.

'Fetch the cat, Jukes; it's in the cabin.'

Then we see him order the pirate, Jukes, into the cabin, obviously to fetch the cat. Jukes goes. Then the music of the pirate song. Hook and pirates sing another verse which evidently, from the action, is about the cat, but before they reach the end of the verse they stop and the music itself stops abruptly. The sudden silence should be among the most impressive moments in the ship scene. This pause is because of a dreadful long-drawn out cry from the cabin, which we need not hear. Evidently the pirates have heard something dreadful. The sudden silence should be very dramatic. After a pause Cecco goes cautiously to the cabin door and looks in. In the semi-darkness we don't see Peter, but we see his shadow standing silent against a wall, a figure of fate. Jukes is seen lying dead on the floor. Hook sees the children looking pleased, and threateningly he orders Cecco into the cabin. Cecco pleads for mercy, then shuddering goes, as dramatically as in the play. All listen intently. There is no more dancing. Then they are again evidently startled by an awful cry. The children delightedly know that Peter must be dealing out death. Then when Hook threatens they dissemble. Starkey, quaking, peeps in at the cabin door, and we now see Cecco's body lying across that of Jukes, Peter's shadow is again seen motionless. Then another picture of the cabin, with now five bodies lying across each other, the topmost a negro. Peter's terrible shadow is still seen.

Next Hook orders Starkey into cabin, but rather than obey Starkey leaps overboard as in the play. All this scene should be very intense. Hook wants to pick out another victim, but the superstitious pirates gather together mutinously. He indicates that he will go in himself.

He lifts a musket, then casts it down, and clawing with his hook (his best weapon) he goes into the cabin.

There is a moment's awful silence, and then he staggers out in a daze. Evidently from his action of clutching his brow someone has struck him a dreadful blow on the head. The pirates talk together mutinously, and while they are doing so Peter, unseen by them, emerges from the cabin. He is carrying cutlasses. He gives them to the boys who begin to cut their bonds. Then another picture of all in same positions as before. Peter comes out: but we see that the boys' bonds are now cut. Wendy seems to be standing against the mast as before, but though the audience (or such of them as don't know the play) are meant to think that this is Wendy, it is really Peter in her cloak with face hidden. The actual Wendy is unseen. The mutinous crew now advance threateningly on Hook.

'Never was luck on a pirate ship wi' a woman aboard. Into the water with her, bullies.'

He indicates Wendy as the Jonah,* and that she should be flung overboard. The pirates think it a good idea. All advance on the supposed Wendy, when suddenly the clock is flung off, and the figure is revealed as Peter Pan, the Avenger. This should be as much a surprise to the audience as to the pirates, who shrink back for a moment from the terrible boy. Wendy now puts her head out of a barrel, which lets us see where she has been hidden.

Now the fight takes place, and instead of, as in the play, its being all on deck and trivial, it should take place in various parts of the ship, and be a real stern conflict.

There are individual contests in which the pirates are killed by Nibs, say, or Tootles, or John. Some pirates leap overboard—and sometimes the boys seem to be the losers, though only wounded. We don't see Peter or Hook just now. Then we see two of the boys pursued up the hatchway by Hook. They are being hard pressed by him.

Suddenly Peter appears and strikes up the swords. He and Hook stand gazing at each other. Their swords describe a circuit, and then the points reach the ground at the same time. Peter is now like a figure of fate. What he has said to the boys is 'Put up your swords, boys; this man is mine.'

'Rash and presumptuous youth, prepare to meet thy doom.'

'Dark and sinister man, have at thee.'

It should be a very real fight now between Hook and Peter, and both must be good fencers. First the one is beaten to his knees, then the other. At one point Wendy tries to save Peter. He flings her across his shoulder and fights with her thus. He knocks Hook's sword from his hand. Hook is at his mercy, but Peter chivalrously presents the sword to him. Wendy is no longer on Peter's shoulder.

Now Peter seems to be lost. He loses his sword. Suddenly he runs up a rope hanging from above (as First Twin does in the acted play). Then as suddenly he lets himself fall plop on Hook who is flattened out.

"'Tis some fiend fighting me. Pan, who and what art thou?'

'I'm youth, I'm joy, I'm a little bird that has broken out of the egg.'

The fight is resumed. Peter drives Hook back, up the ladder on to the poop,* where the plank is. Here they wrestle together, and Peter seems to be getting the worst of it. Suddenly by a piece of ju-jitsu* work he flings Hook over him and Hook comes down with a smash. Hook is now hopeless. Peter indicates sternly to him that he must walk the plank.

'Jas Hook, thou not wholly unheroic figure, farewell.'

Hook shrinks back, and won't obey the order. He shows his teeth. Peter gives an order to a boy who rushes down to cabin and brings Peter the cat-o'-nine-tails. Peter indicates that it will be his painful duty to use the cat if Hook does not at once walk the plank. Thus threatened Hook pulls himself together, and in his last moment is as brave a figure as any Sydney Carton* on the scaffold. Doubtless the 'something' that is said to be part of an Eton education and that can be got nowhere else comes to his help in this unpleasant moment. He has a vision which we see of the 'wall-game',* the most characteristic game of Eton College, and then he sets forth with dignity upon his impressive but brief walk along the plank. Just before the plank goes down the crocodile rears his head in the water below, the great mouth opens wide, and Hook dives straight into it, swallowed in one memorable mouthful. The crocodile waggles its head to get the legs down. They, too, disappear.

Floreat Etona.*

We see the crocodile crawling ashore. He shakes out of his mouth the wooden arm with hook of the late captain. He leaves it lying on the shore and plods away, like one who has lived his great hour and can afford to take the rest of his life more leisurely.

Then we see the deck again with the boys (and Wendy) all more or less wounded and bandaged, gazing in awe at Peter who is off his head with pride in himself and is strutting up and down. He strikes Napoleonic attitudes, but is not dressed as Napoleon.

Next we see Wendy, Nibs, and Tootles in the hold opening a sea-man's chest and bringing clothes out of it: pirate's clothing. Evidently the boys want to wear these clothes. We see Wendy cutting a pair of pirate trousers with scissors so as to shorten the legs for a boy. Then we see Slightly in the cook's pantry of the ship gloating over its attractive contents. He finds a big bottle marked 'Plums' and begins to eat them greedily. Then we see Michael in the hold trying to shave himself with pirate razor. His face is lathered. Then Slightly again, now in stomach pains, but still eating plums. Wendy finds him and destroys plums. Then she finds Michael, and cleans the lather off his face.

Then we see all the boys on deck (except Peter) in pirate clothes, all looking like pirates, and liking it. The clothes don't fit them but have been roughly made smaller.

Then Peter emerges from the captain's cabin and swaggers about. He is dressed in a suit of Hook's cut down but still too big, and is looking as like him as he can. He is drunk with cockiness, and all fear him. He holds a hook in his right hand and threatens Slightly with it. He is smoking Hook's double cigar. He gives an order. Very smartly the boys obey his order, flying to the rigging instead of climbing. Up to now no sails have been set. All sail is set by them now, and the great pirate ship veering round as the sails belly out, with Peter at the wheel, should make a stirring picture. Poor Peter is now, however, feeling squeamish as the result of his smoking. He puts away the cigars, and clutches his head. The other boys to his annoyance gather round him to see what will be the unheroic result of this misadven-ture. Wendy (who is still in the clothes in which she was brought aboard) appears and sees to what catastrophe the incident is tending. She orders the other boys away and then conducts Peter to the side of the vessel, over which he leans and is sick in privacy though we just guess it. Wendy stands near him solicitously but not too near, for she knows that there are moments in heroes' lives when they would prefer to be alone. He is now a little relieved, and she tries to induce him to go to Hook's cabin, of which he has become the tenant, but he won't desert the wheel and he nobly ties himself to it. She gazes at him admiringly and goes away. If possible the ship should be rocking as if in a heavy sea. It is now moving in a narrow channel between rocks that separate it from the open sea. The night is now dark.

Next we see Slightly again in the pantry. He is now eating sardines greedily, though obviously in great pain.

Then the deck scene again with Peter at wheel. Wendy appears with something she is concealing in a cloth behind her back. She doesn't want Peter to see it. We wonder what it is. She sneaks into Peter's cabin with it, and now we see it. It is a hot-water bottle, which she places carefully in the bed. She notices in cabin, as we do, a touching sight, viz. on the floor a little pile of the clothes Peter has taken off and left lying there after the manner of children. She folds them carefully on a chair and goes out. When she has gone Tink pops out of a jug and hops about.

Then we have a picture of the fo'c'sle in which a number of pirates have evidently slept, for here are their bunks. It is a dark, evil-looking place, with horrible pirate weapons still hanging on its discoloured walls. In the bunks lie all the boys except Peter, all asleep, though Slightly is having bad dreams as the results of his greediness. Wendy is sitting on a stool by an oil-stove, darning away as usual. The new conditions don't bother her; she is still a mother. Alternated with this picture we have one again of Peter still lashed to the wheel, spray splashing on him, and the ship heading out of the channel into an open and angry sea. It can be black-dark if this will help the rolling of the vessel; but if it rolls above on deck we must get a similar effect in the fo'c'sle.

<u>After many days the gay and innocent and heartless things reach home.</u>

We have a picture of Westminster and the Thames with a suggestion of the pirate ship there.

Then we see the outside of the Darlings' home once more. Nana goes in at the door carrying a basket in her mouth. Then inside the house and we see Mrs Darling sitting sadly at the open nursery window. She stretches her arms out to window. Nana comes and sits sympathetically with her. She shares Mrs Darling's handkerchief with her, but it should be touching not comic. Mr Darling is sitting dejectedly by the nursery fire. He takes from the mantelpiece a portrait. We see in a close-up that it is of the three children. He is sorrowful.

Evidently he is cold, he shivers, and rises and closes the window, but Mrs Darling opens it at once indicating sweetly that it must always be kept open for them. She goes sadly into another room. Nana is going miserably to her kennel in the nursery, but Mr Darling indicates to her that his armchair is the proper place for her, and that, as a punishment he, himself, must go into the kennel. Nana curls up on chair. Mr Darling goes into the kennel to sleep. Then we see Mrs Darling in the other room, which is the day nursery. There is a picture of Wendy in it, over which she leans unhappily.

Then we see Peter fly in by nursery window. Nana is not there now. Peter is in his familiar garments again. He is excited and quickly bars the window to keep Wendy out.

Here is repeated the vision of Peter arriving at his own nursery window and finding it barred and another child sleeping in his bed.

Then we see from nursery Wendy arriving at the window, and her terror on finding it barred. Peter is hiding and gloating over her discomfiture. She disappears. Peter is grinning and triumphantly going out by the door when we hear 'Home, Sweet Home'* being played on a piano in the day nursery. He steals to the door by which Mrs Darling had gone out and peeps in. The room being the day nursery is furnished as such. We see Mrs Darling at piano playing sadly. We see Peter at the door watching her, but she doesn't see him. He knows what she is sad about, but for a time he is defiant. Soon she breaks down. The picture of Wendy is in her hands and she kisses it. She is crying. He tries to be defiant still. She is now sobbing on the piano stool. He begins to cry, too, in the night nursery sitting against John's bed. At last he nobly flings the window open and goes away in a 'What care I!' manner.

Again we see Mrs Darling, her shoulders heaving as she leans against the piano.

Now we see Wendy flying in, and then Michael on John's shoulders. They are in their familiar clothes. They are gleeful as they point out their old beds, etc. Michael peeps into the kennel and calls the others. They all peep at their father asleep there. They just grin. Then the piano is heard again.

They gaily peep at Mrs Darling from the door. They feel ashamed as they watch her grief.

Then Wendy has a bright idea which she explains to them in dumb show.

They get merrily into their beds and lie beneath the blankets, covering their heads.

Mrs Darling comes to the door. She has heard nothing. Mrs Darling looks from one bed to another, but does not believe she really sees them.

'So often in my dreams their silver voices call me that I seem still to hear them when I am awake, my little children, that I shall see no more.'

The last of her words are from a chair. She stretches out her arms, thinking they are again to fall empty by her side, but the three creep to her and the arms fall on them. Rapture comes as she realises what has happened.

Mr Darling comes out of the kennel and Nana and Liza rush in at door. There is a scene of riotous happiness, with Peter looking on from the window, a lonely figure.

Wendy indicates that she has a surprise for her parents. She opens the door, and all the other boys come in sheepishly, one at a time. They are in their pirate garments, now very soiled and torn, and are a ragged, dirty, woeful-looking lot. They are afraid of how they are to be received, and the Darlings are at first staggered, but then embrace them. General joy. Peter is again at window. Wendy runs to him and hugs him.

'Hands off, lady. No one is going to catch me and teach me solemn things. I want always to be a little boy and to have fun.'

He is saying this when Mrs Darling goes towards him. Then he flies away.

Then on an evening we see Peter in the street looking up at the nursery window. Wendy opens the window and beckons him lovingly to come up. He heartlessly flouts her entreaties and skips about playing his pipes. She flings him a letter. He runs up a tall London lamp-post to read it. It is shown on the screen in Wendy's handwriting—'Darling Peter, Mother says she will let you come for me once a year to take me to the Never, Never Land for a week to do your spring-cleaning. Your adoredable Wendy.'

At the foot of the page instead of crosses are several thimbles. Peter and she wave to each other and he flies off. Next we see a picture of Wendy, John, and Michael going into a school in London with school satchels, etc. The old humdrum life has begun again.

Then we see Peter and Wendy flying together, through the air but without scenery. Wendy is warmly clad this time. They are evidently off to the spring-cleaning, for Peter is carrying a broom and she carries a shovel.

Very soon they all grew up except one.

It is a business street in the city. A close-up of a doorway shows these names printed on it:—
3rd Floor.
Messrs Twins and Tootles, Kew Cement Co.
2nd Floor.
Messrs Curly Nibs & Co., Commissioners of Oaths.
1st Floor.
Sir S. Slightly, Financier.
Ground Floor.
Darling Bros., Solicitors.
Then we have a brief peep into each of these rooms. First we see Tootles and the twins all on high stools at separate desks writing in ledgers.

Next Curly and Nibs in their office, also on stools, busy over legal documents.

Then Slightly in a finer office. He is standing by the fire with legs outstretched, smoking a large cigar, and drinking out of a tumbler. In a close-up we see printed on tumbler the words 'Brandy and Soda'. Slightly is evidently rather proud of being able to drink this.

Then John and Michael. Michael is dictating to a lady typist. John is putting on an over-coat and silk hat and goes out very professionally with a roll of papers. As soon as he has gone Michael ceases to dictate but looks lovingly at typist instead. Her typing stops, she turns and looks self-consciously at him. That is all, but we guess that it is the old story. They are all now grown up young men, some of them quite tall and stout with moustaches or spectacles but all must be easily recognisable. Their hair is of course short. The effect of height can be got by making the furniture smaller than usual. All are in correct office dress, black coats, etc., Slightly being a bit of a dandy. Peter, who is just as usual, is seen looking through the window of each office and grinning cynically at them, evidently thinking that they made the grand mistake in growing up. But they are all too occupied with their own affairs to see him.

Then we have a picture of Wendy, now a sweet young woman in her wedding-gown and looking her loveliest. Presently she goes to the window, which is open, and gazes out with arms outstretched. Memories of the Never, Never Land come to her, and we see them in a vision. What we see are some of the scenes that have become familiar to us—the home under the ground, the lagoon, the forest, and all these scenes are as real as ever. But the figures are only ghosts, done in the manner which is so effective on the film, i.e. they are pale ghosts of Peter, Wendy, the other boys, Hook, and Tiger Lily. Then we see some dancing gaily in their nightgowns, others flitting through the wood, etc. The last scene is Hook's arm lying among grass. In the hollow made by the hook a little bird has built a nest with eggs in it. This is shown in a close-up. Then Wendy again in her wedding gown is seen as before at window. She cries a little, then bravely pulls down window as a sign that the days of make-believe are ended. She smiles at herself.

Then we see a new nursery with one small bed in it. This bed is in much the same position as Wendy's bed in the old nursery, and in it is sleeping Jane, Wendy's daughter. We just see there is a child sleeping in it, but we don't see her face. There is another larger bed in room, evidently the nurse's, but it is not occupied. Wendy is standing at foot of bed gazing lovingly at Jane, patting her, etc. She is in a semi-evening dress very simple. She goes over to fender on which some childish garments are hanging, and rearranges them. At this point Peter peeps through the window curtains at her and is bewildered and unhappy at seeing her so grown-up. When she has arranged garments on fender she goes quietly out on tip-toe with a last loving look at child. She is never aware of Peter's presence. She also must be as tall as possible but in her case it can't be done with making furniture smaller as this would increase size of Peter and child. It must be done artificially by high shoes, long frock, etc. As she goes out Peter comes after her with arms outstretched to her, but she doesn't see him. When she has gone he is a rather tragic, lonely figure. He lies on floor and sobs precisely as he did on the occasion when he came back for his shadow. What happened then is now repeated. Jane is wakened by his sobbing and sits up in bed. Here there should be a surprise for the audience, for though the picture seems to be continuous, Jane is played by the same actress who plays Wendy. She should make herself a little different from Wendy as by a different arrangement or even colour of hair, and wear a coloured woollen nightgown instead of Wendy's white cotton one. But of course they should still be very much alike.

'Boy, why are you crying?'

Peter in answer to her question rises, comes to foot of bed and bows as he did to Wendy. Jane replies by bowing as Wendy did.

'Girl, what is your name?'

'Jane Wendy. What is your name?'

'Peter Pan.'

'Where is your mother, Peter?'

'Don't have a mother, Jane.'

'Oh!'

The result of this conversation is that Jane does precisely as Wendy did. She jumps out of bed, runs to him, and puts her arms round him. She has evidently taken the mother's place.

Then a picture of Peter and Jane flying through the air carrying broom and shovel, just as we have seen Peter and Wendy doing it. They are very gay. Jane is in the woollen nightgown; so that we see clearly that it is Jane and not Wendy.

Then the scene is again the Never, Never Land, a lovely part of the wood near a pool and waterfall. It is a sunny summer day, and first we see Jane doing Peter's washing in a tub on ground, then flying with it to a rope that is hung high between branches. On this she hangs the garments. She is now dressed in the familiar Wendy garments, but tucked up, etc., in a businesslike way. Tink appears and pulls her hair. While the washing is going on Peter appears on his goat. The flowers are following him just as on the day when they went to the lagoon, and in the same way he orders them to go back.

Then he relents and lets them come. He tethers his goat. He sits on a mossy bank playing his pipes. For a little time we see Peter and Jane thus engaged. Another vague figure appears and watches them from behind a tree unseen by them. It is the ghost of the grown-up Wendy in long dress, who has somehow got here to see that her child is safe. She is just a shadow. She watches the two sweetly, but being grown-up, she cannot join in the adventure. Tink, however, discovers her and pulls her hair. Wendy goes away sadly. The crocodile comes and tries to dance to Peter's pipes—so do bears and other friendly animals. Soon the pool and waterfall are alive with mermaids who play games, splash each other, etc. Peter continues playing his pipes and Jane attending to his washing.

Then we have the final picture, which should also be the most beautiful. It is the last moment of the acted play, but much can be done with it that is impossible in the play. The time is now sunset. We see the Tree Tops with the Little House now perched high among them. All around are tiny fairy houses (not nests as in the play, but absurd little houses of thatch and moss, each with a window and a chimney). The exact nature of these fairy houses is for future consideration. As moon-light comes, these houses light up, and at the doors, and flying about among the trees and tree-tops, are innumerable fairies, gossiping, quarreling and playing about. The music of this should all be as it is in the play,* where it is excellent, and mixed up with it should be the bells to indicate much chatter among the fairies. The scene goes on with changes of lighting, etc. After the Little House lights up it is sometimes in one place, sometimes in another, sometimes near, sometimes far away—once it is sailing on the lagoon, and the mermaids are pulling it about in fun—then the fairies capture it and take it back to the tree-tops. We see Peter and Jane at the door waving their handkerchiefs to us. Finally there is no girl, and he is alone. There are no animals. The fairies have gone to their houses; their lights go out (not simultaneously, but fitfully). Now there are only lights from moon and stars, and Peter is seen in silhouette alone, playing his pipes.

THE END

PETER PAN

or

The Boy Who Would Not Grow Up

(1928)

CHARACTERS

(in order of appearance)

Nana (a dog and the children's nursemaid)

Michael

Mrs Darling

John

Wendy

Mr Darling

Peter Pan

Liza

Tinker Bell

Slightly

Tootles

Nibs

Curly

First Twin

Second Twin

Captain Hook

Cecco

Bill Jukes

Cookson

Gentleman Starkey

Skylights

Mullins

Noodler

Smee

Tiger Lily

Panther

Cabby and Friend

Animals and Fairies, Pirates, Indians, Mermaids, Bird

TO THE FIVE*

A DEDICATION

Some disquieting confessions must be made in printing at last* the play of *Peter Pan*; among them this, that I have no recollection of having written it. Of that, however, anon. What I want to do first is to give Peter to the Five without whom he never would have existed. I hope, my dear sirs, that in memory of what we have been to each other you will accept this dedication with your friend's love. The play of Peter is streaky with you still, though none may see this save ourselves. A score of Acts had to be left out, and you were in them all. We first brought Peter down, didn't we, with a blunt-headed arrow in Kensington Gardens? I seem to remember that we believed we had killed him, though he was only winded,* and that after a spasm of exultation in our prowess the more soft-hearted among us wept and all of us thought of the police. There was not one of you who would not have sworn as an eye-witness to this occurrence; no doubt I was abetting, but you used to provide corroboration that was never given to you by me. As for myself, I suppose I always

FIGURE 3 J. M. Barrie, photograph of Michael Llewelyn Davies aged 6 dressed as Peter Pan (1906).

knew that I made Peter by rubbing the five of you violently together, as savages with two sticks produce a flame. That is all he is, the spark I got from you.

We had good sport of him before we clipped him small to make him fit the boards.* Some of you were not born when the story began and yet were hefty figures before we saw that the game was up. Do you remember a garden at Burpham* and the initiation there of No. 4* when he was six weeks old, and three of you grudged letting him in so young? Have you, No. 3, forgotten the white violets at the Cistercian abbey in which we cassocked our first fairies (all little friends of St Benedict), or your cry to the Gods, 'Do I just kill one pirate all the time?' Do you remember Marooners' Hut in the haunted groves of Waverley, and the St Bernard dog* in a tiger's mask who so frequently attacked you, and the literary record of that summer, *The Boy Castaways*,* which is so much the best and the rarest of this author's works? What was it that made us eventually give to the public in the thin form of a play that which had been woven for ourselves alone? Alas, I know what it was, I was losing my grip. One by one as you swung monkey-wise from branch to branch in the wood of make-believe you reached the tree of knowledge. Sometimes you swung back into the wood, as the unthinking may at a cross-road take a familiar path that no longer leads to home; or you perched ostentatiously on its boughs to please me, pretending that you still belonged; soon you knew it only as the vanished wood, for it vanishes if one needs to look for it. A time came when I saw that No. 1, the most gallant of you all, ceased to believe that he was ploughing woods incarnadine,* and with an apologetic eye for me derided the lingering faith of No. 2; when even No. 3 questioned gloomily whether he did not really spend his nights in bed. There were still two who knew no better, but their day was dawning. In these circumstances, I suppose, was begun the writing of the play of Peter. That was a quarter of a century ago, and I clutch my brows in vain to remember whether it was a last desperate throw to retain the five of you for a little longer, or merely a cold decision to turn you into bread and butter.

This brings us back to my uncomfortable admission that I have no recollection of writing the play of *Peter Pan*, now being published for the first time so long after he made his bow upon the stage. You had played it until you tired of it, and tossed it in the air and gored it and left it derelict in the mud and went on your way singing other songs; and then I stole back and sewed some of the gory fragments together with a pen-nib. That is what must have happened, but I cannot remember doing it. I remember writing the story of *Peter and Wendy* many years after the production of the play, but I might have cribbed that from some typed copy. I can haul back to mind the writing of almost every other assay* of mine, however forgotten by the pretty public; but this play of Peter, no. Even my beginning as an amateur playwright, that noble mouthful, *Bandelero the Bandit*,* I remember every detail of its composition in my school days at Dumfries. Not less vivid is my first little piece, produced by Mr Toole.* It was called *Ibsen's Ghost*,* and was a parody of the mightiest craftsman that ever wrote for our kind friends in front.* To save the management the cost of typing I wrote out the 'parts,'* after being told what parts were, and I can still recall my first words, spoken so plaintively by a now famous actress,—'To run away from my second husband just as I ran away from my first, it feels quite like old times.' On the first night a man in the pit found *Ibsen's Ghost* so diverting that he had to be removed in hysterics. After that no one seems to have thought of it at all. But what a man to carry about with one! How odd, too, that these trifles should adhere to the mind that cannot remember the long job of writing Peter. It does seem almost suspicious, especially as I have not the original MS of *Peter Pan* (except a few stray pages) with which to support my claim. I have indeed another MS, lately made, but that 'proves nothing.' I know not whether I lost that original MS or destroyed it or happily gave it away. I talk of dedicating the play to you, but how can I prove it is mine? How ought I to act if some other hand, who could also have made a copy, thinks it worth while to contest the cold rights? Cold they are to me now as that laughter of yours in which Peter came into being long before he was caught and written down. There is Peter still, but to me he lies sunk in the gay Black Lake.

Any one of you five brothers has a better claim to the authorship than most, and I would not fight you for it, but you should have launched your case long ago in the days when you most admired me, which were in the first year of the play, owing to a rumour's reaching you that my spoils were one-and-sixpence* a night. This was untrue, but it did give me a standing among you. You watched for my next play with peeled eyes, not for entertainment but lest it contained some chance witticism of yours that could be challenged as collaboration; indeed I believe there still exists a legal document,* full of the Aforesaid and Henceforward to be called Part-Author, in which for some such snatching I was tied down to pay No. 2 one halfpenny daily throughout the run of the piece.

During the rehearsals of Peter (and it is evidence in my favour that I was admitted to them) a depressed man in overalls, carrying a mug of tea or a paint-pot, used often to appear by my side in the shadowy stalls and say to me, 'The gallery boys* won't stand it.' He then mysteriously faded away as if he were the theatre ghost. This hopelessness of his is what all dramatists are said to feel at such times, so perhaps he was the author. Again, a large number of children whom I have seen playing Peter in their homes with careless mastership, constantly putting in better words, could have thrown it off with ease. It was for such as they that after the first production I had to add something to the play at the request of parents (who thus showed that they thought me the responsible person) about no one being able to fly until the fairy dust had been blown on him; so many children having gone home and tried it from their beds and needed surgical attention.

Notwithstanding other possibilities, I think I wrote Peter, and if so it must have been in the usual inky way. Some of it, I like to think, was done in that native place* which is the dearest spot on earth to me, though my last heart-beats shall be with my beloved solitary London that was so hard to reach.* I must have sat at a table with that great dog* waiting for me to stop, not complaining, for he knew it was thus we made our living, but giving me a look when he found he was to be in the play, with his sex changed. In after years when the actor who was Nana had to go to the wars he first taught his wife how to take his place as the dog till he came back, and I am glad that I see nothing funny in this; it seems to me to belong to the play. I offer this obtuseness on my part as my first proof that I am the author.

Some say that we are different people at different periods of our lives, changing not through effort of will, which is a brave affair, but in the easy course of nature every ten years or so. I suppose this theory might explain my present trouble, but I don't hold with it; I think one remains the same person throughout, merely passing, as it were, in these lapses of time from one room to another, but all in the same house. If we unlock the rooms of the far past we can peer in and see ourselves, busily occupied in beginning to become you and me. Thus, if I am the author in question the way he is to go should already be showing in the occupant of my first compartment, at whom I now take the liberty to peep. Here he is at the age of seven or so with his fellow-conspirator Robb,* both in glengarry bonnets.* They are giving an entertainment in a tiny old washing-house that still stands. The charge for admission is preens, a bool, or a peerie* (I taught you a good deal of Scotch, so possibly you can follow that), and apparently the culminating Act consists in our trying to put each other into the boiler, though some say that I also addressed the spell-bound audience. This washing-house is not only the theatre of my first play, but has a still closer connection with Peter. It is the original of the little house the Lost Boys built in the Never Land for Wendy, the chief difference being that it never wore John's tall hat as a chimney. If Robb had owned a lum hat* I have no doubt that it would have been placed on the washing-house.

Here is that boy again some four years older, and the reading he is munching feverishly is about desert islands; he calls them wrecked islands.* He buys his sanguinary tales surreptitiously in penny numbers.* I see a change coming over him; he is blanching as he reads in the high-class magazine, *Chatterbox,** a fulmination against such literature, and sees that unless his greed for islands is quenched he is for ever lost. With gloaming* he steals out of the house, his library bulging beneath his palpitating waistcoat. I follow like his shadow, as indeed I am, and watch him dig a hole in a field at Pathhead farm* and bury his islands in it; it was ages ago, but I could walk straight to that hole in the field now and delve for the remains. I peep into the next compartment. There he is again, ten years older, an undergraduate now and craving to be a real explorer, one of those who do things instead of prating* of them, but otherwise unaltered; he might be painted at twenty on top of a mast, in his hand a spy-glass* through which he rakes the horizon for an elusive strand.* I go from room to room, and he is now a man, real exploration abandoned (though only because no one would have him). Soon he is even concocting other plays, and quaking a little lest some low person counts how many islands there are in them. I note that with the years the islands grow more sinister, but it is only because he has now to write with the left hand,* the right having given out; evidently one thinks more darkly down the left arm.

Go to the keyhole of the compartment where he and I join up, and you may see us wondering whether they would stand one more island. This journey through the house may not convince any one that I wrote Peter, but it does suggest me as a likely person. I pause to ask myself whether I read *Chatterbox* again, suffered the old agony, and buried that MS of the play in a hole in a field.

Of course this is over-charged. Perhaps we do change; except a little something in us which is no larger than a mote in the eye, and that, like it, dances in front of us beguiling us all our days. I cannot cut the hair by which it hangs.

The strongest evidence that I am the author is to be found, I think, in a now melancholy volume, the aforementioned *The Boy Castaways*; so you must excuse me for parading that work here. Officer of the Court, call *The Boy Castaways*. The witness steps forward and proves to be a book you remember well though you have not glanced at it these many years. I pulled it out of a bookcase just now not without difficulty, for its recent occupation has been to support the shelf above. I suppose, though I am uncertain, that it was I and not you who hammered it into that place of utility. It is a little battered and bent after the manner of those who shoulder burdens, and ought (to our shame) to remind us of the witnesses who sometimes get an hour off from the cells to give evidence before his Lordship. I have said that it is the rarest of my printed works, as it must be, for the only edition was limited to two copies, of which one (there was always some devilry in any matter connected with Peter) instantly lost itself in a railway carriage. This is the survivor. The idlers in court may have assumed that it is a handwritten screed, and are impressed by its bulk. It is printed by Constable's (how handsomely you did us, dear Blaikie*), it contains thirty-five illustrations and is bound in cloth with a picture stamped on the cover of the three eldest of you 'setting out to be wrecked.' This record is supposed to be edited by the youngest of the three, and I must have granted him that honour to make up for his being so often lifted bodily out of our adventures by his nurse, who kept breaking into them for the fell purpose of giving him a midday rest. No. 4 rested so much at this period that he was merely an honorary member of the band, waving his foot to you for luck when you set off with bow and arrow to shoot his dinner for him; and one may rummage the book in vain for any trace of No. 5. Here is the title-page, except that you are numbered instead of named—

THE BOY
CASTAWAYS
OF BLACK LAKE ISLAND

Being a record of the Terrible
Adventures of Three Brothers
in the summer of 1901
faithfully set forth
by No.3.

LONDON
Published by J. M. Barrie
in the Gloucester Road
1901

There is a long preface by No. 3 in which we gather your ages at this first flight. 'No. 1 was eight and a month, No. 2 was approaching his seventh lustrum,* and I was a good bit past four.' Of his two elders, while commending their fearless dispositions, the editor complains that they wanted to do all the shooting and carried the whole equipment of arrows inside their shirts. He is attractively modest about himself, 'Of No. 3 I prefer to say nothing, hoping that the tale as it is unwound will show that he was a boy of deeds rather than of words,' a quality which he hints did not unduly protrude upon the brows of Nos. 1 and 2. His preface ends on a high note, 'I should say that the work was in the first instance compiled as a record simply at which we could whet our memories, and that it is now published for No. 4's benefit. If it teaches him by example lessons in fortitude and manly endurance we shall consider that we were not wrecked in vain.'

Published to whet your memories. Does it whet them? Do you hear once more, like some long-forgotten whistle beneath your window (Robb at dawn calling me to the fishing!) the not quite mortal blows that still echo in some of the chapter headings?—'Chapter II, No. 1 teaches Wilkinson* (his master) a Stern Lesson—We Run away to Sea. Chapter III, A Fearful Hurricane—Wreck of the 'Anna Pink'—We go crazy from Want of Food—Proposal to eat No. 3—Land Ahoy.' Such are two chapters out of sixteen. Are these again your javelins cutting tunes in the blue haze of the pines; do you sweat as you scale the dreadful Valley of Rolling Stones, and cleanse your hands of pirate blood by scouring them carelessly in Mother Earth? Can you still make a fire (you could do it once, Mr Seton-Thompson* taught us in, surely an odd place, the Reform Club*) by rubbing those sticks together? Was it the travail of hut-building that subsequently advised Peter to find a 'home under the ground'? The bottle and mugs in that lurid picture, 'Last night on the Island,' seem to suggest that you had changed from Lost Boys into pirates, which was probably also a tendency of Peter's. Listen again to our stolen saw-mill, man's proudest invention; when he made the saw-mill he beat the birds for music in a wood.

The illustrations (full-paged) in *The Boy Castaways* are all photographs taken by myself; some of them indeed of phenomena that had to be invented afterwards, for you were always off doing the wrong things when I pressed the button. I see that we combined instruction with amusement; perhaps we had given our kingly word to that effect. How otherwise account for such wording to the pictures as these: 'It is undoubtedly,' says No. 1 in a fir tree that is bearing unwonted fruit, recently tied to it, 'the *Cocos nucifera*,* for observe the slender columns supporting the crown of leaves which fall with a grace that no art can imitate.' 'Truly,' continues No. 1 under the same tree in another forest as he leans upon his trusty gun, 'though the perils of these happenings are great, yet would I rejoice to endure still greater privations to be thus rewarded by such wondrous studies of Nature.' He is soon back to the practical, however, 'recognising the Mango (*Magnifera indica*) by its lancet-shaped leaves and the cucumber-shaped fruit.' No. 1 was certainly the right sort of voyager to be wrecked with, though if my memory fails me not, No. 2, to whom these strutting observations were addressed, sometimes protested because none of them was given to him. No. 3 being the author is in surprisingly few of the pictures, but this, you may remember, was because the lady already darkly referred to used to pluck him from our midst for his siesta at 12 o'clock, which was the hour that best suited the camera.* With a skill on which he has never been complimented the photographer sometimes got No. 3 nominally included in a wild-life picture when he was really in a humdrum house kicking on the sofa. Thus in a scene representing Nos. 1 and 2 sitting scowling outside the hut it is untruly written that they scowled because 'their brother was within singing and playing on a barbaric instrument. The music,' the unseen No. 3 is represented as saying (obviously forestalling No. 1), 'is rude and to a cultured ear discordant, but the songs like those of the Arabs are full of poetic imagery.' He was perhaps allowed to say this sulkily on the sofa.

Though *The Boy Castaways* has sixteen chapter-headings, there is no other letterpress;* an absence which possible purchasers might complain of, though there are surely worse ways of writing a book than this. These headings anticipate much of the play of *Peter Pan*, but there were many incidents of our Kensington Gardens days that never got into the book, such as our Antarctic exploits when we reached the Pole in advance of our friend Captain Scott* and cut our initials on it for him to find, a strange foreshadowing of what was really to happen. In *The Boy Castaways* Captain Hook has arrived but is called Captain Swarthy, and he seems from the pictures to have been a black man. This character, as you do not need to be told, is held by those in the know to be autobiographical. You had many tussles with him (though you never, I think, got his right arm) before you reached the terrible chapter (which might be taken from the play) entitled 'We Board the Pirate Ship at Dawn—A Rakish Craft—No. 1 Hew-them-Down and No. 2 of the Red Hatchet—A Holocaust* of Pirates—Rescue of Peter.' (Hullo, Peter rescued instead of rescuing others? I know what that means and so do you, but we are not going to give away all our secrets.) The scene of the Holocaust is the Black Lake (afterwards, when we let women in, the Mermaids' Lagoon). The pirate captain's end was not in the mouth of a crocodile though we had crocodiles on the spot ('while No. 2 was removing the crocodiles from the stream No. 1 shot a few parrots, *Psittacidae*,* for our evening meal'). I think our captain had divers* deaths owing to unseemly competition among you, each wanting to slay him single-handed. On a special occasion, such as when No. 3 pulled out the tooth himself, you gave the deed to him, but took it from him while he rested. The only pictorial representation in the book of Swarthy's fate is in two parts. In one, called briefly 'We string him up,' Nos. 1 and 2, stern as Athos,* are hauling him up a tree by a rope, his face snarling as if it were a grinning mask (which indeed it was), and his garments very like some of my own stuffed with bracken. The other, the same scene next day, is called 'The Vultures had Picked him Clean,' and tells its own tale.

The dog in *The Boy Castaways* seems never to have been called Nana but was evidently in training for that post. He originally belonged to Swarthy (or to Captain Marryat?*), and the first picture of him, lean, skulking, and hunched (how did I get that effect?), 'patrolling the island' in that monster's interests, gives little indication of the domestic paragon he was to become. We lured him away to the better life, and there is, later, a touching picture, a clear forecast of the Darling nursery, entitled 'We trained the dog to watch over us while we slept.' In this he also is sleeping, in a position that is a careful copy of his charges; indeed any trouble we had with him was because, once he knew he was in a story, he thought his safest course was to imitate you in everything you did. How anxious he was to show that he understood the game, and more generous than you, he never pretended that he was the one who killed Captain Swarthy. I must not imply that he was entirely without initiative, for it was his own idea to bark warningly a minute or two before twelve o'clock as a signal to No. 3 that his keeper was probably on her way for him (Disappearance of No. 3); and he became so used to living in the world of Pretend that when we reached the hut of a morning he was often there waiting for us, looking, it is true, rather idiotic, but with a new bark he had invented which puzzled us until we decided that he was demanding the password. He was always willing to do any extra jobs, such as becoming the tiger in mask, and when after a fierce engagement you carried home that mask in triumph, he joined in the procession proudly and never let on that the trophy had ever been part of him. Long afterwards he saw the play from a box in the theatre, and as familiar scenes were unrolled before his eyes I have never seen a dog so bothered. At one matinee we even let him for a moment take the place of the actor who played Nana, and I don't know that any members of the audience ever noticed the change, though he introduced some 'business' that was new to them but old to you and me. Heigh-ho, I suspect that in this reminiscence I am mixing him up with his successor, for such a one there had to be, the loyal Newfoundland who, perhaps in the following year, applied, so to say, for the part by bringing hedgehogs to the hut in his mouth as offerings for our evening repasts. The head and coat of him were copied for the Nana of the play.

They do seem to be emerging out of our island, don't they, the little people of the play, all except that sly one, the chief figure,* who draws farther and farther into the wood as we advance upon him? He so dislikes being tracked, as if there were something odd about him, that when he dies he means to get up and blow away the particle that will be his ashes.

Wendy has not yet appeared, but she has been trying to come ever since that loyal nurse* cast the humorous shadow of woman upon the scene and made us feel that it might be fun to let in a disturbing element. Perhaps she would have bored her way in at last whether we wanted her or not. It may be that even Peter did not really bring her to the Never Land of his free will, but merely pretended to do so because she would not stay away. Even Tinker Bell had reached our island before we left it. It was one evening when we climbed the wood carrying No. 4 to show him what the trail was like by twilight. As our lanterns twinkled among the leaves No. 4 saw a twinkle stand still for a moment and he waved his foot gaily to it, thus creating Tink. It must not be thought, however, that there were any other sentimental passages between No. 4 and Tink; indeed, as he got to know her better he suspected her of frequenting the hut to see what we had been having for supper, and to partake of the same, and he pursued her with malignancy.

A safe but sometimes chilly way of recalling the past is to force open a crammed drawer. If you are searching for anything in particular you don't find it, but something falls out at the back that is often more interesting. It is in this way that I get my desultory reading, which includes the few stray leaves of the original MS of Peter that I have said I do possess, though even they, when returned to the drawer, are gone again, as if that touch of devilry lurked in them still. They show that in early days I hacked at and added to the play. In the drawer I find some scraps of Mr Crook's delightful music,* and other incomplete matter relating to Peter. Here is the reply of a boy whom I favoured* with a seat in my box and injudiciously asked at the end what he had liked best. 'What I think I liked best,' he said, 'was tearing up the programme and dropping the bits on people's heads.' Thus am I often laid low. A copy of my favourite programme of the play is still in the drawer. In the first or second year of Peter No. 4 could not attend through illness, so we took the play to his nursery,* far away in the country, an array of vehicles almost as glorious as a travelling circus; the leading parts were played by the youngest children in the London company, and No. 4, aged five, looked on solemnly at the performance from his bed and never smiled once. That was my first and only appearance on the real stage, and this copy of the programme shows I was thought so meanly of as an actor that they printed my name in smaller letters than the others.

I have said little here of Nos. 4 and 5, and it is high time I had finished. They had a long summer day, and I turn round twice and now they are off to school. On Monday, as it seems, I was escorting No. 5 to a children's party and brushing his hair in the ante-room; and by Thursday he is placing me against the wall of an underground station and saying, 'Now I am going to get the tickets; don't move till I come back for you or you'll lose yourself.' No. 4 jumps from being astride my shoulders fishing, I knee-deep in the stream, to becoming, while still a schoolboy, the sternest of my literary critics. Anything he shook his head over I abandoned, and conceivably the world has thus been deprived of masterpieces. There was for instance an unfortunate little tragedy which I liked until I foolishly told No. 4 its subject, when he frowned and said he had better have a look at it. He read it, and then, patting me on the back, as only he and No. 1 could touch me, said, 'You know you can't do this sort of thing.' End of a tragedian. Sometimes, however, No. 4 liked my efforts, and I walked in the azure that day when he returned *Dear Brutus* to me with the comment 'Not so bad.' In earlier days, when he was ten, I offered him the MS of my book *Margaret Ogilvy*. 'Oh, thanks,' he said almost immediately, and added, 'Of course my desk is awfully full.' I reminded him that he could take out some of its more ridiculous contents. He said, 'I have read it already in the book.' This I had not known, and I was secretly elated, but I said that people sometimes liked to preserve this kind of thing as a curiosity. He said 'Oh' again. I said tartly that he was not compelled to take it if he didn't want it. He said, 'Of course I want it, but my desk——' Then he wriggled out of the room and came back in a few minutes dragging in No. 5 and announcing triumphantly, 'No. 5 will have it.'

The rebuffs I have got from all of you! They were especially crushing in those early days when one by one you came out of your belief in fairies and lowered on me as the deceiver. My grandest triumph, the best thing in the play of *Peter Pan* (though it is not in it), is that long after No. 4 had ceased to believe, I brought him back to the faith for at least two minutes. We were on our way in a boat to fish the Outer Hebrides (where we caught *Mary Rose**), and though it was a journey of days he wore his fishing basket on his back all the time, so as to be able to begin at once. His one pain was the absence of Johnny Mackay, for Johnny was the loved gillie* of the previous summer who had taught him everything that is worth knowing (which is a matter of flies) but could not be with us this time as he would have had to cross and re-cross Scotland to reach us. As the boat drew near the Kyle of Lochalsh pier I told Nos. 4 and 5 it was such a famous wishing pier that they had now but to wish and they should have. No. 5 believed at once and expressed a wish to meet himself (I afterwards found him on the pier searching faces confidently), but No. 4 thought it more of my untimely nonsense and doggedly declined to humour me. 'Whom do you want to see most, No. 4?' 'Of course I would like most to see Johnny Mackay.' 'Well, then, wish for him.' 'Oh, rot.' 'It can't do any harm to wish.' Contemptuously he wished, and as the ropes were thrown on the pier he saw Johnny waiting for him, loaded with angling paraphernalia. I know no one less like a fairy than Johnny Mackay, but for two minutes No. 4 was quivering in another world than ours. When he came to he gave me a smile which meant that we understood each other, and thereafter neglected me for a month, being always with Johnny. As I have said, this episode is not in the play; so though I dedicate *Peter Pan* to you I keep the smile, with the few other broken fragments of immortality that have come my way.

ACT 1

THE NURSERY

The night nursery of the Darling family, which is the scene of our opening Act, is at the top of a rather depressed street in Bloomsbury. We have a right to place it where we will, and the reason Bloomsbury is chosen is that Mr Roget* once lived there. So did we in days when his *Thesaurus* was our only companion in London; and we whom he has helped to wend our way through life have always wanted to pay him a little compliment. The Darlings therefore lived in Bloomsbury.

It is a corner house whose top window, the important one, looks upon a leafy square from which Peter used to fly up to it, to the delight of three children and no doubt the irritation of passers-by. The street is still there, though the steaming sausage shop has gone; and apparently the same cards perch now as then over the doors, inviting homeless ones to come and stay with the hospitable inhabitants. Since the days of the Darlings, however, a lick of paint has been applied; and our corner house in particular, which has swallowed its neighbour, blooms with awful freshness as if the colours had been discharged upon it through a hose. Its card now says 'No children,' meaning maybe that the goings-on of Wendy and her brothers have given the house a bad name. As for ourselves, we have not been in it since we went back to reclaim our old *Thesaurus*.

That is what we call the Darling house, but you may dump it down anywhere you like, and if you think it was your house you are very probably right. It wanders about London looking for anybody in need of it, like the little house in the Never Land.

The blind (which is what Peter would have called the theatre curtain if he had ever seen one) rises on that top room, a shabby little room if Mrs Darling had not made it the hub of creation by her certainty that such it was, and adorned it to match with a loving heart and all the scrapings of her purse. The door on the right leads into the day nursery, which she has no right to have, but she made it herself with nails in her mouth and a paste-pot in her hand. This is the door the children will come in by. There are three beds and (rather oddly) a large dog-kennel; two of these beds, with the kennel, being on the left and the other on the right. The coverlets of the beds (if visitors are expected) are made out of Mrs Darling's wedding-gown, which was such a grand affair that it still keeps them pinched.* Over each bed is a china house, the size of a linnet's nest, containing a night-light. The fire, which is on our right, is burning as discreetly as if it were in custody, which in a sense it is, for supporting the mantelshelf are two wooden soldiers, home-made, begun by Mr Darling, finished by Mrs Darling, repainted (unfortunately) by John Darling. On the fire-guard hang incomplete parts of children's night attire. The door the parents will come in by is on the left. At the back is the bathroom door, with a cuckoo clock over it; and in the centre is the window, which is at present ever so staid and respectable, but half an hour hence (namely at 6.30 p.m.) will be able to tell a very strange tale to the police.

The only occupant of the room at present is Nana the nurse, reclining, not as you might expect on the one soft chair, but on the floor. She is a Newfoundland dog, and though this may shock the grandiose, the not exactly affluent will make allowances. The Darlings could not afford to have a nurse, they could not afford indeed to have children; and now you are beginning to understand how they did it. Of course Nana has been trained by Mrs Darling, but like all treasures* she was born to it. In this play we shall see her chiefly inside the house, but she was just as exemplary outside, escorting the two elders to school with an umbrella in her mouth, for instance, and butting them back into line if they strayed.

The cuckoo clock strikes six, and Nana springs into life. This first moment in the play is tremendously important, for if the actor playing Nana does not spring properly we are undone. She will probably be played by a boy, if one clever enough can be found, and must never be on two legs except on those rare occasions when an ordinary nurse would be on four. This Nana must go about all her duties in a most ordinary manner, so that you know in your bones that she performs them just so every evening at six; naturalness must be her passion; indeed, it should be the aim of every one in the play, for which she is now setting the pace. All the characters, whether grown-ups or babes, must wear a child's outlook on life as their only important adornment. If they cannot help being funny they are begged to go away. A good motto for all would be 'The little less, and how much it is.'*

Nana, making much use of her mouth, 'turns down' the beds, and carries the various articles on the fire-guard across to them. Then pushing the bathroom door open, she is seen at work on the taps preparing Michael's bath; after which she enters from the day nursery with the youngest of the family on her back.

MICHAEL *(obstreperous)* I won't go to bed, I won't, I won't. Nana, it isn't six o'clock yet. Two minutes more, please, one minute more? Nana, I won't be bathed, I tell you I will not be bathed.

(Here the bathroom door closes on them, and Mrs Darling, who has perhaps heard his cry, enters the nursery. She is the loveliest lady in Bloomsbury, with a sweet mocking mouth, and as she is going out to dinner to-night she is already wearing her evening gown because she knows her children like to see her in it. It is a delicious confection made by herself out of nothing and other people's mistakes. She does not often go out to dinner, preferring when the children are in bed to sit beside them tidying up their minds, just as if they were drawers. If Wendy and the boys could keep awake they might see her repacking into their proper places the many articles of the mind that have strayed during the day, lingering humorously over some of their contents, wondering where on earth they picked this thing up, making discoveries sweet and not so sweet, pressing this to her cheek and hurriedly stowing that out of sight. When they wake in the morning the naughtinesses with which they went to bed are not, alas, blown away, but they are placed at the bottom of the drawer; and on the top, beautifully aired, are their prettier thoughts ready for the new day.

As she enters the room she is startled to see a strange little face outside the window and a hand groping as if it wanted to come in)

MRS DARLING Who are you? *(The unknown disappears; she hurries to the window)* No one there. And yet I feel sure I saw a face. My children!

(She throws open the bathroom door and Michael's head appears gaily over the bath. He splashes; she throws kisses to him and closes the door. 'Wendy, John,' she cries, and gets reassuring answers from the day nursery. She sits down, relieved, on Wendy's bed; and Wendy and John come in, looking their smallest size, as children tend to do to a mother suddenly in fear for them)

JOHN *(histrionically)* We are doing an act; we are playing at being you and father. *(He imitates the only father who has come under his special notice)* A little less noise there.

WENDY Now let us pretend we have a baby.

JOHN *(good-naturedly)* I am happy to inform you, Mrs Darling, that you are now a mother. *(Wendy gives way to ecstasy)* You have missed the chief thing; you haven't asked, 'boy or girl?'

WENDY I am so glad to have one at all, I don't care which it is.

JOHN *(crushingly)* That is just the difference between gentlemen and ladies. Now you tell me.

WENDY I am happy to acquaint you, Mr Darling, you are now a father.

JOHN Boy or girl?

WENDY *(presenting herself)* Girl.

JOHN Tuts.

WENDY You horrid.

JOHN Go on.

WENDY I am happy to acquaint you, Mr Darling, you are again a father.

JOHN Boy or girl?

WENDY Boy. *(John beams)* Mummy, it's hateful of him.

(Michael emerges from the bathroom in John's old pyjamas and giving his face a last wipe with the towel)

MICHAEL *(expanding)* Now, John, have me.

JOHN We don't want any more.

MICHAEL *(contracting)* Am I not to be born at all?

JOHN Two is enough.

MICHAEL *(wheedling)* Come, John: boy, John. *(Appalled)* Nobody wants me!

MRS DARLING I do.

MICHAEL *(with a glimmer of hope)* Boy or girl?

MRS DARLING *(with one of those happy thoughts of hers)* Boy.

(Triumph of Michael; discomfiture of John. Mr Darling arrives, in no mood unfortunately to gloat over this domestic scene. He is really a good man as breadwinners go, and it is hard luck for him to be propelled into the room now, when if we had brought him in a few minutes earlier or later he might have made a fairer impression. In the city where he sits on a stool all day, as fixed as a postage stamp, he is so like all the others on stools that you recognise him not by his face but by his stool, but at home the way to gratify him is to say that he has a distinct personality. He is very conscientious, and in the days when Mrs Darling gave up keeping the house books correctly and drew pictures instead (which he called her guesses), he did all the totting up for her, holding her hand while he calculated whether they could have Wendy or not, and coming down on the right side. It is with regret, therefore, that we introduce him as a tornado, rushing into the nursery in evening dress, but without his coat, and brandishing in his hand a recalcitrant white tie)

MR DARLING *(implying that he has searched for her everywhere and that the nursery is a strange place in which to find her)* Oh, here you are, Mary.

MRS DARLING *(knowing at once what is the matter)* What is the matter, George dear?

MR DARLING *(as if the word were monstrous)* Matter! This tie, it will not tie. *(He waxes sarcastic)* Not round my neck. Round the bed-post, oh yes; twenty times have I made it up round the bed-post, but round my neck, oh dear no; begs to be excused.

MICHAEL *(in a joyous transport)* Say it again, father, say it again!

MR DARLING *(witheringly)* Thank you. *(Goaded by a suspiciously crooked smile on Mrs Darling's face)* I warn you, Mary, that unless this tie is round my neck we don't go out to dinner to-night, and if I don't go out to dinner to-night I never go to the office again, and if I don't go to the office again you and I starve, and our children will be thrown into the streets.

(The children blanch as they grasp the gravity of the situation)

MRS DARLING Let me try, dear.

(In a terrible silence their progeny cluster round them. Will she succeed? Their fate depends on it. She fails—no, she succeeds. In another moment they are wildly gay, romping round the room on each other's shoulders. Father is even a better horse than mother. Michael is dropped upon his bed, Wendy retires to prepare for hers, John runs from Nana, who has reappeared with the bath towel)

JOHN *(rebellious)* I won't be bathed. You needn't think it.

MR DARLING *(in the grand manner)* Go and be bathed at once, sir.

(With bent head John follows Nana into the bathroom. Mr Darling swells)

MICHAEL *(as he is put between the sheets)* Mother, how did you get to know me?

MR DARLING A little less noise there.

MICHAEL *(growing solemn)* At what time was I born, mother?

MRS DARLING At two o'clock in the night-time, dearest.

MICHAEL Oh, mother, I hope I didn't wake you.

MRS DARLING They are rather sweet, don't you think, George?

MR DARLING *(doting)* There is not their equal on earth, and they are ours, ours!

(Unfortunately Nana has come from the bathroom for a sponge and she collides with his trousers, the first pair he has ever had with braid on them)

MR DARLING Mary, it is too bad; just look at this; covered with hairs. Clumsy, clumsy! *(Nana goes, a drooping figure)*

MRS DARLING Let me brush you, dear.

(Once more she is successful. They are now by the fire, and Michael is in bed doing idiotic things with a teddy bear)

MR DARLING *(depressed)* I sometimes think, Mary, that it is a mistake to have a dog for a nurse.

MRS DARLING George, Nana is a treasure.

MR DARLING No doubt; but I have an uneasy feeling at times that she looks upon the children as puppies.

MRS DARLING *(rather faintly)* Oh no, dear one, I am sure she knows they have souls.

MR DARLING *(profoundly)* I wonder, I wonder.

(The opportunity has come for her to tell him of something that is on her mind)

MRS DARLING George, we must keep Nana, I will tell you why. *(Her seriousness impresses him)* My dear, when I came into this room to-night I saw a face at the window.

MR DARLING *(incredulous)* A face at the window, three floors up? Pooh!

MRS DARLING It was the face of a little boy; he was trying to get in. George, this is not the first time I have seen that boy.

MR DARLING *(beginning to think that this may be a man's job)* Oho!

MRS DARLING *(making sure that Michael does not hear)* The first time was a week ago. It was Nana's night out, and I had been drows-ing here by the fire when suddenly I felt a draught, as if the window were open. I looked round and I saw that boy—in the room.

MR DARLING In the room?

MRS DARLING I screamed. Just then Nana came back and she at once sprang at him. The boy leapt for the window. She pulled down the sash quickly, but was too late to catch him.

MR DARLING *(who knows he would not have been too late)* I thought so!

MRS DARLING Wait. The boy escaped, but his shadow had not time to get out; down came the window and cut it clean off.

MR DARLING *(heavily)* Mary, Mary, why didn't you keep that shadow?

MRS DARLING *(scoring)* I did. I rolled it up, George; and here it is.

(She produces it from a drawer. They unroll and examine the flimsy thing, which is not more material than a puff of smoke, and if let go would probably float into the ceiling without discolouring it. Yet it has

human shape. As they nod their heads over it they present the most satisfying picture on earth, two happy parents conspiring cosily by the fire for the good of their children)

MR DARLING   It is nobody I know, but he does look a scoundrel.

MRS DARLING   I think he comes back to get his shadow, George.

MR DARLING   *(meaning that the miscreant has now a father to deal with)* I dare say. *(He sees himself telling the story to the other stools at the office)* There is money in this, my love. I shall take it to the British Museum* to-morrow and have it priced.

(The shadow is rolled up and replaced in the drawer)

MRS DARLING   *(like a guilty person)* George, I have not told you all; I am afraid to.

MR DARLING   *(who knows exactly the right moment to treat a woman as a beloved child)* Cowardy, cowardy custard.*

MRS DARLING   *(pouting)* No, I'm not.

MR DARLING   Oh yes, you are.

MRS DARLING   George, I'm not.

MR DARLING   Then why not tell? *(Thus cleverly soothed she goes on)*

MRS DARLING   The boy was not alone that first time. He was accompanied by—I don't know how to describe it; by a ball of light, not as big as my fist, but it darted about the room like a living thing.

MR DARLING   *(though open-minded)* That is very unusual. It escaped with the boy?

MRS DARLING   Yes. *(Sliding her hand into his)* George, what can all this mean?

MR DARLING   *(ever ready)* What indeed!

(This intimate scene is broken by the return of Nana with a bottle in her mouth)

MRS DARLING   *(at once dissembling)* What is that, Nana? Ah, of course; Michael, it is your medicine.

MICHAEL   *(promptly)* Won't take it.

MR DARLING   *(recalling his youth)* Be a man, Michael.

MICHAEL Won't.

MRS DARLING *(weakly)* I'll get you a lovely chocky* to take after it.

(She leaves the room, though her husband calls after her)

MR DARLING Mary, don't pamper him. When I was your age, Michael, I took medicine without a murmur. I said 'Thank you, kind parents, for giving me bottles to make me well.'

(Wendy, who has appeared in her nightgown, hears this and believes)

WENDY That medicine you sometimes take is much nastier, isn't it, father?

MR DARLING *(valuing her support)* Ever so much nastier. And as an example to you, Michael, I would take it now *(thankfully)* if I hadn't lost the bottle.

WENDY *(always glad to be of service)* I know where it is, father. I'll fetch it.

(She is gone before he can stop her. He turns for help to John, who has come from the bathroom attired for bed)

MR DARLING John, it is the most beastly stuff. It is that sticky sweet kind.

JOHN *(who is perhaps still playing at parents)* Never mind, father, it will soon be over.

(A spasm of ill-will to John cuts through Mr Darling, and is gone. Wendy returns panting)

WENDY Here it is, father; I have been as quick as I could.

MR DARLING *(with a sarcasm that is completely thrown away on her)* You have been wonderfully quick, precious quick!

(He is now at the foot of Michael's bed, Nana is by its side, holding the medicine spoon insinuatingly in her mouth)

WENDY *(proudly, as she pours out Mr Darling's medicine)* Michael, now you will see how father takes it.

MR DARLING *(hedging)* Michael first.

MICHAEL *(full of unworthy suspicions)* Father first.

MR DARLING It will make me sick, you know.

JOHN *(lightly)* Come on, father.

MR DARLING Hold your tongue, sir.

WENDY *(disturbed)* I thought you took it quite easily, father, saying 'Thank you, kind parents, for——'

MR DARLING That is not the point; the point is that there is more in my glass than in Michael's spoon. It isn't fair, I swear though it were with my last breath, it is not fair.

MICHAEL *(coldly)* Father, I'm waiting.

MR DARLING It's all very well to say you are waiting; so am I waiting.

MICHAEL Father's a cowardy custard.

MR DARLING So are you a cowardy custard.

(They are now glaring at each other)

MICHAEL I am not frightened.

MR DARLING Neither am I frightened.

MICHAEL Well, then, take it.

MR DARLING Well, then, you take it.

WENDY *(butting in again)* Why not take it at the same time?

MR DARLING *(haughtily)* Certainly. Are you ready, Michael?

WENDY *(as nothing has happened)* One—two—three.

(Michael partakes, but Mr Darling resorts to hanky-panky)

JOHN Father hasn't taken his!

(Michael howls)

WENDY *(inexpressibly pained)* Oh father!

MR DARLING *(who has been hiding the glass behind him)* What do you mean by 'oh father'? Stop that row, Michael. I meant to take mine but I—missed it. *(Nana shakes her head sadly over him, and goes into the bathroom. They are all looking as if they did not admire him, and nothing so dashes a temperamental man)* I say, I have just thought of a splendid joke. *(They brighten)* I shall pour my medicine into Nana's bowl, and she will drink it thinking it is milk! *(The pleasantry does not appeal, but he prepares the joke, listening for appreciation)*

WENDY Poor darling Nana!

MR DARLING You silly little things; to your beds every one of you; I am ashamed of you.

(They steal to their beds as Mrs Darling returns with the chocolate)

MRS DARLING Well, is it all over?

MICHAEL Father didn't——*(Father glares)*

MR DARLING All over, dear, quite satisfactorily. *(Nana comes back)* Nana, good dog, good girl; I have put a little milk into your bowl. *(The bowl is by the kennel, and Nana begins to lap, only begins. She retreats into the kennel)*

MRS DARLING What is the matter, Nana?

MR DARLING *(uneasily)* Nothing, nothing.

MRS DARLING *(smelling the bowl)* George, it is your medicine!

(The children break into lamentation. He gives his wife an imploring look; he is begging for one smile, but does not get it. In consequence he goes from bad to worse)

MR DARLING It was only a joke. Much good my wearing myself to the bone trying to be funny in this house.

WENDY *(on her knees by the kennel)* Father, Nana is crying.

MR DARLING Coddle her; nobody coddles me. Oh dear no. I am only the breadwinner, why should I be coddled? Why, why, why?

MRS DARLING George, not so loud; the servants will hear you.

(There is only one maid, absurdly small too, but they have got into the way of calling her the servants)

MR DARLING *(defiant)* Let them hear me; bring in the whole world. *(The desperate man, who has not been in fresh air for days, has now lost all self-control)* I refuse to allow that dog to lord it in my nursery for one hour longer. *(Nana supplicates him)* In vain, in vain, the proper place for you is the yard, and there you go to be tied up this instant.

(Nana again retreats into the kennel, and the children add their prayers to hers)

MRS DARLING *(who knows how contrite he will be for this presently)* George, George, remember what I told you about that boy.

MR DARLING Am I master in this house or is she? *(To Nana fiercely)* Come along. *(He thunders at her, but she indicates that she has reasons not worth troubling him with for remaining where she is. He resorts to a false bonhomie)* There, there, did she think he was angry with her, poor Nana? *(She wriggles a response in the affirmative)* Good Nana, pretty Nana. *(She has seldom been called pretty, and it has the old effect. She plays rub-a-dub* with her paws, which is how a dog blushes)* She will come to her kind master, won't she? won't she? *(She advances, retreats, waggles her head, her tail, and eventually goes to him. He seizes her collar in an iron grip and amid the cries of his progeny drags her from the room They listen, for her remonstrances are not inaudible)*

MRS DARLING Be brave, my dears.

WENDY He is chaining Nana up!

(This unfortunately is what he is doing, though we cannot see him. Let us hope that he then retires to his study, looks up the word 'temper' in his Thesaurus, and under the influence of those benign pages becomes a better man. In the meantime the children have been put to bed in unwonted silence, and Mrs Darling lights the night-lights over the beds)

JOHN *(as the barking below goes on)* She is awfully unhappy.

WENDY That is not Nana's unhappy bark. That is her bark when she smells danger.

MRS DARLING *(remembering that boy)* Danger! Are you sure, Wendy?

WENDY *(the one of the family, for there is one in every family, who can be trusted to know or not to know)* Oh yes.

(Her mother looks this way and that from the window)

JOHN Is anything there?

MRS DARLING All quite quiet and still. Oh, how I wish I was not going out to dinner to-night.

MICHAEL   Can anything harm us, mother, after the night-lights are lit?

MRS DARLING   Nothing, precious. They are the eyes a mother leaves behind her to guard her children.

(Nevertheless we may be sure she means to tell Liza, the little maid, to look in on them frequently till she comes home. She goes from bed to bed, after her custom, tucking them in and crooning a lullaby)

MICHAEL   *(drowsily)* Mother, I'm glad of you.

MRS DARLING   *(with a last look round, her hand on the switch)* Dear night-lights that protect my sleeping babes, burn clear and stead-fast to-night.

(The nursery darkens* and she is gone, intentionally leaving the door ajar. Something uncanny is going to happen, we expect, for a quiver has passed through the room, just sufficient to touch the night-lights. They blink three times one after the other and go out, precisely as children (whom familiarity has made them resemble) fall asleep. There is another light in the room now, no larger than Mrs Darling's fist, and in the time we have taken to say this it has been into the drawers and ward-robe and searched pockets, as it darts about looking for a certain shadow. Then the window is blown open, probably by the smallest and therefore most mischievous star, and Peter Pan flies into the room. In so far as he is dressed at all it is in autumn leaves and cobwebs)

PETER   *(in a whisper)* Tinker Bell, Tink, are you there? *(A jug lights up)* Oh, do come out of that jug. *(Tink flashes hither and thither)* Do you know where they put it? *(The answer comes as of a tinkle of bells; it is the fairy language. Peter can speak it, but it bores him)* Which big box? This one? But which drawer? Yes, do show me. *(Tink pops into the drawer where the shadow is, but before Peter can reach it, Wendy moves in her sleep. He flies on to the mantelshelf as a hiding-place. Then, as she has not waked, he flutters over the beds as an easy way to observe the occu-pants, closes the window softly, wafts himself to the drawer and scatters its contents to the floor, as kings on their wedding day toss ha'pence to the crowd. In his joy at finding his shadow he forgets that he has shut up Tink in the drawer. He sits on the floor with the shadow, confident that he and it will join like drops of water. Then he tries to stick it on with soap from the bathroom, and this failing also, he subsides dejectedly on the floor. This wakens Wendy, who sits up, and is pleasantly interested to see a stranger)*

WENDY *(courteously)* Boy, why are you crying?

(He jumps up, and crossing to the foot of the bed bows to her in the fairy way. Wendy, impressed, bows to him from the bed)

PETER What is your name?

WENDY *(well satisfied)* Wendy Moira Angela Darling. What is yours?

PETER *(finding it lamentably brief)* Peter Pan.

WENDY Is that all?

PETER *(biting his lip)* Yes.

WENDY *(politely)* I am so sorry.

PETER It doesn't matter.

WENDY Where do you live?

PETER Second to the right and then straight on till morning.

WENDY What a funny address!

PETER No, it isn't.

WENDY I mean, is that what they put on the letters?

PETER Don't get any letters.

WENDY But your mother gets letters?

PETER Don't have a mother.

WENDY Peter!

(She leaps out of bed to put her arms round him, but he draws back; he does not know why, but he knows he must draw back)

PETER You mustn't touch me.

WENDY Why?

PETER No one must ever touch me.

WENDY Why?

PETER I don't know.

(He is never touched by any one in the play)

WENDY No wonder you were crying.

PETER I wasn't crying. But I can't get my shadow to stick on.

WENDY It has come off! How awful. *(Looking at the spot where he had lain)* Peter, you have been trying to stick it on with soap!

PETER *(snappily)* Well then?

WENDY It must be sewn on.

PETER What is 'sewn'?

WENDY You are dreadfully ignorant.

PETER No, I'm not.

WENDY I will sew it on for you, my little man. But we must have more light. *(She touches something, and to his astonishment the room is illuminated)* Sit here. I dare say it will hurt a little.

PETER *(a recent remark of hers rankling)* I never cry. *(She seems to attach the shadow. He tests the combination)* It isn't quite itself yet.

WENDY Perhaps I should have ironed it. *(It awakes and is as glad to be back with him as he to have it. He and his shadow dance together. He is showing off now. He crows like a cock. He would fly in order to impress Wendy further if he knew that there is anything unusual in that)*

PETER Wendy, look, look; oh the cleverness of me!

WENDY You conceit; of course I did nothing!

PETER You did a little.

WENDY *(wounded)* A little! If I am no use I can at least withdraw.

(With one haughty leap she is again in bed with the sheet over her face. Popping on to the end of the bed the artful one appeals)

PETER Wendy, don't withdraw. I can't help crowing, Wendy, when I'm pleased with myself. Wendy, one girl is worth more than twenty boys.

WENDY *(peeping over the sheet)* You really think so, Peter?

PETER Yes, I do.

WENDY I think it's perfectly sweet of you, and I shall get up again. *(They sit together on the side of the bed)* I shall give you a kiss if you like.

PETER Thank you. *(He holds out his hand)*

WENDY *(aghast)* Don't you know what a kiss is?

PETER I shall know when you give it me. *(Not to hurt his feelings she gives him her thimble)* Now shall I give you a kiss?

WENDY *(primly)* If you please. *(He pulls an acorn button off his person and bestows it on her. She is shocked but considerate)* I will wear it on this chain round my neck. Peter, how old are you?

PETER *(blithely)* I don't know, but quite young, Wendy. I ran away the day I was born.

WENDY Ran away, why?

PETER Because I heard father and mother talking of what I was to be when I became a man. I want always to be a little boy and to have fun; so I ran away to Kensington Gardens and lived a long time among the fairies.

WENDY *(with great eyes)* You know fairies, Peter!

PETER *(surprised that this should be a recommendation)* Yes, but they are nearly all dead now. *(Baldly)* You see, Wendy, when the first baby laughed for the first time, the laugh broke into a thousand pieces and they all went skipping about, and that was the beginning of fairies. And now when every new baby is born its first laugh becomes a fairy. So there ought to be one fairy for every boy or girl.

WENDY *(breathlessly)* Ought to be? Isn't there?

PETER Oh no. Children know such a lot now. Soon they don't believe in fairies, and every time a child says 'I don't believe in fairies' there is a fairy somewhere that falls down dead. *(He skips about heartlessly)*

WENDY Poor things!

PETER *(to whom this statement recalls a forgotten friend)* I can't think where she has gone. Tinker Bell, Tink, where are you?

WENDY *(thrilling)* Peter, you don't mean to tell me that there is a fairy in this room!

PETER *(flitting about in search)* She came with me. You don't hear anything, do you?

WENDY I hear—the only sound I hear is like a tinkle of bells.

PETER That is the fairy language. I hear it too.

WENDY It seems to come from over there.

PETER *(with shameless glee)* Wendy, I believe I shut her up in that drawer! *(He releases Tink, who darts about in a fury using language it is perhaps as well we don't understand)* You needn't say that; I'm very sorry, but how could I know you were in the drawer?

WENDY *(her eyes dancing in pursuit of the delicious creature)* Oh, Peter, if only she would stand still and let me see her!

PETER *(indifferently)* They hardly ever stand still.

(To show that she can do even this Tink pauses between two ticks of the cuckoo clock)

WENDY I see her, the lovely! where is she now?

PETER She is behind the clock. Tink, this lady wishes you were her fairy. *(The answer comes immediately)*

WENDY What does she say?

PETER She is not very polite. She says you are a great ugly girl, and that she is my fairy. You know, Tink, you can't be my fairy because I am a gentleman and you are a lady.

(Tink replies)

WENDY What did she say?

PETER She said 'You silly ass.' She is quite a common girl, you know. She is called Tinker Bell because she mends the fairy pots and kettles.

(They have reached a chair, Wendy in the ordinary way and Peter through a hole in the back)

WENDY Where do you live now?

PETER With the lost boys.

WENDY Who are they?

PETER They are the children who fall out of their prams when the nurse is looking the other way. If they are not claimed in seven days they are sent far away to the Never Land. I'm captain.

WENDY What fun it must be.

PETER *(craftily)* Yes, but we are rather lonely. You see, Wendy, we have no female companionship.

WENDY Are none of the other children girls?

PETER Oh no; girls, you know, are much too clever to fall out of their prams.

WENDY Peter, it is perfectly lovely the way you talk about girls. John there just despises us. *(Peter, for the first time, has a good look at John. He then neatly tumbles him out of bed)* You wicked! you are not captain here. *(She bends over her brother who is prone on the floor)* After all he hasn't wakened, and you meant to be kind. *(Having now done her duty she forgets John, who blissfully sleeps on)* Peter, you may give me a kiss.

PETER *(cynically)* I thought you would want it back.

(He offers her the thimble)

WENDY *(artfully)* Oh dear, I didn't mean a kiss, Peter. I meant a thimble.

PETER *(only half placated)* What is that?

WENDY It is like this. *(She leans forward to give a demonstration, but something prevents the meeting of their faces)*

PETER *(satisfied)* Now shall I give you a thimble?

WENDY If you please. *(Before he can even draw near she screams)*

PETER What is it?

WENDY It was exactly as if some one were pulling my hair!

PETER That must have been Tink. I never knew her so naughty before.

(Tink speaks. She is in the jug again)

WENDY What does she say?

PETER She says she will do that every time I give you a thimble.

WENDY But why?

PETER *(equally nonplussed)* Why, Tink? *(He has to translate the answer)* She said 'You silly ass' again.

WENDY She is very impertinent. *(They are sitting on the floor now)* Peter, why did you come to our nursery window?

PETER To try to hear stories. None of us knows any stories.

WENDY How perfectly awful!

PETER Do you know why swallows build in the eaves of houses? It is to listen to the stories. Wendy, your mother was telling you such a lovely story.

WENDY Which story was it?

PETER About the prince, and he couldn't find the lady who wore the glass slipper.

WENDY That was Cinderella.* Peter, he found her and they were happy ever after.

PETER I am glad. *(They have worked their way along the floor close to each other, but he now jumps up)*

WENDY Where are you going?

PETER *(already on his way to the window)* To tell the other boys.

WENDY Don't go, Peter. I know lots of stories. The stories I could tell to the boys!

PETER *(gleaming)* Come on! We'll fly.

WENDY Fly? You can fly!

(How he would like to rip those stories out of her; he is dangerous now)

PETER Wendy, come with me.

WENDY Oh dear, I mustn't. Think of mother. Besides, I can't fly.

PETER I'll teach you.

WENDY How lovely to fly!

PETER I'll teach you how to jump on the wind's back and then away we go. Wendy, when you are sleeping in your silly bed you might be flying about with me, saying funny things to the stars. There are mermaids, Wendy, with long tails. *(She just succeeds in remaining on the nursery floor)* Wendy, how we should all respect you. *(At this she strikes her colours*)*

WENDY Of course it's awfully fas-cin-a-ting! Would you teach John and Michael to fly too?

PETER *(indifferently)* If you like.

WENDY *(playing rum-tum* on John)* John, wake up; there is a boy here who is to teach us to fly.

JOHN Is there? Then I shall get up. *(He raises his head from the floor)* Hullo, I am up!

WENDY Michael, open your eyes. This boy is to teach us to fly.

(The sleepers are at once as awake as their father's razor; but before a question can be asked Nana's bark is heard)

JOHN Out with the light, quick, hide!

(When the maid Liza, who is so small that when she says she will never see ten again one can scarcely believe her, enters with a firm hand on the troubled Nana's chain the room is in comparative darkness)

LIZA There, you suspicious brute, they are perfectly safe, aren't they? Every one of the little angels sound asleep in bed. Listen to their gentle breathing. *(Nana's sense of smell here helps to her undoing instead of hindering it. She knows that they are in the room. Michael, who is behind the curtain window, is so encouraged by Liza's last remark that he breathes too loudly. Nana knows that kind of breathing and tries to break from her keeper's control)* No more of it, Nana. *(Wagging a finger at her)* I warn you if you bark again I shall go straight for master and missus and bring them home from the party, and then won't master whip you just! Come along, you naughty dog.

(The unhappy Nana is led away. The children emerge exulting from their various hiding-places. In their brief absence from the scene strange things have been done to them;* but it is not for us to reveal a mysterious secret of the stage. They look just the same)

JOHN I say, can you really fly?

PETER Look! *(He is now over their heads)*

WENDY Oh, how sweet!

PETER I'm sweet, oh, I am sweet!

(It looks so easy that they try it first from the floor and then from their beds, without encouraging results)

JOHN *(rubbing his knees)* How do you do it?

PETER *(descending)* You just think lovely wonderful thoughts and they lift you up in the air. *(He is off again)*

JOHN You are so nippy at it; couldn't you do it very slowly once? *(Peter does it slowly)* I've got it now, Wendy. *(He tries; no, he has not got it, poor stay-at-home,* though he knows the names of all the counties in England and Peter does not know one)*

PETER I must blow the fairy dust on you first. *(Fortunately his garments are smeared with it and he blows some dust on each)* Now, try; try from the bed. Just wriggle your shoulders this way, and then let go.

(The gallant Michael is the first to let go, and is borne across the room)

MICHAEL *(with a yell that should have disturbed Liza)* I flewed!

(John lets go, and meets Wendy near the bathroom door though they had both aimed in an opposite direction)

WENDY Oh, lovely!

JOHN *(tending to be upside down)* How ripping!

MICHAEL *(playing whack on a chair)* I do like it!

THE THREE Look at me, look at me, look at me!

(They are not nearly so elegant in the air as Peter, but their heads have bumped the ceiling, and there is nothing more delicious than that)

JOHN *(who can even go backwards)* I say, why shouldn't we go out?

PETER There are pirates.

JOHN Pirates! *(He grabs his tall Sunday hat)* Let us go at once!

(Tink does not like it. She darts at their hair. From down below in the street the lighted window must present an unwonted spectacle; the shadows of children revolving in the room like a merry-go-round. This

is perhaps what Mr and Mrs Darling see as they come hurrying home from the party, brought by Nana who, you may be sure, has broken her chain. Peter's accomplice, the little star, has seen them coming, and again the window blows open)

PETER *(as if he had heard the star whisper 'Cave'*)* Now come!

(Breaking the circle he flies out of the window over the trees of the square and over the house-tops, and the others follow like a flight of birds. The broken-hearted father and mother arrive just in time to get a nip from Tink as she too sets out for the Never Land)

ACT 2

THE NEVER LAND

When the blind goes up all is so dark that you scarcely know it has gone up. This is because if you were to see the island bang* (as Peter would say) the wonders of it might hurt your eyes. If you all came in spectacles perhaps you could see it bang, but to make a rule of that kind would be a pity. The first thing seen is merely some whitish dots trudging along the sward,* and you can guess from their tinkling that they are probably fairies of the commoner sort going home afoot from some party and having a cheery tiff* by the way. Then Peter's star wakes up, and in the blink of it, which is much stronger than in our stars, you can make out masses of trees, and you think you see wild beasts stealing past to drink, though what you see is not the beasts themselves but only the shadows of them. They are really out pictorially to greet Peter in the way they think he would like them to greet him; and for the same reason the mermaids basking in the lagoon beyond the trees are carefully combing their hair; and for the same reason the pirates are landing invisibly from the longboat, invisibly to you but not to the redskins, whom none can see or hear because they are on the war-path. The whole island, in short, which has been having a slack time in Peter's absence, is now in a ferment because the tidings has leaked out that he is on his way back; and everybody and everything know that they will catch it from him if they don't give satisfaction. While you have been told this the sun (another of his servants) has been bestirring himself. Those of you who may have thought it wiser after all to begin this Act in spectacles may now take them off.

What you see is the Never Land. You have often half seen it before, or even three-quarters, after the night-lights were lit, and you might then have beached your coracle* on it if you had not always at the great moment fallen asleep. I dare say you have chucked things on to it, the things you can't find in the morning. In the daytime you think the Never Land is only make-believe, and so it is to the likes of you, but this is the Never Land come true. It is an open-air scene, a forest, with a beautiful lagoon beyond but not really far away, for the Never Land is very compact, not large and sprawly with tedious distances between one adventure and another, but nicely crammed. It is summer time on the trees and on the lagoon but winter on the river, which is not remarkable on Peter's island where all the four seasons may pass while you are filling a jug at the well. Peter's home is at this very spot, but you could not point out the way into it even if you were told which is the entrance, not even if you were told that there are seven of them. You know now because you have just seen one of the lost boys emerge. The holes in these seven great hollow trees are the 'doors' down to Peter's home, and he made seven because, despite his cleverness, he thought seven boys must need seven doors.

The boy who has emerged from his tree is Slightly, who has perhaps been driven from the abode below by companions less musical than himself. Quite possibly a genius, Slightly has with him his home-made whistle to which he capers entrancingly, with no audience save a Never ostrich which is also musically inclined. Unable to imitate Slightly's graces the bird falls so low as to burlesque them and is driven from the entertainment. Other lost boys climb up the trunks or drop from branches, and now we see the six of them, all in the skins of animals they think they have shot, and so round and furry in them that if they fall they roll. Tootles is not the least brave though the most unfortunate of this gallant band. He has been in fewer adventures than any of them because the big things constantly happen while he has stepped round the corner; he will go off, for instance, in some quiet hour to gather firewood, and then when he returns the others will be sweeping up the blood. Instead of souring his nature this has sweetened it and he is the humblest of the band. Nibs is more gay and debonair, Slightly more conceited. Slightly thinks he remembers the days before he was lost, with their manners and customs. Curly is a pickle,* and so often has he had to deliver up his person when Peter said sternly, 'Stand forth the one who did this thing,' that now he stands forth whether he has done it or not. The other two are First Twin and Second Twin, who cannot be described because we should probably be describing the wrong one. Hunkering on the ground or peeping out of their holes, the six are not unlike village gossips gathered round the pump.

TOOTLES Has Peter come back yet, Slightly?

SLIGHTLY *(with a solemnity that he thinks suits the occasion)* No, Tootles, no.

(They are like dogs waiting for the master to tell them that the day has begun)

CURLY *(as if Peter might be listening)* I do wish he would come back.

TOOTLES I am always afraid of the pirates when Peter is not here to protect us.

SLIGHTLY I am not afraid of pirates. Nothing frightens me. But I do wish Peter would come back and tell us whether he has heard anything more about Cinderella.

SECOND TWIN *(with diffidence)* Slightly, I dreamt last night that the prince found Cinderella.

FIRST TWIN *(who is intellectually the superior of the two)* Twin, I think you should not have dreamt that, for I didn't, and Peter may say we oughtn't to dream differently, being twins, you know.

TOOTLES I am awfully anxious about Cinderella. You see, not knowing anything about my own mother I am fond of thinking that she was rather like Cinderella.

(This is received with derision)

NIBS All I remember about my mother is that she often said to father, 'Oh, how I wish I had a cheque book of my own.' I don't know what a cheque book is, but I should just love to give my mother one.

SLIGHTLY *(as usual)* My mother was fonder of me than your mothers were of you. *(Uproar)* Oh yes, she was. Peter had to make up names for you, but my mother had wrote my name on the pinafore I was lost in. 'Slightly Soiled'; that's my name.

(They fall upon him pugnaciously; not that they are really worrying about their mothers, who are now as important to them as a piece of string, but because any excuse is good enough for a shindy.* Not for long is he belaboured, for a sound is heard that sends them scurrying down their holes; in a second of time the scene is bereft of human life. What they have heard from near-by is a verse of the dreadful song with which on the Never Land the pirates stealthily trumpet their approach—

> Yo ho, yo ho, the pirate life,
> The flag of skull and bones,
> A merry hour, a hempen rope,
> And hey for Davy Jones!*

The pirates appear upon the frozen river dragging a raft, on which reclines among cushions that dark and fearful man, Captain Jas Hook. A more villainous-looking brotherhood of men never hung in a row on Execution Dock.* Here, his great arms bare, pieces of eight* in his ears as ornaments, is the handsome Cecco, who cut his name on the back of the governor of the prison at Gao. Heavier in the pull is the gigantic black who has had many names since the first one terrified dusky children on the banks of the Guidjo-mo. Bill Jukes comes next, every inch of him tattooed, the same Jukes who got six dozen on the Walrus from Flint. Following these are Cookson, said to be Black Murphy's brother (but this was never proved); and Gentleman Starkey, once an usher in a school; and Skylights (Morgan's Skylights);* and Noodler, whose hands are fixed on backwards; and the spectacled boatswain, Smee, the only Nonconformist* in Hook's crew; and other ruffians long known and feared on the Spanish main.

Cruellest jewel in that dark setting is Hook himself, cadaverous and blackavised,* his hair dressed in long curls which look like black candles about to melt, his eyes blue as the forget-me-not and of a profound insensibility, save when he claws, at which time a red spot appears in them. He has an iron hook instead of a right hand, and it is with this he claws. He is never more sinister than when he is most polite, and the elegance of his diction, the distinction of his demeanour, show him one of a different class from his crew, a solitary among uncultured companions. This courtliness impresses even his victims on the high seas, who note that he always says 'Sorry' when prodding them along the plank.* A man of indomitable courage, the only thing at which he flinches is the sight of his own blood, which is thick and of an unusual colour. At his public school* they said of him that *he 'bled yellow.' In dress he apes the dandiacal associated with Charles II, having heard it said in an earlier period of his career that he bore a strange resemblance to the ill-fated Stuarts. A holder of his own contrivance is in his mouth enabling him to smoke two cigars at once. Those, however, who have seen him in the flesh, which is an inadequate term for his earthly tenement, agree that the grimmest part of him is his iron claw.*

They continue their distasteful singing as they disembark——

> Avast, belay, yo ho, heave to,*
> A-pirating we go,
> And if we're parted by a shot
> We're sure to meet below!

Nibs, the only one of the boys who has not sought safety in his tree, is seen for a moment near the lagoon, and Starkey's pistol is at once upraised. The captain twists his hook in him.)

STARKEY *(abject)* Captain, let go!

HOOK Put back that pistol, first.

STARKEY 'Twas one of those boys you hate; I could have shot him dead.

HOOK Ay, and the sound would have brought Tiger Lily's redskins on us. Do you want to lose your scalp?

SMEE *(wriggling his cutlass pleasantly)* That is true. Shall I after him, Captain, and tickle him with Johnny Corkscrew? Johnny is a silent fellow.

HOOK Not now. He is only one, and I want to mischief all the seven. Scatter and look for them. *(The boatswain whistles his instructions, and the men disperse on their frightful errand. With none to hear save Smee, Hook becomes confidential)* Most of all I want their captain, Peter Pan. 'Twas he cut off my arm. I have waited long to shake his hand with this. *(Luxuriating)* Oh, I'll tear him!

SMEE *(always ready for a chat)* Yet I have oft heard you say your hook was worth a score of hands, for combing the hair and other homely uses.

HOOK If I was a mother I would pray to have my children born with this instead of that. *(His left arm creeps nervously behind him. He has a galling remembrance)* Smee, Pan flung my arm to a crocodile that happened to be passing by.

SMEE I have often noticed your strange dread of crocodiles.

HOOK *(pettishly)* Not of crocodiles but of that one crocodile. *(He lays bare a lacerated heart)* The brute liked my arm so much, Smee, that he has followed me ever since, from sea to sea, and from land to land, licking his lips for the rest of me.

SMEE *(looking for the bright side)* In a way it is a sort of compliment.

HOOK *(with dignity)* I want no such compliments; I want Peter Pan, who first gave the brute his taste for me. Smee, that crocodile would have had me before now, but by a lucky chance he swallowed a clock, and it goes tick, tick, tick, tick inside him; and so before he can reach me I hear the tick and bolt. *(He emits a hollow rumble)* Once I heard it strike six within him.

SMEE *(sombrely)* Some day the clock will run down, and then he'll get you.

HOOK *(a broken man)* Ay, that is the fear that haunts me. *(He rises)* Smee, this seat is hot; odds, bobs, hammer and tongs,* I am burning.

(He has been sitting, he thinks, on one of the island mushrooms, which are of enormous size. But this is a hand-painted one placed here in times of danger to conceal a chimney. They remove it, and tell-tale smoke issues; also, alas, the sound of children's voices)

SMEE A chimney!

HOOK *(avidly)* Listen! Smee, 'tis plain they live here, beneath the ground. *(He replaces the mushroom. His brain works tortuously)*

SMEE *(hopefully)* Unrip your plan, Captain.

HOOK To return to the boat and cook a large rich cake of jolly thickness with sugar on it, green sugar. There can be but one room below, for there is but one chimney. The silly moles had not the sense to see that they did not need a door apiece. We must leave the cake on the shore of the mermaids' lagoon. These boys are always swimming about there, trying to catch the mermaids. They will find the cake and gobble it up, because, having no mother, they don't know how dangerous 'tis to eat rich damp cake. They will die!

SMEE *(fascinated)* It is the wickedest, prettiest policy ever I heard of.

HOOK *(meaning well)* Shake hands on't.

SMEE No, Captain, no.

(He has to link with the hook, but he does not join in the song)

> HOOK Yo ho, yo ho, when I say 'paw,'
> By fear they're overtook,
> Naught's left upon your bones when you
> Have shaken hands with Hook!

(Frightened by a tug at his hand, Smee is joining in the chorus when another sound stills them both. It is a tick, tick as of a clock, whose significance Hook is, naturally, the first to recognise. 'The crocodile!' he cries, and totters from the scene. Smee follows. A huge crocodile, of one thought compact,* passes across, ticking, and oozes after them. The wood is now so silent that you may be sure it is full of redskins. Tiger Lily comes first. She is the belle of the Piccaninny* tribe, whose braves would all have her to wife, but she wards them off with a hatchet. She puts her ear to the ground and listens, then beckons, and Great Big Little Panther and the tribe are around her, carpeting the ground. Far away some one treads on a dry leaf)

TIGER LILY Pirates! *(They do not draw their knives; the knives slip into their hands)* Have um scalps? What you say?

PANTHER Scalp um, oho, velly quick.

THE BRAVES *(in corroboration)* Ugh, ugh, wah.

(A fire is lit and they dance round and over it till they seem part of the leaping flames. Tiger Lily invokes Manitou;* the pipe of peace is broken; and they crawl off like a long snake that has not fed for many moons. Tootles peers after the tail and summons the other boys, who issue from their holes)

TOOTLES They are gone.

SLIGHTLY *(almost losing confidence in himself)* I do wish Peter was here.

FIRST TWIN H'sh! What is that? *(He is gazing at the lagoon and shrinks back.)* It is wolves, and they are chasing Nibs!

(The baying wolves are upon them quicker than any boy can scuttle down his tree)

NIBS *(falling among his comrades)* Save me, save me!

TOOTLES What should we do?

SECOND TWIN What would Peter do?

SLIGHTLY Peter would look at them through his legs; let us do what Peter would do.

(The boys advance backwards, looking between their legs at the snarling red-eyed enemy, who trot away foiled)

FIRST TWIN *(swaggering)* We have saved you, Nibs. Did you see the pirates?

NIBS *(sitting up, and agreeably aware that the centre of interest is now to pass to him)* No, but I saw a wonderfuller thing, Twin. *(All mouths open for the information to be dropped into them)* High over the lagoon I saw the loveliest great white bird. It is flying this way. *(They search the firmament)*

TOOTLES What kind of a bird, do you think?

NIBS *(awed)* I don't know; but it looked so weary, and as it flies it moans 'Poor Wendy.'

SLIGHTLY *(instantly)* I remember now there are birds called Wendies.

FIRST TWIN *(who has flown to a high branch)* See, it comes, the Wendy! *(They all see it now)* How white it is! *(A dot of light is pursuing the bird malignantly)*

TOOTLES That is Tinker Bell. Tink is trying to hurt the Wendy. *(He makes a cup of his hands and calls)* Hullo, Tink! *(A response comes down in the fairy language)* She says Peter wants us to shoot the Wendy.

NIBS Let us do what Peter wishes.

SLIGHTLY Ay, shoot it; quick, bows and arrows.

TOOTLES *(first with his bow)* Out of the way, Tink; I'll shoot it. *(His bolt goes home, and Wendy, who has been fluttering among the tree-tops in her white nightgown, falls straight to earth. No one could be more proud than Tootles)* I have shot the Wendy; Peter will be so pleased. *(From some tree on which Tink is roosting comes the tinkle we can now translate, 'You silly ass.' Tootles falters)* Why do you say that? *(The others feel that he may have blundered, and draw away from Tootles)*

SLIGHTLY *(examining the fallen one more minutely)* This is no bird; I think it must be a lady.

NIBS *(who would have preferred it to be a bird)* And Tootles has killed her.

CURLY Now I see, Peter was bringing her to us. *(They wonder for what object)*

SECOND TWIN To take care of us? *(Undoubtedly for some diverting purpose)*

OMNES* *(though every one of them had wanted to have a shot at her)* Oh, Tootles!

TOOTLES *(gulping)* I did it. When ladies used to come to me in dreams I said 'Pretty mother,' but when she really came I shot her! *(He perceives the necessity of a solitary life for him)* Friends, good-bye.

SEVERAL *(not very enthusiastic)* Don't go.

TOOTLES I must; I am so afraid of Peter.

(He has gone but a step toward oblivion when he is stopped by a crowing as of some victorious cock)

OMNES Peter!

(They make a paling* of themselves in front of Wendy as Peter skims round the tree-tops and reaches earth)

PETER Greeting, boys! *(Their silence chafes him)* I am back; why do you not cheer? Great news, boys, I have brought at last a mother for us all.

SLIGHTLY *(vaguely)* Ay, ay.

PETER She flew this way; have you not seen her?

SECOND TWIN *(as Peter evidently thinks her important)* Oh mournful day!

TOOTLES *(making a break in the paling)* Peter, I will show her to you.

THE OTHERS *(closing the gap)* No, no.

TOOTLES *(majestically)* Stand back all, and let Peter see.

(The paling dissolves, and Peter sees Wendy prone on the ground)

PETER Wendy, with an arrow in her heart! *(He plucks it out)* Wendy is dead. *(He is not so much pained as puzzled)*

CURLY I thought it was only flowers that die.

PETER Perhaps she is frightened at being dead? *(None of them can say as to that)* Whose arrow? *(Not one of them looks at Tootles)*

TOOTLES Mine, Peter.

PETER *(raising it as a dagger)* Oh dastard* hand!

TOOTLES *(kneeling and baring his breast)* Strike, Peter; strike true.

PETER *(undergoing a singular experience)* I cannot strike; there is something stays my hand.

(In fact Wendy's arm has risen)

NIBS 'Tis she, the Wendy lady. See, her arm. *(To help a friend)* I think she said 'Poor Tootles.'

PETER *(investigating)* She lives!

SLIGHTLY *(authoritatively)* The Wendy lady lives.

(The delightful feeling that they have been cleverer than they thought comes over them and they applaud themselves)

PETER *(holding up a button that is attached to her chain)* See, the arrow struck against this. It is a kiss I gave her; it has saved her life.

SLIGHTLY I remember kisses; let me see it. *(He takes it in his hand)* Ay, that is a kiss.

PETER Wendy, get better quickly and I'll take you to see the mermaids. She is awfully anxious to see a mermaid.

(Tinker Bell, who may have been off visiting her relations, returns to the wood and, under the impression that Wendy has been got rid of, is whistling as gaily as a canary. She is not wholly heartless, but is so small that she has only room for one feeling at a time)

CURLY Listen to Tink rejoicing because she thinks the Wendy is dead! *(Regardless of spoiling another's pleasure)* Tink, the Wendy lives.

(Tink gives expression to fury)

SECOND TWIN *(tell-tale)* It was she who said that you wanted us to shoot the Wendy.

PETER She said that? Then listen, Tink, I am your friend no more. *(There is a note of acerbity in Tink's reply; it may mean 'Who wants you?')* Begone from me for ever. *(Now it is a very wet tinkle)*

CURLY She is crying.

TOOTLES She says she is your fairy.

PETER *(who knows they are not worth worrying about)* Oh well, not for ever, but for a whole week. *(Tink goes off sulking, no doubt with the intention of giving all her friends an entirely false impression of Wendy's appearance)* Now what shall we do with Wendy?

CURLY Let us carry her down into the house.

SLIGHTLY Ay, that is what one does with ladies.

PETER No, you must not touch her; it wouldn't be sufficiently respectful.

SLIGHTLY That is what I was thinking.

TOOTLES But if she lies there she will die.

SLIGHTLY Ay, she will die. It is a pity, but there is no way out.

PETER Yes, there is. Let us build a house around her! *(Cheers again, meaning that no difficulty baffles Peter)* Leave all to me. Bring the best of what we have. Gut our house. Be sharp. *(They race down their trees)*

(While Peter is engrossed in measuring Wendy so that the house may fit her, John and Michael, who have probably landed on the island with a bump, wander forward, so draggled and tired that if you were to ask Michael whether he is awake or asleep he would probably answer 'I haven't tried yet.')

MICHAEL *(bewildered)* John, John, wake up. Where is Nana, John?

JOHN *(with the help of one eye but not always the same eye)* It is true, we did fly! *(Thankfully)* And here is Peter. Peter, is this the place?

(Peter, alas, has already forgotten them, as soon maybe he will forget Wendy. The first thing she should do now that she is here is to sew a handkerchief for him, and knot it as a jog to his memory)

PETER *(curtly)* Yes.

MICHAEL Where is Wendy? *(Peter points)*

JOHN *(who still wears his hat)* She is asleep.

MICHAEL John, let us wake her and get her to make supper for us. *(Some of the boys emerge, and he pinches one)* John, look at them!

PETER *(still house-building)* Curly, see that these boys help in the building of the house.

JOHN Build a house?

CURLY For the Wendy.

JOHN *(feeling that there must be some mistake here)* For Wendy? Why, she is only a girl.

CURLY That is why we are her servants.

JOHN *(dazed)* Are you Wendy's servants?

PETER Yes, and you also. Away with them. *(In another moment they are woodsmen hacking at trees, with Curly as overseer)* Slightly, fetch a doctor.* *(Slightly reels and goes. He returns professionally in John's hat)* Please, sir, are you a doctor?

SLIGHTLY *(trembling in his desire to give satisfaction)* Yes, my little man.

PETER Please, sir, a lady lies very ill.

SLIGHTLY *(taking care not to fall over her)* Tut, tut, where does she lie?

PETER In yonder glade. *(It is a variation of a game they play)*

SLIGHTLY I will put a glass thing in her mouth. *(He inserts an imaginary thermometer in Wendy's mouth and gives it a moment to record its verdict. He shakes it and then consults it)*

PETER *(anxiously)* How is she?

SLIGHTLY Tut, tut, this has cured her.

PETER *(leaping joyously)* I am glad.

SLIGHTLY I will call again in the evening. Give her beef tea* out of a cup with a spout to it, tut, tut.

(The boys are running up with odd articles of furniture)

PETER *(with an already fading recollection of the Darling nursery)* These are not good enough for Wendy. How I wish I knew the kind of house she would prefer!

FIRST TWIN Peter, she is moving in her sleep.

TOOTLES *(opening Wendy's mouth and gazing down into the depths)* Lovely!

PETER Oh, Wendy, if you could sing the kind of house you would like to have.

(It is as if she had heard him)

WENDY *(without opening her eyes)*

> I wish I had a woodland house,*
> The littlest ever seen,
> With funny little red walls
> And roof of mossy green.

(In the time she sings this and two other verses,* such is the urgency of Peter's silent orders that they have knocked down trees, laid a foundation and put up the walls and roof, so that she is now hidden from view. 'Windows,' cries Peter, and Curly rushes them in, 'Roses,' and Tootles arrives breathless with a festoon* for the door. Thus springs into existence the most delicious little house for beginners)

FIRST TWIN I think it is finished.

PETER There is no knocker on the door. *(Tootles hangs up the sole of his shoe)* There is no chimney; we must have a chimney. *(They await his deliberations anxiously)*

JOHN *(unwisely critical)* It certainly does need a chimney.

(He is again wearing his hat, which Peter seizes, knocks the top off it and places on the roof. In the friendliest way smoke begins to come out of the hat)

PETER *(with his hand on the knocker)* All look your best; the first impression is awfully important. *(He knocks, and after a dreadful moment of suspense, in which they cannot help wondering if any one is inside, the door opens and who should come out but Wendy! She has evidently been tidying a little. She is quite surprised to find that she has nine children)*

WENDY *(genteelly)* Where am I?

SLIGHTLY Wendy lady, for you we built this house.

NIBS and TOOTLES Oh, say you are pleased.

WENDY *(stroking the pretty thing)* Lovely, darling house.

FIRST TWIN And we are your children.

WENDY *(affecting surprise)* Oh?

OMNES *(kneeling, with outstretched arms)* Wendy lady, be our mother! *(Now that they know it is pretend they acclaim her greedily)*

WENDY *(not to make herself too cheap)* Ought I? Of course it is frightfully fascinating; but you see I am only a little girl; I have no real experience.

OMNES That doesn't matter. What we need is just a nice motherly person.

WENDY Oh dear, I feel that is just exactly what I am.

OMNES It is, it is, we saw it at once.

WENDY Very well then, I will do my best. *(In their glee they go dancing obstreperously round the little house, and she sees she must be firm with them as well as kind)* Come inside at once, you naughty children, I am sure your feet are damp. And before I put you to bed I have just time to finish the story of Cinderella.

(They all troop into the enchanting house, whose not least remarkable feature is that it holds them. A vision of Liza passes, not perhaps because she has any right to be there; but she has so few pleasures and is so young that we just let her have a peep at the little house. By and by Peter comes out and marches up and down with drawn sword, for the pirates can be heard carousing far away on the lagoon, and the wolves are on the prowl. The little house, its walls so red and its roof so mossy, looks very cosy and safe, with a bright light showing through the blind, the chimney smoking beautifully, and Peter on guard. On our last sight of him it is so dark that we just guess he is the little figure who has fallen asleep by the door. Dots of light come and go. They are inquisitive fairies having a look at the house. Any other child in their way they would mischief, but they just tweak Peter's nose and pass on. Fairies, you see, can touch him)

ACT 3

THE MERMAIDS' LAGOON*

It is the end of a long playful day on the lagoon. The sun's rays have persuaded him to give them another five minutes, for one more race

over the waters before he gathers them up and lets in the moon. There
are many mermaids here, going plop-plop, and one might attempt to
count the tails did they not flash and disappear so quickly. At times
a lovely girl leaps in the air seeking to get rid of her excess of scales,
which fall in a silver shower as she shakes them off. From the coral
grottoes beneath the lagoon, where are the mermaids' bed-chambers,
comes fitful music.

One of the most bewitching of these blue-eyed creatures is lying
lazily on Marooners' Rock, combing her long tresses and noting
effects in a transparent shell. Peter and his band are in the water
unseen behind the rock, whither they have tracked her as if she were
a trout, and at a signal ten pairs of arms come whack upon the mermaid to enclose her. Alas, this is only what was meant to happen, for
she hears the signal (which is the crow of a cock) and slips through
their arms into the water. It has been such a near thing that there are
scales on some of their hands. They climb on to the rock crestfallen.

WENDY *(preserving her scales as carefully as if they were rare postage
stamps)* I did so want to catch a mermaid.

PETER *(getting rid of his)* It is awfully difficult to catch a mermaid. *(The
mermaids at times find it just as difficult to catch him, though he sometimes
joins them in their one game, which consists in lazily blowing their bubbles
into the air and seeing who can catch them. The number of bubbles Peter
has flown away with! When the weather grows cold mermaids migrate to
the other side of the world, and he once went with a great shoal of them
half the way)* They are such cruel creatures, Wendy, that they try to
pull boys and girls like you into the water and drown them.

WENDY *(too guarded by this time to ask what he means precisely by 'like
you', though she is very desirous of knowing)* How hateful!

*(She is slightly different in appearance now, rather rounder, while John
and Michael are not quite so round. The reason is that when new lost
children arrive at his underground home Peter finds new trees for them
to go up and down by, and instead of fitting the tree to them he makes
them fit the tree. Sometimes it can be done by adding or removing garments, but if you are bumpy, or the tree is an odd shape, he has things
done to you with a roller, and after that you fit.*

The other boys are now playing King of the Castle, throwing each other
into the water, taking headers and so on; but these two continue to talk)*

PETER Wendy, this is a fearfully important rock. It is called Marooners' Rock. Sailors are marooned, you know, when their captain leaves them on a rock and sails away.

WENDY Leaves them on this little rock to drown?

PETER *(lightly)* Oh, they don't live long. Their hands are tied, so that they can't swim. When the tide is full this rock is covered with water, and then the sailor drowns.

(Wendy is uneasy as she surveys the rock, which is the only one in the lagoon and no larger than a table. Since she last looked around a threatening change has come over the scene. The sun has gone, but the moon has not come. What has come is a cold shiver across the waters which has sent all the wiser mermaids to their coral recesses. They know that evil is creeping over the lagoon. Of the boys Peter is of course the first to scent it, and he has leapt to his feet before the words strike the rock—

> 'And if we're parted by a shot
> We're sure to meet below.'

The games on the rock and around it end so abruptly that several divers are checked in the air. There they hang waiting for the word of command from Peter. When they get it they strike the water simultaneously, and the rock is at once as bare as if suddenly they had been blown off it. Thus the pirates find it deserted when their dinghy strikes the rock and is nearly stove in by the concussion)

SMEE Luff, you spalpeen,* luff! *(They are Smee and Starkey, with Tiger Lily, their captive, bound hand and foot)* What we have got to do is to hoist the redskin on to the rock and leave her there to drown.

(To one of her race this is an end darker than death by fire or torture, for it is written in the laws of the Piccaninnies that there is no path through water to the happy hunting ground. Yet her face is impassive; she is the daughter of a chief and must die as a chief's daughter; it is enough)

STARKEY *(chagrined because she does not mewl*)* No mewling. This is your reward for prowling round the ship with a knife in your mouth.

TIGER LILY *(stoically)* Enough said.

SMEE *(who would have preferred a farewell palaver)* So that's it! On to the rock with her, mate.

STARKEY *(experiencing for perhaps the last time the stirrings of a man)* Not so rough, Smee; roughish, but not so rough.

SMEE *(dragging her on to the rock)* It is the captain's orders.

(A stave has in some past time been driven into the rock, probably to mark the burial place of hidden treasure, and to this they moor the dinghy).

WENDY *(in the water)* Poor Tiger Lily!

STARKEY What was that? *(The children bob.)*

PETER *(who can imitate the captain's voice so perfectly that even the author has a dizzy feeling that at times he was really Hook)* Ahoy there, you lubbers!*

STARKEY It is the captain; he must be swimming out to us.

SMEE *(calling)* We have put the redskin on the rock, Captain.

PETER Set her free.

SMEE But, Captain——

PETER Cut her bonds, or I'll plunge my hook in you.

SMEE This is queer!

STARKEY *(unmanned)* Let us follow the captain's orders.

(They undo the thongs and Tiger Lily slides between their legs into the lagoon, forgetting in her haste to utter her war-cry, but Peter utters it for her, so naturally that even the lost boys are deceived. It is at this moment that the voice of the true Hook is heard)

HOOK Boat ahoy!

SMEE *(relieved)* It is the captain.

(Hook is swimming, and they help him to scale the rock. He is in gloomy mood)

STARKEY Captain, is all well?

SMEE He sighs.

STARKEY He sighs again.

SMEE *(counting)* And yet a third time he sighs. *(With foreboding)* What's up, Captain?

HOOK *(who has perhaps found the large rich damp cake untouched)* The game is up. Those boys have found a mother!

STARKEY Oh evil day!

SMEE What is a mother?

WENDY *(horrified)* He doesn't know!

HOOK *(sharply)* What was that?

(Peter makes the splash of a mermaid's tail)

STARKEY One of them mermaids.

HOOK Dost not know, Smee? A mother is—— *(He finds it more difficult to explain than he had expected, and looks about him for an illustration. He finds one in a great bird which drifts past in a nest as large as the roomiest basin)* There is a lesson in mothers for you! The nest must have fallen into the water, but would the bird desert her eggs? *(Peter, who is now more or less off his head, makes the sound of a bird answering in the negative. The nest is borne out of sight)*

STARKEY Maybe she is hanging about here to protect Peter?

(Hook's face clouds still further and Peter just manages not to call out that he needs no protection)

SMEE *(not usually a man of ideas)* Captain, could we not kidnap these boys' mother and make her our mother?

HOOK Obesity and bunions,* 'tis a princely scheme. We will seize the children, make them walk the plank, and Wendy shall be our mother!

WENDY Never! *(Another splash from Peter)*

HOOK What say you, bullies?*

SMEE There is my hand on't.

STARKEY And mine.

HOOK And there is my hook. Swear. *(All swear)*. But I had forgot; where is the redskin?

SMEE *(shaken)* That is all right, Captain; we let her go.

HOOK *(terrible)* Let her go?

SMEE 'Twas your own orders, Captain.

STARKEY *(whimpering)* You called over the water to us to let her go.

HOOK Brimstone and gall, what cozening is here? *(Disturbed by their faithful faces)* Lads, I gave no such order.

SMEE 'Tis passing queer.

HOOK *(addressing the immensities)* Spirit that haunts this dark lagoon to-night, dost hear me?

PETER *(in the same voice)* Odds, bobs, hammer and tongs, I hear you.

HOOK *(gripping the stave for support)* Who are you, stranger, speak.

PETER *(who is only too ready to speak)* I am Jas Hook, Captain of the *Jolly Roger*.

HOOK *(now white to the gills)* No, no, you are not.

PETER Brimstone and gall, say that again and I'll cast anchor in you.

HOOK If you are Hook, come tell me, who am I?

PETER A codfish, only a codfish.

HOOK *(aghast)* A codfish?

SMEE *(drawing back from him)* Have we been captained all this time by a codfish?

STARKEY It's lowering to our pride.

HOOK *(feeling that his ego is slipping from him)* Don't desert me, bullies.

PETER *(top-heavy)* Paw, fish, paw!

(There is a touch of the feminine in Hook, as in all the greatest pirates, and it prompts him to try the guessing game)

HOOK Have you another name?

PETER *(falling to the lure)* Ay, ay.

HOOK *(thirstily)* Vegetable?

PETER No.

HOOK Mineral?

PETER No.

HOOK Animal?

PETER *(after a hurried consultation with Tootles)* Yes.

HOOK Man?

PETER *(with scorn)* No.

HOOK Boy?

PETER Yes.

HOOK Ordinary boy?

PETER No!

HOOK Wonderful boy?

PETER *(to Wendy's distress)* Yes!

HOOK Are you in England?

PETER No.

HOOK Are you here?

PETER Yes.

HOOK *(beaten, though he feels he has very nearly got it)* Smee, you ask him some questions.

SMEE *(rummaging his brains)* I can't think of a thing.

PETER Can't guess, can't guess! *(Foundering in his cockiness)* Do you give it up?

HOOK *(eagerly)* Yes.

PETER All of you?

SMEE and STARKEY Yes.

PETER *(crowing)* Well, then, I am Peter Pan!

  (Now they have him)

HOOK Pan! Into the water, Smee. Starkey, mind the boat. Take him dead or alive!

PETER *(who still has all his baby teeth)* Boys, lam into* the pirates!

(For a moment the only two we can see are in the dinghy, where John throws himself on Starkey. Starkey wriggles into the lagoon and John leaps so quickly after him that he reaches it first. The impression left on Starkey is that he is being attacked by the Twins. The water becomes stained. The dinghy drifts away. Here and there a head shows in the water, and once it is the head of the crocodile. In the growing gloom some strike at their friends, Slightly getting Tootles in the fourth rib while he himself is pinked* by Curly. It looks as if the boys were getting the worse of it, which is perhaps just as well at this point, because Peter, who will be the determining factor in the end, has a perplexing way of changing sides if he is winning too easily. Hook's iron claw makes a circle of black water round him from which opponents flee like fishes. There is only one prepared to enter that dreadful circle. His name is Pan. Strangely, it is not in the water that they meet. Hook has risen to the rock to breathe, and at the same moment Peter scales it on the opposite side. The rock is now wet and as slippery as a ball, and they have to crawl rather than climb. Suddenly they are face to face. Peter gnashes his pretty teeth with joy, and is gathering himself for the spring when he sees he is higher up the rock than his foe. Courteously he waits; Hook sees his intention, and taking advantage of it claws twice. Peter is untouched, but unfairness is what he never can get used to, and in his bewilderment he rolls off the rock. The crocodile, whose tick has been drowned in the strife, rears its jaws, and Hook, who has almost stepped into them, is pursued by it to land. All is quiet on the lagoon now, not a sound save little waves nibbling at the rock, which is smaller than when we last looked at it. Two boys appear with the dinghy, and the others despite their wounds climb into it. They send the cry 'Peter—Wendy' across the waters, but no answer comes)

NIBS They must be swimming home.

JOHN Or flying.

FIRST TWIN Yes, that is it. Let us be off and call to them as we go.

(The dinghy disappears with its load, whose hearts would sink it if they knew of the peril of Wendy and her captain. From near and far away come the cries 'Peter—Wendy' till we no longer hear them.

Two small figures are now on the rock, but they have fainted. A mermaid who has dared to come back in the stillness stretches up her arms and is slowly pulling Wendy into the water to drown her. Wendy starts up just in time)

WENDY　Peter! *(He rouses himself and looks around him)* Where are we, Peter?

PETER　We are on the rock, but it is getting smaller. Soon the water will be over it. Listen!

(They can hear the wash of the relentless little waves)

WENDY　We must go.

PETER　Yes.

WENDY　Shall we swim or fly?

PETER　Wendy, do you think you could swim or fly to the island without me?

WENDY　You know I couldn't, Peter; I am just a beginner.

PETER　Hook wounded me twice. *(He believes it; he is so good at pretend that he feels the pain, his arms hang limp)* I can neither swim nor fly.

WENDY　Do you mean we shall both be drowned?

PETER　Look how the water is rising!

(They cover their faces with their hands. Something touches Wendy as lightly as a kiss)

PETER　*(with little interest)* It must be the tail of the kite we made for Michael; you remember it tore itself out of his hands and floated away. *(He looks up and sees the kite sailing overhead)* The kite! Why shouldn't it carry you? *(He grips the tail and pulls, and the kite responds)*

WENDY　Both of us!

PETER　It can't lift two. Michael and Curly tried.

(She knows very well that if it can lift her it can lift him also, for she has been told by the boys as a deadly secret that one of the queer things about him is that he is no weight at all. But it is a forbidden subject)

WENDY　I won't go without you. Let us draw lots which is to stay behind.

PETER　And you a lady, never! *(The tail is in her hands, and the kite is tugging hard. She holds out her mouth to Peter, but he knows they cannot do that)* Ready, Wendy!

(The kite draws her out of sight across the lagoon.

The waters are lapping over the rock now, and Peter knows that it will soon be submerged. Pale rays of light mingle with the moving clouds, and from the coral grottoes is to be heard a sound, at once the most musical and the most melancholy in the Never Land, the mermaids calling to the moon to rise. Peter is afraid at last, and a tremor runs through him, like a shudder passing over the lagoon; but on the lagoon one shudder follows another till there are hundreds of them, and he feels just the one)

PETER *(with a drum beating in his breast as if he were a real boy at last)* To die will be an awfully big adventure.*

(The blind rises again, and the lagoon is now suffused with moonlight. He is on the rock still, but the water is over his feet. The nest is borne nearer, and the bird, after cooing a message to him, leaves it and wings her way upwards. Peter, who knows the bird language, slips into the nest, first removing the two eggs and placing them in Starkey's hat, which has been left on the stave. The hat drifts away from the rock, but he uses the stave as a mast. The wind is driving him toward the open sea. He takes off his shirt, which he had forgotten to remove while bathing, and unfurls it as a sail. His vessel tacks, and he passes from sight, naked and victorious. The bird returns and sits on the hat)

ACT 4

THE HOME UNDER THE GROUND

We see simultaneously the home under the ground with the children in it and the wood above ground with the redskins on it. Below, the children are gobbling their evening meal; above, the redskins are squatting in their blankets near the little house guarding the children from the pirates. The only way of communicating between these two parties is by means of the hollow trees.

The home has an earthen floor, which is handy for digging in if you want to go fishing; and owing to there being so many entrances there is not much wall space. The table at which the lost ones are sitting is a board on top of a live tree trunk, which has been cut flat but has such growing pains that the board rises as they eat, and they have sometimes to pause in their meals to cut a bit more off the trunk. Their seats are pumpkins or the large gay mushrooms of which we have seen an imitation one concealing the chimney. There is an enormous fire-place which is in almost any part of the room where you care to light it, and across this Wendy has stretched strings, made of fibre, from which she hangs her washing. There are also various tomfool* things in the room of no use whatever.

Michael's basket bed is nailed high up on the wall as if to protect him from the cat, but there is no indication at present of where the others sleep. At the back between two of the tree trunks is a grind-stone, and near it is a lovely hole, the size of a band-box,* with a gay curtain drawn across so that you cannot see what is inside. This is Tink's withdrawing-room and bedchamber, and it is just as well that you cannot see inside, for it is so exquisite in its decoration and in the personal apparel spread out on the bed that you could scarcely resist making off with something. Tink is within at present, as one can guess from a glow showing through the chinks. It is her own glow, for though she has a chandelier for the look of the thing, of course she lights her residence herself. She is probably wasting valuable time just now won-dering whether to put on the smoky blue or the apple-blossom.*

All the boys except Peter are here, and Wendy has the head of the table, smiling complacently at their captivating ways, but doing her best at the same time to see that they keep the rules about hands-off-the-table, no-two-to-speak-at-once, and so on. She is wearing romantic woodland garments, sewn by herself, with red berries in her hair which go charmingly with her complexion, as she knows; indeed she searched for red berries the morning after she reached the island. The boys are in picturesque attire of her contrivance, and if these don't always fit well the fault is not hers but the wearers', for they con-stantly put on each other's things when they put on anything at all. Michael is in his cradle on the wall. First Twin is apart on a high stool and wears a dunce's cap, another invention of Wendy's, but not wholly successful because everybody wants to be dunce.

It is a pretend meal this evening, with nothing whatever on the table, not a mug, nor a crust, nor a spoon. They often have these suppers and like them on occasions as well as the other kind, which consist chiefly of bread-fruit, tappa rolls, yams, mammee apples and banana splash, washed down with calabashes of poe-poe.* The pretend meals are not Wendy's idea; indeed she was rather startled to find, on arriving, that Peter knew of no other kind, and she is not absolutely certain even now that he does eat the other kind, though no one appears to do it more heartily. He insists that the pretend meals should be partaken of with gusto, and we see his band doing their best to obey orders.

WENDY *(her fingers to her ears, for their chatter and clatter are deafening)* Si-lence! Is your mug empty, Slightly?

SLIGHTLY *(who would not say this if he had a mug)* Not quite empty, thank you.

NIBS Mummy, he has not even begun to drink his poe-poe.

SLIGHTLY *(seizing his chance, for this is tale-bearing)* I complain of Nibs!

(John holds up his hand)

WENDY Well, John?

JOHN May I sit in Peter's chair as he is not here?

WENDY In your father's chair? Certainly not.

JOHN He is not really our father. He did not even know how to be a father till I showed him.

(This is insubordination)

SECOND TWIN I complain of John!

(The gentle Tootles raises his hand)

TOOTLES *(who has the poorest opinion of himself)* I don't suppose Michael would let me be baby?

MICHAEL No, I won't.

TOOTLES May I be dunce?

FIRST TWIN *(from his perch)* No. It's awfully difficult to be dunce.

TOOTLES As I can't be anything important would any of you like to see me do a trick?

OMNES No.

TOOTLES *(subsiding)* I hadn't really any hope.

(The tale-telling breaks out again)

NIBS Slightly is coughing on the table.

CURLY The twins began with tappa rolls.

SLIGHTLY   I complain of Nibs!

NIBS   I complain of Slightly!

WENDY   Oh dear, I am sure I sometimes think that spinsters are to be envied.

MICHAEL   Wendy, I am too big for a cradle.

WENDY   You are the littlest, and a cradle is such a nice homely thing to have about a house. You others can clear away now. *(She sits down on a pumpkin near the fire to her usual evening occupation, darning)* Every heel with a hole in it!

(The boys clear away with dispatch, washing dishes they don't have in a non-existent sink and stowing them in a cupboard that isn't there. Instead of sawing the table-leg to-night they crush it into the ground like a concertina, and are now ready for play, in which they indulge hilariously.
A movement of the Indians draws our attention to the scene above. Hitherto, with the exception of Panther, who sits on guard on top of the little house, they have been hunkering in their blankets, mute but picturesque; now all rise and prostrate themselves before the majestic figure of Peter, who approaches through the forest carrying a gun and game bag. It is not exactly a gun. He often wanders away alone with this weapon, and when he comes back you are never absolutely certain whether he has had an adventure or not. He may have forgotten it so completely that he says nothing about it; and then when you go out you find the body. On the other hand he may say a great deal about it, and yet you never find the body. Sometimes he comes home with his face scratched, and tells Wendy, as a thing of no importance, that he got these marks from the little people for cheeking them at a fairy wedding, and she listens politely, but she is never quite sure, you know; indeed the only one who is sure about anything on the island is Peter)

PETER   The Great White Father is glad to see the Piccaninny braves protecting his wigwam from the pirates.

TIGER LILY   The Great White Father save me from pirates. Me his velly nice friend now; no let pirates hurt him.

BRAVES   Ugh, ugh, wah!

TIGER LILY   Tiger Lily has spoken.

PANTHER Loola, loola! Great Big Little Panther has spoken.

PETER It is well. The Great White Father has spoken.

(This has a note of finality about it, with the implied 'And now shut up,' which is never far from the courteous receptions of well-meaning inferiors by born leaders of men. He descends his tree, not unheard by Wendy)

WENDY Children, I hear your father's step. He likes you to meet him at the door. *(Peter scatters pretend nuts among them and watches sharply to see that they crunch with relish)* Peter, you just spoil them, you know!

JOHN *(who would be incredulous if he dare)* Any sport, Peter?

PETER Two tigers and a pirate.

JOHN *(boldly)* Where are their heads?

PETER *(contracting his little brows)* In the bag.

JOHN *(No, he doesn't say it. He backs away)*

WENDY *(peeping into the bag)* They are beauties! *(She has learned her lesson)*

FIRST TWIN Mummy, we all want to dance.

WENDY The mother of such an armful dance!

SLIGHTLY As it is Saturday night?

(They have long lost count of the days, but always if they want to do anything special they say this is Saturday night, and then they do it)

WENDY Of course it is Saturday night, Peter? *(He shrugs an indifferent assent)* On with your nighties* first. *(They disappear into various recesses, and Peter and Wendy with her darning are left by the fire to dodder parentally. She emphasises it by humming a verse of 'John Anderson my Jo,'* which has not the desired effect on Peter. She is too loving to be ignorant that he is not loving enough, and she hesitates like one who knows the answer to her question)* What is wrong, Peter?

PETER *(scared)* It is only pretend, isn't it, that I am their father?

WENDY *(drooping)* Oh yes. *(His sigh of relief is without consideration for her feelings)* But they are ours, Peter, yours and mine.

PETER *(determined to get at facts, the only things that puzzle him)* But not really?

WENDY Not if you don't wish it.

PETER I don't.

WENDY *(knowing she ought not to probe but driven to it by something within)* What are your exact feelings for me, Peter?

PETER *(in the class-room)* Those of a devoted son, Wendy.

WENDY *(turning away)* I thought so.

PETER You are so puzzling. Tiger Lily is just the same; there is something or other she wants to be to me, but she says it is not my mother.

WENDY *(with spirit)* No, indeed it isn't.

PETER Then what is it?

WENDY It isn't for a lady to tell.

(The curtain of the fairy chamber opens slightly, and Tink, who has doubtless been eavesdropping, tinkles a laugh of scorn)

PETER *(badgered)* I suppose she means that she wants to be my mother.

(Tink's comment is 'You silly ass.')

WENDY *(who has picked up some of the fairy words)* I almost agree with her!

(The arrival of the boys in their nightgowns turns Wendy's mind to practical matters, for the children have to be arranged in line and passed or not passed for cleanliness. Slightly is the worst. At last we see how they sleep, for in a babel* the great bed which stands on end by day against the wall is unloosed from custody and lowered to the floor. Though large, it is a tight fit for so many boys, and Wendy has made a rule that there is to be no turning round until one gives the signal, when all turn at once.

First Twin is the best dancer and performs mightily on the bed and in it and out of it and over it to an accompaniment of pillow fights by the less agile; and then there is a rush at Wendy)

NIBS Now the story you promised to tell us as soon as we were in bed!

WENDY *(severely)* As far as I can see you are not in bed yet.

(They scramble into the bed, and the effect is as of a boxful of sardines)

WENDY *(drawing up her stool)* Well, there was once a gentleman——

CURLY I wish he had been a lady.

NIBS I wish he had been a white rat.

WENDY Quiet! There was a lady also. The gentleman's name was Mr Darling and the lady's name was Mrs Darling——

JOHN I knew them!

MICHAEL *(who has been allowed to join the circle)* I think I knew them.

WENDY They were married, you know; and what do you think they had?

NIBS White rats?

WENDY No, they had three descendants. White rats are descendants also. Almost everything is a descendant. Now these three children had a faithful nurse called Nana.

MICHAEL *(alas)* What a funny name!

WENDY But Mr Darling—*(faltering)* or was it Mrs Darling?—was angry with her and chained her up in the yard; so all the children flew away. They flew away to the Never Land, where the lost boys are.

CURLY I just thought they did; I don't know how it is, but I just thought they did.

TOOTLES Oh, Wendy, was one of the lost boys called Tootles?

WENDY Yes, he was.

TOOTLES *(dazzled)* Am I in a story? Nibs, I am in a story!

PETER *(who is by the fire making Pan's pipes with his knife, and is determined that Wendy shall have fair play, however beastly a story he may think it)* A little less noise there.

WENDY *(melting over the beauty of her present performance, but without any real qualms)* Now I want you to consider the feelings of the unhappy parents with all their children flown away. Think, oh think, of the empty beds. *(The heartless ones think of them with glee)*

FIRST TWIN *(cheerfully)* It's awfully sad.

WENDY But our heroine knew that her mother would always leave the window open for her progeny to fly back by; so they stayed away for years and had a lovely time.

(Peter is interested at last)

FIRST TWIN Did they ever go back?

WENDY *(comfortably)* Let us now take a peep into the future. Years have rolled by, and who is this elegant lady of uncertain age alighting at London station?

(The tension is unbearable)

NIBS Oh, Wendy, who is she?

WENDY *(swelling)* Can it be—yes—no—yes, it is the fair Wendy!

TOOTLES I am glad.

WENDY Who are the two noble portly figures accompanying her? Can they be John and Michael? They are. *(Pride of Michael)* 'See, dear brothers,' says Wendy, pointing upward, 'there is the window standing open.' So up they flew to their loving parents, and pen cannot inscribe the happy scene over which we draw a veil. *(Her triumph is spoilt by a groan from Peter and she hurries to him)* Peter, what is it? *(Thinking he is ill, and looking lower than his chest)* Where is it?

PETER It isn't that kind of pain. Wendy, you are wrong about mothers. I thought like you about the window, so I stayed away for moons and moons, and then I flew back, but the window was barred, for my mother had forgotten all about me and there was another little boy sleeping in my bed.

(This is a general damper)

JOHN Wendy, let us go back!

WENDY Are you sure mothers are like that?

PETER Yes.

WENDY John, Michael! *(She clasps them to her)*

FIRST TWIN *(alarmed)* You are not to leave us, Wendy?

WENDY I must.

NIBS Not to-night?

WENDY At once. Perhaps mother is in half-mourning* by this time! Peter, will you make the necessary arrangements?

(She asks it in the steely tones women adopt when they are prepared secretly for opposition)

PETER *(coolly)* If you wish it.

(He ascends his tree to give the redskins their instructions. The lost boys gather threateningly round Wendy)

CURLY We won't let you go!

WENDY *(with one of those inspirations women have, in an emergency, to make use of some male who need otherwise have no hope)* Tootles, I appeal to you.

TOOTLES *(leaping to his death if necessary)* I am just Tootles and nobody minds me, but the first who does not behave to Wendy I will blood him severely.

(Peter returns)

PETER *(with awful serenity)* Wendy, I told the braves to guide you through the wood as flying tires you so. Then Tinker Bell will take you across the sea. *(A shrill tinkle from the boudoir probably means 'and drop her into it'.)*

NIBS *(fingering the curtain which he is not allowed to open)* Tink, you are to get up and take Wendy on a journey. *(Star-eyed)* She says she won't!

PETER *(taking a step toward that chamber)* If you don't get up, Tink, and dress at once—— She is getting up!

WENDY *(quivering now that the time to depart has come)* Dear ones, if you will all come with me I feel almost sure I can get my father and mother to adopt you.

(There is joy at this, not that they want parents, but novelty is their religion)

NIBS But won't they think us rather a handful?

WENDY *(a swift reckoner)* Oh no, it will only mean having a few beds in the drawing-room; they can be hidden behind screens on first Thursdays.*

(Everything depends on Peter)

OMNES Peter, may we go?

PETER *(carelessly through the pipes to which he is giving a finishing touch)* All right.

(They scurry off to dress for the adventure)

WENDY *(insinuatingly)* Get your clothes, Peter.

PETER *(skipping about and playing fairy music on his pipes, the only music he knows)* I am not going with you, Wendy.

WENDY Yes, Peter!

PETER No.

(The lost ones run back gaily, each carrying a stick with a bundle on the end of it)

WENDY Peter isn't coming!

(All the faces go blank)

JOHN *(even John)* Peter not coming!

TOOTLES *(overthrown)* Why, Peter?

PETER *(his pipes more riotous than ever)* I just want always to be a lit-tle boy and to have fun. *(There is a general fear that they are perhaps making the mistake of their lives)* Now then, no fuss, no blubbering. *(With dreadful cynicism)* I hope you will like your mothers! Are you ready, Tink! Then lead the way.

(Tink darts up any tree, but she is the only one. The air above is sud-denly rent with shrieks and the clash of steel. Though they cannot see, the boys know that Hook and his crew are upon the Indians. Mouths open and remain open, all in mute appeal to Peter. He is the only boy on his feet now, a sword in his hand, the same he slew Barbicue with; and in his eye is the lust of battle.*

We can watch the carnage that is invisible to the children. Hook has basely broken the two laws of Indian warfare, which are that the redskins should attack first, and that it should be at dawn. They have known the pirate whereabouts since, early in the night, one of Smee's fingers crackled. The brushwood has closed behind their scouts as silently as the sand on the mole; for hours they have imitated the lonely call of the coyote; no stratagem has been overlooked, but alas, they have trusted to the pale-face's honour to await an attack at dawn, when his courage is known to be at the lowest ebb. Hook falls upon them pell-mell, and one cannot withhold a reluctant admiration for the wit that conceived so subtle a scheme and the fell genius with which it is carried out. If the braves would rise quickly they might still have time to scalp, but this they are forbidden to do by the traditions of their race, for it is written that they must never express surprise in the presence of the pale-face. For a brief space they remain recumbent, not a muscle moving, as if the foe were here by invitation. Thus perish the flower of the Piccaninnies, though not unavenged, for with Lean Wolf fall Alf Mason and Canary Robb, while other pirates to bite dust are Black Gilmour and Alan Herb, that same Herb who is still remembered at Manaos for playing skittles with the mate of the Switch for each other's heads. Chay Turley,* who laughed with the wrong side of his mouth (having no other), is tomahawked by Panther, who eventually cuts a way through the shambles with Tiger Lily and a remnant of the tribe.

This onslaught passes and is gone like a fierce wind. The victors wipe their cutlasses, and squint, ferret-eyed, at their leader. He remains, as ever, aloof in spirit and in substance. He signs to them to descend the trees, for he is convinced that Pan is down there, and though he has smoked the bees it is the honey he wants. There is something in Peter that at all times goads this extraordinary man to frenzy; it is the boy's cockiness, which disturbs Hook like an insect. If you have seen a lion in a cage futilely pursuing a sparrow you will know what is meant. The pirates try to do their captain's bidding, but the apertures prove to be not wide enough for them; he cannot even ram them down with a pole. He steals to the mouth of a tree and listens)

PETER *(prematurely)* All is over!

WENDY But who has won?

PETER Hst! If the Indians have won they will beat the tom-tom; it is always their signal of victory.

(Hook licks his lips at this and signs to Smee, who is sitting on it, to hold up the tom-tom. He beats upon it with his claw, and listens for results)

TOOTLES The tom-tom!

PETER *(sheathing his sword)* An Indian victory!

(The cheers from below are music to the black hearts above)

You are quite safe now, Wendy. Boys, good-bye. *(He resumes his pipes)*

WENDY Peter, you will remember about changing your flannels,*
won't you?

PETER Oh, all right!

WENDY And this is your medicine.

*(She puts something into a shell and leaves it on a ledge between two of
the trees. It is only water, but she measures it out in drops)*

PETER I won't forget.

WENDY Peter, what are you to me?

PETER *(through the pipes)* Your son, Wendy.

WENDY Oh, good-bye!

*(The travellers start upon their journey, little witting that Hook has issued
his silent orders: a man to the mouth of each tree, and a row of men between
the trees and the little house. As the children squeeze up they are plucked
from their trees, trussed, thrown like bales of cotton from one pirate to
another, and so piled up in the little house. The only one treated differently
is Wendy, whom Hook escorts to the house on his arm with hateful politeness. He signs to his dogs to be gone, and they depart through the wood,
carrying the little house with its strange merchandise and singing their
ribald song. The chimney of the little house emits a jet of smoke fitfully, as
if not sure what it ought to do just now.*

   *Hook and Peter are now, as it were, alone on the island. Below, Peter
is on the bed, asleep, no weapon near him; above, Hook, armed to the
teeth, is searching noiselessly for some tree down which the nastiness of
him can descend. Don't be too much alarmed by this; it is precisely the
situation Peter would have chosen; indeed if the whole thing were pretend—. One of his arms droops over the edge of the bed, a leg is arched,
and the mouth is not so tightly closed that we cannot see the little pearls.
He is dreaming, and in his dreams he is always in pursuit of a boy who
was never here, nor anywhere: the only boy who could beat him.*

Hook finds the tree. It is the one set apart for Slightly who being addicted when hot to the drinking of water has swelled in consequence and surreptitiously scooped his tree for easier descent and egress. Down this the pirate wriggles a passage. In the aperture below his face emerges and goes green as he glares at the sleeping child. Does no feeling of compassion disturb his sombre breast? The man is not wholly evil: he has a Thesaurus in his cabin, and is no mean performer on the flute. What really warps him is a presentiment that he is about to fail. This is not unconnected with a beatific smile on the face of the sleeper, whom he cannot reach owing to being stuck at the foot of the tree. He, however, sees the medicine shell within easy reach, and to Wendy's draught he adds from a bottle five drops of poison distilled when he was weeping from the red in his eye. The expression on Peter's face merely implies that something heavenly is going on. Hook worms his way upwards, and winding his cloak around him, as if to conceal his person from the night of which he is the blackest part, he stalks moodily toward the lagoon. A dot of light flashes past him and darts down the nearest tree, looking for Peter, only for Peter, quite indifferent about the others when she finds him safe)

PETER *(stirring)* Who is that? *(Tink has to tell her tale, in one long ungrammatical sentence)* The redskins were defeated? Wendy and the boys captured by the pirates! I'll rescue her! I'll rescue her! *(He leaps first at his dagger, and then at his grindstone, to sharpen it. Tink alights near the shell, and rings out a warning cry)* Oh, that is just my medicine. Poisoned? Who could have poisoned it? I promised Wendy to take it, and I will as soon as I have sharpened my dagger. *(Tink, who sees its red colour and remembers the red in the pirate's eye, nobly swallows the draught as Peter's hand is reaching for it)* Why, Tink, you have drunk my medicine! *(She flutters strangely about the room, answering him now in a very thin tinkle)* It was poisoned and you drank it to save my life! Tink, dear Tink, are you dying? *(He has never called her dear Tink before, and for a moment she is gay; she alights on his shoulder, gives his chin a loving bite, whispers 'You silly ass,' and falls on her tiny bed. The boudoir, which is lit by her, flickers ominously. He is on his knees by the opening)* Her light is growing faint, and if it goes out, that means she is dead! Her voice is so low I can scarcely tell what she is saying. She says—she says she thinks she could get well again if children believed in fairies! *(He rises and throws out his arms he knows not to whom, perhaps to the boys and girls of whom he is not one)* Do you believe in fairies? Say quick that you believe! If you believe, clap your hands! *(Many clap, some don't, a few hiss. Then perhaps there is a rush of Nanas to the nurseries to see what on earth is happening. But Tink is saved)* Oh, thank you, thank you, thank you! And now to rescue Wendy!

(Tink is already as merry and impudent as a grig,* with not a thought for those who have saved her. Peter ascends his tree as if he were shot up it. What he is feeling is 'Hook or me this time!' He is frightfully happy. He soon hits the trail, for the smoke from the little house has lingered here and there to guide him. He takes wing)

ACT 5

SCENE 1

THE PIRATE SHIP

The stage directions for the opening of this scene are as follows:—1 Circuit Amber checked to 80. Battens, all Amber checked, 3 ship's lanterns alight, Arcs: prompt perch 1. Open dark Amber flooding back, O.P. perch open dark Amber flooding upper deck. Arc on tall steps at back of cabin to flood back cloth. Open dark Amber. Warning for slide. Plank ready. Call Hook.*

In the strange light thus described we see what is happening on the deck of the *Jolly Roger*, which is flying the skull and crossbones and lies low in the water. There is no need to call Hook, for he is here already, and indeed there is not a pirate aboard who would dare to call him. Most of them are at present carousing in the bowels of the vessel, but on the poop Mullins* is visible, in the only great-coat on the ship, raking with his glass* the monstrous rocks within which the lagoon is cooped. Such a look-out is supererogatory, for the pirate craft floats immune in the horror of her name.

From Hook's cabin at the back Starkey appears and leans over the bulwark, silently surveying the sullen waters. He is bare-headed and is perhaps thinking with bitterness of his hat, which he sometimes sees still drifting past him with the Never bird sitting on it. The black pirate is asleep on deck, yet even in his dreams rolling mechanically out of the way when Hook draws near. The only sound to be heard is made by Smee at his sewing-machine, which lends a touch of domesticity to the night.

Hook is now leaning against the mast, now prowling the deck, the double cigar in his mouth. With Peter surely at last removed from his path we, who know how vain a tabernacle is man, would not be surprised to find him bellied out by the winds of his success, but it is not so; he is still uneasy, looking long and meaninglessly at familiar objects, such as the ship's bell or the Long Tom,* like one who may shortly be a stranger to them. It is as if Pan's terrible oath 'Hook or me this time!' had already boarded the ship.

HOOK *(communing with his ego)* How still the night is;* nothing sounds alive. Now is the hour when children in their homes are a-bed; their lips bright-browned with the good-night chocolate, and their tongues drowsily searching for belated crumbs housed insecurely on their shining cheeks. Compare with them the children on this boat about to walk the plank. Split my infinitives, but 'tis my hour of triumph! *(Clinging to this fair prospect he dances a few jubilant steps, but they fall below his usual form)* And yet some disky* spirit compels me now to make my dying speech, lest when dying there may be no time for it. All mortals envy me, yet better perhaps for Hook to have had less ambition! O fame, fame, thou glittering bauble, what if the very——*(Smee, engrossed in his labours at the sewing-machine, tears a piece of calico with a rending sound which makes the Solitary think for a moment that the untoward has happened to his garments)* No little children love me. I am told they play at Peter Pan, and that the strongest always chooses to be Peter. They would rather be a Twin than Hook; they force the baby to be Hook. The baby! that is where the canker gnaws. *(He contemplates his industrious boatswain)* 'Tis said they find Smee lovable. But an hour agone I found him letting the youngest of them try on his spectacles. Pathetic Smee, the Nonconformist pirate, a happy smile upon his face because he thinks they fear him! How can I break it to him that they think him lovable? No, bi-carbonate of Soda,* no, not even——*(Another rending of the calico disturbs him, and he has a private consultation with Starkey, who turns him round and evidently assures him that all is well. The peroration of his speech is nevertheless for ever lost, as eight bells strikes and his crew pour forth in bacchanalian orgy.* From the poop he watches their dance till it frets* *him beyond bearing)* Quiet, you dogs, or I'll cast anchor in you! *(He descends to a barrel on which there are playing-cards, and his crew stand waiting, as ever, like whipped curs)* Are all the prisoners chained, so that they can't fly away?

JUKES Ay, ay, Captain.

HOOK Then hoist them up.

STARKEY *(raising the door of the hold)* Tumble up, you ungentle-manly lubbers.

(The terrified boys are prodded up and tossed about the deck. Hook seems to have forgotten them; he is sitting by the barrel with his cards)

HOOK *(suddenly)* So! Now then, you bullies, six of you walk the plank to-night, but I have room for two cabin-boys. Which of you is it to be? *(He returns to his cards)*

TOOTLES *(hoping to soothe him by putting the blame on the only person, vaguely remembered, who is always willing to act as a buffer)* You see, sir, I don't think my mother would like me to be a pirate. Would your mother like you to be a pirate, Slightly?

SLIGHTLY *(implying that otherwise it would be a pleasure to him to oblige)* I don't think so. Twin, would your mother like——

HOOK Stow this gab.* *(To John)* You boy, you look as if you had a lit-tle pluck in you. Didst never want to be a pirate, my hearty?

JOHN *(dazzled by being singled out)* When I was at school I—what do you think, Michael?

MICHAEL *(stepping into prominence)* What would you call me if I joined?

HOOK Blackbeard Joe.

MICHAEL John, what do you think?

JOHN Stop, should we still be respectful subjects of King George?*

HOOK You would have to swear 'Down with King George.'

JOHN *(grandly)* Then I refuse!

MICHAEL And I refuse.

HOOK That seals your doom. Bring up their mother. *(Wendy is driven up from the hold and thrown to him. She sees at the first glance that the deck has not been scrubbed for years)* So, my beauty, you are to see your children walk the plank.

WENDY *(with noble calmness)* Are they to die?

HOOK They are. Silence all, for a mother's last words to her children.

WENDY These are my last words. Dear boys, I feel that I have a message to you from your real mothers, and it is this, 'We hope our sons will die like English gentlemen.'

(The boys go on fire)

TOOTLES I am going to do what my mother hopes. What are you to do, Twin?

FIRST TWIN What my mother hopes. John, what are——

HOOK Tie her up! Get the plank ready.

(Wendy is roped to the mast; but no one regards her, for all eyes are fixed upon the plank now protruding from the poop over the ship's side. A great change, however, occurs in the time Hook takes to raise his claw and point to this deadly engine.* No one is now looking at the plank: for the tick, tick of the crocodile is heard. Yet it is not to bear on the crocodile that all eyes slew round, it is that they may bear on Hook. Otherwise prisoners and captors are equally inert, like actors in some play who have found themselves 'on' in a scene in which they are not personally concerned. Even the iron claw hangs inactive, as if aware that the crocodile is not coming for it. Affection for their captain, now cowering from view, is not what has given Hook his dominance over the crew, but as the menacing sound draws nearer they close their eyes respectfully.

There is no crocodile. It is Peter, who has been circling the pirate ship, ticking as he flies far more superbly than any clock. He drops into the water and climbs aboard, warning the captives with upraised finger (but still ticking) not for the moment to give audible expression to their natural admiration. Only one pirate sees him, Whibbles of the eye patch,* who comes up from below. John claps a hand on Whibbles's mouth to stifle the groan; four boys hold him to prevent the thud; Peter delivers the blow, and the carrion is thrown overboard. 'One!' says Slightly, beginning to count.

Starkey is the first pirate to open his eyes. The ship seems to him to be precisely as when he closed them. He cannot interpret the sparkle

*that has come into the faces of the captives, who are cleverly pretend-
ing to be as afraid as ever. He little knows that the door of the dark
cabin has just closed on one more boy. Indeed it is for Hook alone he
looks, and he is a little surprised to see him)*

STARKEY *(hoarsely)* It is gone, Captain! There is not a sound.

(The tenement that is Hook heaves tumultuously and he is himself again)

HOOK *(now convinced that some fair spirit watches over him)* Then
here is to Johnny Plank——

> Avast, belay, the English brig
> We took and quickly sank,
> And for a warning to the crew
> We made them walk the plank!

*(As he sings he capers detestably along an imaginary plank and his
copy-cats do likewise, joining in the chorus)*

> Yo ho, yo ho, the frisky plank,
> You walks along it so,
> Till it goes down and you goes down
> To tooral looral lo!

*(The brave children try to stem this monstrous torrent by breaking into
the National Anthem)*

STARKEY *(paling)* I don't like it, messmates!

HOOK Stow that, Starkey. Do you boys want a touch of the cat*
before you walk the plank? *(He is more pitiless than ever now that he
believes he has a charmed life)* Fetch the cat, Jukes; it is in the cabin.

JUKES Ay, ay, sir. *(It is one of his commonest remarks, and it is only
recorded now because he never makes another. The stage direction 'Exit
Jukes' has in this case a special significance. But only the children know
that some one is awaiting this unfortunate in the cabin, and Hook tram-
ples them down as he resumes his ditty:)*

> Yo ho, yo ho, the scratching cat
> Its tails are nine you know,
> And when they're writ upon your back,
> You're fit to——

(The last words will ever remain a matter of conjecture, for from the dark cabin comes a curdling screech which wails through the ship and dies away. It is followed by a sound, almost more eerie in the circumstances, that can only be likened to the crowing of a cock)

HOOK What was that?

SLIGHTLY *(solemnly)* Two!

(Cecco swings into the cabin, and in a moment returns, livid*)

HOOK *(with an effort)* What is the matter with Bill Jukes, you dog?

CECCO The matter with him is he is dead—stabbed.

PIRATES Bill Jukes dead!

CECCO The cabin is as black as a pit, but there is something terrible in there: the thing you heard a-crowing.

HOOK *(slowly)* Cecco, go back and fetch me out that doodle-doo.

CECCO *(unstrung)* No, Captain, no. *(He supplicates on his knees, but his master advances on him implacably)*

HOOK *(in his most syrupy voice)* Did you say you would go, Cecco?

(Cecco goes. All listen. There is one screech, one crow)

SLIGHTLY *(as if he were a bell tolling)* Three!

HOOK 'Sdeath and oddsfish,* who is to bring me out that doodle-doo?

(No one steps forward)

STARKEY *(injudiciously)* Wait till Cecco comes out.

(The black looks of some others encourage him)

HOOK I think I heard you volunteer, Starkey.

STARKEY *(emphatically)* No, by thunder!

HOOK *(in that syrupy voice which might be more engaging when accompanied by his flute)* My hook thinks you did. I wonder if it would not be advisable, Starkey, to humour the hook?

STARKEY I'll swing* before I go in there.

HOOK *(gleaming)* Is it mutiny? Starkey is ringleader. Shake hands, Starkey. *(Starkey recoils from the claw. It follows him till he leaps overboard)* Did any other gentleman say mutiny?

(They indicate that they did not even know the late Starkey)

SLIGHTLY Four!

HOOK I will bring out that doodle-doo myself.

(He raises a blunderbuss* but casts it from him with a menacing gesture which means that he has more faith in the claw. With a lighted lantern in his hand he enters the cabin. Not a sound is to be heard now on the ship, unless it be Slightly wetting his lips to say 'Five.' Hook staggers out)

HOOK *(unsteadily)* Something blew out the light.

MULLINS *(with dark meaning)* Some——thing?

NOODLER What of Cecco?

HOOK He is as dead as Jukes.

(They are superstitious like all sailors, and Mullins has planted a dire conception in their minds)

COOKSON They do say as the surest sign a ship's accurst is when there is one aboard* more than can be accounted for.

NOODLER I've heard he allus boards the pirate craft at last. *(With dreadful significance)* Has he a tail, Captain?

MULLINS They say that when he comes it is in the likeness of the wickedest man aboard.

COOKSON *(clinching it)* Has he a hook, Captain?

(Knives and pistols come to hand, and there is a general cry 'The ship is doomed!' But it is not his dogs that can frighten Jas Hook. Hearing something like a cheer from the boys he wheels round, and his face brings them to their knees)

HOOK So you like it, do you! By Caius and Balbus,* bullies, here is a notion: open the cabin door and drive them in. Let them fight the doodle-doo for their lives. If they kill him we are so much the better; if he kills them we are none the worse.

(This masterly stroke restores their confidence; and the boys, affecting fear, are driven into the cabin. Desperadoes though the pirates are, some of them have been boys themselves, and all turn their backs to the cabin and listen, with arms outstretched to it as if to ward off the horrors that are being enacted there.)

Relieved by Peter of their manacles, and armed with such weapons as they can lay their hands on, the boys steal out softly as snowflakes, and under their captain's hushed order find hiding-places on the poop. He releases Wendy; and now it would be easy for them all to fly away, but it is to be Hook or him this time. He signs to her to join the others, and with awful grimness folding her cloak around him, the hood over his head, he takes her place by the mast, and crows)

MULLINS The doodle-doo has killed them all!

SEVERAL The ship's bewitched.

(They are snapping at Hook again)

HOOK I've thought it out, lads; there is a Jonah* aboard.

SEVERAL *(advancing upon him)* Ay, a man with a hook.

(If he were to withdraw one step their knives would be in him, but he does not flinch)

HOOK *(temporising)* No, lads, no, it is the girl. Never was luck on a pirate ship wi' a woman aboard. We'll right the ship when she has gone.

MULLINS *(lowering his cutlass)* It's worth trying.

HOOK Throw the girl overboard.

MULLINS *(Jeering)* There is none can save you now, missy.

PETER There is one.

MULLINS Who is that?

PETER *(casting off the cloak)* Peter Pan, the avenger!

(He continues standing there to let the effect sink in)

HOOK *(throwing out a suggestion)* Cleave him to the brisket.*

(But he has a sinking that this boy has no brisket)

NOODLER The ship's accurst!

PETER Down, boys, and at them!

(The boys leap from their concealment and the clash of arms resounds through the vessel. Man to man the pirates are the stronger, but they are unnerved by the suddenness of the onslaught and they scatter, thus enabling

their opponents to hunt in couples and choose their quarry. Some are hurled into the lagoon; others are dragged from dark recesses. There is no boy whose weapon is not reeking* save Slightly, who runs about with a lantern, counting, ever counting)

WENDY *(meeting Michael in a moment's lull)* Oh, Michael, stay with me, protect me!

MICHAEL *(reeling)* Wendy, I've killed a pirate!

WENDY It's awful, awful.

MICHAEL No, it isn't, I like it, I like it.

(He casts himself into the group of boys who are encircling Hook. Again and again they close upon him and again and again he hews a clear space)

HOOK Back, back, you mice. It's Hook; do you like him? *(He lifts up Michael with his claw and uses him as a buckler.* A terrible voice breaks in)*

PETER Put up your swords, boys. This man is mine.

(Hook shakes Michael off his claw as if he were a drop of water, and these two antagonists face each other for their final bout. They measure swords at arms' length, make a sweeping motion with them, and bringing the points to the deck rest their hands upon the hilts*)

HOOK *(with curling lip)* So, Pan, this is all your doing!

PETER Ay, Jas Hook, it is all my doing.

HOOK Proud and insolent youth, prepare to meet thy doom.

PETER Dark and sinister man, have at thee.

(Some say that he had to ask Tootles whether the word was sinister or canister.

Hook or Peter this time! They fall to without another word. Peter is a rare swordsman, and parries with dazzling rapidity, sometimes before the other can make his stroke. Hook, if not quite so nimble in wrist play, has the advantage of a yard or two in reach, but though they close he cannot give the quietus* with his claw, which seems to find nothing to tear at. He does not, especially in the most heated moments, quite see Peter, who to his eyes, now blurred or opened clearly for the first time, is less like a boy than a mote of dust dancing in the sun. By some impalpable stroke Hook's sword is whipped from his grasp, and when he stoops to raise it *a little foot is on its blade. There is no deep gash on Hook, but he is suffering torment as from innumerable jags*)*

BOYS *(exulting)* Now, Peter, now!

(Peter raises the sword by its blade, and with an inclination of the head that is perhaps slightly overdone, presents the hilt to his enemy)

HOOK 'Tis some fiend fighting me! Pan, who and what art thou?

(The children listen eagerly for the answer, none quite so eagerly as Wendy)

PETER *(at a venture)* I'm youth, I'm joy, I'm a little bird that has broken out of the egg.

HOOK To't again!

(He has now a damp* feeling that this boy is the weapon which is to strike him from the lists of man; but the grandeur of his mind still holds and, true to the traditions of his flag, he fights on like a human flail. Peter flutters round and through and over these gyrations as if the wind of them blew him out of the danger zone, and again and again he darts in and jags)

HOOK *(stung to madness)* I'll fire the powder magazine.* *(He disappears they know not where)*

CHILDREN Peter, save us!

(Peter, alas, goes the wrong way and Hook returns)

HOOK *(sitting on the hold with gloomy satisfaction)* In two minutes the ship will be blown to pieces.

(They cast themselves before him in entreaty)

CHILDREN Mercy, mercy!

HOOK Back, you pewling* spawn. I'll show you now the road to dusty death.* A holocaust* of children, there is something grand in the idea!

(Peter appears with a smoking bomb in his hand and tosses it overboard. Hook has not really had much hope, and he rushes at his other persecutors with his head down like some exasperated bull in the ring; but with bantering cries they easily elude him by flying among the rigging.

Where is Peter? The incredible boy has apparently forgotten the recent doings, and is sitting on a barrel playing upon his pipes. This may

*surprise others but does not surprise Hook. Lifting a blunderbuss he
strikes forlornly not at the boy but at the barrel, which is hurled across the
deck. Peter remains sitting in the air still playing upon his pipes. At this
sight the great heart of Hook breaks. That not wholly unheroic figure
climbs the bulwarks murmuring 'Floreat Etona,'* and prostrates himself
into the water, where the crocodile is waiting for him openmouthed. Hook
knows the purpose of this yawning cavity, but after what he has gone
through he enters it like one greeting a friend.*

    The curtain rises to show Peter a very Napoleon on his ship. It must
not rise again lest we see him on the poop in Hook's hat and cigars, and
with a small iron claw)*

SCENE 2

THE NURSERY AND THE TREE-TOPS

The old nursery appears again with everything just as it was at the
beginning of the play, except that the kennel has gone and that the
window is standing open. So Peter was wrong about mothers; indeed
there is no subject on which he is so likely to be wrong.

Mrs Darling is asleep on a chair near the window, her eyes tired
with searching the heavens. Nana is stretched out listless on the floor.
She is the cynical one, and though custom has made her hang the
children's night things on the fire-guard for an airing, she surveys
them not hopefully but with some self-contempt.

MRS DARLING *(starting up as if we had whispered to her that her brats
are coming back)* Wendy, John, Michael! *(Nana lifts a sympathetic
paw to the poor soul's lap)* I see you have put their night things out
again, Nana! It touches my heart to watch you do that night after
night. But they will never come back.

    *(In trouble the difference of station can be completely ignored, and it is
not strange to see these two using the same handkerchief. Enter Liza,
who in the gentleness with which the house has been run of late is perhaps a little more masterful than of yore)*

LIZA *(feeling herself degraded by the announcement)* Nana's dinner is
served.

(Nana, who quite understands what are Liza's feelings, departs for the dining-room with an exasperating leisureliness, instead of running, as we would all do if we followed our instincts)

LIZA To think I have a master as have changed places with his dog!

MRS DARLING *(gently)* Out of remorse, Liza.

LIZA *(surely exaggerating)* I am a married woman myself. I don't think it's respectable to go to his office in a kennel, with the street boys running alongside cheering. *(Even this does not rouse her mistress, which may have been the honourable intention)* There, that is the cab fetching him back! *(Amid interested cheers from the street the kennel is conveyed to its old place by a cabby and friend, and Mr Darling scrambles out of it in his office clothes)*

MR DARLING *(giving her his hat loftily)* If you will be so good, Liza. *(The cheering is resumed)* It is very gratifying!

LIZA *(contemptuous)* Lot of little boys.

MR DARLING *(with the new sweetness of one who has sworn never to lose his temper again)* There were several adults to-day.

(She goes off scornfully with the hat and the two men, but he has not a word of reproach for her. It ought to melt us when we see how humbly grateful he is for a kiss from his wife, so much more than he feels he deserves. One may think he is wrong to exchange into the kennel, but sorrow has taught him that he is the kind of man who whatever he does contritely he must do to excess; otherwise he soon abandons doing it)

MRS DARLING *(who has known this for quite a long time)* What sort of a day have you had, George?

(He is sitting on the floor by the kennel)

MR DARLING There were never less than a hundred running round the cab cheering, and when we passed the Stock Exchange the members came out and waved.

(He is exultant but uncertain of himself, and with a word she could dispirit him utterly)

MRS DARLING *(bravely)* I am so proud, George.

MR DARLING *(commendation from the dearest quarter ever going to his head)* I have been put on a picture postcard, dear.

MRS DARLING *(nobly)* Never!

MR DARLING *(thoughtlessly)* Ah, Mary, we should not be such celebrities if the children hadn't flown away.

MRS DARLING *(startled)* George, you are sure you are not enjoying it?

MR DARLING *(anxiously)* Enjoying it! See my punishment: living in a kennel.

MRS DARLING Forgive me, dear one.

MR DARLING It is I who need forgiveness, always I, never you. And now I feel drowsy. *(He retires into the kennel)* Won't you play me to sleep on the nursery piano? And shut that window, Mary dearest; I feel a draught.

MRS DARLING Oh, George, never ask me to do that. The window must always be left open for them, always, always.

(She goes into the day nursery, from which we presently hear her playing the sad song of Margaret.* She little knows that her last remark has been overheard by a boy crouching at the window. He steals into the room accompanied by a ball of light)

PETER Tink, where are you? Quick, close the window. *(It closes)* Bar it. *(The bar slams down)* Now when Wendy comes she will think her mother has barred her out, and she will have to come back to me! *(Tinker Bell sulks)* Now, Tink, you and I must go out by the door. *(Doors, however, are confusing things to those who are used to windows, and he is puzzled when he finds that this one does not open on to the firmament. He tries the other, and sees the piano player)* It is Wendy's mother! *(Tink pops on to his shoulder and they peep together)* She is a pretty lady, but not so pretty as my mother. *(This is a pure guess)* She is making the box say 'Come home, Wendy.' You will never see Wendy again, lady, for the window is barred! *(He flutters about the room joyously like a bird, but has to return to that door)* She has laid her head down on the box. There are two wet things sitting on her eyes. As soon as they go away another two come and sit on her eyes. *(She is heard moaning 'Wendy, Wendy, Wendy'.)* She wants me to unbar the window. I won't! She is awfully fond of Wendy. I am fond of her too. We can't both have her, lady! *(A funny feeling comes over him)* Come on, Tink; we don't want any silly mothers.

(He opens the window and they fly out.

It is thus that the truants find entrance easy when they alight on the sill, John to his credit having the tired Michael on his shoulders. They have nothing else to their credit; no compunction for what they have done, not the tiniest fear that any just person may be awaiting them with a stick. The youngest is in a daze, but the two others are shining virtuously like holy people who are about to give two other people a treat)

MICHAEL *(looking about him)* I think I have been here before.

JOHN It's your home, you stupid.

WENDY There is your old bed, Michael.

MICHAEL I had nearly forgotten.

JOHN I say, the kennel!

WENDY Perhaps Nana is in it.

JOHN *(peering)* There is a man asleep in it.

WENDY *(remembering him by the bald patch)* It's father!

JOHN So it is!

MICHAEL Let me see father. *(Disappointed)* He is not as big as the pirate I killed.

JOHN *(perplexed)* Wendy, surely father didn't use to sleep in the kennel?

WENDY *(with misgivings)* Perhaps we don't remember the old life as well as we thought we did.

JOHN *(chilled)* It is very careless of mother not to be here when we come back.

(The piano is heard again)

WENDY H'sh! *(She goes to the door and peeps)* That is her playing!

(They all have a peep)

MICHAEL Who is that lady?

JOHN H'sh! It's mother.

MICHAEL Then are you not really our mother, Wendy?

WENDY *(with conviction)* Oh dear, it is quite time to be back!

JOHN Let us creep in and put our hands over her eyes.

WENDY *(more considerate)* No, let us break it to her gently.

(She slips between the sheets of her bed; and the others, seeing the idea at once, get into their beds. Then when the music stops they cover their heads. There are now three distinct bumps in the beds. Mrs Darling sees the bumps as soon as she comes in, but she does not believe she sees them)

MRS DARLING I see them in their beds so often in my dreams that I seem still to see them when I am awake! I'll not look again. *(She sits down and turns away her face from the bumps, though of course they are still reflected in her mind)* So often their silver voices call me, my little children whom I'll see no more.

(Silver voices is a good one, especially about John; but the heads pop up)

WENDY *(perhaps rather silvery)* Mother!

MRS DARLING *(without moving)* That is Wendy.

JOHN *(quite gruff)* Mother!

MRS DARLING Now it is John.

MICHAEL *(no better than a squeak)* Mother!

MRS DARLING Now Michael. And when they call I stretch out my arms to them, but they never come, they never come!

(This time, however, they come, and there is joy once more in the Darling household. The little boy who is crouching at the window sees the joke of the bumps in the beds, but cannot understand what all the rest of the fuss is about.

The scene changes from the inside of the house to the outside, and we see Mr Darling romping in at the door, with the lost boys hanging gaily to his coat-tails. So we may conclude that Wendy has told them to wait outside until she explains the situation to her mother, who has then sent

Mr Darling down to tell them that they are adopted. Of course they could have flown in by the window like a covey of birds, but they think it better fun to enter by a door. There is a moment's trouble about Slightly, who somehow gets shut out. Fortunately Liza finds him)

LIZA What is the matter, boy?

SLIGHTLY They have all got a mother except me.

LIZA *(starting back)* Is your name Slightly?

SLIGHTLY Yes'm.

LIZA Then I am your mother.

SLIGHTLY How do you know?

LIZA *(the good-natured creature)* I feel it in my bones.

(They go into the house and there is none happier now than Slightly, unless it be Nana as she passes with the importance of a nurse who will never have another day off. Wendy looks out at the nursery window and sees a friend below, who is hovering in the air knocking off tall hats with his feet. The wearers don't see him. They are too old. You can't see Peter if you are old. They think he is a draught at the corner)

WENDY Peter!

PETER *(looking up casually)* Hullo, Wendy.

(She flies down to him, to the horror of her mother, who rushes to the window)

WENDY *(making a last attempt)* You don't feel you would like to say anything to my parents, Peter, about a very sweet subject?

PETER No, Wendy.

WENDY About me, Peter?

PETER No. *(He gets out his pipes, which she knows is a very bad sign. She appeals with her arms to Mrs Darling, who is probably thinking that these children will all need to be tied to their beds at night)*

MRS DARLING *(from the window)* Peter, where are you? Let me adopt you too.

(She is the loveliest age for a woman, but too old to see Peter clearly)

PETER Would you send me to school?

MRS DARLING *(obligingly)* Yes.

PETER And then to an office?

MRS DARLING I suppose so.

PETER Soon I should be a man?

MRS DARLING Very soon.

PETER *(passionately)* I don't want to go to school and learn solemn things. No one is going to catch me, lady, and make me a man. I want always to be a little boy and to have fun.

(So perhaps he thinks, but it is only his greatest pretend)

MRS DARLING *(shivering every time Wendy pursues him in the air)* Where are you to live, Peter?

PETER In the house we built for Wendy. The fairies are to put it high up among the tree-tops where they sleep at night.

WENDY *(rapturously)* To think of it!

MRS DARLING I thought all the fairies were dead.

WENDY *(almost reprovingly)* No indeed! Their mothers drop the babies into the Never birds' nests, all mixed up with the eggs, and the mauve fairies are boys and the white ones are girls, and there are some colours who don't know what they are. The row the children and the birds make at bath time is positively deafening.

PETER I throw things at them.

WENDY You will be rather lonely in the evenings, Peter.

PETER I shall have Tink.

WENDY *(flying up to the window)* Mother, may I go?

MRS DARLING *(gripping her for ever)* Certainly not. I have got you home again, and I mean to keep you.

WENDY But he does so need a mother.

MRS DARLING So do you, my love.

PETER Oh, all right.

MRS DARLING *(magnanimously)* But, Peter, I shall let her go to you once a year for a week to do your Spring Cleaning.

(Wendy revels in this, but Peter, who has no notion what a Spring Cleaning is, waves a rather careless thanks)

MRS DARLING Say good-night, Wendy.

WENDY I couldn't go down just for a minute?

MRS DARLING No.

WENDY Good-night, Peter!

PETER Good-night, Wendy!

WENDY Peter, you won't forget me, will you, before Spring-Cleaning time comes?

(There is no answer, for he is already soaring high. For a moment after he is gone we still hear the pipes. Mrs Darling closes and bars the window)

We are dreaming now of the Never Land a year later. It is bed-time on the island, and the blind goes up to the whispers of the lovely Never music. The blue haze that makes the wood below magical by day comes up to the tree-tops to sleep, and through it we see numberless nests all lit up, fairies and birds quarrelling for possession, others flying around just for the fun of the thing and perhaps making bets about where the little house will appear to-night. It always comes and snuggles on some tree-top, but you can never be sure which; here it is again, you see John's hat first as up comes the house so softly that it knocks some gossips off their perch. When it has settled comfortably it lights up, and out come Peter and Wendy.

Wendy looks a little older, but Peter is just the same. She is cloaked for a journey, and a sad confession must be made about her; she flies so badly now that she has to use a broomstick.

WENDY *(who knows better this time than to be demonstrative at part-ings)* Well, good-bye, Peter; and remember not to bite your nails.

PETER Good-bye, Wendy.

WENDY   I'll tell mother all about the Spring Cleaning and the house.

PETER   *(who sometimes forgets that she has been here before)* You do like the house?

WENDY   Of course it is small. But most people of our size wouldn't have a house at all. *(She should not have mentioned size, for he has already expressed displeasure at her growth. Another thing, one he has scarcely noticed, though it disturbs her, is that she does not see him quite so clearly now as she used to do)* When you come for me next year, Peter—you will come, won't you?

PETER   Yes. *(Gloating)* To hear stories about me!

WENDY   It is so queer that the stories you like best should be the ones about yourself.

PETER   *(touchy)* Well, then?

WENDY   Fancy your forgetting the lost boys, and even Captain Hook!

PETER   Well, then?

WENDY   I haven't seen Tink this time.

PETER   Who?

WENDY   Oh dear! I suppose it is because you have so many adventures.

PETER   *(relieved)* 'Course it is.

WENDY   If another little girl—if one younger than I am——*(She can't go on)* Oh, Peter, how I wish I could take you up and squdge* you! *(He draws back)* Yes, I know. *(She gets astride her broomstick)* Home! *(It carries her from him over the tree-tops.)*

(In a sort of way he understands what she means by 'Yes, I know,' but in most sorts of ways he doesn't. It has something to do with the riddle of his being. If he could get the hang of the thing his cry might become 'To live would be an awfully big adventure!' but he can never quite get the hang of it, and so no one is as gay as he. With rapturous face he produces his pipes, and the Never birds and the fairies gather closer, till the roof of the little house is so thick with his admirers that some of them fall down the chimney. He plays on and on till we wake up.)

APPENDIX I

'ON THE ACTING OF A FAIRY PLAY' (1904)

1. The difference between a Fairy Play and a realistic one is that in the former all the characters are really children with a child's outlook on life. This applies to the so-called adults of the story as well as to the young people. Pull the beard off the fairy king,* and you would find the face of a child.

2. The actors in a fairy play should feel that it is written by a child in deadly earnestness and that they are children playing it in the same spirit. The scenic artist is another child in league with them.

3. In England the tendency is always to be too elaborate, to over act. This is particularly offensive in a fairy piece, where all should be quick and spontaneous and should seem artless.

4. A very natural desire of the actor is to 'get everything possible out of a line'—to squeeze it dry—to hit the audience a blow with it as from a hammer, instead of making a point lightly and passing on as if unaware that he had made a point. There are many tricks of the stage for increasing this emphasis, and they are especially in favour to strengthen the degraded thing called 'the laugh' which is one of the curses of the English stage. Every time an audience stops a play to guffaw, the illusion of the stage is lost, and the actor has the hard task of creating it again. Don't force the laugh. An audience can enjoy itself without roaring—as the French know.

5. In short, the cumulative effect of *naturalness* is the one thing to aim at. In a fairy play you may have many things to do that are not possible in real life, but you conceive yourself in a world in which they are ordinary occurrences, and act accordingly. Never do anything because there is an audience, but only and entirely because you think this is how the character in that fanciful world would do it.

6. No doubt there should be a certain exaggeration in acting, but just as much as there is in stage scenery, which is exaggerated, not to *be* real but to *seem* real.

J.M.B.

APPENDIX II

J. M. BARRIE'S PRODUCTION NOTES
FOR *PETER PAN* (1908)

PETER PAN, or The Boy Who Would Not Grow Up is a play for children and for 'those who once were children', by an author writing as a child. In our childhood we pretend by day to be pirates and redskins and mothers, and dream such things again by night; but there is also a strange, magical half hour between day and night, between wakefulness and sleep, when the child lies solemn-eyed in bed, and the playing and the dreaming meet in his mind as one, and the world of make-believe becomes real. It is this half hour that this play seeks to recreate. 'Conceive yourself a child again', it says to the 'grown-ups', 'and I will try to bring back to you a little of what you once thought you were, and some of the things you once thought you did. It may make you both laugh and sigh. But you must help me by first journeying back to that half-hour of twilight, where I am writing for you.'

Of Peter himself you must make what you will. Perhaps he was a little boy who died young, and this is how the author conceived his subsequent adventures. Perhaps he was a boy who was never born at all—a boy whom some people wished for, but who never came. It may be that those people hear him at the window more clearly than children do, and he is very elusive. As he says of himself, 'I am youth, I am joy, I am the little bird that has broken out of the egg'. And that is what he means to be for ever and ever; the one thing he is afraid of is 'to grow up and learn solemn things and be a man.' Wendy is simpler; she loves the fireplace; she loves the spirit of adventure; she loves to be 'the little mother'—she loves this so much that she hopes one day she will grow faster than the other little girls. We can take her in our arms and hug her; but try to touch Peter and you will discover that he is untouchable, because he is not there...

APPENDIX III

'WHEN WENDY GREW UP: AN AFTERTHOUGHT' (1908)

CHARACTERS

Peter Pan
Wendy
Jane (her Daughter)
Nana

The Scene is the same nursery, with this slight change—Michael's bed is now where Wendy's was and vice versa, and in front of John's bed, hiding the upper part of it from the audience, is a clothes horse on which depend* (covering it), a little girl's garments to air at the fire. Time early evening. Lights in.*

Wendy emerges from bathroom. She is now a grown-up woman, wearing a pretty dress with train, and she sails forward to fire in an excessively matronly manner. She comes straight to audience, points out to them with pride her long skirt and that her hair is up. Then takes a child's nightgown off fireguard and after pointing it out with rapture to audience exit into bathroom. She comes out with her little daughter Jane, who is in the nightgown. Wendy is drying Jane's hair.

JANE *(naughty)* Won't go to bed, Mummy, won't go to bed!

WENDY *(excessively prim)* Jane! When *I* was a little girl I went to bed the moment I was told. Come at once! *(Jane dodges her and after pursuit is caught.)* Naughtikins! *(sits by fire with Jane on her knee warming toes)* to run your poor old Mother out of breath! When she's not so young as she used to be!

JANE How young used you to be, Mummy?

WENDY Quite young. How time flies!

JANE Does it fly the way you flew when you were a little girl?

WENDY The way I flew. Do you know Darling it is all so long ago. I sometimes wonder whether I ever did really fly.

JANE Yes you did.

WENDY Those dear old days.

JANE Why can't you fly now, Mother?

WENDY Because I'm grown up sweetheart; when people grow up they forget the way.

JANE Why do they forget the way?

WENDY Because they are no longer young and innocent. It is only the young and innocent that can fly.

JANE What is young and innocent? I do wish I were young and innocent! *(Wendy suddenly hugs her)*

WENDY Come to bed, dearest. *(Takes her to bed right, down stage)*

JANE Tell me a story. Tell me about Peter Pan.

WENDY *(standing at foot of bed)* I've told it you so often that I believe you could tell it to me now better than *I* could tell it to you.

JANE *(putting bed clothes round them to suggest a tent)* Go on Mother. This is the Little House. What do you see?

WENDY I see—just this nursery.

JANE But what do you see long ago in it?

WENDY I see—little Wendy in her bed.

JANE Yes, and Uncle Michael here and Uncle John over there.

WENDY Heigh ho! and to think that John has a beard now, and that Michael is an engine driver. Lie down, Petty.*

JANE But do tell me. Tell me that bit—about how you grew up and Peter didn't. Begin where he promised to come for you every year, and take you to the Tree Tops to do his Spring Cleaning. Lucky you!

WENDY Well then! *(now on bed behind Jane)* On the conclusion of the adventures described in our last chapter which left our heroine, Wendy, in her Mummy's arms, she was very quickly packed off to school again—a day school.

JANE And so were all the boys.

WENDY Yes—Mummy adopted them. They were fearfully anxious because John had said to them that, if they didn't fit in, they would all have to be sent to the Dogs' Home.* However they all fitted in, and they went to school in a bus every day, but sometimes they were very naughty, for when the conductor clambered up to collect the fares they flew off, so as not to have to pay their pennies. You should have seen Nana taking them to church. It was like a Collie herding sheep.

JANE Did they ever wish they were back in the Never Never Land?

WENDY *(hesitating)* I—I don't know.

JANE *(with conviction)* *I* know.

WENDY Of course they missed the fun. Even Wendy sometimes couldn't help flying, the littlest thing lifted her up in the air. The sight of a hat blown off a gentleman's head for instance. If it flew off, so did she! So a year passed, and the first Spring Cleaning time came round, when Peter was to come and take her to the Tree Tops.

JANE OO! OO!

WENDY *How* she prepared for him! *How* she sat at that window in her going-away frock—and he came—and away they flew to his Spring Cleaning—and he was exactly the same, and he never noticed that she was any different.

JANE How was she different?

WENDY She had to let the frock down two inches! She was so terrified that he might notice it, for she had promised him never to have growing pains. However, he never noticed, he was so full of lovely talk about himself.

JANE *(gleefully)* He was always awful cocky.

WENDY I think ladies rather love cocky gentlemen.

JANE So do I love them.

WENDY There was one sad thing I noticed. He had forgotten a lot. He had even forgotten Tinker Bell. I think she was no more.

JANE Oh dear!

WENDY You see Darling, a fairy only lives as long a time as a feather is blown about the air on a windy day. But fairies are so little that a short time seems a good while to them. As the feather flutters they have quite an enjoyable life, with time to be born respectably and have a look round, and to dance once and to cry once and to bring up their children—just as one can go a long way quickly in a motor car. And so motor cars help us to understand fairies.

JANE Everybody grows up and dies except Peter, doesn't they?

WENDY Yes, you see he had no sense of time. He thought all the past was just yesterday. He spoke as if it was just yesterday that he and *I* had parted—and it was a whole year.

JANE Oh dearie Dear!

WENDY We had a lovely time, but soon I had to go back home, and another year passed, and Spring Cleaning time came again. And oh the terror of me sitting waiting for him—for I was another two inches round the waist! But he never came. How I cried! Another year passed, and still I got into my little frock somehow, and that year he came—and the strangest thing was that he never knew that he had missed a year. I didn't tell him. I meant to, but I said to him 'What am I to you Peter?' and he said 'You are my mother'—so of course after that I couldn't tell him. But that was the last. Many Spring Cleaning times came round, but never Peter any more. 'Just always be waiting for me' he said, 'and then some time you will hear me crow', but I never heard him crow again. It's just as well Sweetie, for you see he would think all the past was yesterday, and he would expect to find me a little girl still—and that would be too tragic. And now you must sleep. *(Rises)*

JANE I am fearfully awake. Tell me about Nana.

WENDY *(at foot of bed)* Of course I see now that Nana wasn't a *perfect* nurse. She was rather old-fashioned in her ideas—she had too much faith in your stocking round your throat, and so on—and two or three times she became just an ordinary dog, and stayed out so late at night with bad companions that father had to get up at two in the morning in his pyjamas to let her in. But she was so fond of children that her favourite way of spending her afternoons off was to go to Kensington Gardens, and follow careless nurses to their homes and report them to their mistresses. As she's old now I have to coddle her a good deal and that's why we give her John's bed to sleep in. *(Looking left)* Dear Nana! *(Flings kiss to the hidden bed)*

JANE Now tell me about being married in white with a pink sash.

WENDY Most of the boys married their favourite heroines in fiction and Slightly married a lady of title and so he became a lord.*

JANE And one of them married Wendy and so he became my Papa!

WENDY Yes and we bought this house at 3 per cents* from Grand-Papa because he felt the stairs. And Papa is very clever, and knows all about Stocks and Shares. Of course he doesn't really know about them, nobody really knows, but in the mornings when he wakes up fresh he says 'Stocks are up and Shares are down' in a way that makes Mummy very, very proud of him.

JANE Now tell me about *me*.

WENDY At last there came to our heroine a little daughter. I don't know how it is but I just always thought that some day Wendy would have a little daughter.

JANE So did *I*, mother, so did *I*! Tell me what she's like.

WENDY Pen cannot describe her, she would have to be written with a golden splash! *(Hugs her)* That's the end. You *must* sleep.

JANE I am not a bit sleepy.

WENDY *(leaving her)* Hsh!

JANE Mother, I think—*(pause)*

WENDY Well dear, what do you think? *(Pause again—Wendy goes and looks and sees that Jane has suddenly fallen asleep)* Asleep! *(Tucks her in bed, removes the clothes on screen, leisurely, folds and puts them away and then Nana is revealed lying asleep in John's bed beneath the coverlet. She puts down light and sits by fire to sew. Pause—then the night-light over Jane's bed quivers and goes out. Then Peter's crow is heard—Wendy starts up breathless—then the window opens and Peter flies into the room. He is not a day altered. He is gay.* Wendy gasps, sinks back in chair. He sees Nana in bed and is startled. Nana moans, he comes forward avoiding Nana's bed, sees Wendy's dress, thinks she's playing a trick on him)*

PETER *(gaily jumping in front of her)* Hulloh Wendy! *(She turns lamplight away from her)* Thimbles! *(He leaps on to her knee and kisses her)*

WENDY *(not knowing what to do)* Peter! Peter, do you know how long it is since you were here before?

PETER It was yesterday.

WENDY Oh! *(He feels her cheek)*

PETER Why is there wet on your face? *(She can't answer)* I know! It's 'cos you are so glad I've come for you. *(Suddenly remembers Nana—jumps up)* Why is Nana in John's bed?

WENDY *(quivering)* John—doesn't sleep here now.

PETER Oh the cheek! *(Looking carelessly at Jane's bed)* Is Michael asleep?

WENDY *(after hesitating)* Yes. *(Horrified at herself)* That isn't Michael! *(Peter peeps curiously)*

PETER *(going)* Hullo, it's a new one!

WENDY Yes.

PETER Boy or girl?

WENDY Girl.

PETER Do you like her?

WENDY Yes! *(Desperate)* Peter, don't you see whose child she is?

PETER Of course I do. She's your mother's child. I say, I like her too!

WENDY *(crying)* Why?

PETER 'Cos now your mother can let you stay longer with me for Spring Cleaning. *(Agony of Wendy)*

WENDY Peter. I—I have something to tell you.

PETER *(running to her gaily)* Is it a secret?

WENDY Oh! Peter, when Captain Hook carried us away—

PETER Who's Captain Hook? Is it a story? Tell it me.

WENDY *(aghast)* Do you mean to say you've even forgotten Captain Hook, and how you killed him and saved all our lives?

PETER *(fidgeting)* I forget them after I kill them.

WENDY Oh, Peter, you forget everything!

PETER Everything except mother Wendy. *(Hugs her)*

WENDY Oh!

PETER Come on Wendy.

WENDY *(miserably)* Where to?

PETER To the Little House. *(A little strong)* Have you forgotten it is Spring Cleaning time—it's you that forgets.

WENDY Peter, Peter! By this time the little house must have rotted all away.

PETER So it has, but there are new ones, even littler.

WENDY Did you build them yourself?

PETER Oh no, I just found them. You see the little house was a Mother and it has young ones.

WENDY You sweet.

PETER So come on. *(Pulling her)* I'm Captain.

WENDY I can't come, Peter—I have forgotten how to fly.

PETER I'll soon teach you again. *(Blows fairy dust on her)*

WENDY Peter, Peter, you are wasting the fairy dust.

PETER *(at last alarmed)* What is it, Wendy? Is something wrong? Don't cheat me mother Wendy—I'm only a little boy.

WENDY I can't come with you, Peter—because I'm no longer young and innocent.

PETER *(with a cry)* Yes you are.

WENDY I'm going to turn up the light, and then you will see for yourself.

PETER *(frightened—hastily)* Wendy, don't turn up the light.

WENDY Yes. But first I want to say to you for the last time something I said often and often in the dear Never Never Land. Peter, what are your exact feelings for me?

PETER Those of a devoted son, Wendy. *(Silently she lets her hand play with his hair—she caresses his face, smiling through her tears—then she turns lamp up near the fire and faces him—a bewildered understanding comes to him—she puts out her arms—but he shrinks back)* What is it? What is it?

WENDY Peter, I'm grown up—I couldn't help it! *(He backs again)* I'm a married woman Peter—and that little girl is my baby.

PETER *(after pause—fiercely)* What does she call you?

WENDY *(softly, after pause)* Mother.

PETER Mother! *(He takes step towards child with a little dagger in his hand upraised, then is about to fly away, then flings self on floor and sobs)*

WENDY Peter, Peter! Oh! *(Knows not what to do, rushes in agony from the room—long pause in which nothing is heard but Peter's sobs. Nana is restless. Peter is on the same spot as when crying about Shadow in Act 1. Presently his sobbing wakes Jane. She sits up)*

JANE Boy, why are you crying?

(Peter rises—they bow as in Act 1)

JANE What's your name?

PETER Peter Pan.

JANE I just thought it would be you.

PETER I came for my mother to take her to the Never Never Land to do my Spring Cleaning.

JANE   Yes I know, I've been waiting for you.

PETER   Will *you* be my mother?

JANE   Oh, yes. *(Simply)*

(She gets out of bed and stands beside him, arms round him in a child's conception of a mother—Peter very happy. The lamp flickers* and goes out as night-light did)

PETER   I hear Wendy coming—Hide!

(They hide. Then Peter is seen teaching Jane to fly. They are very gay. Wendy enters and stands right, taking in situation and much more. They don't see her)

PETER   Hooray! Hooray!

JANE   *(flying)* Oh! Lucky me!

PETER   And you'll come with me?

JANE   If Mummy says I may.

WENDY   Oh!

JANE   May I, Mummy?

WENDY   May I come too?

PETER   You can't fly.

JANE   It's just for a week.

PETER   And I do so need a mother.

WENDY   *(nobly yielding)* Yes my love, you may go. *(Kisses and squeals of rapture, Wendy puts slippers and cloak on Jane and suddenly Peter and Jane fly out hand in hand right into the night, Wendy waving to them—Nana wakens, rises, is weak on legs, barks feebly—Wendy comes and gets on her knees beside Nana)*

WENDY   Don't be anxious Nana. This is how I planned it if he ever came back. Every Spring Cleaning, except when he forgets, I'll let Jane fly away with him to the darling Never Never Land, and when she grows up I will hope *she* will have a little daughter, who will fly away with him in turn—and in this way may I go on for ever and ever, dear Nana, so long as children are young and innocent.

(Gradual darkness—then two little lights seen moving slowly through heavens)

CURTAIN

APPENDIX IV

'THE BLOT ON PETER PAN' (1926)

I HAD been asked to keep them quiet for an hour, as it was a wet day. 'Well, then, you four shrimps,' says I, 'once upon a time I was asked by some children to tell them what is the Blot on Peter Pan. Then once upon another time the children of those children asked me to tell them what is the Blot on Peter Pan. Is that clear? Then, this brings us to to-day; but still I don't see why I should tell you what is the Blot, when I have so long kept it secret.'

'Because you love us,' suggested Billy.

'No, no, Billy,' said I, annoyed at being caught out, 'there can be no love without respect. Jane, either put your shoe definitely on or take it definitely off. Lay down those matches, Sammy. Sara dear, get off my knee; surely you know by this time that I see through your cheap blandishments. I wish you children had not such leery faces, but I suppose it is your natural expression.'

'Peter is rather a leery one,' said Sammy.

'You have found that out, have you? Well, when I made him up he was the noble youth I should like you to be, though I have given up hoping. He would have scorned then to brag to that girl whom he took with him to his island, and he was always obedient, polite and good.'

'What changed him?'

'I did, Sara, because I had become a cynic.'

'What is a sinsik?'

Here I got in the deadliest thing I have said for years. 'A cynic,' says I, 'is a person who has dealings with children.'

'What made you a sinsik?'

'It was a boy called Neil.'*

'I don't know any Neil,' said Billy.

'You could not have known this boy, he was born so long before you.'

'I daresay I could have licked* him,' said Billy.

'Before you were born?'

'Well, if he had waited.'

'You could not have licked him in any case,' I said rather hotly. 'No one of his age could have stood up to that boy. He was a wonder.'

'So you were fond of him?'

'On the contrary, this story is to be the exposure of him.'

'Funny way to begin,' muttered Billy. 'How old was he?'

'At the time he did for me he was seventeen hundred days* old.'

Sammy whistled.

'That may seem old to the more backward of you,' I explained, 'but those who have got out of beads into real counting should be able to discover his age with a pencil. If any of you has got out of pencil into ink you should be able to do it with a pen.'

Jane was the quickest to work it out (with a pencil), and she found that Neil at that time was the same age as Sara is now, which made Sara simper.

'Before we come, however,' I continued, 'to the advanced age at which Neil laid me out, there is a reason why I should describe his christening, for if it had been a different kind of christening, P. Pan would be a different kind of boy. In the thirty days or so before you are christened it scarcely matters whether you are good or bad, because in the eyes of the law you are only a bundle without a name, or such name as you have is written thus — — which is easy to write but more difficult to pronounce. A boy called Mr. Macaulay* remembered the day he was born, but if you are only ordinarily nippy you get a pass by remembering your christening. Neil could not remember even raising his head at the christening to catch what his name was.'

'I remember raising mine,' said Billy.

'Neil, however, remembered something of far greater class,' I said haughtily; 'he remembered seeing the fairy godmothers sitting on the rim of the font.'

At this there were exclamations, Billy's being the most offensive.

'I had his word for it,' I said.

'But if you had only my word for it——' Billy began and stopped, so we shall never know what he was going to say.

'Did you see them?' asked Jane, speaking like a needle.

'I wasn't there.'

'Weren't you invited?'

'Certainly I was invited; I was Neil's godfather. But when the time came round I could not remember what a godfather wears at christenings.'

'I wouldn't have let that keep me away,' said Sammy.

'You would have risked going in the wrong waistcoat!' I shrieked. 'No, I consulted the best books of reference—fairy tales, of course—and I made the extraordinary discovery that all a godfather does at a christening is to stay away. Though these books are full of godmothers there is not a single godfather in them. I offer a shilling for every fairy godfather you can produce.'

They made a brief search in the books (during which I had rather an anxious time), but not a godfather could they find.

'So I bit my lips,' I told them, 'and stayed away. Among the early arrivals at Neil's christening were the clergyman and the parents and — — himself; and then came the usual rabble of fairy godmothers, who took up their places in a circle on the rim of the font.'

'So they were really there?'
'So Neil did see them.'
'Did the clergyman see them?'
'He is so used to them that if they behave he scarcely looks. If they misbehave he wipes them off the rim with his sleeve. But I don't blame you, Billy, for not having seen them at your christening. They cannot be seen clearly now-a-days because of a shocking thing that happens at their own christenings. An ogre who hates them and is called Science——'
'Why does Sams hate them?'
'Sams is a better name for him. He hates them because they prevent children from joining in the forward movement.'
'Golly, what's that?'
'It is Progress. The fairies see to it that the newly-born of to-day are not a whit more advanced than their predecessors, and so the latest child is just as likely as the first one (dear little Cain*) to ask a poser that has never been asked before. As a result Sams naturally hates the fairies, and he goes to their christenings and tries to rub them out. Don't cry, Sara, he doesn't entirely rub them out; he leaves quite a pretty blur. He also rubs away at their voices, which in consequence have become very faint. If Sara doesn't stop crying I shall stop the story.
'The christening seemed to those present to be quite uneventful. First the clergyman did his dipping and said, "I name this child Neil, and if anyone objects let him for ever after hold his peace." Then the fairy godmothers gave their gifts, qualities such as Beauty, each at the same time copying the clergyman (for they are very imitative) and letting fall one drop of water on Neil's face, always aiming (if I know anything about them) at the eye. The people then went home to rejoice with sandwiches, thinking all was well.'
'And wasn't it?'
'Alas, as the years revolved (which they do because the earth is round) we discovered that the fairies had made a mess of things. What do fairy godmothers usually do at a christening? You know the stories better than I do.'
'All the godmothers are good,' Jane said, 'except one whom the parents forget to invite, so she comes in a rage and mischiefs the child.'
'Exactly, Jane. And it does seem rather dense of parents. One would think that there must have been here and there in the history of the ages a father and mother who learned from the wrecks around them to send an invitation to the bad fairy. Nevertheless, we must admit that she performs in her imperfect way a public function, for if you were entirely good there would be no story in you; and the fairies are so fond of stories that they call giving you one bad quality "Putting in the story."

'I daresay the good godmothers meant to do the right thing by Neil, but on their way to the church there was a block, and the bad one overtook them, and was so impertinent to the policeman that he put her in his pocket, meaning to report her later. This flustered the others, and they got separated. Some of them were not heard of again till they were quite old (they get old by night-time) and several swopped qualities with other godmothers and went to the wrong church and gave Neil's gifts to the wrong child. Oddly enough (not at all) his one valuable quality came from his bad-godmother, who had been released with a caution and arrived at the church in a chastened spirit.

'The qualities implanted in Neil by the godmothers who should have been good were:

The Quality of Beauty
The Quality of Showing Off
The Quality of Sharp Practice
The Quality of Copy Cat
The Quality of Dishing* his Godfather.

'Of course you are all wanting to know what was the bad godmother's gift; but wait, wait. As you will soon hear, P. Pan knows.

'We quickly discovered that Beauty was one of Neil's gifts, but we never guessed at the others till he was seventeen hundred. Let us now blow ourselves out* for a moment and compare the parents of past and present in relation to their offspring. The parents of long ago had a far easier time than the parents of to-day, for they could hear the godmothers announcing the child's future, and so knew for certain what he would grow into, and that nothing could possibly harm him until, say, he plucked a blue rose, when he would be neatly done for. They had no responsibilities, scarcely needed to send him to school——'

'By gum!' exclaimed Billy.

'——and could smile placidly when he swallowed father's watch or came out in spots. How different is the position of the parents of to-day, who cannot hear the fairies' words, and therefore can only guess at the gifts which have been given. They don't know what quality, good or bad, is to pop out of you presently, but they watch for it unceasingly, ready to water it or to grub it up. Thus children who were certainties in the old times have now become riddles. You, O Sara, though outwardly agreeable if somewhat too round, are still only a riddle to your mother. The one sure thing she knows about you is that there you are. Don't cry, Sara.

'Ah me, we guessed very wrongly about Neil. His parents did not extol him in public, but visitors who were equally reticent were not asked back. We thought his gifts were Sweetness, Modesty, Goodness and Blazing Intelligence. We even believed, Heaven help us, that he had Moral Grandeur.

Not being able to find a bad godmother's handiwork in him we concluded that the noble little Neil had bitten it in the bud.'

'Like I bit off that wart,' volunteered Billy, much interested.

'Don't be nasty, Billy, at a time like this,' said Jane, obviously his sister.

I thanked Jane and continued. 'To be present at Neil's brushing of his teeth when in his fifteen hundreds was regarded as a treat; he looked at you over the brush as he did it to see whether you were amazed, and you were. On his first day at school he returned home with a prize. He seemed to like me best. *Always to do the same what godfather does* was a motto he invented, and I little understood its fell significance. Is it any wonder that I was deceived? We now come to the fatal seventeen hundredth day, which was also the day of the production of Peter Pan.'

A shiversome silence fell upon the room, and Sara was hanging on to my leg. 'Give me air!' I cried hoarsely.

They were all very sorry for me. 'What a beast of a fellow Neil must have been!' Billy shouted.

'None of that!' says I sternly.

'There you go, sticking up for him again.'

'The next one who interrupts unnecessarily,' I said, 'I shall ask to spell "unnecessarily." The original performance of Peter Pan was not given in a theatre, but in a country house, and then only the first two acts, the acts that made so small an impression on you, Billy my boy.'

This was a deserved sneer at Billy who, on being asked in the theatre at the end of the second act how he was enjoying Peter Pan, had replied that what he liked best was tearing up the programme and dropping the bits on people's heads.*

'Not so silly as Sara, at any rate,' Billy growled, and then it was Sara's turn to look abashed. Before the performance I had taken her to a restaurant and discovered later that she thought the meal was Peter Pan. For such persons do great minds stoop to folly.*

'The performers were incompetent little amateurs like yourselves, but owing to his youth and other infirmities Neil was not one of the company, to which indignity he was at first indifferent, but a change came over him when he discovered that acting was a way of showing off. He then demonstrated for a part with unmanly clamour, and one of the mistakes of my life was in not yielding to him. I let him, instead, sit beside me and watch my interesting way of conducting rehearsals. Soon he was betraying an unhealthy interest in the proceedings. He could not read nor write nor spell, though he did know his letters, but after seeing a few rehearsals he could have taken my place as producer had I had the luck to fall ill and be put to bed with a gargle.

'At this time there were thunder and galloping horses and the sound of the sea in Peter Pan, though I cut them out after the performance in that house for reasons which will soon be obvious to the dullest of you. I am not sure which of you that is. As soon as Neil saw and heard those marvellous imitations they went straight to his temperature and his eyes glared and he had to be given a powder. Our thunder was made with a sheet of tin, and our galloping horses were two halves of a cocoa-nut rubbed together, and our sea was sago rolled up and down in a tray. Neil daily cut himself on the thunder, bleeding disgustingly, and every night the sago had to be plucked out of him like ticks. His nurse, whom I shall always suspect, despite her denials, of having been his red-handed accomplice in the affair of the seventeen hundredth day, told me that it was no longer an actor that he wanted to be but an author and producer like his godfather.

' "In his sleep," she said, "he writes plays in the air and calls out 'Speak my words and not your own, dash you!' just as you do, sir, at rehearsals, and I have to give him the dictionary to hug in bed instead of his golly-wog,* because he saw you getting the words out of it. If that innocent could spell."

'I admitted that spelling is the dramatist's big difficulty, but could not see how Neil was to get round it.

' "If he doesn't it will be the first thing he hasn't got round," she said darkly, so darkly that I should have taken heed.

'Well, ladies and gentlemen, the night of the performance came round. It wasn't really night, but we helped night along by pulling down the blinds and turning up the lights. All the chairs and sofas and tables and even the mantelpiece were occupied by the public, who had first been filled to repletion with cake and cyder so as to take away their faculties. I was not present myself. I was walking up and down in the garden, listening for approving sounds and gnawing my moustache.

'Out there in the garden I could not hear the words, but I could hear the thunder and the galloping of the horses and the lonely lash of the sea; and, my dear Sara, I could hear the extraordinarily sweet music that is made by the ecstatic clapping of hands. I had not expected much enthusiasm so promptly, because, as you all have often pointed out, Peter Pan opens rather quietly.'

'I expect,' says Billy, meaning no offence, 'they were cheering the cocoa-nuts. Was it really like horses?'

'Far more like than horses are. Well, the applause was so prodigious that I felt it would be churlish to delay any longer giving the audience a sight of me, so I slipped in among them. What I saw I wish to describe to you in the simplest words and with as little emotion as possible, for, after all, it happened many years ago. Still, hold my hand, Sara.

'The first thing I noticed was that the curtain was down though the play had been in progress for but a dozen minutes. Simultaneously I knew that the air was being rent with cries for "Author! author!" I must confess that for the moment I presumed my success to be so epoch-making that the prompter, bowing to the popular will, had taken the unusual step of deciding to present me to my kind friends in front in the middle of the first act.

'Speedily I was undeceived. "They can't have come to the end of the first act yet," I whispered to a neighbour, who happily did not know me.

'"It was all in one act," he explained, "and just lasted a few minutes, but they were glorious minutes, author! author!"

'"Are you speaking about Peter Pan?" I asked with the strangest sinking.

'"No, no," he said, "we haven't come to that yet. This is the curtain-raiser that astonishing little chap has written, author author, author, author."

'Then the curtain went up and Neil came forward in his kilt and made his bow amid a hurricane of idolatry. Made his bow is indeed an inadequate way of expressing it. There was not about him a vestige of the affected modesty that at such a moment so well becomes an author. He carried a toy gun and strutted up and down the stage, leering shockingly and stopping occasionally to join in the applause. I scorn to tell the calls he got. When the audience's hands were benumbed he came on again and again without being called, and in the end he had to be carried off the stage kicking.'

'But he hadn't really written it,' my listeners exclaimed incredulously; 'you said he could neither write nor spell.'

'But I said he knew his letters, Billy. A miracle had happened. The boy who was unable to read, write or spell on Monday was a dab at them all by Tuesday. You may say "Oh, rot!" but it is true. Give me the pencil and I'll show you.'

MACCD

MNO

OSAR

'This was a problem in three lines and a glass bowl that I had given to some youthful onlookers at that luckless Monday's rehearsal and it stumped them as it had stumped me when propounded to me once by a friend. I see it also stumps you, but debase yourselves sufficiently and you will find it reads:

Emma sees de Goldfish

'Em no goldfish,

Oh ess A are Goldfish

'You follow? I agree with you that 'tis but a tiny joke, and at once it passed out of all our minds save one. That mind was the awful mind of Neil.

Though none was in the secret but his Nannie it was suddenly revealed to him how plays are written; quick as a lucky one may jump through a paper hoop and come out on the other side a clown, he had gained access through that friend of mine to a language which he could read, write and spell. With thrills that would have bitten through any thermometer, and bagging that bowl of goldfish, he evolved a powerful drama, and he wrote it in ink; he jumped, Sammy, over Beads and Pencil straight into Ink; indeed, for days, though I suspected naught, his right hand seemed to be encased in a torn black mitten. So far as I can recollect, this is an accurate reproduction of his MS., all of it out of his own noddle except the first three lines:

MACCD

MNO

OSAR

LMECD

LNINOCD

MAYUNOCD

MNO

R

OOOUiiiiI8D

OG

U8MUI

SSS

OUINTK8

YU8MUNTK8YYY

OLNUCIMTNICMNI8M4T

4RTLRDI

4IDINTFS

LOLOLO

NTK88MLRDI

LOLOLO

LMEDI

B4UDISA99

9999

ICD

NICD

SNICD

'Can you stagger your way through it, Jane? Probably not, and yet the audience understood every word, the acting makes such a difference. I heard also that Neil was a superbly severe stage-manager, copying with relish all my ways, including my expletives. He did not act himself (because the other author did not act); but from the wings he worked the thunder and the sea and the horses. The scene was laid in the Peter Pan nursery, thus taking all the novelty out of it. As presented by some of his young friends this was how his play came to life:'

[SCENE—*a nursery with beds in it. Then a tremendous peal of thunder ending in a clatter as if someone had dropped the sheet of tin. Then the galloping of a horse. Then* ENTER EMMA, *the horse-woman, without her horse. She examines critically a glass bowl full of water. Then so much galloping that it seems as if the play can make no further progress. Then* ENTER SUSAN, ELLEN *and* TOM. TOM *is riding on a dog called Nana*].

ELLEN. [*Fondly expectant of a similar treat for herself*] Emma sees de Goldfish.

SUSAN. [*Sneering*]. 'Em no Goldfish.

ELLEN. Oh, ess A are Goldfish.

TOM. [*Riding forward*] Lemme see de Goldfish.

EMMA. [*Breaking it to them sadly*] Ellen, I no see de Goldfish.

SUSAN. [*Fearing the worst*] Emma, why you no see de Goldfish?

EMMA. [*Indicating two breadcrumbs which are the sole occupants of the water*] 'Em no Goldfish.

TOM. [*A defender of the weak*] Are Goldfish.

[*There is more thunder, a horse is heard approaching and* AUNT KATE ENTERS *with a guilty conscience. One glance around shows her that they are on her track. With bowed head, for she is not wholly bad, she makes her dreadful confession*].

AUNT KATE. Oh, oh, oh, you four little ones, I ate de Goldfish. [*They draw away from her*].

TOM. [*Expressing the general feeling*] Oh, gee.

EMMA. [*Gasping like a Goldfish*] You ate 'em, you big one?

AUNT KATE. [*Covering her face*] Ess, ess, ess.

SUSAN. Oh, you bad one, Auntie Kate.

ELLEN. [*Giving her a last chance*] Why you ate 'em, you Auntie Kate, why, why, why?

AUNT KATE. [*Broken*] Oh, Ellen, you see I empty 'n I see 'em n I ate 'em for tea.

TOM. [*With a withering cry*] For 'er tea. [*Sternly*] Le 'er die.

[*Terrific thunder here to intimate that sentence has been pronounced, followed by the break of the surf on some lonely shore to express the helplessness of the goldfish*].

AUNT KATE. [*Waiting patiently for these noises to cease*] 'Fore I die 'ant to confess.

[*At this dark moment a horse's hoofs are heard.* ENTER A DOCTOR].

DOCTOR. [*Taking in the situation at a glance*] Hello, hello, hello.

EMMA. [*Coldly*] Auntie Kate ate 'em. Le 'er die.

DOCTOR. [*A man of few words*] Hello, hello, hello.

AUNT KATE. [*Getting into the papers at last*] Lemme die.

DOCTOR. [*Putting his stethoscope to the erring woman's mouth and pushing her head over the bowl*] Before you die, say 99.

AUNT KATE. [*Without much hope*] 99, 99.

[*A wondrous thing happens: the goldfish swim down the stethoscope into the bowl*].

EMMA. I see de goldfish.

ELLEN. 'n I see de goldfish.

TOM. Ess, 'n I see de goldfish.

[*All are again riotously happy, but none perhaps quite so happy as the goldfish. The* DOCTOR *marries* AUNT KATE. *The curtain falls and rises, with an enlarged copy of* NEIL'S *MS. pinned to it. The audience spell it out and learn how the play was written. The enthusiasm is now louder than the thunder*].

'In the meantime, of course, Billy, my play had gone to pot.'*

'Didn't they act it?' he asked with cheerful brutality.

'Oh yes, they played it, and it was received with mild approval. What they seemed to admire far more, however, was Neil's cleverness in prigging so much from me. At every fresh proof of this they guffawed crudely.'

'Did you wallop him?' asked Billy, whose thoughts frequently run in this direction.

'Ah me, I was deprived of that gratification, because, you see, Neil was unconscious of evil-doing, he had kept his play a secret from me in order to give me a lovely surprise, and he came running to me for praise. *Always to do the same what godfather does*, you remember. I was unfortunately his favourite, and he was so confident of my praise, whoever else might fail him. One may rob or kill, Billy my boy, and yet not be so hard-hearted as to destroy the confidence of a child.'

'You don't mean to say you praised him?'

'I had to be civil to him.'

'It looks to me as if instead of hating him you were just beastly fond of him.'

'That's right, Billy,' says I, 'strike a man while he's down. No doubt I should have taken some of the stuffing out of Neil next day, but another misfortune happened then; mumps or measles, or some other trick of childhood jumped out of the box, and I had to rush him away from infection.'

'Couldn't his father and mother have took him?' asked Jane, who has sometimes a tendency to pertness.

'You don't any of you understand the law about godfathers,' I explained with infinite patience. 'I took Neil to a country inn. Of course I would not have taken him if I hadn't thought I could trust to his honour.'

'What was he up to this time?' enquired Billy, licking his lips.

'He was so fond,' I said, 'of his thunder and horses and hoary ocean that he would not be parted from them, and, to my horror, I found them in his box when I unpacked at the inn. I was in such a fury that I nearly threw them into the road.'

'Why didn't you?'

'That foolish question just shows, Billy, how little thought you have given to the position of a gentleman left alone in a country inn, with a boy who refuses to undress without the accompaniment of thunder and the galloping of horses. I couldn't undress him; his garments were so unexpected. What was worse, nothing could lull him to sleep but the break of waves upon some desolate shore. I had to use a drawer from the wardrobe to roll the sago in, and a heavy drawer it was. Once at breakfast in the inn I heard a man at the next table telling a lady that, though we were so far inland, he had distinctly heard the sound of the sea from his bedroom. I was afraid there might be an inquiry, so of nights, when Neil was at last asleep, I spent æons of time searching the cracks in the drawer for sago, before I could get to work on Peter Pan.'

'What were you doing to Peter?'

'In the burglarious* silence I was altering him, making him more like Neil.'

'Gosh.'

'You may well use that terrible word, Billy; but it was evident that Neil was the kind of boy the public wants. I see that the weather has cleared, so I now release you, begging you to reflect at your leisure on the not untragic picture of an author who wanted to do better but had to give in to circumstances. To save the life of my young hero I was compelled to abstract the humility from him and thus make room for the bad fairy's gift with which Neil had witched humanity. The boy who doesn't have it might as well be a man.'

'Oh, do tell us what it is!' they cried, knowing quite well, but wondering whether an adult had found out.

'Of course it is Cockiness,' I answered. 'One must admit, Billy (however reluctantly), that there is to children a rapture in being cocky which is what keeps this old world smiling.'

They leered.

'And is cockiness the Blot on Peter Pan?' asks Billy.

'Alas,' said I.

'But you gave it to him. Hello, are you Peter's bad fairy?'

I hung my head. Sara at any rate felt for me.

'And when you were blotting Peter was Neil lying asleep in his bed?' she enquired.

'Sometimes in his bed, Sara, and sometimes in the drawer, dreaming children's plays that were far beyond my compass.'

They thanked me primly for my story, as instructed by their wretched mothers, and then all scooted away into the open except Sara. Sara is the very last baggage I shall bother with.

'Is it all true?' she asked.

'No, it is not all true, Sara, but some of it, here and there.'

'Do you love me?'

'Yes, Sara.'

'But you love Neil more, don't you?'

'A hundred thousand million times more, Sara.'

'Is he a man now?'

'No, he is not a man.'

'Where is he?'

'Be off with you into the sunshine, Sara, and bring me some butter-cups at one o'clock. I bet you'll forget.'

'I bet I won't.'

She very nearly forgot, but she ran back for them.

APPENDIX V

'CAPTAIN HOOK AT ETON:*
A STRANGE STORY' (1927)

THIS talk with you arises out of a sort of challenge from the Provost.*
I was here this year on June 4, and in a speech at luncheon the Provost
challenged me to disprove this terrible indictment, 'James Hook, the pirate
captain, was a great Etonian but not a good one.' Now in my opinion Hook
was a good Etonian though not a great one, and it is my more or less
passionate desire to persuade you of this—to have Hook, so to speak,
sent up for good—that brings me here this afternoon in spite of my
better judgment.

To prove my case I have of late been trying to collect facts regarding
Hook's early days, and it must be admitted that he is an Old Boy about
whom Eton has preserved few traditions. We should not even know that he
had been an Etonian but for the statement 'Eton and Balliol'* in a work
that is probably largely unreliable. On the same doubtful authority we learn
that his last words were 'Floreat Etona.'*

Concerning Hook at Balliol, I have pursued few inquiries, feeling
that Eton is more important. He was certainly in residence there for
several terms, and we know that he borrowed from the library a number
of books, all of them, oddly enough, poetry and mostly of the Lake
school.* These volumes may still be occasionally picked up at second-
hand bookstalls, with the name 'Jacobus Hook' inserted as the owner.
Thus his mind was already turning to the classics. Athletically I find
that he was not specially notable at Balliol, but there is a curious record
that when hurt on the football field he 'bled yellow.' His best sporting
performance seems to have been that he was 12th man in the College
100 yards.* Like so many subsequently famous he left Oxford one
morning.

A dry bob youth

At Eton he was a dry bob,* contrary to what one might have expected, as
his future was to be on the sea, but, boy or man, he hated the touch of
water, and he was always the last to leave his ship. He won many colours at
Eton—he had many colours.* His Aunt Emily, whom I succeeded in
tracing, showed me three of his caps hanging very honourably over her
mantelshelf. Being an outsider I don't know what they stand for, but you
will know—one was red and blue, a second was claret and blue, and the
other was all pale blue.* She told me that he had got them specially made at

a little place in the city. Again, I have proof that in his last year at school he was a member of what is perhaps the most exalted assemblage in the world—the Eton Society, or Pop. This society consists of the 30 or so leading persons in the school, who are chosen entirely on account of their mental equipment. The Pops are the chief sight of Eton, and parade on great occasions in sock and spat,* arms linked, six or eight abreast, and two yards in front of the Sun and Moon.* Legend (always untrustworthy) says that Hook's election was a great surprise to the other members, who alone have the right of voting, and that James must have manipulated the ballot-box. But even if so, what ardour to excel, how indomitable is the particle, man. The page in the books of the Society recording his election has been mysteriously destroyed, and for some time I suspected that this could be explained in only one of two ways—either the authorities did it because they thought his subsequent career (meteoric as it was) reflected (on the whole) no credit on the school, or the dilapidations were made by autograph hunters. I have since discovered the true explanation, surely one of the most sombre, yet glorious, tales in the history of Eton. Of that night I will tell you anon and make, in so doing, I hope, a triumphant reply to the Provost, who can hardly grudge this tardy rehabilitation of his old fag-master.*

I hear you asking impatiently what were Hook's intellectual attainments. Here we are on firm ground; he was in the First Hundred.* He also contributed to one of the journals of original matter known locally (one wonders why) as Ephemerals.* His contribution which I have heard is entitled 'A Dissertation upon Roast Pig' and seems to me to have merit, but for some unexplained reason his tutor interfered to prevent his being paid for it. Here is a discovery, which must move those of you who have not hearts of flint, if any such there be. After the fatal affair, culminating in James's decease, a search made in the cabinet of his floating hulks brought to light that throughout the years of his piracy he had been a faithful subscriber to the *Eton Chronicle*.* Hundreds of copies of it, much thumb-marked, were found littering his bunk.

Appearance and manners

Of James's personal appearance and manner when at Eton I have contradictory accounts. According to his Aunt Emily he was a sweetly pretty boy and pious, with much of the courtliness that afterwards so struck his victims on the high seas while he was prodding them along the plank. The soul of honour, she said also, and so sensitive that she urged the powers that be not to cane James but to cane some adjacent piece of furniture, which had the same effect on the parts of the impressionable boy. This advice was not followed, and she feels that the harsher treatment fretted his dark spirit.

The few of his contemporaries whom I have had the privilege of consulting were impressed less favourably. They admit an air of cheap distinction, of which he seems to have been pleasantly conscious. But chiefly they recall a gluttonous boy. 'He oozed so unpleasantly through his clothes,' writes one, 'that in the Wall game* if you pushed him against the wall you smeared it with him.' Others dwell on that blood of his, which they describe as 'yellow after the colour has gone out of it.' This blood, I am informed, saved him many lammings from the head of the house, who, though Keeper of the Fives,* fainted at first sight of it—as James knew and bragged about it. When in want of funds he used to cut himself slightly for threepence and considerably for a strawberry mess.* This shows that he was not without admirers. His piety, say his detractors, was merely that he prayed unctuously not to be found out in certain nefarious transactions. The boy, in short, was 'temperamental.'

I tried in vain to get a photograph of Hook as a boy. Those of you who have been to Eton know that boys there, until they have cheque-books of their own, when their characters entirely change, have themselves so much photographed in their hats that the cost must be equal to the rent of a cottage in the country. I wrote to various masters for a picture of James, saying I knew it was customary for boys on leaving to bequeath a selection of their photographs to their tutor and hazarding the belief that when the time came for the tutor to leave he did not take the photographs with him but left them behind in sacks for his fortunate successor. I was told that this was far from being the case; but unfortunately the news of my quest leaked out among the scugs*—the scugs who are the curse of Eton, getting in every person's way—and a number of them—seeking a momentary prominence—sent me their own photographs, signed, 'Yours truly, Jas. Hook.'

We now come to that night which I have been leading up to. It deals with his astounding last visit to Eton, and my chief informant is Mr. G. F. T. Jasparin. Mr Jasparin is one of those much respected Etonians whom love for their old school has gently paralysed. Instead of adopting some profession when they leave the university they return to the pleasant little town of Windsor, which lies under the shadow of Eton, and settle down there, having no connexion with the school except a memory, but trying to believe that they are still happy little scugs. They have a club called The Buttery (formerly Jordan's*), and are perhaps one of the most inoffensive of all exclusive coteries.

Mr Jasparin's adventure

Mr Jasparin writes me that on that night he was walking to the club in Keate's-lane from his lodging in Windsor (which he has furnished exactly like an Eton room, with a picture of a huntsman falling into a stream, a folding bed, and a hat-box for the surreptitious concealment of coal). He was in a dejected mood because it was past the lock-up hour, and he had still, alas! the right to be at large. I shall try to quote his words.

'The street,' he wrote, 'seemed to be deserted, but as I approached the passage leading to the present rooms of the Eton Society, I was conscious of a shadowy figure sitting motionless on the college wall, the low wall on which none may sit save Pops. In a moment, incredible as it may seem, I knew that I was in the presence of Jas. Hook. I had never before seen him in the flesh—and indeed, I know now that "the flesh" is an inadequate term for this man's earthly tenement. He was dressed in modern fashion in the incomparable garb of Pop, and wore a silk hat, from which his long curls (so un-Etonian, but I suppose he had his crew to consider) dripped like black candles about to melt. You may think I knew him from them, but I did not. Instead of a hand an iron hook protruded from the sleeve of his right arm, but it was not even by this that I knew him. His face was of a hue on which blood of the colour said to percolate from him when in conflict would not have been noticeable. I regret to say that I did not actually see him bleed. All these details I observed later in corroboration, but I knew him first as Hook by his extraordinary note of *noblesse oblige*.* I do not merely mean that Etonian was written all over him: there was something even more than that, as if (may I venture) he was two Etonians rolled by the magnanimous Gods into one. In a word, the handsomest man I have ever seen, though at the same time, perhaps slightly disgusting.

'The moon,' Mr Jasparin continues, 'paused for a moment (which it often seems to me to do over Eton), as if awaiting some singular transaction. I watched the Solitary from the passage, and never, I say, could I have conceived a Colossus* so shrunken. It was mournfully obvious that he was gazing with peeled eyes through the darkness of his present to the innocence of his past, from the monster he had become on the Spanish Main* to the person he had been at Eton, and the effect was heightened by the unclean tears that crawled down his face. While I was wondering whether I ought to withdraw a policeman approached on the college side, and I saw the hook rise as if for some dreadful entertainment. I almost cried out, but my fears show how little even I, who also have quaffed an overdose of Parnassus,* know the stuff our persons are made of, even the pirate ones. The policeman flashed his lantern, and this strange colloquy took place.

' "Are you a Pop, Sir?" the policeman asked huskily, for he knew that every stone in the wall was listening.

'The Solitary not only lowered his hook, but, shocking to relate, hid it behind his back. After an agonizing struggle, "No," he said. That is what he said. Once a Pop always a Pop, but for the honour of the Eton Society he denied his proud connexion with it.

' "Then you have no right to sit on that wall," the policeman said. "Get off." Every stone in the wall said, "Get off."

'The Solitary had merely to slew round his right arm to end the fellow, but for the honour of the school he humbly got off the wall—his wall.

' "Are you an OE?" the policeman asked.

' "No," said Jas Hook, being thus the first Old Etonian to deny that dear impeachment. But it was all he could do for the honour of the school.'

He had slunk away when next Mr Jasparin, to whom my thanks are due, was able to look upon the world again, but James was seen later that night by others with whom I have conversed, once seated drearily on Sheeps Bridge and wandering round Dutchman's Farm and again climbing into Agar's Plough,* which I daresay is so called because those who most distinguish themselves there have sometimes difficulty afterwards in passing their examinations.

A small boy's vision

Probably the grimmest experience of the night went, as usual, to a creature in his first or second half* who was largely unconscious of it until inquiries by Mr Jasparin woke him to a sense of his peril and his importance. This boy or lad occupied a chamber in what is now, I think, Mr Headlam's house, which was part of the old meeting place of Pop (now more splendidly housed), and he woke about midnight to find Hook sitting in his room. Addressed indignantly, the Solitary was meditating too profoundly to hear, and the boy was about to make another remark when he fell asleep again. He will never come nearer to being torn apart like a pair of shorts. How Hook obtained access to this room is not known. It is a difficult room to enter quietly, for as soon as you open the door there are several sudden steps down, and it is therefore a sought-after habitation by boys who await visits from their relatives. James, however, was no stranger to the old Pop room, and he must have come and gone as soft as snow. Perhaps he had an old key to the house; one of his hobbies was to collect keys. Whether thinking that this was still part of the club-room of the giants he sought it because he had a deed of awful renunciation to do is matter for surmise, but later that night he certainly did break into the present premises of the Eton Society and destroy the evidence in its books that he had once been a member. To obliterate the memory of himself from the tabernacle* he had fouled was all this erring son of Eton could do for his beloved. In that one moment was he not a good Etonian? As he stole away had he not earned the right to look back once upon the sleeping school and cry, 'Oh that I were the happy dream that creeps to her soft heart!' Thus he vanishes from the scene, and all its doors close against him for ever. Surely a more tortured revisit to Eton never disturbed her shades than that of the humble pirate. No one saw the Solitary depart to resume his awful role. I should have liked to think that the Provost was looking out at his window. Strange to think that there is one ghost he knows not of—the Eton ghost—a one-armed apparition, cadaverous and black-avised* and wan, who is said to return to Eton to haunt it once every year—on the restless night before the match at Lord's, and to sit on Hook's wall, confidently yet not without tremors, awaiting a morrow he shall never see. Tonight those of you whose windows overlook that wall may see in the light of a pale blue moon, with that ghost's yearly message round it, 'May our opponents win some time, but not this time'———

The end of Hook

But no, no, let us end on a less poignant note. Hook's decease must have occurred not long after his last visit to Eton. I can find but the baldest references to it in the newspapers of the period, perhaps because obituary notices invariably begin 'We regret to announce,' and I daresay no one quite liked to say that about James's passing. One feared the worst when he ceased to send a greeting to the school, couched in the Latin tongue which had always been his custom on the 4th of June. Gradually it became known that a little boy—his implacable enemy—had struck Hook from the lists of Man. He had always hated children, and the callous little brutes did for him in the end. This infant was the only person of whom James's aunt could not speak with charity. She always maintained that on securing possession of the pirate ship he dressed in her nephew's clothing (cut down to fit him by the disreputable female of his wanderings), and with a hook in his hand and a cigar-holder in his mouth strutted the deck using disgraceful language, a painful picture of James's conqueror which I have an uncomfortable feeling may be true. Later there came, from a dive in Manaos,* a miscellaneous collection of Hook's pirate hoard and other treasures, the accumulation of a life of toil. They were wrapped up in a shirt, and included bags of doubloons and figures of eight, a battered silk hat with some black wax adhering to it, and a flute, an instrument on which he is said to have been no mean performer. There was also the ship's log-book, containing many cries from the heart that he is alone among uncultured companions and about the barrenness of fame. Not uninteresting to some here might be a comparison he draws in the log-book between the lives of himself and his former fag,* written in the Plutarchian* manner. In this he admits that they reached distinction along different paths, and discusses what might have happened to the school and to the ship if he and that other had changed places. In their mournful cadences these entries in the log-book are not untinged by the melancholy of the Greeks in their greatest period. Compare, for instance, one of the noblest passages in Sophocles with this terrible line, 'Better, perhaps, for Hook that he had never been born.'*

Of more interest to the vulgar, to whom, after all, this talk must make its chief appeal, is James Hook's last will, which was forwarded to his aunt by a land-shark* of Rio. By this James left everything to Eton. But the Governors, it appears had scruples—even about the hat—and so all passed to his aunt Emily, who told me with a faint flush that not to accept them would have been a slight on James's memory.

These are all the facts I have been able to learn about Hook at Eton, and if you agree that once in his life, that night, he did all that such as he could do for his old school I seek to draw no other moral, though surely the proud, if detestable position he attained is another proof that the Etonian is a natural leader of men. Educationally, I gather from the log-book, his sympathies were with the classical rather than the modern side. In politics he was a Conservative. So far as I can learn there never was any woman in his life. His furrow had therefore to be a lonely one. Perhaps if some dear girl—who can tell? or why so bright a morning had to close in such a cataclysm? Perhaps it was just that at Oxford he fell among bad companions—Harrovians.*

And now, &c.*

EXPLANATORY NOTES

THE LITTLE WHITE BIRD (1902)

5 *Kensington Gardens*: originally the private gardens of Kensington Palace in London and now one of the Royal Parks, covering 270 acres of western central London. They are separated from Hyde Park by the Serpentine, an artificial lake that includes the small island where Barrie places Peter Pan. The Barries lived near the Gardens, first at 133 Gloucester Road and then at Leinster Corner, while between 1897 and 1904 the Davies family lived at 31 Kensington Park Gardens.

David: the semi-fictitious child, based on George Llewelyn Davies, whose antics fascinate the narrator in *The Little White Bird*.

the King: Edward VII, who had succeeded Queen Victoria in 1901.

never-ending line of omnibuses: the Bayswater Road marks the northern limit of Kensington Gardens; one of the area's distinctive horse-drawn omnibuses is depicted in George William Joy's painting *The Bayswater Omnibus*, exhibited at the Royal Academy in 1895.

6 *Figs*: the area to the west of Broad Walk known as The Figs is now the Diana, Princess of Wales Memorial Playground, located next to the Elfin Oak.

commonalty: common people.

full fig: full uniform or best clothes.

Miss Mabel Grey's gate: i.e. Palace Gate, opening into Kensington Road and Hyde Park Gate.

Broad Walk: the main promenade of the Gardens, passing between Kensington Palace and the Round Pond.

mad-dog or Mary-Annish: reckless or effeminate.

Cecco Hewlett's Tree: named after the son of Barrie's friend the novelist Maurice Hewlett. Cecco was one of the children Barrie regularly met in the Gardens; he reappears in *Peter and Wendy* as 'the handsome Italian Cecco, who cut his name in letters of blood on the back of the governor of the prison at Gao'.

7 *Big Penny*: the white marble statue of Queen Victoria, crowned and holding a sceptre, located in front of Kensington Palace; Barrie's nickname refers to the resemblance between it and depictions of Britannia on penny coins.

Baby's Palace: Kensington Palace, where Queen Victoria was born.

the Hump: a downhill stretch of Broad Walk.

a pattern-child: a model child.

8 *Bunting's Thumb*: no trace of this feature now exists.

8 *St. Govor's Well*: 'This drinking fountain marks the site of an ancient spring, which in 1856 was named St Govor's Well . . . Saint Govor, a sixth century hermit, was the patron saint of a church in Llandover which had eight wells in its churchyard' (inscription on a 1970s stone sculpture now on this site).

chimney-sweep: a popular character in nineteenth-century fairy tales, including Hans Christian Andersen's 'The Shepherdess and the Chimney Sweep' (1845) and Charles Kingsley's *The Water-Babies* (1863).

Yorkers: in cricket a yorker is a ball that is bowled so that it pitches just in front of the batsman, making it extremely difficult to score off.

Round Pond: an ornamental lake in Kensington Gardens created in 1730 by George II; it covers approximately 7 acres, and is still a popular spot for sailing model boats.

10 *'Cowardy, cowardy custard!'*: a traditional insult chanted by children who suspect cowardice; 'custard' is a modern variant of 'costard' (i.e. head), perhaps with the added implication of being 'yellow' (the US meaning of 'faint-hearted' dates from the late nineteenth century).

Porthos: Porthos was Barrie's St Bernard dog, who accompanied him on his walks in Kensington Gardens and appeared in various disguises (e.g. a *papier mâché* tiger mask) in *The Boy Castaways of Black Lake Island* (1901). A chapter of *The Little White Bird* is based on the fantasy that he temporarily becomes a human being named William Paterson.

11 *Salford*: a former market town that grew rapidly during the Industrial Revolution, and now forms part of Greater Manchester; Barrie's description is either nostalgic or ironic, as by the end of the nineteenth century it was notorious for its overcrowded slums.

Dog's Cemetery: Hyde Park's Pet Cemetery is located in the garden of Victoria Gate Lodge on the Bayswater Road. Between 1881 and 1903 over 300 dogs and other pets were interred there, beginning with Cherry, a Maltese Terrier who died of old age; they are commemorated by tombstones such as 'My Ba-Ba—Never Forgotten, Never Replaced', and 'Darling Dolly—My Sunbeam, My Consolation, My Joy'.

worsted ball: a ball made out of yarn.

13 *sward*: area of grass.

Lock-out Time: Kensington Gardens were closed at sunset, which could be as early as 4 pm in the winter.

14 *Queen Mab's palace*: Queen Mab is queen of the fairies; P. B. Shelley's long philosophical poem *Queen Mab*, published in 1813, includes a description of her 'celestial palace' with its 'floors of flashing light' and 'vast and azure dome'.

Lancers: armed cavalrymen.

15 *Solomon*: a joking allusion to the famously wise king of Israel who succeeded his father, King David, *c.*970 BCE; Barrie's choice of name may

have been influenced by the story recounted in 1 Kings 3:16–28, in which Solomon ruled between two women who both claimed to be the mother of the same child.

16 *sough*: murmuring sound.

18 *Shelley*: named after the Romantic poet and political radical P. B. Shelley (1792–1822); Shelley's pregnant first wife Harriet had drowned herself in the Serpentine aged 21 in December 1816.

19 *a competency*: 'a sufficiency, without superfluity, of the means of life' (*OED*).

20 *all Kates are saucy*: an idea reflected in popular Victorian ballads such as 'Saucy Kate'.

21 *puffed*: out of breath.

22 *coracle*: a small wickerwork boat covered with a watertight material such as animal skins.

   Master Francis Pretty: a sailor who twice attempted to circumnavigate the globe, first with Sir Francis Drake (1577–80) and then with Thomas Cavendish (1588). The description of Peter's voyage that follows is a mock-heroic imitation of Pretty's style in his book *The Famous Voyage of Sir Francis Drake into the South Sea, and therehence about the whole Globe of the Earth, begun in the year of our Lord 1577* (1580).

   roomer of the shadows: to 'go roomer' or 'go large' is an old nautical term meaning to adopt a course that is further away from the wind. Peter avoids the shadows by changing the direction his boat is sailing in.

   was fain to hold off, seeking for moorage: i.e. was forced to remain at distance from the shore, while seeking water deep enough to drop anchor.

   pretending: directing his course.

23 *stand to their harms*: be ready to suffer injury.

   he boldly leapt ashore: the spot marked 'where Peter Pan landed' on Arthur Rackham's original map (p. 5) is now the site of the statue 'Peter Pan' by Sir George Frampton, erected in 1912.

24 *Jenny Wren*: a popular name for the wren, sometimes regarded (e.g. in nursery rhymes) as the bride or sweetheart of Robin Redbreast; also the name of a character in Charles Dickens's *Our Mutual Friend* (1864–5).

25 *Baby Walk*: i.e. The Flower Walk, which leads past the Albert Memorial towards West Carriage Drive.

27 *basinette*: more commonly 'bassinet', a wickerwork cradle or pram with a hood over one end. In Oscar Wilde's play *The Importance of Being Earnest*, Miss Prism confesses that she 'deposited the manuscript in the basinette, and placed the baby in the hand-bag'.

28 *fairy ring*: a circular mark on the ground (usually a band of differently coloured grass) supposed to be a magic circle created by fairies.

   linkmen: men employed to carry torches.

29 *berberris*: the berberis or barberry is a large evergreen shrub that produces
    red or dark blue berries.

    Solomon's seals: *Polygonatum*, a genus of flowering plants that produces red
    or black berries; its nickname refers to the depressions on its roots, which
    resemble royal seals.

32 *no second chances*: Barrie later developed this theme in his play *Dear Brutus*,
    in which one midsummer night his characters are given the chance to
    reshape their lives.

33 *The iron bars are up for life*: Barrie would later develop this idea at the end
    of ch. 16 of *Peter and Wendy*.

34 *leary*: i.e. leery: wide-awake or knowing.

    combinations: tight-fitting underwear consisting of a combined undershirt
    and drawers.

35 *ayah*: 'A native-born nurse or maidservant, employed esp. by Europeans in
    India and other parts of South Asia' (*OED*).

37 *pelisse*: a cloak or other garment designed for outdoor wear.

38 *'Well-a-day'*: an exclamation of sorrow.

    jagged: cut or gashed.

    compel you to nurse their children: in ch. 15 of *Peter and Wendy*, Starkey is
    captured by the redskins and forced to nurse their papooses.

39 *Brownie*: 'A benevolent spirit or goblin, of shaggy appearance, supposed to
    haunt old houses, esp. farmhouses, in Scotland, and sometimes to perform
    useful household work while the family were asleep' (*OED*); in Charlotte
    Brontë's novel *Jane Eyre* (1847), the heroine asks Rochester for a comb to
    help tame his 'shaggy black mane', explaining that 'You tell of my being
    a fairy, but I am sure you are more like a brownie'.

42 *boon*: gift or blessing.

44 *forcing-houses*: i.e. greenhouses.

49 *kettle-holder*: a piece of fabric used to protect the hand when lifting a hot
    kettle.

51 *tombstones*: in fact these stones mark the boundaries between the Parish of
    Westminster St Mary's and the Parish of Paddington. Barrie's darkly
    playful alternative, which is that they marked the graves of babies who
    had fallen from their perambulators, would later be developed in his
    explanation of how the Lost Boys come to live in Neverland.

A PLAY (1903–4)

56 *a tin*: i.e. of bath salts.

57 *Wendy*: the name was Barrie's invention, a recollection of his friendship
    with Margaret Henley, the young daughter of poet W. E. Henley. She
    called him 'my friendly', but as she could not pronounce the letter 'r',

'friendly' became 'wendy'. In his memoir *The Greenwood Hat* (1930), Barrie noted that 'The lovely child died when she was about five'.

59 *go to by-by*: go to sleep.

60 *her*: from this point on, Barrie's stage directions refer to the sex of the character Nana rather than that of the boy playing her.

62 *British Museum*: founded in 1753, and located in Bloomsbury, by 1904 its collection included curiosities gathered from all over the world.

cowardy custard: see note to p. 10.

chocky: i.e. chocolate.

68 *housewife*: a sewing kit.

74 *Cinderella*: the traditional folktale published by Charles Perrault in *Histoires ou contes du temps passé* in 1697, and later by the Brothers Grimm in their popular collection of *Grimms' Fairy Tales* in 1812.

75 *wires*: for flying on stage.

76 *muff*: 'A foolish, stupid, feeble, or incompetent person; spec. one who is clumsy or awkward in some sport or manual skill' (*OED*).

77 *mea culpa*: 'through my own fault', a Latin phrase acknowledging the speaker's guilt or responsibility for some error.

79 *practicable*: i.e. able to be used in practical ways.

a red cloak such as charity-children wear: scarlet cloaks denoted a humble station in life; in 'The Happy Prince' (1888), Oscar Wilde describes some charity children trooping out of a cathedral 'in their bright scarlet cloaks and their clean white pinafores'.

Rabbits of real rabbit size: an echo of Sir Herbert Beerbohm Tree's lavish production of *A Midsummer Night's Dream* at Her Majesty's Theatre in 1900, which featured real rabbits lolloping around on stage.

81 *how dangerous 'tis to drink cold water when you're hot*: a common medical belief; in *The Physician's Holiday* (1852) Queen Victoria's physician Sir John Forbes warned of the 'dangerous and fatal results that have followed the sudden ingestion of cold water by travellers and others who had been undergoing great bodily exertion in hot weather'.

82 *depression*: although 'depression' had been used since the early seventeenth century to mean 'depressed in spirits' or 'dejected', the first modern citation referring to the symptoms of a specific psychiatric disorder is given by the *OED* as 1905.

86 *dastard*: 'one who does malicious acts in a cowardly, skulking way' (*OED*).

88 *chophouses*: cheap restaurants; presumably the implication is that following fashion in home decor is an expensive business.

tall Eton hat: i.e. a top hat.

90 *'Ulysses'*: a play by Stephen Phillips based on Homer's *Odyssey* that was produced at Her Majesty's Theatre in London in 1902, starring Herbert

Beerbohm Tree as Ulysses; a review published in *The Times* (3 February 1902) noted that when he came to slay Penelope's suitors, Ulysses failed to string his bow properly, and 'Antinous had to put the arrow in his own breast'.

91 *house*: i.e. theatre.

93 *Here a little child I stand . . . on us all*: Robert Herrick (1591–1674), 'A Child's Grace'; 'paddocks' are frogs.

Piccaninny: an American Indian child (now considered an offensive term).

95 *progeny*: offspring.

'*Of all the girls that are so smart*': the opening line of 'Sally in our Alley' (see next note).

'*Sally in our Alley*': a popular ballad written by Henry Carey (1687–1743) which begins 'Of all the girls that are so smart | There's none like pretty Sally; | She is the darling of my heart, | And she lives in our alley'; it was also the subject of a 1902 musical and several later films.

96 '*John Anderson, My Jo John*': a song about the continuing love of an old married couple set to words by Robert Burns (1759–96), based on a mildly bawdy eighteenth-century ballad in which a wife berates her husband for his waning performance in bed; 'jo' is a Scots dialect word for 'darling'.

102 *negligée*: 'A woman's light dressing gown, esp. one made of flimsy, semi-transparent fabric trimmed with ruffles, lace, etc.; (also) a nightgown' (*OED*, from 1862).

103 *blacks*: formal clothing.

104 *flannels*: underclothes made of flannel.

107 *practical*: i.e. capable of being used in practical ways.

110 *Stow this gab!*: stop this chatter!

Bully: good friend, fine fellow.

King Edward: see note to p. 394.

buffet: knock him about.

111 *tumble up . . . lubbers*: make haste . . . unseamanlike individuals.

my hearty: 'an affectionate form of address (chiefly used by or to a sailor)' (*OED*).

die like English gentlemen: a standard phrase of the time; in a farewell letter that was found on his body in November 1912, Captain Scott, polar explorer and Barrie's friend, wrote that he and his team would 'die like gentlemen'.

Babes in the Wood: a traditional tale of two children who are abandoned in a wood and covered with leaves by the birds; first published as an anonymous broadside ballad in 1595, in the nineteenth century it became one of the staple plots of the English pantomime.

112 *Avast*: stop.

the cat: the cat-o'-nine-tails, a whip with nine knotted lashes; until 1881 it was an officially approved means of punishment in the British army and navy.

113 *swing*: be hanged.

114 *stark*: stiff, i.e. dead.

Jonah: the subject of the book of Jonah in the Bible; used figuratively to refer to someone who is thought to bring bad luck.

Blackbeard and Kidd: Edward Teach or Edward Thatch (*c.*1680–1718) and William Kidd or Captain Kidd (*c.*1654–1701), notorious English pirates.

115 *Davy Jones*: nautical slang for the bottom of the sea; to be 'sent to Davy Jones's Locker' means to be drowned.

116 *Rule Britannia*: a British patriotic song; originally a poem by James Thomson, it was set to music by Thomas Arne in 1740; the chorus ('Rule, Britannia! rule the waves: | Britons never will be slaves') led to a strong association with the Royal Navy and Britain's colonial expansion overseas.

117 *SCENE 5*: in Barrie's manuscript of *A Play* this is the only scene without a title.

118 *baccy*: tobacco.

119 *'Home, Sweet Home'*: a popular song adapted from John Howard Payne's 1823 opera *Clari, or the Maid of Milan*.

120 *silver*: soft, melodious.

129 *hansom*: a two-wheeled horse-drawn cab holding up to two passengers.

131 *chest protector*: a covering or wrap to protect the chest from cold.

one and six: i.e. one shilling and sixpence.

132 *Eton suits*: consisting of an Eton jacket (i.e. the short black jacket with wide lapels formerly worn by younger pupils at Eton College) with trousers and a waistcoat.

street arab: a homeless child or young person living on the streets; now generally regarded as offensive.

133 *How de do*: How do you do (imitating an upper-class accent).

Clown: in the Harlequinade that formed part of English pantomime tradition, as developed by Joseph Grimaldi around 1800, Clown was a character in white-faced make-up who served as a mischievous foil to the more sophisticated Harlequin; see Introduction, p. xxxi.

red-hot poker: the Clown's traditional comic prop.

swell: a stylishly dressed gentleman; someone of distinguished appearance or social status.

Columbine: in the Harlequinade, Columbine (in Italian 'Colombina', or 'little dove') was a comic servant romantically involved with Harlequin.

134 *bully*: see note to p. 110.

136 *birch*: i.e. holding canes.

137 *practical*: see note to p. 107.

138 *touzle*; i.e. tousle, dishevel.

139 *Pepper's ghost*: a theatrical illusion that appears to show objects appearing or disappearing, or being magically transformed in appearance; it is named after John Henry Pepper (1821–1900), a scientist who demonstrated the technique during a theatrical adaptation of Charles Dickens's *The Haunted Man* in 1862.

PETER AND WENDY (1911)

143 *tiny boxes . . . from the puzzling East*: a nest of containers commonly known as 'Chinese boxes'.

Napoleon: i.e. Napoleon Bonaparte (1769–1821), the French military leader and statesman who rapidly became a byword for ruthless ambition.

144 *one pound seventeen*: i.e. one pound seventeen shillings in pre-decimal British currency (pounds, shillings, and pence); not all of Mr Darling's calculations are accurate.

Newfoundland dog: Nana's physical appearance is based on Barrie's dog Luath, although her character recalls his previous dog Porthos, a St Bernard who was with him when he first met the Davies boys in Kensington Gardens, and who featured prominently in *The Boy Castaways of Black Lake Island* (1901).

145 *footer*: i.e. football, soccer.

George: Mr Darling shares the name of the eldest Davies son; the names of all the other Davies children, apart from the youngest (Nico), also appear in the story as Peter, John, and Michael.

146 *Neverland*: see Introduction, p. xxx.

gnomes who are mostly tailors: a variation on the traditional fairy tale 'The Elves and the Shoemaker', in which some helpful elves make shoes overnight.

princes with six elder brothers: possibly a recollection of 'The Seven Ravens', a story in which seven brothers are turned into birds, although seven is a popular number in traditional folktales.

148 *not to wipe*: i.e. not to wipe his feet.

149 *getting into shirts*: i.e. starting to wear ordinary clothes rather than babywear.

150 *Mea culpa*: see note to p. 77.

154 *cowardy custard*: see note to p. 10.

159 *embonpoint*: attractive plumpness.

kings toss ha'pence to the crowd: a gesture of charity.

161 *housewife*: see note to p. 68.

'You conceit': a Scottish expression meaning 'A quaint or dainty person' (*OED*), used here with the implication of boastfulness.

162 *set*: social group.

at a venture: without due consideration.

163 *give them a hiding*: thrash them.

165 *Cinderella*: see note to p. 74.

167 *a knife with six blades and a saw*: more commonly known from the start of the twentieth century as a Swiss Army knife.

168 *topping*: excellent.

in words of two syllables: i.e. he can read more complicated words than 'the cat sat on the mat'.

169 *Cave*: beware (from the Latin *cavere*), a school slang expression typically used to warn of a teacher's approach.

171 *popped off*: fell asleep.

173 *tiffs*: arguments, squabbles.

175 *anon*: in a short while.

176 *pampas*: treeless plains found in South America.

Blackbeard's bo'sun: see note to p. 114.

Barbecue: nickname of Long John Silver in Robert Louis Stevenson's influential novel *Treasure Island* (1883).

177 *Long Tom*: a generic name for a large cannon or field gun, e.g. the 42-pounder Long Tom that was placed on the American brig *General Armstrong* for use in the War of 1812, or the 155mm Creusot Long Tom that was used as an artillery piece during the Second Boer War.

178 *topper*: i.e. top hat.

181 *a pickle*: a mischievous child (usually a boy).

Execution Dock: located in Wapping, east London, this was the place of execution for pirates and others condemned to death by the Admiralty Court.

pieces of eight: Spanish silver dollars or pesos; each coin was worth eight reals and was marked with the figure 8.

Cecco: see note to p. 6.

Gao: a city in Mali located on the River Niger, although Barrie may have thought the name was his invention.

Guadjo-mo: a fictitious river.

182 *Jukes . . . Flint*: i.e. Jukes received six dozen lashes; in *Treasure Island* the *Walrus* is referred to as 'Flint's old ship', although Jukes is never mentioned in the novel.

moidores: Portuguese gold coins that were valid currency in England and its colonies in the first half of the eighteenth century; each moidore was worth about 27 shillings.

usher: assistant schoolmaster.

182 *Morgan's Skylights*: Henry Morgan (*c*.1635–1688), Welsh privateer, who grew wealthy by raiding settlements and shipping on the Spanish Main, and eventually became Lieutenant Governor of Jamaica.

Irish bo'sun Smee: actor George Shelton, who played the role in the original stage production, recalled in his autobiography how Barrie had said to him and the actor playing Starkey, 'I want you to individualise your two parts.' Shelton replied, 'I'll make an Irishman of mine', and thereafter it became a theatrical tradition that Smee should be played with an Irish accent.

Nonconformist: 'A person who fails or refuses to conform to a particular practice or course of action' (*OED*); the basic idea seems to be that despite serving the charismatic Hook, Smee is still capable of independent thought.

Alf Mason: named after Barrie's friend the novelist A. E. W. Mason (1865–1948).

Spanish Main: the Caribbean coast and Gulf of Mexico, from where enormous wealth was shipped back to Spain during the sixteenth to early nineteenth centuries in the form of gold, silver, gems, spices, and other valuable items; the area attracted many pirates and privateers.

Sea-Cook: another nickname for Long John Silver (his original profession).

blackavised: dark-complexioned, swarthy.

grand seigneur: great nobleman.

raconteur: skilful storyteller.

183 *Piccaninny*: see note to p. 93.

Delawares or the Hurons: North American Indian tribes.

Dianas: i.e. female hunters (in Roman mythology Diana was goddess of the moon, virginity, and hunting).

184 *Davy Jones*: see note to p. 115.

reconnoitre: inspect the enemy's position.

186 *'Odds, bobs, hammer and tongs'*: an oath adapted from the sea ballad in Frederick Marryat's novel *Snarleyyow or The Dog Fiend* (1837): 'Odds, bobs, hammer and tongs, long as I've been to sea, | I've fought 'gainst every odds—and I've gained the victory' (ch. 9).

Unrip: reveal.

193 *a glass thing*: i.e. a thermometer.

194 *capital*: excellent, first-rate.

195 *orgy*: presumably 'An occasion of feasting or revelry' rather than 'group sexual activity' (*OED*).

198 *Queen Mab*: see note to p. 14.

Puss-in-boots: the hero of a fairy tale that was first published in Italian in the sixteenth century, and later became a popular subject for English pantomimes.

Charming the Sixth: a joking allusion to Prince Charming, hero of the traditional fairy tale *Cinderella*.

Margery and Robin: characters in Maria Edgeworth's children's play *Dumb Andy* (1827).

Tiddlywinks: a nonsense name for a shop based on the parlour game that involves flipping counters into a cup.

rampageous: unruly, uncontrollable.

mammee-apples, tappa rolls . . . calabashes of poe-poe: the fruit of the South American mammee tree; rolls of cloth made in the South Pacific by pounding the bark of the paper mulberry tree (this one is either Barrie's mistake or a joke); gourds, made from the fruit of the calabash tree, filled with cooked or fermented breadfruit or banana with coconut milk.

199 *slates*: for writing on; in common use in elementary schools until the twentieth century.

201 *sanguinary*: bloody.

205 *muffled oars*: wrapped up to deaden the sound they make in water.

206 *'Luff, you lubber'*: nautical slang; 'Bring her into the wind, you clumsy oaf.'

209 *'Brimstone and gall'*: an oath roughly equivalent to 'hellfire and poison'.

cozening: cheating.

bully: see note to p. 110.

211 *lam into*: pile into, whack.

pinked: stabbed or pricked with a pointed weapon.

213 *'To die will be an awfully big adventure'*: see Introduction p. xi.

216 *'You dunderheaded little jay'*: 'You foolish little creature.'

217 *barque*: small boat, sailing vessel.

222 *witting*: knowing.

227 *half-mourning*: the second stage of a mourning period, in which black clothing is replaced by colours such as grey or purple.

hanger: a type of short sword, originally hung from the belt.

228 *négligée*: see note to p. 102.

first Thursdays: i.e. the first Thursday of the month, the date of Mrs Darling's regular 'At Home' receptions, when friends could call on her without prior arrangement.

229 *noodles*: fools.

230 *flannels*: see note to p. 104.

232 *happy hunting-grounds*: 'those expected by the American Indians in the world to come; hence, the future state' (*OED*).

232 *Geo. Scourie, Chas. Turley*: these names are private allusions. The year Barrie completed *Peter and Wendy* (1911) he spent his summer holiday with the

Davies boys at Scourie Lodge in north-west Scotland, where Nico made friends with George Ross, the son of the innkeeper. The second pirate's name recalls Barrie's friend Charles Turley Smith (1868–1940), the author of school stories for boys.

233 *fell genius*: wicked cleverness.

235 *distingué*: distinguished in appearance or manner.

236 *blown out*: swollen.

237 *would be*: i.e. wished to be.

morass: bog or marsh.

sward: see note to p. 13.

periwinkle: a plant with glossy leaves and bluish-purple flowers.

lewd: base.

239 *death-dealing rings*: i.e. rings containing poison.

241 *papooses*: North American Indian infants.

243 *Kidd's Creek*: see note to p. 114; Captain Kidd was hanged at Execution Dock on 23 May 1701.

foul to the hull: i.e. ugly from top to bottom.

immune in the horror of her name: safe from attack because of the fear generated by her reputation.

miasma: a cloud of poisonous vapour or night mist.

walk the plank: a notorious form of execution employed by pirates, in which the victim was forced to walk blindfolded along a plank fastened to the side of the ship, until they either lost their footing or were tipped into the water to drown.

bellied out: puffed up.

dogs: wretches, i.e. sailors who are under his absolute control.

244 *famous public school*: i.e. Eton College; Hook's last words in the 1928 play are 'Floreat Etona' ('May Eton Flourish').

good form: i.e. behaviour in line with the codes and values of the school.

house: like most British boarding schools, Eton is divided into 'houses' where pupils live under the supervision of a housemaster—a system that produces tribal loyalties and fierce rivalries between the houses.

vitals: the organs of the body on which life depends, e.g. the heart, lungs, etc.

presentiment of his early dissolution: i.e. a premonition of his early death, with a pun suggesting this would be an appropriate end to a 'dissolute' or debauched life.

245 *sleuth-hound*: a species of bloodhound formerly used in Scotland to track fugitives or pursue game.

Pop: the Eton Society: a prestigious elected club at Eton College; members are allowed to wear checked trousers and waistcoats in any design they choose.

damp: i.e. sweating.

bacchanalian: riotous.

scugs: public school slang; a scug is 'a boy who is not distinguished in person, in games, or social qualities . . . a boy of untidy, dirty, or ill-mannered habits' (C. E. Pascoe, *Everyday Life in our Public Schools*, 1881). Barrie also associated the term with the public school tradition of 'fagging' (see note to p. 439). In 1916, when the two youngest Davies boys were at Eton, he wrote to them enclosing a story entitled *The Room with 2 Beds*, which includes the following gloss on 'scug': 'One of the oldest traditions of Eton is that no senior . . . must let himself get tired or, in the *vox populum*, fagged. He therefore hires a scug (Anglo-Saxon SC∈9, meaning a cheese-paring, or, more accurately, an infinitesimal piece of the rind) to get tired for him.'

246 *'Stow this gab'*: see note to p. 110.

at maths prep: doing his maths homework.

'Rule Britannia!': see note to p. 116.

251 *cat*: see note to p. 112.

252 *'Sdeath and odds fish'*: an oath combining 'God's death' and 'God's fish' (possibly a version of 'God's flesh').

swing: see note to p. 113.

253 *one on board*: i.e. the Devil.

254 *Jonah*: see note to p. 114.

'Cleave him to the brisket': 'Split him to his breastbone.'

255 *reeking*: i.e. blood-soaked.

buckler: small shield.

quietus: release from life.

257 *powder magazine*: gunpowder store.

sent up for good: at Eton this means being summoned to the headmaster to be commended for an outstanding piece of work.

wall-game . . . famous wall: a traditional Eton game that bears some resemblance to rugby union, played on a strip of ground 5 yards wide and 100 yards long; the best place to watch it is from on top of the wall itself, which is 10 feet high.

bulwarks: 'The raised woodwork running along the sides of a vessel above the level of the deck' (*OED*).

259 *rope's end*: used to enforce discipline (Barrie's joke being that this task has been given to the sweetly inoffensive Tootles).

tars before the mast: ordinary seamen; 'tar' derives from Jack Tar, a familiar name for common sailors, and 'before the mast' refers to where their sleeping quarters were located, i.e. in the fo'c'sle (see next note), which was in front of the main mast.

259 *fo'c'sle*: forecastle, a short raised deck at the forward end of a ship.

lashed himself to the wheel: a helmsman might be tied to the ship's wheel in very stormy weather to prevent him from being swept overboard.

piped all hands: summoned the crew on deck (by blowing on the boatswain's pipe).

Gold Coast: a British colony in west Africa from 1867 to its independence as the nation of Ghana in 1957.

Azores: an archipelago of nine volcanic islands in the mid-Atlantic.

round robin: a nautical term for a letter of complaint, in which the signatures are written in a circle to disguise the order of signing.

a dozen: i.e. a dozen lashes with the cat-o'-nine-tails.

take soundings: measure the depth of the sea by casting a weighted line overboard.

261 *jaggy*: sharp, spiteful.

262 *rubbishy*: worthless.

263 *'Home, Sweet Home'*: see note to p. 119.

267 *'WHEN WENDY GREW UP'*: the dialogue of this chapter draws on the theatrical coda (performed only once in Barrie's lifetime) 'When Wendy Grew Up: An Afterthought' (1908), reprinted as Appendix III.

cypher: nonentity.

268 *Hoop la!*: an exclamation of happiness (hoop = whoop).

271 *married ... became a lord*: a joke about the aristocracy's lopsided conventions; a woman who marries a lord becomes a lady, but a man who marries a lady (i.e. a peeress) does not therefore become a lord.

forbid the banns: make a formal objection to an intended marriage.

three per cents: the interest rate of their loan.

272 *when you were a little girl*: in *Margaret Ogilvy* (1896) Barrie claimed that 'to a child, the oddest of things, and the most richly coloured picture-book, is that his mother was once a child also, and the contrast between what she is and what she was is perhaps the source of all humour'.

SCENARIO FOR A PROPOSED FILM OF PETER PAN (1921)

279 *the painting in my possession*: possibly the original of Arthur Rackham's watercolour illustration to *Peter Pan in Kensington Gardens* that depicts Peter playing his pan pipes as 'the fairies' orchestra'.

289 *Fenimore Cooper*: James Fenimore Cooper (1789–1851), bestselling American author, whose historical romances about frontier and American Indian life included *The Last of the Mohicans* (1826).

290 *beau*: fop, dandy.

  Nonconformist: see note to p. 182.

292 *my private film of 'Macbeth'*: *The Real Thing at Last*, a silent film written by Barrie in 1916, satirizing the US entertainment industry and based on the story of *Macbeth*; no copies are known to survive.

293 *Nemesis*: in ancient Greek religion, the goddess who enacted retribution on those who exhibited hubris (arrogance towards the gods); hence a rival or foe.

294 *much as described in 'Peter Pan in Kensington Gardens'*: see pp. 43–4.

  the scene of the play: in the published 1928 version this is 2.1.

298 *basinette*: see note to p. 27.

301 *crow's nest*: 'A barrel or cylindrical box fixed to the mast-head of an arctic, whaling or other ship, as a shelter for the look-out man' (*OED*).

302 *colours*: here meaning the kit worn by members of a sports team; further details of Hook's school colours are given in 'Captain Hook at Eton': see note to p. 434.

  cat-o'-nine-tails: see note to p. 112.

  'Eton Chronicle': the *Eton College Chronicle*, a school magazine written by the pupils, first published in 1863.

303 *what this should be like*: the fairy wedding is described in ch. 5 of *Peter Pan in Kensington Gardens*.

308 *desperado*: 'A desperate or reckless man; one ready for any deed of lawlessness or violence' (*OED*).

  the 'To be or not to be' soliloquy: *Hamlet* 3.1.

  dissolution: possibly an echo of another soliloquy from *Hamlet*: 'Oh that this too too solid flesh would melt | Thaw and resolve itself into a dew' (1.2).

  'Pop': see note to p. 245.

309 *All the business of the play here*: the action is described in Barrie's stage directions to 5.1 of the 1928 version.

311 *Jonah*: see note to p. 114.

312 *poop*: the highest deck on a wooden ship, located towards the stern.

  ju-jitsu: a Japanese form of wrestling characterized by particular holds and techniques for throwing an opponent.

  Sydney Carton: a character in Charles Dickens's novel *A Tale of Two Cities* (1859) who sacrifices himself during the French Revolution to save the life of his lookalike Charles Darnay; his famous final thoughts just before his execution are 'It is a far, far better thing that I do, than I have ever done; it is a far, far better rest that I go to than I have ever known.'

  the 'wall-game': see note to p. 257.

  Floreat Etona: 'May Eton Flourish', an unofficial school motto.

315 *'Home, Sweet Home'*: see note to p. 119.

320 *music . . . as it is in the play*: music for the original production was composed and conducted by John Crook (1852–1922).

PETER PAN, OR THE BOY WHO WOULD
NOT GROW UP (1928)

323 *TO THE FIVE*: the dedication is to the five sons of Arthur and Sylvia Llewelyn Davies: George, Jack, Peter, Michael, and Nicholas (known as Nico). At the time of publication in 1928 two of the boys were dead: George was killed in the First World War in 1915, and Michael drowned in 1921. Barrie's relationship with the Davies family is discussed in the Introduction, pp. xviii–xliii.

printing at last: although the first production of *Peter Pan* had taken place in 1904, the play was not published until 1928, when it formed part of *The Collected Plays of J. M. Barrie*.

324 *We first brought Peter down . . . only winded*: an episode that would later be adapted for Wendy's arrival in Neverland (Act 2 scene 1).

325 *fit the boards*: i.e. become a suitable character for the stage.

a garden at Burpham: in 1901 the Davies family spent their summer holidays at Burpham, a village near to Barrie's new Surrey holiday home Black Lake Cottage. The stories that Barrie and the boys made up that summer were commemorated in *The Boy Castaways of Black Lake Island*; see pp. xx–xxi.

No. 4: throughout the Dedication the numbers refer to the Davies boys in descending order of age.

St Bernard dog: Barrie's dog Porthos, who played with the Davies boys and was photographed by Barrie in various disguises in *The Boy Castaways of Black Lake Island*. Porthos died in 1902 and was replaced by a Newfoundland dog called Luath, who later became the physical model for Nana in the play.

The Boy Castaways: Barrie's photographic record of the adventures he enjoyed with the Davies boys in 1901; see pp. xx–xxii.

ploughing woods incarnadine: i.e. staining the woods with blood as he passes through them (adapting Macbeth's claim that 'my hand will rather | The multitudinous seas incarnadine', 2.2.62).

326 *assay*: attempt, endeavour.

Bandelero the Bandit: Barrie's first play, which he wrote as a pupil at Dumfries Academy; he later described it as 'a melodrama in six scenes and fifteen minutes, in which I played all my favourite characters in fiction, artfully rolled into one'.

Mr Toole: the comic actor, manager, and producer John Lawrence Toole (1830–1906).

Ibsen's Ghost: Barrie's first theatrical success, a one-act parody of Ibsen's *Hedda Gabler* that was performed in 1891.

our kind friends in front: i.e. the theatre audience.

'parts': sections of a script given to each actor containing only their own lines and cues; formerly a common practice in the theatre when producing new plays, usually to avoid the expense of printing complete scripts, but sometimes also to keep the contents of the play secret before opening night (as happened with the first production of *Peter Pan* in 1904).

one-and-sixpence: i.e. one shilling and sixpence.

327 *legal document*: a formal acknowledgement of the supposed contribution of a line by Jack Llewelyn Davies to Barrie's farce *Little Mary* (1903). In 1933, Barrie repeated the joke after he attended Princess Margaret's third birthday party, and later included a version of her line about her presents being 'yours and mine', and she and Barrie being each other's 'greatest friend', in his final play *The Boy David*. By way of compensation, he told Margaret that she would receive a penny every time her words were spoken on stage. The princess did not forget this, and in due course Barrie received a letter from her father, King George VI, to the effect that if Barrie did not pay up he would be hearing from His Majesty's solicitors.

gallery boys: i.e. playgoers who sat in the cheapest seats high up in the auditorium, and were famous for their rowdy behaviour.

native place: Barrie's birthplace, Kirriemuir, a small town in Angus, Scotland, known as 'the gateway to the glens'.

London that was so hard to reach: Barrie came to London as an ambitious young journalist in 1885, when he was 25 years old, but it was several years before he settled permanently in the capital.

great dog: i.e. Luath, Barrie's Newfoundland dog.

328 *Robb*: James Robb, Barrie's childhood friend, who helped him put on plays in the washhouse of his cottage in Kirriemuir.

glengarry bonnets: a Highland cap that was formerly a part of regimental dress.

preens . . . bool . . . peerie: items of low value: pins, a ball, or a marble.

lum hat: chimneypot hat.

wrecked islands: i.e. islands where one could be shipwrecked. In a 1913 preface to R. M. Ballantyne's *The Coral Island* (1858) Barrie wrote that 'To be born is to be wrecked on an island'.

sanguinary tales . . . penny numbers: i.e. bloodthirsty stories published in the cheap periodicals known as 'penny dreadfuls'.

Chatterbox: a weekly magazine for boys founded in 1866 by the clergyman John Erskine Clarke (1827–1920) as a more wholesome alternative to 'penny dreadfuls'.

gloaming: twilight.

328 *Pathhead farm*: a farm near Barrie's childhood home where he claims to have buried his collection of adventure stories.

prating: idly chattering, boasting.

spy-glass: telescope.

strand: coast.

write with the left hand: Barrie was naturally left-handed as a boy, and switched back to using this hand in 1920 after developing severe writer's cramp in his right hand.

329 *Blaikie*: Walter Biggar Blaikie (1847–1928), who worked for the Edinburgh printing firm T. & A. Constable for almost fifty years.

330 *lustrum*: a period of five years; presumably the mistake is a joke at Peter Llewelyn Davies's expense.

Wilkinson: headmaster of the prep school in Orme Square, facing Kensington Gardens, that was attended by the Davies boys; an imposing figure (despite his nickname of 'Milky'), Barrie first satirized him as 'Pilkington' in *The Little White Bird*, and later turned him into the model for Captain Hook.

331 *Mr Seton-Thompson*: Ernest Thompson Seton (1860–1946), author of the adventure story *Two Little Savages* (1903). In Act 2 of Barrie's play *The Admirable Crichton*, Lord Loam is unable to make fire by rubbing two sticks together.

Reform Club: a private members' club on the south side of Pall Mall in central London; Barrie was elected as a member in 1894.

Cocos nucifera: the coconut palm.

hour that best suited the camera: i.e. the time of day that provided the best light for taking photographs (the first commercially produced flashbulb was not available until 1929).

332 *letterpress*: the written contents of an illustrated book.

Captain Scott: the Royal Navy officer and polar explorer Captain Robert Falcon Scott (1868–1912), popularly known as 'Scott of the Antarctic'; Barrie was godfather to his son Peter. The 'strange foreshadowing' refers to Scott's discovery that the Norwegian explorer Amundsen had beaten him to the South Pole in 1912.

Holocaust: a sacrifice wholly consumed by fire.

Psittacidae: the Latin name for the family of birds that includes parrots.

divers: assorted, various.

Athos: one of the heroes of Alexandre Dumas's swashbuckling adventure story *The Three Musketeers* (1844).

Captain Marryat: Frederick Marryat (1792–1848), Royal Navy officer and author of popular sea stories.

333 *the chief figure*: i.e. Barrie himself.

loyal nurse: i.e. Mary Hodgson, the Davies family's long-serving nurse and increasingly Barrie's rival for the boys' affections; she appears in *The Little White Bird* as 'Irene'.

334 *Mr Crook's delightful music*: see note to p. 320.

a boy whom I favoured: i.e. Barrie's godson Peter Scott.

took the play to his nursery: on 20 February 1906, because Michael Llewelyn Davies was ill and could not attend the London production of *Peter Pan*, Barrie took some of the cast to the Davies family home in Berkhamsted to act out scenes for him there. The occasion is recalled in the 2004 film *Finding Neverland*, when Barrie (Johnny Depp) arranges for *Peter Pan* to be performed in the bedroom of the dying Sylvia Llewelyn Davies.

335 *where we caught Mary Rose*: i.e. the holiday inspired Barrie to write his 1920 play *Mary Rose*, the plot of which revolves around the disappearance of a girl on a remote Scottish island.

gillie: one who attends on hunters and fishermen in the Scottish Highlands.

336 *Mr Roget*: Peter Mark Roget (1779–1869), the British physician, natural theologian, and lexicographer, who is best known for his *Thesaurus of English Words and Phrases*, first published in 1852 and now more commonly known as *Roget's Thesaurus*.

337 *pinched*: short of money.

treasures: i.e. valued servants, 'gems'.

338 *'The little less, and how much it is'*: i.e. underplaying is preferable to over-playing, or 'less is more'.

343 *British Museum*: see note to p. 62.

Cowardy, cowardy custard: see note to p. 10.

344 *chocky*: see note to p. 62.

347 *rub-a-dub*: i.e. beats her paws on the ground.

348 *The nursery darkens*: i.e. ready for Tinker Bell's entrance.

354 *Cinderella*: see note to p. 74.

355 *strikes her colours*: surrenders.

playing rum-tum: hitting him rhythmically.

strange things have been done to them: i.e. the flying wires have been attached to them.

356 *stay-at-home*: someone who is not given to travelling about.

357 *'Cave'*: see note to p. 169.

bang: all at once.

sward: see note to p. 13.

tiff: quarrel.

358 *coracle*: see note to p. 22.

pickle: see note to p. 181.

360 *shindy*: row, commotion.

    Davy Jones: see note to p. 115.

    Execution Dock: see note to p. 181.

    pieces of eight: see note to p. 181.

    Cecco . . . Morgan: see note to p. 182.

    Nonconformist: see note to p. 182.

    blackavised: see note to p. 182.

    the plank: see note to p. 243.

    public school: see note to p. 244.

361 *Avast, belay . . . heave to*: nautical terms meaning to stop, to run a coil of rope around something to secure it, and to use the ship's sails to bring it to a halt.

362 *odds, bobs, hammer and tongs*: see note to p. 186.

363 *of one thought compact*: with only one idea in his head.

    Piccaninny: see note to p. 93.

    Manitou: the mysterious life force flowing through all things that was worshipped by certain American Indian tribes, and by extension a term for the magical powers through which it could be accessed.

365 *OMNES*: all.

    paling: a fence made with strips of wood or metal.

366 *dastard*: see note to p. 86.

368 *fetch a doctor*: an episode borrowed from Seymour Hicks's children's play *Bluebell in Fairyland* (1901); see Introduction, p. xxiii.

    beef tea: a food given to invalids, made by simmering beef for a lengthy period in a small amount of water.

369 *woodland house*: in the original version of this song, published with John Crook's music in 1905, this was a 'darling house'; Barrie removed the pun on Wendy's surname from the 1928 text.

    two other verses: in the version published in 1905 there were three additional verses:

> BOYS We've built the little walls and roof
>
>   And made a lovely door,
>
>   So tell us Mother Wendy,
>
>   What are you wanting more?
>
> WENDY Oh! really next I think I'd have
>
>   Gay windows all about—
>
>   With roses peeping in, you know,
>
>   And babies peeping out.
>
> BOYS We've made the roses peeping in,

The babes are at the door,—

We cannot make ourselves you know,

'Cos we've been made before.

festoon: a chain or garland of flowers.

370 THE MERMAIDS' LAGOON: this Act was added to the play in its second season. The previous year the scene change from the arrival in Never Land to 'The Home Under the Ground' had occurred in the middle of Act 2, while a painted front cloth showing the Redskins' Camp was lowered, and Hook was carried on in a sedan chair, from which he made a series of disappearances down a stage trap-door, each time reappearing in the guise of a different actor: Henry Irving, Herbert Beerbohm Tree, and Martin Harvey. Gerald du Maurier was a good impressionist, but the scene was not popular with the critics, and it was dropped after the new Act was introduced.

371 *King of the Castle*: 'A children's game in which one player must keep the others from occupying his or her place at the summit of a hill or other high position' (*OED*).

372 *Luff, you spalpeen*: nautical slang: 'Bring her into the wind, you rascal'.

mewl: whimper or cry feebly.

373 *lubbers*: see note to p. 111.

374 *Obesity and bunions*: a nonsensical oath.

bullies: fine fellows.

376 *lam into*: see note to p. 211.

377 *pinked*: see note to p. 211.

379 *To die will be an awfully big adventure*: a claim allegedly made by George Llewelyn Davies, in relation to Barrie's stories about the dead children whose tombstones were supposed to lie in Kensington Gardens (see p. 52).

380 *tomfool*: foolish, ridiculous.

band-box: a cardboard box for storing collars, caps and millinery.

whether to put on the smoky blue or the apple-blossom: a joke about fairy fashions.

tappa rolls . . . poe-poe: see note to p. 198.

383 *nighties*: i.e. nightclothes.

'John Anderson my Jo': see note to p. 96.

384 *babel*: babble of voices (an allusion to Genesis 11:1–9).

387 *half-mourning*: see note to p. 227.

388 *first Thursdays*: see note to p. 228.

Barbicue: i.e. Long John Silver in Robert Louis Stevenson's *Treasure Island* (1883), who is called Barbecue by his fellow pirates.

389 *Alf Mason . . . Chay Turley*: see note to pp. 182 and 232.

390 *flannels*: see note to p. 104.

392 *grig*: a small eel.

Circuit Amber . . . Call Hook: technical instructions about the staging of the scene. The circuit (i.e. the path from power source to light) is 'checked' (i.e. reduced) to 80 per cent of its power. 'Battens' are lengths of overhead lighting, which here bathe the stage in a lurid amber glow, and 'perches' are lighting positions on both sides of the stage. 'O.P.' (or 'opposite prompt') is stage right as seen from the actor's point of view, i.e. on the opposite side to where the prompter sits. A 'flood' controls the spread of light, and 'arc-lights' are positioned to give fixed light on the 'back cloth' or painted scene at the back of the stage. When everything is ready, the call-boy is instructed to 'call' the actor playing Hook from his dressing-room.

Mullins: Darby Mullins, an Irish pirate hanged alongside the legendary Captain Kidd at Execution Dock in 1701.

raking with his glass: i.e. scanning with his telescope.

393 *Long Tom*: see note to p. 177.

How still the night is: Hook's soliloquy was added during the original 1904 run, and was gradually expanded by Barrie in later productions.

disky: mischievous.

bi-carbonate of Soda: another nonsensical oath.

bacchanalian orgy: drunken revelry, frenzied dancing; for 'orgy' see note to p. 195.

394 *Stow this gab*: see note to p. 110.

King George: Edward VII was king when the play was originally staged, but George V had succeeded him by the time it was published in 1928.

395 *engine*: contrivance.

Whibbles of the eye patch: named after the critic Charles Whibley (1859–1930).

396 *cat*: see note to p. 112.

397 *livid*: unnaturally pale.

'Sdeath and oddsfish: see note to p. 252.

swing: see note to p. 113.

398 *blunderbuss*: a short gun capable of firing a large number of slugs at once.

one aboard: i.e. the Devil.

Caius and Balbus: another nonsensical oath; 'Caius' is an abbreviation of Gonville and Caius College, Cambridge, and 'Balbus' (literally 'stammerer') was the name of several powerful families in ancient Rome.

399 *Jonah*: see note to p. 114.

Cleave him to the brisket: see note to p. 254.

400 *reeking*: see note to p. 255.

 buckler: see note to p. 255.

 hilts: sword handles.

 quietus: see note to p. 255.

401 *jags*: see note to p. 38.

 damp: see note to p. 245.

 fire the power magazine: i.e. blow up the ship by setting its store of gunpowder alight.

 pewling: whining or wailing (a variant of 'puling').

 road to dusty death: alluding to a speech in *Macbeth*: 'Tomorrow, and tomorrow, and tomorrow | Creeps in this petty pace from day to day | To the last syllable of recorded time, | And all our yesterdays have lighted fools | The way to dusty death' (5.5.19–23).

 holocaust: see note to p. 332.

402 *'Floreat Etona'*: see note to p. 312.

 The curtain rises . . . Napoleon on his ship: the original production included a tableau that showed Peter posing as Napoleon in imitation of Sir William Quiller Orchardson's painting *Napoleon on Board the Bellerophon* (exhibited 1880), which depicts Napoleon standing on deck and gloomily staring out to sea while en route to his final exile on St Helena.

404 *sad song of Margaret*: probably the traditional English ballad 'Fair Margaret and Sweet William', which is about two lovers one or both of whom die of heartbreak (there are several different versions).

410 *squdge*: squash, hug tightly.

'ON THE ACTING OF A FAIRY PLAY' (1904)

411 *fairy king*: traditionally Oberon or the Erl-King.

'WHEN WENDY GREW UP: AN AFTERTHOUGHT' (1908)

413 *depend*: i.e. hang.

 Lights in: i.e. the lamps have been brought in and lit.

414 *Petty*: i.e. little one (from the French *petit*).

 Dogs' Home: Battersea Dogs Home was established by Mary Tealby (1801–85) in Holloway in 1860 as the Temporary Home for Lost and Starving Dogs; it moved to its present location in 1871.

416 *Slightly . . . became a lord*: see note to p. 271.

 3 per cents: see note to p. 271.

417 *gay*: i.e. merry.

420 *The lamp flickers*: a lighting effect intended to help with the attachment of flying wires to Jane.

'THE BLOT ON PETER PAN' (1926)

421 *Neil*: the young hero of Barrie's earlier short story 'Neil and Tintinnabulum', which appeared in Cynthia Asquith's 1925 anthology *The Flying Carpet*, and describes how the male narrator's godson is absorbed into the life of a public school.

licked: beaten in a fight.

seventeen hundred days: i.e. just over four and a half years old.

422 *Mr. Macaulay*: probably Thomas Babington Macaulay (1800–59), the British historian and Whig politician; as a young child he astonished adults with his precocious learning and retentive memory.

423 *Cain*: one of the two sons of Adam and Eve. Genesis 4:1–16 describes how he kills his brother Abel; when God asks him where Abel is, he replies 'I do not know: am I my brother's keeper?'

424 *Dishing*: cheating or getting around.

blow ourselves out: praise ourselves, brag (cf. 'blow one's own trumpet').

425 *what he liked best . . . on people's heads*: in 1914 Barrie took his 5-year-old godson Peter Scott (son of the Arctic explorer) to see the tenth revival of *Peter Pan*; when he asked the boy which part he had liked best, he was told that 'What I think I liked best was tearing up the programme and dropping the bits on people's heads' (Dedication to *Peter Pan*, 1928).

great minds stoop to folly: an allusion to Oliver Goldsmith's poem 'When Lovely Woman Stoops to Folly' in *The Vicar of Wakefield* (1766).

426 *gollywog*: 'A name invented for a black-faced grotesquely dressed (male) doll with a shock of fuzzy hair' (*OED*).

431 *gone to pot*: deteriorated, gone to pieces.

432 *burglarious*: burglar-like.

'CAPTAIN HOOK AT ETON: A STRANGE STORY' (1927)

434 *Eton*: Eton College, the public (i.e. independent) school near Windsor founded in 1440 by Henry VI. George, Peter, Michael and Nicholas ('Nico') Llewelyn Davies were all pupils here.

Provost: appointed by the Crown and Eton's equivalent of a headmaster; in 1927 the Provost was M. R. James (1862–1936), medievalist scholar and author of popular ghost stories.

Balliol: founded in 1263, Balliol is one of the largest and oldest colleges of the University of Oxford; the former prime minister H. H. Asquith (1852–1928) once described the College's students as possessing 'the tranquil consciousness of an effortless superiority'.

'Floreat Etona': see note to p. 312.

Lake school: a group of Romantic poets living in England's Lake District at the turn of the nineteenth century; they included William Wordsworth (1770–1850), S. T. Coleridge (1772–1834) and Robert Southey (1774–1843).

12th man in the College 100 yards: a sporting joke; in cricket the twelfth man is a reserve selected in addition to a team of eleven players.

dry bob: a boy who devotes himself to land-sports such as cricket and football (Eton slang).

he had many colours: i.e. he presented many different faces to the world.

red and blue . . . claret and blue . . . pale blue: caps awarded for various sports at Eton, respectively the 'Mixed Wall', i.e. the Wall game played between eleven Collegers (boys who lived in College) and eleven Oppidans (boys accommodated in the town), Fives, and 'The Eleven', i.e. the first cricket team.

435 *sock and spat*: socks and gaiters, worn together in a way that was seen by some as classy and by others as merely flashy; in Barrie's play *Shall We Join the Ladies?* (1928) Mr Vaile is described as 'a perfect little gentleman, if socks and spats can do it'.

Sun and Moon: possibly a joke about two popular pupils, although there used to be a public house known as The Sun (the building at 12 High Street still has a sun painted on its door).

fag-master: a senior pupil at a public school for whom a junior pupil carries out chores.

First Hundred: the top one hundred pupils measured by exam performance.

Ephemerals: short-lived magazines produced by pupils, often with the aim of making money; an article on 'The Reappearance of the Ephemeral' published in the *Eton College Chronicle* (7 October 1915) noted that 'However bad the Ephemeral, it is always bought'.

Eton Chronicle: see note to p. 302.

436 *Wall game*: see note to p. 257.

Keeper of the Fives: i.e. captain of the Eton Fives, a handball game played at the school.

strawberry mess: a dessert made from strawberries, broken meringues, and whipped cream, also known as 'Eton mess'; it is traditionally served at the annual cricket match against the pupils of Harrow School.

scugs: see note to p. 245.

Jordan's: named after the Jordan, a stream running under the Slough Road and into the Thames.

437 *noblesse oblige*: 'Noble ancestry constrains one (to honourable behaviour); privilege entails responsibility' (*OED*).

Colossus: a giant statue, the most famous example being the Colossus of Rhodes, one of the Seven Wonders of the Ancient World, which stood approximately 70 cubits (33 metres) high and depicted the Greek sun-god Helios.

Spanish Main: see note to p. 182.

Parnassus: Mount Parnassus in central Greece, home of the Muses and popularly regarded as the source of poetic inspiration.

438 *Dutchman's Farm . . . Agar's Plough*: two of Eton's sports fields, with a pun on 'ploughing' as school slang for failing an exam.

half: a school term.

tabernacle: a sanctuary or meeting place.

black-avised: see note to p. 182.

439 *Manaos*: an older name for Manaus, a city in Brazil.

fag: a junior boy at an English public school who performs certain duties for a senior boy.

Plutarchian: resembling the style of the Roman author Plutarch (*c.* AD 46–120), whose best-known work is *Lives of the Noble Greeks and Romans*, also known as *Parallel Lives* or *Plutarch's Lives*.

'*Better . . . never been born*': adapting the most famous line from Sophocles' tragedy *Oedipus at Colonus*.

land-shark: 'one who makes a livelihood by preying upon seamen when ashore' (*OED*).

440 *Harrovians*: pupils at Harrow School, one of Eton's main rivals and their opponents at the annual cricket match held at Lord's.

And now, &c.: a way of introducing a toast or inviting applause.

ILLUSTRATION CREDITS

F. D. Bedford's illustrations to the first edition of *Peter and Wendy* (Hodder & Stoughton, 1911) reproduced on pp. 142, 157, 170, 174, 196, 204, 214, 236, 250, 256, and 275: Bodleian Library.

HENRY ADAMS	The Education of Henry Adams
LOUISA MAY ALCOTT	Little Women
SHERWOOD ANDERSON	Winesburg, Ohio
EDWARD BELLAMY	Looking Backward 2000–1887
CHARLES BROCKDEN BROWN	Wieland; or The Transformation and Memoirs of Carwin, The Biloquist
WILLA CATHER	My Ántonia O Pioneers!
KATE CHOPIN	The Awakening and Other Stories
JAMES FENIMORE COOPER	The Last of the Mohicans
STEPHEN CRANE	The Red Badge of Courage
J. HECTOR ST. JEAN DE CRÈVECŒUR	Letters from an American Farmer
FREDERICK DOUGLASS	Narrative of the Life of Frederick Douglass, an American Slave
THEODORE DREISER	Sister Carrie
F. SCOTT FITZGERALD	The Great Gatsby The Beautiful and Damned Tales of the Jazz Age This Side of Paradise
BENJAMIN FRANKLIN	Autobiography and Other Writings
CHARLOTTE PERKINS GILMAN	The Yellow Wall-Paper and Other Stories
ZANE GREY	Riders of the Purple Sage
NATHANIEL HAWTHORNE	The Blithedale Romance The House of the Seven Gables The Marble Faun The Scarlet Letter Young Goodman Brown and Other Tales

ANTHONY TROLLOPE

The American Senator
An Autobiography
Barchester Towers
Can You Forgive Her?
Cousin Henry
Doctor Thorne
The Duke's Children
The Eustace Diamonds
Framley Parsonage
He Knew He Was Right
Lady Anna
The Last Chronicle of Barset
Orley Farm
Phineas Finn
Phineas Redux
The Prime Minister
Rachel Ray
The Small House at Allington
The Warden
The Way We Live Now